Praise for 'The Black Arrow'

A RIPPING TALE

"Suprynowicz on the loose. Hide the women and children. Evidence that Robert Louis Stevenson and Ayn Rand didn't practice safe sex that night? There's a delicious 'comic book' feel to 'The Black Arrow' that frames beautifully, by contrast, the serious messages posited herein. It's a masterful technique of white-on-black that none but Suprynowicz could dare or achieve. A delightfully demanding gut-check of political reality and literary assumption. Buckle your swash and diss your belief: This tale doth rip!"

BEATS BATMAN ANY DAY

"Vin shoots a wild, bright spark of freedom into a dark, stylized, near-future America. The book's got it all: a freedom underground (literally), and plenty of sex and rock 'n roll. Think Tim Burton's treatment of Batman's Gotham City and you'll come close to the ambience of "The Black Arrow." But for a freedom lover, Vin's hero beats Batman any day."

SUPERHERO STYLISHNESS

"Vin Suprynowicz is undefeated as a Free-Market.Net Freedom Book of the Year winner; his two nonfiction books handily took the prize. Now he's poised to win it again, this time with his first novel, 'The Black Arrow.' Suprynowicz has a reputation for being a master wordsmith — 'The Black Arrow' adds a new dimension to his well-deserved acclaim. I picked up the first page and was almost immediately immersed into the world Vin has created. Simultaneously substantial and stylish, 'The Black Arrow' weaves a compelling story around believable characters. ... As I read the early chapters of 'The Black Arrow,' I became increasingly restless, until the tears started to flow. ... Anyone whose goals including living in a free society needs to read 'The Black Arrow.' "

Praise for 'Send in the Waco Killers'
(FreeMarket.net's 1999 "Freedom Book of the Year")

THE LYRICS TO FREEDOM'S SONG

"This volume by Suprynowicz is why words exist. It is the seminal work of the past five decades. It will change lives. It will direct nations. Unlike the firm big-government hand, offered ostensibly to hoist us out of the mire of day-to-day indecision (while leading us deeper into the swamp), the hand of Suprynowicz only points. But it points to the high ground. It points to hope and the brilliant possibilities alive in the human heart. It points past race and religion, past dogma, past atomizing welfare-state dependency. It does what words were meant to do: inspire and teach. This book works a slow magic. Suprynowicz has given us the lyrics to freedom's song. It is up to us to make the music."

— BILL BRANON, AUTHOR OF "LET US PREY"
(A NEW YORK TIMES NOTABLE BOOK OF THE YEAR),
"DEVIL'S HOLE," "SPIDER SNATCH," AND "TIMESONG."

Praise for 'The Ballad of Carl Drega'
(FreeMarket.net's 2002 "Freedom Book of the Year")

KNEE-CAPPING BIG BROTHER

"Fighting for liberty is not fun. That is, unless you are reading Vin Suprynowicz's latest book, 'The Ballad of Carl Drega.' ... You'll read it, and you will keep reading it, until the deep understanding overcomes you. You will set the book down, knowing exactly why you still fight for liberty against incredible odds."

— RICHARD W. STEVENS, JEWS FOR THE PRESERVATION
OF FIREARMS OWNERSHIP

UNRELENTING ... UNAFRAID

"Written by award-winning Libertarian columnist Vin Suprynowicz, 'The Ballad of Carl Drega' is a scathing examination of the constraints the American government under successive Republican and Democratic authorities has placed on individual and human freedoms, and upon those who martyred themselves to resist the tyranny of bureaucracy. Unrelenting in vehemence, unafraid of controversy, and unambiguously speaking his mind, Suprynowicz warns of oppression in America's past and paints a dark picture for the future. ..."

— THE MIDWEST BOOK REVIEW

THE
BLACK ARROW

Mountain Media non-fiction books by Vin Suprynowicz
Send in the Waco Killers
The Ballad of Carl Drega

Order at http://www.LibertyBookShop.us
Or use coupon at back of this book.

THE
BLACK ARROW
a tale of the resistance

Vin Suprynowicz

A Mountain Media Book
Las Vegas

This is a work of fiction. The names, characters, businesses, organizations, places, events and incidents portrayed are either products of the author's imagination, or are used fictitiously. Any resemblance to actual events, locales, or persons, living or dead, is purely coincidental.

THE BLACK ARROW — A TALE OF THE RESISTANCE

A Mountain Media book
Published by Mountain Media
3172 N. Rainbow Boulevard, Suite 343
Las Vegas, Nev. 89108

www.LibertyBookShop.us
www.TheLibertarian.us

Library of Congress Control Number: 2004098213

ISBN trade paperback 0-9762516-0-4
ISBN leatherbound 0-9762516-1-2
First edition: April, 2005

Cover design: Scott Bieser
Page design: Blain Keyes
Printed in the United States of America

ACKNOWLEDGMENTS:
A number of patient readers spent time with early drafts of this work, offering valued suggestions. My thanks to Claire Wolfe and Ed Silberstang, to Rick Tompkins and Don Doig and Iloilo Jones, to A.D. Hopkins, to Bill Branon, and especially to Lynn Clark. Any mistakes are mine. This book would also not have been possible without the participation of Dan Steninger, Randy and Virginia Paulsen, Rick Tompkins, Marc Victor, and David and Lorrie and Kristin Dorn.

To Madison, wherever you are.

The martyrs will be avenged.

INTRODUCTION

This is the story of a dream.

Whose dream it turned out to be, and whether it was a good dream, you must judge for yourself.

I can only tell you this: the dream really happened.

Some may hold my tale too full of passion. I can only say that this is a tale of freedom and fertility, of rebellion and revenge. And none of these things ever fought its way back into the world without some measure of blood, and joy, and pain.

The Black Arrow may be a symbol, but he is not a myth. I knew the Black Arrow. This is his story.

— Cassandra Trulove

SUPRYNOWICZ

CHAPTER 1

THURSDAY, JAN. 9, 12:35 A.M.

Madison walked alone.

The sidewalk was old, like the city, its textures quilted and worn.

The metropolis soared above her, its half-seen spires dark and looming, empty in the night save the whispering ghosts of braver times.

She did not know, then, how much of the city lay beneath her feet — a world that knew neither day nor night, alive and humming with a very different purpose.

That was all to come.

The only sound was the echo of her footsteps. A black car coasted to a stop across the street. The driver shut off the engine, then the lights.

A stylishly dressed couple got out. The man, who was starting to go bald, was barely an inch taller than his date. Slightly unsteady on spike heels, stylish lady shivered from the cold. He put his arm around her as they walked. She did not pull away.

Caught up in more important things, they ignored the passing pedestrian.

The balding man escorted his date to a parked red convertible. They stopped and talked. She leaned into him. They kissed in a way that said they had not kissed before. Would she get in that car and drive away, or not?

The young observer kept on her way. But she looked back over her shoulder as she turned the corner.

A moment's inattention.

From a long block further east, along the avenue, distant lights and attenuated taxi horns and occasional snatches of piano music carried on the crisp night air.

But now the portal, its blue light buzzing, stood between her and the avenue.

Shit.

Madison spun to head back the way she came. But it was too late.

A Gray trooper with a black German subgun stepped out of a darkened doorway. He was positioned to cut off anyone who came around the corner and then tried to make a break.

He gestured toward the portal.

"I'll have to ask you to step this way," he said.

They always started out polite.

Merely turning away to avoid a portal search was a crime. And she was carrying the disc.

"Empty your pockets and put the contents in the tray," said the bored old guy sitting at the table, as though anyone who'd ever traveled through an airport or a bus station didn't know the routine.

The streetlights overhead drained most of the color from their faces, so they looked like old engravings of hollow-cheeked witch hunters. Their eyes seemed dead.

Usually it would have been a woman at the table. It would have been better if it was a woman. All guys on the night shift.

She didn't carry much. The disc stayed where it was. The pouch was inside her thigh, and there was no real metal; there was a good chance the meat of her leg would shield it. Even if it did register and they scanned it, it would look like just another Japanese porn cartoon — the data was stegged into the white noise at the margins.

The data of the program whose name she wasn't even supposed to know. Subroutine, really. Just a small tributary flowing to the great river of the Queen of Codes.

She did a quick catalog in her mind. No gun or knife; no bootleg software if they didn't find the disc — and even that wasn't illegal, unless they had a way to dig out the code, which they didn't. No illegal drugs, no expired prescriptions, no prescriptions in anyone else's name. She might make it.

Sure enough, she passed through without setting the thing off. The guy who'd been ready to run the wand across her chest and up inside her crotch looked disappointed.

But they weren't going to let it go at that. A boring night, and she was ripe fruit.

"Not carrying much," the supervisor said, as though he was making idle conversation.

"Nope."

"Where do you live?"

She named an address that would match her ID as she reached to try and scoop the stuff up, get it back into her pockets.

"But you're not from around here, originally."

He'd noticed her accent was Irish. She didn't answer. It hadn't been a question.

"Awful late to be out alone."

"That's why I'm going home."

"No wallet? No change purse?"

He didn't sound like he really cared. He pawed through her belongings before she could get hold of them, picked up an orange plastic prescription bottle, held it up close to his eyes to read the label by the streetlight, looking for a pretext.

"I've got my ID. That's all I'm required to have."

5

"Required," he said, as though she'd voiced a deeply suspicious notion. Then, "This prescription is expired."

"No it's not."

"Yes it is."

The mother fuckers. If they couldn't come up with anything legit, they just made something up.

Up above, a slight breeze was bringing in the evening mist off the river. The watcher on the rooftop had been hoping she'd make it. But it had never really been likely.

Soon she was backing away, turning to run. And then they had hold of her, two of them muscling another "random selectee" into the side alley for "a full body search."

The portals had become commonplace on the bustling thoroughfares, where pedestrians walked past them with studied nonchalance, hoping not to be singled out and waved into line for a search with the peremptory motion of a gun barrel. You never knew what you could be handcuffed and led away for. You also never knew who would come back ... and who wouldn't.

The "busy work" arrests kept the Lightning Wagons running back and forth, but they weren't likely to generate the big headlines, or the big funding hikes. The smugglers and black marketeers had learned to avoid the better-traveled streets. That explained the new campaign to randomly set up portals at odd times and places. Like here.

The young woman was almost as tall as her captors — five foot eight, maybe. Skinny as a rail — if you'd pulled up her shirt her ribs probably would have shown. Shoulder-length dark hair. And she wasn't pleading. She stood tall and twisted her shoulders, arguing with a slight accent — Scottish? No, Irish — "You sons-of-bitches, you've got no right. No, dammit ..." as she was half-led, half-wrestled 40 yards deep into the alley. Her two captors were armed only with their service pistols, snapped down in their holsters. That meant they'd left their slinged subguns behind at the portal for safekeeping. Too easily grabbed and used against them by this wild a cat, perhaps.

And why not? What did they have to fear from one un-armed girl? Make that young woman. Full grown.

They reached a point where they could pull her behind a dumpster. Far enough. They tore her shirt open, popping the buttons. She made a noise of defiance, pulled a hand free and punched one of them.

Way to go, little one.

One of her captors punched her back, hard. She was rocked but stayed on her feet, shaking her head to clear it. With a little training, this one might make a fighter.

The bra was quickly sliced through with a belt knife. The trooper who would go second moved around behind the young woman to hold her arms now, as his partner cupped and mas-saged her well-shaped breasts, leaning over to lick and then bite a nipple. With the troopers dressed in their dark gray night uniforms, the white of the young woman's flesh was easily the brightest thing in the alley, which lacked even the scattered sodium bulbs of the larger street behind. The sole illumination here came from the full moon to the southeast, haloed with a promise of frost and filtered through a light haze. From the look of her breasts, it was unlikely she had yet fed children.

Such a romantic setting. From the dumpster wafted the acrid aroma of rotting garbage, too well encrusted to be re-moved with anything less than a steam hose.

Behind the small tableau, on the rooftop of one of the adjoining two-story buildings, a pebble rattled, coming to rest with a clink against an already fractured emerald beer bottle. The young troopers paid no heed.

They should have.

One of the shadows on the rooftop was moving. It ducked low as it crossed the face of the moon. Its head was silhou-etted, briefly. But, involved in matters which they considered more urgent, the troopers again failed to notice. Two mistakes — three, if you counted joining the Lightning Squads in the first place. All they got.

In the distance, a foghorn sounded intermittently down the river, like a lonely sea creature bellowing for its mate.

The black-and-white night was an old wolf, biding his time. But his ribs were showing through his winter coat. He would not miss a chance to feed beneath this moon. Any hunter would have sensed it.

The trooper standing behind the girl was now using pressure where he gripped her wrists to force her down to her knees. His partner unzipped his uniform trousers and indicated the service he required.

The young woman said "No," and half rose to her feet again. A firm, short-stroke punch to the jaw left her partially dazed. It was delivered with some expertise, the amount of force measured to keep her at least partially conscious. The one holding her from behind pushed his own knee into the back of one of hers. With one of her knees no longer locked, she went down fast. They'd done this before.

Good girl. Down you go. Further. All the way down on your knees. Good. A shot from the roof would go a bit high to begin with, due to the downhill angle. They had Hideki working on a narrower, heavier warhead that would have better penetration of the Kevlar vests most of the Grays had taken to wearing. But as of tonight only the traditional, broad triangular hunting heads were available. Not that an arrow to the Kevlar wouldn't do some serious damage. Especially now that they'd taken to dipping them in what was possibly the deadliest poison readily available at your neighborhood convenience store — essence of chewing tobacco.

But to get sure penetration on some of the newer vests, even with the powerful Black Eagle, you wanted to be within 50 or 100 feet. He was a bit beyond that.

Aim high on the back, then, and let the downslope pull the shot a tad high, at the collar line. It was counterintuitive, but arrows went high when you shot downhill.

The main thing he didn't want to do was overpenetrate into the girl. Her kneeling down had taken care of that. A slow breath. Induce the rock calm. I am the sea beneath his wave; the storm passeth over me but leaveth me unmoved; let God guide my flight. He allowed the gradual release to surprise him when it came.

The arrow's travel made no more noise than the fluttering of a bat. The penetration of the neck was slightly louder, like a piece of meat being whacked by a butcher's cleaver that doesn't quite go through to the chopping block. The shooter had lined up so an overpenetrating warhead could actually go on and penetrate the chest of the second assailant, standing behind the kneeling girl. But the warhead ended up slicing through most of the third cervical vertebra on its way through. This absorbed a considerable amount of its kinetic energy.

And so it stopped, only a few inches of jet-black shaft and that nasty triangular razor-blade warhead protruding from the front of the erect trooper's throat just above the breastbone. The arrow dripped a black fluid which would have appeared red in daylight.

The girl would not realize what had happened, at first. Her assailant took a step forward to catch his sudden forward momentum, feeling as though someone had taken a fist and pounded him on the back of his neck. He looked down in confusion at the ridiculous black arrow protruding from the front of his chest, and tried to speak. Then he began to shudder in an epileptic convulsion. Normally at this point he might urinate or defecate. But if he'd had an erection at the time he was struck, the sphincter muscles might hold. Impossible to tell from the rooftop.

Death would be from blood loss, as well as nicotine narcosis, if they didn't get him quick treatment. At least partial paralysis was also likely, however, from that substantial an insult to the spine. The girl dropped to her butt and scuttled over against the alley wall, crablike, as she grasped what was happening, probably first alerted by the spray of warm blood. Smart pusheen. Clear the line of fire.

Showing evidence of at least some measure of training, the unwounded trooper presented his sidearm, thumbed off the safety, and assumed a crouched shooting stance. He quite correctly tracked his front sight along the roofline of the building above. Not bad.

The archer had turned his bow to the horizontal and pressed it down on the parapet. Actually, his head was not fully concealed and might have been visible, though he wore tight-fitting black clothing and a black mask covering the top half of his face and head. But the trooper was squinting into the full moon, scanning an uneven roof line with which he was unfamiliar. And the outline of the roof was rendered even more unclear by the shifting haze off the river, now throwing pink-grapefruit haloes around the lights out in the street. The terrified trooper was unlikely to spot anything but movement. And the experienced hunter above him was careful not to move.

The Gray should have scattered a half-dozen rounds to force the assailant's head down and to alert his comrades in the street. He did not. Instead, with his buddy writhing on the ground and now probably foaming pink at the mouth as well as wetting himself with what could clearly be smelled as warm urine, finding that nothing immediately presented itself to shoot at, and with the girl long forgotten, the trooper suddenly appeared to realize he was alone, but less than 50 yards from help. He took one step backward, then two. Then he spun and ran for the front of the alley.

Which was the chance the archer had been waiting for.

"The Black Arrow!" the young trooper shrieked in an unintentionally high falsetto as he approached the apparent safety of the sidewalk, the streetlights, and his companions. "He got Dirk! It's the goddamned Black Arrow! It's him!"

The second flight was as quiet and nearly as short as the first. It was purposely low, positioned for the left thigh or buttocks, which would never be armored. The runner missed his step and tumbled headlong into the street, reaching around to grab the stinging cold projectile behind him. He tried to pull it from his left ham. As he reached around, his face was well lit by the streetlights. Standing, the archer loosed a quick third shot which he would not usually have allowed himself. It was this shot that clinched his identity in the minds of the forensic team that would later measure distances and weigh the testimony of the witnesses from the now shorthanded Lightning Squad.

They didn't like to admit it, but they were well aware there were now a lot more than one archer out there in the night, choosing an ancient method of attack which rendered their vast SonicNet gunfire detection grid about as useful as the ancient Maginot Line. Had to be. From the similarity of their methods, they were organized, perhaps even recruited and trained by the one they now called Black Arrow Prime.

But there was still only one, or so they hoped and believed, who could have gotten off that third shot fewer than three seconds after the previous. At a moving target. At nearly 50 yards. Into the left lower jaw, up through the palate and into the soft underbelly of the cerebrum. Dead by the time he slid to a stop.

The archer lost interest in the running target after loosing his third shaft, which left the bow sweet. He glanced down to see if there was time or need to also send another shaft into his first target. He decided against it. The troopers would be hesitant about entering the alley, but they had good communications ... so far. One of the increasingly rare helicopters would soon be spotlighting this roof and every other rooftop for a block around.

The young woman had regained her feet and was staring directly at him as she pulled her shirt-front closed.

Standing with her shoulders thrust back, there was something striking about this one. Shoulder-length dark hair, a high forehead, oval face, hollow cheeks that said she sometimes didn't get enough to eat — unless she just didn't bother to eat. A strong nose. Not too long, but still it made her look, what, part Polish? Romanian? The archer had the feeling he'd seen her somewhere before.

When she caught sight of him he was silhouetted against the glowing moon, a tall, masked man with powerful arms and shoulders and thighs. He was a black stallion, all muscle and sinew, rearing up to claim all he surveyed.

Her heart slowed in her chest, then. Her breathing went ragged. Time expanded. There was a strange keening in her ears that she knew was not of this time or place, but of the other world. It was a vision she was having, a waking dream that would long haunt her, drive her in ways unexplained, change her life. In the dream she stood beside that man on the roof. They each had great bows. And though all the world came at them, they would not be moved.

She knew then that, for better or worse, she would never forget this moment ... or this man.

He pantomimed urgently that the alley she was in would lead her away, take her back to the street she'd come from.

Poor man must take her for one of God's innocents, standing here puzzling. She looked at him for another moment, transfixed, memorizing the way he looked. Then she went.

Smart girl. With luck, her adrenalin would carry her a good ways before she stopped to puke, or whatever struck her appropriate. The archer certainly couldn't stand here playing bodyguard much longer. He had less than three minutes to be out of sight. They would expect lateral flight over the roofs, but so what? He was sure-footed, fast enough to enjoy the wind in his face. No one could catch him.

Given life by the moonlight, the other shadows bent to embrace him as he ran, sighing their ancient secrets.

Less than three rooftops away — having cleared two 10-foot alleys without a thought — the creature of the shadows reached a propped-open stairway access door. Pausing, he could hear in the distance the echoing clatter of the approaching helicopter — too late and a block short. Smiling, he kicked away the piece of brick holding the door open, and was gone.

As the young woman, who went by the name of Madison, reached the street and turned to put as much room as possible between herself and what was left of the portal squad, she noticed something, and smiled. The black compact car was gone, but the bug-eyed little red convertible was still on the street, locked and dark.

Good going, bald man. So the tipsy lady decided to go home with you, after all. Bald man was out getting laid, convertible gal would finally get out of those damned uncomfortable shoes and perhaps find the love of her life, she herself was alive and free, and the Black Arrow had cut down another piece of trash — maybe two.

And they said there was no justice in this world.

The Black Arrow *himself,* she smiled.

Now, if *he'd* been the one who wanted to lick her josies ... she cut herself off in mid-thought. She'd gotten into this mess in the first place by letting her mind wander. *Dammit* she should have had the big blade with her. Why had she bought it if she wasn't going to carry it?

Because of the portals, of course. But this was it. She'd had enough. She resolved to be ever on the alert from here on, never to take another blind corner. She would flit like a mouse, stay under their radar, but she vowed she'd been pulled into an alley for the last time. Her job was to avenge her family, not end up like them. If they ever grabbed her again she was going to cut her way through, she swore it. If she went down, fine, but she'd take some of the bastards with her. She had read once that a fighter who no longer planned on surviving could clear the planet of a lot of them while her blood still pumped.

She would work. She would train. She only had to find someone to teach her how to fight with a blade.

Slowing her pace so as not to draw attention, holding her heavy flannel shirt closed by overlapping and tucking in the tails, appearing more to casual eyes like a casual power walker, she reached down to touch the foil-lined pocket inside her thigh. The disc was still there. The disc that contained three months' work from the Spring Street cell. Their small part of the project that might yet change their world, if she could ever get it delivered to Joanie Matcham. The virus whose name no one spoke aloud.

Her jaw hurt where she'd been punched. There would be a bruise. Good. It would remind her.

And then a plan began to form in her mind. How many of her bitches could she really trust? Five? Six? Maybe there was some way to operate in a better organized fashion, so none of them would ever be caught out alone, again ...

❧ ❧ ❧

THREE MONTHS EARLIER:
FRIDAY, OCT. 11, THE YEAR 2030

Like many a lady of a certain age, the Gotham Theatre block still had a strong constitution. The possibility even remained that she might blossom again, one final time, if someone would only pay her the attention, demonstrate the patience.

By the time Andrew Fletcher strode briskly up her three wide marble steps and pulled open one of her chromed Art Deco lobby doors, she had long since given up hope that any such December suitor would arrive.

Still, this one had a firm grip. Massive shoulders, professionally tailored clothes. None of that paunch some of them showed as they entered their 40s. A man at ease with himself. Comfortable in his skin.

Andrew Fletcher was on his way to an antique store several blocks west, in which he held a controlling interest. He had an appointment there with another of the endless parade of city tax assessors, or inspectors, or whatever they called themselves now. The antique shop was too upscale for its present location, though the classic guitars did well. It was a block this side of Chin's Chinese restaurant. That would give him a chance to stop by and see how Mrs. Chin and her brood were faring in their ongoing battle with the Redevelopment Agency. But it was a pleasant autumn day in the city, so he'd decided to stop by the Gotham on his way, look up his old friend Bob. Bob ran the newsstand in the lobby.

The noise of traffic and taxi horns was cut off as the solid door eased closed behind him. Inside the old lobby it was cool and hushed. His echoing footsteps on the pink marble floor reflected not only the building's solid construction but also the fading of its popularity as an office address. Not many tenants left. The place smelled of floor wax and carpet that had been too long damp.

The Gotham Theatre itself, an Art Deco silent movie house of historic architectural status, had been boarded up for 60 years. The rest of the building wasn't doing much better. He was surprised Bob still held on with his newsstand concession, especially after the health department cracked down and stopped him from making a few extra bucks selling the sandwiches his mother made at home each day. Here the old lady was getting up at 4 a.m. to make a few dozen sandwiches, and the city told Bob that if she wanted to continue his mom would have to install a N$100,000 professional kitchen with double stainless steel sinks and certified fire-control hoods, all the usual.

"Hi, Bob."

"Hey, Mr. Fletcher! Great to see you! Boy, it's been so slow, it's actually great to see anyone. What'll you have?"

This approached a joke. Bob was already starting to draw

Andrew's hot chocolate as he asked.

"London Telegraph?"

"Yeah, 10 days out of date. And I'm embarrassed at the price, but that's only marking it up 10 percent. You'd think they brought 'em in by submarine from Corregidor or something. Have a seat, wontcha?"

"All ones," he said as he paid and sat down to glance through the paper. It wasn't really a lunch counter. There were only a couple of stools, usually dragooned as resting places for additional piles of papers. But Andrew had long since been told he should clear one off and pull it up to the counter whenever he came. Bob enjoyed a chat.

"Listen, Mr. Fletcher, there's something I've been meaning to talk to you about. We're pretty much alone here, right?"

"I trust your ears as much as I do my eyes, Bob."

"Yeah, well. Never hurts to check. Sometimes people stand real still to kind of test me. If it's busy I can lose track. It's about this building."

"Yes?"

Bob proceeded to outline the ownership situation of the building, the delinquent taxes the holding company owed, the way the latest change in the tax laws made the property less attractive as a write-off. He updated Andrew on two more offices that had closed upstairs. Then he gave him an impressively detailed report on the state of the repair of the old theater.

"What's unusual, see, is that the Gotham was originally an opera house, and then it was converted to be a vaudeville house as well as a movie theater. So there's a lot of space backstage — wings, flies, all that stuff. And a full basement for your dressing rooms, costume rooms, all that. The carpet would have to be replaced, and the seats reupholstered; the historic preservation people would love it if you went with the original red velvet. But the seats themselves are good, all but a couple of 'em that the kids must have jumped up and down on once too often. You know the tax exemptions are still on the books for renovating anyplace that shows up on the Historical Register?"

"Yes."

"So I was thinking, if you'll pardon me, rock 'n roll."

"What?"

"Rock concerts. That's a business you know, right? And with Rebel Records' talent lineup, you could really kick the place off with a bang. Heck, maybe even open with a reunion concert of the Rockin' Rebels. THAT would sure draw some attention to the old place!

"It's what they call a mid-sized venue. But I don't need to tell you that. Nice big interior lobby, so you could capture the refreshment market — you know, four newbucks for an orange-ade, eight-dollar cocktails, whatever. A little over twelve hundred seats with the balcony, if you can avoid handicap requirements for the balcony, which you can, because of the Historic Register exemption. Ground level you could make some wheelchair room at the back, and you've got all those emergency exit doors along the side to the alley, so they can't hold you up on fire safety.

"And under all that grime, the lighting fixtures are original 1920s and all that gold gilt is still up there on the columns and the ceiling. I had Jimmy climb up and make sure. You'll want to meet Jimmy the janitor, he's an interesting guy if you can ever get him to come out of the basement long enough to talk.

"Clean this building up a little, and it'll look like a damned Palace of the Pharaohs, if you'll pardon my French. I've got a lot of newspaper clippings from when it first opened, my mom helped me collect 'em— Rudolph Valentino and Theda Bara and Vilma Banky. The Arts section of the Mirror would eat it up. And the queers would love it."

"Concert venue."

"Good subway access. Not so great for parking, but who drives in this city, anymore? Plus if the city condemns and seizes some of the blocks to the west, like they're talking about, they'll put in more parking garages whether we like it or not.

"Then the upstairs in this building is a treasure, Mr. Fletcher. The floors are really more like a story and a half, by today's standards. Steel and concrete and cast iron, place is built like a bunker. So it's quiet, see, no vibration. Most places, when a truck goes by outside, the whole building shakes. Not here.

"Put a walk-up martial arts studio on the second floor, turn the third floor into a recording studio, or else use the rest of the second floor — you've already got those thick concrete walls. Offices above that, and up at the roof is a loft that'd make a great penthouse apartment, complete with skylights and a balcony. And the elevators are weird. Two at the rear of the lobby here, of course, but there's another one at the back of the building, a big freight elevator, like. You could set that one up so it'd be an express elevator to the penthouse or the basement; you can shut off the lobby elevators so they don't go to those floors if you like. Flexible access restrictions, see. Jimmy knows how."

"You've got my attention, Bob."

"So, you want me to mention to certain parties that you might be interested if the price is right?"

"No, Bob. I want you to do just the opposite. Don't talk to anyone but Mark Calhoun. You remember Mark?"

"Your lawyer, sure."

"He'll drop by to write down all the stuff you just told me. But don't mention my name to anyone, that'll only drive the price up ... *if* we decide this can be done. Mark has brokers we work with who can make a clearance sale offer, imply they might knock the old place down; save us millions if they don't know anyone has any particular plans for the place."

"OK, Mr. Fletcher, I get it. You really think it might work?"

"Bob, I think this might be the beginning of a beautiful friendship."

"Ah heck, Mr. Fletcher, we've been friends a long time already."

"Say hi to your mom, Bob."

"I sure will!"

❖ ❖ ❖

The taxman was named Jerry Westheimer and he was here about the City Council's new assets tax.

"We have no payments on file, and no self-assessment forms from you, either, Mr. Fletcher. You were sent multiple notices, the last two by certified mail."

"Yes," Fletcher answered calmly, looking through the round-shouldered man with the short red hair. "I told Katia to throw them away."

Boris and Katia pretended to stay busy out front, dicking around with the knick-knacks. He was sure they could hear everything. The place smelled strongly of whatever Katia had been burning to cover up whatever she'd been burning. Sandalwood, he decided.

"You threw them away," the taxman glared. He momentarily lost the superior, Cheshire Cat demeanor he'd been trying to project. "And would you care to explain why you did that?"

Jerry Westheimer did a good glare, though it was less effective when it tended to show he was close to losing control. Besides, there was something wrong with Jerry Westheimer's eyes. They were blue, and should have been attractive, but the whites of the eyes were red and watering, as though irritated. Some kind of a health problem. Possibly chronic drug use, in which case the prime suspect would be plain old alcohol.

"When I agreed to invest in this shop we inquired into all the licenses, fees, permits, and taxes that were required to open a business here," Andrew explained. "If you'll count the tax collection and business license forms and certificates framed on the wall over there, you'll find there are 17. Seventeen. I pay them all. That's our arrangement. I pay all these extortions, even though the city does virtually nothing for me in return. In exchange, the city told me that was all I had to pay. Those were the conditions under which I agreed to open for business.

"Now you want to charge me rent not just on my premises, which you do nothing to maintain, but also on everything I own. In order not to have my belongings seized, I have to pay a percentage of what they're worth, every year, to people who had no role in helping me acquire them.

"My property isn't really mine — even when I buy it with after-tax newdollars and pay a sales tax on top of that. You believe my property actually belongs to the state and I get to keep it only so long as I pay you rent for the privilege. But that was never part of our deal."

"I don't know what 'deal' you're talking about, Andrew." The taxman turned from scrutinizing a period portrait of Isabelle D'Este in a heavy gold-gilt frame as he slid smoothly into using the Christian name. It was supposed to shift the listener into regarding them as a "friendly adviser," though in actual practice it made Jerry Westheimer sound like a schoolmaster lecturing a petulant child. Were they taught that, or did they just pick it up?

"Why not do the smart thing? You get to declare the value of your own assets. Voluntary self-assessed valuation — don't you see?"

"Of course I see. You lure us into lying about how much our belongings are worth. That way, we're allowed to figure we're getting away with something. But we also begin to pay the tax. Later, you'll come around and do those mandatory re-assessments anyway, and charge us penalties for our under-assessments, which you're now winking and implying will be OK.

"Then when we try to protest the validity of the tax it'll be too late; your courts will rule we waived the right to protest when we started paying the tax."

"Andrew, I'm sorry you find it inconvenient to pay your fair share like everybody else. But we are going to collect it. We did a little checking on you when we found out you owned this place. Not only are you the heir to Fletcher Industries, you're the same Andrew Fletcher who made millions as a rock 'n roll star some years back — 'The Rock 'n Roll Rebels,' I believe."

He got it wrong, of course.

"You own your own record company. I wish I had just what you spend on your places in Maui and Ireland."

Information from some magazine feature, then. Not a FINCEN scan. Amateur.

"You're a wealthy man, Andrew. Paying this tax should be about as hard as paying your dry-cleaning bill. So why don't you just make this easy on everyone, and tell your accounting department up there in the Fletcher Towers to send in a check?"

"You see this shop?" Andrew answered after waiting to make sure the weasel was done chattering and licking its whiskers. "It's an antique shop. Not junk reproductions. These are treasures of the centuries, those few that have miraculously survived fire, flood, war and the worm. There are things here that are almost literally priceless, things worth millions of dollars."

The tax man jotted a note in his notebook, recording this valuable admission as though Andrew had just admitted being the last person to see Jimmy Hoffa or Jane Fonda alive.

"The tax is only 2 percent now," Andrew continued. "But it will never produce as much revenue as you figure. Anyone subject to the tax will alter their behavior to minimize their liability, the way sensible people always do. Of course, millions of dollars will be paid to lawyers and bankers and accountants *finding* those loopholes, and more millions wasted doing things people otherwise wouldn't have to do.

"In the end, it won't generate as much revenue as your bosses are hoping, so they'll increase it to 3 percent and then 4 percent and then 5 percent. If I pay you 5 percent of the value of my inventory every year, in 20 years you'll own the inventory. What kind of deal is that? What do I get in return? Might as well just take it all right now, the way the Communists did."

"Now, there's no need for name-calling, Andrew. You keep saying you don't get anything for your taxes, but that's just not true. The city provides you with police protection, and many other services you couldn't get from any other source."

"Really? Police protection? Can I get a written guarantee that the police won't allow any thefts or robberies? I can count on them to reimburse me the full value of anything stolen? I can drop my private insurance?"

"Now you're being ridiculous, Andrew. You know perfectly well the city isn't in the insurance business; that would be illegal. And I'm sure you also realize that, no matter how hard they try, the police can't be everywhere; they can never guarantee a zero crime rate, ..."

"What's your name, again?"

"My name is Jerry Westheimer, Special Tax Assessment Officer Jerry Westheimer. That was my signature on all the letters you've been throwing away, Andrew."

Actually, they'd been rubber-stamped in blurred red ink. But he already had the weasel's card, anyway.

"I suggest you get in touch with your lawyers and accountants and ask them what's likely to happen if you don't get yourself in compliance very, very soon, Andrew. I suggest you do that. Because I'll be seeing you again, and you're not going to enjoy my next visit nearly as much. You have a nice day, now."

Andrew watched him go — carefully, to make sure he'd recognize the man again, even in different clothing.

Katia and Boris were amused and attentive. Good. They'd been part of the Fletcher family long enough; they knew there'd be work — and the antiques, that was the most important thing for them — no matter how Andrew decided to play this.

Heck, they could move the whole operation to Sao Paulo or Dublin or even Prague within a couple weeks, if it came to that.

Boris had learned the import-export trade in Russia and Turkey, dealing with a lot more serious commodities and a lot more serious enforcement types — not to mention competitors — than they generally encountered here. Andrew paid him and Katia well, was always coming up with new challenges, and kept them isolated from some of the more "established" elements of his corporate empire. Parallel redundancy and need-to-know. They were a slim and elegant pair with expensive tastes. There were people in this world who would have killed just to have Boris and Katia's shoes.

Their loyalty stemmed from the fact Andrew had once bailed Boris out of a deal gone very wrong, and then sent what amounted to an Immigration special forces team into the Ukraine to bring Katia out on a fiancee visa ginned up in record time — without even trying to hit on her. That and the fact that he was willing to both fund and turn a blind eye to their tastes in drugs as well as clothes and caviar. In exchange, they were, in essence, the world's best personal shoppers. If you wanted it, and it existed, the only question was "How much?" Barred from export as a "cultural treasure?" Yeah, right.

There was plenty of money, of course — either to pay the absurd tax, or to bribe someone for a certificate of compliance, or exemption, or whatever the going scam might be.

But Andrew had not been lying. The rules were the rules. If the people in power thought they could endlessly bend and change the rules, they were like spoiled children — they would never stop, till someone made sure they got the very serious tummyache they deserved.

"Business as usual through the end of the day," he said. "Then we'll talk."

"Moving day?" asked Boris, blowing his nose.

"Mark's been studying their bogus tax ordinance. As usual, it has enough special exemptions to drive a bus through. He's been focusing on the museum exemption. Seems the arts crowd went batshit, demanded an exemption for museums. The assets tax will apply to museum gift shops, but not museum holdings. You're even allowed to 'de-acquisition' a certain portion of the holdings every year."

The phone rang. It was little Timmy Chin.

"He's very upset," Katia said. "I can't make it all out." Andrew took the phone. They were tearing down the Chin block.

"I'm heading over there," he said after he hung up. "Have Mark call me. I'll get back to you on the other matter — we'd better not leave it too long. I get the feeling Mr. Westheimer is the kind of guy who just loves guns and police dogs in the dawn's early light, flashing his badge like Dick Tracy, showing everybody who's boss."

⚜ ⚜ ⚜

The wrecking ball slammed into the walls and the bulldozers moved in to knock down what remained of the block which — till this morning — had housed Chin's Chinese restaurant. The concussions actually hurt the onlookers' ears. The air filled with concrete dust till you wanted to sneeze.

Carole Chin paced back and forth outside the temporary orange plastic mesh fence they'd strung up. And as each new blow fell she threw herself at the fence, as though she could will herself through its clammy, flexible embrace, uttering involuntary cries like a mother cat watching strangers bash in the

24

brains of her kittens right there in front of her — in plain sight but just out of her protective reach.

Timmy Chin, the grandson, spotted Andrew when he got there. Carole's daughter and son — Timmy's mom and uncle — had just arrived, as well. As each new sympathetic soul put in an appearance, Carole Chin ran to them, waving her sheaf of papers till the bedraggled stack of documents came to resemble the flopping limbs of a kid's doll. Tears streamed down her cheeks and onto the pages as she tried to read them in her broken English to anyone who would listen. The city had declared the Class A restaurant "blighted" and was seizing the entire block under its power of eminent domain.

"A month, it say I have a month," she kept insisting. "They deliver the papers Monday, four days ago. Is this a month? It say I have a month!"

Tim raced over to greet Andrew — he could move faster on his crutches than most kids could walk.

"Hi, Tim."

"Hi, Andrew."

"Not a very good day, hunh?"

"No. Not a good one."

"You hang in there. There'll be other days."

"You think so?"

"I guarantee it."

Andrew reached his attorney on the cell phone. Mark was good, he dropped everything and got through to someone he knew in the city legal department. The redevelopment attorneys had pulled an old stunt. The cover sheet of the stack of papers did indeed say the property was condemned under eminent domain and could be torn down after 30 days. This had the clear purpose of leading the recipient to believe she had a week or two to find an attorney, still well within the 30-day deadline.

But buried three-quarters of the way down in the stack was an "emergency order" to expedite the property seizure, citing a clause in the statute originally intended to allow municipalities to take quick action when raw sewage was flowing into the water supply.

Under that grant of emergency powers — duly signed by a District Court judge who'd previously headed up the city's main redevelopment law firm — the city was authorized to move in as little as 48 hours. By that measure, they were actually a couple days late.

The Chin children had different reactions. Daughter Annie was practical about things — they'd hire an attorney and make sure the city paid, but in the meantime she needed to get her mother away somewhere she could calm down before she had an embolism right on the spot. Their grief should be private.

Son Jimmy's reaction was different. Jimmy just stood there, short and wiry, hands in pockets, watching his family's dreams systematically torn to the ground by the very people to whom they had dutifully paid their taxes and fees all these years.

Occasionally Andrew's gaze met Jimmy's. He had seen that expression — the set jaw, the half smile — before. It was the look soldiers wanted to see on a buddy's face before they moved out on a night mission.

Jimmy nodded at Andrew. He was acknowledging something. At first Andrew wasn't sure what. The he realized: Jimmy Chin must be seeing the same expression on Andrew Fletcher's face.

He spoke to Jimmy Chin briefly. Jimmy accepted a business card.

Then the reporters and the TV crews started showing up. That was generally Andrew's cue to make himself scarce. When he saw one of them was Cassandra Trulove, though, he decided to hang around.

The photographer from the Mirror took a picture that would end up on the front page, of Mrs. Chin standing by the orange plastic fence with tears in her eyes, clinging to her sheaf of papers and pointing at the bulldozers destroying the block her husband had built. The bulldozers were also orange.

Mrs. Chin had grown up in Red China. She told Cassandra she knew about governments and how they talked about the good of the people, when what they really wanted was to take anything that was good away from the people. She had thought America was different, she said. Cassandra told her it once had been.

Cassandra Trulove wasn't like most of them. On previous visits in happier times, Mrs. Chin had showed the columnist all her grandchildren's pictures. And Cassandra had remembered their names. A busy girl like that, who must meet so many people.

But Mrs. Chin knew there was something wrong. Miss Trulove had no man in her life, although she was a beautiful girl. Mrs. Chin had never been beautiful, but she was old and wise; she'd seen this before. Cassandra Trulove was too beautiful, and too smart; she scared the men away. She did not lower her eyes and smile and hold her peace and let the men think they were the smart ones.

It would take a special man to tame this one. She had always wanted to introduce Cassandra Trulove to that nice Mr. Fletcher. They would make a good match.

Now she mentioned to Cassandra Trulove how Andrew Fletcher had tried to help, and how he had been here, just a few minutes ago. Where had he gone?

"You're Andrew Fletcher," Cassandra said as she approached the man with the shoulders, turned half away from her. His arm was around the kid on crutches — one of the Chin grandchildren. She had to raise her voice over the noise of the bulldozers.

"Yes."

"Mrs. Chin says you tried to help her."

"Not enough. I didn't know till today she'd been

served."

And now he turned to face her. "Cassandra Trulove, isn't it?"

He drew one foot back as he turned, shifting his balance in practiced elegance, like an athlete or a warrior turning to face a new threat head-on. He balanced on both feet, relaxed yet able to move in either direction. Not an accidental move. His hand and forearm were strong, sinewy and browned as he shook her own suddenly limp extremity.

Cassie found herself struggling to draw a breath to respond to whatever it was he'd just said. What the heck had just washed over her? She actually felt like she was going to need to sit down. Yet there he stood, relaxed, smiling, supremely confident. He was only a few inches taller than she — not many men were taller at all. He reminded her of one of those great cats whose muscles ripple, seem so loose and relaxed, until they unexpectedly spring, to land daintily on a tree branch further up in the air than you could possibly reach, for all the world as though they'd been settled there by the hand of some unseen woodland god.

Was Andrew Fletcher out of his jungle, or *was* this his jungle?

His brown hair had a tousled look, as though someone had just run her fingers through it. Oh, dangerous thought. He had eyes that looked like he was always amused about something. He wore no decoration or jewelry except a colorfully embroidered wide leather belt, buckled to the left rather than in front.

Cassie just sighed.

Which was something completely different. Cassandra had seen men react to *her* in this way often enough, lurching like clumsy puppies, blurting out the first idiocy that popped into their clouded brains. Testosterone, the Liquid Plumber of the cerebellum.

So this was the reclusive billionaire Andrew Fletcher, former teen heart-throb — she could understand that part — only guy in living memory to have been drafted into the NFL and said "No thanks" — a man rich enough to walk away from pro sports saying he didn't want to finish walking up stairs with canes the rest of his life, thought he'd try music instead.

"What?" she said, stupidly.

"I see you're as beautiful as they say ... and as brave," Andrew Fletcher was saying, possibly for the second time, as the buzzing in her ears faded and she could start to isolate his voice. It seemed to carry just the slightest Celtic accent.

Was that his natural voice? Could anyone else hear that? And what was that musky aroma that was opening her nasal passages? She noticed Andrew Fletcher had a 5 o'clock shadow, found herself wondering what it would be like to watch him shave.

"Brave?" she asked. "I just write down other people's stories."

"Stories that can't make you terribly popular in the corridors of power. I suspect you could prove a valuable ally — or a fierce opponent."

"We've only just met," she found herself replying. "You don't really sort all your casual acquaintances into allies and enemies, first thing, do you?"

He smiled then, and she let out the breath she'd been trying to hold, realizing he still had hold of her hand — or was she holding his?

She was still holding onto his hand. Cassandra Trulove was taller than he'd expected from her pictures, but every bit as beautiful: red hair falling in thick waves, square shoulders, strong jaw, perfect nose, stacked as a bad card game. If she'd once been a model, as he'd heard, she'd clearly quit on her own terms.

OK, the hips were a little fuller than a schoolgirl's. But who was it who'd decided grown women should look like teen-age waifs? A full-grown woman was fine by him.

For a moment, she watched his eyes search hers. Not the eyes of a predator, she thought — at least they didn't make

29

her feel like his next meal. There was an intelligence there. It seemed to ask whether it had found another of its kind.

"I have no casual acquaintances," said Andrew Fletcher, after a brief pause. She believed him.

But now Cassandra felt herself growing feisty.

"Well, Andrew Fletcher, you're either one of the most arrogant men I've ever met, or else the love of my life."

His eyes sparkled, then. Fire opals. Oh God, no, no, not The Smile. Not the dimples.

"Why don't we give that a little more consideration over lunch?" he suggested, producing a card like a magician.

She traded him one of hers. "I'd like that," she agreed.

"If you'll excuse me, I need to ask Mrs. Chin one more question," he said.

Funny, that was usually her line. And wasn't there something else she'd come over to ask this guy? What was wrong with her today?

Timmy Chin stood smiling at Cassie. Smitten.

Annie Chin was helping her exhausted mother into the car. Andrew caught them just in time.

Who had delivered the papers — arranged so cleverly, with the 48-hour emergency order buried deep within — he needed to know.

A man named Jerry, the old woman said. A red-haired man with short hair — a crewcut.

"Jerry Westheimer?"

"Yes, that was the name."

So. What confluence of fates had decided it should start with Special Tax Assessment Officer Jerry Westheimer? No matter. Andrew had delayed putting the plan into action, probably too long. It was always hard to know precisely when to make a beginning. But now his path was clear, and strangely he felt a weight lifting from his shoulders. He had wished many times, since Nicole, that he were dead. Now, he realized, in a strange way, he had been.

The path having been chosen, it was as though he was

just finishing up a few things before the undertaker called. An ending, and a beginning. He was deathly calm. He could not see all of the road ahead. But he could see its shape, now. He saw many things unfolding, of his doing but largely beyond his ability to change, once the first stone had been set rolling. He saw love and death, blood and battle, a half-naked woman, bathed in sweat, dancing with a sword. He saw grief and he saw joy. These images spilling back out of a half-known future washed over him, yet he was able to view them with an odd detachment.

He watched Cassandra Trulove depart with the rest of the news crews. Then he made two calls. First, he needed some information on a city employee — home address, work schedule. With the resources of Fletcher Communications, Rebel Records, and the billion-newdollar Fletcher Group of Companies, it was easy enough not merely to get this done, but to get it done without leaving any tracks.

Westheimer the tax collector actually hadn't a clue about the size of the Fletcher fortune, since it was not well known how much of the family enterprises Andrew had moved into Third World gold mining and Indian and Irish technology stocks a decade past, even before the big dollar collapse and revaluation.

Then he called Boris with the news they'd been waiting to hear:

"Close tonight at six as usual. No unusual preparations before then. But I need you both back at midnight."

"We're going?" Boris asked.

"To the bare walls."

"Into the warehouse?" he sniffed.

"For now. But I may have a line on the building we've been looking for. Not far away, actually."

"Cool."

THE BLACK ARROW

CHAPTER 2

The great object is, that every man be armed. Everyone who is able must have a gun.

— PATRICK HENRY (1736-1799), 1788

If they want to have a war, let it begin here.

— DUBIOUSLY ATTRIBUTED TO CAPT. JOHN PARKER, MASSACHUSETTS MILITIA, APRIL 19, 1775, LEXINGTON.

SUNDAY, OCT. 13, THE YEAR 2030

The park was out by the airport, at the end of the subway run. It was the only place big enough. One weekend a year the entire place was taken over by the Renaissance Faire.

It was a huge draw, and an endless source of snide amusement to European visitors, who found vast irony in the fact that a nation of immigrants — most descended from plowmen who could never have afforded more than a single set of homespun — now enjoyed celebrating an idealized medieval heritage where the ancestors of these jumped-up nouveau riche would have been lucky to clean the boots and boil the parsnips of the kind of aristocrats they now spent small fortunes impersonating.

There were a couple separate grandstands set up, ringed by bales of hay, where the re-enactors could stage their medieval battles in full chainmail and steel armor — though the cutting edges of the weapons had been dulled, or in many cases replaced entirely with bamboo and rattan, to reduce the ambulance calls.

It was dress-up fun, these days, not training for actual combat. Which was not to belittle the skill of anyone who could still maneuver a huge Shire plowhorse around the arena with knee and foot alone. The horse had to respond to knee commands, of course, so the riders' arms would be free to whack at each other with lance, sword, or morning star — vicious spiked balls on the ends of short chains.

The smell of the hay and the horse dung were pervasive, but not unpleasant. Tens of thousands of years had hard-wired the smells of the barnyard into something familiar — even reassuring.

From the sales booths across the greenway drifted the lilting melodies of pre-recorded New Age harpsichords and dulcimers.

It was the sheer size of the show — and the number of participants willing to put time and money into assuming an intricately costumed alter ego from an earlier age — that took a little absorbing.

The early fall weather was still a few degrees warm for the wool plaid baggy trousers and tam o'shanters and leather knee boots ... not to mention all the velvets. But the chill of the oncoming evening would fix that.

A beer company had simply backed a tanker trailer up to one of the main grassy pedestrian thoroughfares, from which lasses in fluffy white German bierhall costumes now sold plastic cups of Miller Lite off the thin camouflage of a stack of hay bales.

Not to be outdone, StatesEast Bank had backed up a gray armored car with automatic teller machines positioned on the tailgate, accessible up a little flight of metal stairs, up which a line of gussied-up medieval courtiers had already formed.

Other stalls sold ready-made medieval costumes; amethysts and crystal balls in a range of sizes with small pewter wizards already attached. And the whole of the commercial enterprise was supervised with undisguised superciliousness by a little Capucin monkey in red satin, holding out his cup for change.

A small group of boys pounded past, chasing some gamboling fat-bellied pygmy goats who had escaped from the petting zoo. Gold-chain belts shifted languorously across the pale bellies of wenches in low-slung skirts being led around on ropes, winking at the modern age's rather different take on "bondage," proving Political Correctness held little sway out here among the feasting, swaying, breeding classes.

Andrew attracted considerably less notice than the slave girls as he moved through the crowd, clad in Lincoln green and brown leather Robin Hood regalia — complete with a stylish matching green mask across his eyes.

His nondescript green jerkin and flannel trousers were practical. They allowed full freedom of movement, and the pants covered soft brown suede boots that generated no sound signature as he passed.

By an indirect route, Andrew ambled up to the tent and sales table of Hideki the bladesmith.

"Greetings, masked man."

"Good to see you, blademaster."

A few young men had been admiring Hideki's wares, handling with admiration those lesser models which were set out within easy reach. But they quickly blanched at the bladesmith's answer when they asked about prices, retiring around the corner to a booth which offered mass-produced pseudo-swords in a far more entertaining range of fanciful shapes and handguard treatments, stamped sheet-metal jobs with fake glass rubies in the pommels in the N$100 range, brand new from the Indian subcontinent.

"How's business?" asked the archer, without additional introduction.

"Ah, so it's you," replied the swordsmith. "I should have recognized the bow."

"Not sure you've seen this one before."

"The fact that it was live, I mean, not some plywood prop. That one of the Oneidas?"

The fact that the compound bow's gearing was well inside the limbs made it distinctive — and a little less hypermodern in appearance, at least to a casual observer.

"Oneida Black Eagle."

"Never thought I'd see you carry a weapon you didn't mean to use."

The archer smiled a joyless smile beneath his mask.

Hideki's long sideburns came to a point below the ears. His hair was swept back and tied behind. He was full-blooded Japanese, but spoke with no discernible accent. With his full dark mustache and goatee, he looked a positive devil.

"Business poor?"

"My last year. Probably would be, even if Councilwoman Janes wasn't about to nail down the twenty-sixth vote for her 'Weapons of Terror' ordinance. I don't even bring the best katana any more. They all balk at the prices. But of course they only want them to hang on the wall between the extra refrigerator and the neon beer sign."

"No appreciation of craftsmanship."

"None."

"Maybe you should come work for me."

"Doing what?"

"What you do. Teach some self-defense classes at my new dojo. Set up a new forge and make me some live steel."

"A new dojo," he contemplated. "But how much live steel could you need?"

"With their new SonicNet, they're confident no one can

offer any resistance. Even a single gunshot is supposed to bring them down on us by the busload. The time will come to show them just what a useless white elephant they've built. But for now, there may actually be an advantage to be gained there. The thing to do is to start out stealthy, use the old ways, something they won't be looking for. Picking the time and place, a small group of fighters operating on familiar ground can demoralize a much stronger foe, and never make a noise. In fact, silence would be far more demoralizing."

"How small a group of fighters?"

"You and me, to start with." The archer shifted the quiver on his shoulder. With old eyes, the swordmaster noted the shafts did not shift around, the way they would have if the points buried in the depths of the quiver had been target points — those thin, tubular steel sleeves designed to give enough weight for proper flight but lacking any barbs, facilitating easy removal from a straw target. Instead, the arrows held stiff, as though planted in Styrofoam. Warheads.

"But let's say we had 20. What kind of sword would you use to arm 20 men to fight a silent resistance, in the dark, in the parking garages?"

"Sten guns."

Andrew laughed. "OK. I agree we'll have to move to firearms eventually. Although I wouldn't limit us to 9 millimeter.

"But just for the sake of argument: We want to show people there's hope. Show them this SonicNet is useless if the enemy is determined. Frustrate the hell out of the Grays, shove their billion-dollar sonic Maginot Line right back in their faces. We want maximum psychological impact on a class of people who've never felt threatened with any kind of personal repercussions for their crimes. If death is silent, it can lurk anywhere. Make them afraid of the dark."

"Then I'd arm them with the sword Alexander the Great used, the kopis, but in steel. It's a very effective chopper; can't thrust worth a damn. The kopis or the Spanish falcata, the sword from which the Gurkha kukri is descended. It eventually evolved into the Turkish yatagan, as well. Totally pragmatic, like a big recurved butcher's cleaver. Designed to chop off limbs through light armor, no finesse needed, no years of training.

"The reason the Japanese blade requires so much training is that it'll chip or break if you try to use it like a cleaver. That's why we spend so much time teaching how to slice, and in traditional swordsmanship you never use the edge to parry.

"The katana was state-of-the-art for the 12th century, but then the Japanese stopped, they just froze in place while the Europeans kept adapting.

"The European blades are softer, springier, so you don't have that chip-out problem. A European hand-and-a-half sword is 38 inches long, and it'll take a side of beef in half. You can use a good European sword to chop all day. Make them out of 5160 steel with just 75 points of chrome, just enough."

"You can make a lot of them?"

"As many as you need. Run us two hundred, three hundred newbucks apiece, if you're counting something for the labor. You're actually going to do it?"

"Think we should wait a few more years?"

"No. No." The old Japanese smith cocked his head, thinking. "You're here today just to talk to me?"

"No. Hoped I'd run into you. But I have information someone else will be here. Got your city business license?"

"Sure do. I went through hell to get it. They won't let me use coal; I can only burn gas in the forge. What do they care whether you can control the temperature as well? Air pollution? Ha! Like I could put out as much soot in a year as one of their half-empty diesel buses does in a day. And then I can't have an apprentice, because OSHA would make me get rid of my drop hammer. Not up to the current code!"

"We'll move you somewhere where you can have apprentices. And your hammer. But I mean, have you got your business license with you, here today?"

"Sure. Those guys can be assholes, fine you for not hav-ing it with you anywhere you set up, even if you can prove it's home on the wall." Hideki reached under the table and pulled out his framed city business license, complete with multiple official-looking signatures and a fancy gold seal.

"Yeah. That's good. Keep that handy."

"Why?"

As if on cue, voices were raised briefly at the lemonade stand across the way. A man dressed in brand new creased bluejeans and a rugby shirt — a government employee's idea of "plainclothes" — was writing the proprietor a citation for not having his business license with him. Or not having it at all; impossible to tell at the distance.

The man writing the citation had a crewcut, and bright red hair.

"Tax inspector?"

"Mmm-hm."

"Someone you know?"

"Could be."

The smaller man just nodded.

"I'm going to make myself scarce for a little while. Is there a back entrance to your tent, there?"

"Tied shut."

"But you could untie it."

"Consider it done."

"And maybe you could leave this bag inside where I could find it."

"Spare shirt, in case you get that one dirty?"

"Something like that."

"No problem."

"Could make you an accessory."

"About time somebody got this party started."

When the next set of gawking lads stopped by to fondle Hideki's shortswords, he was alone at his table.

Andrew Fletcher chose his position carefully. He was behind some currently abandoned tents — their occupants away participating in some part of the ongoing festivities.

Nearby, some local archers were demonstrating their 40-pound recurved wooden bows to a few kids who had wandered by, showing them how to hit the traditional colorful bulls-eyes tacked up on hay bales at 30 yards.

A far cry from the 150-pound longbows real medieval archers had somehow pulled, downing the French knights at Crecy and Agincourt at ranges out to 300 yards, generating some considerable ill feeling on the continent for centuries to come.

The amateurs were shooting shorter shafts with different colored fletching than the black hunters Andrew carried in his quiver. He hadn't thought of it, but that was actually better — the innocent local archers would be able to convincingly prove their noninvolvement in short order.

He was on the side away from the entrance flaps to the tents, but sandwiched close up against a storage area where some extra hay bales had been carelessly stacked, whether by the archery folks or someone with a horse to feed was not immediately clear. No, wait — he could smell horse droppings nearby, now that he was paying attention.

He lounged there, his slightly shopworn Robin Hood get-up allowing him to easily pass for a festival participant who'd been hitting the mead too hard and had merely sought out a quiet area for a late afternoon nap. In fact, he'd seen a number of exhausted fighters in just such postures behind other tents in the encampment, taking advantage of the warm afternoon rays.

The sun was still a good hour off the horizon when he saw Jerry Westheimer, clutching his citation book, hold up his hand against the glare and peer westward toward the archery range, trying to determine whether any money was changing hands there. Sharks look for wounded seals; Jerry Westheimer looked for commercial activity with some blood still remaining to suck.

It looked like he might bypass the archers without actually demanding to see a license. Fine. Better to take him when he wasn't actually engaging someone in conversation. But that meant it had to be now.

The man in the Robin Hood mask was kneeling behind a hay bale as he drew a black arrow from his quiver with studied casualness. He briefly inspected the skeletal, pyramid-shaped, razor-sharp warhead for symmetry, making sure it hadn't picked up any spare crud that could affect its flight.

This was it, then. Andrew Fletcher, a wealthy man who could have taken his millions and lived out his life in peace on some obscure Pacific island, or among a dozen Thai concubines and an equal number of hired bodyguards somewhere in the Golden Triangle, was about to kill in cold blood a man who had not attempted to harm him ... at least not by the operative definitions of most modern judges and prosecutors.

This was not a legislator who made the laws, nor a judge who enforced them, nor a prosecutor who'd built a career railroading the innocent on perjured testimony purchased with sentence reductions. Though their time was coming, he smiled to himself, grimly. No, this wasn't even a cop who shot innocent people for owning guns or "resisting" rubber-stamped search warrants in their homes.

Jerry Westheimer was just a tax man, a medium-level cog in a very big machine. He knew people did not like him, but he did not expect to be killed for what he did, which was merely to steal the property of the productive class, a little at a time, gradually driving his own country deeper and deeper into the sinkhole of socialist corruption and induced redistributionist poverty.

They had had their lessons. They had seen what such a system had done to Russia and all of Eastern Europe. But they would not stop. Someone else would have to stop them. Someone else would finally have to say "No." And it would not be the courts, or the legislatures, or the prosecutors, or the police.

Someone else.

The man now poised at the end of his black shaft like a beetle on a pin was in all likelihood a husband and father who loved his dog and spent his weekends doing carpentry or watching the game with his poker buddies, saving up to put a kid through college. By what right did Andrew Fletcher take his life? He was just a foot soldier of tyrants, "only doing his job; just following orders."

He had gone over it a thousand times. But these foot soldiers of the Great and Poisonous Leech had been feeding on people like Andrew Fletcher and the widow Carole Chin for generations — assuming that no one would ever fight back.

And what did you do, finally, with a leech?

In the background, the practice arrows lodged in the straw targets with a rhythmic "Thump, thump."

And calmly, without further hesitation — focusing his memory on Carole Chin, hurling herself at an orange plastic fence — he drew the bow full, shot tax inspector Jerry Westheimer through the chest, and it began.

The tax man did not fall dead at once, of course. He looked down at the few inches of feathered shaft still protruding from his chest with an expression of puzzlement. Andrew Fletcher had lowered his bow and leaned back out of sight after releasing his shot, so if the recipient of his black carbon fiber gift looked up in the direction from which the arrow had come he would see nothing of note.

Jerry Westheimer touched the arrow, as though to make sure it was real. He took a step. Then he dropped to his knees. Some young girls who were walking past — their faces painted in bright primary colors — looked at him, laughed and pointed at what they presumed was another piece of re-created medieval play-acting. They walked on by.

"Help me," Jerry Westheimer said, not very loudly, as though he were slightly embarrassed. "Help me; I've been shot."

It was one of the men operating the nearby archery exhibition who spotted him and came running. Recognizing real blood when he saw it, he called for help from a woman with a cell phone.

Moving around the abandoned tents to place them between himself and the minor stir now developing around the downed taxman, the archer unobtrusively slung his bow over his shoulder and sauntered calmly along an arcing path which would eventually bring him back to Hideki's tent. The last thing he wanted anyone to see — even to recall later on — was a masked bowman rushing toward an exit, in a beeline from the scene of the shooting.

Slipping in through the untied rear flap to Hideki's tent, he quickly unstrung his bow and piled it in with a bunch of unmounted blades and pole weapons that he'd help Hideki carry out to his van in good time, after sunset. No one unfamiliar with the sport was likely even to recognize it as a bow, in such an unstrung condition. He then ditched the mask, and changed out of his Lincoln green outfit and into a full red Elizabethan doublet, form-fitting snow white leggings, flapped knee-high black velvet boots and a huge, shapeless, jaunty black velvet cap with a white feather. Finally, a gold mesh collar draped over his neck and shoulders. He now looked precisely like Sir Walter Raleigh. In drag.

"Perfect," Hideki smiled when he emerged to show off his new duds.

"I look as queer as the Queen of Diamonds," Andrew replied.

"Just what I meant."

The archery demonstration range was visible in the distance from Hideki's sales table. They sat sipping cold sweet cider out of pewter mugs. Cold enough that a dew precipitated out of the humid air onto the sides of their tankards. By watching calmly from the distance, Andrew learned a good deal.

The first surprise was just how little police presence ever showed up. One of the beat cops assigned to patrol the fair seemed to be taking some statements as his lady partner directed the resident ambulance across the grass with arm gestures. Faintly, they could hear the gonging noise the ambulance made as it moved slowly in reverse.

The archers were undoubtedly telling the cop it couldn't have been an accident since the arrow shaft in question bore no relation to their practice arrows — it was even a different color, being a uniform dull black all the way to its fletching. But the officer seemed unmoved. The injury had occurred near the archery area; it involved an arrow; people being hurt was precisely what the cop expected to happen when they let grown-ups fool around with live metal arrows and swords, which would have been banned entirely if he'd had his way.

Any disclaimers to the contrary he would dismiss as the usual "Some Other Dude Done It" crap that he heard on the streets every day.

As far as the officer was concerned it was a civil suit, a matter for the organizer of the event to settle up with his insurance provider.

As for Westheimer the tax collector, he had turned just as the arrow released, with the result that the angle of attack had been more obliquely through the side of the ribcage than the archer had intended.

One of his lungs was collapsed and there was considerable internal bleeding, but neither the heart nor the main arteries to the brain had been destroyed.

In earlier times he would have died of internal bleeding within a few hours — long before the fragments of his shirt carried into the wound would have time to fester and kill him of suppurating infection.

But the miracle of the modern ambulance service did its

work. The taxman was still alive — and cursing a blue streak, despite his shortness of breath — when he reached the emergency room, falling into the hands of a zealous young Indian emergency room surgeon who had actually been reprimanded on occasion for "opening up" too soon, before waiting for proper insurance approvals.

The doctor went in like a dervish, propping Westheimer's chest open and clamping off every bleeder he could find before repairing the gushing venous walls with a combination of old-fashioned stitches and the new "Superglue" technology. Only then did he go to work peeling back the clinging flesh from the triangular warhead and getting the invading object out of there.

A very lucky tax collector would survive, returning to restricted duty in less than a year.

The case didn't remain open ... because there was no "case." A pro forma inquiry revealed no specific recent death threats against the victim. He was not involved in any messy divorce or custody battle. No one had taken out any new life insurance policies on him in the past year. He'd been on duty, so insurance covered all his treatment and rehabilitation, which was everyone's main concern. And of course he didn't die, which meant it never went to Homicide.

He was never even officially identified as the Black Arrow's first "victim." He tried to make such a claim numerous times in later days, pointing out the arrow that had struck him was black ... asking quite sensibly how the authorities would have reacted to the incident only a few months later.

Inevitably, his laughing friends would point out the Black Arrow's almost infallible reputation, in the months to come, for deadliness. If he'd been shot by the Black Arrow, why was he still alive?

It was a question even Jerry Westheimer would never be able to answer.

Back at Hideki's sales table, a couple of giggling young

women in their early 20s — if that — came up and started asking Hideki about the blades. Slim. Full of the energy of youth. Though the taller one had something else. Old eyes. Eyes that looked out from somewhere else.

They both had lilting Irish accents. The bladesmith soon warmed to his subject and began explaining the problems with traditional Japanese blades.

"You're not from around here," Andrew observed.

"No, we're just off the cruise boat," said the taller, strikingly pretty one with lips dark as wine and the heavy eyebrows, her voice a little throaty. "Got lost looking for Lord & Taylor. Is Fifth Avenue near here, aroon?"

The huge brown eyes laughed as she spoke. They were almond shaped, turning down slightly at the outside, with tawny eyelids — if they were painted that color it wasn't obvious. An oval face, slightly cleft chin. Her brown hair was parted in the middle, hung to her shoulders, a few lighter highlights out here in the sun. A straight nose, not long, but wide. Her hollow cheeks said she sometimes didn't get enough to eat. Yet here she was pricing N$400 swords

Oddly enough, given their earlier conversation, she focused right in on the Gurkha kukris — the serious choppers.

"And what would you be planning to do with a weapon that size, Miss?"

"Kill Grays."

Everyone nodded soberly, considering.

"I didn't ask that question," the swordsmith said.

"I didn't answer it," she agreed. "But which is the best for practical use? You know ... chopping things. Not taking fencing lessons for the school play. Something you can grab with both hands, should the need arise."

Hideki recommended a nice pattern-welded blade. She tried hanging it at her side, then had her friend measure it for concealment across her back. The Kukri itself wasn't quite straight enough for a draw from the shoulder. The falcatas filled the bill, but the longer ones were a full 25 inches, she'd need something a little shorter to fit in a back sling.

"How much for this one?" she asked, hefting one that ran 18 inches or so — the length of the ancient Roman gladius, most powerful short sword ever devised. Andrew could see her testing her muscles against its weight. She wasn't strong enough to wield it confidently or long ... yet. But she might have the makings, if she applied herself.

"The better blade is 400. It takes longer to make."

Andrew had seen Hideki charge good customers a lot more for a piece with that much extra fit-and-finish work.

"But all these blades will stop anything that gets within range," Hideki's sales pitch lacked hype, but it was information rich. Most American kids got bored, stared off into space, cut him off before he went 20 seconds. These two listened.

"The hilts are cut to fit the tangs, mounted while the metal is hot, then I hammer the pommel down to lock them on while it's still hot ... not that loose, rolling pin stuff you get on the cheap reproductions. If it ever breaks or comes loose, which it shouldn't, bring it back and I'll fit a new one, no extra charge. Keep them clean, keep them oiled, you can leave them to your kids. Your grandkids."

"Yeah, I'm about to kittle. We just took a break from buying the baby furniture to stop by here. It's gonna be all matching. Persimmon."

"Fuschia," the smaller one corrected her. She was a petite blonde — a real one, judging from her pale eyebrows and translucent skin — arms so thin she looked like she'd break in a tumble.

"I don't have 400. How about these?"

"Two hundred fifty."

"You import these from India, or what?"

"I forge them by hand."

"Like, red hot, with a hammer?"

"Exactly."

"All by yourself, by hand?"

"We use a drop hammer for some of the work now."

She looked a question.

"A piece of machinery. Cuts down on the muscle work ... since I don't have a couple of loyal apprentices with sledge-hammers. But they all still get hammered by hand, the old fashioned way. Takes days. These are the real thing. Live steel."

"Wow. I'd like to learn that."

Hideki plucked one of his business cards from the agate ashtray in which a stack lay virtually untouched, handed it to the young woman, who read it, looked him in the face, tucked it away. Then she looked at Andrew, stuck her chin out to size him up better. This time, they did not speak.

"I'd like the good one," she said, turning back to Hideki. "But I don't have 400. I don't even know if I have three. Raitch, you got a hundred newbucks?"

"Yeah, I've got a hundred bucks. I got it from the maid this morning. Oh, wait, I spent it all on that corn dog."

"So that means I've got like, two hundred. Can you give me the cheaper one for 200? And do you know someone who can teach me to use it? You know, classes or something?"

Hideki looked at the blade and thought. Andrew picked up the better, pattern-welded blade with the dark hardwood handle and used it to replace the less fancy sword in his old friend's hand. The pattern of the weapon made it look as though it had been embossed in a white and gray geometric pattern down the center, though in fact what you were seeing was a cross-section of a blade that contained up to seven different hardnesses of crystal-patterned steel, after being folded and re-forged dozens of times.

"I haven't done much business here today," Hideki said, wistfully. "If you really mean to take care of this blade, and learn how to use it, call me and I'll find you a class. A serious class for serious people, not stage-acting. And I give you the better blade for two hundred. It needs a good home."

She tilted her head then, measuring the old bladesmith. Then she fixed Andrew Fletcher with the same gaze. "That's it? A four hundred dollar sword for two hundred and we walk away?"

It was Andrew who nodded, returning the stare of those dark eyes, now gone quite serious again. And now she knew where her discount was really coming from.

"Two hundred for the falcata ... and the scabbard," Andrew said. Without raising an eyebrow, Hideki dug around and found a fringed leather scabbard that fit the blade. Two brass snaps closed the top, near the hilt.

"Fringe?" she sneered, her eyes smiling.

"Fringe is practical on leather," Hideki explained. "If you get things wet the fringe carries the water away; it evaporates faster. And you will get it wet, if you mean to use it. Keep it oiled. Even steel will rust, eventually."

"Gotta be fifty newbucks worth of hand-sewn leather here," she said.

"Weekend special," Hideki smiled.

"Cool," she said, turning back to Andrew. "Who are you?"

"My name is Andrew ... alanna." He looked friendly enough. Kind of rough-and-tumble comfortable, actually. Brown hair that needed a comb, a big square jaw, eyes that looked like they were always smiling. That was to the good. Otherwise he would have seemed ... larger than life.

"Andrew. Glad to meet you, Andrew. I'm Madison."

They shook hands. Her grip was strong. She sized him up again, with those dark eyes, as though trying to place his face. Her smaller friend, Andrew noticed — the natural blonde — was staring at him with eyes the size of ping-pong balls, a smile frozen on her face, saying nothing. He'd been made.

Then the taller one shrugged and paid cash and the ladies walked away. Andrew wondered if he should have taken it further.

"I think I'm in love," Rachel said when they were out of earshot.

"The Japanese guy?"

"Yeah, right. The one with the arms and shoulders, dude. That was Andrew Fletcher, the rock star. What a dreamboat."

"From the Rockin' Rebels? That was my mom's favorite band. I knew I'd seen him before. But he didn't look old enough. Guy would have to be 40, anyway. You sure?"

"Why do you think I couldn't even talk? He's famous. And a zillionaire, owns his own record company now. And he noticed you."

"You think so?"

"He noticed you."

"Think I should have hauled him back in the tent, offered him a ride and a rasher? A bit of the bold thing?"

"A hammer job? An Irish marathon?"

"Fucked him blind?"

"Such a mouth, on a sweet pusheen like you, I'm shocked. Is that how they taught you to speak in that fine English finishing school?"

"Aye, I got finished in school. And watch who you're calling a shoneen, jewel. So you don't think he's a smuggler, a jinny-ass?"

"Aye, he dresses like a queen. That velvet! I wish I had a dress in it."

"The velvet and the tights."

"Sizin' up the langer on that article, were you?

They both laughed.

"But no, not the way he looked at you, alanna. That was serious. They're all dressed up funny here today, aren't they? It's all for show. And he wanted you to have the big blade. None of this 'What's a delicate creature like you want with the likes o' that?' You should go back and get his number, ionuin. He'd keep you up nights, he would. And pay your rent, too.

"Are you peddling me in the streets, now?"

"Oh, pardon me. I forgot we was dining on the fancier side of the alley tonight. Could have afforded to give you the blade for free, that one."

"And why would he? He'll pay his friend half, as it is; I think that's all the favor I want right now. Anyway, an article like that'll already have a lady."

"Did. And she died, didn't she?"

"Did she?"

"It was in all the papers, jewel."

"Well, I've got his friend's number."

"Oh, aye. That's good, then."

The one carrying the heavy blade in its new leather scabbard punched her in the shoulder, and they both laughed again, They broke into a trot as they dashed past a band of Roman centurions, kicking up dust, sweat-stained and dragging ass after a measly half-hour of mock battle — made you wonder how their ancestors had gone at it four and five hours at a whack.

"That one saw you," Hideki told his old friend as the girls strode away, joking and punching one another, the fragrance of harpsichords and dulcimers and vanilla wafting in their wake.

"Saw me shoot? I had the mask on."

"No, not that. She marked you. She means to see you again."

"Doubt that. It's a big world."

"Maybe so. But you remember I told you. If that one finds you again, she'll give you cause to remember."

"Good or bad?"

"Who can tell? But we'll hear from her again. And from that sword. Only one like it I ever made. What did she say her name was?"

"Madison," Andrew answered. And then Hideki gave him a sly smile.

"What, because I remembered her name? So?"

Shortly, the little Capucin monkey in the red satin outfit came bounding across the grass, an escapee avoiding pursuit.

Without a moment's hesitation he scrambled up Andrew's leg like he was a tree trunk and took up residence on his shield-side shoulder, hissing and baring his teeth at anyone who tried to remove him.

The creature had sharp little claws.

Andrew talked to him like an old friend, offered him some pieces of apple that Hideki obligingly sliced off for him. Finally his owner came over to negotiate; promised he wouldn't have to pass the cup anymore if he'd come home for supper. The small creature cackled once or twice, giving him a piece of his mind, before scrambling down. He came back to shake Andrew's hand, then loped away with considerable dignity.

A modern jet, flaps down for landing and painted an unlikely red and blue, came drifting along the fence line on final approach. Its inability to be heard over the ambient hubbub of the fair gave it the appearance of a giant balloon being pulled past by a child too short to be seen and almost ready for his nap.

Sitting on a fence rail in the foreground, a tonsured medieval monk in a brown cassock completed the fracture of the time continuum as he turned to give the apparition a casual glance, puffing on a technically illegal filter cigarette.

As they folded the tent and carted Hideki's wares back to his van on a little wagon, someone set off a black-powder cannon in celebration of today's victories in the arena. The shock wave set off three separate car alarms in the parking lot of the McDonald's across the street.

On their last trip out to the van the full moon was rising in the East, just as the sun set in the West. It always worked that way, though it was surprising how few people knew it.

What folks didn't realize here in the tree-lined lands where there were always clouds — what you'd realize only after you'd spent time at sea or among the wide, empty horizons of the desert West, where the nation's main battle for freedom was now being fought — was that the full moon rose in a pale, pastel echo of the sun fading at the opposite end of the sky. It was actually born a bright cantaloupe orange, fading quickly through salmon pink to lemon yellow as it rose, its progress surprisingly swift while there was still the benchmark of the horizon near at hand to measure it against.

Finally — two moonwidths off the horizon — it had reached its traditional ivory, goatcheese color by the time it got noticed by the off-duty medieval peasants, folding their own tents and preparing to steal away into a neon night. A few of the women pointed with their illegal filter cigarettes and oohed and aahed. But the now-vanished colors of the newborn moon remained Andrew's secret. He stored them away in his heart, treasures to be recovered and spent in some future time of need.

SUPRYNOWICZ

CHAPTER 3

We want one class to have a liberal education. We want another class, a very much larger class of necessity, to forgo the privilege of a liberal education and fit themselves to perform specific difficult manual tasks.

— WOODROW WILSON (1856-1924), ADDRESSING A GROUP OF BUSINESSMEN SHORTLY BEFORE THE FIRST WORLD WAR

Give me four years to teach the children and the seed I have sown will never be uprooted.

— VLADIMIR ILYICH LENIN (1870-1924)

When an opponent declares, "I will not come over to your side," I calmly say, "Your child belongs to us already. ..."

— ADOLF HITLER (1889-1945)

A tax-supported, compulsory educational system is the complete model of the totalitarian state.

— ISABEL PATERSON (1886-1961)

They ran half an hour late. Everything had to be pushed back while Tony U re-initialed the operations orders. The SonicNet had to know who was where, in case they met resistance and gunfire broke out.

Hey, it happened.

Tony was now in command, moving up to replace Jerry Westheimer, who was in the hospital — injured in some freak Robin Hood accident at the fairgrounds over the weekend.

Finally all the paperwork passed muster, and they were good to go.

It went down with military precision. It was a thing of beauty.

Two combat vans roared in from opposite directions at exactly 10 a.m., screeching to a halt directly in front of the building. The three-axle moving van, assigned to haul the building contents to the warehouse, came rumbling up behind, careful to park out of the line of fire.

A dozen members of the municipal tax collection Special Units, ponderous in black Kevlar helmets, plastic riot shields and full Navy blue bulletproof armor, stormed out like a double line of circus elephants on parade, accompanied by three excited canine units.

Three men and one of the dogs lumbered up the side alley to cover the rear door. Without bothering to try the lock, the two-man entry team hit the front door with their battering ram, throwing the door inward to land on the floor with a dust-raising bang.

Everyone else poured in, pistols and black combat shotguns at the ready.

Everyone but Tony Ulasewicz. Tony took his time, looking up and down the street, making sure there were no threats to their flanks. Then he sauntered into the building, to find his men ... standing around.

The inside of the building had been stripped to the bare walls. There wasn't so much as a desk or a phone.

Come to think of it, there wasn't even a sign hanging outside. Had they even taken the sign?

"What's up, Tony?"

"Double-check the front door against the address on the warrant," he said. "Call and double-check everything."

Not that it'd do any good. Tony U wasn't new to this. You didn't haul a full unit of men half way across town to bust a building on the wrong goddamned street. He could imagine trying to live that down.

No, he'd double-checked.

This was supposed to be an antiques store, contents estimated at more than a million dollars. And he'd purposely brought his biggest guys. They were no ballerinas, even before they put on their vests and combat boots.

Tony U's standing goal was to make sure the deadbeats saw his guys break or seriously damage stuff valued at more than the overdue tax assessment right before their eyes, before they even got the stuff as far as the trucks. Teach 'em a lesson the old-fashioned way. Let 'em file all the court papers they wanted, after that. To Tony, there was no sweeter sound than the tinkling of broken glass inside a sealed pasteboard box.

"Runners?" Liddy asked.

"Looks like."

Somehow the deadbeats had gotten word of what was coming. Probably Westheimer had been out here the week before, rubbing their noses in it. He loved to do that.

"Have the canine guys check that back office and the bathrooms. Look for paper with anything written on it."

But this had all the signs of a dry hole. He checked his clipboard. A briar patch of holding companies, with a margin note that said "Fletcher Group?" Enough to keep the lawyers busy for years.

One of the guys took his dog out front to pee the fire hydrant. Tony wandered out behind him, pausing to enjoy the sunshine. Out on the sidewalk, a little Chinese kid on crutches was watching everything, eyes wide.

"Know where they went?" Tony asked him.

"Who, sir?"

Polite kid.

"The people who ran this antiques store."

The kid looked in through the window at all of the empty, as though it was just sinking in.

"No," the kid said. "But he'll probably be back in touch."

That was weird.

"Hey, Tony." It was Liddy again.

"Yeah?"

"Anyplace good around here for lunch?"

❖ ❖ ❖

STILL OCTOBER ...

Jean-Claude Renaud fought in three wars for three armies on three continents in three decades. Then he grew his hair out and retired.

A soldier of fortune generally doesn't find it easy to save money. But the European welfare states were good about sending Jean-Claude his small pension checks. And his grandfather had taught him from an early age to send some modest part of his pay to the family banker in Switzerland, with instructions to invest it in nothing but rifle factories, gold coins, and gold-mining shares.

When the American dollar and the Japanese yen plummeted to the worth of inflated toilet paper, those who held gold in lieu of being lured into dollar- and yen-denominated securities with the ever-renewed (and ever more desperate) promises of that "Bull Market Right Around the Corner" found themselves the equivalent of one-eyed men in the land of the blind.

It didn't matter so much whether their holdings had increased in value — though in fact they had, through the mechanism of increased demand for a limited product. The point was simply that, faced with 400 percent paper-money inflation, someone who started with a dollar-denominated $8,000 might now have $10,000 — a lovely 25 percent return on paper — but would find that sum now commanded a buying power of only $2,500. While someone who started with 20 ounces of gold worth $8,000 still had 20 ounces of gold ... now valued on paper at $32,000.

And that was just the bullion. Jean-Claude had also bought mining stocks, which tended to go up in multiples of the bullion price as desperate investors, watching their paper securities disappear down the drain, raced to the shelter of precious metals no matter what the price.

Jean-Claude was still not wealthy, by the measure of the kind of people who owned mansions and yachts. But he had plenty for his simple needs — and to buy a piece of land.

And by then he had met his Louise — a tall, slim, simple country girl given to long skirts and sweaters who had wanted precisely what he wanted, to marry and move out into the woods and live a simple life and have babies.

They had bought the old cabin in the wooded hills far above the tony beach towns of southern California, up a dirt road on a parcel of land surrounded on three sides by state and national parks. Well, they were called "parks," though in fact they were little but an impenetrable maze of trees, thorns and underbrush allowed to go rampant. A people who had built a nation by "taming the wilderness" now believed the rights of toads and mosquitoes to be left undisturbed trumped the need for human housing, even overruling the obvious need to clear dead brush from a forest to reduce the chance of fire.

But the isolation suited Louise and Jean-Claude just fine. Some of his old service buddies had settled down the coast not far away, and would occasionally come to visit and practice their shooting — which drove the park rangers crazy, of course, though it was still perfectly legal on private land.

The Men in Green sicked every kind of zoning code enforcement team they could find onto Jean-Claude, contending he was running some kind of "militia compound." (Ironically, of course, militia practice was the specific reason cited in the Bill of Rights for guaranteeing every American the right to own and carry around their military arms.) They claimed the old wooden pipe which had been there when he bought the property — bringing water to the house from a nearby waterfall — constituted an "illegal and non-permitted water system." The authorities checked, determined it was a permitted "grandfathered" use which pre-dated any such regulations. Told the parks guys to go hump sand.

Jean-Claude proceeded to improve the house and property by his own handiwork, adding an upstairs loft bedroom, a solar-heated shower fed by the aforementioned old wooden pipeline run downhill from the waterfall — and, when the first baby boy arrived, a nursery.

Louise kept a kitchen garden. In the mornings, she would carry the baby out with her and leave him to play on a blanket as she pulled the weeds from the dew-softened ground. The birds sang. Animals as large as raccoons and skunks would sit at the edge of the woods and watch Louise work, staring in fascination as she hummed softly in her contentment, a scene out of some old Disney cartoon. Their friends warned them they should fence the garden, or her little "friends" would clean them out. But Louise didn't mind sharing, and it wasn't as though they really needed to raise any huge crop to subsist.

By the end of the first year the raccoons would come within her arm's reach, and she knew them by name. They left her herbs and most of her flowers alone, and if they helped themselves to some of the tomatoes and the maize ... well, it was an arid climate; Louise's sparse vegetable crop wouldn't have fed them many meals, anyway.

Jean-Claude promised to build her some sluice ditches so she could irrigate with stream water the following year. She even said she'd let him fence part of the plot next spring — finally agreeing with a laugh like falling water that "sharing" didn't mean you had to let them eat *all* the squash the day before it was ripe.

They were very happy.

Then they noticed the new antenna arrays being erected on the national park property. The area, it turned out, was perfectly sited to receive data from the Pacific Missile Test Range. It seemed like a strange use for park lands — no private company would have been allowed to build such structures without a decade of fights over "environmental and endangered species impact" — but Jean-Claude didn't much care. He figured if he left them alone, they'd leave him alone.

And that, of course, is the very thing the modern state cannot bring itself to do. No one can be left alone. "Quiet enjoyment of one's property" might as well be a fading inscription carved in the hieroglyphs of some long-lost jungle temple.

The parks people approached Jean-Claude on several occasions, asking him to sell his property. Seems they just couldn't stand to look at their maps and see that incursion of private land into their delightful green blob. It represented the cancer of capitalism. These people drove an *internal combustion engine*. They ate *meat*. And they were *breeding*.

Jean-Claude said he had chosen the site carefully, and he liked it just fine; no thanks.

How large a role the National Security Agency and NASA's Rocket Propulsion Laboratories played in what happened next, no one was ever sure. At least, no one who was talking.

Stymied in their attempt to buy the Renaud property, the parks agencies hit on an alternative plan. Contending an officer had seen "marijuana plants growing under the trees" during a drug-seeking overflight (though they were unable to produce any photos, which would normally have accompanied the request for a warrant), 30 agents from various jurisdictions gathered quietly outside the locked gate to the Renaud homestead in the morning mists of Wednesday, Oct. 16, 2030.

Of the 30 law enforcement officers present, 13 were from the Los Angeles Sheriff's Department, five from the Los Angeles Police Department canine unit, three from the National Guard, three from the National Park Service, two from the U.S. Forest Service, two from the California Bureau of Narcotic Enforcement (BNE), and two from the federal Drug Enforcement Administration. Also present were two "researchers" from the Rocket Propulsion Laboratories (RPL) in Pasadena. Two of the Los Angeles Sheriffs deputies were from the asset forfeiture unit.

After cackling over the maps of the 200 acres of prime land they were told they'd be able to grab under federal asset seizure laws should they find as few as 14 marijuana plants, this mismatched gang — only the park and forest rangers wearing any recognizable "uniforms" — cut the chain on the gate with bolt-cutters and raced the half-mile up the dirt drive to the ranch, complete with police dogs.

(The lead investigating officer — Los Angeles County Sheriff's Office narcotics detective Gary Daumer — would get a cash percentage of the total value if the land could be seized.)

Louise Renaud was out in her garden, a short distance from her infant son, who only occasionally uttered a matching rhythmic noise as he pounded his wooden toy onto the blanket. The child was blond. He would grow up to look like his father, she knew.

Jean-Claude had wide cheekbones. His eyes were either blue or gray — just when she'd made up her mind, they always seemed to change again. But the strong chin was probably his most prominent feature. It had that deep dimple in the middle.

His long hair was sandy blond and he nearly always managed to look like he'd just started re-growing his beard a week before.

Jean-Claude's son was a contented child, bright and curious about the world around him, rarely fretful. She was so happy they'd found a place where he could be raised away from the terrors of the city.

There were cucumbers ready to pick — but maybe she'd leave them till afternoon, pick them for their salad. An early morning bee buzzed sleepily in the rosemary. If she closed her eyes and took deep breaths, she could identify most of her herbs, even from 10 feet away. The rosemary, the mint, the thyme ... even the basil. So different from the pale gray powders, a year in the bottle, that commanded such enormous prices down at the store.

Something was moving down by the driveway. One of the raccoons? Had the dog scared up a bear? Then she realized with alarm that there were too many footsteps, pounding too fast. Running. Deer being chased up the drive by dogs? No. The puppy was in the house with Jean-Claude. She did hear a dog bark — a strange dog — but there were also men, lots of men.

She didn't have to stop to wonder if that was good; it couldn't be good. Jean-Claude kept the gate chained and locked — friends called ahead or at least honked to let you know they were coming.

She yelled Jean-Claude's name — he was taking his morning shower in anticipation of the arrival of three friends for a morning of shooting — as she ran to pick up the child and rush him inside. She heard the shower turn off, so she yelled again, her voice rising in pitch. The house, which had always seemed so close, suddenly felt an enormous distance away. Jean-Claude insisted they carry a gun whenever they went into the deep woods — Louise felt silly about it but agreed because of the child, for she knew there were cougars — but she had always scoffed at the idea of going armed to her own garden. After all, this was no longer the Wild West.

But now dozens of strange men in plaid shirts and blue-jeans and brandishing guns — there were no badges or warrants in evidence, so she knew these must be criminal invaders of some kind — came swarming up the drive, shouting things in hoarse voices which she could not understand.

She screamed for Jean-Claude one last time as she turned her back on the approaching gunmen and bent over to pick up her child. But the infant was playing with a piece of his dad's woodworking equipment — an old wooden plane from which the blade had been removed. Not familiar with the object, an agent behind Louise later testified the woman had disobeyed their shouted direct orders to freeze and raise her hands, that he believed at that point he was dealing with a drug plantation guard who had stooped over to pick up her gun. Two agents opened fire, hitting both mother and child with several rounds of softpoint .40 Smith and a single round — the killer — of .223.

Jean-Claude Renaud, still naked from his shower, grabbed an antique cap-and-ball pistol as the closest thing to hand as he heard the gunshots and came running out of the house in answer to his wife's screams.

His golden retriever, an overgrown year-old pup with huge paws, came with him. Reading his master's unmistakable emotions, he was up to top speed in seconds, fangs bared, snarling and charging for the invaders.

The dog had launched himself at the throat of the nearest officer, was already in mid-air, when they opened fire. They hit him at least once in the spine. His momentum knocked down the nearest attacker, but the pooch was only able to slash a single four-inch gouge in the left shoulder before hitting the ground with a thump. The cop crabbed away on his back, firing into the dog, which was still dragging himself forward with his forepaws, growling, when he died.

They shot Jean-Claude, too, as he tried to run to his wife. Louise dropped first to her knees among the cucumber vines, then flat onto her stomach, clutching her screaming child to her breast, turning part way to the side to protect him as she fell.

Louise heard a droning sound in her ears. She had disturbed a little honeybee amongst the last of the season's star-shaped yellow cucumber blossoms. But the bee did not try to sting her, for the little worker had grown accustomed to the larger creature's presence there, did not regard the slow-moving woman as a threat to herself or the hive.

The cucumber blossoms were beautiful. She hoped Jean-Claude remembered to pick the cukes now, at their most tender. She reached out to stroke her son's golden hair. Why was he shrieking so? He had never been a fretful child. And why was there so much blood? She had never seen so much blood. Where could it all be coming from?

A photograph of two of the plainclothes cops (County Sheriff's Deputy John L. Bean, Jr. and Los Angeles County Sheriff's Office narcotics Detective Gary R. Daumer, also identified by government investigators as the shooters) later displayed on a New Columbian Web site, showed the two men smiling and pretending to blow smoke from their gun barrels as they stood, each with a foot on one of the shoulders of the very recently dead Louise Renaud. (She was struck in the throat, completely blowing out her carotid artery. Brain death under such circumstances takes less than two minutes.) Though out of focus, in the background Jean-Claude can be seen, kneeling on the ground with his hands cuffed behind his back, as agents kick out several of his teeth while demanding to know "where the fucking pot is."

About 10 minutes after the raid began, Jean-Claude's service buddies Quart Low Cavanaugh and Airburst Barnes, along with a mutual friend from back east, former Australian Army medic Dr. Helmut Stauffer, arrived at the Renauds' front gate for their scheduled morning of shooting. Spotting no fewer than 10 official police vehicles from such a wide array of agencies — parked and empty at the front gate, which hung ajar with its chain bearing a shiny new silver cut-through — they feared the worst.

"You gentlemen should probably wait out here," volunteered Quart Low, as he dug his M-1A out of its soft black case, chambered a round, engaged the safety, and checked his extra magazines. "But it looks to me like Jean-Claude and Louise are in trouble. He's told me before how these guys want to grab his land; I don't have much doubt that's what they're up to, probably in there planting drugs on him or something. So I'm going in, and I'm going in armed, and if you guys want to turn around and walk out, no one'll mention you were here; there's no need for you to be a part of this."

Quart Low had still been called "charming" by ladies 20 years his junior. The leprechaun twinkle in his eyes, probably. But his close-cropped hair — more like peach fuzz, really — had turned almost entirely from from red to silver, now.

"I thought we came out here for some shootin'," answered Airburst Barnes, moving his five-shot Smith belly gun up to the dashboard and pulling out his own rifle, a heavy-barrelled .308 built on one of the old hammer-forged receivers from LRB on Long Island. Where Quart Low had kept his military haircut, Airburst had gone in the opposite direction, now sporting a full white beard and glossy, slightly wavy locks cascading well down over his collar. Many a child had mistaken him for Santa Claus, despite the lack of any appreciable paunch on his six-foot, three-inch frame. "I'm in."

"Helmut?"

"Well, yes, I would love to help, of course, but with these American rifles, I'm not sure how useful —"

"Actually, we brought a FAL for you."

"A FAL?"

"A Sturmgewehr-58."

"With the Steyr barrel?"

"Yep." Quart Low pulled it out for the visiting doctor's inspection, careful not to cover anyone with the muzzle.

The Belgian-designed .308-caliber FN-FAL, with its distinctive pistol grip, had been manufactured under license in a number of NATO countries. The Austrian version was designated the Sturmgewehr-58, for its year of adoption. The one Quart Low now handed the good doctor had been stripped down to parts in Austria, whereupon its receiver had been destroyed with a welding torch. Then, under America's wise and sensible federal gun-control regime, the parts had been shipped to America and reassembled on a Brazilian receiver, which made the whole thing perfectly legal. Had the original rifle simply been imported intact, of course, everyone involved would have gone to prison. This apparently made sense, if you were a member of Congress.

"Well, then. This is different," Stauffer said, cranking down the rear sight to point blank range on the superior Austrian version of the Fusil Automatique Legere, and joining them in setting out full 20-round magazines where they could reach them.

They were about to barrel up the drive when Airburst had a thought. "Wait a minute. If we leave your truck here outside the gate, and take one of these police carpool vans, they'll think it's more of their own guys comin' in, give us an element of surprise. Then on the way out, we can park their van to block the exit, get clean away in yours. That way, nobody will have seen your vehicle or your plates."

Sure enough, they found the keys tucked under the sun visor of one of the cops' Suburban Assault Vehicles.

Crunching up the driveway at medium speed, they found no one paid them any attention. What had happened was clear enough. Jean-Claude was down on his knees just outside his front door, wet and stark naked, his hands cuffed behind him and blood still oozing from a nasty gunshot wound to the shoulder as two interrogators punctuated their questions by kicking out several of his teeth in a spray of saliva and blood. Over by the garden, the unit photographer was taking trophy photos of two of their proud shooters, each with one foot resting on Louise's still-warm body. (Yes, it seemed hard to believe. But FBI agents had done precisely the same thing atop the cremated corpses of the women and children at Waco. And German soldiers had sent home thousands of such photos — smiling Wehrmacht enlisted men each posed with one foot on the corpses of dead, unarmed civilian Jews, Gypsies, and Slavs — as they moved through Eastern Europe in the early 1940s. The instinct to claim a trophy from a successful hunt seems to have been hard-wired down through the millennia. In this regard, about the only good thing to be said about photography is that it has largely supplanted the practice of cutting off body parts.)

The Renauds' infant son, also shot, lay still on the ground where Louise had tried to shelter him with her own body as she went down.

Airburst Barnes from the front seat and Dr. Stauffer from the rear with the STG-58 opened up with softpoint .308 as they drove past. Only seven or eight of the original 32 attacking officers were in plain sight. The rest were apparently out scouting around, looking for the phantom marijuana plants which the park rangers had claimed they could see growing under the trees. (Not a single stem of marijuana was ever found.)

The cops were carrying nothing of anywhere near the power of these full-sized, semi-automatic battle rifles. Within seconds two government men were down and five others had beat a hasty retreat, firing scattered rounds over their shoulders as they fled. Airburst jumped out, frisked Jean-Claude's two dead torturers for their handcuff keys, and released his friend. He started to lead Jean-Claude, still naked and bleeding, toward the back seat of the van. But Jean-Claude wasn't having any of that. He broke away and ran to his wife, kneeling beside her, pulling her still-warm body up into his arms.

"Honey? Honey?" He smoothed her hair, searched her face for any sign of life, put his ear to her lips to see if she was breathing.

"I am sorry," said Dr. Stauffer, as soothingly as he could. He'd already done all the cursory examination that was necessary. "They have shot away her throat and carotid artery. There is no pulse. I understand it's hard, but even if we were at the hospital, there is nothing I could do for her. All we can do now is get you and the child away from here as quickly as possible. She would want you to save the child. Here: hold your son. Quartlow, you need to get me my bag from the back; I'm afraid this is very serious."

"No!" Jean-Claude grabbed the doctor's rifle, leapt to his feet and scanned the horizon, looking for someone to kill. But then he stumbled to one knee, barely conscious himself — the blood loss from the gunshot wound now abetted by having several teeth knocked out. He let out one more incoherent bellow, like a large animal in its death throes, and sagged to the ground, cutting his elbows on the large wood chips Louise had used as garden mulch as he still tried to crawl forward toward their tormentors.

The nakedness of his well-tanned body revealed the white jagged scars of a half-dozen combat wounds long since stitched, healed, and forgotten. The garden around him smelled of rosemary and fresh tomatoes. No birds sang.

With Airburst's help they got Jean-Claude under the armpits and managed to wrangle him, the badly injured baby, and their long guns all back to the vehicle. Quart Low Canavaugh could still move surprisingly quickly over short stretches, despite his stiff-legged gait. Too many broken kneecaps and dugout bullets over a long career of jumping out of perfectly good speedboats and airplanes in the service of the United States Navy.

By now they were under fire again. The cops regrouped and began to pepper their borrowed government vehicle with

9mm slugs that sounded like heavy hailstones as they hit. Quart Low got the vehicle in gear and skidded through as fast a U-turn as he could manage.

As badly off as Jean-Claude was, the doctor ignored him and spent all his efforts trying to stop the blood loss from the child. The single round of .223, after penetrating the mother's throat, had carved a wound cavity in the infant that might have been survivable in an adult. But in a child that small, it had simply torn away too much of the chest.

Down at the gate, Quart Low skidded the vehicle side-ways between the gate posts to block the exit for any pursuers. (It would also slow down access for any ambulance, but no ambulance was going to do Louise any good, now.) As they jumped out, he took the big SAV's keys and distributor cap with him for good measure.

The five of them transferred back into Quart Low's vehicle — Quart Low hobbling pretty good by now — and made a clean getaway.

Jean-Claude's first and only child died before they could get him down the hill to a hospital. They buried him high in the forest to keep him out of the hands of the government jackals that had killed him.

As it was, the cops tried to claim Louise had been shot by Jean-Claude's dangerous militia buddies during their "ambush and counterattack." When the cops refused to release the results of their ballistic tests, however, the public quickly figured that one out. And then, of course, the "trophy" police photographs of the triumphant hunters posing with their feet on Louise's corpse surfaced on the Web.

Ventura County District Attorney Michael Herbert, af-ter a six-month investigation into the Louise Renaud killing, concluded a voluminous report by branding the fatal raid "a land grab by the (L.A.) Sheriffs Office." He confirmed the odd fact that "Two researchers from Rocket Propulsion Laborato-ries in Pasadena" were also present for the so-called drug raid, and asked in his conclusion, "Did the National Park Service orchestrate the investigation or killing in order to obtain the land?"

Not a single marijuana seed or stem was ever found: "All they had to show for their trouble was the body of a dead young wife and mother on the ground by her garden," reported the Los Angeles Times.

The multiple government agencies ended up settling a wrongful death suit filed by Louise's parents for N$5 million.

A year later, parks personnel refused to allow fire engines to enter the property to dig a firebreak. County firefighters later testified with tears in their eyes that they'd arrived in plenty of time to dig a firebreak which would probably have kept the blaze away from the ranch, but the National Parks representative denied the firemen permission to do so, since "It violates our rules to disturb the natural beauty of the land."

The cabin Louise and Jean-Claude had loved — so much of which he had built with his own hands — burned to the ground.

No officers were ever charged in Louise Renaud's death.

⚜ ⚜ ⚜

Helmut Stauffer nursed Jean-Claude back to health — well, physical health — in a remote fishing cabin that Airburst Barnes maintained not far from the little town of Bishop, high in the Sierras. The air was so clear you could see a hundred miles, the rock faces standing out in red and blue and brown, etched in textures as sharp as an old Maxfield Parrish print. They could look down on the rainstorms as they moved up the valleys, distant lightning strikes cleaving the pearl and purple clouds.

The air was so clear that the rain and lightning actually

had their own smells. The rain smelled sweet, like new-mown grass, like the mint and thyme in Louise's little garden. And the lightning created a sharp tang in your nose that was not unpleasant, stinging slightly of ozone and iodine.

Airburst and Quart Low had both seen men die. Both had suffered losses in their time. But nothing to rival the sheer insane evil that their old friend Jean-Claude had just experienced. They sat with him, walked with him, fed the fire in the cabin's old fieldstone fireplace, careful not to say they understood ... for they had seen enough summers to realize they could never understand.

Who could understand the cruelty men would inflict on the innocent in the name of "law and order" — afterwards posing and smiling and handing each other promotions and awards?

It might have been better if Jean-Claude had yelled and screamed and tried to tear down the rock fireplace with his bare hands. They'd seen all that.

Instead, he moved like a ghost, as though each step, even a turn of his head, took a deliberate effort of the will, required careful concentration.

When he was able to talk at all, he talked of Louise's love for their child, for her garden, for the animals. The way her hair would shine in the morning sun. And every time he saw something move out of the corner of his eye he would jerk his head around, expecting it to be Louise, bringing him something she had found outside, a bird's feather, an oddly shaped stone, or — if it was a movement down near the floor — their son, crawling someplace where he might get into harm's way.

His intellect knew they were gone, but his senses had not adjusted — could not possibly adjust — so quickly. Every time he woke up he reached out, found no one next to him, wondered what could be wrong that had led Louise to get up so early. Was she sick? Was the child sick? Would he find her in the kitchen, stirring a cup of coffee?

And then he had to remind himself, all over again.

Yet there in that place, for all Jean-Claude's pain, it was hard not to sense the hand of God in the diaphanous curtains of distant rain, suspended beneath the dark pregnant bellies of the mother-of-pearl clouds, backlit by a golden sun.

Was this a God who simply did not care? Or was there some terrible hidden purpose here, beyond what any of them could comprehend?

Jean-Claude's gunshot wound was not life threatening once the .223 slug was removed and the immediate risk of infection was past. What they did not have access to, however, was any proper amalgam to create for him a new and aesthetically pleasing front tooth. Fortunately, Quart Low Cavanaugh had graduated Johns Hopkins as a dentist, long before the Navy discovered he could swim with a knife in his teeth. In fact, they'd recruited him as a killer precisely because he was a tooth fairy, a trained professional who could blithely spend an afternoon cracking wisdom teeth out of the mouths of anaesthetized young recruits, competing with the guy across the hall to see who could wear out his chisel first.

But that was a whole 'nother story.

In the end, Airburst donated an old $10 eagle to the cause, and between them Quart Low Cavanaugh and Helmut Stauffer crafted Jean-Claude's temporary replacement teeth the way it would have been done a century before — out of 90 percent gold.

They walked the high ridges. Jean-Claude had always had a fear of heights, so it worried them a little, the way he now prowled the cliff-edges like a mountain goat. They decided never to let him go alone — though given that he could cover ground at twice their pace, the notion that either of these old-timers could keep him from harm by puffing along 50 yards behind was touching, at best.

They lived on wild asparagus and jerky and little spotted native trout from the stream and heavy sweet Paiute bread that Quart Low hauled from the Dutch bakery in Bishop. It would have been an interlude in paradise, in happier times. But the nights were already cold enough to form a disc of ice atop the left-over coffee in their mugs if they set them down for long — they couldn't stay any longer without proper provision for the winter.

They were startlingly beautiful, but these were not casual mountains; they were serious, life-and-death mountains. The three of them were lucky the passes hadn't snowed in already.

Initially it had seemed their best options were either to head down to Old Mexico or else to offer their services to the forces of New Columbia, currently fighting the much-degraded U.S. Army to a standstill in Montana and Wyoming.

Jean-Claude favored a more direct and personal form of retribution, back in L.A. County. At first all his plans started with him driving his pickup at high speed through somebody's plate glass window. Then, over time, he spoke less of specifics, and spent more time disassembling and cleaning the rifles.

Oddly enough, it was their visitor, Helmut Stauffer, who finally offered the plan.

"They will be looking for us in either of those directions. By now they will know Airburst and Quart Low have not been around, and they will start putting two and two together. You know, when I left Gotham to come here, it was only as a stop-over. I had planned to join some members of my family who are still in Australia, since I can no longer openly practice my profession in this country.

"But if Jean-Claude wishes to fight, let me make a suggestion. In Gotham City lives a rather wealthy man — quite wealthy, I think — who helped fund my defense through the courts. Where, as you know, I actually won an acquittal from my jury ... much good that turned out to do me.

"No one will expect us to go there, especially by car. And if we take turns driving, we can be there in, what, three or four days? Let us see if my benefactor will finance our efforts, and perhaps suggest a line of action where we may be able to do more than just take out a few secretaries and desk clerks, before dying in a shoot-out with some pathetic rent-a-cop."

"And what is this mysterious benefactor's name?" Jean-Claude asked.

"I promised not to tell anyone about his generosity. But if you will agree to come meet him, then of course you will learn his name."

True to his word, it was not until they arrived back in Gotham and he had contacted his old friend that Dr. Stauffer told the others the name of the man he hoped would help them find a way to channel their anger as well as their talents — or, all else failing, fund a new start for all of them in another, freer land:

Andrew Fletcher.

⚜ ⚜ ⚜

THE NEXT YEAR: FEBRUARY, 2031 ...

Jack Brackley would have preferred to go into the Army, like his dad. He had his doubts about the War in the West — those people were far away, and they could go live however they wanted as far as he was concerned. The argument that they just didn't want to pay for their government services didn't make much sense, since they obviously didn't *want* any of New Washington's so-called "services," most of which seemed to involve sending them back some reduced portion of their own tax payments, with a whole bunch of new strings attached.

The argument that a divided country would no longer be the world's unrivaled superpower made more sense ... if you really enjoyed knowing your country was feared and hated from Lima to Liberia.

But his dad had served, and he felt like it was the least he could do. Sure beat sitting in college reading ancient poetry about fields and trees while other guys were out changing the world.

His dream had been to serve in his dad's old unit. But his uncle ran the family now. His uncle had been good to Jack, never made him do without. So he figured he owed his uncle. Everyone said the smart thing to do was to listen to the voice of experience. And his uncle said the Army was a dead end, especially with the War in the West going the way it was. War was expensive and dangerous ... especially when half the stuff turned out not to work when it finally arrived at the front.

No, the thing to do was to sign up with the Homeland Defense Special Forces, better known as the Lightning Squads, his Uncle Dan had said. They were actually more elite than the Army — more selective. The lightning slashes carried a lot of prestige, and prestige was what would be important in his future career, Uncle Dan insisted. Plus, you were less likely to come home with a leg blown off. Uncle Dan always tried to take the long view.

Besides, even though the Grays were technically under federal control, they essentially became the personal bodyguard of any local politician who wielded the kind of political power his Uncle Dan did. Promotion, he was told with a smile, would not be a problem.

So Jack had joined the Grays. Though so far, that "elite" part largely escaped him.

Oh, morale was high. This bunch was rarin' to go kick some rebel ass. But it struck Jack it was a lot easier to talk the big talk when you knew you'd spend tomorrow guarding the airport, or busting some poor mom for not getting her kids their shots, than if you knew you were gonna be out patrolling some God-forsaken ridge in Wyoming, where the enemy snipers could hit from 800 yards — closer to a mile with their damned .50-cals — rendering a grunt's life expectancy in Indian Country something short of 100 days.

Jack had taken his usual share of ribbing about being the mayor's nephew. Of course, that also meant he was the son of the late Tom Brackley, hero of the Battle of Denver. So that was OK. Mostly, it turned out the guys expected he'd be getting some kind of special white-glove treatment. When it turned out he was a regular guy, not some kind of snitch, that he insisted on pulling his share of KP and all the other shit details, things smoothed out pretty good.

Except that guy Judson, who had kept on his case in Basic. Jack had tried to laugh it off for days, especially since the guy was actually smaller than he was. Was it true most bullies were small? Finally Jack just beat the shit out of him, put him in the hospital with quite a few things broke. Judson had quietly been transferred out and that had been the end of that.

After that, Jack Brackley had done real well in training. OK, some of it was a little weird: the late afternoon slide shows that the guys took to calling "Blood and Gore, I Want Some More" — 30 minutes of full-color dead-terrorist-blown-apart crime scene photos always followed by pizza and beer and a busload of Ladies of Easy Acquaintance, some second-rate psychologist's idea of "desensitizing the troops to images of violence."

But Jack liked the physical training part of it, the running and the obstacle courses and helping whip the other guys into believing they could do it, too. That part just came natural.

Jack Brackley was pretty big. He had smiling blue eyes, a smooth broad dome of a forehead, and brown hair sun-bleached to blond at the top. No one was ever likely to call him a pretty boy — maybe "ruggedly handsome."

He'd been nominated for officer training after basic, though he suspected that was because of his name. So he said he'd rather see some action first; come talk to me again next year.

And so he'd found himself assigned to Gotham's new

SonicNet. The latest and greatest, everybody said.

In fact, he was starting to have some doubts about the whole crew here.

The new Homeland Security headquarters on the east side of midtown Gotham — better known as SonicNet HQ — was an impressive eight-story edifice. Its blast-proof golden windows added to the impression of inscrutable power, reflecting the light and allowing no mere mortal to glimpse what was going on inside — the same effect that state troopers got by hiding their eyes behind mirrored shades, making them look like huge predatory beetles.

Of course, the place was headquarters for a whole lot more than the SonicNet. This was also regional security and interrogation headquarters — you weren't even supposed to ask what happened to people who got taken up to the seventh floor — and this was also the regional nerve center of the Total Information Awareness Program.

Thanks to the TIA, basically no one in this city could do anything that involved an electronic transaction — e-mail, a phone call, a credit card purchase, even an ATM withdrawal — without Big Brother taking notice. And the nerve center was right here.

That kind of power could go to your head. Jack decided to keep quiet and learn what he could.

Today, Biff Harder was finishing up his orientation on the Net monitoring screens.

"Afternoons used to be dead time here," Biff was explaining. "Now they're picking up, which is great."

More activity meant more people needed on the afternoon shift, which meant Biff got to spend more time at night with his wife Darla and his three-year-old daughter Cindy.

In the old days, most of the work monitoring the Violence Intel and Sensing Array — better known as the SonicNet, since "VISA" was already taken — had been concentrated in the early morning hours, Biff explained. That was when the SWAT teams staged most of their raids on the city's remaining criminal element, and when those remaining criminals, of course, also favored committing their crimes.

The job of the monitors seemed simple enough when it was explained to the visiting schoolkids, though of course there was a lot more nuance to doing the job — spotting a bogey quickly enough to save someone's life — than might be apparent at first glance.

Whenever a firearm was discharged — or any substantial chemical explosion occurred — almost anywhere in the city, the sensitive combination of sonic sensors and chemical sniffers which now covered the city in an intricate gridwork started a red flasher on Biff's screen — or the screen of one of the 77 other monitors who could conceivably be on duty at peak hours.

The operator could then toggle through any of the street-corner video cameras in range, looking for an image that would show what was going on.

Meantime, the automated computers quickly went to work, cross-indexing that event against the mission plans filed by police agencies staging SWAT raids at that time, along with the occasional legitimate blasting operations to dig trenching for new water mains and so forth.

Officers on the beat also carried weapons nowadays which would quickly send coded telemetry to the sensors, verifying that the perp, resister or shaker who had just been downed was a righteous police shooting.

In all these cases, the red flashers would quickly change to green — legitimate shootings.

The machines were also supposed to be able to discern and identify trucks backfiring, sonic booms from aircraft, and all kinds of other miscellaneous industrial clutter, showing those noise sources as whites — neither red nor green.

Needless to say, this didn't always work, and the biggest open secret around here was that the techs were continually mounting new screening software so they wouldn't keep sending out so many units to arrest some poor nudge with a jackhammer which the SonicNet insisted was a terrorist with a 30-caliber machine gun.

The gift of the skilled operator was to be able to judge as quickly as possible when a red flasher was NOT shifting to green or white quickly enough, indicating the unauthorized use of an illegal, unregistered weapon ... while developing almost a sixth sense about false alarms.

Just now, for instance, a telltale rash of flashers — indicating flashbang grenades deployed at the beginning of one of the increasingly common afternoon SWAT raids — shifted quickly from red to green as the computer matched them to a properly filed police tactical plan. This was followed quickly by a brief rash of gunfire. Officers disarming and canceling resisters ... or bad guys making a last stand, which could demand a quick deployment of back-up units?

Biff toggled to the best video image — the sensors automatically zooming and centering the camera on the motion which that camera hadn't "normalized" based on a weighted score of recorded vehicle or pedestrian traffic — and then to the search warrant: Both showed a Lightning Squad was backing up the black-clad SWAT Team of the borough Child Welfare Department, storming an unregistered, unlicensed child day care center — perhaps even a hotbed of anti-government militia propaganda.

Sure enough, here came the telemetry, properly coded with this day's Operations password — the burst of automatic fire had been entirely from the Grays, with no return fire — everything well in hand.

"A day-care center?" Jack asked.

"Yep."

"Like ... little kids?"

"Don't they cover this in Basic, anymore? It may not sound like it, but an unlicensed day-care center or so-called 'private school' is one of the most dangerous operations we face. If this place wasn't licensed that means these kids probably never got their shots, which means they travel around the city like little Typhoid Marys, threatening to infect your kids and mine. People like this pay no taxes, and given time they teach those kids to hate the government, to hate everything that's good and decent about our civilization. Hell, they hate television. Hearing nothing else all their lives, what chance do they have to grow up as anything but murderers and drug-addicted terrorists?

"Because of what those guys are doing out there today, thousands of other parents who were thinking about saving a little money and taking the easy way out, turning their precious kids over to the religious nuts and the resisters, may think again, and start their kids out on the right path, the path to being decent citizens like you and me."

"Uh ... yeah." Jack sat down at the panel and Biff coached him through the routine process of tracking and logging. Simple. A kid could do it.

Company Leader Delgado came in, looked around, spotted Jack, and came over.

"Good news, Brackley. You've been looking for an assignment to an active duty squad. Well, I've got an opening tomorrow and you're it. Roll call at oh-800, we start running sims in the box house at oh-930, operation starts anytime after noon o'clock."

"What is it, Sarge?"

"Classified, Brackley. But it's a full-fledged op, I can assure you. Plenty of action."

As he left, Jack and Biff looked at each other and nodded. Day care center.

❖ ❖ ❖

It was a semi-detached building right next to a crosswalk that led to an elementary school across the street. Smart. That way the number of little kids coming and going wouldn't attract too much attention. Someone had noticed, though, and called it in to Silent Witness for the anonymized reward.

Everything went pretty much the way they'd practiced it. The Initial Entry Team was four guys stacked on either side of the door — Jack was last on the left — with weapons charged and safeties off. When everybody clicked off "Ready," the Sarge banged three times on the door, shouted, "Police, Warrant!" and then signaled for the four guys on the battering ram to take the door off its hinges.

There was a lot of yelling and shrieking and scrambling inside as they tossed in the disorienting flash-bangs and the eight-man IET poured in right behind. One of the guys over on the right tripped over the heels of the trooper in front of him, put out his hand to break his fall as he went face-down, tripped off a three-round burst from his Heckler & Koch MP-5, managing to put one round through his own left hand.

The rest of the team was scanning the room looking for signs of resistance, watching for pistol or rifle barrels. When they heard the 9mm go off they naturally opened up on everything that moved, just like they had in all the simulation runs. Took less than 15 seconds before everyone inside the place was down.

As the gunfire sputtered out, leaving behind the noise of the brass empties clinking and rolling across the floor, Jack surveyed the main room of the day care center with a certain amount of consternation. None of his guys were hit, that was good. It wasn't clear who'd started firing, but what was clear was that it had not been the occupants of the room; he saw no evidence of a single firearm among the dead and moaning wounded scattered across the floor.

There appeared to have been three caretakers in the large

main room, all overweight young women in casual — make that frumpy — clothes. They'd been in the process of trying to gather about 20 kids under the age of eight or so into groups near the back of the room, whether to protect them or herd them toward the exits or just to get them away from what they knew was coming, Jack couldn't tell.

Jack had never been in a slaughterhouse, so he wasn't prepared for what that much spilled blood actually smelled like. It had a strong, overripe, metallic smell that would have made him want to vomit, if he'd been in the mood to allow himself to feel anything.

Beneath that, the room smelled the way these places always smelled — poster paints and that weird waxy green sawdust they used to sweep the floors. And something else. Tuna fish?

And the room seemed to be overheated. Why did all places that dealt with children seem to keep their thermostats up at about 76 degrees? It was stifling. Probably all the fat women had circulatory disorders from eating too much brown rice and bean curd, or something.

Maybe a third of the occupants of the room appeared to be dead or dying. Most just lay there, moaning. Unlike in the movies or on TV, where people sprayed with subgun fire always lie down and cooperatively die right away, in real life the human body could take quite a few rounds and survive, assuming the victim got some prompt medical attention and hadn't been hit in the brain or a major artery. Months of rehab and, for some, a life of intractable, chronic pain? Sure. But half a dozen dead out of the 20 would be unusually high.

Their training was supposed to get them used to what it looked like, though the slide shows had always featured grown-up dead terrorists on the floor, not little kids.

The bad ones, actually, were the kids who had gone into what appeared to be epileptic seizures after being hit. They thrashed around, their eyes rolled back in their heads, spurting

83

blood and uttering weird buzzing and clicking vocalizations that would haunt Jack's dreams. Not as bad as what Waco and Bennington were supposed to have been like, mind you. Incendiary ferret rounds to set the plywood compounds on fire after you spray in the tear gas in a flammable aerosol, snipers to pick off anyone who tried to leave, fire engines held a mile away from the makeshift crematoriums till all the women and children were done to a crisp; no more terrorist breeding camp.

But right now Jack couldn't be thinking about that. He concentrated on keeping all the emotional stuff well clamped down. That was the kind of self-indulgent crap that got people killed. Focus on those rear doorways. Somebody could come around one of those corners with a rifle blazing any second now. Small comfort to have them write on your tombstone, "But it wasn't very likely." Fuck that. Kill first; feel bad later.

"Bloom, Mahoney, move right, check that opening, looks like the kitchen," ordered Company Leader Delgado. "Brackley, Keller, left wall, see where that corridor leads. Use your clearance drill." The group leader then turned to deal with the back-up squads now entering the room to clear for weapons and 'sterilize and contain' the suspects. And to deal with the radio man of one back-up squad that seemed to have taken a wrong turn and ended up at the wrong building entirely.

Jack bent his back and moved briskly to the wall beside the corridor he'd been instructed to clear — a wall decorated, he noticed, with posters displaying portraits and quotations from people like Washington and Jefferson. One had a black-and-white photo from the 1920s, some guy with a cigar and short hair parted in the middle. He read it as he passed:

"The aim of public education is not to spread enlightenment at all; it is simply to reduce as many individuals as possible to the same safe level, to breed a standard citizenry, to put down dissent and originality." — H.L. Mencken, Baltimore Sun.

But mostly his attention was divided between the threatening empty hallway ahead of him and trying to step over the writhing, gagging wounded as well as the silent dead, slipping only briefly in a small but growing pool of crimson blood on the green linoleum floor. He was pretty particular about his footing. You weren't going far without good footgear. One of the blood-soaked infants lying disturbingly still was so small Jack could hardly believe the kid was old enough to walk. Jack managed not to step on him. From the look of things it wouldn't have mattered; he just didn't want to hear anything go crunch.

But when he turned to see whether Keller was ready to move down the corridor in pattern with him, he saw the strutting young recruit leaning with one hand against the wall in the corner, vomiting his guts out.

Standard procedure called for him to shout for another backup. But that would draw attention to Keller's behavior. Probably no official notice would be taken, though Jack couldn't be sure. He glanced back to the company leader, who was busy with other stuff. Bullshit, he thought, no one here was armed with so much as a nail file. He moved down the corridor alone, pulling up at the next bend, holding his weapon vertically at the ready, sliding one eye around to see whether anyone waited in ambush.

Presumably she could have gotten out through the clearly marked exit door just behind her. Instead the little brunette was down on one knee just this side of the door, tying strips of what looked like kitchen towel around the bleeding leg of a young black boy about five or six years old who, from the glazed look in his eyes and generally listless behavior, was rapidly going into shock.

Jack moved cautiously forward, reminding himself to swing his head from side to side to scan for anyone who might be poised in ambush.

"Here to finish the job, trooper?" she said quietly, without looking up.

She had a short haircut. Parted high on one side, the bangs combed down across one eyebrow. She wore a single Bjorn silver pendant earring and had some kind of metal stud in her nose that made Jack dizzy — whether it was iridescent or holographic he wasn't sure. Other than that, she would have reminded him of Nicole deBoer from "The Dead Zone." Or *had* Nicole deBoer worn a Bjorn earring on one of those Star Trek spinoffs? This was making his head hurt.

He did notice she wore a leather jacket, cut stylishly short, and parachute pants, not that different from his own. Mobility, storage, the heavy polynylon fabric offered good protection if you had to lay it down. That and the short haircut meant this one actually could be a fighter. Cute ass.

"How bad is he?"

She looked up then, but only briefly, before returning to her work on the boy's left calf. Blue eyes, wide jaw, perfect mouth, high ears that made her look like some kind of elf. She was so petite her head actually looked big for her body. Just his luck for her to be cute as a doll.

"Muscle's shot to hell. Semi-jacket hollowpoints, I presume. Listen, if you're going to kill me, try to make it a little cleaner. Your marksmanship here today has really not been up to your outfit's ill-deserved reputation. Recruiting right off the streets, now? And promise me afterwards you'll get this boy to a real doctor, OK?"

The young woman's conversational tone seemed perfectly natural, which under the circumstances only made the scene all the more disorienting. Behind him Jack could still hear wounded women and children moaning and crying out for help, and the heavy bootsteps of his comrades, who he could picture moving among them, rolling over bodies to search for hidden weaponry which they knew damned well they weren't going to find. But procedure was procedure; it was for everyone's safety; never assume ..."

They'd be up behind him in another minute, give or take.

"No one's going to kill you," he said.

"Really? You have something more creative in mind?"

Jack was about to assure her that kind of thing didn't happen in the Lightning Squads. Then he thought back over what he'd seen in the past two weeks, recalled the rumors he'd heard about things that went on in the interrogation rooms on the seventh floor.

No, getting a little overly familiar with a prisoner who was going to be beaten or worse for whatever information she possessed would hardly be out of the question for a bunch of guys who'd been taught they were immune from the rules that applied to everyone else. Especially when they got an eyeful of this little babe. Not much of a chest, from what he could see, but a very nice little ass, and a face right out of the shampoo ads. Just as cute as hell. Were those freckles?

He suddenly had a vision of her, small, naked and bleeding, chained to an old radiator in a dark room that contained nothing else but a stained mattress. He didn't like it.

"Where's that door lead?" he asked.

"I have no idea," she said.

"What?"

"I don't work here. I was just helping fix the computers. You guys backtrack everything if it's not routed offshore, you know. How the hell would I know where the fire exits lead? Out to some alley, I assume."

"That kid gonna survive long enough to get to a hospital?"

"You missed the big artery. But he won't last the night without some kind of attention. Assuming you mean for him to last the night."

"Pick him up. Open the door. Now."

Surprisingly enough, given what a snide piece of attitude she seemed to be generally, she did pretty much as told, standing with the boy in her arms. There was blood on her own leg.

"You hit too?"

She looked down. "I don't know."

"Brackley! Keller!" came the company leader's voice behind him. "All clear in there?"

"No joy!" He said to his own collarbone, tripping his throat mike with a shrug of his neck. "There's a door — I'll clear it."

"Wait for back-up!" The sarge responded.

Now or never. Jack slung his weapon over his shoulder, cut off his mike again, strode forward past the girl (who stood still as a statue, holding the roughly bandaged child), and palmed the pressure bar on the exit door. It opened with a loud click and a gust of cooler, fresher air. Outside was a landing and concrete stairs leading down to the rear alley. Through some thoroughly predictable screw-up, the backup units which should be covering the rear of the building were not in immediate sight.

"Go, go."

She went, but stumbled on the stairs, barely catching herself with her elbow on the frigid steel banister, her hands being occupied with the kid.

"Here," he said, taking the boy, who couldn't weigh more than 40 pounds. Were all kids this tiny? "We gotta move, babe. Make it around that corner?"

"No problem." Once they were out of sight around the corner of the first building he pushed her up against the wall without a lot of explanation — she lifted a fist as though she was going to fight him, but then thought better of it — he probably outweighed her by at least 70 pounds. He handed her the kid, whose breathing had gone shallow, and bent down to wrap a pressure bandage from one of his thigh pouches around her wounded leg.

"I'm fine," she said.

"I know you are. You're leaving a blood trail."

"Oh," she said, giving him a close look for the first time. He wasn't skinny — more like "powerful." Blue eyes. Not a pretty boy. She checked his nametag.

"You're gonna get in a world of hurt, helping me, even if your name is Brackley," she said.

He could see her breath in the cold.

"How do you know my name?"

"It's on your pocket. Plus I'm not deaf. I don't know what your company leader thinks he needs a mike for, if he's gonna yell like that."

He took the child back.

"Where we going?" she asked.

"You said the kid needs medical attention. There's a hospital near here, should be a couple blocks northwest."

They took off down the alley at a slow trot. Behind him he heard someone shouting his name from the top of the rear stairway.

"Northwest," she noticed out loud. "Not 'uptown.' You're not from around here."

⚜ ⚜ ⚜

They paused while there were still some parked ambulances and a bedraggled line of shrubbery between them and the main Emergency Room entrance. The self-important guard diverting folks from parking in front of the door seemed to be some kind of private rent-a-cop in an ill-fitting Day-Glo vest. He'd be no problem. But manning the table just inside the door were a couple of real enough GPD cops scanning everybody's subdermal chips.

"So, I wouldn't be going out on a limb here if I assumed this kid has no chip in his arm, right?"

"Practically guaranteed." She reached in the kid's shirt pocket, pulled out a piece of paper with a hand-written phone number on it. "This is all we've got."

"Keep ahold of that. We run him in there without a chip they'll isolate him, give him a temporary tag that flashes 'illegal' every time he walks past a scanner, and hold us for questioning to boot. I might stare 'em down alone, but I assume you're no better than the kid?"

"Leaving aside the 'better' versus 'worse' question, Trooper Brackley, the fact is I'm tagged up to beat the band. I'm just slumming, you see. I'm actually the daughter of a high-society industrialist; I can walk right onto any military base in the country."

Oh, great. Went without saying all her ID would be crooked. But she was slick, talked like a college girl, so at least it would be the best and latest knock-off stuff out of Nagoya or Prague, none of this drive-in flea market stuff they sold the Africans for 40 newbucks, lucky if it'd get you through the Food Stamp line.

"It's explaining what the two of us are doing here *together* that could get interesting. In a pinch, though, tell them I'm working undercover."

"This might be easier if I go in alone," he said.

"Not going to happen," she smiled.

"Anybody ever tell you you're a pain in the ass?"

"Constantly," she smiled.

"OK, there've got to be other doors. Let's try around the corner."

Sure enough, a gaggle of staff were exiting an employee door right around the corner. They spotted Jack's uniform and held the door for the three of them without even giving them a close look, resumed their getting-off-duty conversation as they breezed past. In Jack's experience this was typical for any "secure" building, right up to the level of U.S. Embassy.

The inside was a maze of dark and indistinguishable hallways until their eyes started to adjust. Jack had an excellent built-in sense of direction, though, and as they started to work their way back toward what should be the rear of the ER he noticed that among the colored lines painted on the floor they seemed to be following the red one.

They passed freight elevators, signage directing them to Pediatrics and the OR quad, storage rooms, finally some kind of lab complex. And now, sure enough, from the bustle ahead of them, what had to be the rear of the Emergency Room.

Entering from the wrong direction, they went completely unnoticed. The place smelled of rubbing alcohol. Some kind of 24-hour news broadcast droned from a TV in the corner over by the front entrance, where several people slept in chairs molded out of thin plastic in an unlikely palette of Play-Doh colors. Jack sized up the staff as quickly as he could. There were several young nurses and aides who he thought might be most sympathetic. One, with a shorter skirt, held definite promise. His new companion proceeded to poke him in the ribs as he checked out the thighs. But then, his mind racing, he realized the younger ones were his own age, had gone to the modern government schools, received precisely the same government indoctrination he had. So, swallowing hard, the child now lolling pale and unconscious in his arms, he marched across the room to the oldest, stoutest, sternest looking woman he had ever seen.

"You're in charge here?" he asked.

"I'm the charge nurse. That child is bleeding. Where's his wristband? Where's his chart? Take him over to the scanning desk. You're bleeding all over my floor. He needs immediate attention, young man; where'd you come from?"

"I'm a member of the Lightning Squads."

"I can see that. Our procedures are the same for everyone. Get moving; he's lost a lot of blood."

Jack gritted his teeth, dropped his volume. "An hour ago I went out on a raid of an unlicensed day care center."

"You must be very proud."

"We shot this child. Someone on my team. Well, who the hell knows who shot him."

The stern old woman tilted her head, said nothing.

"I could be in big trouble just bringing him here. This child isn't registered. Never chipped. If we run him through admissions and his parents ever do try to claim him they'll be arrested. So you're not going to scan him, see? You're going to treat him under the ID of some other kid who was discharged earlier today, or who died, or something. And when he's better, you're going to call the number on this slip of paper." His young companion with the blue eyes and the silver earring dutifully held it up before tucking it back in the boy's shirt pocket. "That's all we have, is this number. His parents won't even know he's alive or dead, till you call."

"What you're asking me to do could get me and my supervisor thrown in jail," the old woman said.

"Yep. You gonna save his life, or not?"

She paused another second, reading his eyes, and his nametag. Then she had the child in her arms, staining the front of her white uniform jacket. "Johnson, what the hell are you doing? Can't you see we need a crash cart here? Put down that God-awful paperwork and ring Dr. Pawlahvi. Tell them we've got a bleeder for OR 3. Roberts, how many times have I told you to keep the chart with the patient? Send me Tomas the janitor. Not later, Roberts. Drop that. Go get Tomas now. Go."

Of course. The janitors could go anywhere, no questions asked. They'd have easy access to wristbands and chip scans from the morgue or wherever such stuff went when a patient was discharged. Quickly there was a swirl of activity around the boy, who had apparently been invisible to everyone because he hadn't arrived through the normal channels, but who was now laid on a white-covered gurney.

"Punch an I.V. right now, Johnson. The other right arm, please. Start saline. Draw for a blood test. You: Get some pressure on that wound."

A short, dark young doctor almost flew into the room, his white lab coat streaming out behind, and immediately got the whole pod of swirling activity started back through one of the swinging doors at the rear, his hand on the saline bag hanging on the extended arm over the gurney. The big charge nurse grabbed the slip of paper with the phone number just as the boy was swept away, did not even turn to look at Jack's face as she brushed past him. "You still here?" she asked. "Visitors are not allowed in my Emergency Room."

"Thank you."

"You'd best wash off in the men's room before you go dripping any more blood on my floor. And don't let that door hit your ass on the way out. We'll do everything we can." And she was gone.

On the way out, Jack and his companion stopped to watch a breaking news report on the TV mounted to a bracket on the ER waiting room wall. The breathless bimbo in the bronze hairspray helmet was reporting from a scene of tragedy downtown this afternoon, where three staff members at an illegal, unlicensed day-care center apparently attempted suicide, taking three young children with them, and injuring at least a dozen more.

As ambulance crews wheeled gurneys out of the now-familiar building across the street from the elementary school a couple blocks downtown, Company Leader Delgado held up two bloody submachine guns which he said had been used by the weird religious cult in their ritual murder-suicide, despite the best efforts of his boys to break in and bring a halt to the carnage.

"Jesus," Jack said. "There were no guns there."

"You new to this, kid?" asked his companion, pushing the bangs away from her huge blue eyes. But this time, she was not smiling.

⚜ ⚜ ⚜

Outside, the city seemed different. Brighter; louder.

In part this was the effect of what Jack and his young companion had just been through. The combination of the noise and the adrenalin pump of a gunfire incident left the senses partly shut down. It was a measurable neural effect — the attention focused very tightly on the problem at hand; ambient noise and other sensory input were filtered to a minimum.

Their race to the hospital with the bleeding child in their arms had allowed no let-up in those adrenalin levels, which had thus persisted for nearly an hour. Now, finally, the resulting adrenalin drain left them exhausted, allowed all the outside sensory input to race back in and fill the void.

All this was true. And yet it did not completely explain how different the world looked to Jack Brackley now. He had acted on instinct; he felt he had done the right thing. Yet circumstances had forced him to act on the feelings of doubt and dislike he was developing for the Lightning Squads — to act far earlier and more quickly than he had ever imagined he would be driven to. He had no idea precisely where this left him, but it was not part of his nature to worry how much trouble he was in with his superiors, how he might be punished, anything like that. All that stuff was secondary to his need to process how he felt now — what had happened, what he'd figured out (if anything) — what he intended to do next.

It was in this context that he felt he was looking and listening to the city for the first time.

In the distance, sirens seemed to be wailing, somewhere, almost constantly. He knew from his training that anti-terror forces in Israel had determined sirens could be a psychological deterrent to would-be terrorists. Was it possible it had now become policy to simply keep sirens going, somewhere in the city, at all times during daylight? Or did this simply reflect a level of chaos and instability which they had now come to accept as so normal that the hurrying passers-by no longer even

94

noticed — at least at a conscious level?

Add the sirens to the almost constant noise from patrol helicopters, fighter aircraft — stationed to escort or shoot down any commercial aircraft whose passengers got up from their seats or made the mistake of telling a bomb joke — and the extremely high-pitched whine of the unmanned aerial Predator and Skyhawk surveillance vehicles, and what your senses were telling you was that this was not a city at peace, but the economic capital of a nation under siege.

But under siege by whom? Where was the enemy?

Just from where they were standing, on the street corner outside the hospital, makeshift concrete anti-truck barricades and new rows of huge concrete tank traps disguised as planters could be seen blocking motor vehicle access to the lobbies of any nearby government building. The HS video cameras were ubiquitous, four to each street corner, supposedly just scanning for accidents and traffic blockages ... as though anyone really believed that. Additional surveillance cameras scanned automatically or could be manually directed by remote operators from the rooftops of nearby office buildings, and in glass bubbles disguised as street lamps, now accompanied by the inevitable omnidirectional microphones of the SonicNet grid.

Half a block uptown he could see a knot in the pedestrian traffic where another Lightning Squad was randomly selecting passers-by to run through one of their portable search portals.

Most of the traffic in the streets, of course, consisted of taxicabs and delivery trucks. But now outnumbering private cars — or so it seemed — was the combination of dark-windowed black SUVs representing the agents of one federal "civilian" police agency or another, and the brown-and yellow "camouflaged" HumVees of the various military and Homeland Security units now assigned to "stabilization" duty in the city, many of them sporting .30- or even .50-caliber machine guns on their roofs.

Now, up at the checkpoint, a young man dressed in dark,

nondescript clothes which appeared to be several sizes too large for him — his pant cuffs spilling unhemmed around his shoes — started to lean rapidly back and forth where he stood in line, second or third from the front. Then his nerve broke completely, and he darted like a rabbit across the street, making a break for it.

Probably a draft dodger losing confidence that his fake ID would get him through, or that his Selective Service implant had been fully disabled or removed.

The closest Lightning Trooper shouted for him to halt and fired a warning burst at the back of the fleeing man's knees. He started to limp but kept going, gaining the far sidewalk.

Now a brown-and-yellow HumVee with tinted windows arced out into the street with surprising speed, cutting off a taxicab that screeched on its brakes, fishtailing to a stop.

The gunner popped up and spun the fleeing suspect with a deadly accurate burst of .50-cal, probably not more than seven rounds. The vehicle sat there, idling, till the corpse had stopped twitching. Then the gunner dropped back down and the driver put it in reverse, the HumVee whining at a far more stately pace back to its original guard position.

Once the shooting was over, everyone on the street went very deliberately back about their business, ignoring the new corpse on the sidewalk as though it was a bag of spilled popcorn. Someone would be called in to clean it up. Meantime, a group of pigeons landed nearby, bobbing their heads as they approached to check out the new pickings.

Jack and his companion had paused near the stairway that led down to a subway entrance. Stray sheets of newsprint and other paper trash blew in small circles as the breeze moved it up and down the stairs past the hurrying pedestrians. The wind carried the smell of hot peanuts from a nearby vendor's cart.

The sale of newspapers had now been banned in the stations — the newspaper vending machines boarded up lest anyone place a bomb there — though Jack couldn't remember a single reported case of such a crime actually occurring in Gotham. Trash piled up on the subway platforms; waste containers on the concourses had also been banned. Recorded announcements regularly and sternly instructed passengers in the stations to report anyone who looked "suspicious."

At least the prevalence of hobos, winos, and shopping cart ladies seemed to have been visibly reduced. Jack felt that was an improvement, though you occasionally heard whispered questions about just where they'd all gone. If they'd only been driven underground — the term of choice now seemed to be "Mole People" — it was hard to see how that was any long-term solution.

But the most surprising thing, as you looked around, was the way people had adjusted. Was there nothing that could faze them? They didn't look particularly happy, mind you. But neither were the people of the city unusually sullen. Basically, the passers-by looked the way they'd always appeared in this town — in too big a hurry to worry about it.

The city's unofficial motto might just as easily be, "That's the way it is; step over it and go on about your business."

The two of them made a relatively awkward looking couple, standing here by the subway entrance — the Lightning trooper in full tac uniform with subgun slung and pointing down at the sidewalk, the young woman who wasn't really his prisoner, both their exposed hands and faces starting to turn red from the cold, despite the pale winter sun.

"I've gotta get back," Jack said, a little reluctantly.

"Will it go hard on you ... letting me go?" She crossed her arms and hugged herself, shivered a little from the cold.

"I never caught up with you, see. I'll get my ass chewed for violating procedure, but I'll survive. You'll want to get a little further away first, but you need to have that leg looked at. If there's a bullet still in there it'll hurt like hell in about an hour."

"As opposed to what it feels like now?"

"Hurtin' pretty good?"

"Hell yes. You ever been shot?"

"No, actually, I haven't. You want to go back in and see Nurse Ratchit?"

"I think that would be pushing our luck. Anyway, we've got doctors, Trooper Brackley."

"Listen, I know this is strange ... I don't suppose there's a way I can reach you? I don't even know your name."

Her lip curled as she smiled, but the smile was still like sunshine breaking through clouds. Jesus, she was cute. "Is this how you usually pick up your dates, breaking into their places of business and shooting them?"

"We don't have time to go into how I ended up in the Grays, right now. I could get into some pretty deep shit for letting you loose, you know."

"I'm sorry — I don't know your first name, either."

"I'm Jack."

"Ah. So you really are the famous son of the famous late Colonel Tom Brackley."

"Yeah, guilty to that."

"Hello, Jack Brackley. I'm Joan."

"Joan. Well. I don't know if getting out of the Lightning Squads is gonna be quite as easy as getting in, but let's just say I don't think I'll be attending any more kiddie shooting galleries real soon. Sorry about your leg and all. It wasn't me, just for the record. Still got a full magazine. Somehow I never spotted any of those hostiles everybody else was shooting at."

"Listen ... if you've really changed your mind about things ..." she said, not looking at him but at the crumpled body of the draft dodger up the street, which everyone else was so studiously ignoring.

And then she sobbed, her voice catching in her throat so that she had to start again.

"... maybe you don't want to get out of the Grays just yet. Maybe you can do more good ... from the inside. Why don't you give me a way we can reach you?"

"We?"

She just smiled. Jesus. So she was part of the resistance. And not just some day-care worker — a computer programmer. How high up in their organization? A few days ago he might have dreamed of making a catch like that.

"I'm not going to sell out my friends," he said. "But I would like to hear from you. I've got a lot of stuff to think through." He jotted a phone number on a torn piece of newspaper blowing past them, handed it to her.

"I may not be the one to call. If someone calls with a message from your friend at the hospital, don't hang up. We'll figure out a safe way to meet."

"I'd like that ... Joan."

She looked at him for a moment. Then she threw her arms around his neck and pulled herself up and kissed him. He'd actually been thinking the same thing, although he wouldn't have dared. And this wasn't some little schoolgirl peck. She forced his mouth open and pretty much cleaned his teeth. Passers-by were smiling. Shades of V-J Day. The hero home from busting the dastardly church-schoolers. Oddly enough, he could tell precisely the moment she was going to pull away and stop. Because it was about two seconds before she was going to jump up and wrap her legs around him. Now, how did he know that? Who was this girl?

"You're a brave and good person, Jack Brackley. Thanks for saving that boy. I think we'll meet again."

She turned and walked away, making a brave effort not to limp. He watched her go, wondering many things. Not that there was much chance he wouldn't watch her walk away. So it was a foregone conclusion he'd still be staring at the swaying of the nicest little butt in town when he saw her confronted by another member of the Lightning Squads not half a block away, motioning with his gun butt that she should get into line for the portal search up ahead.

Without stopping to think about it, Jack was up to them at a trot.

"Good work, Carnieri," he said, reading the name sewn onto the pocket of his fellow enforcer of Truth, Justice and the American Way ... glad to see he wasn't outranked. "You spotted the bandage on her leg, right? She just escaped custody, I'm taking her back to have her ID run."

"I'm not supposed to let anyone out once they're in line," answered Carnieri, a little guy with a big Adam's apple, though his voice betrayed a detectable level of uncertainty.

"You did good work here, trooper," Jack said, employing the command voice and shoving his chest and nametag in front of the shorter man's eyes. "Don't think we didn't notice how quickly you alerted on that draft dodger when he made a break for it."

Young Carnieri smiled proudly, then made his best effort to straighten his face into something more closely approaching aw-shucks modesty.

"I'm on a Class One Tactical, which takes priority," Jack said, using a voice from the training films. "You've just apprehended an important fugitive. I'll see your name is mentioned in the report. Two in one day; not bad at all. Maybe you've heard MY name before."

"Jeez. Yes, sir. OK, sir."

Jack clenched his teeth and stuck his jaw out, gave the little dweeb a serious look and a nod, half picked up Joan by the back of the neck, quick-stepped her back the way they'd come.

"Thanks," she said under her breath. "And also ouch. But I might have made it."

"Bleeding from a bullet wound?"

"That's a hell of a command voice you've got. Your name must help a lot, too. Can we slow down just a little, that hurts."

He complied. "Don't like doing that. Always hated the

way people expected me to ask for special treatment."

"Hey, you use what you've got."

He scowled.

"I'm joking. Thanks, really. OK?"

By the time they'd made their way back to the subway entrance, he saw two more Lightning Troopers coming up the avenue from the other side — the direction from which they'd originally come from the day care building with the gunshot little kid. And these were men from his own squad, still in full combat rig.

Jesus Christ. Never rained but it poured. "They're gonna spot us for sure," he said.

This time it was Joan who moved quickly, grabbing his arm and yanking him down the stairs into the subway entrance.

"Brackley! That you?" came a shout, half a block behind.

At the bottom of the stairs, Jack looked left and right, figuring they could head back up to the surface by some different flight of stairs, exit onto one of the cross streets, hopefully shake pursuit that way. But Joan pulled him off to one side, headed for a gray door marked "Maintenance," shouting, "Come on!"

Surprisingly, the door wasn't locked. They found themselves in a narrow corridor running parallel to the tracks, a janitor's closet, a white mop and some blue rags hung up to dry, then a room full of electrical circuit breakers off to their left. Everything smelled damp. At the end was another door with a pressure bar, marked in large red letters, "Emergency Exit: Alarm Will Sound." Joan reached up and did something with a couple of wires held together with colored tape at the top of the door — she was so small she could barely reach the top of the door — and pushed it open. No alarm sounded.

Ahead of them was a three-foot drop to the dirt and cinder tunnel floor, and then the tracks themselves. The lights of the station were off to their right, while to the left the tracks vanished into the gloom, illuminated only by a series of red lights along the walls.

"Are you nuts?" he asked. "People get killed down here."

"Your people," she answered. "By my people. You want to wait here?"

"No, they'll search the whole station."

"OK then. You know about not stepping on the middle rail, right? Lots of lovely volts."

They jumped, turned left, scrambled along the tracks.

"The switchmen have a name for that," he said.

"For what?"

"It's on the tip of my tongue. That pattern of lights along the wall — three red, stacked one above the other."

"Lady in red."

"That's it. 'Trouble ahead, lady in red, take my advice or you'll be better off dead.'"

As if on command — as though summoned by the words of the old children's song — a low rumble came from the darkness ahead of them. They could feel it through the soles of their shoes. And it was getting louder.

"Switchman's asleep," Joan picked up the old refrain, "and train Hundred and Two ... Oh, shit."

"Run!" Jack spotted the black opening of a perpendicular tunnel ahead and to the right, apparently large enough to duck into. But Joan was lagging now, her limp becoming more pronounced. Mercilessly, he grabbed her upper arm with one hand, put the other arm around her and yanked her along behind him, almost pulling her off her feet. The headlight of the approaching train came into sight, the noise growing quickly to an almost intolerable level in the confined space as the monster roared around the bend directly at them, the noise filling their world as the beast hurtled toward them like some deepsea behemoth in a panic to sound for the safety of the depths.

The train was actually slowing for the station, sparks flying off its shrieking wheels as the engineer hit his brakes — or
was that all done by computer now? But the rate at which it
was closing would still make their reaching the dark oval doorway a close-run thing. Now the bow wave of wind off the front
of the train buffeted them head-on, surprisingly cold, threatening to slow their progress even further. On pure brute strength,
Jack actually did pull Joan off her feet, swung her around so he
was carrying her in his arms the way he'd carried the little kid
up the street, hurled them both into the shelter of the dark oval
doorway, only seconds to spare as the thundering train hurtled
past, its brakes continuing to shriek as the wheels sparked and
squealed.

He tried to swing her back to land on her own feet, then,
but immediately the floor of the tunnel into which they'd
lunged fell away beneath them. Just his luck. Some kind of
goddamned drainage tunnel, and completely black. They slid
a good dozen feet, struggling to stay upright and gain some
kind of traction ... finally tumbling head over heels into a black
abyss.

CHAPTER 4

It is impossible to give the soldier a good education without making him a deserter. His natural foe is the government that drills him.

— HENRY DAVID THOREAU (1817-1860)

When the state is corrupt then the laws are most multiplied.

— CORNELIUS TACITUS (A.D. 55-117)

Criminal means, once tolerated, are soon preferred.

— EDMUND BURKE (1729-1797), "REFLECTIONS ON THE REVOLUTION IN FRANCE," 1790

It was some days later that the phone rang. The woman who answered the phone had obviously been crying. "Hello?"

"I don't know your name and I don't want to know your name. Don't tell me anything," said the voice of an older white woman. "I found this number on a slip of paper in the hand of a little boy. About five years old, I'd say, light brown, curly hair. Needs a haircut."

"Oh my God. My Deion. Is he ...?"

"He's going to be fine. Some scars, but they won't show outside his clothes. He's walking. It was serious, took some work, but he'll be fine. Maybe a slight limp. He was shot."

"Oh thank God. Deion is alive, he's alive," she said to someone else in the room. Then "Shot? Who is this?"

"Don't be stupid. Name a street corner that's less than three blocks from where you are."

"What?"

"Try to pull it together here, sister. We don't want to be on this phone call a whole long time. Name a major street corner that's two or three short blocks from where you live, from where you are right now. No closer."

She did.

"OK. I'll call you back in a few minutes at this number and tell you a place near there. Are you alone or is the father there?"

"He's here."

"Do you both look like the child?"

"What?"

"Are you both the same color as the child?"

"My husband is darker than me."

"Just the two of you, then. Don't call anyone else. Don't talk to anyone else. If I call back and this line is busy, I will NOT call again. Understand?"

"Oh please. We'll wait for your call. God bless you."

The curly-haired little boy was wearing a new sweater — well, a cast-off sweater, actually, a little too large for him — walking hand-in-hand with a large white woman, her gray hair in a severe bun, when he spotted his parents sitting on the bench and ran shrieking to embrace his mother.

It was a bright winter day. The large white woman stopped to watch them for a moment, then began to walk on. The father folded the paper he'd been pretending to read and half rose from his seat to speak to her; her steely glare sat him down more effectively than a bat across the knees. As they were on their way home, though, suddenly the large woman was there again, falling in to walk beside them.

"God bless you, ma'am. We thought we'd never see you again."

"You won't. And I'd prefer it if you didn't remember my face, either."

"Of course."

"If you'd been followed, I would have been grabbed by now. I'm only going to risk talking to you once. If you follow my advice, you'll get that child and yourselves out of this city. It's not safe."

"But things are changing. The Black Arrow —"

"Is one man. The trouble he's stirring up creates an opportunity to get out. He or others like him may even win in the end, but it also means in the near term they'll be cracking down. They already are. Your boy was seriously injured. A very brave or very stupid young member of the Lightning Squads managed to get him some top-notch medical care. God knows who or what guided him to the right place. Maybe you're the kind of people who believe in prayer."

"The Lightning Squads? But ..."

"We didn't ask. But you were very lucky, more lucky than a lot of parents who had children there that day, from what I heard."

"It was terrible. Three of the children died. And the rest ..."

"Yes. And now you're going to have another child?" They both looked suddenly drawn; no one else had noticed the wife was showing, yet. Had this woman been checking up on them? No, she'd said she didn't want to know anything about them, had been very specific about that. So she was a midwife or a doctor, then, that was it. There must be signs only a person like that would notice.

"You're going to expose her to all this?" the older woman

asked. "The government vaccinations, the indoctrination, the pre-school child outreach bureaucracy? Or are you going to go on trying to hide them both in the attic, like Anne Frank?"

They both took deep breaths. She couldn't really know about the attic. It had to be just an expression. Still ...

"We've talked about getting away to the free lands in the West, but it's so far away. We have very little money; we don't know anyone along the way who we could trust, except my sister in —"

"You weren't really going to tell me where your sister lives, were you?"

"No. No."

"They'd have no reason to check the child's ID on a train trip to Hartford. You buy the tickets all the way through to Hartford, that's important. And you only take what you'd normally carry for a weekend trip. Try to move the family furniture and you might as well not even bother. Don't make a big show of giving it all away, either. You just leave instructions for someone to handle things two weeks after you're gone. Pay the bills up through then. No forwarding addresses, no calling to cancel magazines and your Christmas dinner reservations, for God's sake.

"Ticket through to Hartford, but after you change in New Haven, you get off at a little station called Meriden. Walk west, then turn right half a block. Look for the coin store, there's only one. You're thinking of starting the boy in on coin collecting, see, plus it's an investment. You ask for some advice about that. Ask about Krugerrands, from South Africa. You could even make a joke — black folks, South Africa. Arrive in the middle of the week, by the way; coin dealers travel to coin shows on the weekends. The man will tell you Canadian Maple Leaves are better. Don't say anything else till he mentions Canadian Maple Leaves."

"You're with the underground railroad."

"There's nothing romantic about this. You have to make

your decision in a businesslike way. But what that boy deserves is your courage. You can go or not; it's your call. Can you remember what I've told you?"

"Tickets through to Hartford, but we get off before that, in ..."

"For God's sake, pay attention. Meriden."

"In Meridian."

"Close enough."

"West to the coin store. Mid-week."

"And ask about ..."

"Krugerrands, South Africa."

"But you won't know everything is OK until he talks to you about ..."

"Canadian Maple Leaves."

"Good. Don't write it down, or someone could die. Just repeat it back to one another after you get home, till you're sure you both remember. Now this is goodbye. You're a brave boy, Deion. You grow up and be strong, you hear?"

"Thank you, Auntie Mame."

"Deion, don't say the lady's name."

"It's OK. That's a special name just for Deion."

"God bless you, doctor."

The large woman almost smiled. Anyway she didn't look quite so gruff, just for a moment. She turned to go.

"Wait — the sweater."

"It's a gift," she said. "Belonged to another child, long ago." Then she crossed the street, stared down a taxicab that braked to a short stop, and was gone. They never knew her real name.

Two weeks later they were in Vermont, and free. Little Deion would always limp, just enough to keep him from playing soccer. He was told the story of Auntie Mame many times through his childhood, in part because his parents wanted him to know that many of the people who had helped them had been whites and Indians, and no one had ever mentioned a word about their color, or about payment. Deion grew up to attend medical school in the mountains of Alberta, and to become a renowned surgeon among the freedom fighters. Later, after the wars, he was chosen for the office of High Constable in his canton of New Columbia. He died peacefully in his sleep, grandfather of nine grandchildren, three of them doctors, after practicing medicine for 64 years.

Without a license.

⚜ ⚜ ⚜

Cassandra read over her fourth — fifth? — attempt at the novel they kept telling her she should write, resisted the urge to tear it into little shreds. Instead she allowed the pages to slide gracefully into the wastebasket.

Seized with rage, she spanned the keyboard with her long, slender, apparently totally talentless fingers, and launched into a parody of her own drivel:

"Dick Bruiser thrust himself into the car and drove to the place where he was going. Along the way, he noticed it was raining. Insert tedious simile comparing the rain to a prize-fighter pummeling the city with rabbit punches even though he was near the end of his career and knew the fight game would get the best of him in the end. Oh, the ennui of it all. Insert medium dose of additional ennui, wrapped in a phantasmagory of drug-warped neon reflecting off the darkened oil slicks of the rain-swollen gutters of a corrupt city's collective resignation and regret."

Hey, not bad. Maybe she should have been a poet. Oh, wait, she was a poet. So the billboards and the house ads said. Poet of the oppressed. Lady Lancelot of the forlorn and the downtrodden. Commentaries and compassion on demand, in carefully pre-measured dollops, like storefront pizza by the thousand-word slice.

"Dick Bruiser got out of the car and went into the place where he was going. There, he found the person he wanted to see, even though in real life the person you're looking for is NEVER there ... and you'd never find a place to park within two blocks, in the first place, you asshole, especially if it was goddamned raining. Now insert two pages of snappy, hard-bitten dialogue which also advance the plot. Pick up some Spaz magazines and throw in some trendy street jive about the homeboys, including some up-to-the-minute drug slang. Try to avoid having all the characters call each other by their first names all the time as though they're wearing a wire and want the FBI transcript to be easier to follow. ..."

Her eyes welled up with frustration. What was this "fiction" crap, anyway? Making up bedtime stories, when there were more heart-rending real-life tales than she could get to?

How could any made-up crap ever compare with the stack of columns she was going through on her bed, trying to winnow down a handful to enter in the annual auto-erotic journalism awards contest? Pathetic, shattered fragments of a city under the rule of a faceless, power-mad, lockstep bureaucracy.

How did you capture, anyway, the sadness, the inescapable futility, the hopelessness of life, on a written page? And if you ever could capture that little piece of moonlight in a bottle, what then? What people wanted was escape, diversion, vicarious adventure no matter how unlikely, the hero scales the wall of a castle full of armed men to rescue the imprisoned damsel and miraculously survives unscathed.

Who was going to pay to be reminded how useless were their pathetic struggles against a world they couldn't begin to understand — a world that had seen them coming and trained the clever, double-talking judges to overrule their arguments before they could even get them out of their tongue-tied mouths?

Not germane. Point not at issue. Already stipulated to in

the preliminary motions. Bring it up on appeal.

The society these men had built made a mockery of the principle that men should be free to control their own lives, their own labor, the property they bought with the sweat of their brow. In little more than a century these politicians had eaten out all that was good, like beetles eating out a granary from the inside, till there was nothing left in the land but broken promises, empty husks of dreams recited now in cynical sarcasm and empty parody.

Yet God forbid she should mock and ridicule *them*. Isn't it your job to give us hope and uplift us and give us something inspiring? Can't you ever look at the bright side? Why don't you include an address we can use to do something useful, like sending a letter to our Congresscritter?

You're just trying to show how smart you are and make everyone else feel small, Cassie. Over their heads. Fancy talk about obscure things in history and Dead White Males.

Why do you want to be so depressed all the time? You don't have to have principles and walk around under a cloud in a blue funk *all* the time. People would like you better if you cheered up. You seem like such a nice person when people meet you in person, why do you have to write this stuff that makes everyone angry and upset?

Brain-damaged trolls. Selling a heritage of freedom for a warm plate of cheese nachos and the NBA playoffs.

Yeah but, Cassandra, those nachos you're making fun of have sour cream and sliced jalapenos and bacon bits, have you tried them? they would laugh. And she would laugh too. And the party would go on and the novel would lie unwritten because nobody wanted to read that stuff, anyway. Spurs over the Mavericks in five games on the strength of some seven-foot African guy who guarded the basket like ... you were going to try and remember the names of the hounds that stand chained at the gates of hell, weren't you? You were actually going to look it up. Always too intellectual, sweetie.

Cassie went back to the hideous job of sorting people's lives in thousand-word swatches, like choosing upholstery for the new couch.

She'd been putting it off for weeks. But the incorrigibly chipper Alana from Promotions had done her job, tracking her down where she hid out on the floor of the library, digging through the heaps of freebies rejected by the book reviewers. Alana — vocative of the Gaelic leanbh, child: "the fair one" — reminding her the contest deadlines had arrived, just as they did every year around this time, thank a merciful God for the awesome rhythms of nature.

And if Cassie didn't submit her handful of columns, Alana would choose, probably that piece of crap on the first robin of spring she'd filed on a holiday Friday last year when the only people returning her calls were dingbats convinced the CIA was spreading plague germs in the subways.

The journalism award contests were humiliating enough, but winning with a bad column would be far worse than losing with a good one.

They were always judged by some bored crew of retired socialist journalism professors hoping to get through the pile of entries in time for the free catered croissant lunch in bucolic Medicine Hat, Delaware or Deer's Knob, Pennsylvania. Cassie had never been sure whether it was more embarrassing to just barely beat out what passed for her local competition here in the city, or to actually come in second behind some photo-feature by a kid two years out of J-School in upstate Peekskill, writing on the Disease of the Week.

But Promotions wanted to celebrate their "award-winning journalists" on billboard, newsstand, and cereal box. And needless to say, they'd rather have glamorous Cassie Trulove up there, leering like a loon, than bald John with the weekly fishing report.

And so the game of narcissism and self-delusion ran on.

Cassie had dumped 10 or 15 likely candidate columns to

the printer and gathered them up on her way out the door this evening. Now she slid into her rattiest bluejeans, brewed herself a hot cup of Bigelow's Constant Comment, redolent of cloves and orange peel and forever betraying her New England roots, and plopped herself on the huge pink leather couch to play Sift-and-Sort.

The pile of candidate columns went on a pillow beside her, not on her lap. Anyone who lived for any time at all with a 20-pound fur person soon realized laps were not so much private property as open ground, eligible for immediate homesteading.

Sure enough, although the monster had been nowhere in sight, presumably sleeping it off somewhere in the deepest recesses of the luggage heap in the bedroom closet, by the time Cassie had turned on a Wilson sisters CD, positioned her mug of tea on the seriously misnamed coffee table, turned her knees and snugged her feet beneath her still reasonably pert little butt, she barely had time left to tense her stomach muscles — thank you, company-paid gym membership — before the air was magically full of gray blur and 20 pounds of Graymalkin were making their always astonishingly delicate four-point landing in her lap, already kneading and purring.

"My God, you're a moose. You are definitely going on the low-cal food tomorrow," she said. He closed his eyes in a smile. Saw right through her.

So. How close to the top of the heap should she place the case of Yuri Petrov, railroaded into prison on perjured testimony for "conspiracy to manufacture marijuana" when all Yuri and his wife Tanya really did was run an irrigation supply store known to be frequented by folks who grew pot in their basements? Their real crime, clearly, had been not merely refusing to help the narcs entrap their customers, but actually going ahead and blowing the whistle on the cops' ham-handed efforts, tipping off the TV stations to the millions of dollars being wasted staking out customers, running license plates, etc.

Her columns about Melinda DeWitt, the juror charged with jury tampering for discussing with her fellow jurors in the jury room the possible sentence their victim was likely to get for "possession of drug paraphernalia," were more important, since the end of the independent juror was precisely what facilitated tragedies like Yuri Petrov being sent to prison for 20 years for selling hoses and sprinklers.

But the DeWitt columns presented a few problems. First, the case had dragged out more than a year. So how were you supposed to pick just one or two columns to tell the whole story?

Second, DeWitt had managed to stay free on bail. Not to be too callous about it, but there was less pathos there than seeing Yuri Petrov, an infantry veteran of the First Western War, separated from his bride and childhood sweetheart for the first time in 12 years of marriage to be sent up the river for selling drip valves.

And last, of course, you had to use up precious space trying to explain to a populace dumbed down by four generations of government schooling why jurors free to vote their conscience and judge the law as well as the facts were vital to a free nation.

Reluctantly, she slid the two best Melinda DeWitt columns to the bottom of the stack.

Ah, here was her old friend Tyler McCallan, who choked to death on his own vomit after the federal judge refused to let him use the medical marijuana that helped him keep his chemo drugs down ... even *after* the people of his state had legalized the stuff by referendum, 59-41.

How to rank that against her columns on Dr. Helmut Stauffer, subjected to a criminal trial for writing "too many pain-killer prescriptions" for a patient list that included a man with a back curved 90 degrees from spinal arthritis, 40-year-old men with cancer of the testicles?

Miraculously, the jury had acquitted Helmut Stauffer. Not

that it had ended there.

In the end, Cassie decided the story of Yuri and Tanya Petrov trumped them all. She'd called it "The great sprinkler conspiracy":

Yuri and Tanya Petrov didn't grow marijuana. They didn't buy or sell marijuana. Yet today Tanya's husband sat in a federal pen in Connecticut, awaiting the imposition of a sentence which was likely to see him doing hard time for a decade ...

... or until we end the War on Drugs, whichever comes first.

What the Petrovs did was operate a store in suburban Long Island, called Northern Waters. They sold irrigation pipe and valves and timers for people who wanted to grow plants indoors. Some of their customers — a small minority — used that equipment to grow marijuana.

Yuri Petrov is a hydraulic engineer. His dream was to leave Russia and start his own business in America. He did.

When the Petrovs learned they were drawing the attention of the federal drug police, they checked with an attorney. They were told the irrigation systems, the hoses and valves and flow meters and regulators Yuri designed and sold, did not constitute "drug paraphernalia" — even if some people chose to use them to grow pot — so long as they had other, legitimate uses. Otherwise, the local attorney laughed, the folks who manufacture various sizes of plastic sandwich bags would be in a world of hurt.

The Petrovs' mistake was in assuming the federal drug police would pay any attention to the law. The federals don't care what the law says.

The amount of money the federal Drug Enforcement Administration, the state Department of Investigation, and various other action-hungry government agencies spent to nail the Petrovs remains untallied. But the following numbers may give us some idea:

The narcs staked out the Petrovs' store for two years. At times there were as many as 15 government personnel involved in videotaping people as they went in and out of the store, and writing down the license plate numbers of customers' cars. The government ran some 1,000 license plate numbers. Then they started investigating the 1,000 people who owned those cars. But in at least one case they spent time and money investigating a woman who bought a car two weeks *after* it was spotted in the Petrovs' parking lot.

They secretly subpoenaed residential water bills, using provisions of the new anti-terrorism acts to bar the water departments from even telling their customers which bills had been grabbed. They used high-tech government equipment to take "thermal imaging" pictures of these suspects' homes, hoping "hot spots" would show up to indicate where indoor marijuana was being grown. They sorted through these people's garbage. Then they subpoenaed their electric bills, without their knowledge, to see who might be using suspiciously large amounts of electricity.

(Of course, the reason people grow marijuana indoors, even in areas like Long Island with soil and climate ideal for *outdoor* hemp cultivation, is that the government already takes sophisticated aerial thermal images to determine what crops are growing outdoors on private property. Apparently this no longer constitutes *enough* of an invasion of privacy.)

RAIDED 80 HOMES

Finally, the government raided 80 homes. They made 29 federal cases for growing marijuana. Although some of the remaining 51 were turned over to state authorities for disposition, a fair number turned out to be people who had bought their irrigation systems to raise orchids or tropical fish. That means 36 percent of those raided, and fewer than 3 percent of those investigated, turned out to be worth prosecuting for this heinous federal crime.

But it was enough to make the conspiracy case against the Petrovs — "conspiracy to manufacture" all the marijuana seized, if only a few of those 29 could be convinced to testify that the Petrovs had talked with them about growing marijuana.

Why would anyone testify to such a thing? Simple. They were promised reduced sentences, or in some cases promised that

SUPRYNOWICZ

charges would be dropped entirely, in exchange for their testimony. Dropping the charges was "absolutely" part of the deal that
motivated government witness Vivian Kostic, who was busted
growing pot for a husband with multiple sclerosis, to testify that
Yuri Petrov knew she was growing the marijuana, according to
defense attorney Michelle Sanangelo.

And so they seized the Petrovs' life savings, out of their
bank accounts and their safe at home — using the fact that Russian immigrants tend to mistrust banks and keep much of their
savings in cash as further "evidence" they must be drug dealers
... and meantime depriving them of the means to fund a proper
defense.

"What they ought to require is that when these government
witnesses testify, they put them on the stand and have a U.S. marshal stand right there with a gun to their heads," says Joe Crosby
of the local chapter of the Fully-Informed Jury Association, himself a Marine Corps combat veteran. "That's the only way the jury
would get a clear picture of their motivation."

But why would the federals sacrifice real "marijuana criminals" — people who were actually caught with the goods — and
expand the definition of "conspiracy" so near the breaking point,
contending people who sell sprinkler systems and potting soil
"conspire" to grow all the pounds of marijuana which may sprout
under those nozzles over the years, just to jail some sprinkler
salesmen?

'NO FRIEND OF THE GOVERNMENT'

"Because the Petrovs dissed them," says the Petrovs' attorney, using the current ghetto slang to indicate a purposeful demonstration of disrespect. Instead of quietly closing their business
and slipping out of town when they learned they were under surveillance, the Petrovs, emboldened by the knowledge they were
committing no crime in this new Land of the Free, "stayed open
for two years while they were staked out. They called the newspapers, they called their congressman, they went on (FNN's) Police
Beat."

It all comes down to whether you're considered a "friend of

the government." And U.S. Attorney Valerie Dunhill told Judge James McNair that Yuri Petrov is "no friend of the government."

The judge and prosecutor pre-screened the jury to eliminate anyone who might be fed up with the War on Drugs and its insane excesses. The result was fore-ordained.

Awaiting sentencing, Yuri Petrov writes me that he finds himself surrounded in the federal lockup by "doctors, lawyers, publishers, professionals and intellectuals, mostly first time offenders, who are in many ways victims like myself," most guilty of violating bureaucratic edicts, not felonies. "Yet some are serving prison terms of up to 15 years. That's longer than served by many murderers and rapists!

"We are turning into a new type of totalitarian state and we don't even know it. ... For much of my life I endured the oppression of Eastern Europe. Now I am reliving the experience in my new home where I came in search of Justice and Liberty.

"Unfortunately, most Americans are blind to the greatest threat to this country since the American Revolution," he says, "their own government raging out of control."

Yeah. The Petrovs went on top of the pile.

⚜ ⚜ ⚜

Mayor Daniel Brackley was pissed off, so angry he wanted to kill somebody.

Not that this was a temporary condition, you understand. This was pretty much his permanent state of mind.

His success was due to his drive, and what drove him was his anger, his barely suppressed raw fury. And who was he mad at? At the whole fucking world, thank you very much.

All his work, and how was he treated? Did anyone acknowledge the careful dovetailing of his well-thought-out plans of civic improvement? Nooo.

"Brackley shreds Constitution"; "Brackley's War on Property Rights"; "Mayor Plays Political Favorites in Redevelopment Scheme."

But nooo, he wasn't supposed to blame the world in general for his troubles, was he? Didn't make any sense to blame "the world." You had to take responsibility for your own life, for your own happiness, didn't you? No sense weeping and moaning over spilt milk and blaming everyone else for our problems when it was really in our own hands, was it, Danny?

His mother had told him that, a thousand times. And you know what Danny Brackley had to say to that? Fuck you, and the horse you rode in on. He wished the old bitch would take another world cruise. In the meantime, he'd bought her a place so far out on the island that if you went any further you'd have to do the backstroke.

He'd taken responsibility for his own life, OK. About 30 years too late.

He could remember when he was going away to boarding school. He had to have been what, eleven? "You have to work hard now, do you know what this is costing us? Have to get good grades, have to study hard, have to keep that scholarship. No beer and cigarettes and fast cars and fast girls like those no-account boys in town, no. That was going to ruin their lives. Little Danny was going to be different; Little Danny was going to study hard and be a good boy and learn to conjugate his Latin verbs and make his mother proud and never mess around with those tramps and get some little bitch in trouble and have to get married and ruin his life, was he? No, he was going to play by the rules and have a good life, wasn't he?

Well you know what happened? Those other kids, the tall good-looking kids with the blond hair and the perfect teeth, you know what happened to them? They got drunk and they got high and they got laid, that's what happened to them. They got the fast cars and they got the girls. They had all the rip-roaring good times that little Danny missed because he was hitting the books and being a good boy and baby-sitting his brat baby brother who grew up taller than he did. And when those bad, hot-rodding, pot-smoking kids got caught do you know what happened? Everybody chuckled and said, "Boy, that Todd, that Lance, he sure is a rowdy character, boys will be boys, and if I were his age, I'd have a car and a half-naked little babe squirming around in my lap just like him. Wink wink, good going, son. In like Flynn."

He heard from them all the time. They'd gotten miserable test scores while little Danny had been studying and studying, no drunken weekend revels for him, no holiday vacations, studying away like Ebeneezer fucking Scrooge. But did they suffer? In fact it seemed to Danny Brackley a lot of them got awfully good year-end grades without even trying, especially the guys on the starting varsity. Funny how that worked.

So they got the cheerleader pregnant and they got married and had two kids and then they got caught screwing her sister so they got divorced and then they married their secretary or their nurse so they had trouble paying the child support from the first marriage so the second wife said the first wife was a cold hard bitch who didn't want to let him have a life.

And were they miserable then? Was there at least some justice in the world? No! They went into banking and real estate and law and made three times what Danny Brackley made. Hell, five times. They complained about being in debt up to their eyebrows but they STILL drove nicer cars that looked like huge polished tanks and lived in nicer houses than Danny Brackley, had those hot blonde wives with the long-stemmed American Beauty legs that just brought tears to your eyes and if there was any price to be paid *he'd* never seen it. Sure, their kids were brats, but at least they had the chance to screw them up.

And meantime what had little Danny Brackley's life turned out like? How had he been rewarded for being a good boy and always playing by the rules? He could remember going out shopping for the trunk full of clothes that he'd take away with him to boarding school. They shopped from a list the school sent you. The blazers would be blue and the slacks would be gray flannel or else they'd be chinos and the ties would be in the school colors and the shirts would be either white or blue and they'd have button-down collars. And his mother and the sales lady had pored over the lists and selected the clothes and held them up to him, he was just supposed to stand there like a clothes horse, like a fucking little dummy. He didn't like wool because it itched. Too fucking bad. It was cold where he was going and mother knew best and besides the list said wool, so wool it was. And finally they asked him if there was anything he saw that *he* liked. And yes, there was a mint green sports coat and a coarse-knit orange tie that he thought were simply beautiful and both the women had laughed and patted him on the head, laughed at how stupid he was, "No, I don't think so." "I'm glad to hear you agree," ha ha ha, stupid crewcut 11-year-old dwarf, thinking he could know what he ought to wear, and then his mother had taken him to the fancy restaurant on the mezzanine of the store with the big parking lot in the swank suburb where all the best dentists lived and he'd wanted a cheeseburger with bacon but they'd had cucumber sandwiches with the crusts cut off instead, "Isn't it clever, dear, how they cut the crusts off? Oh, this place is so refined."

And his mother had chosen a suitable girl for him to marry, not one of those sluts with their hip-hugger pants and a tattoo of a butterfly in the small of her back that he liked and the big boobs barely covered up, sashaying down the street and giving you the eye like whores but instead a prim and proper upstanding Christian girl who would make him a good wife and mother except Barbara hadn't actually made such a good fucking mother, had she? Hadn't really been very interested in sex, certainly not in the morning or during the daylight hours or anywhere but in bed with the lights out so you didn't have to look at exactly 11:40 p.m. because you had to wait till the talk show monologue was over and certainly not interested in doing any of those nasty things where you actually touched each other in bad places. So after awhile he gave up and just masturbated in the bathroom after she drank herself to sleep. She never got pregnant and she never had any kids and she turned into a grouchy old fat unhappy woman who drank and drank and drank herself to sleep every night although everyone said he was so lucky, she was so charming and proper and always socially correct and chose the *nicest* furniture and knew how to dress and how to set the table just so, although Danny Brackley would have given all those years of having the table set just so for two years and two kids with some tramp with a tattoo who'd fucking well let him screw her over the kitchen table and then Barbara had gotten sick.

And he had never cheated on her, had he? No, Danny Brackley was still a good little boy even when he was 45, working his way up through the Byzantine city bureaucracy, carrying the water buckets and cleaning up other people's messes and heading up the committees on toilet paper and fire extinguishers and setting the mileage reimbursement rate, committees no one else wanted to head up and going without his vacation time to make extra money to pay the medical bills as he nursed his sick wife.

Did he cheat on her, even then? Nooo. Did he dump her when she got sick and go marry some young bimbette who could give him the hot sex and the children he wanted? Nooo. Because Daniel Brackley was a good little boy and he played by the rules and he always did what he was supposed to do the way his mother had always told him because eventually that would give him a good life while all those wild kids who drove the fast cars and hung around with those trampy girls would pay, they would pay in the end, his mother told him so.

But did they ever pay? Not that Danny Brackley ever saw. The ones he hated most of all were the pretty boys, the tall ones with the athletic builds and the shock of pretty red or blond hair and the perfect teeth. They were always the easy, graceful Kennedys to his grubby, pouting, hard-working Richard Nixon with the 5 o'clock shadow that the cartoonists loved to make fun of. Everything was so easy for them, they lived on credit while Dan Brackley was scrimping and saving and they always knew the bright, slick things to say and he was always left standing in the doorway watching everyone else head off shrieking and giggling for cocaine and skinnydipping, tubby little Danny Brackley, balding little Danny Brackley, be sure to lock up when you leave, stuttering and stepping on his dick.

All the golden boys had to do was flash a smile and the girls came running, and what did little Danny Brackley get? He got to clean up after the party when everyone else was out getting laid. He was the also-ran, the club treasurer, the chief of staff, while the pretty boy, Mr. Prep School, Mr. Fraternity Brother, Mr. Class President ended up getting elected to the City Council where all the payoffs were and getting the trophy wife and getting rich.

Yes, rich! That was the most galling part. Because no matter how hard Danny Brackley worked, he was still never handed the insider deal that came from the developer or the lawyer or the banker calling up the Golden Boy and saying, "Hi, Todd, we're putting together a limited partnership to buy this redevelopment parcel out on the island that we think the city is going to buy up for a park; we've got the developer all lined up to turn it into a public golf course, you know him, he's *very* well connected, but we think you can probably help us make all this happen, Mr. Golden Boy, so how about if we cut you in for 5 percent? That could be worth millions when the whole thing closes in about eight months, what do you say?

"What's that? How much would you have to put in? Wellll, now, why don't you just not worry about *that?* You help us make sure we don't run into any snags with the pesky zoning commission, get that flood zone waiver, and you can just pay us back your buy-in out of your portion of the profits when the whole deal closes next year; how's that sound?"

Little Danny Brackley had watched it happen again and again. He was the one who carried the water and did the dirty work and made sure everything went through like shit through a goose, but did *he* get cut in for 5 percent? Nooo. That went to one of the Golden Boys, since it was Mr. Frat House who could get elected, not little Danny Brackley, who was now going to turn 50 and would never be tall and would never have those perfect, gleaming teeth and would never have all his hair again.

Barbara had died and left him with medical bills and her credit card bills and closets full of shoes and half-used cosmetics. Even to sell the house he'd had to invest in new carpets and new paint because no one wanted to buy a house that looked like a *used* house, and by the time he was done selling the house it only just covered all the bills so he'd moved into an apartment and started again from scratch at the age of 45. Forty-five years and nothing to show for it but his job as deputy city manager, still working late and doing the dirty work for the real players.

But you know what? Little Danny Brackley had a lot of time on his hands while he'd been nursing his sick wife, and Little Danny Brackley had finally got smart.

Because if they went to Danny Brackley to do the mule work it stood to reason he'd also become their go-to guy when they had a little mess to clean up. And Danny did clean them up, oh yes. He picked up some friends on the vice and homicide squads and at the newspapers, made sure they were well paid to tip him off when things were happening and also to make sure certain files and stories went away when it was necessary. When you were assistant city manager it was surprising what you could do with overtime pay and no-bid contracts and putting girlfriends on the payroll, and it wasn't even illegal. You just had to understand the budgeting process, and Danny

Brackley knew that budget inside out, oh yes. So Danny was always able to clean up a mess when one of the Golden Boys slapped around one of his whores too hard or developed a little problem with an underage boyfriend who'd gotten into drugs and was threatening to blow the whistle on the city council-man's little dalliances with those underage Filipino lads down at the Ramrod Cafe.

Little Danny Brackley cleaned up the messes so spot-lessly and asked for so little in exchange, he would just say, "Oh, don't mention it, someday you'll be able to do me a favor in turn." Only what the golden boys didn't realize was that the files and the photos and the notarized statements and the addresses where he relocated the bought-off witnesses never actually went away, they just went into the files Danny Brack-ley started keeping.

Files on everyone.

When no one else wanted to give the speech at the rib-bon-cutting for the disabled veterans or the new Hispanic Studies Center, Danny Brackley went. He started to store up some political favors. Then he'd found Oliver Oates slaving away at the community college, organizing Save-the-Whale rallies. But Oliver was smart, he knew how to run computer analysis of voter information, he knew where to put the money — where most of the other guys were wasting money reaching voters who had either already decided or just weren't going to turn out on election day no matter what you told them.

With Oliver Oates' help he started building a political machine, though he was careful never to call it that or let it look like that. His people were parked in "Community Ser-vices" or the Elections Department warehouse, jiggering the machines, or else they went to work for non-profit outfits with names like "Project Safe Streets" that seemed to stay busy do-ing worthy things like organizing gun buy-backs and passing out AIDS literature to make sure more gay black men went on AZT therapy — that was a brilliant one, the big pharmaceutical houses were willing to subsidize those efforts up the ass, made something like N$1,800 a week off every single faggot who went on the program, a program which generally killed them off in a couple of years, thank God they never seemed to run out of faggots, you'd think they'd notice the ones who never went on AZT were living years longer than the ones who took the medicine, but they never did — as a matter of fact, anyone who pointed that out was called a "homophobe." And in the meantime what Danny Brackley was really doing was building a machine, a machine with salaried staff and phone banks and everything he needed.

He bided his time, and then finally the time came when it was going to be Councilman Brackley, and Mayor Brackley. The golden boys had laughed at him, of course, patted him on the head, said he was so valuable behind the scenes, why did he want to go out and face defeat at the polls? As though the goddamned idiot voters decided anything, as though it wasn't all campaign contributions and pulling a file on any viable op- ponents till they steered clear of running against him for fear of their fucking lives and knowing how those fancy new elec- tronic voting machines he'd bought on a sole-source contract were programmed.

And when they finally saw he was serious and they asked how dare he think of challenging them, the men who had made him what he was, the world's champion water-bucket boy, he ought to be happy with what he had and keep his place, that's when Dan Brackley's hired cops from vice and homicide came calling, threatening to show the files and the photos to their wives and their kids, and everyone realized then that Danny Brackley knew where all the skeletons were buried, didn't they?

And the ones he liked best were the ones who *didn't* fall into line right away and say "Yes, sir, Mr. Brackley sir, and thank you for keeping me on your team, Mr. Brackley, and would you like your boots licked now, Mr. Brackley?" Because those were the ones he could use as examples for the rest, not just destroying them politically, but setting them up to have their houses and bank accounts seized under the organized crime and racketeering laws, making sure they lost their homes, their families — if Danny Brackley himself didn't fuck their trophy wives and get them crying and asking for more on the camera hidden behind the mirror he damn well saw to it that someone else did, someone *very* large and ugly.

No, once he got started on one of the college boys there were no plea bargains, he got his friends on the newspaper editorial pages to bray "An example must be set! This embarrassing wave of corruption must end!" and they went to prison, goddammit, where Danny Brackley had the contacts to make sure they got buggered every night, the little preppie milksop wimps. Didn't like it so much when it was little Danny Brackley asking, "Oh, has life not been *fair* to you, Mr. football star?"

And then his goddamned brat little brother had come home from the wars out West with all his medals. Danny had met with him and told him there was a place all carved out for him, see, those medals would be worth their weight in gold, they'd be a team, see, there was no political substitute for that kind of credential. And what had his little brother said?

He was going to come out against the War! Two years out West and he'd gone completely native, said the rebels were right, the government was trying to impose a fascist police state, blah blah anarchist bullshit right up the ass. Oh sure. These goddamned snake-handling, child-molesting yahoos in Montana and Idaho and Alberta were the equivalent of Tom Paine and Mahatma Gandhi and the Minutemen of Lexington and Concord all rolled into one. And it wasn't like he was just going to restrict himself to spouting all this secessionist bullshit in private, talking about how they should goddamned recognize New Columbia and let Texas go, too, if that's what they wanted.

No, he was planning to go *public*.

Danny had tried talking to him, hadn't he? He'd tried to tell him it didn't matter what he believed as long as he'd keep his damned mouth shut, the gravy train was all laid out. Congress, the Senate, the governorship, his war hero little brother could have had his pick. But no, he had to keep mouthing off about some organization of Communist nuns that was going to hold a pray-in at City Hall, exposing some damned conspiracy theory about corrupt government contracts for rebuilding war-torn Denver. Oh yes, little brother Tom was bound and determined to blow the lid off the whole corrupt, imperialist war machine.

And did he care what this would do to Danny Brackley's carefully laid plans, so long in the making? He did not. He didn't care the slightest bit. He'd found God, he'd found a mission, he was like Joan of Arc, possessed of the Holy Spirit. Well his big brother had tried to tell him what had happened to Joan of Arc, hadn't he? He'd tried to warn him what would happen.

What a tragedy. What a loss. His only brother.

And meantime, how had the sweet little bitches of this fair metropolis rewarded Danny Brackley for being such a good boy, such a fine, upstanding fellow? After his two years of mourning and taking flowers to place on his dead wife's grave every weekend he'd found himself 47 years of age, at which point he figured it must be time to try and find himself SOME kind of a life again. And guess what?

He promptly discovered that life had passed him by. The kind of women a short, fat, balding 50-ish man can meet are divided into three classes, Danny Brackley soon discovered. The first class were women well past 40 themselves, bitter divorcees, who either came with their own raft of bratty, spoiled, brain-damaged children in tow, behind on their dental work, barely literate thanks to the fine government schools, refusing to accept discipline from anyone, snarling "You're not my dad and I don't have to do anything you say and if you touch me I'll have you arrested for child molest," or else their kids were in college and any inquiry as to whether the mom in question was still fertile and might be interested in having another child got you laughed out of the room. "Go through babies and diapers *again?!*" After all, it would interfere with their jogging and their evening bingo, wouldn't it?

The second class of women were hard-as-nails broads in their thirties, strippers and whores and professional grifters and con women who still looked damned good but who had seen it all and who'd proceeded to play an eager middle-aged novice like Dan Brackley for a fool till all his available money was gone, at which point they'd had their real boyfriends or "brothers" beat him up, steal his stereo and skip town.

And finally there were the young girls in their 20s who got hired as clerks and secretaries down at City Hall, fresh out of school, traveling around together in little gaggles like geese, laughing and gossiping and twittering incomprehensibly. Did any of them ever say, "Gosh, Mr. Brackley, it certainly is great how you never cheated on your wife and you nursed her through sickness and in health just like you said in your vows. That's so romantic and mature and stable of you. Why, you're just the kind of stable and mature man my mother says I should look for in a husband, instead of these immature young studs with the beautiful hair and the beautiful teeth and the flashy cars and the gold chains who keep inviting me out to parties where I can wear my sexy new dress that's about the size of a handkerchief that shows off the top half of the new tattoo on my ass because they just want to get me drunk and get into my pants. Of *course* I'd love to join you for dinner and a movie, Mr. Brackley, a serious fellow like you."

"Not," as the young people were wont to say. Not a fucking chance in the world, to put a little finer point on it. In fact they laughed in his face, looked at his balding head and his paunch and laughed at him in ridicule and disbelief that he would have the *nerve,* older than their fathers, ran to tell all their friends till he was embarrassed to even show his face in the office for a week. Dirty old man, trying to steal children from the cradle, you know what's on HIS mind.

Yes. Marriage and children, an undertaking pretty much limited to ladies under 40, last time he'd checked his high school biology text. Pretty fucking sordid, eh? Pretty fucking stupid to think any of the rules he'd grown up believing in and following so scrupulously would do him any good now — that a fertile young woman might be interested in a stable older guy with a new-bought house and a steady job and no desire to roam.

Oh, the rules had been great when they called for Little Danny to be patient and not act immature and do everybody else's bidding and wash everybody else's dirty laundry and act like he was already 50 when he was still 20 and could get a hard-on just looking at the department store models in the Bali bras in the Sunday paper. But when it was supposed to come payoff time and he was supposed to be rewarded for a lifetime of stability and maturity, no whoring around, no drugs, no good times?

Turned out it was all just a big joke, and the joke was on him. The sports car roared by, the naked broads giving blowjobs to the coke dealer in the front seat, and there was Danny Brackley, standing by the roadside eating dust, splashed with mud, watching the world laugh as it sped by.

But you know what? Once he'd learned to turn the tables on those pretty college boys, those prep-school Kennedy lookalikes, once it became known that he had what it took — not just the files and the evidence but the WILLINGNESS, the DETERMINATION, the KILLER INSTINCT — to go after anyone who crossed him, even his own little brother for God's sake, to ruin them, not just cost them their political careers but to see to it they actually went to PRISON, and that once there he could arrange to have them buggered every night for months by a big bald stud who made them wear frilly aprons around the cell ... once the lovely wives and daughters found out he'd really done that to someone they knew and he had the power to do that to their beloved hubbies and daddies who were now caught up in the government money-laundering and conspiracy prosecution sausage machine, it was just AMAZING how suddenly more attractive chunky, balding little Danny Brackley became. Oh, the THINGS they would come to him and offer to do if only he'd let their blessed hubby off the hook.

And you know what? Danny Brackley found out he liked it that way. None of this always trying to look right and smell right and not fart after dinner and hold their doors for them and send them flowers, as though he was still playing assistant waterboy in charge of cleaning up other people's messes. Because now HE was in charge, God damn it, and when they came to him like that it delighted him to tell them, "OK bitch, take off your clothes and kneel down like a suntanned little doggie, and I don't want to hear anything out of you but, 'Oh, master, that hurts so much, won't you do it to me harder?' "

And when they thought they'd paid the price and that was the end? Son of a bitch if it didn't turn out there was VIDEO of their being ridden like bitches down at the No-Tell Motel, whining for Danny to do it harder, close-ups of their faces and their tits bouncing on the floor or the bed, their legs spread wide and Dan Brackley massaging their thighs and riding those pretty wide-open rocking pussies like the Lone Ranger riding off into the sunset, wearing nothing but his orange necktie, and if you don't want that sweet hubby of yours and all his partners in the preppie law firm to spend their lunch hours watching this great piece of video every day for the next month, oh, turn up the sound, yeah, I'll see you again next Tuesday, same time, same place, and be sure to bring your kneepads and your harness.

And so he kept his stable of very expensive doggie whores; they discovered they had to keep coming across whenever he wanted it, because otherwise those videos just went into the package with Danny's face carefully edited out and they'd go down right along with their dirty hubbies.

Oh, it was sweet. But it wasn't enough. No. Because now on top of everything else Mayor Daniel Brackley's plans were being fucked up by this Black Arrow character, this goddamned Order of the Arrow terrorizing his people, actually TAKING THE LAW INTO THEIR OWN HANDS and killing perfectly innocent public servants who were only doing their jobs, people with wives and mistresses until the resignation letters and the requests for extended sick leave started to pile up, and when he called down to get something done it was always the same story, "We're short-handed, we can't keep up," whine whine whine.

In short, he was still pissed off and he still wanted to kill someone, or at the very least ruin an enemy, and today would be as good a time as any. He went to buzz for his trusty assistant — but of course Milton buzzed him just before he could reach the button. He ALWAYS did that. DAMMIT.

"Yes?!"

"Sir, it's Mrs. Petrov."

"Who?"

"Her husband was sentenced in a drug case. The sprinkler store?"

"Oh yes. Right. Send her in."

He remembered her as he saw her walk in. She seemed hesitant, of course. He routinely had courthouse surveillance photos of the wives and daughters delivered to him. No, he hadn't made a mistake with her. Tanya Petrov was dressed a little dowdy, in a matching skirt and jacket that looked like they'd been made out of some brightly colored bedspread. Belonged upholstering an old sofa in someone's basement rec room.

But Daniel Brackley had too good an eye to be fooled. He wasn't hiring fashion sense, here. Ample breast, great legs, a nice curve to the butt. Even the face was prettier than most. Oh, yeah. This one went on the "A" list. Cute little upturned nose. A little too much cornfed Odessa farmgirl for his normal taste, but that would only make it all the more delicious to ride her like a squealing pig, make her beg for more, if she decided to come across. A surprising number of them did.

She was probably 10 or 15 pounds heavy, but even there the stress she'd been under had helped. They didn't tend to eat real well when the government took away the house and put the kids in foster care and dragged hubby around for photo ops in manacles and an orange jump suit so everyone would know he was guilty long before the hand-picked jury rubber-stamped the government's case. "What's that, Prospective Juror Number 8? You think drugs should be *legalized?* Oh, ha ha. Thanks for your honesty; you're excused." Funny how all your friends stopped taking your calls when hubby was identified as a major drug kingpin on the TV news.

Especially the drug cases. Once the bank accounts were seized as "illicit drug proceeds" they were left penniless, dependent on a public defender who was, of course, an employee of the state. Oh yeah, they had a GREAT chance at that point.

Did this one have kids? He couldn't remember. Didn't really matter.

"Mr. Mayor," she said, standing and holding her purse nervously in front of her. The office was designed to make people nervous. It was big, full of windows and sunlight and big red leather chairs with brass studs, the walls sparkling with awards, certificates, and photographs framed in gleaming stainless steel. Daniel shaking hands with the senator. Daniel shaking hands with the other senator. Daniel shaking hands with the last president — the new one hadn't come through town, yet. Anybody's guess whether he'd live long enough. Two assassination attempts already. Why did anyone even *want* the job?

Jesus, what was that purse made of, white imitation leather? The woman probably served lime Jell-O with fruit in it. Did they have Jell-O in Russia? Milton pulled the door discreetly closed behind her. Good lad.

"Your Honor," she corrected herself. "I don't have anywhere else to turn. My husband, Yuri Petrov, is a good man ... a military veteran. We've never been in trouble with the law a day in our lives. This is the first time we've been apart since we were married. The police tried for years, they sent in undercover agents with recorders, tried to get us to talk about how you could use our equipment to grow marijuana. It never worked. We never talked about that, because that would be illegal. That's all we sell — sold, is irrigation equipment. Not even potting soil. You can grow anything with our equipment; orchids, fruit trees. There's nothing about it that specifically lends itself to drugs. The lawyer proved that. But it turns out that does not matter. The law does not matter."

Nice voice. Not shrill. Kind of melodic. What did the old song say? "She speaks good English and she'll take you upstairs to her room."

"They said no one else could help me now, that you might be able to talk to the judge and get the sentence reduced. You know they copied down the license plates of the people who came to our store, raided their homes at night? Most of them just had vegetable gardens. Even then, the ones who were growing pot wouldn't lie and say we told them how. They only got poor Mrs. Kostic to lie about us by telling her they'd put her in prison and her husband would die. He has multiple sclerosis ..."

She had started to sob, dug a Kleenex out of her purse. This is where they always expected Daniel Brackley to leap to his feet, pull them up a chair, listen to their crap for another hour or so, put on a somber expression and nod sympathetically. Last time he checked, totally useless sympathetic nodders with medical degrees got a couple hundred newbucks an hour to look up every 15 minutes and ask "And how did *that* make you feel?" Time to nip this crap in the bud.

"Mrs. Petrov — Tanya!" he said, sharp enough that she jumped a little and looked him in the eye. Suddenly the tear machine seemed to be drying up a bit. She looked at the mayor closely now, for the first time. He had a prominent nose and jaw. He had strong, even teeth, and pale blue-gray eyes. He did not appear to be very tall. He made no attempt to disguise his bald head — what was left of his hair was straight, light brown, swept back cleanly above either ear.

"I'm not a lawyer and I don't write a sob-sister column for the newspapers and I really don't have time for the whole tale of woe, OK? There are other people who are paid to listen to this crap. All the stories start to sound the same, believe me, and they all run to the hundreds of pages. 'And then the judge refused to hear our challenge of the Terry frisk and the Hannah priors.' Everybody's innocent. The only thing is, they had their trial and they were convicted, so whether your husband was innocent or not doesn't really matter. Are you listening to me? Do you hear what I'm saying?"

"Yes."

"I'm sure he's a wonderful guy and he never leaves the seat up on the john, but whether I'm going to help you doesn't have anything to do with whether he's innocent, so save your story and write it up for the Barbed Wire Gazette, write a letter to the Civil Liberties Union, Xerox it up and send it out as your family Christmas letter, I don't care. If you want to talk about how he's innocent and how he doesn't deserve this, thanks for coming by; I'm a busy man."

"Oh," she said. But she didn't leave.

"What you're asking is expensive. I have friends, but they're not my friends because we're old fraternity brothers, or because I set the place on fire when I sit down to play the piano at parties, OK? The judges who do me favors do me favors because my police officers have agreed to ignore certain indiscretions on their part, or because we helped them against a political opponent, and we're going to give them even more help when that next shot at an appointment to a higher bench comes open. OK? That's how politics and power work, Tanya. Everything has a price, and I'm the broker.

"You're here because I'm a powerful man. But power doesn't come free. It's expensive to maintain my friendships. It's an ongoing expense. I don't give it away for free. You've been to see the free Legal Aid people. I'm sure they've got some law student who hopes to start shaving soon with fat lips and moles and hair like a Brillo pad already working real hard on your case, don't they?"

"Do you know Joel?"

"It's all worth exactly what you pay for it. His briefs will look real good gathering dust on a shelf someplace. Throw him an extra 12 bucks for a nice binder."

"Oh."

"Now, I've looked over the case file. I can't spring your husband tomorrow, or next week. No one can do that, with this many conspiracy charges and sentence enhancements for non-cooperation."

"They wanted us to name other people. But we couldn't name other people, because we've never even seen a pound of marijuana, let alone — "

"Tanya, honey. Shut up."

She did.

"He's going to serve some time. But can we put in a word, get the sentence reduced, get him put into a minimum security country club instead of sending him to a really bad place where he'll be lucky to see the sun for an hour a day inside a fenced exercise kennel, the kind of place where he'd have to defend himself with a shiv in the daytime and he'll have a bald-headed roommate named Bubba to pay special attention to him every night? That's where he's going and that's the stuff the Public Defender doesn't bother to tell you about, Tanya. Can I help him out, there? Yes. Quite possibly I can do that.

"But in the real world, justice is expensive, Tanya. What

can you pay? What are you willing to pay?"

"I'm ... They broke us. The bank accounts — the house is gone. They said it was 'bought with drug proceeds,' which means all the money we saved. I'm staying with my sister. We really don't have anything. I could probably put together a few hundred new dollars ..."

"Tanya." He sighed for dramatic effect. "I had someone talk to you before you came here. That man isn't stupid, and he told me you didn't appear to be stupid. You're here because you're pretty, and you're not too fat, yet, and you have a great ass, if you don't mind my saying so. We're not here to talk about money. When you offer an official money, that's called a bribe."

"No, I didn't mean — I'm sorry."

"Good. Now I'm going to make this real easy for you, Tanya. Either you're going to leave now, and write to your husband every week in prison, and listen to some jerk-off law student in the Drug Amnesty Project tell you how he's real sure one of their appeals on Ninth Amendment grounds which has never gone any further than the courthouse dumpster is bound to get a hearing one day real soon, right about the time pigs fly, and you're going to become an old maid pining away for your lost youth, or else you're going to wipe your eyes and stop playing Shirley Partridge and say, 'I'll do anything you tell me if you can get my husband's sentence reduced so I can see him again before he's 55. If you can get his sentence cut in half, I will do anything.'"

She had stopped blubbering.

"This is one of those important moments, Tanya. No one's going to make you murder anyone. No one's asking you to cut off your arm. But no one's going to twist your arm, either. This is a completely voluntary choice on your part. You have tried all the other avenues. I won't contact you again. I'm a very busy man. You're not the only decent-looking woman who's ever come here asking if there was anything I could do. There is something I can do, there's quite a bit I can do. We're not talking miracles but you could add years to your Yuri's life. His free, after-he-gets-out-of-prison life. But this isn't kindergarten; you've only got one thing left to barter that's of interest to a serious man.

"You're a grown-up woman. You know what we're talking about. Now you're free to say 'No thanks' and walk away and wonder whether there was any more you could have done. Or you can take my proposition and pay to help your Yuri in a way that no one else but you CAN help him, now, in a way that no one else but you CAN pay. One or two evenings a week, you tell your sister you've got a date or you're sitting up with a sick friend or you're taking an aerobics class, whatever. But this is the point where you have to decide, Tanya."

Tanya's knees felt weak. Her stomach churned. She wanted to sit down but he hadn't offered her a chair. That was on purpose, she realized. She was not here as a friend, as any kind of social equal. She was here as a supplicant, and he was demonstrating to her who had the power — the power to help Yuri, but also the power to name his own price.

How could she have been such a fool? The man who had approached her to invite her here — the handsome young man with the long hair and the thin mustache and the mincing manners — had spoken of the possibility of "an arrangement." He had told her the mayor had expressed "a personal interest." Even if she didn't quite understand all this business about "arm twisting," her English was not so bad that she should have missed those cues. But she was just so caught up in the case, reaching out to anyone she could talk to about it. She had been so desperate ... she had not listened closely for the meaning of the words.

She was familiar with stories of such dealings in the old country, of course. Foolishly, she had believed such things could not happen here in America. But men — especially men in power — were the same everywhere, weren't they? They all wanted the same things. Why should anyone be surprised that, once you allowed them to gather a certain amount of power, some of them would decide to use their power to satisfy their personal appetites?

She was here alone, now. She had no one to advise her, and no one as a witness. He would deny everything if she complained, of course. But he had presented it all so firmly, with such ease. No hemming and hawing, no false starts, no beating around the bush. Clearly it was not the first time he had made such a proposal. Oh, far from the first. So, did the other women accept?

Of course they did. Enough of them, anyway. He wouldn't continue if it didn't succeed. And why wouldn't they, if they were desperate enough, if all other hope was gone?

"Tanya?"

She shivered at the sound of her own name. The room felt suddenly very cold, despite the bright winter sun pouring in the windows. "What?"

"You can walk away, or you can tell me you want me to help Yuri. It's up to you."

There was his clear-eyed girl, now. The eyes narrowed a little. The jaw set. Brain in gear. "I want you to help Yuri — if you really can."

"And you will do anything I ask you to do, in exchange for that help."

She didn't answer.

"Tanya, you have to say 'I will do anything you ask.' "

"I — I don't know. I need time to think."

He leaned forward, handed her a slip of paper. "All right. You have the rest of the day to decide. That's a street address and a room number, also a phone number for a cab, and an account number to charge the ride. I recommend the cab, but there's also a parking garage. Be there at 9 o'clock tonight and bring an overnight bag. Come alone. If you're not there by 9:30 ..." he left the sentence unfinished, gave her a quick smile, and turned back to the work on his desk.

She took the paper and stood there, uncertain what to do next.

At this point, of course, Daniel Brackley wanted to leap to his feet, take her in his arms, comfort her, assure her he was going to help her, that everything would be all right. He WAS going to help her, after all, wasn't he? He wasn't such a bad person, really. Had he invented this War on Drugs? No. Had he told this young couple to foolishly go into the sprinkler and irrigation supply business, surely knowing some of their customers had to be growing dope? Of course not. Had he told them to thumb their noses at the cops, commit the crime of Making the Officers Look Stupid, calling the TV stations to complain about their store being staked out? Had he told them to do any of those stupid things? What did they THINK was going to happen to people who embarrassed their betters in such a way, when the other side had the unlimited funds and patience of The Government on their side?

Now she needed help trying to get her husband a better deal. And Daniel Brackley was in a position to offer that help — he'd gone to a lot of trouble to make SURE he was in that position. She'd also be needing someone to fill that void in her life that her missing man had left, wouldn't she? Why should a warm, vibrant, healthy young woman like this have no lover to warm her bed and keep her complexion clear?

But Daniel Brackley did not jump up and attempt to embrace and comfort her, of course. No, no, no. He hadn't been doing this for years without learning SOMETHING. To do so would only give her another, better chance to push him away, to reject him, to cause a ruckus that would have the secretaries wondering what was going on ... assuming he still retained anyone who didn't know enough to look straight ahead and keep their damned mouths shut.

No, either she would accept his offer — take his deal — or she would not. And once she had, there would be no pushing away, no refusal to do ANYTHING he required of her. Once she arrived with her little bag.

It was a hard discipline Daniel Brackley had imposed on himself, to show no tenderness or mercy. But it was a discipline these women themselves had taught him, with their beckoning ways and then their cold rejection, one following the other as the night follows day, always leaving HIM looking like the clown with the red nose, the floppy shoes, and the embarrassing boner. But he had learned. Oh, yes. He might be a slow learner, but he had figured out how to turn things his way, eventually. He would remain sternly in control, in charge.

And what was so wrong with that? Every animal had to develop its own reproductive strategy. Biology rewarded those who succeeded, not those who sat home trying bunko hair re-growth formulas and exercise treadmills and whining and bitching about how unfair life was.

"You can go now, Tanya," he said, trying to sound a bit more kind and gentle. "I'm sure I don't need to tell you the authorities still have a case against you, which they're holding open in case you give us any trouble. So I'd suggest you not talk about this with anyone. What you're doing here right now is technically illegal. It's an attempt to suborn a public official. But I'm going to overlook that, because you're really a very special girl, with something very special to offer. If we come to develop some affection for each other — well, they can't make it illegal to make a few phone calls, to help a friend.

"Make some excuse to your sister; you need to get away in the mountains for a day or two, whatever. Everything's going to be just fine as long as you keep this a private arrangement between the two of us. You understand?"

"Yes. I do."

"Good girl. Run along now. 9 o'clock tonight."

She only hesitated a second, and then she turned to go. Women. They were really the more practical half of the species, by far. Once they found out the weeping and the moaning weren't doing any good, several layers of bullshit could disappear with amazing speed.

"Oh, and Tanya?"

"Yes?"

"Nice ass, really." And then, just before she left, he gave her his nicest smile. And they said he'd never make a politician.

The door clicked softly closed.

Daniel Brackley knew he was a little bit nuts, of course. But didn't he have good reason to be nuts? Couldn't he recall with crystalline clarity every detail of the things that had made him nuts, things he'd gone over in his memory again and again, locking them away as evidence of the way the bitches had treated him as his eager and well-meaning passion had gradually turned to bitterness, hatred and a determination to be revenged on the evil subspecies known as woman?

He hadn't had a woman for a year and a half when the lovely Carmilla, who he'd been trying to ask out for months, finally called and invited him over to her new co-op to help her hang some pictures. She'd met him at the door barefoot and beautiful in a white T-shirt and tight blue jeans that showed off the physique of a gal who was manic about running and bicycling, talked endlessly about the endorphin high she got when she first broke a sweat and felt her skin cooled by the rushing wind. A divorced lady with a grown child and the money to buy a huge new apartment, she was no innocent virgin, ignorant of the ways of love or the world.

Her makeup wasn't overdone, but she'd clearly put it on just for him; some blush on her cheeks, and that thing she did with her eyes, painting a little black triangle at the outside of her eyelids so they looked oriental when she closed them. Subtle, beautiful, just for him.

She was cooking a Thai dish, eggplant and peppers in coconut milk, and she invited him to stay. Clearly the minimal work of helping her hang a few heavy pieces on the wall was a pretext for getting him over to her place for conversation and whatever might develop. She bubbled with enthusiasm, pulling stuff out of the cupboard and refrigerator to show off the various Asian foodstuffs she'd bought the day before at the new Asian market she'd discovered.

Carmilla had always put him off before, claiming she had a boyfriend, but where was this boyfriend to help her move into her new place?

With growing excitement, Daniel Brackley realized her excitement at the market the day before had been over the prospect of having a new man for whom to buy her coconut milk, so viscous and suggestive as it flowed into the pan ... a new man named Daniel!

She invited him into the bedroom — the bedroom — to help her choose a wine from the wine rack, kneeling and swaying to the music on the player as they languorously chose a Petite Sirah. She poured big glasses and sniffed the aroma with undisguised sensual pleasure, laughing musically as they discussed whether you could smell the essences of black pepper and currants and raspberries that the wine reviewers claimed to be able to detect there. Soon the bottle was gone and she opened a second — *a second bottle of wine* — without his even having to suggest it. She scampered up the ladder to help him position a heavy clock on the wall, her fingers and breast and eyelashes brushing against him so casually, so accidentally. He watched her educated fingers as they slowly slid the plug of the electric clock into the wall, the same sensual elegance with which those fingers had peeled the eggplant and sliced the peppers, just for him.

She came and sat by him on the black wrought-iron stools at the kitchen counter, brought hard Gruyere to go with their wine. He leaned forward and gently kissed her lips. She did not pull back. In fact, she kissed him back, and then demurely lowered her eyes and thanked him. Soon they were on the rug in front of the fake gas fire, which was all his new air pollution regs allowed in new construction, anymore.

She brought the meal in bowls with chopsticks, but the food sat largely forgotten as he kissed her deeply and well, lowering her to the floor. She shuddered and moaned with long-suppressed desire as he bit her ear and neck, dragged his fingers across her still-covered breasts. She explained the boyfriend was "in transition," separated from his wife but still involved in an interminable three-year divorce — there was a lot of money involved.

Daniel understood. This ripe, live, fertile woman needed a man, and the rich man she wanted wasn't there to satisfy her needs. Well, Daniel wasn't proud. He was willing to be the second choice, the consolation prize, even if only for a while. Who was he to demand any more? He was sure the missing boyfriend was only stringing Carmilla along, of course — no divorce takes three years. Probably lying about being separated, for that matter. Or he'd surely be here to take advantage of the wonders of Helping Carmilla Move In.

She repeatedly said "Oh, this is so dangerous," as she giggled and kissed him back with her tongue, her mouth wide open and panting with desire. He picked her up and carried her into the bedroom, his strength immeasurable in the heat of his passion, laid her gently on the bed as they talked and talked and kissed. He gave her a back massage. She rolled over and spread her legs and he lay between them.

"Oh, I'd like to tell you to just fuck the beJesus out of me," she said, "Just drill me." He laughed and joked about her still using the conditional tense. "I'm right here, baby, all you have to do is ask," he'd said. She talked about how she got so frustrated sometimes she used a vibrator, how she was so uptight back when she was married that she'd never been able to tell her husband things like that, for fear he'd take offense. Daniel took her hand and put it between his own still-clothed legs and told her he had a spare that she was welcome to use, that his was a superior model; it came with teeth and shoulders.

She talked then about how she loved to cuddle and how she loved to make love in the morning when she was still half-asleep. Daniel was used to women who had no desire to cuddle with him, and who would never satisfy his morning hard-on, instead insisting they had to jump out of bed and get ready for work, why did he have to be such a bother and a pest at inappropriate times and places? His mind soared to thoughts of long and languorous weekends of endless, creative, gasping, moaning love in this bed. He laughed and asked if perhaps, their tastes in wine and food and ... other matters ... being so similar, they'd been separated at birth.

He'd called her "honey" and she'd laughed with delight and asked him to call her that again and again.

She'd laughed and kissed him back. He had gone to unfasten her belt and pull off her pants, figuring he'd already waited longer than must be considered usual, didn't want to seem like he lacked confidence or didn't know what he was doing. And that's when his world and the very sky had collapsed in around him. She sat up then and slapped him and said, "No, and no means No."

She'd told him she had a boyfriend, after all, hadn't she? He was out of town, that was all. It'd all been a joke, a mistake. She'd just been fooling around and he should have known it was just because the wine had gone to her head.

She turned on the light and asked him to leave. It was in Daniel Brackley's mind to throw her down on the bed right then and do her anyway. He knew his passion had given him the strength to force her if he wanted. And this was not some naive high school girl, his astonishment reminded him, but an experienced 40-ish divorcee who already had a teen-age child, away at school somewhere. But instead, to his endless regret and shame, he'd been such a wimp, such a coward, such a cowering eunuch.

He'd been afraid she'd call it rape; the fucking feminists had the courts and the prosecutors convinced the woman was always right. It was always rape if the woman said so, there was no defense. And even if he were to be acquitted at trial on such a charge, any such trial would be the end of the fledgling political career he had struggled so long to build.

And so he had let his main chance to be a real man slip by; he had left humiliated, but still determined she must want him, she had to want him. Hadn't he felt her shudder and sigh under his kiss, giggle and urge him to "say it again, say it again," when he'd called her "honey"?

It was all just part of the mating game. It had to be. She clearly wanted him to pursue her. She was holding it back only so he'd grow harder and harder, his desire building up until he could erupt inside her like a volcano of love when she finally relented and said Yes.

He wasn't blind. There were no man things around her apartment from this supposedly absent boyfriend. For all Daniel Brackley knew she'd invented him out of thin air as a way to put off unwanted suitors; she wore no rings on her fingers.

During the weeks that followed he had e-mailed her and tried to call her and see her. But instead of continuing to flirt with him now she went cold and said he was frightening her and that she'd call the police if he didn't stop. He tried to send her little presents and she told him she threw them away un-opened for fear she'd find "a sheep's heart inside, or something."

Why? What had Daniel Brackley done wrong? He'd been polite and respectful, obviously an adequate kisser, reasonably amusing in conversation, never done any more than she'd invited him to do, as she gaily laughed and moaned and flirted with him in the warmth of her ripe and warm and shuddering female need and fertility.

She kept saying she was sorry. He kept saying he didn't want her to be sorry; he wanted to fill her up with the joy of his love, a love she clearly wasn't getting from the Absent Boyfriend. But that's what she wanted, she lied — no commitments, just the never-seen, absent boyfriend to come and see her occasionally and not interfere with her wonderful life of ... what? Working overtime and running and bicycling? Classic paths to divert frustrated sexual energy, if Daniel Brackley knew anything about human psychology and physiology.

But what could he do? She threatened to call the police if he didn't leave her alone, and he was smart enough to know what that meant. The accused stalker was always presumed guilty, a sex-driven perverted maniac forcing his unwanted attentions on the demure and innocent virgin.

He had screamed with fury into the empty nights. Were they all mad? Who in their right mind would endorse giving a large male animal a taste — not just a sniff but a whole mouthful — of what it wanted most in the whole world, and then snatching it away? And then blaming HIM if the hormones pumping inside him told him to knock down walls, if that's what was required, in order to get to the object of his honest and appropriate and righteous desire?

It wasn't just about getting laid. He tried to masturbate, but that wasn't the point. He wanted HER. He wanted to satisfy HER needs. He wanted to feel that shudder and sigh of desire again when he bit her ear. Of course he wanted sex with her, but it was so much more than that. He wanted to provide for her, to protect her, to LOVE her. Yet HE was in the wrong?

What did they expect would happen? Any lion tamer could tell you what would happen. Ask Siegfried & fucking crippled Roy, for God's sake. In Alaska, bull moose were known to charge speeding locomotives that entered their territory during the rut. That was the kind of power the male mating instinct was understood to command in the wild. But HE was the one in the wrong? HE was the one who'd be seen as a lunatic stalker?

In his frustration, Daniel Brackley had cried like a child. He had wished he had the courage to take his own miserable life, or cut off his own balls, now useless burdens to him anyway. He knew what it was. The missing boyfriend was tall, wasn't he? Tall and slim with a tiny waist and a tight little butt and a full head of hair and perfect teeth and huge, hulking shoulders. A bright, charming college fraternity boy who knew all the right people and which fork to use with his salad. In Daniel Brackley's mind as in hers, Missing Boyfriend became the ideal man Daniel Brackley could never, ever be, no matter how he tried.

Bitches, bitches, bitches, with their fluttering eyelids and downcast faces, their techniques of attraction passed down over the generations, their elegant and educated fingers, their demure and subtle smiles, promising what he could never have. Well, he'd find a way. He'd put himself in a position where HE was in charge, god damn it, where HE was dominant. Let THEM squeal and complain about how unfair the world was, how they didn't *deserve* to be put in a position where they had to hike up their skirts and kneel down on the floor whenever he fucking felt like it.

Daniel Brackley decided then and there he would never again let himself be made ridiculous in such a way — a stupid, short, balding clown with everyone pointing and laughing at an inappropriate hard-on that he couldn't make go away. From now on, before he started to make love to a woman, he would make sure she was in no position to say no, that she was his slave and whore. Drugs, chains, blackmail, more subtle and more insidious methods of control and coercion that might occur to him later, he didn't give a damn, but from now on HE would be in control, damn it. Miserable flirting whores.

His favorite song came on the office radio, and Daniel Brackley turned up the volume, his Song for Carmilla:

Well I'd rather see you dead, little girl
Than to see you with another man.
You better keep your head, little girl
Or you won't know where I am.

You better run for your life if you can, little girl,
Hide your head in the sand, little girl.
Catch you with another man
That's the end, little girl.

Bitches.

Where was Newby? Christian Newby was his jack-of-all-crimes, a handsome young devil even if he was of uncertain sexuality, that long hair always falling down over his ears. Or maybe he drew all that attention precisely because no one was really sure — who could say? He had an assignment for Newby. He went to buzz for Milton. But of course Milton buzzed him just before he could reach the button.

"Sir?"

"YES?!"

"Christian Newby and Group Leader Heydrich are here to see you."

Well of course they were. Why did they ALWAYS DO THAT?

"And Mr. Oates is on the phone about the new polling."

Oliver Oates was a genius with numbers, but he was also becoming increasingly tiresome. Daniel had to keep reminding him they didn't poll to find out what to DO — they knew what they were fucking well going to DO — they polled to find out the best way to put it over, what kind of spin would work best. Did the new asset tax get the best numbers when it was sold as "building more schools and hospitals" or when it was promoted as "finally making the pampered heirs and heiresses pay their fair share"? But more and more, Oliver wanted to talk about the "long-term economic consequences of our taxing and spending policies," like he was back in his old classroom, evaluating the balance sheet of some African peanut farm.

"Have Oliver turn over the polling data to Bonnie," Daniel instructed Milton through the intercom. Bonnie was an assistant city manager for whom he had high hopes. Her face had some acne scarring, but she had a trim figure, quite adequate honkers, and the nicest green eyes. "Then set them up with a morning slot in a couple days to come present." That would help keep Oliver focused on the job at hand. "And send Christian in."

He would have brought Heydrich, of course. Heydrich was a useful man, but he gave Daniel the creeps.

SUPRYNOWICZ

CHAPTER 5

School-days, I believe, are the unhappiest in the whole span of human existence. They are full of dull, unintelligible tasks, new and unpleasant ordinances, brutal violations of common sense and common decency. It doesn't take a reasonably bright boy long to discover that most of what is rammed into him is nonsense, and that no one really cares very much whether he learns it or not.

— HENRY LOUIS MENCKEN, OF THE SUN (1880-1956))

If you have ten thousand regulations, you destroy all respect for the law.

— WINSTON CHURCHILL (1874-1965)

Exhausted from their breakneck escape and 20-foot tumble, Jack and Joan lay panting for some minutes at the bottom of the darkened drainage tunnel. Behind and above them they could still hear air venting from the train's brakes. Its engine thrummed as it idled, taking on passengers. Otherwise they seemed to be alone now; the beating of their hearts was the only sound.

At least they'd landed sitting pretty much upright. Joan

was leaning against him. Moving gingerly, Jack did a quick inventory, failed to discover any broken bones. They were sitting in almost an inch of some kind of stinking water; he hoped it wasn't anyone's blood. They were sheltered from the wind, down here, but the water was still chilly. Finding they were still holding onto one another's hands, he slipped free and gave her a quick pat-down, as well.

"I find you attractive, too, Jack. But do you really think this is the time and place?" came her voice from the darkness, surprisingly close to his throat.

"You OK? Nothing broken?"

"Only my heart."

"I'm gonna have to give up meeting girls this way."

"Oh that's nice. We've only just met, this is the first time you've felt me up, and you're already making plans to go looking for other women? Am I so unattractive that you need someone else in your life, Jack Brackley? Those will get bigger after you get me pregnant, you know."

He realized where his hands had come to rest and quickly removed them.

"Unattractive? You're the most beautiful girl I've ever met. Or woman. Whatever. But you're also kind of a force of nature."

"Is that bad?"

"I don't think you and I are shaping up to have that great a future, Joan."

"No?"

"In case you haven't noticed, we're sitting in a pitch black storm sewer, you've been shot, I'm out of a job and probably about to find myself on several Most Wanted lists. We'll be lucky if we can both get up and walk; from the smell of it whatever this ooze is we're sitting in is probably going to infect your leg wound, and in about half an hour there are gonna be a hundred guys down here searching for us, probably with police dogs. And on top of that ..."

"I'm a rebel and I'll never, ever be any good?"

"... on top of that, my uncle Daniel is trying to marry me off to some high society bitch who spends all her time shopping and hobnobbing with the social set out in the Hamptons."

"Oh. Is she pretty, this pampered princess of yours?"

"I've never even met Miss High-and-Mighty Eustace Summers, who I have no intention of marrying. Some things I'll do for honor, country, and Uncle Dan, but, I dunno, I think of marriage as kind of personal. Something that might involve someone you actually like and find attractive. Come to think of it, I'm starting to have serious questions about Uncle Dan's advice to join the Grays, too. But I can tell you right now, no fancy society bitch has got anything on you, Joan ... Do you have a last name, Joan?"

"Have you decided not to arrest me, Jack?"

"A bit late for that."

"I'm known in the tunnels as Joan Matcham."

"Well, Joan Matcham. Aside from this being-part-of-a-terrorist-underground thing, you happen to be the bravest, most beautiful female person I've ever met."

"Oh, Jack!" She reached up and kissed him again, pretty seriously if his physical response was any gauge. Which was completely ridiculous under the circumstances. Though he liked it enough not to complain. Except right at the end he could tell, even in the dark, she was wincing from the pain in her leg.

"That leg is starting to hurt you."

"Yes."

"It'll stiffen up if we stay here. Can you walk?"

"Nothing to do but try. I don't suppose the well-equipped modern Lightning Trooper carries a flashlight?"

On a day raid they hadn't drawn full-sized MagLite head-bashers. The little pen light attached to his belt showed they were in a circular drainage pipe with a diameter of about 10 or 12 feet, running parallel to the track above and behind them. At least they could stand upright.

"Which way?" he asked as he disconnected his earphone and throat mike.

"Here," she replied with surprising certainty, leading him left, which would probably be north.

"How do you know?"

"How do you think we get around this town?"

" 'We' being ..."

"The deadly assassins of the terrorist revolutionary underground, silly. The Order of the Arrow."

That figured.

After 70 yards or so the tunnel had widened out considerably and Jack noticed a dim blue daylight was filtering down through vertical feeder pipes from storm grates set at regular intervals about a story and a half overhead. He experimented with turning his pen light off and on, decided they could see OK without it, shut it down to save the pathetically small batteries in case a more urgent need should arise.

Now they moved through a dimly lit cavern of deep cerulean blue, bathed in a pale but almost iridescent light. The air itself seemed to glow, though whether that was caused by reflections off lingering smoke particles or suspended dust he couldn't be sure.

It was definitely chilly — no problem yet, though it would presumably get a lot colder when the sun went down. Other than the sloshing of their feet and the occasional, distant rumble of truck traffic high overhead and another train passing on the parallel subway line, the main sound was a persistent drip of water relentlessly insinuating its way down into the main tunnel.

How far the shaft stretched in each direction was also rendered unknowable by the way the light faded into an impenetrable gloom after 60 yards or so, creating the eerie impression they were deep in the bowels of some alien spacecraft or beneath the ruins of some ancient, undiscovered jungle temple.

Jack tried to shake it but he just couldn't lose the feeling there was some kind of ominous presence here. He'd heard stories of people who went down into the tunnels and never came back. He'd never been afraid of any enemy he could size up face-to-face, but this gave him the creeps.

"It's drier up here away from the middle of the tunnel," he recommended.

"No, stay in the water."

"And the reason we'd want to keep getting our feet soaked in the lovely cold smelly slime would be ..."

"You're the one who mentioned police dogs."

"Oh."

"Still not used to thinking about *not* being found, are you?"

"You're right." He was silent for another minute as they slogged along. Then he spoke again. "Those kids back at the day care center ..."

"Yes?"

"They were getting indoctrinated with anti-government propaganda."

"They were being taught to read, Jack. You know — books?"

"But kids learn to read in the public schools."

"Just barely."

They walked on awhile. Aside from the distant rumble of traffic high above, the only sound was their sloshing, and the persistent dripping of the water. From time to time, ahead of them, the leader of one of the small packs of brown rats as long as your forearm would stand on his hind legs to size up the interlopers, yellow eyes flaring as he sniffed the air. Then he would drop back to all fours and lead his harem out of sight — with disturbing nonchalance, Joan thought.

"Yeah, but ... if kids don't go to school they never get socialized. Plus, these kind of people never even get their kids their shots. If you let kids go without their shots they could spread infection through the whole city."

She sighed. "Jack, if vaccinations work and everyone else's kids are vaccinated, how could it hurt anyone else if an un-vaccinated kid got sick? Their vaccinations would protect the vaccinated kids a hundred percent. Wouldn't they?"

"Um ... never thought of that."

"The mercury in vaccines and the old dental fillings caused that huge epidemic of autism in the '80s and '90s, everybody knows that. And the pertussis vaccine kills hundreds of kids every year."

"That sounds a little paranoid."

"The federal government admits it, Jack. Why do you think there's a Vaccine Injury Compensation Program? When the Japanese stopped giving the shots to any kid under the age of two, crib death disappeared over there. Just disappeared.

"When we have children, Jack, do you really want them born in a government hospital like that one back there, where they'll be numbered and chipped so the government can track them everywhere and seize two thirds of their income every day of their lives? Do you want their eyes burned with silver nitrate because they won't trust me to be honest when they ask if I have syphilis? Do you really want their tiny little immune systems shot up with infected horse pus and toxic mercury without our being asked? Hospitals are for treating sickness, Jack. Do you think pregnancy is a sickness?"

"I'm sorry, did you say 'When we have children?' "

"I certainly hope so. I'm healthy; you look healthy. Did I mention I'm a firm believer in having sex every day; more on the weekends? I think sex with the person you care about is wonderful, don't you? There are so many things I can't wait to try with you. I hope you're not one of those people who wants the lights turned out all the time. Unless you have some physical infirmity you haven't told me about, Jack."

"Did I pass out for awhile back there, and propose to you while I was in a coma, or something?"

"Jack, you surprise me sometimes. Who gets the final say on whether a boy and girl are going to get married, the boy or the girl?"

"Um ... the girl."

"There. See how easily things resolve themselves when you just think them through logically?"

She gave him another hug, after which she didn't let go. She was definitely needing some help walking.

"You can't go much further, kid. I need to at least pour some antibiotic on that wound and rewrap it. Let's look for a dry place to stop."

"We turn right here."

"You sure?"

"Yep."

Soon the smaller, lateral tunnel dumped into a larger intersection. They turned left again. Here water was flowing a little more freely, only about six inches deep but still generating enough force that you had to watch your footing. And it was freezing cold. The already dim light was fading — darkness falling on the city above. And then, off to the right, the yellow light of a fire, smoke and the delicious smell of something cooking.

Jack urged caution. Joan assured him they'd be fine. And she was nearly played out.

Six men sat around the makeshift fire, brewing up who-knew-what in a small kettle. A lantern slung on a pole provided some additional light. Gas or battery, Jack couldn't tell for sure. He noticed they'd positioned themselves on a high spot where a kind of chimney led to storm grates high above, creating a natural draft to draw the smoke from their fire.

As the pair sloshed haltingly into view, several of the men moved their hands to the hilts of the good-sized knives they carried in their belts. This was hardly an unexpected response to the sight of Jack's spiffy gray-and-black uniform with the sparkling silver lightning flashes on the collar. He'd heard

159

about these Mole People. Anyone who spent their life hiding down here in the tunnels was likely to be a petty thief at least, more likely a smuggler or trafficker in one or more serious forms of contraband.

It was Joan who spoke up, attempting to damp down the tension.

"I'm Joan Matcham," she said, as though they might recognize the name. "Hi, Ratzo. This is my friend Jack. Jack helped me escape from a Lightning Squad raid on a day care center a little ways downtown. He saved me, and he saved a little boy who we took to the hospital. He's with me. OK, guys?"

"Men dressed in that uniform are not usually welcome here in the dark. As a matter of fact, I don't believe one has ever gotten this far ... and lived to tell about it." smiled one of the men, apparently the leader, as the firelight glinted off a gold front tooth.

It was not a warm smile. His speech sounded like English was not his first language, though the underlying accent was hard to place. French or German, maybe. His English was excellent but outdated by a generation or two, like someone who'd learned the language by reading old books before he actually spoke it with the natives. This character had long dirty blond hair, tied behind, and was wearing a couple days growth of beard, though Jack could still tell he had a strong chin with a deep dimple in the middle, like one of those old movie actors. Viggo Mortensen? Burt Douglas? He was always getting them mixed up.

"As long as he's the one holding the gun, Miss Joan, I can't guarantee his safety down here indefinitely. But it looks like you've been hurt. You're both welcome to share our fire, so long as your friend here doesn't try arresting anyone."

The other men around the fire actually chuckled at this notion, as the one who spoke — the one with the gold tooth — stood and helped Joan settle in close to the flames. The heat

even of the small fire was welcome in the gathering gloom
— ice would form on the water in these tunnels tonight. Jack
was careful to keep his hand away from the grip of his MP-5,
which he still wore slung close to his chest, as he stooped to
join them.

"Dish up for two more, will you, Airburst?"

"I'm going to look at that leg," Jack said, waving off his
proffered bowl of stew.

"Time enough after she's got something warm in her belly, young trooper. And you, too. It ain't rat, I promise. Not this
time, anyway. Best Dinty Moore beef stew, straight from the
can."

The old-timer he'd called Airburst — the tallest of the
bunch, with a flowing beard and head of white hair that made
him look like Santa Claus on a weight loss program — dug
the empty can with the familiar label out of his plastic bag
and held it up. They all laughed as Jack smiled, shrugged, and
agreed to share their supper.

⚜ ⚜ ⚜

They didn't eat much, but it seemed to help Joan relax a
little. As she recounted the outlines of how they'd spent their
day, Jack slit her pants leg with his knife and examined the
wound. An area the size of a good-sized orange was red and
swollen around an entry wound that was only weeping a little,
now. Didn't look like enough tissue destruction for an expand-
ing slug, but there was sure something in there — maybe a
ricochet.

He looked up as she paused in her account. The men were
scraping their plates, looking at him but trying not to be obvious about it. Wondering what kind of guy would shoot up a
room full of little kids, maybe. He shrugged; he didn't feel any

need to defend himself to this lot.

"Listen, I took about two days of Medic, and all I know is, if you're within a couple hours of a doctor, you'd rather have a doctor probe this than me. Without anaesthetic there's no way you're going to hold still, and with nothing but this knife I'm likely to do more harm than good. If we were three days out in the bush I might give you something to bite on and tie you down and take the chance, but not here in town. I am going to open it just enough to squeeze in the antiseptic before I wrap it up again, and even that's gonna hurt a little. Any of you guys know any different?"

"Sounds about right, young trooper," said an old-timer whose close-cropped red hair had now gone mostly snowy white. The geezer hobbled to his feet, circled around the fire, and squatted down on arthritic knees, feeling Joan's leg with confident hands that were nonetheless surprisingly gentle. Jack wondered if he might actually have been a doctor, in some former life up top. A corpsman, anyway.

"Whatever's in there has to come out, and I wouldn't give it too many more hours. You watch for a red line of infection to start moving up towards the heart; that'd be a bad sign, though I don't see it yet. Problem is, this is no operating room. Ratzo can get you to a real doctor inside an hour, but you may need our help carrying her."

"I can walk," Joan insisted.

"I can put a stick of morphine in that leg that'll let you walk," Jack volunteered. "The main risk is that you'll push yourself to do more than you should, make it worse. I'll only do it if you're sure we're no more than an hour out. Otherwise you should take them up on their offer."

"You carry morphine?"

"Little half-grain syrettes. Combat kit."

"Is that what that was back there: combat?"

Jack saw no way to win that argument. "All I know is, if I hadn't been there, that raid would still have happened, and you'd be someplace a lot worse, right now."

"I know that, Jack. I'm sorry. Stick me, baby." She tried to smile. It wasn't completely successful. But she was still cute enough to eat. The big eyes, the bangs, just a hint of some freckles, that exotic single earring and whatever that dazzler was she wore in her nose. God, he hoped she wasn't just messing around. Jack was old enough to know plenty of young men who met the love of their life every two weeks. He'd never been like that. If this one was really serious ...

"You're not allergic to real opiates?"

"Oh God no. Love them."

A single one-and-a-half cc dose wouldn't kill the pain completely, but anything that would do that could leave her unsteady on her feet. It would help, anyway. She still gave a little involuntary cry as he opened up the wound enough to squeeze in the little tube of antiseptic gel before tying the leg up again.

"You're a brave little dame."

"I am, ain't I?"

They all looked up as a young boy came sliding down the tunnel wall above them — Jack had no idea where he'd come from or how long he'd been up there.

"Four blues in the service tunnel this side of the D line," he said without preliminaries, pointing with his head. "With dogs."

With an alacrity Jack would have judged unlikely from their languorous poses, all six men were on their feet.

The old-timer who'd come over to look at Joan's leg moved away to their left, stiff-kneed as though his legs had fallen asleep as he'd squatted down, probably off to take a leak downstream. None of them said a word as the lanky, white-bearded cook scuffed the fire out with his boot — not only was drinking water valuable but it made smoke. Even so the air was suddenly full of the acrid smell of ashes, as a third man tossed aside a ragged blanket which had been spread out on the tunnel

163

floor behind them.

Jack had assumed one or more of the hobos had been about to turn in and get some sleep. But beneath the blanket, arranged in military precision, were five neatly arrayed compound hunting bows with accompanying fixed-storage quivers.

"Jesus Christ," Jack said, leaping to his own feet as he recognized from his training the silent weapon of choice of the urban resistance, a sight to strike terror into the breast of all but the most foolhardy politician or government agent, these days. IRS, AFE, DEA, the judges, the prosecutor's office, the goddamned Department of Motor Vehicles, for heaven's sake — there was hardly a state or federal agency that wasn't growing tired of funeral parades behind hearses as black as these tools of silent death.

The weapons were matching Oneida Black Eagles, clean, well maintained, and jet black, only visible now by the light of the remaining single lantern and the blue glow of some mercury vapor lamp high above, its dim light filtering down two stories from the street to glint off the crisp edges of these ancient but newly re-engineered engines of death.

The pulleys of the modern compound bow were there, but set in tighter, not out at the far ends of the bow but at the top and bottom of the slab-like central handle. Outside them, a more traditional pair of recurved arms swept back sleekly toward and then away from the shooter, marrying the look of the traditional recurve with the advantages of the modern, compound hunting bow.

The last time Jack had checked, such professional weapons went for over a thousand newbucks apiece — and just to own one in this city could now be worth your life.

Here were no amateur wanna-bes, these men who now picked up these bows and slung them over their shoulders with near-military precision. It also dawned on him they could not merely have stumbled on these men — if they had one boy scouting and standing lookout away in the shadows there would doubtless be more, in several directions.

No, Jack and Joan had been allowed to approach like flies drawn to a spider web — not by a gaggle of toothless winos and derelicts, not to a campfire of down-on-their-luck hobos — though a careful effort had been made to present that appearance — but rather by a squad of the deadliest professional guards of the underworld.

"What is this?"

"An army of resistance, young trooper," snarled the one with the gold tooth. "You didn't think you could take away a people's property, their freedom, finally their lives, even shooting up their children in their day care centers, and not mobilize a rebellion, did you? What kind of people did you think we were?"

And now, with a suppleness that added to Jack's list of surprises, Gold Tooth spun about and was suddenly hissing in Jack's face.

"The only reason you're not dead yet, young trooper, is that the lady here spoke for you. She's known here in the dark — known by many names. But that only goes so far. Now it's decision time. If you're going to use that thing, the dance starts now. What name should we put on your marker, boy?"

Jack looked down to see that the taller man had drawn the knife — a Bowie large enough to kill a boar — from his belt and now held it poised mere inches from Jack's belly. He realized he had instinctively tightened his own grip on his loaded subgun as he rose. He could kill a few of them, no doubt, but he'd surely be knifed for his trouble. And how would Joan fare in such a quick, no-holds-barred firefight?

But that hadn't been his intention, anyway. He had reacted purely on instinct and training. After the massacre at the day care center, Jack was feeling seriously confused about a lot of what had been drilled into him in his months of training with the Lightning Squads.

"This pistol is on full auto," he said, "And I know how to use it. If you want to dance, after it slices you in half we could leave it to Miss Matcham here to count how many others will share a headstone with Jack Brackley. But you shared your fire with us; I won't be the one to break the truce ..."

Slowly, deliberately, he lowered the muzzle of his weapon toward the ground, pulled his hands away and let the 9mm hang harmless on its sling. "... today. The young lady and I are headed in a different direction, I think."

The other men were straightening in surprise by then, strangely enough, mumbling his name, several pulling off their caps in a strangely old-fashioned gesture of deference. Gold Tooth, as well, straightened as though an electric shock had run through his body. As quickly as it had come out, his broad Bowie knife was off Jack's belly.

"Is that true, Miss Joanie? That his name?"

"Yes, this is the long absent Jack Brackley, and I'll thank you not to stab him; I've got a prior claim. Both of you stop this right now."

"My apologies, then, young Brackley." The big knife went back in its sheath.

"I don't want any special treatment because my uncle's the mayor."

"The only special treatment you'd get for that would be a one-way trip down the sea sluice. But most of these men served with your father in the war, one time or another. Not a one as wouldn't give his life for the son of Tom Brackley."

"You knew my father?"

"Proud to say it."

"He was a hero in the West."

"Hero, yes, if by that you mean a man who'd go any distance, face any hardship, to avoid the unnecessary waste of his men's lives."

"But if you served with my father you're heroes of the war, too. What are you doing ..."

"Rotting away in the tunnels?"

"Well ... yeah."

"We stick our heads out occasionally. But in case you haven't noticed, it's a dangerous thing to know too much about the War in the West. Coming back and wanting to tell the truth about what they saw there has gotten a lot of men killed ... men not nearly as famous as your dad."

"I don't understand. My father was killed by rebel agents."

Strangely, the six men who had shown such respect a moment before — and even their boy watchman — now hooted and laughed.

"You'll have to look a lot closer to home to find your father's killer," said Gold Tooth. "And you'll have to learn a lot more about what he was saying about that war, to get to the bottom of his murder."

"What do you mean by that? You know who killed my father?"

"There's things you wouldn't believe coming from my lips, boy, that you'll have to find out for yourself. Maybe the big guy can tell you something more. I've already said more than I should."

"Alright. We'll talk more about that, one day. Right now, my problem is that if I let those canine officers get ambushed without warning, it'll be like I betrayed them. I'm still wearing a uniform, no matter how I feel about it right now. They're probably only down here looking for me, in the first place. So either you take Joan where she's going and I go surrender to them — turn them back to save their lives — or I want the same deal for them that you're giving me. Your word as a soldier they pass unharmed today, same as us — tomorrow can take care of itself."

The man with the gold tooth smiled, then. "OK, young trooper," he said. Behind him Jack heard a rustle of clothing and froze for a moment as he realized the sixth man — the

167

one with the short red hair gone mostly white who'd moved stiff-legged out of his range of vision to the left, the one who'd helped him check Joanie's wound — had silently circled behind him as they spoke. He heard a long knife going back into a hard plastic sheath as the man behind him stood down at a nod from Gold Tooth. So he would have faced a second blade in his back, as well as the one at his front. He'd have to remember that.

"You've got balls, as well as loyalty ... however misplaced," laughed the man with the big chin. "I see a lot of your father in you, Jack Brackley. It's just the kind of pain-in-the-ass behavior I would have expected from him.

"We'll lay low and spare whoever's coming, be it Grays or Blues, providing they don't come any further than this, which is highly unlikely, seeing how it appears you two were smart enough to stick to the water. Meantime, Ratzo, can you show these two youngsters on their way?"

"Where to?" asked the shortest of the six men, as the one who had held the knife to Jack's back now circled back into his field of vision. Jack saw the one they called Ratzo was the only one without a bow, as the others shifted theirs into place on their shoulders. Another latecomer to the campfire, then — though clearly he was a known man.

"They've got to go uptown, anyway. Can you take them to the caverns to see the big guy?"

"I can probably find the way," the short fellow said, the others chuckling at a joke that Jack didn't follow.

Jack wasn't sure he liked the sound of meeting "the big guy." It occurred to him he could still take out most of these guys with his subgun. The rest might scatter; he and Joan could work their way back to the four transit cops who were trying to locate them with the dogs.

But not without putting Joan at risk. Anyway, what if she took their side? Was he ready to shoot her? The question answered itself. And did he really want to take it on himself to kill in cold blood — to open fire on unsuspecting civilians for the second time in a day ... on men who'd shared their fire, hadn't actually done him any harm?

Besides, if these people — these rebels, he corrected himself — knew something about his father's death, well ... in for a penny, in for a pound.

"Go in peace in your father's name, Jack Brackley," Gold Tooth said as his men started to blend into the shadows along the tunnel wall, working their way back to keep an eye on the canine cops. "I hope the next time we meet you've re-thought which side you're really on. If not, stay out of my tunnels. I'd hate for it to be my arrow that ends the Brackley line."

"My uncle is still alive," Jack retorted.

"So far," Gold Tooth sad with a very unsettling smile. And then, like so many wisps of silent smoke swirling into the deeper gloom, they extinguished their single lantern, were heard for a further moment only as some irregular sloshing in the nearby stream, and were gone.

In the semi-darkness, Jack could make out the silhouette of the unkempt and misshapen creature who was now their sole companion. This "Ratzo" produced from a kind of shoulder holster what appeared to be a battery lantern far larger than Jack's. He flicked it on, its beam cutting through the gathering gloom like a glowing blue knife.

Then, in a ludicrous parody of a medieval courtier, the creature made an exaggerated bow, ending with a roll of his wrist which swept the beam of his light in the direction Jack and Joan were to proceed — deeper into the tunnels.

Out of the frying pan, Jack found himself thinking.

❖ ❖ ❖

Tanya was five minutes late. Which meant she'd probably

walked past the door and started back down the stairs at least twice. Her knock was soft. He didn't let her wait long. Patience was one thing, but you didn't want to lose the fish right at the net.

"Come on in."

She'd brought a little zipper bag, as instructed.

"I'm drinking Scotch. But I can do you a Black Russian, or a rum and tonic," he said, turning to the bar. It was an expensive suite with plenty of hangings and accoutrements in different textures and fabrics. The carpet was red paisley. There was quite a bit of precious extra space, it was not one of those cheap claustrophobic shoeboxes that was all bed and scratchy carpet with no lid on the toilet. Real class. He even had some candles and incense burning. Not sandalwood. Rose.

"No. No thank you. Maybe an icewater."

"Tanya, I know this is new to you. Take a deep breath now, and relax. I opened the window to let in a little fresh air. But you're not going to drink icewater, at least not without a kicker. If you're not used to Scotch, I recommend either a black Russian, or a rum and Coke. The black Russian is sweeter. Unless you'd prefer something to smoke. But I —"

"No."

"I didn't think so. So your drink —"

"Oh. The 'black Russian,' please." She smiled a little as she said the name, which she apparently considered slightly ridiculous. That was fine — anything to break the ice.

"Good girl. Put your bag down. And lock the door, would you?" It was always best to have THEM lock the door. With his back turned, pouring the drinks, she would think about leaving. Instead, he heard her throw the deadbolt. Right. And ... they're off.

Daniel handed her the drink. She tasted it.

"Take off your shirt and sit down on the bed."

"What? Oh." She set down her glass and started to obey, then paused. Jesus, it was like getting a dog to learn its first trick. He had to remind himself to maintain a proper mix of patience and firmness. Now she was going to make sure he had the doggie treat in his hand for her if she performed her little tricks as required.

"You're sure you can help Yuri? The lawyer says it's important to get a good pre-sentencing report ..."

"That's all bullshit, Tanya, and I think you've got that figured out by now. You wouldn't be here if you were a dummy. You've been going through all the motions the way the public defender tells you. He's paid by the government, right? He's there to make it look like everything was done according to form. He puts the big red bow on the package as they send Yuri up the river, and he gets paid very well for it. By someone other than you. If you hadn't already gotten the picture you wouldn't have come to see me today, would you?

"Now, I already made the first call today. Whatever that public defender tells you the sentence is going to be, I can get it cut in half. I can also get the hold released on one of the bank accounts, enough so you won't have to sell apples in the street, you can start to pay a little rent to that sister of yours, buy a few new clothes, look nice like you want to. Providing you're a smart girl and you remember why you're here. As long as you're planning on being a good girl and doing what needs to be done, this can be relaxing and fun for everyone. I mean, every girl has fantasies of doing it with a stranger, right? Right?"

"Yes, I guess so."

"Here, turn around and let me help you with that."

She let him help her out of her jacket, of course. Learned response. She stiffened a little when he also undid the blouse buttons down her back. Some kind of sensible no-iron cotton-rayon blend. He kissed her neck, stayed there to breathe for a second, then pulled away so she wouldn't feel smothered.

She obeyed — well, partially. She stripped down to her bra, laying her shirt carefully across a chair, and had a seat, crossing one leg demurely over the other and straightening her back into a proper ladylike posture. Jesus, she had great tits.

Considerately, Daniel Brackley turned off the bright overhead light so the room was lit only by the gentler lamps and the candles. At least a few lights had to remain on, of course, both so the light-sensitive video camera behind the mirror would catch all the action, from which his own face would later be carefully masked if he needed to use the discs ... and because he simply liked it better with the lights on. He liked them to see exactly what was happening to them. It was about control, and honesty. He liked an honest relationship.

He also had to remember to keep her turned so she was facing that camera at least part of the time, so it could catch those lovely tits swaying and bouncing, especially when he would later instruct her to beg for more and make it sound real convincing.

Some of the reluctant little whores got the impression their bill was paid up after just one session. He had no idea where they got that impression — he was careful never to say such a thing. In fact, he always mentioned "one or two evenings a week," so they'd get the idea. It was like joining a bowling league, see?

But for those who hesitated to maintain their regular schedule of appointments — or to remain on call at his pleasure, however he cared to set it up — an anonymously mailed copy of the edited video from that hidden camera behind the mirror, their pretty faces clearly visible, their ample tits bouncing up and down or cupped in the stranger's hands, another man spreading their ass and thrusting and thrusting as they cried and begged for more — with a little note that this would be playing on all their friends' home video theaters tomorrow night and might even find its way to dad or hubby in the joint, unless they kept that important next appointment — generally did the trick.

"You're not used to being with anyone but your husband,"

he said.

"No, never."

"Finish your drink, Tanya. Here, take one of these." He handed her a little white pill.

"What is it?"

"Something to help you relax."

"Drugs?"

"I have a prescription, Tanya. Here, I'm taking one, too." He mixed her another drink as soon as she'd downed the powerful muscle relaxant, twice the dose he'd taken. And of course, he was used to them.

"You love your husband very much."

"Yes, I do."

"That's why you're here."

"Yes. It is."

"I want you to take off your bra and close your eyes, and rub your breasts the way he would, Tanya." Daniel Brackley turned off another light, then, turned a chair back-first and straddled it so he could watch. Easier for her to start if she saw there was a physical barrier between them, no matter how transient and inconsequential. Really, it was like training dogs. Intriguing but at the same time kind of tedious.

Sometimes he longed for a real whore who knew her trade. Not that there wasn't a reward for his efforts, when these amateur wives and daughters finally let go and he felt those shudders of resistance ended, surrender acknowledged, the reluctance to take pleasure finally abandoned — sometimes abandoned with downright enthusiasm. No, he could never have gotten all that from a pro. A close simulation, maybe. Nothing real.

But there were really no surprises, here. They all knew what they'd come for — a man's hotel room late in the evening, carrying an overnight bag, for Christ's sake, you weren't there to sell Tupperware. Some even came to enjoy it, he knew. The forbidden affair with the masked stranger, abandoning yourself to a passion over which you had no control, doing dirty, shameful, wonderful things you would never dare do with that upstanding Boy Scout who mowed the lawn at home every Saturday morning. It was, in its way, every woman's dream. Oh, the stuff he was going to teach this one.

She seemed to shiver a little, but she did as she was told. Almost.

"Tanya, you seem to be having a little trouble getting into the spirit of the thing. It's my fault; I was wrong to rush you. Here, let me give you a back rub and get you a little bit relaxed. You didn't have any trouble finding the place?"

Get her talking. Ask her about her sister's kids and her recipe for apple-cranberry cobbler or sour cream borscht or whatever it was they ate and pretty soon she'd be chattering away like you were an old school chum.

"I'm not here to hurt you," he said finally, in her ear. "It's not so bad, having someone to hold you, is it?"

"No."

"What you have to do now, Tanya, is to get yourself nice and warm and and wet, so later when you're kneeling on top of me and rocking up and down as fast as you can and we're fucking like rabbits it's all going to be nice and wet and smooth and it's going to feel wonderful for both of us. That's it. That's better. Now rub your breasts with one hand and put your other hand down between your legs and make yourself nice and wet. You know how. Here, let me help a little. There are no secrets here, Tanya. That's it. Let's get that skirt off and slide your panties down, honey. Spread your legs a little wider, that'll make it easier for you. That's right. Start out slow. Here, let's pull those pillows up behind you so you can lean back if you need to."

Daniel Brackley reached over and flipped on the stereo, pre-set, playing the low, throbbing love songs he'd carefully chosen through a highly scientific screening process. They were from the years when Tanya Petrov would have first met and slow-danced with and married her husband, who truth be told was headed for a minimum-security country club before Daniel Brackley even picked up the phone.

Though he could indeed call in a few favors, have some "cooperated by identifying co-conspirators who unfortunately fled the jurisdiction" crap entered in his file to justify Judge McNair reducing the absurdly long sentence to one that was at least within the limits of human imagination. After all, Daniel wanted this little wife waiting anxiously at home, still readily available to service Mayor Brackley on demand, not running off with the doctor or the insurance man.

One of the problems with this kind of bogus case was that there were no actual seized drugs to spread around among the various agencies; this guy was such a Dudley Do-right there hadn't even been a fancy red sports car or a high-speed cigarette boat to dangle as a reward for someone helping to bend the rules.

He was pleased to see Tanya Petrov was finally starting to get into the spirit of the evening. She'd picked up her pace considerably now that the clothing was out of the way, had gradually shifted her position and leaned back; her eyes were squeezed tight shut as she remembered the old song she and the hubby had once danced to, in happier days. She was even starting to breathe in short, hot breaths and make little involuntary whimpering noises. Oh, yeah. This was "A" list stuff, for sure. Just look at those magnificent, all-natural tits.

Daniel Brackley slid out of his own pants, which were starting to feel tightly constricted around his now-engorged and swollen member. When she looked up he was kneeling over her in all his stiffened glory.

"That's a great start, honey. Now roll over and kneel on the floor next to the bed with your butt up. Actually, let's put some pillows under your knees. That's it. Your knees a little further apart, honey. Further." The bed had been chosen for its height, with this in mind.

"Very good. You know," he said as he knelt on the floor between her legs and slid languorously into her now wonderfully hot, wet cunt, grabbing the points of her hips and pulling them back toward him, "I think I could get to like you, Tanya. You really do have the sweetest ass."

As he dragged his fingernails across the now-taut flesh of that wonderfully articulated, spread-out bivalve butt, he could tell from her little electric shiver that no one had ever done her this way before. Ah, the things he would teach her before they were through. In fact, if you looked at it properly, these little adventures of his were really quite philanthropic in nature. Continuing the education of a deprived class of otherwise shut-in felons' wives and daughters.

He never failed to appreciate the marvellous symmetry of their design. The grand matched hemispheres of the female buttocks, here now within his easy reach. The smaller, matching hemispheres of the breasts, coming into view as she lifted herself when he reached to slide his hands up beneath her warm, smooth belly. And finally the much smaller hemispheres of the labia, opening to kiss his erect manhood with a promise of such delights within.

Though he would have to instruct her to shave her pussy. Yes. Not that it was bad this way. It was more a power thing, so she'd remember every day just whose pleasure she served. And she would be just a little prettier that way, he thought. Just for him, of course. Ohhhhh yes.

With her face turned away now and buried in the pillows, she started to sob quietly, as she wished and imagined it was her Yuri, or whatever the hell his name was, ramming his way into her precious little pussy over and over again, thrusting and throbbing.

But that was OK. She was sobbing for her lost man. Women were emotional, they had to go through a period of mourning for their lost love as they came to realize they had a new master now, who'd be screwing them once — no, he reconsidered, this one was damned good and shapely once her clothes were off, and literally quite hot — twice a week.

On many occasions Daniel Brackley had noted with some degree of wonder just how resilient the female of the species was, how quickly they adapted to new circumstances, accepted those changed circumstances as normal, actually starting to put up curtains in their cell, as it were.

Psychiatrists talked about the Stockholm Syndrome, how hostages after a couple of days would start to sympathize with their captors' motivations, try to explain to the authorities how they really weren't such bad people. After all, they were providing food and water and letting their hostages use the bathroom, and all the kidnappers wanted in return was the release from death row of a few of their comrades from the Fifth Route Army, who had doubtless been placed there for selling underweight Girl Scout cookies or some such technical violation. What could be more reasonable?

And so tonight Tanya lay here sobbing as he was churning to a climax in her sweet, steaming pussy, and in a couple of weeks she'd be calling him by secret pet names and bringing home-baked cookies to their assignations, coyly asking him if he thought her new, bright red, push-up bikini underwear was too shocking.

He loved the liquid, slapping noise it made as he rammed it into her.

"You're so beautiful, honey, now that you're all warm and wet and delicious. You're really an unusually good lay, you know. I hope you don't take any offense if I come inside you for the first time pretty soon, here, Tanya. You can put it down to your just being so plain delicious." He grabbed for a firmer grip on her luscious hips, then, to give himself more leverage as he picked up his pace, leaning back and slamming it up under her lovely butt as strongly and as deeply as he could.

"But don't be disappointed, now. After we rest awhile we'll go again, I promise you, and that won't be such a quickie.

I mean, what kind of a host would I be, just irrigating a lady once, without giving you a chance at some of the moaning and shuddering? Mmm. Now doesn't that feel good, honey? Say it feels good."

"Yes, it feels good."

"It feels good, DANIEL."

"It feels good, Daniel," she said through her sobs.

"Oh yes, Oh yes. Here we go now. I think we're going to have to do a lot more of this, little Tanya. I mean, it's not like I'm the kind of guy to fuck and run. Not while the evening is still young. Oh yes, we're going to do some wonderful things tonight. In fact, I think this could be the start of a beautiful — oh yeah — friendship. Maybe next time, I'll even, oh, oh, let you be on top. Ohhhh yesss."

⚜ ⚜ ⚜

Dominic Cantari — just promoted to CHIEF Inspector with the State Department of Investigation, thank you very much — had personally ramrodded the Yuri & Tanya Petrov prosecution. Fortunately, after the Petrovs, those assholes, had called the TV reporters who in turn had exposed the undercover surveillance of their parking lot, his superiors realized the reputation of the entire agency was on the line, and authorized additional millions of dollars for the helicopter surveillance and all the simultaneous busts.

Even then, none of the guilty drug-dealing assholes would admit the Petrovs talked to them about how to grow their pot. So it was Dominic himself who finally focused in on Mrs. Kostic, whose husband had Multiple Sclerosis and would die without her being there to change his diapers, or whatever it was she did. It was Dominic who put the pressure on, convinced the old bat the only way she wasn't going to prison was if

178

she implicated the Petrovs. Even then, her initial "admission" didn't quite meet all the requirements of the conspiracy statute, so he'd had to have the U.S, attorney's guys rewrite it for her signature.

But in the end it all worked out fine, their annual budget increased by all the extra money he'd spent. And now, finally, he had his gold shield.

They'd made his promotion official as part of the after-dinner presentations. Now, at the bar, Dominic was showing uncharacteristic restraint, in part because he was anxious to get across town and cheat on his wife, who had gone home early. And so he waved his hand in solemn rectitude at the incessant demands of the lesser wannabes that he stay for another night-cap at the bar, joked that "I'm a man of sober responsibilities now; I'm in *management*" — which set them all laughing a little harder than he really considered appropriate, considering it was true — and instead walked away in a far more sober condition than usual, punching the elevator to take him down to the parking garage.

It was chilly in the garage — should have worn his heavy wool coat. Place smelled the way they usually did — old motor oil soaked into dusty concrete. He was still concentrating on locating the proper key for his big Lexus — fanciest one they made, thank you, and in metallic green — when he caught a hint of motion out of the corner of his right eye.

Turning his chin, he pushed his forehead down and squint-ed, furrowing his brow, to figure out what the figure he'd spot-ted down at the end of the row of cars was doing. The lights in the garage were uneven and this character, who appeared to be dressed all in black, was standing in a pool of partial shadow, 40 yards away. What was strange, actually, was the fact that he *was* standing — just standing. People move through parking garages, coming or going ... they don't just stand in them. Not normally.

The guy wasn't close enough to pose any immediate problem, even though he seemed to be holding some kind of stick, holding it upright. A panhandler? Chief Inspector Cantari was about to turn back to unlocking his car when he heard a noise that his ears struggled to place. Something moved between him and the standing-still man in black, just a flash, as though there'd been a spark of static electricity, or maybe the beam of a slow-moving car several levels above or below them in the garage had reflected and flickered off the chrome of one of the intervening cars, a reflection of a reflection, barely seen, like an 8-ball banked off three cushions in a darkened room. What color was an 8-ball?

He knew what the noise reminded him of, now. It sounded like the hiss of air escaping from the pneumatic cylinder of one of those spring-loaded doors that's set up so it won't slam closed too hard.

He should have paid more attention to the object moving between him and the standing-still man in black. But it would not really be correct to say Dominic Cantari began to wonder about that. For before the thought that there might be a problem here could actually form in his mind, the 34-inch, black anodized epoxy resin/carbon fiber arrow shaft had driven the 150-grain, three-blade warhead — its usually bright and silvery razor surfaces in this case acid-treated to a lustrous blue-black — into and through his right ocular orbit, destroying the structural integrity of all the ocular tissues (from cornea to retina, and everything in between) before smoothly penetrating into and through the lacrimal bone and then the bulk of the cerebrum and exiting the rear of the skull just above the occipital.

There was a pause of somewhat under a second, though it must have seemed far longer to Dominic Cantari, who began to raise his right hand toward his eye to see what had begun to cause him some discomfort there, before his body actually responded to this compound insult to his circulatory and particularly his autonomous nervous system. Patients have actually survived major traumatic head wounds providing the offending projectile cuts a neat swath without substantially destroying any major brain structures — something a smaller-caliber bullet can do fairly easily if it manages to penetrate the skull without tumbling and without collapsing any of the major bone structures.

But the broadhead point of the arrow in question was a full inch across, and the cross-section not merely knife-shaped but triangular. The shock of that much tissue destruction was simply more than the organism could compensate for through any of the re-routing of signals it briefly attempted, especially since it cut quite close to the mid-line between the right and left brain.

After a momentary pause, blood spurted out of the front of Dominic Cantari's right eye — or what had been his right eye. Even prior to that, of course, a substantial amount of gray dura matter propagated out of the rear of the skull, spraying in a cone-shaped pattern around the still present arrow shaft onto the car behind him.

Though surviving family members are often told out of compassion that death was "instantaneous," it is seldom that. Chief Inspector Dominic Cantari's body now began to shudder violently. Then, as he spun, took a step, and overbalanced to the floor of the parking garage — his depth perception and balance being completely shot, of course — the head and fore-shaft of the arrow, which had come to rest protruding a full foot from the back of his head, caught the hood and fender of the car behind him.

Resisting the dead weight of his 230-pound body falling toward the garage floor, this had the same effect on the arrow shaft now neatly segmenting his head from front to back as if someone had grabbed it and thrust one end downwards while pulling the other up, in an attempt to lever the top of Dominic Cantari's skull off.

The skull remained intact and the arrow in place, in the

event, but the exit wound was now extended upwards by another full inch. As he spun the rest of the way to the ground, Dominic Cantari's body gave up trying to control his bladder and sphincter, and the faint odor of human waste and urine began to waft from his dying form, as it lay thrashing on the concrete floor up against the left front tire of his Lexus, in the throes of what would have appeared to any passer-by to be a grand mal epileptic seizure ... except for the back half of the black-feathered arrow shaft still sticking up out of his right eye, of course.

While it would thus not be true to say that Chief Inspector Dominic Cantari died "instantly," it would indeed be true to say that, in any literal sense, he never knew what hit him.

The masked archer who had fired the arrow now stepped around the back of the car which had been Dominic Cantari's but which now to all intents and purposes belonged to his estranged son Toby, or would, as soon as the younger Cantari got out of prison on charges of hijacking that entire semi trailer full of frozen turkeys the previous Thanksgiving. Brilliant move, storing them in the walk-in-freezer of old man Paterno's grocery without getting anyone's permission.

The figure in the tight-fitting black outfit had a second arrow nocked and the black compound bow drawn back, ready to release a second shaft if necessary. But watching the body thrash for a moment and sniffing the telltale odor of death, he decided the follow-up shot would not be necessary. He eased back the bowstring, deftly returned the second shaft to the quiver on his back, slung the bow over his shoulder.

He'd had a little speech ready for Dominic Cantari, He'd planned to tell him — right about now, in a calm and conversational tone — that he'd just been executed for telling poor Mrs. Kostic they were going to put her in prison and that her husband would die with no one to take care of him, unless she got up on that witness stand and lied and said what they needed her to say about the Petrovs.

He had it all worked out.

But now, what was the point? Dominic Cantari wasn't going to remember. He wasn't going to tell anyone. Killing someone did not teach them a lesson. It was just the final "F" posted on the hallway bulletin board.

Till you'd seen it first hand, the bladder and bowels letting go as the eyes turned inward, the brain devoting its last energy to seeking some way to recover control and succeeding only in a spastic shuddering, body parts rattling like dry corn husks in a gust of wind, it was hard to grasp the finality of death.

How could a sane man take this power on himself and not wonder, pacing and snarling in the claustrophobic night, "What if I made a mistake?"

Had Dominic Cantari deserved some lesser punishment? But that was the problem with those who committed their crimes in the name of the consolidated state. What black-robed judge would impose any lesser sentence? What jailer would enforce it?

The archer licked his lips. He ought to say something. At least, "Congratulations on your promotion, chief inspector. It'll mean a bigger funeral; hope you enjoy it." In the movies they always said something ironic or amusing.

But in the end, it wasn't Dominic Cantari's dignity that demanded silence. It was the radiant dignity of the third presence, there in that cold concrete cavern, smelling of rock dust and old motor oil. It was the majesty of what approached now, stately on dark velvet wings, that choked the words in Andrew's throat.

He had summoned it. It was a companion he must now learn to live with — no matter which turned out to be the servant, and which the master. But still he could not bear to gaze upon its shining perfection.

And so he turned his back on the still-shuddering corpse of Dominic Cantari, and walked away.

SUPRYNOWICZ

CHAPTER 6

Some of these days they are going to remove so much of the "hooey" and the thousands of things the schools have become clogged up with, and we will find that we can educate our broods for about one-tenth of the price and learn 'em something that they might accidentally use after they escape.

— WILL ROGERS (1879-1935)

The flames kindled on the 4th of July 1776, have spread over too much of the globe to be extinguished by the feeble engines of despotism; on the contrary, they will consume these engines and all who work them.

— THOMAS JEFFERSON (1743-1826),
LETTER TO JOHN ADAMS, SEPT. 12, 1821

The strange creature who had been selected to guide Jack and Joan on the next stage of their journey into the underworld had a long nose, long, unkempt hair, and a tendency to bend from the waist and thrust his head forward as he walked.

There was little doubt why they called him "Ratzo."

He proved a cheerful enough guide. If anything, excessively so. But he also appeared to be a fellow not much used to human company. He was given to long periods of silence, broken only by an endless string of bad jokes that seemed to pop into his head pretty much at random.

He appeared to know the tunnels from memory. He used his sturdy three-battery flashlight till he'd led them up a half-story ladder and through a gray steel door into a somewhat smaller tunnel of rectangular cross-section, full of insulated, humming water pipes.

From there on most of their route was well lit by traditional overhead bulbs — the air still chilly but drawing enough heat from the water pipes to stay above freezing.

And what a route it was.

Jack couldn't figure out how on earth he remembered where to turn, when to lead them into a ladder-well with painted-over stainless steel rungs that carried them half a story up or down, without ever consulting any kind of map or any wall markings that Jack could spot — occasionally doubling back a short distance to pick up another tunnel leading in their main direction of travel, but never hesitating for even a moment.

"Does he *live* down here, or what?" Jack asked Joanie.

She smiled, though the strain was starting to show.

Occasionally Ratzo would stop to let Joan rest her leg for a few minutes. There was a price to be paid, however.

"So a union guy is in town for a big convention," Ratzo offered the first time they stopped, apropos of nothing discernible. "He's looking for some entertainment, so he goes out to a local whorehouse. He asks if they're unionized, but they're not, see. So he says, 'I'm sorry, I cannot patronize a non-union establishment that exploits its workers.' He goes to a second whorehouse, asks if they're unionized. The madam tells him no they're not, so he says 'I'm sorry, I cannot patronize a non-union establishment that exploits its workers.'

"Now he's getting a little discouraged, but he walks a little further down the street, goes into a third whorehouse, and the girls here are really beautiful. So he asks if they're unionized. And the madam says, 'We certainly are. We're affiliated with the AFL-CIO.' Well, the guy can't believe how lucky he is, he says, 'You're a union shop and you've got the most beautiful girls in town! I'd like to spend some time with that young red-head right there at the bar, the one with the big tits.' The madame says, 'I bet you would, sir.' She waves her hand and this wrinkled little 80-year-old lady who's been doing her knitting at the table comes hobbling over, and the madame says, 'But Ethel here has seniority.' "

Soon they'd heard about the gay guy who came into the bar after the bartender got so tired of hearing the guys arguing about who had the biggest dick that he had them lay them out on the bar to be measured. Gay guy says he doesn't want a beer, he'll just have the buffet. Next it was the three Paddys trying to haul a truckload of garbage to the dump but the tarp they used to cover the load keeps blowing off. Finally two of the Paddys get out and lie on top of the tarp to keep it from blowing off while the third Paddy drives. Truck goes under a bridge and one of the guys walking overhead says, "Look at that, somebody threw away two perfectly good Irishmen."

"Yeah," Ratzo added. "We used to tell that joke about three niggers, but then we had to change it 'cause they decided it was racist."

"That's, uh ... that's good," Jack said.

"Is there any way to make him stop?" he asked Joan the next time their guide had pulled far enough ahead to be out of earshot.

"Hey, Ratzo, tell him how you know the tunnels," Joan said, as she stopped to steal a drink from Jack's canteen. "I think it'll be OK. Besides, it's a great story."

It was.

A skinny kid who wore eyeglasses and read books, Jimmy "Ratzo" Rizzolo had not been exactly the most popular kid in school. In fact, he matter-of-factly related that getting beaten up on the playground was something he could look forward to, pretty much daily. His mother had taught him not to fight back, that it was better to turn the other cheek. So both his cheeks got turned into pretty regular punching bags.

He was small, and there was no one to teach him to fight, so Ratzo just learned to avoid the other kids. Instead he spent time in the library, or wandering around alone, collecting things.

"Collecting what?" Jack asked.

"Anything. Stamps, old coins, matchbook covers. Beetles and bugs. When there was a construction project I'd even dig around in the rocks looking for fossils, although it turns out this place isn't a very good place for fossils. More out on the island. You need limestone and shale deposits, see?"

Other kids enjoyed playing basketball in the playgrounds or in the streets. When Jimmy tried they just knocked him down. He looked it up in the rulebook and showed them where it said you weren't supposed to knock each other down; that was called a "foul." They laughed at him and knocked him down more.

So Jimmy "Ratzo" Rizzolo had retreated to a magical world of his own where there was no one to break the rules. His mother worked long hours to support them and drank when she was home, so there wasn't exactly much of a home life. (He didn't say this critically. Drinking meant his mom was committing suicide, but slowly enough that she'd last till her son was grown. If that was the best she could do, Jimmy appreciated it. He was not bitter.) Instead Jimmy would play in the basement of his building, fantasy games involving a hunt for lost treasure buried in the realm of the trolls.

But in searching for stuff for his collections, Ratzo had discovered an unlocked door from the basement into the tunnels — and suddenly his fantasy world came very much to life.

The door led to a ladder which in turn gave way to the tunnel through which the steam lines from one central furnace and power plant linked three adjoining buildings. At first he was excited merely to learn one of the passageways led under the street to an old theater which had fallen on hard times and become a tawdry strip joint, where he could spy on the half-naked dancers in their basement dressing rooms.

Needless to say, the attraction of spying on the strippers as they changed costumes was substantial to a young teen-age boy. But he immediately grasped this was a bigger discovery than that. Yes, he could explore the club late at night when everyone had left, snitch some leftover cake and cold coffee from the girls' refreshment table. But the fact that these basement doors could stand unlocked and ignored for such long periods of time drew him to explore how much further the tunnels might lead.

He discovered security in the tunnels was minimal. Only janitors and electricians and other service and repair personnel ever went down there. And they didn't like the duty much, so none of them ever seemed to explore any further than they needed to. Indeed, their general attitude was that there was nothing worth stealing and it would be a pain in the ass to put locks everywhere. So things were generally wide open.

His next big discovery was that the tunnel adjacent to the basement of the geology building of the nearby branch of the city college held a treasure trove of rock and mineral samples — not little things but huge pieces of malachite and amethyst geodes sometimes heavier than he could lift, slices of rock as big as tabletops revealing petrified birds, dragonflies ... the surplus from the department's little museum had simply been stacked in the heating pipe tunnel outside the basement access door as the years went by, the janitors and professors obviously confident *they* needed a key to open that door, never realizing that coming from the *outside* Ratzo could open that door at night, cover the bolt with a piece of masking tape so it wouldn't latch should it slide closed (he usually propped the door open with an additional matchbook or something else unobtrusive, as a double safeguard) and explore to his heart's content.

It was a wonderland, like discovering a secret fairy treasure cave with a hidden door right in your own basement. Even the public libraries — storehouses of the world's knowledge, guarded by alarms and bars and floodlights from ground-level incursions — stood wide open when you climbed up the access ladders from the tunnels.

From the start his instinct, which would have warmed the heart of any archeologist, was not to steal these things. Where would he have put them if he'd hauled them away, after all? That would be like stumbling on the Mammoth Cave and immediately starting to whack down all the stalactites so you could carry them home and hide them in a box under your bed, where they'd just be a bunch of rocks, never nearly so impressive as in their original setting.

Young Jimmy felt that in a kind of gratuitous grace he'd been transported to Valhalla. You wouldn't start out stealing the shields off the walls in Valhalla. And because he stole nothing — except the occasional unguarded candy bar or can of soda pop — he remained undetected and virtually undetectable. He left no footprints, literal or figurative. He was the perfect phantom.

Only years later did it occur to him that he probably could have found a way to steal rare books and framed wall hangings for re-sale. At the time, it simply never crossed his mind — any more than he would have had the slightest motivation to commit any kind of random vandalism. What was exhilarating to him was simply gaining access to places to which the adult world thought he should not be trusted with access — the ability to tiptoe freely through twilit buildings that made him feel like the hero of one of those science fiction movies he loved, where the rest of mankind has mysteriously vanished in some plague, leaving all their treasures unguarded for the Last Man on Earth.

Jimmy wished he was the Last Man on Earth.

What's more, most of the tunnels were surprisingly dry

and well lit. Yes, eventually he found access points to the storm sewers and the subway system, where on occasion the junkies and the Mole People would seek shelter and foul their own lairs. Those places he avoided. But they were far away from the places that interested him.

At the deepest levels were the giant water mains, bringing the city its pure water from reservoirs far upstate. Jimmy rarely went that deep — "the deep blue," he called it, where dark shadows moved, accompanied by weird clanking noises, creatures too long shut away from the light, whose nature and purpose he had no desire to learn.

As the weeks and months went by, young Jimmy expanded the range of his explorations. One of his first concerns, of course, was simply locating access points from which he could safely emerge into a basement which held an unlocked men's room, or vending machines where he could conveniently buy soda pop, snacks, and hot chocolate — he was far too young to have developed a taste for coffee.

Oddly enough, he never encountered a guard dog. Dogs were messy and could bring liability suits; they might be used far out in the suburbs, but here in the urban snugness the only domestic animals he encountered were cats — mascot cats of office buildings and theaters and other places who were almost universally excited to have new human company at a time of day when they'd been accustomed to wandering their twilit haunts in solitude. And so he made many friends among the fur people — especially once he learned to bring snacks.

And in carrying food for them it occurred to him it would be wise to set up small caches of supplies for himself — all well sealed against rodent incursion, of course, and stored somewhere high and out of sight.

It was almost as an afterthought, as police security began to increase aboveground, that he realized he'd discovered an alternative method of moving about the city, of accessing much of the world without dealing with doormen, bouncers, admission charges, guest lists, taxicabs, inclement weather ... or the more and more pervasive police portals.

And so the tunnels — the tunnels and a guide who could open them up like opening the pages of a favorite book — had lain waiting. Waiting for the Black Arrow.

⚜ ⚜ ⚜

Finally they reached a point where Ratzo paused.

"The problem is," he explained, "where we're going now, and this is no joke, if you know how to find it, they might decide to kill you."

Jack nodded.

"So, if you've got something Joanie can tie around your eyes for a blindfold, it's really for your own good."

Jack produced another rolled bandage out of one of his thigh pockets, and Joan wrapped him up till he certified he couldn't see a thing. Their progress was a lot slower then, especially since it was mostly downhill, by what seemed to be not regular man-made stairsteps, but rather some kind of twisting rabbit hole. At some points either Joan or their guide had to literally place his hands on each handhold, and his feet on each resting place. The air grew warmer, strangely enough, and there was a noticeable breeze in his face.

Finally Ratzo announced himself satisfied with their progress, and told him he could remove the blindfold.

The scene that opened up before him should have been impossible.

Gotham was primarily a granite island; everyone knew that. That's why you could build skyscrapers on it without having them settle and lean over like those famous Italian towers.

There weren't supposed to be natural caverns in such a geologic formation — those were supposed to show up only in the limestone creek country of Kentucky and New Mexico.

Yet here it was, a fully enclosed natural cavern hundreds of feet deep and who-could-tell how long in extent, formed through millions of years of erosion by an underground stream and the gradual percolation of surface water, leaching away this giant bubble of limestone and other, softer rocks that had somehow been trapped inside the larger mass of the granite island back in the mists of ancient geologic time, long before the last Ice Age.

What's more, you always expected to come upon such a formation from the bottom, by following the bed of the stream that had gradually eaten its way down through the pockets of softer rock — to discover the abyss of open space towering above your head.

Here, instead, they'd entered the cavern from near the top, emerging onto a natural gallery or ledge of rock which Ratzo had stumbled onto years ago, his greatest discovery, yet one he had dared show no one, till he offered to lead the Black Arrow here, in search of a refuge.

The formation had been pitch dark when Ratzo had first stumbled into it, of course. There was still too little light to make out its full expanse. But over the months a few strings of electric bulbs had been run along the major access paths, and — from far below, now — came the additional noise and glowing orange light of Hideki's drop-hammer forge, echoing and casting an eerie glow as though they were indeed looking down into the legendary workshops of Hades.

The forge didn't put out enough warmth to explain the temperature. Jack realized it wouldn't be correct to call it "warm," actually — it was probably about 55 degrees. But the cavern, being essentially sealed off but for a few narrow and winding access points, maintained a constant temperature which certainly felt warm compared to the fast-freezing February night outside.

And the combination of the pale strings of white electric

lights and the orange glow of the distant forge were enough — as their pupils adjusted — to reveal a glittering wonderland of stalactites, stalagmites, huge formations of ruby and saffron and even translucent beryl flow-stone that flashed an occasional opalescent rainbow, shaped into forms that resembled melting wax pipe organs. There must be copper ores, too, for in a wide band below them spread formations that looked like throne rooms of the gods, carved in the sparkling blue agates of malachite and chrysocolla.

It was too wondrous a moment to last.

"Don't move," said the black-clad archer who rose from behind a smaller formation not 40 yards down the trail — a young red-haired woman and no giant, from the sound of her voice ... though her drawn Oneida bow and the blue steel razor at the end of her arrow looked dangerous enough.

"That you, Caelan?" Ratzo asked, squinting to make out a face.

"It's Kiera. I'm not alone. Now stand away from that Gray, so we can kill him for you. Unless I hear some objection."

⚜ ⚜ ⚜

The Japanese guy and the young woman working the forge in their heavy denim aprons seemed to be in charge, from the way Kiera and her fellow Amazon deferred to them after bringing Jack and Joan in.

Joan had spoken up quick enough in Jack's defense, but the one named Kiera still wouldn't let them come any further until Jack agreed to let Joanie carry his MP-5 and his combat knife. It seemed a reasonable compromise. He wasn't planning on shooting anybody just now, anyway.

The path to the cavern floor had been worked on, first by Ratzo — gradually, laboriously — and now by a larger num-

194

ber of willing hands. A heavy knotted rope had been strung to provide handholds; natural shelves and steps had been deepened or reinforced with new pieces of rock from the tumbled piles far below or with rough-hewn beams that appeared to be undersized railroad ties, probably scavenged from old subway lines long since abandoned or replaced.

The lights were dim, but just stretching enough of them to illuminate that long and winding a trail had taken considerable manpower and resources. Jack couldn't hear the whine of any diesel generator, so they'd obviously tapped into some existing electric mains — that meant someone knew how to safely step down 220 to 110.

But most of all what impressed him was the sheer scope of the place. In this television age mankind had grown used to thinking of himself in close-up. Here, by the time he widened his field of view to take in the entire grandeur of the place — the twisted, fanciful rock formations only partly visible in the gloom — Jack and his companions took on the proportion of tiny insects, facing an hour's work as they struggled across the irregular surface, hoping to reach the far side of some depraved giant's sculpture gallery by sunrise.

They called the young woman Madison. She was clearly a leader of some kind. Exactly where the Japanese guy working the forge fit in, he couldn't be sure. Guy didn't say much.

She had lots of shoulder-length brown hair, parted in the middle.Five foot eight, maybe.

Once she'd turned to decide Jack's fate she stood with her shoulders thrust back. A high, domed forehead, oval face, huge brown eyes like almonds that turned down a little at the outside. She had a cleft chin and a lilting Irish accent ... tempered by at least a few years Stateside.

"They could have set up the whole thing to get him in here," she said — addressing Joanie as though Jack wasn't standing right next to her.

"Jack's OK," Joan answered. "Otherwise I would have

killed him."

The strange thing was, not only did she sound serious, but the Amazon from the forge didn't seem to find anything amusing about it.

Jack loved Joanie.

Finally she turned to face Jack directly. "You a spy?" she asked. "Assuming you live, what do you plan to do if they ask you to lead 'em back here?"

Funny how few people would think to simply ask. His esteem for these people kept going up.

"I plan to lie. Looks to me like I got into this thing on the wrong side. But that doesn't mean I'm ready to sell out my unit, either. Tell you the truth, I don't know what the fuck I'm gonna do. Not meaning to offend anyone's tender ears, you understand."

The Japanese guy coughed and covered his mouth with his hand. Finally Madison smiled, too. She had a real pretty smile, he found himself thinking. Big dimples. Joan punched him on the arm. How did they do that?

"Now that is too stupid to be a lie," was the judgment of the lady from the forge. "Kiera, you're fastest. You know where to find the doc?"

"Yep."

"Ask him to come look at Joan's leg, hell's hammers. And bring me back three more bows, jewel. One to help keep an eye on our guest till we send Joanie home, two more to scout back with Ratzo along the route they came in, make sure nobody else got through."

Ratzo opened his mouth to object. Madison looked at him and tilted her head about an inch. The sentence died in his throat.

"Then get word to himself, he's gonna have to make a final decision about our new friend 'Jack.' "

Kiera re-slung her bow and took off at a trot. Jack was impressed.

They were taught that civilian criminals and irregulars invariably squabbled and whined. That's not what he was seeing here. There was an ease among these folks. This Madison gave an order and there was no argument, no hostility. This was especially impressive with the copper-haired Kiera, who appeared to be the prettiest of the lot. A young woman in command would often give a prettier subordinate a hard time — not that this Madison would exactly break your mirrors. A young commander who would instead surround herself with the best and the brightest could be a force to be reckoned with. Fifty fighters with this kind of discipline could be a real problem. And these were the girls.

"Rachel, back off a little, find someplace comfortable to hunker down. In the dark, jewel. You're on guard and I want you out of sight if anyone else shows up. You guys want to stay by the fire; it's warm and the light's good here. Rachel, you got any clean points?"

"No."

"You hear that, Joan? Your friend know what that means?"

"No, I don't," Jack answered for himself.

"Rachel doesn't have any untreated points. Any trouble breaks out here, her first arrow is for you. And it'll kill you. Curare or tobacco, whatever they're carrying. We got real tired of so many assholes surviving, after all the trouble we went to to shoot 'em. So if you need to use the Porta-Potty or anything, tell us now."

He did, actually. They had Joan frisk him. "Oh my," she said.

"Weapon?" Madison asked.

"Not the kind I'm going to share with you, honey," Joan responded. Then they settled in to watch Hideki pound his steel and wait for the doctor to arrive.

⚜ ⚜ ⚜

197

Madison disappeared somewhere behind them, presumably setting up some kind of medical treatment area in one of a series of low-ceilinged chambers or "rooms" where they seemed to have strung most of their lights.

Hideki — that was what they called the blacksmith — wore a heavy apron over bib overalls and a T-shirt tied around his head as a headband as he worked a bar of cherry red steel in an open-ended gas oven, occasionally pulling it out with his tongs and placing it under his power hammer, which he could work with either a foot pedal or an electric toggle switch. The thing dropped at a rythmic three or four strikes a second.

The echoes of the hammer were faint and distant enough to give a further sense of the vastness of the cavern, only a portion of which was revealed by the lights slung here in the "inhabited" area, and along the winding path leading up to Ratzo's Doorway.

Jack asked how hot the glowing red steel was. "2350 to 2450 degrees," the old-timer answered matter-of-factly, using Fahrenheit. "You look for that bright cherry orange, that's right at the temperature where I weld."

And the mechanical hammer?

"They used to run off the jack line in the mills. This is the 25-pound 'Baby.' They also made the 50-pound Boy, the 100-pound Man, the 250-pound Giant, and the 500-pound Jumbo."

Seeing as how the Baby could obviously smash your thumb to a pulp if you didn't have your hand out of there when you tripped the hammer, Jack didn't even want to think about what would happen to a body part caught under the 500-pounder.

"In 1910 to 1915 they introduced the cone clutch. This one's from 1897. It's better. It's got the wood blocks. Lem Lillymeyer bought 'em all up, in Minnesota. He's making replacement parts for 'em. But if you have an employee you can't use 'em any more. OSHA regulations."

As he spoke, occasionally Hideki would stomp one foot and say "Ow" as a spark found its way through a hole in his pants. Oxidized gray-white slag came off the sides of the bar as he hammered it.

"You make Japanese blades? Samurai swords?" Jack asked.

"Yes. But why is everybody fixated on the Japanese blade? Oh, it has its aura. But they *would* break, that's why form is so important in Japanese swordsmanship. With a Japanese blade you have to slice through, not chop like a European sword. You want to chop off body parts through light armor? The European sword might be better.

"Forty to 45 points of carbon gets you a hardness of 50 to 55 Rockwell, and 55 is as high as you want to go. The Japanese blades run 53 to 59, where the European blades will run 48 to 52. They're softer, springier, so you don't have the chip-out problem.

"In the European sword you want weight to carry through. In the European style swords there's no evidence they did any refractory hardening at all."

"In a Japanese blade you'll see chips, called kisu, right out of the martensite, the edge. If they're polished down too far, the blade gets tired. You polish past the tempering. My Japanese brothers are very closed-mouthed about all this. We would temper and harden in one step, in the quenching. But for practical use, a shinshinto blade made in the 1920s is probably better than an antique."

"They're made out of more than one type of steel?"

"There are up to five or six types of steel in a Japanese-hardened blade, defined by the crystal structure, which gives you different properties. We temper and harden in one step, in the quenching. Which types of steel form where is controlled by coating the blade with varying thicknesses of clay before you temper, which affects the way the heat penetrates. That's the art, because it's all done at once. Austenite is the softest,

199

'I'm kinda laid back.' Then there's pearlite, 'I'm kinda pissed off.' Then your martensite is really angry."

Why did he keep refolding the hot steel, Joan asked.

"Every time we weld we lose 7 to 12 percent of the mass, that's why you need to start with a big bar of steel. If you get up to 27 layers and you fold them five more times, you'll reach 800 layers. You want to end up with 5,000 layers, which is pretty much homogeneous, which is what you want. The ancient Europeans would weld three or four bars into a pattern, and then do cementation, hardening down 15 to 20 thousandths of an inch. The Sutton Hoo find was eight bars with edging applied. That had 16 to 65 layers per bar, so it was really quite coarse."

People kept forgetting that steel was a crystal, the old ironsmith said, warming to his subject as he continued to hammer, pausing occasionally for a sip of water which he drew from a bucket with a dipper. "The rivets on the Titanic were rolled 90 degrees against the grain, which is why they popped so easily when the ship hit something, you got lateral shearing force and they popped like buttons off a shirt. You've got to roll steel rivets with the grain; steel is a crystal. Or take the famous Wilkinson blade. People forget Wilkinson made its reputation in the Crimean War because they were the only blades not breaking, they had British swords even breaking along the long axis, which is really bad. They forgot there was a reason people had been folding that steel so many times, to get rid of the directional grain."

Joan was obviously exhausted, kept looking like she wanted to doze off, but the leg wouldn't let her. Finally Kiera came back with the doctor, tall German guy with longish gray hair. Jack would have said he actually looked a little unkempt, but he was businesslike enough as he examined the leg, declared they were going to have to concentrate some lights on a table in the sleeping area, "Whatever's in there has got to come out, and I think we can do it right here if Madison can rig up a clean area for me, plug in the autoclave, and — I know this sounds like an old Western movie — but perhaps boil us some nice clean water."

"Already on it," said Madison.

❖ ❖ ❖

Jack started to wander off and have a look around — after asking Madison for an escort so he wouldn't get shot — sensing he would only get in the way. He'd been raised to believe surgery was a private and rather intimate affair. But the doc— someone had called him Stauffer— obviously did not agree.

"Get back here, young man. Tie on a mask and don't touch anything unless I tell you. You should see what a bullet does, it will advance your education."

No one else seemed to consider it the slightest bit odd when a fat orange cat climbed up on a nearby stool, tucked in his forepaws, and proceeded to settle in and watch the goings-on with evident equanimity.

The doctor pricked the area around the wound with a needle, asked Joan if she could feel that, got a mumble and finally a rather distracted "No." Joan was pretty well out of it after being shot up with whatever the doc had given her. Jack was tempted to ask if he was a real M.D., but decided it wasn't his place.

"Good." The gangly old German started cutting into the wound with an alacrity that made Jack pull back involuntarily, though his stomach held OK. Nothing compared to what he'd seen on the floor of the day care center. Had that really been only this afternoon? Besides, he cared for this girl. So if the doctor said he could be of some use, this was no time to go worshipping at the porcelain altar.

"Hm," Stauffer said, using a long pair of tweezers off his

tray to draw some clump of bloody material out of the now freely-bleeding hole in Joan's leg, as Madison and the one they called "Brawny" applied white gauze to soak up most of the overflowing blood.

"What did you shoot her with, 9 millimeter?"

"I didn't shoot her personally."

"We have to proceed rather briskly here, young man. I need useful information, not exculpatory testimony. A 9 millimeter bullet?"

"Yes."

"115 grain?"

"Federal Hydra-shok, semi-jacketed hollowpoint, 124 grain."

"Hm." He set down the object he'd pulled out of Joan's leg — obviously a bullet from the way it clinked in the metal pan — and went back to work, digging and cutting a lot deeper than Jack would have expected was necessary.

"Is that bad?"

"As you can see, the wound is, if anything, shallower and less severe than we might expect. Of course, most of my experience has been with 30-caliber rounds, especially the seven-six-two by thirty-nine, which do considerably more damage than your pistol rounds, even if they don't expand quite so attractively, due to some technicality of the Geneva Convention by which you policemen apparently do not feel yourselves bound.

"If you can do so now without actually shooting anyone else, please strip a round of 9 millimeter off the top of one of your magazines. Then pick up this bullet I have just removed and compare the weight.

"Pick it up?"

"Come, come, young man, we are both in the business of blood, you know. You shoot them up, I patch them back together, two ends of the same business. Don't be squeamish, now. I'm sorry I have no time to sterilize it for you. Pick it up.

Compare."

Even with the brass cartridge case still attached to the round from one of his spare mags, Jack could tell the difference. "It's too light."

"Correct. What we have removed from the wound is too light. Also, it does not penetrate as far as we might expect, given that it does not appear to have struck the bone, and it shows no evidence of expansion. She probably didn't even realize, at first, that she'd been shot."

"No, she didn't. So this is — "

"A bullet fragment. About half of the bullet, I would estimate."

"And that's ... bad?"

Joan made a noise, sounded like concern. She wasn't completely out, of course, and could presumably hear most of their conversation. The doctor had explained he had no safe way to administer a general anaesthetic by himself, and would have waited a few more hours after their meal of beef stew with Gold Tooth and his guards, anyway. So he'd settled for a combination of a local and some kind of sedative.

"No, no, this is going to be fine. Actually, the bullet did very little damage. There will be a small scar, a little white line, but we will try to take a little care and use a smaller needle when we stitch the young lady up, so it will hardly be noticeable. I dare say she likes to show off these legs in a bathing suit from time to time. Ah, yes. I see you care for our Joanie."

"I do. She says she's going to marry me."

"Really? And what do you say, young man?"

"Joan says the girl gets to decide."

"Well, if you will take the advice of an old man who has seen war and troubles on several continents, you will not let this one get away. This is a very special young woman we are dealing with here. She is very smart and, as we now know, very brave. You know she has been in considerable pain all day, I suppose."

"She didn't let on."

"A very brave young woman. As I said, the bullet did very little permanent damage, although we've certainly done the right thing to get it out of there." He was now scraping material out of the inside of the wound, applying what Jack assumed were a couple different kinds of antibiotic or antiseptic, one of which frothed and bubbled as he poured it on.

"The reason we're being so thorough here is that we don't know where that bullet had been, what it might have passed through, including the clothing, before it came to rest here. So we're cleaning everything up very well, and then we'll follow up with two antibiotics, one a broad spectrum, I believe I have some amoxicillin, and then a specific antibiotic called Augmentin that we use when we think there's any chance foreign tissue may have been transported into a wound, actually we call it the cat-scratch antibiotic, since that's the major use.

"You'll make sure she has the wound checked daily for any signs of secondary infection, but it appears to me we've gotten everything. Just a little more cleaning up, here, and then perhaps one of you young ladies will reach into my bag and hand me some needle and thread, one of the smaller needles, so we can make some nice small stitches. You didn't know I was a seamstress as well, did you?"

"Is there some kind of form you have to fill out, when you treat a gunshot?"

The two assistants looked at Jack as though he was a congenital idiot.

"Oh, yes, yes. Forms for the gunshot, forms for the sedatives, forms for the procaine anaesthetic, all in triplicate. They used to make quite a considerable pile, let me tell you. But you know what? No matter how many times I ask if they can tell me one life that has ever been saved by these forms, they cannot answer. Because these are not medical forms, you understand. A bullet wound is not a communicable disease. You can't catch a gunshot from the patient in the next bed. The government doesn't give a damn whether I'm prescribing an opiate which is contraindicated by something else on the patient's chart. This is not what they care about.

"No, no, these are police forms, nothing else, intended to restrict the practice of medicine, to limit the availability of these drugs to patients who need them, and to help them track the gun owner who shot the burglar, so the homeowner who was defending his family can be arrested. My only suggestion to them about these forms is that they should print them on some softer sort of paper, so they would be much more useful to us when we take them with us into the bathroom."

Dr. Stauffer's eyes were twinkling as he sewed.

"Will she be in pain when she comes out of it?"

"No, no. I suspect she will sleep a bit now, and then she'll be feeling much better. The young heal very quickly. Though we should probably get her out of this damp cave, up someplace where there's fresh air and sunlight. But she will suffer no pain at all, because we will give her as much painkiller as she needs. That's what we have doctors for, young man. In the old days, of course, doctors used to tell their patients a certain amount of pain was normal, it built character, that we should just grit our teeth. But they were barbarians. Today we know that pain actually causes stresses on the heart, stresses which can slow the healing process, and so we give the patient whatever she needs."

"Really?

"Yes. Well, this is what good doctors do." He turned to Jack, removing his mask and giving him a big smile. "And I am a very good doctor."

⚜ ⚜ ⚜

Jack must have dozed off for an hour. It seemed like no time before they had Joanie up and about. Two of Madison's

Bitches — that seemed to be their official unit designation — changed into somewhat more colorful street clothes and prepared to escort her "topside" to her daddy's townhouse in the city, where she said she'd be safe recuperating for a few days — apparently she'd been telling the truth about being the daughter of some wealthy industrialist, up there in that other world.

Their farewell was brief.

"I'd like to see some more of you. Really," he said.

She replied by delivering a much more thoughtful, lingering kiss than she'd shown him in the past. She didn't seem to want to stop breathing the same air. It was very ... intimate. "I'm glad to hear that," she smiled. Though he could tell she was still pale and woozy.

"How do I reach you?"

"That wouldn't be smart, silly. You'll hear from us."

"You sure?"

"Yes. I am."

Then they were heading up the trail, Jack already missing her in a very physical way ... and then, as Jack turned around, he had a much more pressing concern.

"Himself" turned out to be a big guy in a mask, dressed all in black, with a black bow and quiver. Arms and shoulders like tree trunks. It was The Black Arrow, no doubt about that. And he appeared to have popped up out of nowhere, right in front of Jack. How had he done that?

"Pistol in your pocket, or you just glad to see me?"

"I just met the girl I'm going to marry, if it's any business of yours."

"Congratulations." The masked man just stood there, then, studying his face. Jack wasn't sure why some people did that, but he was from a military family; he knew the drill. You stared right back. Apparently liars and scam artists couldn't do this without shifting their eyes or blurting something out. It was weird, but if standing still for a minute could convince some people you weren't a face-dancer ... well, he'd done a lot more boring things in his young life.

He could not help considering, during this minute of silent scrutiny, that if he could figure out a way to kill this guy, he'd be hailed as a hero. Well ... a way to kill this guy and get away alive.

And then Jack discovered something about himself. He discovered he couldn't actually tell you whether he'd consider being hailed as a hero to be a good thing, until someone could answer the question, "hailed as a hero ... by who?"

"You're Jack Brackley?"

"Yes."

"You present us with a bit of a quandary."

"Sorry about that."

The blacksmith joined their conversation. The girl they called Madison did not. This told Jack something about their chain of command.

But since no one was doing any obvious posturing, things didn't take as long as he might have figured. They'd decided not to kill him, which meant they pretty much had to take him at his word that he really hadn't decided which side of this thing he was going to end up on — he just knew he wasn't going to betray Joan and he also wasn't going to be shooting up any more day-care centers.

Anyway, he had a bigger priority now: finding out who'd really killed his father. He asked if they knew. There was a pause in the conversation.

"You have to understand something about my friend," Hideki explained. "He's ... direct. You shouldn't ask him a question if you don't really want to know the answer."

"I want to know the answer," Jack replied.

Still the Black Arrow stared at him for long seconds. Then, softly, "You mean a lot to our Joanie."

"She means a lot to me."

"I hope so. Because it wouldn't be doing her any favor

if you went rushing off without a plan and got yourself killed. Plans have to be developed. They have to mature. Finding out the truth is one thing. Figuring out how to use it is something else again."

"You haven't answered my question."

"Daniel Brackley had his brother Thomas killed."

"That's impossible."

"You know it's not. But you also can't act on my say-so. You have to confirm it for yourself."

"How do I do that?"

"Don't act too rashly. Your uncle's campaign manager, Oliver Oates, knows what happened. But this is dangerous ground, young friend. Your father was killed because he was going to publicly denounce the War in the West. We believe he'd prepared a written statement, maybe even a video disc. If you threaten to locate and go public with those documents — if they so much as know you're looking for them — there are men on the other side who won't hesitate to kill again. You. Joanie. Whoever. So don't get too headstrong. If you're serious about our Joan, I don't want to see her widowed before her honeymoon."

Funny. Up in the regular world, people would snicker and "Oh sure" you at the notion that you intended to marry someone you'd just met. What was different down here? Combat. That had to be it. These people lived in a perpetual state of combat. Time was compressed; emotions had to be fast and true. You learned to trust your instincts, because those with bad instincts were either dead already, or headed there soon.

"You need to go slow," the Black Arrow continued. "Let us help you when we can. You trust Joan. We'll put her in touch with you, get you as much additional information as we can. Maybe there are ways we can help each other, without your having to break your oath to your unit. But maybe not. Eventually, you may face decisions that aren't easy or comfortable, Jack Brackley."

"Wherever the truth leads."

"Good. That's what I needed to hear."

They proposed giving Jack an anaesthetic, tying him up and dumping him in the alley next to the Homeland Security SonicNet headquarters with a note pinned to his chest warning the Grays to "Stay Out of Our Tunnels." That would piss 'em off and divert their attention to some kind of exercise, demonstrating to everyone that government forces could enter the tunnels at will, like a kid proving he could eat all the candy he wanted. Anything that drove the enemy to waste resources on useless gestures was inherently good.

"I disagree," Jack said.

"Oh?"

"The sooner I get back the better. My only goal was to get Joan someplace safe. Since I have no intention of leaving the country or living down in this cave for the duration, I've got to go back, and the shorter the time I'm gone the easier it'll be to explain."

"Yes."

"But if I come back without my weapon it'll be obvious I was captured. Right away they're going to wonder why I wasn't held for ransom or a prisoner exchange. Once someone gets captured and released unharmed they've always got to wonder if he's turned; they'll always keep a closer watch on him, never trust him — maybe even set traps where they slip him bad information and see if it finds its way to the other side."

The kid wasn't admitting that coming back without your weapon was tantamount to an admission you'd turned tail and run in the heat of battle — no one would want to do it, if it could be avoided. But he was showing he was smart, and could think fast. That was good.

"You have some alternative?"

"Blindfold me till I'm well out of the caverns so I can't find my way back here, even if I tried. Then give me back my

MP-5 and set me loose somewhere near a subway station. I take a train back to headquarters, tell them I chased the girl down into the subway system but I lost her down there, at which point I had to lay low to evade a bunch of guys with bows and arrows. Since I was never captured, I don't know anything, and no one has to wonder why I was released."

"And when they ask you to lead them back to where you saw all these resistance fighters?"

"I got so turned around down there, I have no idea which direction was which ... sir."

"But why were you gone so long? Why didn't you come back right after you lost the girl?"

"Like I said, I got lost. The rebels move in bands of six; I figured it was better to escape and look for reinforcements than to take on that many on my own. So I spent a lot of time hiding. Green recruits are taught to withdraw and re-establish contact."

"How'd the girl get away from you if she was shot?"

"She didn't run like she was shot. Who said she was shot?"

"You were seen running down into the subways with her."

"I'd caught her, at that point, but she pulled away and ran down into the subway entrance. I wasn't with her; I was giving chase. Slippery little bitch; she knew every twist and turn."

The Black Arrow thought it over. He was hard to read, behind that mask. "Works for me," he said.

✤ ✤ ✤

Everyone else had gone their separate ways. Hideki's forge had long since fallen silent. Madison should probably have quit long ago, too. Sometimes she tried something, though, and she just had to keep going till she got it right. Or gave it up entirely. She was one stubborn bitch, basically. And that had been her criterion in selecting her gallai. Stand up for yourself, you're a bitch. Stand up for your sisters, you're a bitch. And all Madison wanted was cold, hard bitches. Size wasn't the main thing. Strength — physical strength, anyway — wasn't the main thing, or Rachel wouldn't have been in. Some of them were crossover Irish, American born. But out on the streets, the Irish Bitches was the nicest thing they got called. So that was their name. Wanna do something about it?

She was hitting the target OK with the big Oneida black eagle, but she was still trying to understand what he'd said about the way you should feel before the arrow released. Funny how she thought of him with just the third person pronoun, now. He. Him. Not The Black Arrow. Just ... Himself.

A sense of calm, he'd told them. Her right arm was getting sore and she seemed to be getting worse instead of better. Far from calm, she was just getting more angry and exasperated. That couldn't be right. Hopeless Madison, trying to shoot like the Black Arrow, because of some stupid vision she couldn't get out of her head. Probably just delayed teen-age lust, imagining the big guy huge and hard as a stallion, grabbing her and cleaving her like the prow of a ship through the waves.

Stop it. Concentrate.

Finally she decided she'd draw the bow, moving both arms the way he'd taught them, close her eyes, hold it steady, and not release at all. Concentrate, concentrate, concentrate. Calm, calm, calm. Strangely, the soreness in her arm seemed to ease. In fact, she couldn't feel her arm at all. And then she heard the arrow fly. Oh great! Her fucking right arm had gone so numb the shaft had slipped, under no control at all, probably end up killing somebody.

Fortunately, the thing struck the target.

"Finally," said the voice behind her, closer than she would

have believed anyone could sneak up on her, any more.

"Jesus, will you not sneak up, I could have —"

"Killed me?"

It was the Black Arrow.

"Oh. Sorry. I thought I was alone. Don't you always make that 'whoosh' sound when you show up?"

"Sometimes silence is more dramatic."

"Well, you're pretty dramatic, I'll give you that. Is that a major goal, though? Being dramatic?"

"Yes," the Black Arrow replied, seriously. Not that he was ever anything but serious. " 'Dramatizing' is a perfect description. Hundreds of books have been written over the years, demonstrating with charts and graphs and detailed case histories that taxation and all the other forms of collectivism don't work, that they can only be enforced through ever-increasing tyranny and centralized control, which destroys incentives and price signals and leaves everybody impoverished and enslaved — starving while the turnips rot in the fields.

"And what happens to those books? More people watch the average TV comedy than have ever read all those books combined. They shrug and say, 'What we're doing isn't collectivism; what we're doing can't be tyranny; it's all nurturing and compassionate and good, because this is America.'

"So we have to dramatize it to them, show them that any agent of the tyrant may have to pay the ultimate price at any time for living on stolen funds and helping to keep this coercive system going, whether you're a prosecutor or a judge or a schoolteacher or a meter maid.

"We wouldn't choose what we're doing as the best way to kill a whole lot of them. Just poisoning the office water cooler or the coffee machine would kill more in a single day. Or you just nuke New Washington, the way they kept nuking Old Washington.

"But because those methods are indiscriminate, they wouldn't have much exemplary value. Stalin said one death is a tragedy; a thousand deaths are a statistic. We're teaching lessons by example, one at a time, to people who refuse to do the reading on their own. And we're doing it with limited resources. So the examples we set have to be dramatic."

"Yeah. OK."

There was no sarcasm in her voice. He liked that about this Madison, who'd just shown up one night with her seven-member all-girl band, escorted by a high-tailed orange cat, as though finding these caverns was child's play, asking if they could hang around, serve as Hideki's apprentices at the forge, whether someone would teach them the sword and the bow and let them help kill Grays. God, they hated the Grays. He didn't even want to ask why. It said a lot about the respect the Bitches had for Joanie Matcham — who had vouched for Madison right at the start — that Jack Brackley hadn't been brought in limp, cold and cockless.

The average government-school graduate would ask you an inane question designed to make you repeat everything you'd just said. Then they'd try to parrot it back to you, which made a third time through the same material — all designed to make it seem like remembering stuff was really hard. But these same kids could recite popular songs and 10-minute snatches of movie dialogue, word perfect, after hearing them once.

The basic deal was so simple it had taken a century of hard work to screw it up. In the real world as it existed before the government youth camps, you waited to explain something till someone asked. When they asked, you explained it. While you explained it, since they were the ones who had asked, they did you the courtesy of listening. Once.

Somehow, this Madison had remained unspoiled. She watched your mouth and eyes, like what you were saying was actually important to her. If she disagreed, she spoke right up. Otherwise, it was "OK," and move along. It was like finding someone who could ice skate after years of watching the poor moon calfs slog through mud. He realized he was smiling. Not

213

SUPRYNOWICZ

in character, at all.

Taking advantage of the silence, she found the courage to tell him, her voice notably throaty. "You don't remember, but you saved my ass one night."

"Oh?"

"A couple of Grays had me in an alley off Spring Street, down near Mott. You were on the roof. Took care of 'em real good. That was you, right?"

"I remember. I hope you were OK."

"Better than OK. That was the night I decided to track down Hideki, learn about swords. That was the night that led me here. You probably didn't know it, but I was carrying a piece of Joanie's code that night."

"Actually, we did know she was expecting a courier. It's one reason we were out. But that's not the main reason I killed those two."

She tilted her head. He was silent, looking in her eyes. Oh, God. It changed the way she breathed. She felt no desire to be anywhere else. He didn't look at her tits, although she was expecting him to.

"When the arrow decided to fly, a minute ago, it surprised you?"

"Damn right," she said. By speaking again, he'd broken a kind of spell. She'd been thinking about that night, and her vision. He meant he'd killed them because he didn't want anyone else fucking with her.

Again, he didn't say anything. Conversations with Himself could get a little one-sided. But that was OK. Just standing here next to him, breathing, was fine with her.

"You said the arrow decided to fly. That was good?" she tried.

"What do you think?"

"Kind of nuts. My eyes were closed."

"And was the shot better than your others, or worse?"

"About the same."

"Would you have believed, a week ago, that you could hit that target with your eyes closed?"

"Just luck."

"Shoot another one with your eyes closed."

"Sounds like a good way to lose a perfectly good arrow."

"For me, Madison."

Had anyone else ever said her name that way?

"But this time, pay attention to the way your left arm feels, the muscle memory of your left arm. Close your eyes before you draw."

She concentrated, willed her left arm to feel the same, breathed, waited, released. When she opened her eyes she saw the shot was high and left.

"No better," she acknowledged. Odd, she was somehow divorced from any ego, from feeling like Madison was screwing up. It was just an interesting experiment, like cutting up a dead frog or something. And he's said she should do it for him. She wondered if he knew how much she'd do for him.

"With your eyes open again, now, but hold the draw, don't release."

She usually hated following orders, but this was interesting.

"Shift the left arm so you're aimed high and left. Feel that?"

"Yes."

"Now shift so you're aimed low and right. Feel the difference?"

"Yes," she almost laughed. It was so simple.

"Swing your arm back and forth between high left and low right. Now bring it back on target. And wait for the arrow to want to fly; we've got all night."

Bullseye. Though it shouldn't count, of course, since she hadn't been thinking about the shot. She'd been thinking completely inappropriate thoughts about the phrase "We've got all night."

"Are you still angry?"

"What? No." How did he know she'd been angry?

"Now close your eyes, and duplicate that shot. Slowly. Wait for the arrow to be ready to fly."

She knew before she opened her eyes. Solid black, right next to the others.

"Whoa. I can kill in the dark."

"Yes, you can."

"How do you do that?"

"Shoot?"

"No. Teach someone else."

He smiled again. For it was the right question, the question only one in a hundred would think to ask.

"I don't. Galileo said, 'You cannot teach a man anything; you can only help him to find it within himself.' "

She smiled back. "Galileo." This time with her trademark irony.

"Galileo. Come see me in a few days; we'll start you shooting at things that make noise in the dark. And tell Hideki I said to speed up your training with the blade."

"Come see you? What do you have, office hours?" The mouth on me, she thought.

"Hideki can usually get word to me. But there's another way. And it's time we hooked you and your ladies up with some real-world jobs, anyway, give you a way to move around topside."

"Jobs?" Madison was automatically suspicious.

"Money for food and lodging. A place to be around competent people, doing useful things. You have to have people in your life; the problem is finding the right ones. Looks to me like you and your girls have been struggling, a little."

"It's always a struggle. Nothing new there."

"If you're going to help us, you shouldn't have to worry about where your next meal is coming from. And it's a good cover, lets you move back and forth. Not too far from here, up top, is the Gotham Theatre block. It's being renovated. Lot of businesses setting up there, or just across the street. Restaurants, a theater, the new recording studios for Rebel Records. There's also a dojo — a martial arts school — where Hideki teaches.

"He generally teaches only the advanced students, but he mentioned if you came by he'd like to be your tutor, start training you to teach some of the less advanced students. Sometimes the fastest way to learn is by teaching someone else. There's a young woman there named Caitlin, the nutritionist, who I think you'll like. Of course, there's a price to be paid. You may end up facing a lot of vitamin shakes and cod liver oil.

"There are some other people there I think you know, already. Jimmy — Ratzo? — started out as the janitor at the Gotham. Jean-Claude and some of his men work in the theater there. They also handle building security, which is another place you and your ladies could help out.

"It's an interesting place. I think you'd fit in. But what I want you to do, is go there alone the first time — "

"Disguised as an old prospector?"

He smiled. Oh, good smile. "Introduce yourself to a guy named Bob, who runs the newsstand in the lobby. Buy something from him. Wait till he isn't busy, introduce yourself, ask if you can pull up a stool and talk to him a little. Bob hears everything; he knows who's looking for help. And Bob is the other way you can get word to me."

"Gotham block, Bob at the newsstand."

"I'm glad you found us, Madison." Stepping close behind her, he put his hand on her shoulder, actually gripped her for a moment. It seemed kind of dramatic, but it didn't feel fake. As a matter of fact, it felt something else entirely. His hand was warm. His whole body was warm. And strong. "We can use you in this fight."

Then he turned and strode away. There was that little whooshing noise, and he was gone in the gloom. How did he *do* that?

Her shoulder, where he'd touched it, tingled with electricity. Was this what it felt like to find a place you were actually wanted, she wondered — where people actually thought you were worth something? People you could trust with your life?

Madison had been a long time looking.

CHAPTER 7

*The evils of tyranny are rarely seen but by him
who resists it.*

— JOHN HAY (1838-1905), 1872

*Unless we put medical freedom into the Constitution,
the time will come when medicine will organize into an
undercover dictatorship. ... To restrict the art of healing to
one class of men and deny equal privileges to others will
constitute the Bastille of medical science. All such laws
are un-American and despotic and have no place in a
republic. ...*

— BENJAMIN RUSH (1746-1813), M.D. UNIVERSITY OF
EDINBURGH, SIGNER OF THE AMERICAN DECLARATION OF
INDEPENDENCE

They all tried to keep their composure, but the excitement
was spreading, there beneath the ornate 19th century dome in
the ancient dark wood Senate chamber of the state Capitol.
More and more members of the party were gravitating toward
Bambi's seat, their smiles starting to break through, preparing
to congratulate her.

The fascist right-wingers — almost every one of them a
male, of course — were going down to the wire, marshaling

their forces to the floor to make sure everyone voted. But one thing Bambi Fiducci had learned was how to count votes. And the majority's floor managers were even more efficient.

Her people were all here, as well. And as the roll call proceeded ponderously on, Bambi saw the progressive side was picking up virtually every one of the "questionables" and "undecideds."

Their strategy had worked perfectly. Unless you were in an absolutely safe upstate Republican district, who on earth was going to vote against protecting little babies from loose guns lying around near their cribs? The Anthony Fiducci Firearms Safe Storage and Child Protection Act was going to win not just the 32-vote majority — she'd known they had that — but the 42 votes necessary to override any veto.

And then it was done. The majority leader was reading the results, the gavel was sounding, a recess was called, and the smiles and celebrations were no longer masked.

They hugged Bambi. They patted her on the back. They danced in the aisles. Safe storage was law.

Bambi Fiducci had always hated guns. They were the tools of the oppressor, part of the whole cult of machismo that had allowed men to keep women down for so many millennia. To keep women pregnant and uneducated, sex slaves in their own homes. But now there would be a new era, an era of fairness and justice and peace, a clean, hygienic age when there would be no need for those smelly oily steel tubes of spitting death and all the pain and misery and slavery they caused.

Her friends had always told her she could go far in politics. But she'd never seriously considered seeking office till the Samoan had killed Anthony on that suburban commuter train.

Of course, she and Anthony had actually been separated — at the time of his death, she hadn't seen him in months. But the press generally didn't mention that part. What difference did it make?

She'd declared for the state senate seat, against that slimy country club gun nut with his white plastic belt and his false teeth and his bad comb-over. And she had run on just the single issue: ban the guns that had killed all those people on the train.

Oh, the NRA had made fun of her, the housewife in tennis shoes out walking the district. They'd poured in the money against her, said she didn't have a chance. They actually had the nerve to argue Charles had died precisely because of all the gun laws already in effect.

Can you imagine? There obviously hadn't been enough gun laws to stop the Samoan, yet they argued there were too *many?*

By the time he shot Anthony, the Samoan had stopped to reload twice. If the law had permitted Anthony or any other passenger on that train to legally carry a concealed weapon, the gun nuts argued, they could have shot back and killed the Samoan. That's the way it would have happened among the breakaway rebels of New Columbia, they'd argued.

And that had sunk them, right there. The nerve, suggesting the suburbs of Gotham City should be like some Wild West shooting gallery, where honest, law-abiding citizens had to carry guns and get involved in shoot-outs every day just to defend their lives, like this was Idaho or Alberta, full of gun-slinging, snake-handling white supremacist cowboys who kept their women chained barefoot in the kitchen!

They truly were insane. She'd won by a huge margin, and had set about banning the very kinds of guns the Samoan had used.

Now, it turned out the Samoan had actually violated numerous existing firearms laws in acquiring and transporting and using his weapon. She couldn't very well get credit for passing laws that were already on the books.

But soon some more experienced hands took her aside and explained how it worked.

The male-dominated courts still refused to let them ban guns completely, based on the archaic Second Amendment, written when people still thought they needed muskets to wage genocide against the Indians and kill defenseless animals for food.

In reality, of course, the Second Amendment only guaranteed the right of the *states* to arm the National Guard — it had nothing to do with individuals being allowed to run around with machine guns. Anyone but an inbred hillbilly could see that. Go ahead and do a poll on legalizing machine guns like the AR-15 or the Mini-14 — the latter so-named because you could hide it in a coat pocket. Why, you'd be lucky to find 2 percent support.

But there was a huge lobby of gun and ammunition manufacturers dedicated to keeping alive the Militia Myth — an earlier and far more profitable version of the penis enlargement pill.

So, you just worked around it.

Even the gun-lugging troglodytes couldn't very well oppose some moderate, reasonable *safety* laws. All you had to do was assure them you weren't trying to ban guns — you thought it was just fine for a legitimate hunter to have a hunting rifle locked in the gun closet at home, take it out one week a year to travel up to the north woods and shoot himself a trophy rabbit or raccoon or whatever. As long as they fingerprinted you when you bought your five-shot box of bullets. But how could such legitimate, law-abiding hunters *possibly* object to a law that was merely intended to keep cheap Saturday Night Specials and rapidfire rat-a-tat assault rifles away from defenseless *children?*

And so she had brainstormed with her new political allies, and come up with the state's first "Safe Storage Law," providing prison terms for any adult who left his firearms unlocked and accessible to minor children while he was away from home.

They'd found a case in which two little kids playing at home had found daddy's gun and the boy had shot and killed his little sister. OK, it turned out this kind of crime happened only four or five times a year in the whole United States. But they'd only needed one.

Now, this particular law would not have actually stopped the Samoan, of course — he'd bought his weapon at a legitimate gun store using fake ID.

But the point was to gradually make gun ownership more difficult and expensive, especially for the smelly, farting, blue-collar illiterates who owned most of them. Gun locks alone could drive up the price of the average Instrument of Death by 50 newbucks. Soon Bambi and her allies would require personalized ID chips like the cops were using — that would add another hundred and fifty.

Little by little: that was the key. Make them expensive, and make the wife-beating thugs worry that just leaving the damned thing in the wrong place for a few minutes could get them sent up the river for years. Brand gun owners as aberrant. Make gun ownership more of a hassle, more and more risky and unusual, till they could finally get their friends in the psychiatric profession to define gun ownership itself as a mental illness.

They'd get there. But in the meantime, Bambi was going to savor today's victory.

"Prime-time face time tonight!" shouted Mary Beth Campbell, flexing her biceps and giving Bambi the thumbs-up.

Indeed there would be television time. What a perfect opportunity for Bambi to announce that she was ready to step up to the next level — taking this victory in hand and marching on, throwing her sneakers in the ring for the Fourth District seat in the U.S. Congress!

❖ ❖ ❖

Cassandra could remember interviewing Dr. Helmut Stauffer. People who'd known him said they could hardly recognize the good doctor, after the government regulators had been at him for a few years, like pack dogs hounding a starving bear.

They described a hale and hearty man, a strapping fellow with a sparkling wit who played French horn in the local community orchestra.

But by the time Cassie sat to interview him in a local diner Helmut Stauffer had lost 30 pounds. He had a shambling gait. His hair kept falling in his eyes as he searched nervously through his pockets for one tattered news clipping or another.

Cassie could picture him now, even as Graymalkin purred and kneaded her sweater. Cassandra was only supposed to be sorting the old columns for the contest, not re-reading them. Like that ever happened. It was headlined "No such thing as 'innocent' " ...

Most Americans probably figure if you manage to get a dispute with a government regulator into court, and if 12 good (wo)men and true then proceed to unanimously acquit and exonerate you, that's an end to the matter. The citizen walks out of the courtroom a free man; the bureaucrats slink back to their burrows licking their wounds; justice is triumphant.

America, meet Dr. Helmut Stauffer.

A native of what is now the Czech Republic, Helmut Stauffer escaped to the West with his family while still a youngster, in 1968, under fire by the Red Army. Though he still speaks with a discernible German accent, the family actually emigrated to Australia, where Helmut received his medical degree, later serving a stint with a M.A.S.H. unit in Iraq, suffering honorable wounds. He now practices in Gotham. At least, he did until recently.

Helmut Stauffer is a general practitioner. But over the years, he developed a bit of a specialty, as most GPs will. Those with acute non-cancer pain seek out Dr. Stauffer.

"I've talked to his patients, and they say 'This is the most wonderful doctor, he'll spend so much time with me,' " says Gotham attorney David Stills, one of a slew of lawyers with whom Dr. Stauffer is obliged to spend a lot of his time these days, instead of with his patients. "But he does prescribe based on what he sees their needs as, and that has got him set up for some trickery, for some skullduggery, by the government," Stills continues.

NURSE TURNED INFORMANT

Dr. Stauffer's problems with the federal Drug Enforcement Administration seem to have begun in 2026, when a secretary in his employ was caught calling in unauthorized prescription renewals to local pharmacies. Stauffer says there's no doubt the young woman was carrying on the activity on her own, as a profitable business. But the employee apparently told investigators she was acting on Stauffer's orders, and accepted a deal to turn informant, feeding state and federal drug police information about Stauffer's practice, where they believed they saw a pattern: more pain-killer prescription being written than is typical for a GP.

Asked at a later date why they had singled him out for persecution, Stauffer says a DEA investigator told him over the phone "We don't like the way you practice medicine." The DEA wouldn't let me ask the agent in question about that. A PR spokesman for the drug police asked whether I was going to take Dr. Stauffer's word, or a government agent's. I pointed out it was hard to take the agent's word if I wasn't allowed to talk to him.

Dr. Stauffer responds: "He never set foot in my office. He never saw the misery of these people. They stereotyped me. They said there couldn't possibly be a little GP treating all these complicated patients. He ought to be just treating sniffles and hemorrhoids. ..."

Government regulators moved against Stauffer on several fronts. The state medical board held hearings, contacting dozens of his patients. The IRS has been auditing his business and his tax returns. And, most invasively, the DEA sent undercover agents

SUPRYNOWICZ

into his office on numerous occasions in 2027 and 2028, pretending to be patients and asking to be written prescriptions for pain killers ... though of course Helmut Stauffer didn't know that at the time.

"They were calling people who said they had no complaints, they brought in six patients at one hearing, one with a spine curved 90 degrees from spinal arthritis, four others in chronic pain, and the last one was a 40-year-old patient with cancer of the testicles, there were two shoulder injuries, and these members of the medical review board, none of whom will even touch a chronic pain patient, are going to decide if I'm overprescribing pain-killers," Stauffer says.

THE JURY ACQUITTED

Finally, in the spring of 2029, federal drug agents arrested Helmut Stauffer, charging him with 16 counts of improperly distributing prescription drugs. He went on trial in December in Gotham City, on charges of illegally prescribing Valium, Xanax, and Percodan to undercover agents. Prosecutor Patrick Reilly told the jury Stauffer was not so much in the business of medical treatment as he was in the business of "supplying drugs on demand." The 55 newbucks per office visit was "easy money," Reilly contended.

But defense attorney Lathrop Wells successfully pointed out that transcripts of secret recordings made by the agents showed Stauffer often questioned the government plants about their symptoms.

"What they had in there was a guy begging him for pain killers, and he kept saying 'No, we don't do things that way'," adds attorney Stills, who has acted as a general legal adviser to Stauffer, referring him in turn to each of the expensive specialist attorneys he needs to fight each of the layered government actions.

The jury deliberated for only a few hours before acquitting Dr. Stauffer on all 16 counts. "Merry Christmas," prosecutor Patrick Reilly told Stauffer after the Dec. 15 verdict was read. "No hard feelings," responded Dr. Stauffer as he shook Reilly's hand.

But the government did harbor hard feelings. Oh, indeed it did.

Dr. Stauffer believed he would be allowed to go back to the practice of medicine. After all, the jury had spoken, and none of his clients had any complaints; he has never been sued for malpractice in more than 20 years of practice.

But suddenly, in February, a pharmacist called Stauffer's office to report he could not fill a routine prescription. He had been informed by the DEA that Stauffer's DEA license number — required to write prescriptions for any "controlled" drug, including even mild pain medication — had been lifted. Pulled. Canceled.

"I was never notified. That's how I found out, from the pharmacies," Stauffer says

Normally, there was no way they'd have let Cassie talk directly to a DEA Associate Special Agent in Charge like Ed Norton, about a case like Dr. Stauffer's — the Justice Department generally handed off responsibility to some glib media spokesman, safe behind the protection of not really knowing anything. So she'd been surprised when ASAC Norton returned her call in person.

"I understand what he's saying," Norton said, "that it's all a punitive, vindictive act by the government, which is not the case."

"But he was found innocent by a jury."

"Not 'innocent'; he was found 'not guilty.' There's a difference," ASAC Norton told her.

"What?" she'd asked, sensing she was near the heart of the matter.

"They don't use the word 'innocent' in the legal process. It's 'not guilty.' it doesn't necessarily mean the defendant didn't do it. 'Not guilty' can be based on a technicality. I'm not talking about this case in particular, but maybe a confession is thrown out because the defendant wasn't Mirandized.

That doesn't mean he didn't do it, it just means he's found 'not guilty.' Now there's a different evidentiary standard for an administrative process, than there is at trial. Just like a cop can be found innocent at trial, but there can still be administrative disciplinary action taken against him."

"But the policeman has voluntarily entered into a contractual arrangement with the department," Cassie said.

"Yes, and a doctor has entered into a contract concerning the safe handling of drugs as part of a public trust, as well," ASAC Norton replied.

Ah, a voluntary contract. But guess what happens if you decide to practice medicine without "volunteering" to submit yourself to licensing by the government medical authorities?

"For some reason the feds have it in their mind that they want this guy," says David Stills. "Dr. Stauffer has bucked the system, he has a different way of dealing with pain patents. Everyone else is afraid to write prescriptions, and he's not. You want to know why pain is undermedicated in this country? The doctors are afraid to write prescriptions because they'll get crucified, that's why."

"It's a totally unnecessary, insane witch hunt," says Helmut Stauffer. "Young doctors believe pain is non-measurable so it's non-existent. Half of the uninsured are in chronic pain. They're not working because of chronic pain. We send these people in for three, four back operations and it doesn't do any good, they use up all their insurance coverage, so after that the medical profession doesn't want anything to do with them; they abandon them. ...

"The medical boards are responsible for 50 percent of the drug problem in this country. The people buying most of those pilfered drugs are chronic pain patients. The drug problem is becoming definitely worse, there are thousands in jail. They get a scrip for 10 pills, they need more, so what do they do? They break into a house, and they end up in jail. The chronic pain patients are desperate, and no one helps them."

⚜ ⚜ ⚜

Prosecutor Patrick Reilly and Ed Norton, number two man at the Gotham bureau of the federal Drug Enforcement Administration, had known each other long before they teamed up to end Helmut Stauffer's medical career. In fact, they'd come up through the ranks together, double-dated in the days back before Norton's wife Cathy had divorced him and taken the kids and run home to Michigan, declaring Ed an asshole.

Fact was, most people who knew Ed Norton of the DEA said he was an asshole. Pat Reilly couldn't figure out why — which was, in the final measure, the strongest basis of their continuing friendship.

Pat and Charlene Reilly had been there for their friend during those hard times, so it seemed natural for Ed to be around, offering his support, after the Reillys found out Charlene had cancer.

Of course, Ed had never told Pat about how he'd been screwing Charlene on the side all these years, usually on Tuesday evenings when Pat was out at Scout meetings with the boys. And it appeared Charlene would take that little secret to the grave with her, as well. Nothing to be gained by causing Pat any additional worry and concern at this point.

Charlene had had the best treatment federal health coverage could buy. There had been periodic improvements, rallies, and plateaus, but all proved temporary. She was now recovering from what would be her last surgery, before being moved either home or to a hospice — she and Pat had yet to decide. She'd had a good 41 years, but now Charlene Reilly was dying, and everyone knew it.

Pat Reilly and Ed Norton were late arriving at the hospital in Ed's big new chauffeured car — Pat visited daily, of course, but Ed made a point of always joining him on Tuesday evenings, since Ed seemed to have Tuesday evenings free these days, for some reason.

They were late this night because they were both backed up with work, especially with all the new security protocols being put in place in response to the recent wave of assassinations and terror attacks on federal employees. They each carried an issue pistol now — they'd long had authorization to do so, of course, but they were now supposed to be carrying 24-seven.

There'd even been a minor Duel of the Bodyguards earlier in the evening, until Ed had pulled rank, declared they were going to travel together to the hospital in his DEA car, and that the services of his driver — an armed federal marshal — would more than suffice. Pat's lower-ranking gumshoe was sent off to Donutland with the promise he'd be paged as soon as they were ready to head home.

Ed's driver now waited on the ground floor, where he could keep an eye on the car, which was in the doctors' surface lot and not in any parking garage which could conceivably have a basement. He had politely pointed out his "U.S." plates to hospital security and informed them, in the calmest and friendliest of tones, that anyone who walked close enough to that vehicle to so much as place a note on the windshield would be shot.

No one had laughed.

Pat Reilly and Ed Norton agreed all the rigmarole seemed a bit over the top. But they were each secretly glad they'd risen high enough in the ranks to be considered worthy of such extra security. After all, it meant you were important to your country, didn't it?

Visiting hours were almost over when they exited the elevator in front of the nursing station on the third floor. There wasn't much activity on the floor, now. The lights had been dimmed in preparation for the night shift. Down the way, flickering blue patterns played across darkened hallways from TV screens in the patients' rooms.

They presented themselves to the charge nurse and gave Charlene's name and room number. She told them it'd be a minute — staff was in there checking Charlene's bandages and making sure she was set for the night, all perfectly routine.

Ed Norton didn't remember seeing this nurse before. Her perky short white uniform emphasized her trim but muscular thighs and perfectly proportioned cleavage. She had long hair to her shoulders — unusual to see a nurse wear it long that way on duty without tying it back — full lips, a cleft chin and the biggest almond eyes, turning down a little at the outside corners. He watched her stir her coffee and lick her spoon. He very definitely watched her lick her spoon.

"Haven't seen you here before," he said. "Aren't you a little young for this job?"

"Yeah, well, I guess they're desperate," she said, giving him a big smile. Red cape: bull.

Ed leaned on the counter and made more small talk. She laughed softly at his jokes. It was a pleasant sound, like falling water. She lowered her eyes demurely. But not too.

"You know, the boy got the count wrong on the coffees," said the lovely Miss Spoonlicker, whose nametag actually said "Halsey." "I've got three extra, nice and hot. Can I interest you boys in a couple? It's the good stuff; hazelnut from Starbucks."

They accepted — to be sociable, if nothing else. The coffees had come black but she had sugar and actual real refrigerated half-and-half that had once been inside a cow, not that nasty synthetic stuff that never went bad. Really, could anything be good for you that had the shelf life of diesel oil, Ed asked. Ed could start a conversation with a wet mop. He had the gift.

Pat Reilly was distracted, thinking about Charlene, so he left Ed to schmooze Nurse Halsey, sipped his coffee with cream

231

as he tried without much success to focus on reading whatever it was that was posted here on the hallway bulletin board: a scheduled meeting of some support group, an announcement of new municipal water conservation measures, the emergency evacuation plan with red lines showing the perfectly predictable location of the twin stairwells.

Coffee had a little after-taste, actually. He never went for this special, fruit-flavored stuff.

Finally a hefty Filipina girl in scrubs came out of Charlene's room, pushing some little cart, and Nurse Megan Halsey — Ed had gotten the first name out of her by now — told them they could go in now. "Visiting hours are almost over, but you boys can stay a little longer if you like, seeing how it's so slow." Pat Reilly took it at face value. Ed Norton wondered if Nurse Halsey would appreciate someone hanging around later and livening up her slow night.

As soon as they entered the room, both men knew something was wrong. Charlene was pulled up into a little ball, her muscles clenched, facing away from the door.

"Charlene?" Pat asked. "What is it? What's wrong, honey?"

She tried to roll over towards them, but seemed unable to relax her muscles. Her hands were knotted up in fists and her face was one large grimace as she tried to fight down the pain.

"Pat. They say I can't have a shot for another hour. I'm trying to hang on but isn't there anything you can do, hon? It's pretty bad."

An old trooper, she was clearly understating her need. Pat pushed the button for Nurse Halsey but Ed turned around and stomped down the hall to meet the young nurse halfway. Pat held his wife as he heard their voices arguing in the hall. "For God's sake, she's in pain," he heard Ed insisting. He couldn't make out all of what the nurse said in reply, but he heard her tone change from calm explanation to feisty argument. "The regulations are what they are," she said, and then something about triplicate forms for controlled drugs, limited availability at off hours, and something about new regulations.

"Goddammit, I make those regulations," Ed replied, shouting now. "Do you know who I am? I'm the Drug Enforcement Administration, goddammit, and if you don't want this whole place to be in a world of hurt, missy, you'll get that doctor up here right now."

The voices moved back down the hall to the nurse's station, then.

"We'll get this taken care of," Pat assured Charlene, who was crying now. "You just hang on a little while longer, now, babe." He held her head and rocked with her, like she was a baby. His lovely Charlene.

The young doctor showed up, looking haggard. He was small — shorter even than Nurse Halsey — with short hair that stood up like he hadn't slept in 24 hours, which he probably hadn't. His eyeglasses made him look owl-like as he tried to give them the same explanation. Controlled substances, triplicate prescriptions, new regulations designed to cut down on what the DEA contended was an unacceptable level of inventory leakage from the Class 3 medicine lockers. Hadn't they heard about the recent prosecutions of doctors charged with writing "too much" of these kinds of drugs? He'd be the first to testify the rules were absurd, but he had a rationed supply and too many patients in need and he was just doing the best he could.

If he doubled or tripled Mrs. Reilly's meds — which is what she needed, he readily agreed — he'd be essentially stealing those doses from another patient on another floor. Could they get him more morphine or at least more codeine or Oxycontin? Could they give him some kind of "Get-Out-of-Jail Free" letter that would save his ass when the regulators called in his superiors and his superiors called him in for an explanation, threatened to turn him over to the Medical Review Board?

Ed Norton wasn't buying it. And Ed Norton wasn't shouting now. He showed his badge, had Pat show his, explained to the young doctor he didn't give a shit about any regulations, this woman was going to get all the pain relief she needed, right now. She was terminally ill, and they were not leaving here until they were convinced she had enough medication to see her through the night.

The doctor, whose name was Herbert West, called Nurse Halsey back and scribbled a note for her on a piece of paper from his pad.

"But doctor, the pharmacy is closed," she said.

"Take it out of the cabinet," he said.

"But doctor —"

"That's an order, nurse. I gave it to you in writing. If there's any question later, I gave you a direct order and I put it in writing. Enter it on the log in my name."

"Yes, doctor."

Within minutes, the nurse had discharged a syringe into Charlene's I.V. tube. Within two minutes more, the men could see her muscles visibly relax. It was like watching 20 years come off her face. She was still pale and sweaty, and of course her beautiful hair was long gone. But she looked like their lovely Charlene again. She did not pretend the pain was gone completely. But it was manageable, now.

"Ed," his friend Pat Reilly said, tentatively, as Charlene finally dropped off to sleep. "What they said about stealing doses from other patients. Is it really that bad? I mean, there could be dozens of other people in this hospital going through what we just saw Charlene going through."

"It's nothing but sheer incompetence. We have review boards that constantly supervise how much of each Class 3 narcotic is allocated to each hospital. If you give them everything they ask for they double and triple their requests, supposedly to handle emergencies but really so they can sell the stuff on the black market."

The strangest thing was happening. Pat Reilly felt as though his consciousness was somehow rising away from his body, looking down at the three of them in this room through one of those wide-angle, fish-eye lenses. He was picking up intonations in his friend's voice which he realized had always been there, but to which he'd never been sensitive before.

He had no idea what was causing this weird effect, but he could tell — as surely as he knew his own name — that Ed was lying. Ed knew how bad it was, knew that his own agency was causing this, but was so deep into denial and counter-accusation that they had to be skills he'd been practicing for years. My God. Did that mean the jury had been right, that people like Helmut Stauffer weren't drug peddlers, but the last of a dying breed, a rare few doctors still brave enough to risk their careers trying to help legitimate patients facing a life of agony?

He stared at his old friend's face in fascination. The flesh moved in familiar patterns of smiles and reassurance, but it was like watching the flow of some kind of evil simulated flesh scrambling to cover the ghoul-like, rotted skull beneath and never quite accomplishing the job. Fascinating and hideous.

"Pat. What's wrong? wrong?"

"I don't know. I feel so strange." The new vision he'd had of Ed — he could see a different soul inside his old friend's face, working to keep the features looking calm, reasonable, normal, like watching the Wizard of Oz behind his screen, desperately manipulating levers — was now spreading. He looked down at Charlene and saw her in a whole new light, too. A wounded angel, ready to fly home to the peaceful place she deserved, a better place than he'd ever been able to give her. Oh, she'd put up a good front — she did love the boys, he knew that — but he'd never really made her happy. He wondered now what it was he could or should have done differently, while he still had the chance. Should have talked to her, at least, told her she was free to go look for that life somewhere else, if she needed to. And now the walls — the very walls of the room seemed to be rippling, shifting.

"I must be sick," he said. "Something wrong with me." The floor seemed to be rolling under his feet, like the deck of a ship. What could he do to make this end? Maybe he needed to go make himself vomit or something.

And now the pretty nurse was back at the door, speaking to Ed. Her voice was beautiful, deep and throaty, but now it sounded as though she was in some kind of reverberation chamber. "Sir, can you step out here for a moment?... for a moment? ... for a moment?"

Ed stepped out in the hall. The nurse backed away from him, as though she didn't want him to come too close. Then there was a noise, like something flying past your ear, and Ed spun around. Pat Reilly couldn't believe his eyes. Ed looked directly at him, a look of surprise and supplication. Ed needed his help. There was a black arrow sticking out of the right side of his chest. Two. Now a second arrow had struck him, from the same direction but this time in the left side, since he'd turned around. The arrows went most of the way through, so it was actually the arrowheads that stuck out. Never speaking, Ed dropped to his knees. Weirdly, the two arrows sticking out at opposite angles made it look like he had a second set of arms, held out to the side like Jesus on the cross.

Chief Federal Prosecutor Pat Reilly had to do something, or he and Charlene could be next. He drew the unfamiliar pistol from its shoulder holster as he stood up and moved toward the door. He felt like the top half of his body was some kind of helium balloon, dragging along vastly heavy legs and feet which scraped the ground 20 feet below him. What the hell was wrong? He'd been drugged. Some kind of gas being piped into the room?

Flipping off the thumb safety on the pistol, holding it high, he edged cautiously through the doorway, looked left and right. There, to the right, a figure clad all in black was exiting the hallway via the stairwell door, and in a hurry, too. He checked the nurse to make sure she was alright. She nodded that it was OK for him to follow the suspect as she kneeled to help Ed.

He could see the man almost a full floor below him as he started down the stairs. Moving fast, dressed all in black, taking the stairs four or even six at a time.

Pat Reilly didn't count the floors as he pursued as fast as he could without tumbling head over heels. He managed to keep the guy in sight all the way to the lowest door, which was obviously on some basement level. He saw the last of the guy's black outfit disappearing and then the door trying to swing closed on its air spring. Casting caution to the winds he ran through the door, turned, steadied his aim with both hands at the fleeing suspect, who he now saw carried a black bow over his shoulder, and pulled the trigger.

⚜ ⚜ ⚜

The nurse's aide was upset, and seemed to have lost her English at the worst possible time. He couldn't follow much of her Tagalog, either. But combined with hand gestures it was enough for her to indicate where the emergency was. The young resident hurried back to the floor where the two federal assholes had ordered him to give that woman the same dose of painkillers he wished he could give to every patient who needed it. Not that they gave a damn that just doing his job this once might leave him unemployed, tomorrow.

The charge nurse was down on her knees about halfway down the dimly-lit hallway, looking strangely peaceful with her long hair to her shoulders — could that really be regulation? — holding in her lap the head of a fully clothed man in a suit who had fallen on the floor. He recognized him as one of the federal agents with the badges. Except that now he had a long black arrow shaft sticking out from each side of his chest.

"What are you doing?" he asked as he ran up and dropped to one knee beside them, feeling for a pulse. "Have you called the crash cart? We have to get him to surgery."

"No we don't, doctor," she said, as she calmly stroked the dying man's hair.

"What? What's going on here?"

"This is the DEA agent who set up the case against Dr. Helmut Stauffer, put him on trial, and then — after the jury acquitted — pulled his DEA number and drove him out of practice. This man drove away all of Dr. Stauffer's patients; he didn't give a damn what happened to them. Because of him, hundreds of people are dying in pain tonight, just like his mistress there was, until you threw away your career to give her the morphine she needed. By the way, doctor: Thank you. We have a job for you, a job where you can practice the way you were trained to, if you're interested. Working for the patients, instead of for the government. Dr. Stauffer has a lot more than he can handle, now."

"What? Stauffer went to Australia."

"No, he's here with us."

"Us? My God, I knew I hadn't seen you here before. You're —"

"The Order of the Arrow, doctor. The Angel of Death, if you prefer. You see, justice is way overdue for some of these assholes."

"My God. What makes you think I won't turn you in?"

"Because you're one of the good guys."

"I don't care who you are, I can't let this man lie here and die. If you haven't called I've got to —"

"Careful!" she said, as his hand came close to one of the arrows. Small glass ampules had been mounted below each warhead. They had shattered on their way through Ed Norton's torso, releasing their toxic contents.

"Don't touch the glass. It's no use, you see. Those ampules were loaded with curare. Look at his breathing, doctor. He's gone, already."

"Curare? But in a high dose that'll paralyze his involuntary —"

"Yes. And be sure to tell whoever handles the body. But as the attending physician, I recommend you simply write 'Death due to multiple arrow wounds.' It'll raise a lot fewer questions for everyone. People won't start inventorying your pharmacy to see if there's any curare missing — there is, by the way. Besides, 'arrow wounds' is technically true. Anyway, as I'm sure you noticed ... this guy was a real asshole."

"Yes." The young doctor sighed, finally accepting the inevitable, as he'd been having to accept the inevitable far too often, these days. "He really was, wasn't he?"

⚜ ⚜ ⚜

Pat Reilly's pistol didn't even click. It failed to fire. Nothing happened. They did that sometimes. Unlike revolvers, semiautomatics were real sensitive to whether the slide had properly seated the round in the chamber.

Fortunately, although Pat Reilly rarely fired his gun, he'd kept up with his refresher training, and managed to remember what to do. Dropping the magazine into his left hand. he racked the slide to expel the round which had not fired — the stumpy little brass cartridge clattered noisily off the wall and rolled along the floor. Now he racked the slide a second time, just in case anything else was wedged in there. Finally, he reinserted the magazine and racked the slide a third and final time to strip and load a new round off the top of the magazine and into the chamber, hearing it slam home with a reassuring click. Good to go.

Ahead of him, the fleeing archer had pushed through a double swinging door on the left side of the hallway. Reilly now trotted down to those doors, which were marked "Morgue."

They had no handles — the doors were designed to swing open into the room for someone pushing a cart or gurney ahead of him. Taking a deep breath and holding his weapon at the ready, Reilly pushed through.

A few of the overhead lighting panels were lit, some flickering as though ready to burn out. But most were dark. It provided enough light to see, but just barely. And the flickering lights were disorienting, like a strobe light in a carnival funhouse.

Along the right wall were locker doors, behind which he was sure were rows of horizontal cold storage lockers, for longer-term corpse storage. But arranged in an orderly pattern in the middle of the room were six wheeled stainless steel tables — gurneys — covered with sheets.

Or, to be more precise, tables on which rested dead bodies covered with sheets.

Reilly had already been feeling odd. Now his stomach was churning uncharacteristically, and he found he was having some trouble focusing his eyes. It was cold in here. He actually shivered. He shook his head as the noise of the various pieces of machinery — compressors, refrigerators, the hum of the few flickering fluorescent bulbs that'd been left on — seemed to invade his brain and threatened to take over his consciousness. What the hell was wrong with him? He'd figure food poisoning, but he hadn't *had* any supper yet.

And then, taking form against the back wall, as though he had simply materialized out of the gloom, appeared the figure of a doctor in operating room attire — mask, cap, and scrubs — except that they were all as black as the pit of hell.

He seemed half again as tall as a man, and when he moved towards Reilly it seemed he didn't walk so much as glide forward, as though on wheels.

"Pat Reilly," the apparition said. "Your gun isn't working because it's the new government model with the anti-theft safety. To solve a problem that hardy ever happened — cops being shot with their own guns — they put in the electronic safety so it'll only fire when it's within three feet of your personal chip.

"An old-timer named John Comiskey tried to warn them, but they wouldn't listen. The problem is, that system works by radio. Radio signals can be jammed and dampened. In fact, they just couldn't resist, they went ahead and put in a circuit that allows them to shut down individual guns from headquarters, just in case any cop or group of cops ever decided to go rogue on them.

"We located that frequency, Pat. We're running a dampening field here in the building right now that'll shut down every government gun for a quarter mile. The new models won't slam fire, either. So many damn safeties, I'm surprised they work at all. Needless to say, our weapons are not affected."

Reilly aimed and tried to pull the trigger on his gun twice, three, four times. Nothing.

"By now you'll be feeling a little odd, too. I'm afraid I can't tell you exactly how much Di-lysergic acid diethylamide you've had — that's LSD, to the popular press, still the most potent hallucinogen around, and almost completely free of physical side effects, except a little metallic taste in the mouth — because it just depends how much of Nurse Halsey's coffee you actually drank. Could be more than a thousand micrograms, if you were a good boy and drained your cup, in which case your visual field could break down entirely at some point. You should be prepared for that. Kind of a kaleidoscope effect. Scary, but also kind of cool, as long as you're not in the process of driving a car or something.

"It's important you know you've been drugged, Pat. You're not insane. It's a drug. A drug we needed to give you so you could really understand what we have to say to you here tonight. Which I think you'll agree beats being killed, though it does make things more complicated. The drug turns off the filters, if you will. But it'll wear off, usually in 12 hours or so. You need to remember that; it can be an important thing to hang onto. Not that the government schools offer any such hope of reprieve to the kids they dope up for years on *their* speedballs; Ritalin, Luvox, Prozac ...

"Your friend Ed is dead by now. The nurse had some extra syrettes of curare, just in case. But with two warheads in the chest cavity, it was all over for Ed before you even started down those stairs."

"Bastard."

"Yes, he was, wasn't he? But you, Pat, you we decided not to kill.

"Mind you, you're going to have to stop prosecuting drug cases. You did swear an oath to protect and defend the Constitution, and the entire Drug War stands in violation of the Ninth Amendment, as I'm sure you know. If the drug laws were necessary or constitutional, how come we got along just fine without them all the way up to 1914, when Mitchell Palmer started jailing all those foreigners?

"It was all about Chinamen. The 'Yellow Peril.' It was only later they added the nonsense about pot and cocaine making greasers and black bucks 'as strong as 10 men' as they strode around, raping white women in the streets. But you knew that.

"The point is, you played by the rules. When the jury acquitted him, you shook Dr. Stauffer's hand. That counts for something, Pat. Really. There's no evidence you had any part in what your friend Ed did to him after that — after Ed's employers on the jury had spoken and given Ed Norton his unanimous instructions to leave Dr. Stauffer alone and let him go back to helping his patients.

"By the way, your friend Ed had been screwing Charlene every Tuesday night for years."

"That's a lie."

"No it's not. If you'll think about it, I'm sure the pieces will start to click into place. They usually do."

He was right, this Doctor Death. Pat was amazed at how quickly so many things that had never made sense were suddenly falling into focus. It felt like the drug was speeding up his ability to sense things, to recognize patterns and collate seemingly unrelated perceptions, by a factor of a hundred. Nonetheless, he still hoped they were telling him the truth, that it would wear off and not leave him insane.

"What an asshole," Pat Reilly heard himself saying.

"Yeah, we thought so, too. Anyway, Pat, the reason we've brought you here is because there are a few people who want to talk to you.

"You and Ed dedicated your lives to the proposition that a consenting adult has no right to determine his own state of consciousness, no right to decide whether or not he wants to consume drugs. In your world, the state can throw you in prison if you do the wrong kind of drugs, and the state can also lock you up against your will and *administer* whatever drugs it chooses, against your will, so long as some government doctor says it's 'for the good of the patient or society at large.'

"That's wrong, Pat. It's so wrong. You didn't like those rules when you saw what they were doing to your Charlene, did you? We just used your own doctrine when we decided to give you the LSD without asking you — because we could, because we're the ones whose weapons work, tonight. Do you like the feeling that we could do that to you any time, without your having any say in the matter?

"So now we want you to come over to our side, Pat. We want you to acknowledge that an individual has a right to decide for him or herself how much painkiller she needs, or whether or not he or she wants to, let's say, trip out on a thousand mikes of LSD.

"The right to say yes. And also the right to say no.

"You see, there are only two choices. Either a person has a right to decide for himself whether or not he wants to buy and consume any amount of any drug he wants, any time … or someone else can decide for you whether to dose you up, or not let you dose up, even if you're in excruciating pain — an absolute power, exercised at their whim, with no appeal. And tonight, we're the ones who are deciding, Pat, because — well, because we're the ones whose weapons still work.

"And when we're done here tonight, I think you'll agree that's bad, and freedom would be better.

"Now I'd like you to meet a few of Dr. Helmut Stauffer's patients, who didn't experience the kind of pain you saw tonight on your pretty Charlene's face for just an hour or two. Oh no. They had to live and suffer like that for days, weeks, months, till they finally died, writhing and screaming in agony, not shown any mercy by anyone, because of what you and Ed did to them and their doctors — because of what you and Ed do for a living."

And now the apparition of the doctor in black seemed to withdraw back, to simply dematerialize into the shadows and the mists at the far end of this cavernous storeroom of death. And then it happened. At first Pat thought it was just more of the visual hallucination, the way the sheets covering the corpses on the six gurneys seemed to shift and move. But then came the cold, paralyzing moment when he knew it was no optical illusion. They were, indeed, moving. The corpses stirred on their oh-so-cold, shining, stainless steel tables. They sat up, and their sheets began to fall away.

And it was horrible. His blood ran cold. For these weren't the peaceful dead, the kind you saw dressed up with rouge and perfume, resting in angelic repose in their best suit in some funeral home casket. Here were faces twisted in the agony of untreated pain. Their bodies were curled and knotted with their pain until they couldn't walk, but only limped and shuffled and crawled as they slid down off their gurneys and started closing in on him, naked or covered with only the most pathetic, tattered rags, pale and reeking of the corruption of the grave, their faces and limbs marked with dark abscesses, corruption and wounds.

The stench. The rot. Great pieces of their scalp and hair were missing; you could see the cold white bones of their skulls poking through. As they lurched and crawled, more pieces of some of the bodies actually fell off. In some of their gaping black and oozing green wounds, white maggots swarmed.

And their mouths! Their sightless, opaque eyes and their mouths, many with the lips rotted or chewed away, grimacing and moving and trying to form words, though no sounds emerged. Pat Reilly turned and ran for the doors. But somehow the double doors had latched, had locked behind him and sealed him in here with these fiends, these walking, shuffling dead.

He pounded on the doors. He screamed for help at the top of his lungs. Faintly reflected in the glass panels of the doors, he saw an image of his own face that was horribly aged — 30, 40 years older than it ought to be. The lines, the wrinkles, the pores, his hair a gray, disheveled mass ...

He turned back toward the apparitions, throwing his head wildly from side to side in search of another exit.

But it only got worse. Now the putrescent, pale, translucent flesh was flowing off their faces and bodies, dripping and oozing and plopping onto the floor and they crawled and shuffled towards him, their mouths still working in agony, trying to explain to him how they had died, what he had done to them, the weeks and months of unendurable pain to which he and Ed had condemned them when he and his men arrested and jailed the only remaining doctors who would write them prescriptions for the painkillers they needed to live out the remainder of their lives in some kind of peace.

God, no! They had to let him out! He was sorry, he was so

sorry, he'd promise never to do it again, only he couldn't stand this; they had to let him out.

And then one of them touched him, and his own flesh became like theirs. Yes! Progressing from the point where he'd been touched his own flesh, too, began to rot and putrefy and slide from his bones and face. He could feel it! Feel himself rotting away. And the stench! A hundred times worse than that day he'd had to watch them pull that body out of the pile of severed animal parts at the packing plant, and he'd barfed for hours on that one, till his throat was burned raw from his own stomach acids, hadn't been able to eat for days.

But this smell of decay and the grave! Oh God, not this. No no no no no.

Pat Reilly dove for the corner of the room, hid his head in his hands, he moaned and cried and waited for the end. But it wouldn't end.

Racing back into his mind now were all the tales his grandmother had told him about the old country, where Jenny Greentooth, the skeletal, green-skinned Bean-Fionn with her long, stringy green hair, reaching up to drag little children down into the watery depths if they strayed too close to the deep and silent pools where she sheltered in her bog, and of Ankou, king of the dead, scouring the land and collecting the souls to lead them down beneath the dark hills on November Eve.

Oh, God, why hadn't he listened? He prayed now to Gods whose names he could barely remember, to the spirits of the Tuatha De Danaan, the oldest of the still-folk who lived beneath the hills, and to Brigid, the flaming arrow, goddess of healing. How had he brought himself and his lovely Charlene to this? Was there no confession he could make now, no act of contrition that would spare them this end? And now the bony fingers grabbed him, cold and clutching, a vice of steel, and pulled him down, down into the still, cold depths where he would not be able to breathe, where he would surely drown, not that this was any better than he deserved. Oh, how could he have screwed up and wasted all their lives so badly?

Pat Reilly wept. He gave up all hope, closed his eyes, prepared for death, and wept like a child.

❧ ❧ ❧

"Been like that since we found him. Keeps mumbling something about how his gun wouldn't work, but we checked it out, looks A-OK to us," said the uniformed cop who was turning over control of the now brightly lit hospital basement to Deputy Chief Bill Flanagan, who'd been called as soon as they recognized the work of the Black Arrow gang.

"Probably got buck fever, ran into the perp down here and couldn't pull the trigger," Flanagan replied, trying to settle the uniformed cop's nerves as much as his own. "It happens a lot even on the force. Guy like this, a chief prosecutor, probably never had cause to pull his gun in 20 years."

Flanagan's rugged looks hadn't exactly hurt his career. He was big and lanky. Big hands. Sean Connery eyebrows.

"Yeah, but what about the rest of it?" the uniform asked. "He keeps babbling about dead bodies coming alive and coming for him, dead flesh oozing off their bones, really weird shit."

"I don't know, Jackson. This guy's wife is upstairs, pretty sick, dying from what I hear. Then he sees his friend shot dead in front of his eyes. Give him some credit: He gave chase, came all the way down here on his own. Who the hell knows what he ran into? Finding yourself in a morgue would freak a lot of guys out, all by itself.

"But that's the thing, chief. The sign by the door says 'Morgue,' but the janitor says this place hasn't been in use for months. They moved the whole operation into another wing of

SUPRYNOWICZ

the hospital a year ago. No dead bodies down here now, at all. All we found was this, back there on the floor."

The uniformed officer handed him an undersized bed-sheet with some colored residue on it — white, black, pastel green — and a much smaller piece of cloth with strings hanging from it. The second object was an operating room mask, he realized. But not white, not pastel green or blue. This one was jet black.

"What's this stuff on the sheet?" he asked.

"We'll send it for testing. But near as we can tell, it's what they used to call greasepaint — theatrical makeup."

"Weird. I assume there's tunnel access from this level."

"Oh, yeah. All the usual: heating, water, electric. The access doors are locked from this side now, but one of them was probably propped open from the other side till he made his getaway. He, or they. You want us to pursue?"

"Call in the Grays, let them risk their asses. Not that they'll find anything. Clearing for Claymores, they'll be lucky to track them a quarter mile by morning."

Young Dr. Herbert West came over, guy looked like an exhausted owl with those round glasses, explained he'd given prosecutor Reilly a shot to relax him. "We'll get him upstairs and keep an eye on him. What he needs most is quiet and rest; he's been through a lot."

"You think he's gonna be OK, doc? I mean, is he gonna need to ... go away for awhile?"

"Psychiatric observation? No, I think that's premature. Frankly, I think he's been drugged in some way. Let us keep an eye on him for 24 hours. I understand there are two teen-age boys at home?"

"Yeah, that's right."

"They'll probably be OK. You'd know better than I whether these characters ever go after the kids. But I assume you'll still want to send some other family members or people from his department to sit with his boys tonight, let them know their dad is going to be OK. Mrs. Reilly has been asking for me; if you'll excuse me I'm going to go tell her her husband has had a considerable shock but he's going to be fine. I think mostly the man just needs some rest."

Before disappearing, the Black Arrow's nurse had recommended Diazepam or Valium to Dr. West over the more traditional antipsychotics, pointing out what he'd be dealing with in the case of the surviving federal prosecutor wasn't really schizophrenia, and that the benzodiazepines had been shown to work fine in combination with a quiet environment conducive to "talking the patient down," without lowering the seizure threshold like many of the antipsychotics, a theoretical advantage in patients manifesting severe LSD toxicity.

Actually, Herbert West was seriously considering the young woman's offer. It would be refreshing to work around someone competent, again. And to finally be able to treat with whatever was called for, without fear of being arrested, like Dr. Helmut Stauffer ... run out of the profession for nothing more than the proper practice of medicine.

She'd given him a number to call. Depending on how things went when they found out he'd issued the extra morphine to Mrs. Reilly last night ... well, he didn't see how it could be any worse than conditions here.

⚜ ⚜ ⚜

8:45 A.M. THURSDAY, FEB. 20, 2031

When Norbert Bachman pulled his old and well-beaten French Silk Lincoln Town Car into the ice-slick alley beside his Freedom Book Shop on lower Fourth Avenue at 8:45 Thursday morning (Town Cars didn't come in "brown" — they came in "French Silk"), 15 armed Treasury agents had already been there for 10 minutes, executing their search warrant.

What "executing the search warrant" meant was that they were seizing and loading into trucks all his computers, his file cabinets full of records concerning everyone who had bought his books and attended his seminars — even using fork lifts to pick up and haul away the palettes full of books he sold via mail-order from his warehouse.

The creaking wheels of their loading dollies and the pneumatic tailgate jacks of their rental trucks and the electric snarl of their smoking little junior-size forklifts and the repeating gongs that sounded automatically when they backed up made a little symphony for them, rising and falling in the bright morning air. The machinery was all undersized, making the men look like overweight grown-up desperadoes squeezing into the locomotive and coal car of a miniature train ride as they attempted to hijack it from some kids' amusement park.

Norbert Bachman had been fighting the IRS for years. The government was growing desperate as he refused to be intimidated and more and more people had started reading his books, attending his seminars, and — worst of all — asking questions. The government's agent at the Mirror, who posed as "staff writer" David Gay Filmore, had even taken to inserting high up in his stories the formulaic assertion that Bachman's "psychiatrist has determined that he holds a deluded belief that he alone can properly interpret the tax laws," while constantly reminding his readers that Bachman "has twice gone to prison for tax crimes."

The journalistic equivalent of "Do not try this at home. Stunts performed by professional driver on closed course."

This morning Norbert had some pithy and sarcastic comments for the low-level N$130,000-a-year G-men, but he'd dealt with most of them before and knew their attitude was "Hey, it's just a job." To a considerable extent, his loud and boisterous defiance was to reassure his staff.

His bookkeeper and two younger female clerks were standing out on the sidewalk, watching the goings-on in a combination of anger, frustration and fear. Bachman's good-humored abuse of the G-men served to somewhat dissipate the fear, which was precisely what he aimed to do. You had to show everyone they were just stupid bureaucrats. They had no real power. It was all bluff and bluster.

"Yeah, I like that you're taking the books!" he shouted. "You have to give me a full inventory, you know. You have to itemize! Be sure you keep track of how many of each edition!"

The men with the clipboards snarled and said nothing, which means they knew he was right. And that no, they hadn't been keeping proper track. There were different *editions?* No one had told them about that.

"You should also remember where you got each palette, for when the court orders you to bring them back."

"Oh, I don't think we'll be bringing 'em back," smiled one of the stupider G-men, with a sarcastic leer.

Norbert loved it when they rose to the bait, since he was almost always right. After all, he'd been in court a lot more often than any of these goons.

"You haven't stopped to think it through, then, have you?" he smiled. Gosh, he loved it when he knew he had them dead to rights. "What does the government do with seized property? Eh? They auction it off, don't they? Have to, under the federal asset seizure laws. To the highest bidder. Well, I just want you to think what happens when I go on the radio and say, 'What's in my books must be true! You know who's selling them now? The U.S. Treasury Department is selling them by the boxful! Would they sell my books if what's in them wasn't true? You have it on the very best authority! The U.S. government is now my biggest distributor!' "

The G-man stopped smiling.

Norbert Bachman was a jovial bald man with a big nose, an unmistakable Rhode island accent, and a gray Brillo pad of hair above each ear, who appeared to have been born in a tight tweed jacket with brown suede elbow patches. He'd been at it for years. They would never break his spirit.

His bookkeeper, Marge, got so frustrated she lit a cigarette. One of the blue uniformed cops in attendance — Norbert loved the fact they always brought along a city cop or two, since it proved the IRS men had no real police powers of their own — immediately dashed over and asserted his authority by officiously writing her a N$500 ticket for smoking in public. She and Norbert smiled. Norbert asked to borrow a cigarette and lit up, too. He didn't really smoke; he just wanted to see the look on the cop's face.

CHAPTER 8

Whenever the Legislators endeavour to take away, and destroy the Property of the People, or to reduce them to Slavery under Arbitrary Power, they put themselves into a state of War with the People, who are thereupon absolved from any further Obedience ... (Power then) devolves to the People, who have a Right to resume their original Liberty, and, by the Establishment of a new Legislative (such as they shall think fit) provide for their own Safety and Security, which is the end for which they are in Society.

— JOHN LOCKE (1632-1704)

A wise and frugal government... shall restrain men from injuring one another, shall leave them otherwise free to regulate their own pursuits of industry and improvement, and shall not take from the mouth of labor the bread it has earned.

— THOMAS JEFFERSON, FIRST INAUGURAL ADDRESS, MARCH 4, 1801

The moment the idea is admitted into society that property is not as sacred as the laws of God, and there is not a force of law and public justice to protect it, anarchy and tyranny commence.

— JOHN ADAMS, SECOND PRESIDENT OF THE UNITED STATES (1735-1826)

MARCH ...

Bob had come up with the Gotham Block deal, done all the research, so when it closed Andrew brought him a briefcase at the newsstand. Bob thumbed quickly through the stacks of bills.

"Holy cow, Mr. Fletcher, there's got to be 1,500 newbucks here. You didn't have to do that. But I'll tell you, that's gonna make a much merrier Christmas for me and mom this year; I sure appreciate it.'

"It's the usual finder's fee for finding us a deal like this one, Bob. Counting all the theater furnishings and the closeddown restaurant on the corner, which is pretty much intact, we got a huge bargain here picking up the whole block at N$5 million, thanks to you. Even considering its current condition."

"Yeah. They thought someone was gonna tear it down for a parking lot. When they found out you were the buyer and you were gonna restore the place you should have heard the kind of language. I had to cover my ears, I'll tell you. They said they could have gotten four times the price if they'd known. I had to work to put on that long face, believe me."

"With any luck, I think you can count on business picking up here," Andrew said, tying into his hot chocolate. "And I'd like to talk about putting you on retainer to do a little management work for me, too."

"I don't know, Mr. Fletcher. I don't think I'd wanna give up the newsstand. Kind of know my way around after all this time, if you know what I mean."

"Not talking about that. You stay right here and do what you're doing, I send people by to talk to you from time to time, maybe we get you a few more stools, so we can park someone here to see how they act when their guard is down. You get a reading on them and tell me what you think. I'll pay you as a personnel consultant."

"Sure, that's fine. Did you say this dump went for five

million?"

"Counting the pay-off of the back taxes, which is where most of it went. And a bargain at the price, with what New Washington has done to our once-proud dollar. I based your fee for putting the deal together at five million, Bob. If you want some help getting some of that banked in Zurich or Vancouver, just let me know. The bills in the case aren't ones. They're hundreds."

"Hey, OK. I think that calls for another hot chocolate, Mr. Fletcher. On me!"

"Shake on it?"

"OK, Mr. Fletcher."

"Only you've got to call me Andrew, now that we work together."

"Yes sir! So you said all the bills here in the case are ..."

"Hundreds, Bob."

"Hundreds. Yes, sir."

It was the first time Andrew had ever seen his old friend cry.

⚜ ⚜ ⚜

In the old days, a particularly defiant girl of the town might declare the father of her child to have been the 7th Regiment of Foot.

The Thomas Brackley Performing Arts Center and Arena, to be named for the dead war hero who not so coincidentally bore the same surname as the current mayor, had a similarly cosmopolitan parentage.

One father of the arena was Joey "Melon Balls" Cantalupo, owner of the National Hockey League's Shreveport — now Gotham — Seminoles. Cantalupo's peripatetic franchise had started play in south Florida — hence its distinctive name

— but had shifted to a new arena in Shreveport following some rigged voting to create a "Special Use" stadium district tax, unsavory even by the none-too-high standards of that particular state and parish.

Daniel Brackley had then a cut a deal to bring the Seminoles to Gotham for the previous season, though to say Joey Cantalupo was none too happy with the run-down college rink where they'd sited him, across the river in the eastern suburbs, would be an understatement.

Major cities needed major sports franchises as a matter of prestige and to keep the people loyal. Everyone understood that.

Joey was now widely rumored to be negotiating with Indianapolis, which had lost its franchise when that team simply upped and moved in the middle of the night to go play in the new Freedom League in the secessionist Western states, a terrible public relations blow to those who'd been insisting the western rebellion was on its last legs.

And Joey Cantalupo hadn't gotten where he was by writing his requests real nice on a lace doily. He'd made it clear he was outta here unless the city built him a big new stadium with corporate skyboxes which could be leased for big newbucks. The skyboxes were where all the easily launderable cash came from.

Problem was, a hockey team only played a couple dozen home games per season. Any such facility would sit vacant the rest of the year. And even in the rarified atmosphere of government finance, where one of the goals was to flush as much money as possible so a shortage could be declared at year's end, proving the need for more taxes and harsher collection procedures — even in Daniel Brackley's world — the need was seen to create a multi-use facility which would be lit more than 40 nights a year. That would also bring in more constituencies to lobby for the thing as an "artistic and cultural necessity if Gotham is going to remain at the forefront of ..."

whatever bullshit the PR flacks could drum up this time.

Enter David Bilderberg of StatesEast Bank, SA, anxious to build something big and impressive to bear his name, since the Oppressed Arab People's Army had once again blown up his big tower over on the East Side (blaming it on the Jews, of course.)

Bilderberg was a character who enjoyed playing the role of Patron of the Arts, after the model of the Medicis or the D'Estes or whoever all those dead Italians were whose 15th and 16th century portraits adorned his several townhouses. David was particularly desperate to do something grand since his brother, who now chaired the Federal Reserve, had built the new federal complex, which loomed over the downtown financial district in the shape of an enormous 19th century clipper ship, right next to the New Stock Exchange.

So David Bilderberg was on a crusade to build a new home for the symphony and the ballet and the Museum of Television, and Daniel Brackley needed some other tenants for his big hockey arena. A marriage made in heaven.

Or so they figured, till the architects brought in the acoustic engineers to try and explain why hockey teams rarely played in symphony concert halls and symphony orchestras rarely got excited about playing in hockey arenas — something about hockey teams expecting seats in a 360 degree circle around the rink, which played hell with these mysterious "acoustics."

Fortunately, no one in City Hall could understand a word of it. In the end, the committee claimed the facility would pay for itself by scheduling some added high school graduations, rodeos, ice shows and Puerto Rican music festivals. Half the new budget was covered with a sleight-of-hand last minute "grant" from some arts agency that existed only as a board of directors on some hastily-cranked-out stationery.

Unfortunately, this still left the project more than 100 million newbucks short.

That's when Martin Woo stepped forward, proposing a

cost-saving, innovative design for the 300-by-360-foot space-frame roof. The proposed roof consisted of two main layers arranged in 30 by 30-foot grids composed of horizontal steel bars. Four L-shaped steel beams would be bolted together to form each main cruciform composite beam. That is to say, looked at on end, each main beam would appear cross-shaped.

Instead of boundary columns or walls, his roof would be supported by four pylon legs positioned 45 feet inside the corners. The great advantage of the space frame roof, of course, came in the unobstructed views it created.

Critics argued the design, with its main cruciform beams, was inherently less safe than traditional I-section or tube section designs.

Martin Woo's firm clinched the deal by responding that they would employ a state-of-the-art computer analysis to guarantee the safety of their design.

Meantime, a site was needed. Tearing up an existing park went nowhere politically, as each city councilman and borough delegate screamed bloody murder that there weren't enough green spaces down here in Drive-By Corners or Fertility Flats in the first place. So the staff went to work with the city maps, crossing out areas where considerable effort had already been put into creating quaintly labeled historic districts with distinctive gaslights for the benefit of the tourists.

Access to bridges and tunnels had to be considered, to get the suburbanites on and off the island without tying up the crosstown streets for half the night. That crossed big swatches off the map.

More important, of course, was recourse to the secret maps that showed the zones of political influence — properties owned by wealthy banking families or campaign donors or overseas investors with federal protection. More cross hatching, narrowing down the little white squares and triangles close to the freeways and bridges.

Finally, the colored overlays were placed one atop another, and there, standing out like a sore thumb, was a four-block district of mostly Asian merchants southwest of the theater district, just west of the old Gotham Theatre block, which that wild card record executive and real estate heir Andrew Fletcher was restoring.

Best of all, the shops and buildings of this little, mostly-Asian enclave were run-down, insignificant little three- and four-story properties which could be condemned and seized at minimal cost. The Asian minority was far more quiet and complacent than the blacks or Italians or even the Puerto Ricans, and they had no business being there, anyway.

The city's official Chinatown had been officially designated several miles to the southeast — just north of the downtown financial district. It was all neatly marked and colorfully decked out with gateway signage and red-and-gold street signs and little pagoda-shaped phone booths.

(Hardly anyone actually used pay phones anymore. But they were in the redevelopment plan, so they stayed.)

What was this particular gang of Chinamen doing, infiltrating their restaurants and bakeries and Asian travel bureaus and video stores into an area which had traditionally been reserved for Jewish jewelers and camera stores? Didn't they have any respect for the neatly laid out maps of a city proud of its multicultural diversity?

And so, by a simple process of elimination, the Gotham City fathers came to focus on a four-block area on the lower West Side. Owners and residents of three of the blocks were easily intimidated. That left the Chins.

The law left it up to Mrs. Chin — for whom the rents from that block had been the main source of family income for 20 years — to come up with money for lawyers to challenge the price the city was offering for her property — the assessed valuation of N$50 per square foot.

Furthermore, she had to do it without touching a dime of the "purchase price" the city had put in escrow in the bank — if she touched that money, the courts would automatically hold she'd "accepted their offer."

Even though — the city having no other acceptable site for its new hockey arena and performing arts center — a willing seller could have commanded virtually any price she wanted.

Instead, the city simply seized the land under the guise of "public use" and transferred it to a "limited liability corporation" controlled by David Bilderberg and his StatesEast Bank ... which had been in the habit of paying 1,000 newbucks per square foot when it found it necessary to buy land for new projects on the open market.

Councilwoman Jenna Janes owned stock in several Bilderberg-StatesEast ventures. In a meeting required by law to try and "settle" a price for the land already seized, Mrs. Chin explained to Councilwoman Janes that she had never had a vacancy in her 6,000-square-foot building and that she depended on the 6,000 newbucks per month that she received in rent from the property. Councilwoman Janes would not budge from the city's 450,000-newbuck offer (300,000 base plus relocation allowances.) In fact, it was at that point that she famously said, in public, "Mrs. Chin, you have had your property long enough. It's time to give it up!"

❧ ❧ ❧

City Councilwoman Jenna Janes almost laughed at the little Oriental guy who strode up and stood right between her and her new black Mercedes roadster, a little closer than she would have liked. He smelled of some kind of pansy floral aftershave. Or was that a spice? Reminded her of Christmastime. Oil of cloves, maybe.

From the far end of the parking garage came the thrumming of an engine and a squeal of tires. The councilwoman felt safe here. There were other people around, not far away. This was a good part of town. Panhandlers were generally run off.

The guy was neither very big nor very heavy — certainly not one of those sumo wrestlers you saw on TV — though he did have big arms.

There was something ... evil-looking about him, though, with his dark mustache and the goatee outlining his chin. He was dressed in some kind of loose-fitting black pajamas or bathrobe, the legs of his pants too short to cover his skinny ankles above his clumsy-looking black hippie sandals, or clogs, or whatever you called them. Were they wearing those again? His straight black hair, graying at the temples, was pulled back and tied into some kind of knot or ponytail behind. The hair glistened like it was wet, or oiled up.

"What you dressed up for, chief? Halloween?" Councilwoman Janes asked the little Jap, chuckling at her own joke. The girls at the office had always appreciated her quick repartee.

Jenna was in a good mood. She'd just left a big meeting upstairs with the developers of the new Brackley Arena. In exchange for her help in greasing the skids for the eminent domain land-clearance, it appeared they were going to follow through with that six-figure job as an executive vice president of StatesEast Holdings, so she would never have to march in another goddamned freezing St. Patrick's Day parade or kiss another stinking baby. And, if she played it right, she also fully expected to be the next Mrs. David Bilderberg. David seemed *very* interested in her after-hours schedule.

Jenna was no longer 40, but she was still slim and blonde and well-preserved, thanks to a couple surgeons of her acquaintance and a well-maintained eating disorder. More importantly, though, as they'd sounded each other out the way worldly people with an instinct for adventure will, Jenna had picked up strong signals that David, oh, how to put it delicately, liked some sex with his pain.

They hadn't had their first heavy date yet. But when he'd picked her up at her place a few nights earlier she'd oh-so-negligently made sure he caught a glimpse of the leather outfits and animal-training equipment in her closet. Sure enough, he had become instantly aroused, his voice dropping a throaty half-octave.

Yes, this could be the start of a beautiful friendship.

"You are City Councilwoman Jenna Janes?" the little Jap asked, calling her back from her reverie. This was getting tedious.

"Yeah. And I'm afraid I'm late for an appointment. Call my office in the morning."

By the time it occurred to Jenna that it would probably be wise to get a grip on the .40-caliber Glock she carried in her medium-sized brown purse, just in case the need should arise, the little guy had placed his right hand on the hilt of the black scabbard that Jenna only now noticed he wore at his waist — black on black, dammit, and half hidden in that bathrobe, she must be getting slow not to have noticed — and drawn forth a deadly looking blade. Hissed like a snake as it came out of its scabbard. Damned thing must be two and a half feet long if it was an inch, gleaming like polished coal.

The little Jap held it up in the air over Jenna's left shoulder, and it occurred to the councilwoman she should take a quick step back as she shifted her right hand to reach for the Glock in the purse hanging behind her back.

Swords were now strictly regulated. She'd introduced the new "Instruments of Terror" ordinance herself. And it didn't seem likely this asshole was just here with an offer to sell her a war souvenir.

But there was something wrong with her right hand. Looking down at the floor to her right, Jenna saw the damndest thing. There, lying on the floor, was something that looked exactly like a human hand, only smaller than it ought to look, lying there with the lower sleeve and cuff of a blue shirt and a piece of black nankeen jacket still attached. Just like the blue shirt and black jacket Jenna herself was wearing. She looked at her own arm and saw — where the hand should have been — nothing but an abbreviated stump, with red stuff starting to ooze from the end and a neatly sliced protruding piece of bone, gleaming an unlikely bright white.

Had the bastard actually cut off Councilwoman Janes' right hand? But when? He hadn't yet brought his sword down in a cutting blow.

"Son of a bitch," she tried to say, although for some reason the words formed silently on her lips, only the slightest hint of wind emerging behind them.

Damn. She found herself fighting to catch her breath. What the hell was wrong with her? Shouldn't have had the chili OR the three martinis. OK, four, what the hell. Slowing down; getting old; should have taken early retirement last year; God knew she had enough tax-free bag money by this time.

But she'd still teach this little Jap bastard to mess with a fucking elected member of the goddamned Gotham City Council. Hadn't he ever heard of the full force and might of the Gotham City Government?

She again started to step back, away from the little son-of-a-bitch. She noticed the Jap was staring her straight in the eye, unblinking, like a fucking snake, as he lowered the blade slowly back between them, flipping it to shake off some kind of black oil that clung to it, proceeding to draw its length up between his left thumb and forefinger where they still gripped the edge of the scabbard, and then — feeling the point between his fingers when it was reached — silently sliding the whole blade back into its covering.

Jenna actually started to laugh, though, because the little chink hadn't got it down quite as neat as he thought; Jenna had noticed a few drops of blood glistening between the yellow thumb and forefinger where the little gook had evidently cut himself as he slid the blade back into its sheath.

But why would he draw the thing, have Jenna at his mercy, and then put it away? Never one to look a gift horse in the mouth, Jenna decided she wasn't going to ask; it was time to end this damn thing right now. She would take advantage of her assailant's foolish failure to follow up with a killing blow when he had the chance. Typical damned Oriental, catching her with a sneak attack.

Again Jenna Janes tried to take a step back from the little dwarf, this time reaching for her purse and the little pistol with her left hand.

What the hell was wrong now? She felt the strangest stinging along the whole front of her body, in a straight line from her right waistline up under her left armpit. And she still couldn't seem to catch her breath, and her legs didn't seem to be working right, and now there was some more blood running out of the stump of her right arm, though not pulsing out the way she thought it would, if in fact some kind of major artery had been severed. Oh, this bastard was gonna pay. Lawsuit city, man. Loss of a limb; could be millions. It was going to ruin her tennis game, though.

In the end, it was the swordsmith Bizen Hideki nokuni Takahira, of Bizen province, who took two steps back, pressing his hands together and bowing very slightly, giving his adversary time and space to die with whatever small, remaining measure of dignity this half-mummified female could muster.

"This has been done to honor and avenge the women and children whose property you have taken and whose lives you have ruined, Councilwoman Janes. For you have long since become a thief and a brigand who oppresses the defenseless, using the power of your office to destroy those you should have protected," he explained.

"Even though you have long ago disgraced yourself and fallen from the path of discipline, perhaps you will still find it in yourself to thank me for having done this cleanly, and find some grace and honor, at least in the manner of your death.

"In our tradition, you see, there are two techniques for use of the katana, or long sword. Kenjitsu is the discipline for using the sword outside the scabbard. But the discipline of Iai-jitsu was originally developed to give the samurai a technique to use when he was taken by surprise, his sword still in its scabbard.

"As it developed over the centuries, the discipline of Iai-jitsu eventually came to mean that the opponent is cut in half with the same motion which draws the sword from its scabbard at extremely close quarters, killing the opponent with one stroke of the sword, after which it is flipped clean and returned smoothly to its scabbard.

"This art takes considerable practice. Many years. But when it is done properly, as you see, the need for all unsettling struggle and conflict is eliminated. The secret of Iaijitsu is a calm spirit.

"I do you this courtesy of explaining to you why you have been executed, though many would have merely eliminated you, like a rat or a common thief. Have a good journey to your Christian heaven, Councilwoman Janes, if that is the faith you follow. Perhaps you will want to make an act of contrition, even now. For I must inform you that your time is very short."

But City Councilwoman Jenna Janes said nothing further. The nerve impulses from her brain found the thoracic spine severed at the seventh vertebra, and the adhesive qualities of the arterial and venous walls of her lower body began to degrade. Her legs sagged, not quite symmetrically, and the top half of her body pitched and fell forward and to her left. She was still able to instinctively put out her left hand and arm to break her fall, and look back to where the lower half of her torso had made its separate landing. Though she had to gaze through the strangest bright red shower, which was now jetting into the air from the severed main arteries immediately below her heart.

City Councilwoman Jenna Janes did live long enough to

realize — despite the numbing effects of the blessed onset of shock — that the little Japanese swordmaster had, indeed, cut her in half.

And at the end, finally, tears did well up in her eyes. She had *plans,* dammit! This was so *unfair!*

Now the little Japanese stepped forward, drew his blade again, and held it high over Jenna Janes' head in the traditional two-handed execution pose so familiar from the Samurai movies and Hollywood recreations of the Bataan Death March.

"Now, finally, I bring you a message from Mrs. Carole Chin, Councilwoman Janes. Mrs. Chin asks me to say, 'I think you have had your head long enough, Councilwoman. Time to give it up!' "

He stepped back with his left leg as he brought the blade down, so that his strike became a slice rather than a chop. For this was the secret of handling the Japanese blade, which is neither as strong nor as resilient as a European blade, but is rather designed for slicing.

⚜ ⚜ ⚜

"So you're telling me he cut the councilwoman in half, and then sliced off her ... head ... with cops and private security guards less than a hundred yards away on either side, one guy, and nobody heard a thing?"

"Sir, a sword is pretty quiet. The SonicNet never alerted."

"So as long as all the lights on their panels stay green, our guys just keep playing cards and don't notice anything?"

Deputy Chief William Flanagan was not happy. It was late, and the parking garage was cold. Outside it was raining, and the wind was picking up, moaning and banging things around. Ed Dudley hoped the power didn't go out. Added to the questions of protocol the morgue guys had faced in figuring out the right way to cart away the councilwoman's body in several pieces, the scene already reminded him far too much of some old horror movie.

Dudley just shrugged. They both knew once you set up an electronic sensor system the men would put far too much confidence in those green lights — trust them more than they would their own eyes and ears.

"And then he just ran down the stairwell to the basement and got away? All a perp has to do is run down into a basement and we're done, out of options, game called on account of your men are afraid of the dark?"

Dudley had to say something.

"Sir, it would be different if this was out in the suburbs somewhere. Isolate the structure, that's always the first rule in Sunnyvale or Hempstead. But this part of the city is well over a century old. These buildings don't just have basements, they also have ladders down to sub-basements, which give access to the service tunnels for the water mains, the ConEd electric grid. ... It's a fucking maze down there, sir, if you'll pardon my French.

"The water mains have parallel access tunnels for inspection and maintenance. Same thing with the electric and phone cables. Once you're down below the basement level you start running into vertical ventilation shafts for the subway system, some of which carry emergency ladders."

"To which I don't believe the average tour-bus visitor has free access, lieutenant."

"Sir, the main way access is blocked is by the manhole covers, which weigh more than a hundred pounds apiece, and the simple fact that no one knows where these things are and for the most part people are scared of rats and alligators that kids have flushed down the toilet and wouldn't go down there if you paid them. But for the safety of the guys who work down there we can't have keyed locks every 40 yards, there's too much chance somebody could get injured and trapped. The time they're most likely to go down there is when a water main breaks in sub-freezing weather or when there's a fire or something — it's hazardous enough without a lot of locked gates.

"Plus, you've got to remember, sir, when the subways were being dug you had separate competing firms, some of which went bankrupt, very inefficient. And that was 140 years ago. There are whole lengths of tunnels down there that were never even finished, they were just sealed off with headwalls. Over the years there were steam lines installed, pneumatic delivery tubes, cable fiber optics, cable TV ...."

"I get the picture, Dudley. But there must be maps, dammit. Don't we have maps?"

"Yes, sir. A hundred and forty years worth of maps, too damned many maps. Con Ed has a map of its system, the phone company and the water department have their own maps. Rolls and sheafs and drawers of overlapping maps in three different scales. But they tend to be schematic, the indications of actual depth from street are few and far between.

"We've been working on a system to overlay all the available maps of a given block in a holographic matrix where we could rotate it and look at it in three dimensions. But you send a guy down there to spot-check our accuracy and they find things don't look very much like we've projected them, at all. There's been a lot of ad hoc repairs and re-routings over the years when something broke or flooded. ...."

"So once again, lieutenant, what you're telling me is once this guy burrows in, there's nothing we can do? He just runs down to the basement and a police force of 40,000 uniformed personnel and more than 100,000 support and auxiliaries just throws up its hands and waits to see where he pops up next? Dammit, Dudley, I *knew* some of these victims. Mike Ketchum has a pretty young wife, his kid played Little League. I'm just supposed to tell them, 'Nothing can be done because he's hiding in the sewers'? What is this, The Phantom of the Opera?

Has he got a secret Bat Cave down there?"

"Sir, in most cases where a perp drops into the tunnels they've planned a single escape route, and they're out again pretty quick. You stake out the girlfriend, the fence, you have the train stations and the rent-a-car joints watch for his chip.

"But I've been saying for years that if we ever ran into a real tunnel rat, someone who's at home down there, we'd have ourselves a big problem."

"Options?"

"We do have a huge transit police force who can be put on alert, sir, along with the harbor authority and river tunnel cops, even the museum guards. You'd be surprised how far underground some of the museums stretch. Lots of storage vaults. He can't avoid them forever. But the problem is, if he's smart enough to disguise himself as a hobo, a bum, we get lots of them down there, especially in the winter.

"They use the tunnels as a kind of combined outhouse and bunkhouse. We roust 'em on a regular basis but we don't spend a lot of time running their IDs; a lot of them really don't *have* ID. All we can do is move 'em along."

"I didn't just fall off the truck, lieutenant."

"No, sir. So that's the school of fish he can hide in, and the only way to remove that camouflage is to round up these homeless guys and actually hold 'em long enough to do a real background check, really get 'em out of circulation."

"Do it."

"Sir, I'm not sure you realize how many there *are* out there now, what with the economy the way it's been. We'll need new holding facilities, lock 'em up in abandoned high schools or supermarkets or whatever. That means we'd have to feed them. And the ACLU will throw a hissy fit, sir, squawking to the press about how we're abusing the rights of the downtrodden to squat and pee wherever they want. We've already seen it when we just tried to run 'em out of the public libraries. They'll file a lawsuit."

"Come up with a plan, Dudley, and get it on my desk. We'll take it to the mayor and I'll deal with the goddamned ACLU. This damned Black Arrow thing is spreading panic in the work force. The judges will back us up; they understand it's their damned necks, too. But we've got to show we're doing something.

"For God's sake, they're talking about assigning armed federal marshals to escort clerks from the IRS office to the subway stops in the evening, like Atlantic convoys in goddamned World War II. Clerks!

"Write me a plan to clean out the tunnels and throw in the Grays. Get 'em off the streets, anyway. We never should have let this thing spread outside the airports, Dudley. These guys are going to breed us a rebellion, you mark my words.

"And when it comes they're gonna be completely outclassed by any real veterans out there, and whose ass do you think is gonna end up in a sling? Whose job do you think it's gonna be to clean up the mess? When the time comes for those little twerps people won't be drawing any fine distinctions about the color of the uniform, you mark my words."

Bill Flanagan had served in Colorado with Tom Brackley. Not in the same company, but he'd met the man. He'd always felt things would have gone vastly different if the city had been led by someone with a real moral compass, like the younger brother, instead of a manipulative bastard like his older brother, Danny the Dwarf.

"You've seen the headlines, Dudley: 'Tax collectors under siege; last night's body count on page 4.' We've got to do *something.*"

"Yes, sir."

✦ ✦ ✦

Cassie went out with Andrew Fletcher. A number of times.

In the evenings he took her to little cellar hideaways with live musicians who would ask him to sit in for a set. He usually begged off, though once he accepted a guitar and played "Beautiful Tonight" — she thought that was sweet. Another time he pulled a stool up to the piano — that was a surprise — and gave them what he called his Keith Emerson medley, "Blue Rondo 69" followed by "She Belongs To Me."

He liked to eat at little hole-in-the walls. An Indian place with a spicy gosht Vindaloo and a chicken korma to kill for and three kinds of breads on the table with nuts and raisins and sweet cheese baked right in and everyone smiling when he came in and knowing what he liked, catching up on the gossip and the owner coming out from the kitchen to fawn over Cassie.

A Mexican joint run by actual Mexicans named Tomas and Estrella who baked their own corn chips and kept bringing different salsas, red and green and burned-pepper brown; a Jamaican chicken joint with cornbread and fried plantains and little kids who waited on your table. The restored Belmore Cafeteria on the lower East Side, all chrome and Art Deco red and white formica, full of cab drivers and the smell of corned beef and a guy behind the counter who snarled at you if you didn't order quick enough and told you you couldn't have any more, "Three items on the special; you already gotcher three!" all bark and then — for Cassie — a sly smile and a little lagniappe of something extra.

And nearly everywhere people seemed to know Andrew by name and he called them by name. To these people, Andrew was just a guy from the neighborhood, a guy they could joke around with — but a guy who had usually helped them out, one way or another. She had no idea if they even knew who and what he was.

And then she corrected herself: They knew exactly who

271

he was. It was only Cassie who was programmed to assume the definition of "who Andrew was" had to involve limousines and Initial Public Offerings.

Joe Crosby from the Gotham affiliate of the Fully Informed Jury Association came into the Belmore while they were there. Well, to be more accurate, Joe Crosby, who *was* the Gotham affiliate of the Fully Informed Jury Association. Skinny guy with a beard.

"Hi Cassie. Hi Andrew," said Joe, who carried his usual battered book bag full of brochures and other jury-rights literature. He made a beeline for their table, of course.

"Hey, Joe," Cassie smiled. "You two know each other?"

"Oh sure. Andrew is a big donor."

Joe sat down and they discussed the relative hopelessness of trying to keep these modern judges from stacking juries with people sworn in advance not to ask whether the law was constitutional, or even whether it made any sense.

Joe ate green beans and macaroni and cheese — either he was a vegetarian or it was some weird diet. Pretty soon a shout came from the other end of the cafeteria, though, and here came Norbert Bachman, who had spotted Cassie from across the room. She shrugged at Andrew. It often went like this.

"Cassandra, did you get my messages?" the tax gadfly shouted. Though always cheerful, Norbert Bachman only shouted.

"Yes, Norbert. And your faxes."

"So, are you going to print it?"

"Print what?"

"My appeal. We've got 'em dead to rights this time. There's no way we can lose. Once the judge sees my citations, the IRS is completely blown out of the water. They don't have a chance. They'll be completely out of business."

"Norbert, this is Andrew Fletcher, and Joe Crosby from Fully Informed Juries."

"Yeah, I know. Hi, Joe. So, are you going to print it?"

"Norbert, I've told you a dozen times, they only give me a thousand words; I can't run 20 pages of court citations. I've done two columns on your case since they raided you."

"Yeah, but this one can't lose. It's the First Amendment, Cassandra. They've banned me from speaking, from going on the radio, from selling my book. They seized my books, for Chrissakes. My book which is nothing but facts, all court citations, all footnoted. It's the First Amendment! Surely the Mirror can get behind that!"

"We already have, Norbert. I've written columns; the paper has run editorials against what they're doing."

"Yeah, buried on page 27. You've got to understand, Cassie, this time we've got 'em. We're going to win, because they're boxed in a corner. The judge banned a book he never even read. They say I'm misleading people, telling them to cheat on their taxes. Well, where are their expert witnesses? How can they win a hearing where they don't present any evidence and don't put on any witnesses? How can I cross-examine them and prove no one owes this tax if they don't present any testimony in the first place? Don't you see, we've got 'em."

"Norbert. You always say you're going to win, and you always lose. We print these quotes where you say you're going to win, and you always lose, and then you wonder why no one takes you seriously."

"But we only lose because they won't follow the law!"

"I know that, Norbert."

By the intervention of a gracious God, Norbert announced he had to leave for an appointment after only about five more minutes of this, and Joe Crosby tagged along with him, asking if Norbert had any volunteers who could help pass out FIJA brochures during the next tax trial down at the courthouse. Not that there was ever any shortage of tax trials down at the courthouse.

It was right after that that Andrew told Cassandra he'd

set a date for re-opening the Gotham. She was invited to the gala opening. Who would perform, she asked, already mooning like a schoolgirl.

"Just some acts on the Rebel label. Maybe the Veronicas. Me."

"Andrew. Are you telling me you're reopening the Gotham Theatre with a live concert by the Veronicas, who are only, what, the hottest girl act in the country, and ... you? You're coming out of goddamned retirement after 13 years and doing the reunion tour people have offered you how many millions for and you just casually mention this over — what is this stuff?"

"Rasmali is basically goat cheese with cardamom and almonds ..."

"Yeah, yeah. Don't duck the question."

"It's just the one time. Kind of a reunion thing."

"Kind of a reunion of ... the Rockin' Rebels?"

"I've talked to the guys, they're amenable. Joey knows it means a couple weeks on the straight and narrow, but it's amazing how he's cleaned up with the new wife and the baby. We might even come up with one or two new tracks, just to liven things up."

"And you're telling me this off the record? So I can, what ... go disembowel myself in the city room when they break this on RockTV?"

"Oh, right. I keep forgetting I'm talking to the Mirror."

"We went off the record some weeks back, Andrew, as I'm sure you remember. But they'll kill me if I let somebody else break this story. You do have some idea how big this is, right? You'll do a live satellite feed, I assume?"

"60 countries, I think. Have somebody call Sue Weatherford in publicity this afternoon. I'll tell her to make sure we're geared up on ticket availability. If they'll wait a day or two we can get them everything. I'll tell her to make sure the Mirror gets a 12-hour break, if you can get your friend Sullivan to promise us some front-page play."

"Oh, you are good."

"Am I?"

"Like you don't know. This is going to be huge. Especially the fact you'll be up and running months before Brackley's ridiculous combination Arts Center and Mafia hockey rink, which is an over-budget hole in the ground the city just keeps pouring money into. And you did it all without a penny in tax subsidies, I presume?"

"I took advantage of every tax break I could find. ADA exemption for an historic structure. I'm sure the Mirror's editorial page will call those subsidies. But every penny was Fletcher Group money. I certainly didn't seize some old widow's property to build it on."

"They really make you angry, don't they?"

"Anger gets in the way. They just need to be destroyed. It's more like business."

"Andrew, you're priceless. You do realize you were just doing Richard Castellano from 'The Godfather.'

"Al Lettieri, I think."

"Pretty soon you'll be telling me you've got the Black Arrow on the company payroll."

"Couple other acts, too."

"At the opening? Other than the Veronicas and the Rockin' Rebels."

"Yeah. Called in a couple favors, guys we used to open for in the old days."

"No. Don't tell me. Do not tell me anyone is going to be there from England who usually plays Shea Stadium at 300 newbucks a pop. I can't even afford a ticket to this, can I?"

"Was kind of hoping you'd come as my guest. We decided to hand out half the tickets to kids who live in the neighborhood, but I held a few back. I hate those shows where the people in the balcony just clank their jewelry."

"Who said that?"

"John Lennon. He can't make it, unfortunately."

"With you, Andrew, nothing would surprise me."

⚜ ⚜ ⚜

At home that night, Cassie ignored Graymalkin's insistent bleatings to provide him with his accustomed lap, brewed mint tea and paced, contemplating the question of Andrew Fletcher.

Cassie was considered happy enough by everyone who knew her — cheerful, energetic, builds strong bodies 12 ways. And because she was born with the face, the body, everyone assumed she had no shortage of lovers.

In fact, though it had taken her some time, Cassie finally concluded she'd never had a lover. Men, yes, a few, and a surfeit of suitors. Some were boys who meant no harm, dear creatures, eager as puppies, clueless as fawns.

The older men? She took no offense at the ones who were honest enough to propose arrangements on straightforward terms. Enough socializing to make sure she wasn't a grump and could use the proper fork, and then it was down to business. Kept woman or trophy bride, she could have had all ... of whatever it was kept women and trophy brides have.

Cassie had stuck with the ink-stained wretches, and made it on her own.

But lover? Cassie sounded out the word on her tongue: "love-er." Amo, amas, amat. To love. To be loved. To make love to. The guys had a joke: "Making love: What a woman think she's doing while a man is fucking her."

The problem, she knew perfectly well, was that she wanted what she most feared. She wanted to find herself able to let go of all the careful controls she'd put on her life, to take the great risk, throw herself into that great passion with a male animal who would snarl and lurch and bite and heave till everything was in a heap on the floor and you curled up against him, sheltering in his mass, safe and exhausted as a kitten.

They did WANT to be Tarzan, rolling the bitch over the coffee table and tearing her clothes off and spreading her wide and filling her up with hot inside ... didn't they?

Or did they? Was that it? Was THEIR primeval dream gone, too, stolen away and replaced with some simulacrum of financial-planning foppery? Sex on schedule between the evening news and the late show, and what are you doing pawing me in the morning, I'll be late for my meeting with the third vice commissar?

Wasn't it the ultimate insult to deprive her of passion? Why be with someone if you couldn't make them feel like a bull moose in rut, willing to charge a moving locomotive? If I don't make you feel like running into large objects and knocking them over, why are we wasting each other's time?

They didn't believe in magic. That was it. She was the nut case, to believe some huge, rogue wave could still rise up and lift her away, too mighty to resist. Something to throw herself into and not know if she'd ever come up.

When the chance came, would she be afraid — hesitate to take it? She would, wouldn't she?

Oh, but she regretted now the turnings not taken. So many times she'd walked right past that faint sparkle of fairy dust, that magic frame that seemed to freeze for a moment of time and hang there, beckoning, telling you a brief, fleeting chance has arisen to follow the March Hare down some thoroughly unpredictable rabbit hole. Sparkle. Shimmer. Going, going ...

She'd seen it, more than once.

But then someone would reach back and grab her arm, "Hey, Cassie, what's wrong? Schedule to keep here, ticket to punch, baby, career calling." And she always went. Goddamn them, she always went. No, goddamn herself. She always walked on, caught up, went where she was supposed to. Always. Always.

Always.

Was he truly so impossible to find, this man she wanted, who could be a bull, a stallion, a lover ... and still share the music?

Would she know him if she found him? Had that been him, at lunch, today? How were you supposed to know for sure? Would her heart thunder and her legs turn weak and her center turn to liquid fire? Would she run from him in fear and terror? Would she run from the very bull she wanted?

Oh God, please let her recognize him when he came, please don't let me turn and run in fear and miss the One Great Chance.

Please.

⚜ ⚜ ⚜

It was only a matter of weeks since Bambi Fiducci's new "Firearms Safe Storage and Child Protection Act" had gone into effect.

Thomas Scott obeyed the new law. When he and his wife left their rural, upstate home to head into town that Saturday morning, they left Tamlyn, at 16 their oldest, in charge of her younger siblings. And Thomas Scott carefully padlocked the gun closet so none of the children could get at his guns.

It was ridiculous; his kids had all been trained to recognize how powerful a gun was, that it was not a toy, that only a grown-up or someone trained — like Tamlyn — was allowed to use them.

Tamlyn knew how to shoot. Her father had taught her. And there were adequate firearms to deal with the crisis that arose in the Scott home a few hours later, when 27-year-old Mark David Bell came calling.

Tamlyn's four siblings — Elizabeth, 13; Tessa, 11; Amber, 9; and Matthew, 7 — were still in their bedrooms when Bell broke into the farmhouse shortly after 9 a.m.

Bell, an out-of-work telephone solicitor who was armed with a pitchfork — but to whom police were never successful in attributing any motive — had apparently cut the phone lines. So when he forced his way into the house and began stabbing the younger children in their beds, Tamlyn's attempts to dial 9-1-1 didn't do much good.

The phone was dead. The kids were screaming in their bedrooms. The man was naked. Tamlyn couldn't even get herself to look at the dark hair and all the rest between his legs — he would have been the most frightening thing she'd ever seen even if he wasn't chasing the kids, stabbing them with the spade fork, making them scream.

My God, they were all going to die.

Tamlyn ran for where the family guns were stored. A shotgun, even the big Smith revolver. But the gun closet was padlocked, locked up tight.

That stupid new law! Mom and dad had talked to her about it. It couldn't be. She yanked at the chain as hard as she could, seeing if it would give, if she could pry the door open just enough to get her arm in, to reach at least one gun, any gun. Her eyes filled with tears.

Amber made a noise now like Tamlyn had never heard. Even though she'd never heard that noise before, she knew what it meant. He was killing Amber.

"When the 16-year-old girl finally climbed out the window and ran to a nearby house to escape the pitchfork-wielding man attacking her siblings," wrote reporter Lisa Stein of the suburban Daily Knickerbocker, "she didn't ask her neighbor to call 9-1-1. She begged him to grab his rifle and 'take care of this guy.' "

He didn't. Tamlyn ended up on the phone.

By the time police arrived at the home, 11-year-old Tessa and 9-year-old Amber Danielle were dead. Seven-year-old Matthew survived by hiding under the bed. Amber had apparently hung onto her assailant's leg long enough for her older sisters to escape. Thirteen-year-old Elizabeth was wounded but also made it out of the window and survived.

Once the cops arrived, Bell rushed them with his bloody pitchfork. So they shot him dead. They shot him more than a dozen times. With their guns. The guns which proved necessary to solve the problem.

The following Friday, the children's great-uncle, the Rev. John Cronenberg, told reporters: "If only Tamlyn had a gun available to her, she could have stopped the whole thing. If she had been properly armed, she could have stopped him in his tracks."

Maybe Matthew and Amber would still be alive, Tamlyn's uncle said.

"Unfortunately, 17 states now have these so-called safe storage laws," confirmed Yale Law School Senior Research Scholar Dr. Timothy Anwar, when the reporter from the Knickerbocker called him. "Such laws are based on the notion that young children often 'find daddy's gun' and accidentally shoot each other. But in fact only five American children under the age of 10 died of accidents involving handguns in 2027," Dr. Anwar said. "People get the impression that kids under 10 are killing each other. In fact this is very rare. The problem is, you see no decrease in either juvenile accidental gun deaths or suicides when such laws are enacted, but you do see an increase in crime rates."

Daniel Brackley read the story all the way through, a second time.

Then he scanned the bigger, Metro dailies. Nothing. Excellent. They knew better than to run a story that would provide fodder for the gun nuts. This story would never make the national news — TV or print — and people couldn't debate the meaning of what they were never told.

The gun nuts would circulate it through their media, of course. The Internet, talk radio. Little Tamlyn Scott would become the latest darling of the rebels and the sewer rats. They'd declare her younger brother and sister had been "Murdered by Gun Control," or some such crap. They'd probably put a price on ... Bambi Fiducci's head.

Of course. He knew the way their minds worked, by now. Here was a chance, finally, to get ahead of them, instead of endlessly playing catch-up.

Bambi Fiducci was running for Congress. That meant fund-raising. And fund-raising would bring her here, to Gotham, this fall.

The Black Arrow Gang would try to kill her. They wouldn't be able to help themselves. And where an enemy was predictable ... he was defeatable.

Milton buzzed him.

"Yes?"

"Sir, the overgroup leader had asked if he could speak with you. And Christian Newby and Group Leader Heydrich are here."

Perfect.

❖ ❖ ❖

Daniel took the Over Group Leader first. He loved taking these strutting, tight-collared, black-booted officers down a notch.

A pro forma Gray review board had looked into Jack's little Absence Without Official Leave following the day care center raid downtown. They prepared a report that they considered adequately sensitive to the lad's political connections. Basically, they concluded he'd committed no major offenses, though he should of course no longer go running off on his own without benefit of specific orders.

Showing at least a minimal instinct for self-preservation, however, this particular Over Group Leader had wisely shown the report in draft form to the mayor for his approval before signing off.

Brackley did not signal his emotion as the popinjay marched in and clicked his heels. He looked up from scanning the draft report. And then — showing his own particular gift for political theater — Daniel Brackley hit the roof.

"No major offenses! Are you insane?"

The Over Group Leader was dumbfounded. They'd whitewashed the whole incident, for heaven's sake. No harm done ...

"No harm done? Group leader, if you were choosing a man for an important mission, and you saw a performance review that said his work was 'adequate' and that he had 'committed no major offenses,' what would you think?"

"Well ..."

"Compared to a candidate whose review said his performance was exemplary, and in the best tradition of the Squads?"

"But Mayor Brackley, what do you expect us to do?"

"Is my nephew a traitor?"

"No, no, of course not." The Over Group Leader swallowed hard. He loosened his collar. He pulled out his kerchief and wiped his face. What had he walked into, here?

"Did he get anyone killed? Did he show cowardice in the face of the enemy?"

"No, no, Mr. Mayor. Nothing like that."

"In fact, he showed great courage and initiative, chasing after this important suspect, not merely another day care worker but apparently some important resistance leader who happened to be at the location that day, isn't that correct?"

"Yes, yes."

"He showed great personal courage in pursuing her down into the subways, alone, and then great resourcefulness in extracting himself without injury, only after being confronted with locally overwhelming rebel forces, isn't that so?"

"Yes, yes, of course."

"I expect to see a report reflecting these attributes by the end of the day. And, of course, to remove any suspicion that your report has merely been dolled up due to political influence, I think a promotion would also be appropriate."

"A promotion."

"You have too many under company leaders? I could arrange to have a few transferred to Wyoming."

"Yes, yes, a promotion. An excellent idea."

Newby and Heydrich barely suppressed their smiles as the superior officer stormed past them. He was pale and still wiping cold sweat from his face. Probably considered himself lucky to get out of the mayor's office with his own eagle patches intact, from the look of things.

Mayor Brackley was all smiles by the time they were beckoned in for his next audience.

"Gentlemen. Anything to report?"

"Sir."

Newby usually did most of the talking. Just as well. Heydrich gave Daniel the creeps. That pale blond hair and watery blue eyes, and the way his chin and cheekbones protruded — guy looked like a walking skull. A wonder he could always look so smug.

"The surveillance on the newspaper columnist, Trulove, may finally have turned up something," Newby was saying. "She's been spending time with a record company executive, Andrew Fletcher, of the Fletcher Group. We've run him; former rock 'n roll musician. He's financed quite a few right-wing causes. He could well be a conduit to the rebels, maybe even to the Black Arrow Gang itself. We'd like to have him picked up."

"No." The mayor rubbed his chin. "I know about this Fletcher. He's big. He spends money at the state and federal levels. We'll need a lot more on him. Otherwise his legal staff and his political connections will raise hell."

The mayor walked over and looked out the window. The mayor only did that when it was something big. Newby liked it when it was something big.

"He's the one who's renovating that old Gotham Theatre, a couple blocks east of the new arena."

"Yes sir. That's his base of operations, now, due to open up soon."

"See if you can get some agents in there. Get them jobs. Nothing too prominent. Slip them in."

"Yes sir."

"You have some people who can do that?"

"Yes sir, I have a couple of people in mind who'll do fine."

"Mix 'em up. Boy and a girl, maybe a black or an Asian. Couple of people they'd never expect to be working together. And even though we're mostly looking for information, put two people in there who can do some wet work on short notice if it's needed. You understand?"

"Oh yes."

"In the meantime, we need some show trials as evidence for the press and public that we're making progress against these underground terrorists. Call the D.A.; arrange a meeting."

"Yes sir."

"We need a stronger presence in the tunnels. We need to be able to track terrorist movements down there. Set up another meeting with Flanagan, the cop."

"Yes, sir."

"But there's something I don't want you to tell Flanagan, or anyone else — this will remain an exclusive Counter-Intelligence operation."

"Sir?"

"Make contact with Bambi Fiducci's campaign staff, Christian. She's in our party, after all, and running for congress takes a lot of money. Offer our help in setting up some fund-raising dinners for her, here in Gotham this fall. Check out a couple of sites where we can move in and control tunnel access without anyone noticing — maybe the Dupont Convention Center. We want to be intimately involved in planning the logistics of any visits she makes to the city for the rest of the year. You understand?"

"Sir?"

"The Black Arrow is going to try and kill Bambi Fiducci, gentlemen. I know it. And this time, when he does — we'll be ready for him."

⚜ ⚜ ⚜

"We don't know how deeply this Andrew Fletcher and his people are involved in the rebellion."

Christian Newby leaned forward in his chair. He was slim, of medium height. His deep-set, come-hither bedroom eyes flashed an unlikely jet black, seemed to pin you no matter where you walked in the room. He had a square jaw, a thin moustache and long hair worn down over his ears which some considered effeminate. A lot of women seemed to like the look, though. Maybe it was the whole "can't-tell-for-sure" thing.

He noted the two agents he had selected were listening attentively, not interrupting to ask whatever random question popped into their heads. Good. They were pros.

"So the safest thing to assume is that you're going right into the home nest of the terrorists. You'll want to seem reasonably open to some anti-government rhetoric, but don't lay it on too thick. If you're in a conversation and they're sounding you out, you're mildly pissed off at the high taxes, can't see any reason why someone should go to prison for a lousy ounce of pot, that sort of thing. But you're mostly apolitical. If you start quoting the great anarchists like a couple of campus radicals you'll only invite more questions.

"Mostly you're watching and remembering names, faces, relationships. Look for people obviously overqualified for what they're doing, people gone and unaccounted for a lot of the time. Not to mention the obvious — guns, bows, secret meetings, contraband in wholesale quantities, large sums of cash, kids not in school, people working off the books.

"But obviously, don't write anything down. No list of names hidden in your shoe, right?"

They didn't answer. There was no need to.

"Nguyen, we've gone over your cover story already. We're going to see if their security is a little more lax when it comes to workers in that new restaurant they're getting ready to open."

Nguyen nodded. He'd taken his Masters in Oriental languages before attending the FBI academy. His height and strong features argued there must have been an American G.I. grandfather somewhere in his background. He'd go far in the squads. If he survived.

"Your challenge is to be less of a cop. Scuff up your shoes, or wear some nasty suedes. Beat up, not new. Let your hair grow out. Slouch. Take up smoking. If you look like you just came off the parade ground ... "

"I understand."

"Kylie, you're here because of your training in classical music."

"The new Rebel Records studios."

"But I don't want you walking in the door with a neatly typed resume. This isn't the Philharmonic. You'll have to find some other way to start hanging around with the people in that building. When they do finally spot your talent they have to believe it's their own discovery. Understand?"

"I'm a pathetic street musician. Every stop is neatly planned for a poet and a one-man band."

Kylie was tiny, Australian, freckled, with a sharp nose. She looked like a little bird, except the fact that she was already smoking a technically illegal cigarette. Oh, Christian was a genius. Nobody would *ever* suspect these two.

"Now the most important thing. This is deep cover. Don't be trying to get in touch with me every day to report how many eggs they use in the fried rice or the fact that the bass player smokes dope in the boy's room. You're not in there to write traffic tickets. If they want you to join in committing some minor crime as a test, don't hesitate. Do what you have to.

"But communicating is when you're most vulnerable, so don't do it beyond your weekly status reports, unless you have to. If you do hit on something big enough to justify a quicker response, we've gone over how you signal me to be ready for your call. Right?"

They nodded.

"And if that doesn't work, just get out of there; call me from the safe house.

"Meantime, on the assumption these people won't be running metal detectors, I'm authorizing compact pistols. Whether and when you carry them is up to you. But since you're trying to make contact with the criminal element, I've decided it's worth the risk. If they turn them in a search, don't get defensive and make excuses — just the opposite. Get mad and spout some gun-nut rhetoric. Second Amendment. Everybody has a right to shoot the wife and kids. Right?"

They nodded a little more seriously, now. He'd made sure they were both qualified shooters.

"There is, of course, one consideration that outweighs your cover." He paused for effect.

"If you see the Black Arrow, kill him."

SUPRYNOWICZ

CHAPTER 9

Rock 'n roll is sung, and written for the most part, by cretinous goons; and by means of its almost imbecilic reiterations and sly, lewd — in plain fact, dirty — lyrics it manages to be the martial music of every sideburned delinquent on the face of the earth. This rancid-smelling aphrodisiac I deplore.

— FRANK SINATRA (1915-1998), 1957. (SINATRA IN 1963 SURRENDERED HIS NEVADA GAMING LICENSE RATHER THAN HAVE IT REVOKED AFTER REPEATEDLY CALLING STATE GAMING CONTROL BOARD CHAIRMAN ED OLSEN A "MOTHERFUCKER" AND USING OTHER "FOUL AND REPULSIVE LANGUAGE WHICH WAS VENOMOUS TO THE EXTREME" DURING AN INVESTIGATION OF HIS MOB CONNECTIONS).

All of the rock music being aired today is demonically inspired. Any individual listening to it is entering into a communion with a wickedness and evil spawned in hell.

— JIMMY SWAGGERT (1935 -), EVANGELIST, ADULTERER, AND COUSIN OF JERRY LEE LEWIS.

Rock 'n roll is a means of pulling the white man down to the level of the Negro. Rock 'n roll is part of a plot to undermine the morals of the youth of our nation. It is sexualistic, unmoralistic, and ... brings people of both races together.

— NORTH ALABAMA WHITE CITIZENS COUNCIL, 1958

Groups with guitars are on their way out.

— DECCA RECORDS EXECUTIVE DICK ROWE, EXPLAINING TO BRIAN EPSTEIN WHY THE LABEL HAD DECIDED NOT TO SIGN THE BEATLES, 1962.

AUGUST, 2031 ...

Cassandra had hoped to avoid the paparazzi at Andrew's opening gala. She instructed Andrew's driver to drop her 50 yards up the street from where the big black hearses were lined up, waiting to disgorge their celebs and would-be celebs into the media maelstrom directly in front of the Gotham.

The driver — a dangerous looking man with long blond hair spilling over his shirt collar below his chauffeur's cap — had displayed a golden front tooth as he told her in a not quite identifiable foreign accent that he loved her writing.

"Oh, thank you," she replied. "Tell all your friends."

He reluctantly agreed to drop her further up the street, but then opened his own door and stood beside the idling car, watching her till she'd reached the theater door. A fellow who obviously took his responsibilities seriously. Cassie didn't want to think what would have happened to anyone who'd tried to give her any trouble. She didn't generally think of herself as needing any looking after. But it was rather sweet, actually.

The evening air was starting to cool, but the sidewalk was still radiating heat. Her efforts to avoid attention were aided somewhat by the fact the crowd was already huge — good-natured, cavorting and jackdawing about. Since the affair had long since sold out, assigned seating only, there was none of that sullen line-waiting going on.

A handful of young colleens in ponytails inched a frosty white ice cream cart through the crowd, handing out free blue and purple Popsicles. They made monkey faces at Cassie as she walked by.

She smiled. What had been a throbbing violet and salmon sunset, spilling across the horizon like an inverted magma flow, was now fading to pink grace notes on a Technicolor skyblue sky, providing her an entrance out of Jerome Robbins. When you're a Jet you're a Jet all the way.

But even with the celestial display and the excellent cover

provided by the milling throng, Cassie still could not pass unnoticed. She dressed down for the day job, but when invited to be billionaire Andrew Fletcher's date at his million-dollar opening night gala, what was a girl to do, show up in curlers and a horse blanket?

Cassie had red hair which fell in heavy waves, red eyebrows, and — tonight, at least — even redder lips. A little understated rouge quickly turned her skin into what was traditionally called "peaches and cream." She was tall enough to be a clothes horse, and not overweight. Well ... not by much. And some men actually seemed to like the places she put on weight. Her eyes would go either green or blue, depending on what she wore. Tonight was blue.

In fact, it would be within the bounds of acceptable license to paraphrase the poet, and say the dress stole the bright out of the daytime, and turned the nighttime blue. Electric, peacock, off the shoulder, blue.

The dress, which was not sequined but had Mylar fibers woven in to give the same effect, and which had no back to speak of, left no doubt about the shape of Cassie's aureoles. After all, if you had 'em ...

Cassie had come from the manufacturer properly designed to hold up an off-the-shoulder dress (thank you, mom). She'd already had the broad white shoulders at age 15, when they tried to turn her into a runway model. One season of photo shoots trying to look sexy as she stood up to her knees in a thong in some freezing Italian fountain while the wranglers tried to get the pigeons to fly on cue — no, into the wind, "Dal vento, dal vento!" — had convinced her the "world travel" package wasn't all it was cracked up to be. She banked the year's earnings and went to college instead.

Sure enough, the TV pod spotted her coming, the breathless paid celebrity gushers barking at their cameramen to redirect the lights in her direction — much to the consternation of some fox-clad bimbo hired to add glitter to the arm of whatever local video celebrity or dogfood merchant was being re-gurgitated forth out of the limo line at the moment.

They shoved microphones in her face, called her by name to show how well they'd studied their briefing books (it was doubtful most of them actually read the paper) and asked her inane "Are you looking forward to the concert?" questions in lieu of what they really wanted to ask, which would have been, more or less in order, 1) What's the matter, couldn't get a date? 2) Are those your real tits? 3) How did you get invited to this thing when we have to stand around out here breathing super-heated monoxide with the valet parking guys? and 4) Do you date richer guys than we do?

She gave them a big smile and the 8-second, "Yes, really looking forward to the show; I hear they've just done wonders restoring this old place, isn't it beautiful?" that they needed, whereupon they immediately wheeled back towards the curb in hopes of gutting some bigger fish, or catching someone else's dual floppies slipping out of her decolletage.

She felt a gentle hand on her elbow and looked down to see a smiling young Asian teen-ager in what seemed to be the standard manservant's livery for the evening, a loose-fitting silk outfit of red, orange, and gold, accompanied by what appeared to be the kind of broad-bladed sword the eunuchs might once have carried in a Turkish harem. Brass hilt.

"Hello, Miss Trulove, I'm Tommy Chin. I'm supposed to escort you inside to the museum reception."

"You're one of Mrs. Chin's grandkids?"

"That's right, ma'am."

"Well, your grandmother is a very brave woman. How's she doing?"

"Pretty well, thanks to you. And thanks to Mr. Fletcher."

"Oh?"

"Gram's been working real hard supervising the food for this party. Then tomorrow our new restaurant opens, just down there on the corner."

So Andrew Fletcher had found a way to work the Chin family into his redevelopment plans. Just a magnanimous gesture, Cassie wondered ... or another example of the old rock peddler, doing well by doing good? A restaurant of proven quality and reputation right next door could be a huge money machine if his museum and concert venue took off. It would also become a kind of in-house cafeteria for his own employees at the sound studio and martial arts school and gym Andrew had already opened upstairs.

Being just a couple blocks east of Mayor Brackley's new Arts Center and hockey arena wouldn't hurt. And needless to say, Andrew Fletcher would hold the restaurant lease, probably take a share of the profits in exchange for bankrolling the venture. Carole Chin wouldn't have the capital, now that the city had seized and bulldozed her paying properties.

Capitalist synergy.

"I get letters from your grandmother occasionally," she told the youngster as he led her proudly past the similarly clad — but much larger — doormen and bouncers who were checking other people's invitations. (No one asked Cassie for hers. Nice touch. Anytime someone wanted to show around her picture and say, "This lady is special; don't give her any shit," she wasn't going to complain.) "I'm afraid she thanks me for more than I was really able to do."

"No, Miss Trulove," said the boy, meeting her eyes. "You gave my family hope. You let us know someone still cared."

"Are those real swords you guys are carrying, Tommy?"

"Yes, ma'am."

"And do you expect to need them?"

"Mr. Fletcher says the best way to make sure you don't need a weapon, is to make sure everyone knows you have a weapon." Then he smiled. "But we actually wear them just so people won't notice the machine pistols under our shirts."

Cassandra laughed. On the assumption he was joking.

Inside, the glitterati were setting upon mounds of fresh

shrimp the size of disposable razors and ground-up goose innards and all the usual silver bowls of exotically flavored mush resting in heaps of ice on the white tablecloths. More Chin-in-laws and one strikingly handsome Asian fellow — taller than the rest — in white jackets and chefs' hats sliced and served teriyaki London broil and sugared ham and smoked red Pacific salmon presumably smuggled in from New Columbia — not the pale yellow farmed "Atlantic" stuff.

"There's no food in the museum," Tommy confided. "Mr. Fletcher said I should bring you in as soon as possible, but if you want some food first I'll be happy to bring you whatever you want. We won't tell."

"Just something to drink, Tommy. I'm anxious to see Mr. Fletcher, myself. If they run out of deviled eggs, I'll just have to fend for myself later."

"Oh, if you want something later, Miss Trulove, just phone the kitchen and let me know." Like a magician, the young lad snagged her a brim-full straight-up martini from a passing tray.

"Martini OK, ma'am, or did you want an iced tea?"

"The martini is lovely, Tommy."

She sipped as they strolled through the lobby. It was nice and cold and possibly even Bombay — someone was doing good work.

The Gotham Block dated from sometime in the late 19th century, when this had been the far southern anchor of the old theater district and the main original feature of the block — the huge Gothic opera house which squatted like a caged bat, staring threateningly westward across Marion Square — had hosted the great stars of Italy and the Continent, insert appropriate P.T. Barnum rhetoric here.

The building had fallen on hard times during the World War, when Wilson seized the railroads, and in its first and greatest rebirth had been acquired by Marcus Loew and — in the mid 1920s — upgraded into one of the opulent landmark

Art Deco movie palaces of the silent era, an Egyptian-themed temple of dreams designed to display the product of Loew's Metro Pictures, a studio which in 1924 was in the process of merging into Hollywood's Metro-Goldwyn-Mayer. It was the gala re-opening of THAT version of the Gotham that had been graced by Clara Bow and other since-forgotten big names among the Jazz Babies.

Apparently the slightly pyramidal tower behind the theater had been original, giving the whole mass of steel and concrete the look of a brooding, outsized Mayan temple.

Was "outsized" right? Surely the temples of Tikal and Cassie's favorite, Uxmal of the serpent God, all pink stone and shockingly un-dead serpents, weren't more than three or four stories. She made a mental note to have Punda check. Then she made another mental note to stop making mental notes. She was supposed to be here for fun, not writing things up for the Mirror's lame-ass Features section.

The red carpets bore the stylized gold MGM lion. Andrew had gone to considerable expense to conserve and restore the original carpet, having new swatches re-woven where necessary. The gold gilt Egyptian lobby columns had been restored, along with the matching chandeliers and sconces — most of which, Cassie knew, had been found still hiding under nearly a century's worth of soot, smoke and grime.

Cassie and Tommy passed a big colored floor-plan map that showed the new dojo and martial arts academy up the broad staircase to the second floor, the antique and gift shop beyond the museum, Chin's Chinese out at the corner — sure enough, a rear interior corridor also allowed access to the restaurant for building employees without going outside — and of course, the huge theater complex itself. A sizeable area out by the old loading docks at the rear of the building was shaded dark gray on the map, apparently remained vacant.

A smaller plaque announced the new recording studio for Rebel Records upstairs, along with the new executive offices of the record label on four and five.

No signs indicated the building had more than five floors, though Cassie knew it had at least six or seven. From Andrew's invitations to visit — so far politely declined — she knew he'd converted at least one of those top floors into a penthouse.

"I'm amazed at how fast all this has been done."

"Mr. Fletcher likes things to keep moving," Tommy replied. "Lots of people from the old neighborhood working here, now."

"In the theater?"

"In the theater, in the recording studios, in the museum. Then there's the dojo on the second floor."

With the skyrocketing crime rate after the total city ban on all self-defense weapons had come a growing demand from a terrified populace to be taught at least the ancient arts of self-defense which didn't involve the banned knife or gun. Cassie had taken some classes, herself, though she carried a rare licensed hand cannon when venturing into some of the seedier sections of town ... well, that meant most of town, these days.

She reflexively clutched her little blue purse to make sure her smaller, .40-caliber "evening" pacifier was with her; the larger .44 wouldn't fit without bulging.

Come to think of it, how refreshing to enter a public facility and not be hassled with metal detectors at the door. She'd have to remember to ask Andrew why he decided to do without security measures considered routine even at nursery schools, these days.

They climbed a few wide steps past more red-and-gold liveried bouncers and past the sign that said they were entering the inner sanctum of the museum's "private collection" — two large tables for spent dishes and glassware had been positioned beneath the "No Food in Museum" sign. But no one asked her for her martini glass; she was apparently invisible.

They passed through a narrower doorway which could doubtless be gated and alarmed at night.

The lighting seemed more carefully modulated to the somewhat reduced scale of the space, here — pin spots and indirect ceiling panels — the air conditioning was a few degrees cooler and the crowd felt a bit thinner. A large central room gave access to three smaller linked galleries. Since the assets tax had moved Andrew's most valuable holdings into the tax-exempt "museum" category, there were no price tags — though tasteful signage did indicate recent appraised or auction values of similar pieces.

At the far side of the room, the museum fed into the gift shop and antique store, where the real sales and marketing went on. The gift shop was open despite the lateness of the hour, Cassie noticed. Standing sentry duty at that side was a slim, elegant Russian couple who she recognized from Andrew's descriptions as Boris and Katia. They noticed her too, raised their martini glasses and smiled in a silent toast, which she answered with a smile and a nod. Great shoes.

Antiques usually bored Cassandra to tears, all lacquered Chinese mother-of-pearl room dividers and malformed half-ton pots with fantastic pricetags and prancing foppish proprietors who assumed you wouldn't now a Tang Dynasty stone lion from a portrait of one of the D'Este sisters.

Oh, she'd been dragged around some of the finest museums in Europe in between plotting her escape to dance the night away with the dark-chested lads.

It appeared that Andrew acquired only what interested him ... and that a surprisingly wide and eclectic range of stuff "interested" him.

There was the outrageous 1935 Auburn V-12 Speedster sitting on a piece of red carpet in the middle of the room. Probably got mileage to rival an M-1 tank, but it was still to die for, all blond wood and chrome. Old military sniper rifles, 70-year-old guitars, his 18th Dynasty Egyptian crook and flail with matching vulture headdress in beaten gold, inlayed with enamel and lapis lazuli — more than 3,000 years old, assuming it was real. And she'd love to know how and when they'd gotten *that* out of the Middle Kingdom.

What had her own Celtic ancestors, hunkered down in some rocky cave or barrow, been doing more than 3,000 years ago, while the Egyptian craftsmen worked that vulture headdress for their Pharaoh? Actually, how early had the Celts designed in gold? She made a mental note to have Punda check.

Above a wall of electric guitars — many with beautiful sunburst finishes — were the names of the great rock 'n roll bands. One legend read "Rockin' Rebels," the name of the band headlining tonight's reunion concert in the restored Gotham, the band that had single-handedly resurrected the old Eric Carmen-Wally Bryson songbook more than a dozen years before, marking the beginning of the Retro Pop era of which the Jugheads and the Veronicas were now the reigning kings and queens.

RetroPop had seemed like a breath of fresh air after the long and desultory reign of rap, hip-hop, and spaz, which Tode Connors of the Mirror had so appropriately dubbed the "rhythmic chantings of the permanently disgruntled underclass."

Most had figured the trend would fade as fast as this month's supermodel, but it seemed to be hanging on quite resolutely, despite the unsparingly negative reviews of Tode, who saw the whole scene as "depressingly derivative," condemning it as "re-chewed Bubble Gum."

Of course, poor Tode was widely reported not to have gotten laid in years.

In fact, the biggest tectonic shift in 50 years of popular music had been the rediscovery and subsequent elevation of The Raspberries — the quintessential early 1970s Cleveland Rockers, and the band whose songbook Andrew and the Rockin' Rebels had single-handedly revived — into the rock 'n roll pantheon.

And here Andrew was, chatting with a few laughing old silver foxes accompanied by alarmingly slinky young women (one wearing what appeared to be a sprayed-on silver Mylar sheath — was the poor creature's belly actually *concave?*), though whether they were second wives or second-wives-in-waiting was not immediately clear.

Feeling suddenly catlike, Cassie gave them the kind of smile which brood queens reserve for visiting adolescent bitches — the one that says, "How nice to see you; were you about to leave or were you actually looking forward to being ritually disemboweled?"

Andrew embraced her. It was socially acceptable but little more. She got the distinct impression he was keeping her at a little distance. Or was he just responding to the fact that she'd been holding *him* at arm's length? He'd made it clear, over the months, that a more serious invitation was open if she was interested. But now, however subtly, she got a slightly different message. He was friendly, smiling, but ... cooler. Just preoccupied with his upcoming show? No, something more. His invitation might not be open forever. It'd been 10 months, after all. Was she interested or not?

Whether they were just being polite or not, the men attached to the little sex kittens were at least old enough — and educated enough — to have some idea what Andrew was talking about. The girls were just good at pretending.

Cassie liked Andrew. She'd already known that, hadn't she? Why had she held back so long? Afraid of having her heart crushed, of course. He had everything, he couldn't really need her. Unless, of course, she was supposed to be just another lovely acquisition for the collection.

"But I'm boring you with matters of no concern to today's readers," he smiled as he finally turned back to give her his full attention. "Fashion trends and the music of the young people. Gym shoes that flash in the dark."

"No," she protested. "The things in this room speak to you, don't they?"

He gave her the evaluating look again. "Yes, of dead kings

and dead causes. My modest burden, I'm afraid."

Their eyes met, then. Andrew smiled.

The other couples who'd surrounded them wandered off, lured in part by the excellent buffet in the next room, and possibly by something in Cassie's new ... focus. She laughed, she was charming, but she was also feeling a bit ... proprietary.

She quite deliberately slung herself on Andrew's shoulder, smelling him, feeling his warmth, enjoying him. She was his date, after all. If she didn't want someone else moving in on this, she was just going to have to establish her claim, wasn't she? Whatever happened, happened.

"And over here we have a real treasure," Andrew said as they strolled, little Tommy Chin popping up to replace her empty martini glass with a full one, darting off with the empty, despite any written proscriptions to the contrary. Cassie found herself chuckling.

"What?" Andrew asked.

"Nothing. Stray inappropriate thought."

"Between us?"

"I suddenly had a picture of a little Asian serving lad showing up next to your bed with a condom on a silver tray."

"Never use the things," he smiled. "Why make love to a woman who you wouldn't want to bear your children?"

"Well," she said. "Most guys equate knocking you up with thermonuclear war, or at least bankruptcy and an IRS audit."

"Not entirely their fault. Look what they've done to marriage. Marriage is about children and sex, when you strip it down. But the bride and her mom spend more time picking out the bridesmaids' dresses than anyone spends discussing how they're gonna keep the kids out of the government youth camps or how much sex they like or whether the only way she can come is doggie-style.

"The poor guy assumes the kids are gonna be locked out of the master bedroom six evenings a week so they can keep going at it like naked trapeze artists. Then he finds out she wants the kids to have the run of the place till midnight, by which time they're both too tired. It dawns on him he may not have sex again for 20 years, and we wonder why you can see the whites all around the poor kid's eyes, like a steer being led to slaughter."

"Andrew, you're amazing."

"Did I just say that out loud?"

"Have you been sneaking in and spying on my dreams?"

He smiled. She thought he might kiss her, but he didn't. Then he reached up and reverently removed a long Japanese tachi from its holder on a small, spotlit platform.

"This is the O-Takahira. The 'O,' in Japanese, means — "

"The smith's masterwork."

"I'm sorry." He smiled, more warmly, she thought. "Educated people are getting so thin on the ground."

"Among all the useless disciplines available to me, I majored in art history, dear. Anyone who's studied Japanese culture knows that of the historic named blades catalogued by the appraisers of the Shogun what's-his-name in the 18th century, the two really big names are the Dojigiri and the O-Kanehira, of Bizen Province, late Heian," she recited, giddily finding some use for the mind-numbing arcana with which she had once stuffed her brain. "But I've never heard of the O-Takahira."

Glancing to either side to make sure he had clearance, Andrew drew the great blade from its dark blue wood and silk scabbard.

Cassie had developed this habit of sudden and involuntary intakes of breath when Andrew was around, like some schoolgirl with the vapors. But where she'd expected something dull and brown, this iridescent blue blade now flashed as though it'd been forged last week. Down the middle of the great blade ran the hamon — the broad wavy temper mark where two or more completely different grains of steel melded. Here the brittle sharp cutting edge met the more flexible, thicker body of the blade that gave it strength and resilience.

The effect was accomplished through the magic of clay hand-tempering. Without it the masterwork would either hold no edge, or else shatter like brittle glass. And here in this ham-on, in just one turning, she saw intricate pattern of ashi, konie, and nioi, a pattern like a frozen snapshot of the spray of surf along a rocky shoreline.

"My God," she said.

And then he placed the rough white grip in her hand. Under the wrappings, the gnarly skin of a sting ray.

She found herself actually shivering. "So light," she said. She was tempted to swirl her wrist, but she realized this was not only live steel but probably sharp enough to take off an ear as easily as a barber shaves a wayward hair. And a priceless treasure, to boot. Besides, there were other people in the room … weren't there?

"This is more than 500 years old."

"Mid-Heian, actually."

"A thousand, then. This blade was used a thousand years ago." Then she could resist no longer, and did put the blade through a simple wrist-roll. "But so light."

"Nearly all live blades will feel light compared to modern reproductions. It's too costly to trim the blades to proper fineness from a heavy blank, so the modern industrial makers compromise and give us too light a tang. It's the ratio of the blade weight to a too-light tang that we feel as 'heaviness' in nearly all the modern copies."

She passed him back the O-Takahira, which she was glad to see carried no price tag. He sheathed it expertly, she was also glad to see. Such a sword should not be in the care of some mere broker unfamiliar with its ways.

Andrew drew the sword-spine up between his left thumb and forefinger, which sat poised at the scabbard's opening, until he felt the kissaki, the back of the angled tip. Then he slid the blade silently back into its scabbard, without removing his eyes from her face.

"In the Bizen province at that time there were three master swordsmiths," Andrew explained, his voice heated with excitement as though relating some marvel just uncovered on his latest dig, "known as the three hira. A fair number of blades of Kanehira survive, but none as long and broad as the O-Kanehira. A few of Sukehira's swords also survive in Japan, though if there was ever an O-Sukehira, it's unknown.

"But for centuries, it was believed that no work of the third Ko-Bizen smith, Takahira, survived, at all — at least none that he had signed."

"So this sword is not in the great catalogue."

"No. The Kyoho meibutsucho does list a number of 'lost blades,' which were believed destroyed by fire prior to 1719. But there were also named blades held in secret by certain of the daimyo houses, which were not named in the catalogue simply because they were not submitted for inspection. We believe O-Takahira is one of those."

"A thousand years. Can you imagine actually meeting one of those swordsmiths?"

"Ah, you don't know, then. We have one here."

Andrew seemed barely to gesture with his chin, and a shorter man of full Japanese blood, slender but for his muscular arms — Cassie couldn't be sure of his age but wouldn't have made him much more than 50 — walked up with a slightly rolling gate. He had straight black hair pulled into a knot behind his head, graying just at the temples. Long sideburns that came to a point below his ears. With the dark mustache and goatee outlining his chin, he looked a perfect devil. He stopped and bowed his head very slightly.

"Cassandra Trulove, our own Bizen Hideki nokuni Takahira — Takahira of Bizen Province."

"You bear the same name as the great sword."

"I have that honor."

"And from Bizen province, too. You must have been bred

to the craft, then."

"Let us say I have been a swordmaker for ... quite a long time." The old-timer smiled, then. His eyes twinkled. Cassie liked him.

Still, she couldn't help wondering: Long enough to have learned how to make convincing reproductions of an 11th century tachi? She said nothing of the sort, of course. There was some deep water here, she sensed, noting how easily the two men communicated with a minimum of words, how the smith appeared to have been almost waiting to be called ...

"These things speak to you," she said to Andrew — not quite a question.

"They represent a struggle, generations of trial and error. Beauty, perfection of design, still married to utility."

"But no one uses ancient Samurai swords any more," she said.

Hideki the bladesmith smiled and nodded. Especially among the Japanese, this could sometimes mean the listener was too polite to contradict you.

"Have I told you I love that dress, by the way?" Andrew asked. "Works so well with that little carnival purse, which, judging from the weight, tells me you've opted for a compact automatic tonight in ... 9 millimeter? .40 Smith?"

"I'd never depend on the stopping power of a 9 millimeter," Cassie smiled, catlike.

"A lady after my own heart."

Their mouths were tantalizingly close. Hideki drew off, pretending to be intensely interested in something in a glass case.

"You collect beautiful things."

"None as beautiful as a tuned human body, the face of a woman in love, a mother breast-feeding her child. But it flashes by so quickly. The artist wants to capture some element of that joy and beauty. Years of training just so he can wait, spot it, grab it in an instant, like a wing shot. A great Picasso can be a line he drew in seconds. One time in a million, the craftsman captures the essence of something eternal, freezes it there.

"The people who designed and built these things defeated death. They left behind something so compelling you want to go find out where these things came from. Learn about their lives, their discipline, and you learn a little more about yourself.

"Life is a process of sorting. Watching for things that sing and soar, that make you smile. Things you can go to sleep with."

"And do I make you smile? Make you want to tuck me in?"

"You do, Cassandra. I'm sure a lot of men have told you that. The question is, are you ready for something big? I'm ambitious, see. I want big and powerful things. Love and passion are big."

"Am I blushing, yet?"

"In a minute, you'll ask me if I was planning to hang you on the wall."

"Oh, good one."

"The real treasure is the moment that reminds you you're alive. That's the one they can't capture."

"Why, Andrew. I think you may be a poet, after all."

And then came the smile, again. My my my. If this got any worse she'd find herself tossing her hair, putting her hand on her hip, turning her jaw to bare her neck.

They leaned forward, touched their foreheads. And then Tommy Chin was beside them again, tugging Andrew's sleeve.

"Sorry boss," he said. "They've sent up twice from the theater. They let in the crowd and it's less than an hour till showtime, and now Long Shot says he needs to talk to you about the sound system."

It occurred to her then that Andrew never took a call when he was with her. Often enough she'd seen him returning a call as he walked away, but he must turn it off when he was with her. She liked that.

Again, Andrew did little more than lift his chin and the bladesmith Hideki was back at their side.

"Hideki and Tommy will see you get to our seats down front. Try not to look too smug as you pass all the rich people stuck in back. I hope you'll stay and join me for the party at Chin's after the show?" He raised his eyebrows in a question mark. She responded by shifting her weight against his side, slight little wiggle to get herself snugged into the curve between his hip and shoulder. Clear enough, sailor?

"That'll be a while though, so make sure the boys let you graze at the troughs as you amble past."

He kissed her ear and was off, beckoning for one of his serving men, sending the young lad off scurrying with important dispatches, damn Yankees threatening to flank us through the woods.

On her way out, Cassie passed Boris and Katia, deep in conversation with a couple of the distinguished old silver-maned lions Andrew had been talking to when she arrived.

Katia, clearly Ukrainian, bent down as Cassie passed, picking up an orange kitten that was attempting to climb her stockinged leg. Cassie noticed they were standing next to a glass case that seemed to be set up to compare the funeral jewelry of the Mayans, the Egyptians, and the ancient Celts. Boris had his brow furrowed, seemed to be rattling off price estimates and jotting down orders in a small notebook, in between sniffles. Poor dear had a summer cold; must be the air conditioning.

Funny thing, though. Cassie would have sworn it was now illegal to import that stuff.

⚜ ⚜ ⚜

THE BLACK ARROW

The talent lineup was first rate, Cassie had to admit. What you always dreaded was the hallucinogenic prospect of the aging society matrons attempting to dance the evening away, doing the bump 'n grind in their formal gowns as their graying escorts lurched in spastic good spirits alongside them — The Munsters on ketamine. But fate seemed to have intervened to forestall the nightmare.

Except for a small group of seats taped off near the back to provide room for the ushers and ticket girls once their jobs were done, the place was largely packed with enthusiastic folk still this side of middle age.

The half-round pilasters and wall and ceiling light fixtures were all Egyptian themed. They glowed a burnished, antique gold, revealed in a 60-year-overdue cleaning. The red velvet fabric on the old blue-green cast iron seats had an almost corduroy feel to it.

Coming out of retirement, Harry Zimmerman, who must have been 80, led off the show by dedicating "Subterranean Homesick Blues" to "Mayor Daniel Brackley and his Lightning Squads — I think it's still legal to say that."

Then the Crows sauntered on to back him up on a Zimmerman hit they themselves had covered recently. The crowd, needless to say, went bonkers. The Crows played stadiums. They did not generally play back-up for an opening act.

The drunken politician leaps
Upon the street where mothers weep
And the saviors who are fast asleep
They wait for you
And I wait for them to interrupt
Me drinkin' from my broken cup
And ask for me to open up
The gate for you
I want you, I want you

Yes, I want you, so bad ...

Sure enough, the mingling of Stig's pouting, strutting impression of a New Orleans bluesman with Harry's nasal twang was unforgettable, oddly reminiscent of the way good cocaine up your nose made you feel like your brain was puckering up.

To get the crowd on its feet at this early a stage seemed awfully daring. How could this kind of fever pitch be sustained? Most performers would be scared to death to follow this kind of opening act.

"Hello, New York, the blackbirds are back."

The crowd sounded like Zulu warriors, beating their shields.

"I'd like to thank Mr. Zimmerman for inviting us here tonight, and for being nice enough to loan us his song. They've also asked me to tell you our next album is being recorded here at the Gotham Studios; it should be out by summer. Meantime, those of you here tonight be sure to keep your ticket stubs. Tickets for our New Year's Eve concert here at Gotham City's mighty Gotham Theatre go on sale tomorrow, but on your way out, anyone with a ticket stub here tonight can trade it in for a free New Year's Eve ticket.

"Pretty good, eh?

"Maybe we'll be out again later. But first, I know you've all been waiting to see the really big acts. So let me introduce to you ... The Veronicas!"

The biggest female act in the RetroPop firmament were a mixed-race all-girl foursome — three of them being the Jones sisters, Sahara, Flamingo and Tropicana — in skin-tight white vinyl wrapped in what appeared to be iridescent chemically blued barbed wire, backed by the full Rebel Records studio band dressed in ghastly oversized ultraviolet luminescing leisure suits, each in one of the pure primary colors of a children's playground. They opened with their current hit, a straightforward cover of Heart's "Straight On To You," followed by a couple of their upcoming Rebel releases, covering the Beatles' "I Don't Want to Spoil the Party" (the lyric quite emphatically *not* gender shifted, so the girls still sang "I Still Love Her") and the Chiffons' "Sweet Talking Guy."

All Retro, all the time.

The Veronicas threw kisses, bowed a lot, sashayed off stage. But the crowd was given no chance to catch its breath — Jesus, how were they going to wedge in the aphrodisiac commercials? Immediately the curtain reopened, Jim the drummer opened up, and that burning, gonorrheal guitar lead introduced, for the first time live on stage in more than a decade ...

If we were older
We wouldn't have to be worried tonight

Baby oh (oh), I wanna be with you
So bad, (I wanna be with you)

Well tonight's (tonight) the night
We always knew it would feel so right
So come on baby, I just wanna be with you.

The lede guitar lines burned and drilled into your head. The key, Cassie realized, was the juxtaposition of those tight, upbeat vocals with the rocking bass line, full of syncopated triples. It seemed to her now that in the past the bass had always somehow dropped below the register where she could really hear it play a tune — had just sat there as a kind of rhythmic thumping. Here it was a full part of the melodic arrangement, first as a counterpoint, then interweaving intricately, always on target, always a quarter-beat ahead. It straightened your spine. It was chemical, or electrical, or something.

Someday's a long time

And we've been waiting so long to be here

Baby oh (oh), I wanna be with you
So bad ...

Andrew played what must be the Wally Bryson guitar parts on a big Rickenbacher 12-string. His wide guitar sling with its bright geometric patterns — matching the gold and brown sunburst pattern of the guitar — was a match for those beaded or embroidered leather belts he always favored. In addition to the drummer they actually used two other guitarists — five musicians doing the work of the original four as they worked to include all the original guitar parts, so many of which had originally been overdubbed and layered in the studio.

The key to the old Carmen-Bryson-Smalley hits had been the juxtaposition of the band's bright instrumental sound against Eric Carmen's warm, crooning voice, which he would place right up against the microphone — Andrew said it used to drive the engineers crazy. She noticed Andrew's voice combining with the others to exactly the same effect. Made you shiver. The work was basic, carnal, unadulterated — pure Let's-Get-Laid-Before-Mom-and-Dad-Get-Home.

But what the crowd was really waiting for was the twice-again mega-hit, the tune with the secret, which was that the bass player played the lede, giving the whole experience the feel of extremely energetic sex.

And then, just as Andrew and the boys stepped up in unison to launch into "Go All the Way," Cassie got it. It just hit her like a hammer, and she got it.

Andrew stepped to the mike, reached his chin out, looked directly at her, and sang

I never knew how complete love could be

Till she kissed me and said,
"Baby, please, go all the way,
It feels so right (Feels so right)
Being with you here tonight,
Please (Baby please), go all the way,
Just hold me close (Hold me close)
Don't ever let me go"

Sweet Jesus, he was singing it to her. More than a thousand people here, thousands more out on the sidewalk, millions of people around the world watching on satellite TV, and her man was singing this *to her.* She felt blown back into her seat like a pilot pulling multiple Gs. She just melted. Her eyes teared up. For her.

Of course, somewhere higher in her cerebral cortex she understood about 700 other dames and probably a hundred quite snappily dressed gay guys were feeling the same thing right here in the hall. But she didn't care. Hers was real.

And now she finally understood why she got so angry when she heard some 30-year-old rock song turned into elevator music or a popcorn ad.

Here was an anthem of her generation's raw sexual energy, coming directly at her, music to hump by, not just under the covers with the lights out but leaning over the kitchen sink if that's what you felt like, raw and joyous, without artifice or restraint. The raw power of that was simply indescribable. No wonder the old people hated it, screeched that it was too loud, covered their ears and ran from the room, asking why no one could play "Surrey with the Fringe on Top" like Lawrence Welk did anymore. How dare someone who was peddling the MSN "protect your kid from seeing any naked titties" butterfly try and appropriate THAT?

The Bible-thumping assholes had hated it, had fought to put our music down. Cassie knew too much history, that was the problem. They'd tried to ban it from the radio, they'd staged record-burnings. Hell, they would have burned the musicians themselves at the stake if they could have gotten away with it — they sent enough of them to prison for using the drugs favored by the Negro or finding willing young girlfriends the judges and prosecutors would have killed to spend an hour with alone in their chambers — simpering in their righteousness, gotta drive the devil out of these children.

They'd refused to let Elvis be televised below the waist. They'd boycotted John Lennon for saying the Beatles had more fans in their time than Jesus, which was plainly true from population figures alone. How many goddamned people had even spoken Aramaic in 30 A.D.?

But the new generations had fought and won. Fought for their music, for her boyfriend to be able to wear his hair long and a fucking earring if he wanted, to snort cocaine and screw with their boots on and the music blaring, goddamn it, and now these same assholes who'd tried to shut them down and box them into a "Leave It To Beaver" world were getting away with appropriating the anthems of her sexual liberation and turning them into jingles to sell station wagons and potato chips and Ambien.

Well FUCK that. FUCK the bald-headed, self-righteous, fundamentalist, can't-get-it-up-without-a-penis-pill, check with your doctor to see if you're healthy enough for sexual activity assholes! And while she was at it, she was going to fuck Andrew Fletcher tonight, too, if he'd have her, fuck him like a bunny till he pleaded to be allowed to sleep, and then fuck him one more time for good measure. Jesus, he was beautiful. She stood up and screamed.

> *I couldn't say what I wanted to say*
> *Till she whispered, "I love you,*
> *So please go all the way,*
> *It feels so right (feels so right)*
> *Being with you here tonight ..."*

The guitars crunched. She came on a wave of pleasure, pushing her head back into the seat like pulling back the stick on twin Pratt & Whitneys. And as God was her witness, in the breakdown the guitars sounded like trumpets. Why couldn't she see them right, any more? Because you're crying, you helpless loon.

"Thank You. Thank you," Andrew said, after letting them go on cheering ever so long.

Cassie was exhilarated and exhausted. She wondered if she'd actually wet herself. She didn't really care. Sticky was good. The room was alive with joy; it was electric.

"You've been a great crowd, helping make this gala re-opening of the Gotham such a success, and we hope you'll all be back many times as we showcase the considerable talents unearthed by our own Marvin Jones of Rebel Records. Thank you, Long Shot!

The big black man in the V-neck sweater leaned on from the wings, waved casually.

And then everyone who'd been on stage that night trooped back on, plugging in and tuning up. By this time there seemed to be no one in the crowd who failed to realize they'd laid hold of something historic here. This wasn't merely a re-enactment, like costumed stuntmen staging some hoaky Wild West shoot-out for a crowd full of Bermuda shorts and videocams. No, they had really done it. The creature had come back to life, lurched to its feet ... and danced the Monster Mash.

"Have you had enough?" Andrew asked them.

"Nnnoo!"

"Have you had enough?"

"Nnnoo!"

"Well I'm afraid we're coming to the end of our allotted time. We only have the one more, and this has to be good night. Thank you all for coming and being part of this wonderful evening. This one's by the late Phil Everly, I'm sure you know it, feel free to sing along. On the bass, if you would, Dominic."

The Veronicas took the lead as Dom and Mustapha the twin bass players cued them, and then everyone joined in, the close three-part harmony giving the piece the feel of an old church spiritual:

I've been cheated, been mistreated
When will I be loved?
I've been put down.
I've been pushed 'round
When will I - I be loved?

When I find a new man
that I want for mine,
it always breaks my heart in two.
It happens every time
I've been made blue. I've been lied to.
When will I - I be loved?

⚜ ⚜ ⚜

The private party was at Chin's, on the corner of the restored Gotham block, paying homage to the well-recognized need for those who'd put the show together to wind down, vent the adrenalin, recall the evening's close calls.

The new Chin's didn't look like your traditional Chinese restaurant. The establishment had been a steak house with a full bar in an earlier incarnation. Some new paint and green wallpaper had lightened the dark wood look of the joint, somewhat. But the long bar against the south wall had been retained.

Jimmy Chin was tending bar. He poured tall ones for himself, Andrew, and Hideki. "A toast," he said.

"What to?" Andrew asked.

"To Jenna Janes."

"Ah." The other two men nodded soberly, raised their glasses. "To the late Jenna Janes."

"She had her head long enough," Jimmy said.

There was no shortage of booze and other, technically restricted intoxicants. (The more laws they passed, the more generally they were all ignored.) Boris and Katia passed among the crowd like angels of mercy, distributing the powdered and encapsulated hors d'oeuvres out of the pockets of large leather shoulder bags, stopping to sit for a moment and offer a learned consultation if any of the guests had a question about likely drug interactions.

Cassie noticed the man with the gold tooth and the big chin who had driven her here tonight, trying to drink a couple other grizzled old war veterans under the table. They were apparently part of the theater's technical crew, worked the lighting boards while Marvin and his gang from upstairs at Rebel Records handled the sound. They looked like guys you'd rather have on your side than breaking their bottles and turning on you.

Cassie was glowing. She wondered, briefly, how she could ever write about the way she felt. Maybe it was magic precisely because you never could.

Would she just be wasting her time, trying to explain why the Raspberries' stuff had outlasted "Knock Four Times on the Ceiling," or whatever twaddle Andrew said was in the top 10 when Carmen and Bryson and Smalley wrote their stuff, back in — what, 1971?

At some museums they rented you earphones which were cued to play the appropriate narration as you walked past the stuffed saber-tooth tiger — was it a pointless effort to keep trying to stretch the archaic technology of the written description when all you really needed was to stick a 50-cent CD in the book flap, print numbers in the margins, tell them "Put on your earphones and play track 11 while you read this passage so you can hear what the heck I'm talking about ..."?

Cassie noticed someone had let the stray cats in. A half dozen of the sweet young things who had worked the concert as ushers and ticket girls had grabbed a table over by the bar and were now making a show of oh-so-casually displaying their willowy selves, making calf eyes of availability at the lads in the band.

One — a wafer-thin blonde — appeared to be flirting with the handsome Asian chef who'd been slicing the salmon and brisket earlier at the buffet. Another — a copper-haired beauty — had actually snuck in a tiny orange furball of a tiger kitten, all paws and ears, possibly the one Cassie had seen earlier in the museum.

The little ball of fluff was slipping about on their tabletop. The one with the long copper hair swept it off its feet now and tucked it into a large straw bag she'd slung over her shoulder, her outrage only half feigned as she caught her companions trying to get the poor creature to lap a saucer of beer.

As the girls fluttered and chirped, Cassie could understand why the Brits had long called them "birds." Occasionally one would jump up and flit to the bar, checking on something with their obvious leader, a slim brunette who stood apart, leaning on the rail and nursing a pint of something dark.

Funny how such little packs always had a leader — usually the prettiest, though in this case the brunette would have to rank second in that category to the redhead at the table.

As Cassie was eyeing the brunette at the bar — shoulder length hair parted in the middle, a skinny child but with a serious mien and a jaw set with determination — the creature looked up and met Cassandra's eyes. Cassandra actually experienced a little involuntary shudder, so intensely was the young woman looking her a pair of daggers.

What on earth had she ever done to this little creature to

316

engender such hatred? Something she'd written?

No. This was the more ancient thing — the woman thing. The light came, like the sun breaking through clouds. It was Andrew. This little pack had been busy maneuvering for the attentions of the top breeding stallions here, and Cassandra was the interloper, stepping in to block their play.

She gave the little brunette a big smile. The child slammed down her stein, turned on her heel, and stormed out, fuming.

Andrew had joined in the corn chips & chatter long enough to make a good appearance. Now, though, he gave Cassie the look, walking directly back toward her.

She was the most beautiful and desirable doe in the forest. She had run off her own competition, then lured the great bucks in with her scent. She watched, seemingly uncaring, as the great studs clashed and battled for the honor of servicing her. Now her champion stood, having driven all challengers from the field, his chest heaving, the foam of sweat from his triumphs glistening on his flanks and loins, scanning his head from side to side on those bulging neck muscles to see if anyone else dared challenge him.

And so she carefully positioned herself upwind, turned three-quarters away from him so he could see the lovely white fur outline of her sleek little butt, casually nibbled a blade of grass, waited for him to remember why he was here ... Come on, champ ... yes, you're smelling the real thing, the thing you live and die for ... thaaaat's right ...

Andrew's pace was measured, deliberate, inescapable. Being at the focus of that kind of undivided attention was exactly what she needed. What was it the songwriter had said? "It feels so right." Did that make her a rock 'n roll mama? Guilty as charged, your honor. She felt any remaining resistance flowing out of her, replaced by a kind of soft, liquid, golden glow of anticipation. Mutually, they agreed to surrender themselves to biology.

And now that smile lit up his face. It was as though, for

317

him, there was nothing else, no one else, in the room. It was a focus thing. When she looked in his eyes, it was as though the audio dropped out, and she heard nothing but his voice. It took her breath away. How did he do that?

He didn't stop until his very firm pectoral muscle pressed deliberately down on her left nipple, which raised itself, unbidden, to the occasion. Oh my.

"Ready to get out of here?" he asked. "Out of here?" the words echoed in her ears.

She shivered. Not taking her eyes off his face, that fearful symmetry, she reached behind her to grab her purse without a word — what was there to say? — melting against his shoulder as he put his arm around her.

Was it possible to have sex while still upright? Neither of them looked back. They didn't so much walk as glide. His hand was on her hip. That felt nice. He guided her out a back door past the now-dark and deserted restaurant kitchen, down a hallway, to a well-camouflaged elevator door that he keyed with an electronic code. It serviced the penthouse. Good verb.

But the elevator was slow, very slow. Once it started to climb, he leaned forward and kissed her, long but tentatively, sampling her lips the way you'd sip a new bottle of wine. When he was done, she leaned forward and kissed him back, a bit more firmly. On their third or fourth exchange, things got a bit more serious. She found herself wondering why on earth people wore all these clothes.

She got the passing impression the penthouse was large and spacious with a ceiling as far away as the sky, decked out in nice soft rugs in white and brown. Animal colors. Little pools of light from baby spots and track lighting. Skylights and balconies provided some kind of view of a deep maroon night sky and the river and the city lights. But it was all a blur. She kicked off her shoes and dropped her stuff and pretty much glued herself to that mouth. Then she was off her feet, being carried. He lifted her like she was a feather, and Cassie knew

318

she was no feather.

Presumably at the end of this non-stop flight would be a bed, right? Ah, there it was. Bed. About time. A huge bed, plenty of room for rock 'n roll. And she didn't even have to help him with the micro-hook on the back of the dress. (What had she been thinking? Weren't they making outfits that closed with Velcro, these days?) She leaned her head back, turning it to one side and exposing her neck for his bite — yes, there it was, thanks for noticing I needed that — arched her back to raise her pelvis to meet him. With one hand he deftly slid a pillow beneath her butt to hold her there when she relaxed. And when he entered her it was as though someone had pushed a really nice helping of morphine into your hospital I.V. The drug users chased this rush — and found only a pale imitation. And then he was huge inside her without any hesitation, yes, ramming her as hard and steady and irresistible as a jackhammer, yes, just the way she loved it, yes, night without end.

Oh, God, where had this been all her life? Or had it been here all along, waiting for her — had she been the one who'd been Away Without Official Leave?

From somewhere she heard music — ah, what a nice choice ...

Rock and roll mama
Gets her kicks at the hop every Friday night
They know when she walks out the door
She ain't comin' home all night

Rock and roll mama
Wanna take you home with me
Put down my guitar
Just long enough to make you see

I'm gonna hold you like a lover should
Yeah! rock and roll mama

Make you feel so good
All right! all right! ...

✤ ✤ ✤

Cassandra woke in the bed. She felt wonderful. What had made her feel like this? Oh yeah ...

She hugged herself. The waves of pleasure returned. How often did you meet someone who was brilliant, and beautiful, who shared your politics, who correctly answered "both" to the question "Do you like to be on top or on the bottom," who could hump like a bunny all night long?

She didn't remember deciding to stay. She couldn't imagine deciding to leave. Then suddenly she shuddered, her body gave an actual lurch like she'd touched a live electric cable as she realized the arm and shoulder were gone. No, relax, it was OK — he was still here, somewhere. She could still feel his presence. Would it always be like this now, this feeling of connectedness, being able to tell he was nearby, just by pausing to feel for that — what was it — not just warmth. Some kind of electrical field? Or did she hear the rhythm of his breathing without realizing it at any conscious level? God, what would it be like to have this, and then lose it?

Andrew's loft was a mostly wall-less space — a more personalized, more comfortable version of the museum downstairs. A smaller rectangle was walled off in the southeast corner — partly with architectural frosted glass bricks — Cassie correctly guessed this would contain the bathroom, though she hadn't anticipated the outside corner wall also set full of an irregular shape of frosted glass bricks — it must admit an enormous amount of sunlight in the morning — the terraced greenhouse of plants churning out oxygen here, surrounding the giant tub and shower on three sides, hooked up to an automatic system of audible trickling rivulets and drip irrigation like a slow-motion fountain to keep the jasmine and begonias blooming even when Andrew was away. Or did small Asian servants pad around in tabi sandals, primping and pruning? A private tropical forest, for God's sake. And then the sunlight would penetrate on into the apartment proper through more architectural frosted glass in the interior wall, as well ... some of which even appeared to be beveled and faceted.

An opaque wall did screen off the huge bed, though there was no door. No rat warren of guest quarters — this place has never been intended for more than one person ... or two who slept together. Low couches. Big pillows. Fur rugs and deep-piled carpet. The fire in the fireplace — gas — was burning but turned down low. Some waist-high partitions set off the kitchen area with its industrial-size copper and stainless steel stovetop and large hanging mesh wire bins for vegetables. She could smell the onions.

That meant he actually cooked. Why did that not surprise her? Probably a degree from Escoffier or the CIA tucked away somewhere. She could hear a dripolator brewing coffee — he must have tripped it as he went past. Smelled luscious.

But otherwise the loft, occupying the entire top two floors of the building and opening into the skylit tower, just sat there and reeked of the quiet opulence of space in a city where people paid fortunes for a few dozen square feet to park their cars.

An entire area of matted floor and weight benches for when he didn't want to bother heading down to the dojo on the second floor. A section of free-standing glass display cases like a smaller, private museum lit by PAR lights set high on the wall, dimmed now by some rheostat — Cassie picked out what she had no doubt was an original set of 17th century lacquered samurai armor, including a fantastic hawk's-head helmet. The bright colors would say "reproduction" ... if you didn't know Andrew.

And here was the music system and a wall containing not only his own gold and platinum discs and photos of the Rock-in' Rebels in their heyday, but also a separate, smaller section bearing the awards and concert photos and the gold discs of ... Nicole. The late and sainted Nicole, pregnant when the plane went down.

❧ ❧ ❧

He was out on the balcony, watching over his city.

The sliding doors were partly open to the breeze — high enough to provide a welcome cool break from the two-month heat wave. 180-degree view. The city was to her right and left, glittering in the permanent ambient dusk ... though it would be dawn soon, surely. How soon? She had no idea of the time, didn't care, wished it would stop still at this moment, forever.

Straight ahead, tankers thrummed their way up the mighty river to the west, the lap and surge of the tidal race inaudible except for the occasional distant foghorn. The night and the lights, so far way. The noises of the city seemed oddly muted up here, making it feel like miles and miles.

The music still carried from the speakers inside, also muted. "Once I could find my way, But that was yesterday. Believe me, it's not easy, I am waiting."

He sensed as much as heard her coming, reached back to pull her into his island of warmth, face nuzzling her hair, strong arms warming her shoulders. No words. It was so tempting just to let him envelop her. Did it always feel like this? God, it made you so vulnerable. You gave them everything. You gave them — him — the power to explode your world. They could say, "We'll do lunch," and the crystal moment would shatter in irrecoverable shards. Had shattered, so many times. The soulmate you thought was there turned out never to have been there at all. Just your imagination, running away with you. Cell phone. Necktie. Gotta go, luv. Call you.

No. She wasn't letting herself go down that road. No girding the defenses. That only *made* it happen. How dare that pang of loneliness intrude here, reminding her of the danger of handing to some halfway stranger the power to destroy you? Wasn't that what made it precious? If this was a dream, let it last another hour, and she'd never ask any more. Was an hour so much to ask? Maybe a day or two?

"It's beautiful." She craned her neck to measure the roofs of smaller nearby buildings, some bearing ancient wooden water tanks.

"You can't see the Empire State from this side, which makes it harder to orient yourself. You can just make out the Chrysler if you lean out. And this far downtown the bridges are to the East, of course. We're a ways uptown and west of Chinatown."

"Is this the gloaming? Or do you only get a gloaming in the evening?"

"I think there are two. It's like a bonus. Buy one gloaming, get one free. Only we usually don't notice."

So warm under his arm. That melting feeling again. How could she like that so *much?* She felt tears in her eyes.

"The city used to seem brighter," she sighed.

"It was brighter. It peaked in the late '60s or '70s, I think. Animated billboards flashing all night, the cigarette ads actually smoked. This was a city of boundless energy. Marketing and advertising practically invented here. Even the coal companies and the lumberyards had neon signs ... red ones, blue ones.

"But there's less need to compete when your market share is allocated by some central distribution board. Why advertise when people are told where to get their food, where to get their health care ... And collectivism breeds crime, of course. If there are no property rights it becomes a crime to eat anything but your handouts, to own anything Dan Brackley and the Bilderbergs want. You have to grab what you can before the Grays get it. You can spot the areas that are still kept patrolled for the ruling class. The lights are brighter there. But they get smaller every year."

"I know."

"Sorry. I know you know."

"You're not old enough to have been here in the 1960s."

"I'm not?"

"You're not." She snuggled in tighter. Please, let him want her some more. "Are you?"

"My family has been here almost two centuries. Passing on the memories was always something real important. Not just names and dates, but what it looked like, what it smelled like. Voice to voice. Memories are part of a family's wealth. My father would take me by the hand and say, 'In that building there, Murray Rothbard used to have dinner with Ludwig von Mises. Ayn Rand ate in this restaurant. The waiter hated her.' His father had told him, see? That reservoir of direct knowledge is our strength, as much as the investments, the wealth. After awhile, you see it as a continuum, the crowds chasing the latest Ponzi scheme, falling for the latest version of the old 'We're here to protect you' shell game. The way everyone should see history unfolding, if they really taught history anymore. Losing it is like giving up breast-feeding."

"Hm?"

"You stop transferring your natural immunities, leave the young defenseless."

"Oh."

"The Japanese see the world that way. Talk to Hideki. 'On this hill, one of my ancestors pledged his service to the shogun in your year 1685. It was a late summer day. There were dragonflies.' As though they were saying, 'I saw a deer browsing here yesterday.'"

"You don't have any children."

"No."

"No other lady in your life, Andrew? I mean, currently?"

"There is someone who fills my dreams," he said. She felt herself stiffen, trying to control her breathing. Slowly. In and out, regular-like. Be calm. It's all right. You can make it home before you die. Done it before.

"I fell in love with her mind, first — her way of thinking, the way she cared about people. But I figured she was inaccessible. Just a picture on the billboards, on the delivery trucks. A creature that beautiful had to be completely inaccessible, if she really existed at all — if she wasn't just some Photoshop composite. But I figured, what the hell, they used to consider you a charmer. Take the chance. Worst thing that happens is she laughs in your face, calls you a dirty old man, you wait another lifetime. But you can't win if you don't roll the dice."

She exhaled. "There was someone else in your life, once," she said.

"You've been reading up on me."

"It's what I do."

"She died."

"I know." But she didn't want to take him there, not really. "Beautiful song," she said. Don't let me have ruined it. Please.

"It's brilliant. The musical phrase is longer than the words. He sings, 'Believe me, it's not easy, I am waiting,' and the music still has a measure to go. Hear it? It creates a tension. You know there ought to be words there. Then he comes back the next time ..."

As Andrew spoke, the singer did come back — he had not put on his own cover of the tune, she noticed, but the Eric Carmen original. "When love was in her eyes, I had to pass it by. Believe me, it's not easy, I'd been waiting, all my life. ..."

"... and finishes the phrase. 'waiting, all my life.' "

Andrew's cadence was perfect, of course. How long had there been that sigh, that wave of pleasure inside her, when she thought the name "Andrew"? Was that new, or had that been there a while now, unnoticed?

"Relieves a tension you didn't know was there. Without realizing it, you've been ..."

"Waiting," she laughed, softly.

"Yes."

"Was he really the best? Eric Carmen?"

"Incredibly underrated. He wrote this one when he was 12."

"Twelve?"

"The early Eric Carmen stuff belongs right up there with McCartney, and George Gershwin's lovely wife Ira."

She hunched her shoulders. He hugged her tighter. She turned into him. His neck was there. As though it had always been, warm and strong. Maybe it had been. Always there. Einstein said time wasn't always linear, right?

"Ira was George's brother," she sighed.

"Old radio joke."

"Oh." Closer. "Sorry. After awhile you learn to bite your tongue. It's so tedious, being around dolts. I used to think they must just be pretending, or something. And it's not just specialized knowledge. They don't know stuff you could pick up from the *History* Channel."

"It's the government schools. But why are we the ones who try to fit in with them, Halloween in the land of the retards? Life is supposed to be full and rich, and bright, and easy."

"Is it?"

"Yes."

"Easy?"

"Yes." She found his ear. He found her throat. Soon they were doing things inappropriate for open-air balconies. Easily.

Inside, the singer continued.

"She said 'I've been waiting all my life
For love to show his face

When will I know, how will I know
Where to take my place?'

Once I could find my way
But that was yesterday
Believe me, it's not easy
I'll be waiting ... all my life"

"And you," he asked as they paused for breath. "No kids?"

"Not yet."

"Ever gonna do that?"

"Actually, my doctor says I'm as fertile as a bunny. So if we were to be foolish enough to go on like this much longer ..." But she didn't care. Really didn't care. This was her life, right here.

"How exciting." He picked her up off the ground like she was a kitten. She wrapped her legs around his trim and muscular hips. How did he stay so muscular? Well, he owned his own martial arts school downstairs, for heaven's sake. And this place was big enough to stage the sword fight from Robin Hood. The heavy flannel robe she'd grabbed by the bed opened and they slid together like they'd been designed by the same engineer. Which was pretty much true, now that she thought about it.

"Oh God," she said, the tears of joy flowing freely now. "Is there anything about you that's *not* perfect?"

"I'm not tidy," he said.

"I can li -ive with that."

"I was once told I snored, though I haven't had it checked recently."

"I'm glad you ha- haven't. Had it checked, I mean. Ohhh. That feels nice."

"I have some unusual hobbies. Spend some nights out with the boys."

"OK. Hobbies are OK. As long as I'm one-nnh of them. Oh dear. More of that, please.

"Other than that, and the fact that I'm, you know, an international terrorist ..."

"That's OK. I can live with that."

⚜ ⚜ ⚜

Later, as the sun crept slow and gold, the facets in the frosted glass bricks of the bathroom throwing little rainbows around the walls, and from somewhere the smell of new-cooked bacon joined the aroma of fresh-brewed coffee, she stretched, still half-asleep. Back in bed, she saw.

"I like the hanging gardens in the bathroom," she yawned.

"Yuri and Tanya Petrov."

"Oh. I wrote some pieces about them."

"I know."

"You're lucky you weren't busted with the rest of their clientele."

"They tried. But this system was purchased by the Wyoming affiliate of an Andorran company with a delivery address in Seymour, Connecticut. Lotsa luck." He rolled over to her, nibbled at her ear, then started using his tongue. Odd: her ear wasn't the main part of her that started to feel wet as a result.

"There's some bacon on the warmer. I think I've got a cantaloupe that's still good. But if you want a real breakfast I can phone down."

"Phone down? Like, for the servants? Andrew, do you have people on call 24 hours a day?"

"Well, not formally. It's not the Ritz. But a couple hundred people work in this building, off and on. The kitchen at Chin's is open for the guards, even if it's only sandwiches. Bob has coffee going in the newsstand by 5:30. And the dojo and the sound studio can be going any time — if someone wants to lay down a track while it's fresh in their mind you don't tell them to come back later. So there are generally people around."

"It feels completely quiet up here."

"Really thick floors. Plus, this area is isolated from the rest of the building. You may have noticed this elevator only goes to the main floor and back."

Actually, it would also run express to the sub-basement and one of the secret routes to the caverns when he was leaving on a different kind of errand. He didn't mention that.

"Do the ladies usually stay, Andrew? I imagine they do."

"There are very few ladies, Cassandra. Decided long ago I wouldn't waste time with anyone who I wouldn't want to bear my children. Simplifies things enormously."

"You shouldn't propose till the third date, you know."

"There's no surplus of passion in the world, Cassie. If there's something here that looks good to you, grab hold of it. Tight as you like."

"Are you really an international terrorist?"

"No."

"Oh."

"You sound disappointed."

"It did sound exciting."

"I try to be on my best behavior when I'm overseas. I figure I don't have any business overthrowing the governments of *other* countries."

"That shows admirable restraint."

"Thank you."

"So you just overthrow governments here at home."

"I could answer that question, but then I'd have to marry you."

"That would be OK," she said, sounding like Willow Rosenberg from "Buffy the Vampire Slayer," Joss Whedon's favorite character in the seminal TV drama which had just been feted with that big retrospective at the Museum of Television. She even felt like little Alysson Hannigan's Willow, unable to draw breath for a second after the words came out. You weren't supposed to say these things till much later. It was in the rulebook, somewhere. "How Not to Scare Him Away Till Later."

She waited to see if any tenseness crept into his muscles. Instead, he stretched languidly, like a huge cat, half rolled towards her, and bit her neck some more. Only this time, he didn't stop half way. And then she knew she wasn't going home that day, unless he beat her out the door with a stick. And that one way or another, things were never likely to be the same again. And that was a good thing.

"We can't possibly do this *again*," she laughed.

"Why not?" he asked.

Which also turned out to be a good question.

CHAPTER 10

The right of self-defense is the first law of nature; in most governments it has been the study of rulers to confine this right within the narrowest limits possible. Wherever standing armies are kept up, and when the right of the people to keep and bear arms is, under any color or pretext whatsoever, prohibited, liberty, if not already annihilated, is on the brink of destruction.

— St. George Tucker (1752-1827), American jurist and legal scholar, in his annotated 1803 edition of Blackstone's 1768 "Commentaries on the Laws of England."

The spirit of resistance to government is so valuable on certain occasions, that I wish it to be always kept alive. It will often be exercised when wrong, but better so than not to be exercised at all. I like a little rebellion now and then. It is like a storm in the atmosphere.

— Thomas Jefferson to Abigail Adams, 1787.

There's no way to rule innocent men. The only power government has is the power to crack down on criminals. Well, when there aren't enough criminals, one makes them. One declares so many things a crime that it becomes impossible to live without breaking laws.

— Dr. Floyd Ferris, in Ayn Rand's (1905-1982) "Atlas Shrugged," 1957

Cassie and Andrew stayed in bed till noon. By that time they needed a rest, so she borrowed slacks and a shirt from the closet and they headed down to Chin's for lunch.

The new joint was already busy, but Carole Chin managed to find them a booth. The place was done up in pastel shades of green, contrasting with the dark wood — Mrs. Chin said she hated the way everyone went with red and gold, "like Hong Kong chicken house; no taste."

"Rachel?" Andrew was surprised to see one of Madison's best little fighters — and her smallest — getting ready to take their lunch order.

"Annie's out and they were never expecting it to be this busy right at the start, so Mrs. Chin called upstairs to see if anyone could help her with the lunch rush," Rachel explained. "Madison and I were laying down some back-up tracks, but Madison is the one Marvin really wanted, so I didn't mind."

"Backup tracks?"

"Madison keeps saying her voice is too scratchy, but Marvin says we call that 'throaty' and besides she has perfect pitch. Said her voice is just what he needs for a couple of these songs. Isn't this place a trip?"

"So you're getting along OK?"

"Never better. And this is a real kick," she leaned down closer and lowered her voice. "See that asshole in the gray suit over by the window, giving his waitress hell?"

"Yeah." He was a large man with a big neck, a florid face and a comb-over.

"Been like that ever since he came in. First table we gave him wasn't good enough, even though the place is full. Then his menu wasn't clean enough, there was a smudge on it. You know the kind."

"Yep."

"Well, word is that guy has an appointment upstairs in about an hour, where he's going to try and talk the people at

Fletcher Communications into buying his flea-bitten company, which has a balance sheet with so much red on it it looks like a Confederate flag."

"Yeah?"

"So, do you see who his waitress is?"

"Is that Melody?"

"Yep. She heard the call and came down to help out, too." Andrew and Rachel cracked up. Cassandra looked a question at the both of them.

"Melody works upstairs. In accounting," Andrew explained. "As a matter of fact, she's the number two person in acquisitions. So when Mr. Suit opens his briefcase upstairs and starts trying to paint a rosy picture of his dog-eared company, who do you suppose is gonna walk in and sit down and tell him our offer?"

"Oh, jeez. I hope he leaves a good tip,"

"He won't," Rachel smiled.

She took their order and headed for the kitchen, still laughing. Two of the cooks even came out for a gander at Mr. Bigshot, who clearly still didn't have a clue.

One of them was the new guy, Nguyen. As she squeezed past him into the kitchen, Rachel purposely bumped his hip. He smiled and bumped back. Nguyen was tall and dreamy. She thought he had excellent potential.

Hideki the blademaster came in and whispered in Andrew's ear, then withdrew to a polite distance.

"I'm sorry," Andrew said, grabbing a curry puff for the road. "There's an emergency; I have to go."

"Anything I can do?" Cassandra asked.

"Please, finish your meal. You're welcome to stay upstairs; I hope you will. Although I don't know how soon I'll be back. If not, just ask for a car."

He kissed her on the forehead and left. More goons met Andrew and his Japanese companion at the door. Cars pulled up for them. Jesus, she was starting to feel like the girlfriend in some Godfather movie, the one who eventually finds out the upstanding olive oil importer's son she thought she was dating is actually Don Guido Giuseppe, Undisputed Capo of the Five Families.

And now her own phone was buzzing.

"Cassie? It's Glenn." The Mirror's downtown cop reporter. "You asked me to call you."

"Yes?"

"The Grays are calling for backup at the 23rd Street IRT. You anywhere near there?"

"Pretty close."

"Now, I'm not recommending you go down there alone. But you asked me to let you know."

"Thanks, Glenn. I owe you one." She started to roll up her sleeve to wave her chip at the credit reader. "Oh no, ma'am," a passing waitress said in horror. "Mr. Fletcher would never allow that."

Then she was outside, hailing a cab.

❖ ❖ ❖

Cassie got into the subway station just before they cordoned off the entrances. It wasn't hard to figure out where the action was; you just watched which way the Grays were running. Technically she had no more right than any average subway passenger to follow them ... but also no less.

The press was supposed to be allowed to go anywhere the public could go. Any good reporter learned early on that the last thing you wanted to do was show your press card and wait around till they could find a public relations handler to tell you why you couldn't go anywhere or see anything, when just by shutting up and pretending to be Suzy Secretary you could have gone and looked for yourself an hour ago.

Cassie clipped her hair up and pushed past the fleeing bystanders, spotting a gray steel door which stood propped open, leading away from the main passenger platforms. These Grays obviously had something a lot more serious on their minds than keeping stupid rubberneckers out of the combat zone.

She had one close call. She pretended to be barfing into a rare remaining trash container and the squad of running Grays passed her by. After that the weirdest thing was how quiet the access tunnels got. Whenever she came to a fork she chose the way that led deeper. She was about to conclude it was a bum steer when ahead of her she heard the sounds of shouting and running feet.

The tunnels had narrowed and grown more damp as she'd proceeded; this one was lit by a few naked bulbs, shielded inside small wire cages every 30 yards or so. But the pools of near-darkness between them were larger than the pools of light.

Now the running steps grew louder. Behind them came the loud staccato cracks of machine pistol fire. Cassie glanced around in increasing panic, spotted an alcove off to the side — an access point to a steel ladder leading even deeper. She had no idea where the ladder went, so she just climbed partway down, leaving her head exposed above the level of the tunnel floor.

Dashing past her came the legs of a dozen pounding, panting men. She could smell their tangy, acid sweat. They ran at top speed through the shroud of darkness and the shallow pools of light, splashing in the trickle of water on the tunnel floor. The pounding of their running feet echoed and built in volume inside her head. Their silhouetted legs alternately blocked and revealed the blue-white emergency lights reflecting off the tunnel wall till the stroboscopic flashes reach a speed too fast to make out as anything but a random pattern of vengeance and determination.

"Go, go, go!" shouted one of them — a wiry fellow with long dirty blond hair who she thought she recognized, though she couldn't remember from where. Then he called two of his men by name — well, some kind of nicknames, really — instructed them to "Lay back and give us some cover here."

Two of the men responded without argument or hesitation by dropping to their knees, facing back the way they'd come. They twisted their bows off their shoulders and began firing arrows at their pursuers, still invisible to Cassie. Something whooshed back at them through the air and landed nearby with a clatter, began emitting a cloud of thick white smoke. Cassie hoped it was only tear gas. Then she got a whiff and wondered why in hell she'd used the word "only."

Not only did her eyes begin to tear, the mucous membranes in her nose and throat began to swell and clog; she could hardly breathe. She knew from covering many a police "standoff" that the manufacturer only intended this stuff to be used outdoors; they specifically warned it could be toxic in enclosed spaces.

Now with a terrible splatting noise one of the men also took a couple rounds of 9mm, spun to the ground as his blood spattered the far wall. He lay there, struggling for breath, silently moving his mouth like a beached fish. His companion shouldered his own bow, shouted behind him for help. Figuring she didn't want to get stuck here between two fires anyway, Cassie climbed up and helped him get the stricken man onto his unsteady legs.

"Who the hell are you?" the able-bodied bowman asked.

"Innocent bystander," she said, even as she realized there might no longer be any such thing. "Actually, I'm with the Mirror. All the news that fits?"

More bullets clattered and whined off the walls as they helped the wounded man stagger away from the assaulting Grays, whose looming, silhouetted forms and orange muzzle flashes could be partially glimpsed like figures from a dream through the cloud of white and dark gray smoke behind them.

From ahead, now, came more bowmen to aid their wounded colleague. Then Cassandra felt as though someone had punched her in the small of the back, hard. She fell to her knees. There were bright flashes of orange light. More noxious clouds swirled around her. There were more shouts and pounding feet, though they now sounded strangely hollow and far away.

In the history books, battles were always summed up in a way that made them sound orderly and easy to follow. The commanders deployed their troops on a fine, sunny morning, moved them about like brightly colored pieces on a chessboard. Rectangular formations of red or blue or green moved ahead by file or pivoted to the flanks; everyone could easily see the objectives, the crisply defined struggles to attack and defend.

Cassie remembered that before the first Battle of Bull Run, the ladies of Old Washington had packed their parasols and picnic baskets and driven their coaches and surreys out to the hillsides overlooking the grounds of maneuver for what they anticipated would be a stirring few hours' entertainment. They had ended up dashing for home in a panic as the routed and bloody Union forces came pouring directly through them, Confederate shot and shell pounding close on their heels.

But what she was experiencing here made even that seem sane.

She was in a much larger space than the tunnel where she'd started out — some kind of old subway engine switching and repair yard with a ceiling high enough that it was lost in the gloom. The battle sounded further away but it also sounded like someone had brought some heavier firepower to bear.

337

The ground shook to the sound of heavy crumps like explosive shells going off. Somewhere she could hear concrete fragments of tunnel walls and ceilings rumbling and crashing to the ground.

She looked at the man lying next to her. He wasn't young. Somehow she had assumed all soldiers were young. But he was dead. Cassandra had seen dead people before, but never quite so ... intimately. The freshly dead actually looked little different from the living, until you tried to stare into their eyes. It was always a temptation to try to shake and coax them back to life — except for the eyes. They were fixed, and dilated unnaturally, and covered with a little film that seemed thicker than it ought to be. Because it was drying, maybe. It gave you a new appreciation of the word "empty."

She felt oddly calm. It would be easy just to close her own eyes, which still wept and stung. But some internal voice told her that lying quietly among the dead might not be the smart way to go.

She tried to sit up. Her back and her left kidney hurt like hell. She ended up rolling over to get to her hands and knees. She put a hand behind her back. There was considerable blood, some dark purple and clotting, some still fresh and red. Shit. Her own blood.

Well, yes it's your own blood. Duh.

A form came leaping at her out of the mist, legs apart like a ballet dancer or a gazelle. No, not at her — right past her. He was Asian, dressed all in black, with a black headband. Someone was chasing him — a Lightning Trooper in a crisp gray uniform. But the trooper seemed to have too much assorted stuff flopping from his belt. It all got in his way — chains and canisters, a flashlight and a radio, swaying and clanking and knocking his arm so he fumbled with his weapon as he ran, trying to insert a new magazine. His attention temporarily diverted, he nearly tripped headlong over the rebel in black as his

338

quarry turned the tables, dropping to his knees without turning, drawing his long katana blade from his scabbard, bracing it with both hands up through his armpit so it stuck up behind his back.

Head on, in the smoke and the shadow, the narrow blue blade must have been almost invisible. The pursuing Lightning Trooper ran onto it at full speed, came to a halt like a horse balking at the jump, staring down in consternation at this unlikely metal object now sticking out of his chest.

With studied elegance, the ninja withdrew his blade, stood, spun, and took off his erstwhile pursuer's head with a single slice. Cassie felt herself splattered with something liquid and warm.

But here came two more Grays, firing their subguns. The swordsman turned again, running. Cassie thought she saw him lurch from a hit, but then he was gone in the billowing white smoke. Out of that smoke, though, came arrows, black arrows, passing just over her head. One of the remaining Grays fell, gargling blood, skewered through the neck. She lost track of what happened to the other. She looked around for him and he had simply disappeared. Things moved so quickly, they were like images half-glimpsed in a dream.

The bowmen were regrouping at the far end of the switching yard, sheltering behind a pair of long-abandoned, graffiti-covered subway cars ... though whether to stand or withdraw she could not tell. Hell, she couldn't tell what objective they were fighting over. Though it did seem the Grays were on the attack, pushing the rebels back.

Then, as the men in black worked to help their wounded comrades to shelter, there raced forward to cover them on either flank a group of mere girls — high-school girls, from the look of them, quick and willowy — in green sweatshirts with their hair tied back, majestic in their fearlessness.

"Let fly, yeh fine things!" shouted one with a notably

raspy voice. "Did ya wanna live forever?"

Cassie had seen her before. The angry brunette from the cast party at the Gotham Theatre. These girls were like furies. Their arrows flew in clouds, like rockets coming off a line of those Russian rocket launchers in the old black-and-white World War II films. They sparked and rattled like handfuls of deadly pebbles on the wall behind the advancing Grays. It was enough to send the bravest man scurrying for cover.

Now, apparently timed to take advantage of this brief counterattack, snaking down from an overhead gallery where the switching engineers must once have sat watching the trains come through the yard, came spilling a long black rope, not shiny but flat on its surface, like velvet, the near end falling in coils on the floor. And down the rope came ... well, of course.

Springing, he landed on both feet, like a cat, loomed there, larger than life.

Massive thighs and shoulders, and the black mask. His form-fitting black tunic held multiple layers of polykev in lateral bands, overlaying his pectorals and abdominals.

"You're hurt," he said, conversationally.

"Of course I'm hurt. These bastards are trying to kill me."

"Which bastards?"

"The Grays."

"Ah. The other guy's bastards."

He sized up the SWAT team members deploying towards them, systematically charging their subguns and waiting to be sure they were in range. "Stay down," he said.

Then Cassie saw something at the same time so magical and yet bizarre — almost a stylized Kabuki of mortality — that she later wondered if it had really happened as she remembered it at all, or whether the memories were only some hallucinogenic artifact of her warped perception thanks to the smoke and the gas and the loss of blood from her wound, there in that world without sun.

The Black Arrow — there couldn't be a moment's doubt that's who'd finally put in his appearance — thrust out his mighty black Oneida bow toward the advancing troopers, the sinews taut beneath the dark ordered hair on his outstretched arm, the bulging tricep muscle curling around his arm like a fat snake. He reached his right hand behind his neck and drew forth the feathered shaft of an arrow from the quiver snugged there along the line of his back.

He flipped out the black shaft in one fluid motion, nocked, and drew his bow.

And as he drew the great bow it formed an arc, and the arc was the arc of her life, the energy gathered there the potential of all their lives to change themselves, to change the world, all held steady for that brief moment, rock solid in those mighty, unwavering arms.

But as quickly as she saw this truth, frozen in a lightning flash, he released the shaft, which flew so quickly that its blur of motion was not so much seen as heard, by which time another shaft seemed to have leapt into his hand, where it in turn straightened and flew, seemingly of its own accord, in a blur and a sound like a second sparrow taking wing.

At first Cassie figured the strategy must be simply to fill the air with a scatter of arrows without bothering to aim — adding the weight of his fire to that of the green-clad schoolgirls behind them, forming a kind of blind artillery barrage in the general direction of their assailants to force the oncoming Lightning Troopers to break ranks and seek cover, even if such an unaimed volley couldn't possibly be expected to strike more than one or two targets, by the sheerest of accidents.

And she continued to believe that, mind you, for a full two or three seconds, until the first two shafts had struck.

The advancing troopers, moving mechanically in their cumbersome Kevlar helmets and gas masks and bulletproof vests, did not cry out. At least, she didn't think they did. Neither did they clutch at their throats or stagger around in the throes of agony. Instead, the arrows began to strike as though drawn by magnets — Cassie would have sworn she saw more than one of the shafts track in an arc at the last second, like a pitcher's breaking curve ball, anticipating a last-instant attempt by the targeted trooper to lean to left or right — though she managed to convince herself later this had to have been an optical illusion, something to do with parallax.

And where they struck was, in each case, at the base of each trooper's throat. They dropped, then, these heavily laden footsoldiers, in rapid sequence, like bowling pins, each man like a marionette whose strings had been sliced away clean from the control of whomever or whatever held them suspended from above.

Cassie knew enough about anatomy to realize there was only one thing that could do that. Even a brain shot could leave the prey thrashing like the victim of a massive electrical discharge — which was exactly what an injured brain sent out.

No, as surely as the blindingly fast she-cat finds and pierces this same spot on the back of the neck with her long incisor, paralyzing in a flash the prey that will feed both her and her kits, here each arrow in its turn was severing the windpipe and the spine of its prey either just above or just below the third cervical vertebra.

Mother of God, it was terrible.

And so six men died in silence, tossed to the floor like playthings, like abandoned rag dolls no longer commanding the attention of some spoiled pre-adolescent giant.

"No man can do that," she said.

But it wasn't just a man, of course. It was The Black Arrow.

Out of the dark mist — Cassie wasn't sure how much was smoke and how much was a different kind of darkness, closing down her peripheral vision till she could focus only through a narrow tunnel directly ahead — came Hideki the swordmaster. He was accompanied by a strange man who looked almost rodent-like — large nose, a ragged mop of dark hair, bending forward from the waist as he moved with an odd, loping stride.

"They hit us from three sides," said the blademaster. "They've got a lot of strength, must have been infiltrating down here for days. Jean-Claude wants to pull back to the caverns."

"No," said the Black Arrow. "Not while we're engaged this close. We'd lead 'em right in behind us. We need to get clear, then disperse, take the long way around."

"They're going to keep pouring in reserves. And we can't — I've got nothing left. Where else can we go?"

Even Cassie could see their reprieve was going to be brief. A new wave of troopers now scuttled in from the far tunnel, taking up better sheltered positions, firing test bursts which sparked off the wall and the old subway cars behind them as this new batch of Grays methodically adjusted their range.

The girls in green took them under fire and at least got their heads down.

But Cassie realized neither their arrows — nor the supply in the big guy's quiver — could last forever.

"Can you walk?" the Black Arrow asked. He didn't shift his gaze from the approaching enemy, but somehow from the tone of his voice Cassie knew he was talking to her.

"I'm not sure," she said, fighting back the instinct to lie bravely.

"Then put your arms around me and get the best grip you can."

She did just that, and felt herself swept off her feet without discernible effort — later remembered thinking that was a pretty good summary of her life to date. The big guy even smelled good.

"Ratzo, you told me about another level, way down. A

place you'd never gone, a place you called The Deep."

"Never gone and never want to. There's a nasty feeling about that place. Besides, you'd have to get down on ropes or something. It's real deep and real dark, and then when there *is* a light it's this spooky blue glow. It's like — not human."

"And where does it lead?"

"Damned if I know. But I can hear a lot of water moving down there, and some kind of machinery, so it has to have something to do with the big water mains. If there *are* dry service tunnels they'd have to lead uptown."

"That's it, then. Set a rear guard, rolling retreat, send men with Ratzo to put together as much rope as we can find. Take this one."

His last words sounded as if they were in an echo chamber. That's the last she would be able to remember, later. At least, the last that made any sense.

At that point her blood loss must have begun to tell. She felt cold and nauseous, the world began to spin, and the gray clouds and the droning of some distant Gregorian chorale swept back in to block her senses, so that save for a rhythmic jostling which curiously caused her no pain she really had no idea in what direction he carried her.

With the last of her will she kept reminding herself to hang on to the big guy for dear life. And so she had no idea how far they dropped and ran through the darkness deep beneath the city. Try as she might, she would never be able to reconstruct more than fragmentary images of wonders seen and dangers braved — precarious ledges above roaring black rivers; ancient creatures that revealed themselves only as looming, misshapen forms or eerie wailing cries, deep amidst the mighty clanking and whirring machinery of the Morlocks, long-forgotten engines of ancient ingenuity which nonetheless continued to pump the city's lifeblood to an oblivious populace of sleepwalking Eloi far, far above.

She was sure, however, that they plunged deeper into that vast, cold and azure abyss than anyone else would now dare to trespass ... except by permission of The Black Arrow.

❧ ❧ ❧

She was on an operating table, turned inconveniently on her belly. She felt great, which was inappropriate. Morphine, or something like it.

She turned her head to the side. Bright lights and white linens, but the doctor was in street clothes beneath his smock. The background looked like no hospital she'd ever seen. More like the Bat Cave. Hallucinating, probably. Why else would the doctor be humming Franz Liszt? Or was that Mendelssohn?

"Mendelssohn?" she asked.

"Yes, very good," he replied, in a noticeable German accent, as though they were merely picking up a conversation which had been briefly interrupted. "Fingal's Cave Overture, from 'The Hebrides.' But you're not supposed to be with us right now, Miss Trulove. You are supposed to be sleeping, you see. Of course, we sometimes err on the side of caution. Have to keep the patient breathing, you know."

"I was shot."

"Yes, shot. Twice, in fact. I'm becoming unfortunately quite familiar with these 9 millimeter Federal Hydra-Shoks. And I will not pretend you have not offered us a bit of a challenge. Fortunately, Dr. West here was able to assist me. Quite ably, if I may say. He informs me there are parts of this city where Emergency Room practice has long resembled a war zone."

"Hi," came the voice of a younger man from the other side. Cassie was not going to bother turning her head, though.

Too much work,

"A little resectioning, but we got lucky; only a small amount of damage to the liver and kidney. The blood loss was the main concern, but this is now completely controlled. Fortunately, your friend here turned out to be a perfect match for our little transfusion. I will expect a full recovery out of you, young lady."

"I know you."

"Yes, you interviewed me at some length. And I thought your columns were quite good, if I may say so. It was a pleasure to meet someone who made an effort to write down what I actually said."

"You're Helmut Stauffer."

"I trust the next time we meet will be under more pleasant circumstances. Now these young ladies are going to take you someplace a little more quiet, where I really must insist you rest awhile. I assure you there is no need for concern; we have passed the worry of initial infection. And your friend here insists on staying by your side, so you will not be alone."

Friend? Someone was holding her hand, she realized. It was The Black Arrow. How strange. But dreams had their own logic, didn't they?

"Dr. Stauffer went to Australia," she said.

"But this is my Australia," smiled the soft-spoken old practitioner, patting their hands where they joined, "nor am I out of it."

The big guy in black still held her hand. From out in the Bat Cave, beyond the makeshift curtain rigged across the doorway to whatever room or chamber they were in, came a distant ringing or banging noise, which set off a pattern of even more distant echoes. It was regular, about every three seconds — some kind of mechanical hammer, she would guess, unless they were drilling an oil well. Busy little beavers, here in the underground. She tried to refocus her eyes out into the less-well-lit cavern. It was beautiful — the walls seemed to sparkle in opal, beryl, ruby, malachite. Then, in the foreground, a group of six or seven Asian-looking workmen walked by with tools over their shoulders. Short fellows, whistling. For a moment she could have sworn the tune was "Whistle While You Work," but she knew that couldn't be right. It had to be the drugs, which were making her feel very good and warm, only a little queasy in the tummy.

On a footstool about five feet away, contemplating Cassie through half-closed eyes, purring and watching the goings-on with evident aplomb, sat what she knew must surely be a hallucination. Cassie closed and reopened her own eyes, several times, slowly, expecting the apparition either to disappear, or to resolve itself into a pile of brown towels heaped in a suggestive shape. Full-grown marmalade cats weren't allowed in operating rooms, were they?

The cat winked back, slowly.

Whatever these drugs were, she wanted more. She half expected the creature to open its mouth and start intoning homilies in the voice of James Earl Jones.

"Can anyone tell me what that battle was about?" she sighed, closing her eyes.

"What's any battle about?" asked the Black Arrow, who in this dream had a voice just like her Andrew's.

"They're trying to drive us out of the tunnels," he explained. "Some of our guys ran into some of their guys. Everybody called for backup. Since there are more of them than there are of us, today's job was to throw out a screen, recover our wounded, get the hell out of there."

She recognized someone else, standing nearby. A well-lined face, long, dirty blond hair, and that strong, dimpled chin. He had a patch on his arm. Had he been shot, or had he been giving blood? He smiled, and showed the gold front tooth. Of course. Andrew's driver, who had picked her up to take her to the grand opening of the Gotham Theatre.

Was Andrew's driver part of the Resistance? Not just a fighter, but some kind of commander — for surely this was the guy who'd been shouting commands back in the tunnels. But that would mean Andrew was somehow involved, himself. Well, why should that surprise her, given his politics, the kinds of causes he supported? In fact, nothing could be more natural.

There was something else, though. Something nagging at her mind.

"You're going to be fine," Dr. Stauffer was telling her. "A few days of bed rest, and please do me a favor and don't go performing any gymnastics and pulling out my nice stitches. Now, this will help you to sleep."

"No, wait," she was saying. "There's something ..."

⚜ ⚜ ⚜

She knew where she was, now. This was familiar. Andrew's huge bed, high in his pyramid temple to the serpent god. The sun shone in through the frosted glass, casting little rainbows along the far wall. This was a good place, and warm. God, she felt like she'd been cold for so long — the warmth now was delicious. But how had she gotten here?

She was lying on her side, turned almost on her belly. Not the most comfortable position for a full-figured gal. She started to roll over, felt the catch and the pain in her back, remembered what had happened. Dr. Stauffer had patched her up. But then how had she gotten here?

She heard Andrew moving. She could always tell when he was in the room. She looked up ... and flinched. It wasn't Andrew — it was The Black Arrow. Was she still hallucinating? What could he be doing here? He put away a small silver pistol in a dresser drawer. Then he set a cup of tea on the end table near her — she recognized the mug as the one Andrew always made her tea in. He sat down on the bed beside her. She tried to pull away, but the wound in her back made it hard for her to flex her obliques.

"You OK?" he asked. In Andrew's voice. His hand held hers. His hand was Andrew's hand.

"Oh my God."

"You really didn't know?"

"Andrew? Oh my God."

Of course. Those arms. The way he smelled. Of course.

He leaned down and kissed her, softly, tentatively. "You've been through a lot," he said.

She found herself putting her hand tentatively to her own lips. It couldn't be. But it was. Shit. Pieces of the puzzle clicking rapidly into place. How big an idiot could she have been?

For she remembered those six arrows, perfectly placed. This was her Andrew, the man who'd turned down a job as an NFL quarterback — how accurately could *they* hit a moving target?

"My God. Andrew, are you kidding me? Tell me this isn't real."

He pulled off the mask, started to take off the black polykev vest as well. "I told you I spend some nights out with the boys."

"You think this is funny? I almost get killed, you put your own life at risk — my God, you've killed dozens of people. You've started a goddamned revolution, and you think it's all a big joke?"

"OK. I was hoping to start with something more along the lines of 'Thanks for saving my life; stupid of me to go down in those tunnels alone.' But it's still good to have you back."

"You think this is funny? You're the goddamned Black

Arrow and you don't tell me? You're sleeping with me and you sort of forget to tell me this one little incidental detail? 'By the way, I'm the most wanted multiple murderer in seven states'? Do you know what an idiot I feel like?"

"Cassie, I told you there were things about me that I couldn't tell you right away."

"Yeah, like you got drunk and married a hooker in Vegas one weekend, or you knocked up your high school sweetheart, or you own 51 percent of IG Farben, or there are no graves for the Fletcher family men because when you get old you all hike off for a final date with Ayesha and they bury you in the elephant's graveyard or something. Those are the kinds of things you might not want to mention on a first date. But, 'Oh, by the way, I'm the head of a vast terrorist army of murderous assassins who prowl the tunnels beneath the city, popping up to behead the odd federal judge after dinner and a show'? When was that coming, at the wedding rehearsal? Andrew, you murder people."

"I think you'd admit in a calmer moment that, in this day and age, there's a better way to put that."

"What, now you think I'm wired?"

"No, Cassie. The point is, I've been doing what needed to be done; the thing you wanted done, that no one else had the balls or the wherewithal to do. How many times have you screamed at the walls that people would read your columns and never do anything?"

"There are people whose jobs it is to take care of this kind of thing, Andrew. Prosecutors, judges —"

"All of whom are thoroughly corrupt, as you yourself have demonstrated over and over again."

"You can't take the law into your own hands."

"Cassie, maybe we should talk about this after you've slept and had a chance to think things over. You've had surgery with anaesthesia. You know how I feel about people being responsible for what they say, and anybody could tell you this is not a good time for you to be making long-term judgments."

"Don't —"

"You've been through a lot. You've been shot, for God's sake. Give yourself some time to rest and think things through —"

"Don't give me that, Andrew. When did I ever need to be babied? Is that what you think? I'm too shallow a bimbo to handle the truth about what you do, taking the law into your own hands?"

"Where does the law start, Cassie — with the people or with our government masters? They've turned the law and the courts into a rigged game, a maze with no exit, where every cop and every prosecutor holds a magic 'Get Out of Jail Free' card, no matter what they do, no matter who they torture or kill. The one thing left to do WAS to take the law into our own hands.

"What would you suggest? That we put our heads down and march through the portals like obedient cattle, turn in our weapons and obey all the laws and turn in our neighbors if we catch them listening to Radio Free Columbia? Sit home shivering and trembling behind our locked doors while the Grays rape any woman they find on the streets after dark?"

"There are ways to work for reform within the system."

"Is this the same Cassie Trulove who sat here and shook her head about how they've blocked off every single avenue of peaceful reform? Did you want to join the Libertarian supper club and debate platform planks that call for an end to taxation and legalizing heroin and no speed limits on the moon? Pass the hat so we can paint up a few yard signs?

"I think they got 2 percent of the vote the last election before their chairman ended up serving 3 to 5 for purposely getting himself arrested holding up a pistol in the park so he could challenge the gun laws on Second Amendment grounds.

The judge threatened to throw his lawyer in jail if she so much as mentioned the Constitution in his courtroom in front of a jury stacked with stooges who swore in advance to enforce the law as the judge explained it to them, and YOU wrote about it. They meet every third Thursday at the Denny's over on Ninth Avenue, 15 well-meaning, pasty-faced, overweight guys with pocket protectors, I'm sure they're going to figure out a fool-proof letter-to-the-editor that'll win us back our freedoms any week now."

"You used my columns and you did all this behind my back and you never told me."

"That's what's really upsetting you, Cassie. But think about it. When I met you the day they were tearing down Carole Chin's restaurant I should have said, 'Hi, I really love your columns; By the way I'm planning to start killing all the assholes you write about'? That's how I should have started trying to win your heart, convincing you I'm an OK guy?"

"You used me."

"I did not. I never asked you to run down an address for me; I never so much as called you at the office and had you check the spelling of a goddamned name. The stuff you wrote about was sourced with public records; the information in your columns was available to everyone in this city. Whether you ever came here, whether we ever met, whether we ever made love would have had zero impact on what the Black Arrow chose to do."

"You shut me out; you kept me in the dark."

"Cassie, are we really having this conversation? I can hardly believe it. You're the one who seemed to want the extended courtship. I invited you into my life, but you wanted to take everything real slow, like there was some kind of courtship instruction manual. OK, I went with that — I wasn't going to jump you in the cab. 'Let her take her time,' I figured. 'Probably she's been burned before.' I brought you in as fast as

I thought I could, for your own safety. You kind of forced our hands, down there in the tunnels."

"Oh, now it was all for me. I should be so grateful."

"Cassie, your editor at the paper, Sullivan? Didn't he ever ask if you knew anyone from the underground, if you ever slipped any information to the resistance?"

"Yes, he did. And I lied to him; I told him I didn't know anyone like that. Stupid me."

"No, Cassie, when you told him that, you told him the truth. It's only if I'd told you everything all at once that you would have been put in a position of having to lie, or — knowing you — trying to take the Fifth, which would have been a disaster."

"I just feel so used."

She cried into her hands. He tried to hold her. She tried to turn away. She couldn't, because of her bandages, which made her even more frustrated. She pounded on him with her fists.

"You didn't think you could trust me."

"I wanted to trust you; I thought I could trust you. I still do trust you, with my life, with a lot of people's lives. That's why you're here, right now. But the way you're acting makes me wonder. What's this all about, Cassandra?"

She tried to get up.

"Cassie, you have to stay in bed for a week. Now get hold of yourself. If you don't want me here we'll have a nurse and Mrs. Chin come up and look after you. Now, do you want Graymalkin brought here, or do you want someone to stop by your apartment and feed him, in which case you need to show me which key and tell us if the alarm's on. You also need to give me a list of people we should tell you're going to be out for a few days. Or if you want to call people yourself, this phone is encrypted and routed offshore. If you need phone numbers let me know and we'll get them for you."

Cassie lay back on her pillows, curled up her lip, and

snarled. Andrew laughed; he couldn't help it. She wasn't any less pissed off. But she was glad he'd remembered Graymalkin. That was just like Andrew.

✜ ✜ ✜

10 DAYS LATER ...

Hideki was the last to arrive. Downstairs, his men guarded the elevators. There would be no interruptions.

Madison was surprised to be included. A little. And surprised at how it felt. Cold sweat, nervous stomach. Stuff she hadn't experienced since her first competitions, as a kid.

It was like a weight on your shoulders. This was life and death. She worked security, the same as Hideki and Jean-Claude. If anyone else in this room were to tell what was discussed here, she herself might be instructed to kill them. Kill them without question. If you couldn't do that, you had no business here.

Which made Joan Matcham's presence another surprise. She'd known Joan longer than any of the others — known her from that other underground, a world where boot software traded the same as sex or pharmaceuticals or bogus ID chips, where she was such a legend Madison had once believed she might not exist at all — the Mistress of All Codes.

But she'd never thought of little Joan as a fighter.

Andrew. Jean-Claude, who insisted on keeping his gold tooth as a souvenir. Madison. Hideki. Joanie.

She'd never been in Andrew's penthouse before. Rich man's digs, thick carpets and fancy works of art. She didn't even know what some of them were. Cost the world, no doubt. And this was where they said Cassandra Trulove had spent a whole week recovering after she was shot in the big battle in the tunnels.

A whole week. With Andrew.

God, Madison's dreams were pathetic. Why couldn't she just be happy with her place in life?

"You've all done well," Andrew began. "But now they've counterattacked in the tunnels. They'll come up with counter-measures, better security. If it were just the Grays we wouldn't worry. But this cop Flanagan fought in the West. As he deploys more men into the tunnels, our growing numbers start to work against us."

He paused.

"The key there is not to try and hold territory," Jean-Claude interjected. "Ambush. Booby-trap. Keep them dying. Gradual attrition. But don't give them the pitched battle they want. It's not like we *live* down there. We can still transit through, with Ratzo as a guide."

"Yes," Andrew agreed. "Fortunately, they seem to only think in two dimensions. Ratzo has already shown us some par-allel tunnel systems running above and below the ones they're patrolling. But we can't get into a war of attrition down there. We can't trade them one for one, or even one for 10. They can keep throwing in replacements; our flow of new help from the neighborhood clubs is just too slow."

"If we try to speed that up, we risk security problems," Hideki added.

"Exactly," Andrew agreed. "On the bright side, the new headwalls are diverting them away from the caverns. But they'll try air-flow indicators eventually, sonic detection, seis-mometers. If you stay on the defensive, eventually you get tired. You make a mistake; they come up with one more thing you haven't countered. That's why we're here today."

Himself crossed to the big wooden easel and pulled down a piece of blank white paper which had been covering it. Revealed was a large blown-up photograph of a building. Madison had seen it before. Its bulging gold windows reflected the light so it looked like some big alien bug set down in the middle of the city. SonicNet headquarters, uptown on the East Side.

"You all know this building. By the end of the year, the Order of the Arrow is going to attack this building. We're going to give them a much bigger problem to deal with. We're going to destroy the SonicNet."

The prospect of killing Grays would usually have sent the good rush up Madison's spine. But there was something different here. He had said "attack." Some of her girls could die. So this was what it felt like — sitting and making plans that you knew would probably get good people killed. This is what people did to get the medals and the promotions and the gold on their shoulders. Is that what she was doing here? Clawing her way up over the bodies of her bitches? It made her a little sick to think about it. For the first time, she began to understand why Andrew seemed so sad, sometimes.

But he was right. They couldn't just go on killing one clerk at a time. They had to gather their forces and hit back somewhere ... hard.

"A frontal attack?" asked Jean-Claude.

"A lot of circumstances have to change before we can do that," Andrew replied. "We don't have extra bodies to throw against these walls. We'll look at tunnel entry, the back alley, the rooftops."

"Sneak in a demolition team?" Jean-Claude asked.

"Let me get to the point," Andrew said. "We've got a lot of work to put this thing together. You'll all be consulted. We may bring in a few others if we need their expertise. But not without checking with Hideki and me, please."

He paused again. Madison knew his thought, now. He'd just been tempted to remind them of the need for security. But he said nothing. They were not children.

"We're going to take this building down in a way that's noisy and highly visible, even if it costs us casualties. We're going to do that for two reasons.

"First, it's a symbol of New Washington in this city. A mysterious fire that they can blame on some electrical short circuit does nothing to mobilize resistance. We need the Fall of the Bastille. Torches and pitchforks, film at 11.

"But the second reason is what Joan is here to tell you about."

Joan walked up to the map. She looked small next to Andrew, almost childlike.

"It's known as SonicNet headquarters. It is the Gotham nerve center of the Lightning Squads and the SonicNet, that's true. Most of you also know about the interrogation center — the torture chambers — run by Christian Newby and Group Leader Rennie Heydrich on the seventh floor. A lot of us had friends who went in there."

She did not say how many had come out.

"What you may not know is what's here." She pointed to a window centered near the top of the building. "Well, behind this room, actually. The room I'm talking about is closer to the building's core, on the sixth floor. There are no windows. Structurally, it's a big bank vault. It even has a solid steel door, 18 inches thick, which the operators are under orders to close in the event of any trouble. They lock themselves in. They have emergency air, food, and water supplies. They can hold out for days. If you burned the building down they might die. But it wouldn't really matter. The opportunity here is not to kill them; it's to get into that room.

"Inside that vault sit two code operators. The computers largely run themselves now. They're skilled crypto guys, but their main function is to protect the computers.

"They draw on the SonicNet for data, but they're completely firewalled. They're not part of the SonicNet.

"What's interesting about this system is that, by its very nature, since it operates in real time, it's open both ways. It's like an intravenous shunt right into the headquarters of the Defense Advanced Research Project Agency, in New Washington.

"This room is the Gotham nerve center of the Total Information Awareness Net — tracking every American from birth to death. Every paycheck, bank transaction, doctor's visit, prescription. Travel, mortgage, draft status, criminal history, drug use, venereal disease, magazine subscriptions, education, child support, the books you took out of the library, the sex toys and that hookah you bought over the Internet ... it's the Target of all Targets — it's the Target of the Gods."

"You think we can get you in there?" Madison heard herself asking. "You think you can knock out the TIA for all of Gotham?"

"No, love," Joanie smiled. "We don't want to knock it out." She reached into her jacket, pulled out a golden disc, held it up, turning it slowly. Into the eyes of each of them in turn, the little disc flashed a blinding rainbow of refracted sunlight, caught from the skylights overhead. "I want to deliver them a little present."

Sweet Jesus.

"You people seem to know something I don't," said Jean-Claude.

"He'll be asking men to die," Andrew said. "Everyone here has a right to know. But after we leave this room, we don't speak the name out loud, again. We don't write it down. This is need-to-know, and even most of those who think they know ... will believe this is just about ransacking the SonicNet building, date uncertain."

"The last time they nuked Old Washington, DARPA wrote off most of the original TIA computer system," Joan continued.

"They rebuilt it, in New Washington.

"People risked their lives — no, that's not right. Our people sacrificed years off their lives to recover those components, which were very hot indeed. They rebuilt a version of the computer with capabilities very close to those in the system now running. It's given us a target to use for our dry-run attacks. A target they don't know exists. We've been developing a virus that will penetrate that system. More than a virus, a Trojan Horse. It's not enough just to get in, because they have time-delay purges. Our little creature has to be able to get in unnoticed, and nest there, and replicate.

"There's a warning in the Bible story. Samson was unwise in love. Delilah the Philistine learned the secret of the Israelite's strength lay in his hair. So she shaved him bald while he slept. Then Samson was easy to capture, and blind, and enslave.

"The Philistines brought him to their temple at the festival of Dagon, to parade the blind cripple and ridicule their once great enemy. But they'd let his hair grow back. He'd regained his strength. Even though he was blind, Samson pulled down the temple, killing thousands of the Philistines ... and himself.

"Our enemy will still be dangerous, even if this works. But we finally did it. We wrote a code that penetrated the test installation without a trace — our rebuilt version of their old system they left behind in Arlington.

"We call our little creation Samson 6.

"The problem was, we didn't have anyone on the inside at SonicNet with the capability to keep that code room door open till we can get into the building — to get us into that vault. Now, we think we do."

She didn't have to say Jack Brackley's name.

"If he can do that, we're going to load Samson 6 into the TIA computer, and flush him right through to DARPA ... a mainframe that links with every other computer in the federal system."

"Every ... other computer?" Madison asked.

"Oh yes."

"BAFE? DEA? Treasury? Social Security? ... The IRS?"

"Oh yes."

"And if we can get you in there, Samson will ... replicate?"

"Oh yes."

"And then?"

For a moment, Joanie just smiled. Then she said "And when he awoke he could remember not a thing — not the number of his oxen, nor of his herds, nor of his slaves, nor any of their names. He was as a babe fresh from the womb, a rock washed clean by the rain, a slate cleaned for the writing. Thus did he stand on the rock where Moses stood."

"Now, in the meantime," Andrew said, after waiting a moment for that to sink in, "we have to continue enough normal operations that they won't suspect something's up."

"Bambi Fiducci," Madison said.

"Hm?"

"The 'safe storage' gun grabber. My bitches are ready, and we can probably get a lot closer to her than any menfolk. Let me set up a hit."

"She's not here in the city."

"She'll have to come here to do some fund-raising, eventually. We'll draw up contingency plans."

"She's running for Congress, Madison. That means more security."

"And once she's elected to Congress she'll only get harder to reach, not easier," Madison pointed out. "We've canceled three hits in as many weeks because of the increased security. Yeah, we can smother meter maids in their sleep. But you said we need to keep up enough activity that they don't get suspicious we're planning something bigger."

"Hideki?"

"Madison's right about the beefed-up security. And that means they're not going to leave that high profile a target alone in a parking garage or an elevator, any more. We'd have to go at her in a public place. You'll never get close enough for a sure bowshot. Hard to be certain with a small blade. Very high risk. I might be able to do it quickly enough to get away, with an icepick. But anyone else?

"Unless you actually want a big battle. Then I'd send Jean-Claude's boys. Combat experience, and if one or two buy the farm, well; us old guys have had full lives. You need to stop and think how we'd feel if Madison and a couple of her girls ended up dead, or lying in some hospital with a leg shot off, screaming in pain, no painkillers till they talk. Let Madison's team try their wings with some lower-risk missions."

"We'll take her with silenced pistols," Madison said.

"We've got reasons for not using firearms, yet," Andrew replied. "One is to prove their SonicNet is useless ..."

"Silenced pistols won't trigger the SonicNet inside a building," Madison replied, "although it's a little silly to think no one will notice our shooting the senator in the middle of a crowd. Which makes the whole thing a little bit moot."

"... and the other reason is because, when the day does come when we need to use them — like, maybe, getting into SonicNet headquarters, a few months from now — we want it to come as a shock; we want them to get used to thinking we won't or we can't use firearms."

"Nothing else will work in the kind of places we can get access to the senator."

"Then maybe the answer is not to do this one," Andrew said. "Our numbers are still small. We've accomplished a lot with hit-and-run. If we start getting into pitched battles on the enemy's ground, where he can bring superior forces to bear, we could be bled dry in no time."

Madison shrugged, gave a wan smile. She'd tried.

Then, "Are your girls trained on pistols?"

That was a surprise.

"We've already started. Boris got us some nice Para-Ordnance high capacities. With suppressors. We're doing jam and reload and quick-point drills in the caverns, breaking down and reassembling in the dark. We can do this. Besides, if we end up at some fund-raising dinner, I don't know many of Jean-Claude's boys who could pass for a hotel waitress ... no matter how close they shave."

Andrew had the strangest expression, then. She couldn't read it. She'd remember to ask him about it later.

"OK," he said.

❖ ❖ ❖

Thomas Scott couldn't go. He had to work.

They hadn't had any life insurance on the girls, of course. There had been some donations, but burying Tessa and Amber still cost money, more money than they would have expected, and a lot of time off work. The Scotts weren't rich.

Initially, Clarice hadn't wanted to go, either. It was too early. She was afraid she'd lose her composure. And this broadcaster's reputation was unsavory. A "shock jock," always interviewing strippers and porno actresses and circus freaks.

But even without much to compare it to, they'd been surprised by how little coverage the girls' deaths had received down in the city, or nationwide. A naked drug addict with a pitchfork, murdering children. You'd have thought the whole country would be up in arms.

They decided someone needed to tell their story — the real effect Bambi Fiducci's "Safe Storage" law had on two very real, wonderful children when that hideous, sick, deranged Mark David Bell had come calling.

Imagine. They said Bambi Fiducci was likely to get elected to Congress now, where she could do even more harm. Surely she realized her own husband had died only because gun control laws didn't stop criminals — they only disarmed the victims, left them with no way to defend themselves.

Hadn't that been the lesson in England and Australia — anywhere it'd been tried? Violent crime rates skyrocketing when the criminals realized the law had left their law-abiding victims disarmed?

It was Tamlyn who'd finally decided them. Tamlyn pointed out how many listeners this guy had. If he was willing to take a chance when no one else would put them on the air and let them tell their story, then they needed to take a chance, too. She'd go along and offer Mom some support. A few minutes on his TV show and then the promise of a longer interview on the radio. They'd just tell their story, that's all. How bad could it be? There was nothing to worry about if you just told the truth.

Thirteen-year-old Elizabeth was staying with friends. They loaded a picnic basket with sandwiches and drinks — Gotham had famously high prices — and proceeded to load the basket and seven-year-old Matthew in the back.

They considered taking a revolver for self-defense. But they finally decided they just couldn't risk it — the laws down in the city were simply too harsh if you were caught with a gun, any gun, and word was they were now actually stopping and searching cars at random. No search warrants, no probable cause — and the courts said it was OK. Unbelievable.

Clarice wanted to make an early start. She'd always hated driving in the city, anyway — they drove like maniacs, down there. And now with all this extra Homeland Security malarkey, they'd been warned to allow extra time. Hours extra.

But Matthew never seemed to be ready to go. He'd forgotten his video games. Then he had to go to the bathroom again. The last time he came down he brought his big green watergun.

"No way, young man. I told you, we're going into downtown Gotham City. There are a lot of police there and they're very nervous about guns. You think I want to see you get arrested?"

"Mom, it's a squirt gun."

"I don't care. Go put it back inside. Then get in this car; we're late."

Tamlyn was in the front passenger seat. She took her mom's hand. Clarice was so glad they still had their Tamlyn. Not to say she had ever had favorites among her children, that wouldn't be right. But Tamlyn was tall and straight and good and already a great comfort to her parents.

The rear door slammed.

"Are you finally ready?"

"Yes, mom."

Clarice read his face in the rear view mirror. "What are you grinning about?"

"Nothing."

Matthew had put away the big green squirt gun, just like they'd told him. Nobody had said a word about the smaller blue one in his jacket pocket. He'd wait and use it when it would make the funniest surprise. For now, he lowered his head to his portable video game.

The miles swept by. It actually lifted their spirits, being on the open road, away from home. Except for one more bathroom stop on the turnpike, they made good time till they were entering the city.

Then the traffic jams started, just as they'd been warned. Some of it was construction — they seemed to be erecting more barriers and toll gates, which was ridiculous. As though traffic in this city wasn't already an impossible snarl.

But finally, when they were less than a mile from the address they were looking for, traffic simply slowed to a crawl for no apparent reason.

Tamlyn tried to talk and keep her mom amused, to keep her spirits up, chirping on about anything that came to mind. But Clarice was quickly becoming a nervous wreck.

It was live television, for God's sake. You couldn't be late. What was the hold-up? This was so exasperating. If she'd seen a place to park she would even have considered leaving the car and walking the last mile with the kids. But there were yellow "no parking" hoods on all the parking meters, despite which cars and delivery trucks seemed to be double-parked everywhere, with the meter maids darting among the stalled cars in their little carts, festooning the windshields with their manila mail-in cash envelopes.

Finally, fuming, Clarice saw a chance to pull out of traffic, hang a U turn, and head back the other way. They were so close, surely they could find some parallel, alternate route.

And then the Homeland Security trooper in his fancy gray uniform, billed hat, black boots and submachine gun was right in front of them, moving his hand up and down for them to stop. Clarice floored the brake pedal, screeching to a stop. Where had he come from? She'd almost hit him, for God's sake.

And now another one, at the driver's side door, his face red and twisted with anger.

"What the fuck do you think you're doing? Get out of the car!"

"What?" Clarice said, reaching for the power button to roll down the window.

"No getting out of line! Get the fuck out of the car, right now!"

The young man must be deranged.

"Please," she said. "There are children here. We need to

be on Sixth Avenue in half an hour for a broadcast, and this traffic simply isn't moving. ..."

The Lightning Trooper yanked the door open, grabbed Clarice Scott by the shoulder of her shirt and sweater, pulled her from the car so hard that she fell to her knees in the street.

"Are you fucking deaf? NO GETTING OUT OF LINE!"

There were three or four of them around the car now, shouldering their weapons as though preparing to shoot, all screaming different commands at the top of their lungs.

"Young man, we are not criminals." Clarice was confident that if she just remained calm, these young men would realize their mistake, would be shamed into apologizing. "These are my children. This car is properly licensed and registered. If I've broken some traffic ordinance I'm sorry — "

"Mom!" shouted young Matthew, opening his own door and rushing to help his mother, who he'd never seen down on all fours on the ground like that. His hand had tightened around the blue squirtgun in his pocket as the men had started shouting. He didn't realize he had it out in his hand now as he jumped down from the car.

"Gun!" shouted one of the troopers, dropping to a half-squat firing position and blowing five or six rounds of 9mm into the seven-year old. It sounded like a string of Chinese firecrackers going off. Clarice Scott still couldn't believe this was happening. Her son was thrown back against the door jam of the car, where he bounced around as though he'd stepped on a live electric wire. Tufts of his clothing flew off into the air. His face was pale, grimacing in pain.

She started shrieking. She threw herself in front of her son, screening him from the bullets with her own body.

So Clarice was shot as well — three multiple-round bursts from two different machine pistols. The mother and child fell to the pavement next to the car, silent. Still twitching.

Since his standing orders were to keep shooting any assailant until he or she "stopped," and since Clarice was still thrashing around on the pavement — which meant she hadn't "stopped" — one of the troopers stepped forward and stitched the dying Clarice Scott with another burst.

At first Tamlyn froze in horror. Now it occurred to her that, whatever was wrong with these men, no matter whether they had set out to kill her family on purpose or whether it was all some terrible mistake, they themselves might panic now; might not want to leave any witnesses alive.

She opened her own door and started running directly away from the car.

Something caught her around the knees and she fell, cutting her elbows and chin on the pavement. She also bit her tongue; she could taste the blood.

What air remained in her lungs was knocked out of her as someone planted a knee in her back, yanked her arms up behind her, handcuffed them. Then he stayed there, a heavy man, his knee in her back, so she could hardly breathe.

Group Leader Rennie Heydrich had been a short distance away, supervising the car searches up at the head of the line. He strode up and evaluated the scene.

"Trooper?"

"Sir! They pulled out of line and tried to evade the vehicle search, sir! Refused to exit the vehicle when ordered. Then the boy came out with a gun!"

Heydrich used the side of his black boot to push the young boy's body aside. The blue "gun" had a white plug in the back where you poured in the water. Some had leaked out on the pavement.

"A squirt gun, it appears."

"Sir! My men were protecting my life, sir!"

"Read her chip."

The trooper stooped and scanned his portable reader across Clarice Scott's forearm, handed the unit to the group leader, who wore Counterintelligence patches on his shoulders. No messing with these guys; their orders could mean life and death. And he'd heard of this guy Heydrich. Very big medicine. And extremely creepy. Guy's face looked like a big white skull with the skin stretched tight across it.

As it happened, Heydrich recognized the family name. He'd had some of his staff making calls, letting some powerful people at the network know that allowing their rogue talk show host to interview these people on the air was not exactly a prudent course of action. Better to stick with the Man-Boy Love Association and the masturbating circus freaks.

"You know who I am, trooper?"

"Yes sir!"

"Very well. We prefer to handle things a little more discreetly in this part of town. You'll get me the names and numbers of all your men here."

"Yes sir."

"In my office by the end of the shift."

"Yes sir."

"You've lucked out, trooper. Mind you, I'd prefer to see things handled with a little more ... discretion ... in future. And none of your men is to speak of this to anyone. You understand?"

"Yes."

A few pedestrians were gathering to gawk at the scene.

"Have your men move those people along."

The company leader dispatched two of his men back onto the sidewalk with arm gestures.

"But as it turns out, these people are enemies of the state. Remove the plates from this vehicle and have them on my desk at SonicNet Headquarters within an hour. Call this number," he handed the still-shaking trooper a card. Had to be steroids, or one of the newer adrenal amplifiers. Side effects could get very squirrelly. Didn't they give these men physicals any more? "...

and tell them you need this vehicle towed within the hour and crushed. You understand? Not impounded, crushed. Use my name."

"Yes sir!"

"Remove the chips from the mother and child before they go to the morgue; I want the chips on my desk, as well."

"Um ... if they're not dead?"

"They're dead."

"Yes sir. And the other one?"

"What?"

"The girl, sir. Over there."

They circled the car. Heydrich squatted down to get a better look at Tamlyn. Well, well.

He pulled a hypodermic syringe from his pocket, removed the plastic sleeve, pumped the injection into the girl's exposed forearm near the handcuffs.

"She won't give you any trouble, now. Get her over to headquarters right away. Seventh floor."

"Yes, sir."

"And trooper?"

"Yes, sir?"

"Handle with care."

⚜ ⚜ ⚜

Tamlyn woke up. She felt sick. She was lying on her stomach, so it was easy enough to lean over the side of the bed, find the bedpan, vomit into it.

But why was she so close to the floor?

She rolled over. She was naked, in a large white room. There were other patients here. Patients? Prisoners? All girls, anyway, and also all lying on mattresses on the floor. Her own

369

eyes wouldn't focus right, but there was something wrong with these girls. They were quiet. They seemed to be alive, but they weren't making eye contact. One moved, rolled over on her side. But they seemed ... listless, like they were stoned on dope, or something.

Why was she naked? Her ankle hurt. So did her tongue. She'd bitten her tongue when she'd hit the pavement, she remembered that. And her chin. There was a bandage where she'd hit her chin. Must have cut it. But how had she gotten here? And what was this place? Why couldn't she remember?

She tried to bend her knee to reach her ankle, but something stopped it from moving. There was a steel cuff around her ankle. It was attached to a stainless steel chain. The chain led to a large ring that was bolted into the wall. All the other girls were also chained to the wall.

There was some blood between her legs, drying. That was strange. Her period wasn't due for weeks. At least, she didn't think it was. And she hurt down there. Not a sharp pain, but ... sore. She started to reach around for sheets, blankets, something to use to cover herself.

Keys clanked in the lock of the door at the end of the room. She scooted back against the wall, pulled her knees up, made herself into as small a ball as possible to hide her nakedness. A huge man with white hair and red eyes, dressed all in white like a hospital orderly, opened the door and held it for a Lightning Squad officer. The officer came in and the door closed behind him. At least the big monster hadn't come in.

Although the guy who had come in was creepy enough. Jaundiced-looking skin stretched tight over a jutting chin and cheekbones. He was an officer in the full Lightning Squad uniform with the black boots; looked like a goddamned Nazi in the old movies. What was going on? Why was she here? Where was her mom?

Of course. Her mom and little Matthew, shot. Were they

both dead?

"Ah, little Tamlyn," said the officer, as he took off his cap, threw it down on a chair that was probably too far away for her to reach. Then he took off his jacket, hung it on the chair as well.

He was hideous. Blond; pale blue eyes that seemed to be watering all the time. That face, like a skull. And he knew who she was.

"I'm glad to see you're feeling better," he said, eyeing the bedpan where she'd just vomited. He seemed to be amused.

"Who are you? Why am I here? Where's my mother? Did you kill her?"

"So many questions. What you will begin to learn today, Tamlyn, is that what matters here is obedience. Discipline, and obedience. I and one or two of my associates provide the discipline, and you ladies ... provide the obedience."

He was still smiling. Smirking, really.

"What do you want with me?"

"Come, little Tamlyn. You don't appear to be stupid. Surely that's obvious. Actually, I've already done you once. So you see, there's no need to be embarrassed. We're already ... close friends."

She was going to be sick again. She understood now why she was sore between her legs.

"You'll be happy to know I enjoyed it a great deal. You're very pretty, especially when you're opened up like a flower in the sun. But I suspect you'll be a lot more interesting companion if you're not drugged up like these others. Such a spirited child. No, I believe you'll break to the saddle very well. It may take some time, but there's no shortage of that.

"Now," he said, taking off his shirt. As he removed his clothes he switched a brown object which he was holding from one hand to the other. A braided piece of leather with a handle. A riding crop.

"As I said, what I'm here to teach you is obedience. You want food, water, a blanket at night? If you don't yet, I assure you you will. You want not to be beaten? Well, that is to say ... not beaten very hard? Well then. The secret is obedience.

"Now Tamlyn, the first command you're going to learn today is 'Roll over.' Do you think you can do that for me? Roll over?"

CHAPTER 11

*A good militia will always preserve the public liberty. But
in the best constitution that ever was ... if the militia be not
upon a right foot, the liberty of that people must perish. ...
I cannot see why arms should be denied to any man who is
not a slave, since they are the only true badges of liberty;
and ought never, but in times of utmost necessity, to be put
into the hands of mercenaries. ... Is it not a shame that
any man who possesses an estate, and is at the same time
healthful and young, should not fit himself by all means for
the defence of that, and his country, rather than to pay taxes
to maintain a mercenary, who though he may defend him
during a war, will be sure to insult and enslave him in time
of peace?*

— Andrew Fletcher (1653-1716), "A Discourse of Government
with Relation to Militias," 1698

*It does not require a majority to prevail, but rather an irate,
tireless minority keen to set brush fires in people's minds.*

— Samuel Adams, revolutionary (1722-1803)

*The price of freedom is the willingness to do sudden battle,
anywhere, any time and with utter recklessness.*

— Robert Heinlein (1907-1988), "The Puppet Masters," 1951

It had been a pretty good day on the Arts Center job, other than having to waste time listening to another pompous lecture from that little pantywaist Newby from the mayor's office. That had cut a good hour out of the middle of the morning (He was sure Newby considered it "first thing in the morning," probably hadn't even finished his morning seaweed and soy flakes till 8:30), droning on about how things had changed now that he was "in charge" — this from a guy who couldn't find the bathrooms on a blueprint and who got green in the face if he was ever hoisted above the second floor. Which was basically never, thank God for small favors.

Today's lecture had concerned the roof drains. Looking over the prints and thinking ahead, Jerry Burgess' guys had pointed out city engineering specs called for at least 55 drains on a roof as big as the one they were putting together for the Brackley Center — enough to handle the 10-year storm.

Yet the plans called for only eight drains, each 5 inches in diameter. And not only that, their openings were placed 2 inches above the base of the roof. The guys weren't exactly math professors, but they figured this would limit outflow of rain off the roof to about a tenth of a cubic foot per second. The idea was to get the water *off* the roof, right?

Apparently not. Newby had patiently explained to them — Newby believed anyone who didn't wear a necktie needed things explained very slowly — city staff's concern that the aging storm sewers in the area could not keep up with the amount of runoff the Brackley center would produce. Therefore, he explained, the design had been revised to use the arena roof as a "temporary reservoir" during big downpours.

"You're placing a temporary rainwater reservoir ... on the roof?" Jerry had asked.

Yep.

But the guys had made good progress that morning, even while he was having to pretend Newby the Twit could figure out how to build a treehouse. Everybody knew the delays on this job had been caused almost entirely by all the "innovative" architectural crap which had required change order after change order as the guys had dragged themselves back to the command trailer again and again, asking what the geniuses wanted them to do about walls that didn't meet up (forget about "right angles" — what the hell were those?), bathroom plumbing that was apparently designed to flow uphill, weather joins that would let in the rain and snow like a gypsy's tent.

But finally now the guys were in their element, bolting and riveting the steel roof beams, which were being assembled on the ground, to be winched up into position later as a unit.

The biggest breakthrough had come when they'd convinced Newby that a lot of their time was being used up trying to weld the diagonal support braces at the middle of each 30-foot beam.

Problem was, the plans called for those braces to fit snug into the 90-degree interior angles of the cruciform beams, which meant the end of the support brace had to be finish-fit to a 90-degree point, like an arrowhead, and then someone had to get in there and weld both sides of that "arrowhead" into the interior corner of the beam while the whole shebang was held tight at the proper angle. Needless to say, no one up in the penthouse where the architects lived had ever so much as welded an oil pan; they clearly had no idea how long it took to get a weld done right in that kind of constricted space.

Jerry would never forget the blank look on their faces when Lee Gomez had pointed out you couldn't just dangle there by your left arm like a monkey while you were doing those welds, you needed your left forearm free to push your mask up so you could see what you were doing when you knocked slag.

One of the architects had asked why they couldn't hang on with their right arms. Lee Gomez had later theorized that the architects must do their own welding with their torches strapped to their dicks. They'd proceeded to go through three entire pitchers at O'Rourke's that night, speculating on which

375

orifice of their bodies those guys used to hold their welding rods.

In the end, Jerry had asked why they couldn't just insert two thicknesses of steel stub between each pair of the sandwiched L-beams that formed the cruciforms, bend these little stubbies 45 degrees apart where they stuck out from the bottom, and weld the diagonal braces to those. Hell, they could even throw in some bolts, which should make the whole deal even stronger.

Charged with speeding things up, Newby asked how much time it would save, and initialed the change in the "as-builts" without further ado.

But it was too good to be true, of course. Here came Lee, one of his best guys, hat off and wiping his head with his bandana, which was always bad news.

"I don't want to hear it, Lee."

"I know you don't, boss."

"Well?"

"I thought you didn't want to hear it."

"I'd also like the old lady to meet me at the door tonight with a six-pack and take off her shirt and give me a blow job, instead of telling me I have to go to the school play. Now you gonna tell me what it is, or do I have to take you dancing and buy you flowers?"

"Where the north-south and the east-west beams come together at those big octagonal gusset plates?

"What's wrong?"

"The beams all have six bolt holes, like they're supposed to, but the way the holes are spaced, on some of these beams there are only four that actually overlap the plate. The last two holes, you look through and there's nothing but air."

"You're shitting me."

"You can come and look."

"Maybe you got the wrong end."

"We thought of that, so we tried turning 'em around. It's

the same either way. Six holes on the beams, but only four actually overlap the plates. And if you try to shift the gusset plate, it's even shorter for the beam coming in from the far side."

"But you can get a solid footing for four on each end?"

"Sure."

"Jesus Christ." Couldn't anything on this whole goddamned job be a square peg in a square hole? This was EXACTLY the kind of bullshit that had run the whole show six months behind and who knew how many million over budget. Jerry Burgess knew exactly what he OUGHT to do. He OUGHT to go back to the trailer with his hat in his hand and ask pretty please what should he do about the bolt holes that were placed so there was nothing to bolt them to? But he knew fucking well what they'd tell him: it would cost extra weeks to reformulate the beams, and even that would be after they called some guy in Pittsburgh who would insist he'd formulated those beams just the way they looked in the plans and HE wasn't gonna pay if there was a mistake on the plans, which would probably mean two more weeks of arbitration over who made the mistake, which couldn't be resolved until the shop steward of the steelmaker's union was paid off with a lap dance and a weekend in Vegas.

The Arena contract was divided into five subcontracts, with total confusion reigning about who was responsible for the project as a whole. Even though the architect had recommended a qualified structural engineer be hired to oversee the construction, the construction managers — the latest of whom was now Newby, apparently — had consistently refused, saying it was a waste of money and they could just as well inspect the project themselves.

And in the end, if he went trooping back to check with the twerp, what would he be told? That mathematically you didn't really lose 33 percent of your strength when you went from six bolts to four, that the added bolts were really only there to reduce the chance of the whole thing flexing, and since the roof was overengineered by 100 percent, what the hell were you worried about?

And hadn't that asshole Newby just lectured them for the sixth time that they needed to show some initiative, take some responsibility, make some decisions, get this job back on schedule and stop whining back to the architects every time they couldn't read some squiggle on the plans?"

"Four is plenty, Lee. We don't design 'em, we're just paid to bolt 'em together the best we can. Bolt 'em up and let's see if we can't get something finished, for once."

"Yes sir, boss," Lee smiled, always the wise-ass but obviously happy that someone had finally made a decision that would allow them to get on with something they knew how to do.

In fact, the absence of two bolts from each set of six bolt holes would not turn out to be crucial. What would turn out to be crucial was the change which now saw the diagonal braces bolted to the little metal "stubs" sticking out of the bottom of each cruciform beam, instead of being welded snug into the 90-degree receiving angles formed by the side of each beam's cruciform cross-section.

This change invited flexing, where the original design would have been ruthlessly rigid. And ironically, this is the change that Newby had specifically OK'd.

This change, all by itself, had the effect of reducing the force each beam could withstand from 625,000 pounds to 362,000 pounds — almost entirely eliminating the 100 percent safety margin that everyone thought they were working with.

Interestingly enough, Martin Woo had realized his roof design was innovative enough to confuse construction guys who'd never seen it done this way, which is why he'd insisted that the contract call for the week of special training, to be conducted by him personally, during which he would meet with the construction guys during the site preparation stage, to explain the mechanics of his innovative cruciform beam structure — and the importance of the safeguards he had provided to deal with the increased susceptibility of such a structure to buckling.

Martin Woo would doubtless have screamed bloody murder at the cancellation of those training sessions ... had it not been for the unfortunate boating accident which claimed his life in the Virgin Islands the weekend before that decision was made — the boating accident which had curiously spared his wife, who was off water skiing with one of his partners that day, the partner who she happened to marry about six weeks after Martin's untimely demise.

But Jerry Burgess was hardly to know all this. He'd just moved the job ahead by weeks. They'd buy him a round of drinks for that.

❖ ❖ ❖

SEPTEMBER ...

They'd gotten Bob some more stools for his counter, to encourage people to hang out. He also had a refrigerated glass display case with more ready-made stuff — sandwiches, desserts — now that they could be fixed fresh daily over at Chin's, fully satisfying all the bogus Health Department Protection Racket regulations.

A young woman dropped something heavy on the tile as she squeaked up a stool — a guitar in a case.

"Hi," she said, sounding wet and bedraggled.

"Hi there, miss."

"What can I get for a newbuck?" she asked. Many would have heard an English accent. Bob heard Australian.

"You eating or drinking?"

"Well, since I don't feel like a candy bar, better make it

a coffee. No, iced tea. You got iced tea?" She sounded tired. Bob sensed she'd been out in the afternoon drizzle for awhile. An "Irish hurricane," Madison's girls called it. Been doing that for days.

"Sure do. Iced tea and a sandwich, then, one newbuck."

"I can get a drink and a sandwich for a buck?"

"End of the day special. Catch is, you gotta settle for whatever's left in this case here. Pretty well picked over, I'm afraid."

"Sounds good to me. Do I just help myself?"

"Yeah. I can't tell 'em apart, see. Long day?"

"Long day without eating."

"You a musician?"

"I'm — what? What made you think that?"

"Strings on that guitar made a noise when you put down your case."

"Wow."

"Don't see a lot of people carrying around a 12-string."

"OK, I'm impressed. That's not some kind of trick, is it?"

"You working upstairs?"

"I wish. I write letters, I send discs, I go door to door. No one wants to listen to me play."

"You bring that guitar from Australia?"

"The accent's not all gone, is it?"

"I listen real close. You're a singer?"

"Songwriter. Well, I wanted to be."

"I'll listen to you play."

"No, I mean no one will listen to me who's ... Really? You want me to play something? Now?"

"Tell you what. You keep that newbuck. If you move down to the end there and play me a couple tunes, the sandwich is on me, and I'll throw in dessert."

A large black man in a bowling shirt stopped by, picked up a paper and asked Bob for a coffee, stood listening to the girl play her songs for a minute. "Friend of yours?"

"She said nobody would listen to her play; I told her I would."

"Paying her?"

"Lunch."

The man in the bowling shirt listened for another few seconds to the freckled girl with the straight, pointed nose. Then he walked over and laid a five-dollar bill on the counter in front of her. She stared at the bill, half-folded and standing on its edge, trailed off in her song. "Thank you," she said. But she looked sad. It could be a tough town.

As the fellow paid Bob and started across the lobby for the stairs, the girl started playing something else. But this was nothing like the songs she'd been trying to belt out, written in the style of standard two-and-a-half minute pop hits, borrowing all the cliches of the genre. Now, using all her fingers, she played a haunting melody that flowed, seemingly formless, full of diminished sixths. But she played so softly, it was as though she played only for herself.

The man with the coffee and the paper froze, halfway across the lobby toward the wide staircase that curved up to the second floor. He turned around and watched. The girl was oblivious, lost in her music, which was ... ethereal.

He walked back to her, stood silent till she came to an end. She looked much more at ease, now that she'd stopped trying to sing. Her fingers were strong, skilled, etched free of fat by rigorous training. He recognized those fingers. Though as the music swept through her, the muscles in her face relaxed, and he could see just how young she really was. She was petite, freckled, her hair a rusty blonde.

"What was that?" he asked.

She jerked a little. Lost in her reverie, she had apparently forgotten other people were still around.

"Oh, nothing. Sometimes when I'm a little down, the guitar tries to cheer me up, is all. It's not a song or anything.

Sorry."

"Who wrote it?"

"No one. I mean, I guess I did. Except it's nothing, really. It's just something my fingers do."

"When you're tired."

"Yeah."

"Your fingers just play that music."

"Yeah."

"You've had classical training."

"Years and years. Lot of good it does."

"You mean it doesn't help you write hit songs."

"I guess."

"And why do you want to do that?"

"Be a songwriter?"

"There. That's the problem."

"What?"

"Child, you didn't say you needed to write songs. You said you wanted to be a songwriter. That's a hat."

"What?"

"That's putting on a hat. The boy says he wants to be a railroad engineer, but he doesn't really enjoy the heat and the oil and the noise. Fixing the machinery doesn't make his blood sing. He just wants to wear the hat, to be able to say he's the engineer. Your fingers are telling you what you ought to do. You're not a songwriter, child. You're a musician."

"My songs aren't very good, are they?"

"Not that stuff you were playing when I came down. But that's because you haven't been listening for your own song. That last thing you did was your own music — the music that's trying to get out."

"That? That was easy."

"Only for you, child. What on earth made you think you had to write songs like everybody else?"

"The stuff I play when I'm alone doesn't really fit in anywhere."

"And is that the music's fault? Or the fault of the folks who don't know what to do with it because they haven't heard it yet? Or your fault for trying to deny what's inside you? What do you care if it fits in anywhere? Heavens, girl, I hope nobody told you music was a good way to get rich."

"No, I think I got that part figured out."

"What's your name?"

"I'm Kylie."

"Australian."

"Yes. Originally."

"Tell you what. Tuesday and Thursday nights, we set up a microphone and a few amps at Chin's, over on the corner. Around 10 in the evening we play some tracks we're working on, stuff we want to try out in front of a few people. It's no big show; nobody gets paid. But I'll make you a deal. You show up around 9:15, the next couple of nights, you can play a while. None of those made-up songs, though. You just have to promise me to let your fingers sing that music I just heard. Meet a few people. Might even lead to some part-time work, somewhere down the road. What do you say?"

"A job writing songs?"

"No, child. Playing guitar. Depending how things work out, you understand."

"Um, no offense. You're been really nice. But ... do you work there? I mean, if I show up, who do I tell them sent me?"

"No, Miss. I don't work at Chin's. I work upstairs at Rebel Records. If you decide to stop by, you just tell them you're invited — you tell them Marvin asked you to stop by."

The girl watched him walk upstairs.

"He really work at Rebel Records?"

"Depends what you mean by 'work at,' miss."

"Wait a minute. Marvin? Was that —"

"That was 'Long Shot' Jones, Kylie. He kind of runs the place, the way I hear it."

"Long Shot Jones just asked me to come play guitar with some of his guys?"

"That's the way it sounded to me. You ready for that dessert? And by the way, you got a place to stay?"

"What?"

"If you're going to be working with Marvin for a few days, our personnel department will want to make sure you're not sleeping out on the streets. You need a voucher for a motel room or anything?"

"Um ... personnel department?"

❖ ❖ ❖

The elevator to the penthouse opened. It was Hideki.

Andrew had been charting a new bass line for something that sounded like an old Beatles tune. He sat on the piano bench, playing and replaying the same piece of recorded music by rocking a foot pedal. He would try out the new part on his guitar, then lean over to scribble notes on a piece of music paper clipped above the piano keyboard.

He stopped and looked up.

"I've been looking over the plans for The SonicNet raid," Hideki said without preliminaries.

"And?"

"We decided we've used tunnel entry so often they'll be watching for that. That's why we shifted to initial entry over the roof."

"Unh-hunh."

"But that didn't get us enough fighters inside quick enough for the 'fast punch.' That's why we added the North Pole teams, to get a quick breach of the ground floor doors, so we can get more bodies inside faster."

"You're going somewhere with this?"

"That's where I see the problem. We'll be OK if this is all a complete surprise, but what if it's not? What if they're waiting for us?"

"Go on."

"This awards assembly they've scheduled at the new arena is the perfect opportunity. No denying that. But that's got to be obvious to them, too. It practically invites someone to attack their facilities while the staff is at skeleton levels. So what if, as a precaution, they were to put spotters and snipers on the roofs of the buildings adjoining the headquarters, just for that night?"

"Snipers."

"Police snipers would have a clean field of fire against those ground-floor doors. I've gone to take a look. They're naked; no cover from overhead, none at all. Not so much as an awning. Place must have been designed by a German."

"Put someone up there the night before, to take out any snipers as they move into position?"

"I thought the same thing. But I had a look at those rooftops."

That was Hideki for you. He didn't mean he'd asked someone to go check out the rooftops. If he said he'd checked out the rooftops, he meant he'd gotten himself a ladder and put on some kind of painter's jumpsuit and gone and checked the rooftops.

"The problem is, they have too much flexibility in deciding where to place men to cover this building. We don't have the manpower to cover all those positions with counter-snipers, and even if we did, and we started taking them out too soon, they'd be out of radio communication; it would give us away."

"Back to square one."

"Not quite. The Army's doing very badly in the sniper war out West. They've drafted riflemen everywhere — good marksmen get harder to find when a country has spent 40 years indoctrinating the kids that it's a sign of mental illness if you want to touch a gun.

"The Grays themselves don't actually *have* a sniper unit in Gotham. I had Joanie check. When they need shooters they call in Gotham P.D. And at this point, the entire Gotham City police sniper squad is down to six men. Just six.

"If we can set up a situation somewhere at the far end of the city, choose our ground, make them deploy in an area where we can predict exactly where they'll place their snipers ..."

"The timing wouldn't matter. We could clean them out days ahead of time, and they wouldn't immediately link it to the date of the upcoming Lightning Squad award thing."

"Exactly."

"But they could re-staff the unit."

"Before they have their big Wagnerian funeral with the 17-gun salutes? It takes time to train new men to work as a unit. They'll be stunned, nothing like this has ever happened. Police deaths are statistically scattered — no one has ever targeted and eliminated a specific unit, to the man. And they won't see the urgency. They'll have to conduct a review, find a scapegoat, write reports.

"Right. But it sounds complicated. Takes time. You've got to find someone they trust as a snitch to feed them the tip about your location, make it juicy enough that they don't put it on the bottom of the list. Then it's hard to control the timing, how fast they'll respond.

"Picking our own ground, I like that. But you've got to have escape routes for the guys we pre-position on the roofs to take out the snipers, and for the guys you use as bait. Hostage situation? I hate to risk a lot of bystanders."

"Some mixed-use area out in the suburbs," Hideki suggested. "We scout for a location which already has some kind of tunnel access, if not to the buildings directly then something close enough that our men can cut an escape tunnel in advance.

And, if things go well, we might even be able to arrange to take down a helicopter. They tend to grow highly overconfident when they think they've got someone surrounded."

"OK. But you're talking about wet work, up close and personal. Do we have six guys we're sure will cut a throat without you and me freezing our butts up on those roofs for a couple nights, peeing in bottles? Or were you planning on supervising this one up close and personal?"

"If you give us the OK, I'll be there. And yes, Jean-Claude has got more than six real killers. As a matter of fact, Airburst and Quartlow have been getting a little restless. They keep saying we promised them they could take some ears."

"OK, draw it up. But remember, you'll be dealing with regular uniforms, not Lightning Squads."

"I thought we decided we couldn't draw that distinction, any more. The 'regular cops' are deploying in full military gear, now. When the Blues gas and shoot your 'mole people' down in the tunnels, the color of the uniforms doesn't make much difference. These snipers get loaned to the Grays on regular rotations."

Andrew offered no argument. "This will take manpower, and rehearsal time. Spreading us too thin?"

"Let me scout for a location. You can always turn it down after we see how much manpower is needed."

"Talk to Boris about what he can get moving through the pipeline for you. You do want to make sure you get our friend Flanagan's full attention. Maybe a big Barrett .50 at the front door, and something special to bring down your helicopter. Give him a wish list, Boris will tell you how long it'll take."

"Could cost some money."

"The live disc from the grand opening just went platinum. And the Rockin' Rebels are going back into the studio with some new material." Andrew smiled. "We'll try to write you some rockets."

⚜ ⚜ ⚜

OCTOBER ...

Finally the time for Madison's Bitches had come.
Through Joan Matcham, their source close to the mayor
— Madison had no idea who it actually was; that kind of information was need-to-know — reported Sen. Bambi Fiducci
would be speaking at a fund-raising dinner in Gotham. Finally,
a chance to extract the justice for little Tessa and Amber Danielle Scott which the law would never extract. To execute the
senator for violating her oath to protect and defend the rights
of the people, including that inconvenient little "right to keep
and bear arms."

To shoot the bitch.

Ratzo would cover them, waiting below in the tunnels in
case they needed to develop some alternate escape route in a
hurry. There was no map that could compare to his three-di-
mensional knowledge of what lay beneath the city.

Fiducci had been assigned two police bodyguards and a
third, armed policeman as her limo driver for her time in Gotham. In addition, the hotel where she was speaking and especially the parking garage and its basement stairwells — now
recognized as the favorite stalking grounds and escape routes
for the Order of the Arrow — were patrolled by roving pairs
of Lightning Troopers. Not only that, the parking garage was
above ground, and its lighting had been upgraded.

After dismissing the airport — since any getaway there
would likely entail high-speed motor vehicle pursuit, allowing
enemy assets, including helicopter gunships, to gain full traction — three final options were considered:

Killing the state senator and her police guards in the elevator was dismissed, based on the likelihood the guards, even

if severely wounded, could take out one or even two attackers with their sidearms. Though anyone working with the Black Arrow knew they *could* lose their lives, they were not generally given to suicide missions.

Likewise, killing the senator in any of the ladies' rooms she would pass along her route presented problems. First, separate assassins would have to be stationed for long periods in each likely lavatory, risking inquiries. Then, even assuming relatively silent success, a killer, possibly heavily blood-stained, would have to get out past the bodyguard, who would post himself at the door. (None of the hotel restrooms had windows.) And all this was assuming she would even *use* a ladies room, that no doubles would be deployed, and that she wouldn't be assigned a female officer.

This made the banquet hall itself the most likely locale — just as Madison had figured, all along. It was known when the senator would be there. Her guards would be standing some distance away — possibly only one in the room itself. A large number of people would be coming and going, and a young woman dressed in the hotel's fairly generic outfit for waitresses — black slacks, white blouse, burgundy vest — could move around with a tray bearing iced tea or desserts without raising questions from anyone, both in the hall itself and in the kitchen and service corridors.

They considered poison, but the logistics of poisoning only one bowl of soup rather than killing everybody in the hall (or at least at the table) proved cumbersome. Besides, sometimes the speaker spent the dinner hour working the room, simply didn't eat till later.

So it turned out Madison had anticipated correctly there, too. The only way to pull off this hit was with silenced handguns.

⚜ ⚜ ⚜

Rachel came in to see Madison. She'd been crying.

"What is it, babe?" Rachel closed the door to the little office Madison had commandeered from Jean-Claude and his boys off the wings and half a flight down at the back of the theater. Seeing her face, Madison picked up the orange kitten that had been sleeping on the desk and set it down on the floor, where it promptly crawled into a cast-off pasteboard box to resume its nap.

The room didn't look like much, but the whole backstage area was a cascading rat warren of dimly-lit costume rooms, green rooms, dressing rooms ... eventually giving access down to the tunnels and — if you knew the secret — a roundabout route to Ratzo's caverns. Someone was always turning up some intriguing old Elizabethan doublet or Druid's robe or simulated Roman centurion's helmet. Even with its cobwebs and peeling paint, the set-up appealed to anyone who'd ever read with a flashlight under the covers the old stories about hidden treasure caves and dungeons, old castles with secret passages, princesses carried off under the mountains by trolls.

You started to get a feeling for what had drawn Ratzo to his tunnels.

"I don't think I can go," Rachel sobbed. And Rachel was not the kind to break out in waterworks over just any bad day in the bogs.

"The Dupont job."

"I keep trying to tell myself I'll be OK. I ... I know everyone gets nervous and scared. But that's not it."

"This is an all-volunteer outfit, Rachel. We don't shoot deserters."

"It's not that I want to quit. I mean, you'd have every right if you want. To kick me out. It's not that I don't want to earn my keep. This sounds so lame, but it's not that I'm afraid to die. Honest, I've thought about it and thought about it and I don't think that's it ..."

"What is it, Raitch?"

"It's the mission. I don't know if I can kill someone. If it comes time to pull the trigger and I don't, then I put everyone at risk. Right? I keep telling myself, 'Well, everybody feels like this, and when the time comes you'll just do it because you have to.' But then I wake up with these cold sweats, shaking. I wanted to talk to someone about it. I've been seeing Nguyen, but I just didn't feel like I could talk to him about this. He's not family, you know? Mission security and all. How could I explain what it's about? So I got no one to talk to. I just feel like such a rat."

Madison stood up and put her hand on Rachel's shoulder. Rachel had been her best friend, out in the streets. Tiny and conny as she was, she'd never shied from a fight.

Raitch bent her head to lay her cheek across the back of Madison's hand, making no effort to wipe her tears. Madison took her in her arms and hugged her.

"You did right to come to me, allana."

"I don't know."

"There'll be plenty of missions. We'll take Caitlin this time. And you were right not to talk to Nguyen. He can't be vetted for any work outside the building, since he doesn't show up on any of my duty rosters, which is something you need to bring up with Jean-Claude and Bob if you decide things are going to get any more serious, there. Not telling you how to live your life, macushla. You just gotta consider what it'll be like, being with someone you can't talk to about stuff."

"Now I feel like such a piece of shit. What if Caitlin goes and something happens to her? No, never mind. I'll go. I'll be fine." She pulled away, shook herself, pulled out a Kleenex, wiped her eyes.

"No one's questioning your courage, Raitch. This isn't going to leave this room. I don't need to give a reason to change the lineup. Caitlin has some waitress experience. Not as much as Kiera, but some."

"Look, I'm sorry I came."

"Rachel, this one's closed. It took courage to come see me. Butterflies in your stomach is one thing, but when you get a message this strong, you're supposed to listen. It's the only way we survived on the streets as long as we did. Right?"

"That's the way it felt."

"We'll talk more after the mission. We'll find one that's right for you."

"You sure?"

"Subject's closed, babe. Everything happens for a reason. Don't give it another thought."

"We're still OK?"

"We're tight."

Raitch closed the door behind her, quietly.

Nguyen not being on any of the duty rosters wasn't unique — the Chins had brought some other kitchen help with them that weren't involved in resistance work. But Madison had thought they were all family. And Nguyen wasn't Chinese — that was a Vietnamese name, wasn't it? She'd have to remember to ask Bob or Jean-Claude about that.

Right now she had to find a missing kitten, before she forgot and locked him in.

❖ ❖ ❖

3:30 P.M. THURSDAY, OCT. 16, THE YEAR 2031

Daniel Brackley had instructed Tanya to come over to the mayor's mansion in the afternoon to service him before he went off to the big fund-raising dinner for State Senator Fiducci, who they all assumed would be a shoe-in to Congress, what with her strong record on gun control.

Was it shoe-in, or shoo-in? Some of these American expressions still confused Tanya. At least "shoe" was a real word. What was a "shoo"? She wished Yuri were here to ask.

Daniel hadn't invited Tanya to go to the dinner with him, of course. She was just his whore.

Arriving, she had to pull the door closed against a wind that was already starting to lift the first of the autumn leaves in random corkscrews. There was a meeting of the building restoration committee going on in the sunny porch off the kitchen, servants padding around providing coffee and tea and cookies as the ladies discussed the mayor's big Christmas party — the politically correct Americans insisted on calling it the "Holiday Gala," of course — which would be held here at the mansion this year, doubling as a fund-raiser to collect money for yet another renovation of the drafty old barn.

It was warm here, out of the wind. She stuck her head in and said Hi, since she recognized a few faces, including her friend Buffy, who had been sent to approach her shortly after Yuri had gone off to prison.

The resistance knew how she'd been extorted into becoming the mayor's ... Buffy had been too polite, so Tanya had finished the sentence for her.

"Whore."

"And we know you're not the only one."

"Yes, I know that, too."

Then Buffy had explained. The prison where Yuri had originally been sent was in Connecticut. But now, they had learned, he would be transferred to a facility further west ... much closer to rebel territory.

"No!" Tanya was upset at the prospect of no longer being able to visit him twice a month.

"Listen to me," her old friend Buffy had explained to her — amazing Tanya with both her firmness and her intimate knowledge of the current state of the resistance movement. If the petite, fluttering socialite Tanya thought she'd known had

SUPRYNOWICZ

merely been an act on Buffy's part, it had been a damned good one. "This is good news. You can act disappointed when you hear Yuri is being moved — you should — but don't fight it too hard. Create the impression you're much more interested in spending more time with the mayor, now, anyway."

"He'll never believe that."

"Sure he will. Bring him little presents. Buy fancy frilly underwear and ask him if it makes you look pretty. Act like a schoolgirl with a crush on him. Any man will believe this, because it's what they all want to believe. Women are completely inscrutable to them. They look at it like playing a slot machine; they have no idea why their number occasionally comes up, so they never ask why. As far as they're concerned, everyone else you've ever known was a fag, they're the first man to ever show you how good a penis feels, and their number's past due to come up, anyway."

"Why? Why should I do this, when I'd rather kill myself?"

Buffy had explained it, then. They would try to stage a raid and break Yuri out, carry him off to the free states of New Columbia, where Tanya could be sent to join him. But they wanted something in the meantime. They wanted her to spend more time with the mayor, listen and learn what she could, pass along whatever information she gleaned. They wanted her to be a spy.

In the end, it had given her something to live for. It had allowed her to feel she was fighting back, in the only way she could. Tanya had felt nothing when she learned Dominic Cantari, the lead investigator who had helped frame the case against her Yuri, had been killed by the resistance. She couldn't even remember the man's face. He was only one among so many who had conspired to ruin their lives, from the legislators who passed the absurd drug laws through the judge who had sentenced Yuri to more time in prison than they gave murderers and rapists — Yuri, who had never hurt a fly, who didn't even use drugs, let alone grow or sell them.

To her, it had been a faceless mob of oppressors. Daniel Brackley, at least — pathetic and mundane as he was — gave evil a face. And this thing they asked her to do was something she *could* do. It had given her hope.

Now, Buffy smiled and said hello, along with most of the other wealthy, important, idle socialites who had taken it upon themselves to raise some money for needed renovations of the two-century old mayor's mansion, a drafty old Revolutionary era farmhouse which had actually been used to store feed for the zoo animals during the Second World War — a function to which it was much better suited, in Tanya's estimation. There wasn't a warm, properly padded velvet couch in the whole place. What good was it being rich and powerful if you were going to live in a museum made out of hard sticks with no comfortable place to sit? Sometimes these Americans astonished her — it had to have something to do with the Protestant church.

The fresh hot coffee smelled good, though no one offered her any.

She knew the women would give each other knowing looks as she proceeded upstairs to disappear into the mayor's quarters for an hour before he came down to leave for his fancy banquet. Well, so what? None of them was obliged to publicly acknowledge what *they* put up with in private to stay among the wealthy and powerful. Tanya knew at least one of those ladies was married to a judge who preferred little boys in matched pairs; did anyone roll their eyes and ask where *her* children had come from?

Upstairs, she stripped down to the fancy, frilly red underwear she'd bought to surprise Daniel, showed off her curvaceous figure for his approval. He was distracted, talking on the cell phone, showed only the minimum required appreciation before he started to take his pants off. Always so romantic, her Daniel Brackley.

He sat on the bed, beckoned for her to pull off her panties and kneel on top of him, his favored position of late. She had no idea if the bed was as old as most of the furnishings and always wondered if it was going to collapse. Tanya stroked him into a state of arousal and slid her clean-shaven pussy — he had expressed a preference for her to shave — onto his manhood, finally convincing him to put down the phone and place his hands on her chest. Not happy holding her through her red bra, he undid the hooks and started squeezing her naked breasts as she picked up her pace, leaning back and working them both into a sweat.

But of course the phone rang again. A lot going on today, it appeared.

"So they're all in position? In the hotel and in the tunnels? Great. We'll bag 'em like rabbits in a net."

Tanya pretended not to be listening, though she did wonder, idly, if Americans really netted rabbits. Did they drive them on horseback? It didn't sound very efficient. So they were expecting the resistance to try and take out Sen. Fiducci tonight — as well they should. The bitch had won election by promising to take more guns away from the people, while Tanya knew this Fiducci and her young daughter never traveled anywhere themselves — not even to the private school the daughter attended so she wouldn't be turned into a brain-damaged leech like the rest of the populace — without an armed bodyguard.

These Americans, so pathetic. They started out an armed nation, a free people, the most literate nation in the world — they had everything people around the world fought for and dreamed of — and now they gave up their arms and their heritage of real education like sheep. Hadn't they seen what Hitler and Stalin managed to accomplish once the populations were disarmed and the state finished taking over the schools?

"And Newby?" Daniel was asking, paying less attention to Tanya now and starting to lose his erection. "Two of them, inside his headquarters? Excellent. Where? What do you mean he didn't tell you? Goddamn it, I keep telling you, intelligence has to flow *up*. Yes, I know he wants to be sure before he passes stuff along. Get back to him and tell him we need to know as soon as possible. What if something happens to those agents? Tell him to call me after the banquet. Yes, before midnight."

"Darling," Tanya whispered as she licked his ear. "How can I please you if you won't pay attention?"

He clicked off the phone, finally, put his hands on her hips, and helped her get her rhythm going again. She pulled his shirt open and dug her long nails into the hair of his chest. "That's my big boy," she crooned as he took one of her breasts into his mouth and started suckling her. And now she was up to full speed, rocking up and down on him, clutching his stubby penis between her labia and her thighs until she brought him to his climax. Finally.

⚜ ⚜ ⚜

4:43 P.M. THURSDAY, OCT. 16, THE YEAR 2031

"Where you off to in such a hurry?"

It was Daniel. He'd come back into the bedroom. His keys.

"My sister, hon." Tanya's mind raced. "I told you I had to see her this evening. You kept me later than I expected." She raised one eyebrow, smiled at his crotch. Calling him "such a stud" would have been laying it on too thick.

But he was watching her face. Damn it. She usually hugged a pillow, thought of Yuri, took her time getting dressed. Now he knew there was something wrong, even if he wasn't sure what it was. Why the hell couldn't she have waited till he was safely gone? You're such an amateur, Tanya! And now she was not fully convincing him — his antennae were detecting something wrong.

"No," he said, after a long pause. "Evans?" His bodyguard stuck his head around the corner from the hallway. Daniel didn't give a damn if they saw her half-clothed. She was not expected to have any dignity. "Tanya is coming with me to the dinner for Senator Fiducci this evening. Till then she won't be leaving the residence. You understand?"

"Yes sir," said the armed Lightning Trooper.

"Daniel," she said, doing her best to smile with incomprehension. "What's going on? I'd love to go, but you should have told me much sooner. Elena will wonder where I am."

"Well, then," he smiled back, his eyes darting to the phone on the desk. "Just phone her, and make your apologies."

She willed herself not to look at the phone. He had realized she knew too much about what was happening tonight; the trap for the Black Arrow. He was daring her to use the phone to tip someone off. It would be tapped and monitored, of course.

"Darling, I have nothing to wear."

"You've got plenty of outfits in the closet, here."

"Nothing suitable for a dinner at the Dupont Center, love. You have to let me go home and get something appropriate."

He examined her face again.

"No. You'll look lovely, regardless. Just do the best you can. We leave in half an hour." He smiled again, that cold smile, pocketed his keys, and left. He wasn't sure, then, or he would have had her arrested on the spot. But now what? How was she to get the word out? He'd be watching for her to give herself away.

At least he'd closed the door behind him. She continued dressing, now eyeing the phone. Could she get a message out in some kind of code? No, she had nothing pre-arranged, any such attempt would sound stilted and ridiculous and would never be understood before someone came in to cut her off.

Make a break out the window, like some trapeze artist? Equally ridiculous. She'd probably break an ankle, if they didn't find her hanging out there, dangling from the Christmas lights. Later, downstairs, she might manage to slip away. And then what? Run across the stubble of the November fields in her high heels? Flag down a passing car? It was all ridiculous.

There had to be another way. Who else was in the building?

The restoration committee! Was Buffy still here? She dialed downstairs and asked. Just left.

"Oh, gosh, I needed to borrow a pair of shoes she has in her car. Could you just check and see if you can catch her?"

The phone laid down on the table. Waiting. Waiting. Waiting. God, please. And then, an answer to her prayers.

"Tanya, where are you?"

"I'm upstairs, dear. This is so embarrassing. There's a change of plans and I'm going out to dinner with the mayor. But I simply don't have a pair of evening shoes that I'd be caught dead in. And then I remembered you carry a pair in your car. Would you be a darling?" Please. Buffy. Please be smart.

"Well of course, dear. Dinner with the senator, that's wonderful. I don't have much, but let me go see what I dig out of the Magic Bag of Tricks. Shall I come up?"

"No, I'll meet you downstairs. And maybe a wrap, if you have something."

Hose. Something black from the closet. A black dress was always good. She was only supposed to be his dumb Russian whore, after all. As long as it showed off her tits, the men wouldn't know any better. And the women would hate her, anyway. Some black shoes, inappropriately low heeled. And then she was out the door, past the ridiculous guard, who would traipse down the stairs after her like a panting dog.

Buffy was coming in the door as she reached the bottom

of the stairs. Thank God, she had two pair of heels in her hands that might work. Buffy was a petite little thing, of course, not a plowhorse like Tanya. But they were all straps; and what did it matter if her feet hurt? When did they ever not hurt? And she had four or five dresses and wraps over her arm, as well. Men could carry a tire iron and a flashlight and think they were prepared for anything; a woman's emergencies were of a different nature.

"You're a life-saver!" Tanya gushed. "Come, we'll see if I can squeeze into anything." She led her to the downstairs powder room. It was highly unlikely to be bugged, but Tanya turned on the faucet and flushed the toilet to generate a little noise, anyway.

"I know what it's like," Buffy confided. "Men have no idea; think they can change a date from the bowling alley to the Philharmonic on five minutes' notice."

Tanya locked the door. "Buffy, the dinner tonight is a trap."

"What?"

"Make sure you're not tailed as you leave. Then call them off. The banquet room will be stacked with plainclothesmen, and there are Grays in the tunnels."

"Shit." Buffy had not been specifically briefed on any planned hit on Sen. Fiducci. But it made sense.

"It gets worse. There are two spies inside the building."

"The hotel?"

"No, Buffy. Inside the headquarters."

"Whose?"

"His."

"They know where the Black Arrow's headquarters is?"

"Only Newby knows. He's the handler. Can anyone get to him?"

"I don't know. Jesus. *Two* spies? Do you have names?"

"No."

There was a soft rap on the door. Buffy told whoever it

was that they'd just be a minute. Tanya set to work trying on shoes. The dresses would never fit, but with the black high heels and one of the wraps she'd do.

"Will you be OK?" Buffy asked her.

"I would have killed myself months ago if you hadn't gotten to me, given me some hope."

"I've never told you how sorry I am that we had to ask you to ... to do this."

"Buffy, dear, I was already here. You didn't create the situation. Although you have no idea. Sometimes when we're together he even dresses up in a black mask and cape and pretends to be the Black Arrow. I mean, that's all he wears, you understand, the mask and cape, and that orange necktie. Does that make any sense? The Black Arrow stands against everything Daniel represents, right?"

"Tanya, there are things about the minds of people who seek power over others that we can never really understand. They're clever, don't get me wrong. They're brilliant in their own way, and very dangerous. We may even think we have them figured out. But there are depths of madness there that it may not be healthy to even TRY to understand. I'm sorry we've put you in danger."

"I survive. And it's you who'll be in danger, if we don't get you out of here right now."

"Nonsense. Didn't you know? The mayor hopes to marry his nephew off to me — though from what I've heard, that's a young man who's not to be ordered around so easily. Apparently the Brackley organization doesn't get enough of the Summers family fortune every election cycle."

"Don't underestimate Daniel. The man has plans within plans. Now let's get you out of here."

Tanya sent Buffy on her way, gushing thanks for the clothes. A couple stray Lightning Troopers and Tanya's personal warden just rolled their eyes. Women.

Buffy checked her rear-view several times as she drove

away. Fortunately she carried multiple cellulars, encrypted and anonymized through offshore satlinks, thanks to Joan Matcham the computer whiz. No one in the Gotham Building knew Buffy by name. But if it was Joan who called, they'd perk up their ears.

❖ ❖ ❖

5:06 P.M. THURSDAY, OCT. 16, THE YEAR 2031

Andrew and Hideki and Jimmy Chin had taken a late afternoon meeting at a trendy raw food joint way the hell out in Bayside Queens — which meant they were most of the way to Great Neck — with the managers of two of their most far-flung neighborhood dojos — both of whom appeared to be in need of some guidance.

Andrew was briefly interested in the restaurant operation when he saw the prices they were getting for what amounted to fermented beancurd cakes garnished with seaweed and walnuts. With a better location, some proper promotion, and a menu that didn't look like someone had locked their pet monkey in the Xerox room with a whole shitload of green construction paper ...

... but no. When he took a minute to watch a little more closely, he changed his mind.

The place wasn't mobbed, despite the fact it was new and trendy. And "trendy" was a two-edge sword. The high prices were dictated by the low volume and the highly labor intensive food preparation methods. The place was full of what looked like refugees from the Berlin underground. When this pale and pierced flock of dissipated dietary Calvinists moved on and business dropped off there would be staff turnover, and it would be hard as hell to train new staff on the fly to do all this hand-finish work. The owners would end up exhausted wrecks, doing all the work at night and sticking it in the cooler for next-day sale. Marriages had foundered on less.

Andrew hoped for their sakes he was wrong. But he wasn't.

And most of all, Andrew just didn't like the stuff very much. You had to be careful not to fall for all that "Midas touch" publicity that got written about you in the business magazines by folks who had no idea how much detail work went into making it look like you could just wave a magic wand. The secret was rejecting 98 percent of the ideas that came along — only developing the ones that made you chuckle in your sleep.

They shook hands with the two managers and sent them on their way. One of them looked like he was headed for Death Row. Master Liu had spoken warmly about the progress the students were making. But the other fellow, a wiry Armenian who'd married a Filipina girl and come into the business managing a traveling martial arts stage show, had been less talkative. He seemed to feel he was at a disadvantage, though he'd loosened up and answered briskly enough when Andrew asked him a few questions about his financial reports. He was bright and quick ... still in fine physical shape ... but obviously frustrated.

"Are they both loyal?" Andrew asked when they'd gone.

"Yes," said Hideki.

"And Master Liu is liked by his students?"

"Oh, yes. Respected, but also liked. He has endless patience."

"The Armenian is not as patient."

"Just the opposite. And he's smart enough to know it's not working out. His class numbers are down, and that's against his higher rent in Port Washington — he chose a great location but it's not cheap. I don't think he'll be surprised if we tell him we have to close him down, or let him go."

"No." Andrew had decided. "Adajian had his nutrition-ist give free consultations. She suggestion-sold their nutrition products and tripled their volume. And he's done better with the older clientele, which is good business — they have money and they don't move around as much.

"Get back to the two of them separately. Tell Adajian we know he'll be disappointed to give up his direct contact with the students, but we need him to run both his studio and Master Liu's for now — we'll be giving him more studios to manage as quickly as he can expand his staff to handle them. Tell him Master Liu will be promoted as the head instructor for both facilities — he'll be the one with his picture in all the windows. But Master Liu will just be on salary — Adajian runs the busi-ness end, Master Liu works for him. Tell Adajian the challenge will be integrating both the studios to run on the same business model. Stress efficiencies of scale — he can save money by bulk purchasing for both.

"Give Adajian a choice of a raise, or a bigger cut. He's smart, he'll probably take the percentage. Master Liu hires the assistant trainers, but give Adajian complete control of hiring and training everyone else, the nutritionists and especially the sales staff, and setting up their commission plans — tell him when he finds the right people, the sky's the limit. His goal is for his sales people to make at least as much as he makes. More. Do we know the wife?"

"She's good people. And the staff like her."

"Tell him he's free to offer her a good position as his as-sistant if he wants to, but it's up to him. Everything we do has to make it clear to him that he's in charge. If he blossoms the way I think he will, bring both him and the wife down to the Gotham, we'll see if he's not the guy to handle rifle distribu-tion for this part of town, too."

"Taking away Master Liu's studio. He'll be hurt."

"Not if it's presented right to him and to the students. The man knows nothing about running a business. He doesn't even know how much he pays for electricity, for God's sake, so he can't possibly enjoy that part of things. He'll be the master instructor at both dojos — stagger his hours. Gin up some promotion, put his name and picture on some full-color T-shirts. Call Sue Weatherford at Rebel Records PR and tell her we want some of the magazine writers she knows to do features on Master Liu — an ancient discipline at the crossroads of the modern age.

"Make a big deal about this, you have to sell it with some excitement. Tell him we understand he's a modest man, but it's for the good of the school. Also tell Master Liu he needs to start picking a few of his most advanced students and groom them to become instructors in their own right, so eventually he can supervise the training staff at even more facilities by placing his star pupils there. The ability to promote his best students will mean much more to him than money for himself. Tell him his time is much too valuable to waste hiring janitors and paying the electric bill — we're going to let Adajian take those tiresome burdens away so Master Liu can concentrate on passing along his art."

Jimmy Chin and Hideki smiled and nodded. This wasn't just tinkering around the edges. It had drama, yet no one had to be fired. Finding people's strengths was just what Andrew always preached. But to actually do it ... Jimmy Chin wondered if he would ever have the boldness.

They talked about the food as they settled up to leave. A passing comment brought up the subject of Nguyen, the new cook at Chin's.

"You mean he's not a blood relative of yours?" Andrew asked.

"Oh, no. But I went to elementary school with him," Jimmy Chin replied.

"So you've known him all these years? You know where his mother lives? You've always been close?"

"No, not really. He moved away when we were eight. It

was a big surprise when he came around, asking if we needed any help in the new restaurant."

"But you recognized him right away as your old childhood friend."

"After all these years? No, he had to remind me who he was."

"And you were out of touch all that time? The last time you saw him had been ... more than 10 years? You have no idea where he went to high school, whether he went to college?"

"No. Do we have a problem here? He remembered a lot about where we used to live."

"Who hired him?"

"My mom."

"But I was very clear about that, Jimmy. Family is OK; anyone else has to go through Bob, and then Jean-Claude for a security check. No one else checked out this Nguyen before your mom hired him?"

"I guess not. You think he's trouble?"

Andrew was already on his phone as they reached the sidewalk, dialing Jean-Claude. But he couldn't get through. Bob's newsstand would be closed by this time of day, and Madison was off running a mission. Quart Low Cavanaugh was taking some time off to visit his family — you tended to forget these guys had real families out there in the real world, grown children leading normal lives as architects or engineers or federal prison inmates — or even boot-strapping new businesses into existence "across the line" in tax-free New Columbia.

"He's unusually tall and well-groomed to be working as a cook, isn't he?"

"Yes, we've even joked, he looks more like a guy who should be in some junior executive program ...""

"Yeah."

"Oh my God."

"Is he seeing any of the girls?"

"What?"

"Has he started dating any of the girls in the building?"

"Rachel is pretty sweet on him; everybody talks about it. You think ..."

"They're taught to do that. You can learn more in one night of pillow talk then a month listening at the water cooler."

"You think he's not Nguyen at all?"

"They could have interviewed the real Nguyen, gotten all the background they needed for this guy to convince you. Or maybe he *is* the kid you knew years ago. More than a decade goes by, a guy can go into the military, the police, all kinds of things can happen. Call us a cab, Jimmy. Somebody's been leaking information on our plans, and if they've got someone inside the building now, everyone could be in jeopardy."

Several of the Chin grandchildren were now driving cabs around the city. It gave the outfit mobile eyes on the streets; no one would get curious about seeing a cab almost anywhere. It also amounted to a private limousine service, far faster than calling in someone who'd have to fight his way out of a garage, into traffic, and across town.

Tommy Chin had dropped them off and had remained cruising the area east of the Van Wyck Expressway. He said he could be there for the pick-up in minutes, but warned them it was now past 5. Between fighting rush-hour traffic across the bridges and avoiding the new security checkpoints, they'd be at least an hour getting back to the Gotham Block — could be 90 minutes.

And now the call came in from Joan Matcham. Two spies — not one but two — expected to report the location of the Black Arrow's headquarters before midnight. The Fiducci hit at the Dupont Center a trap. Andrew told her to hold one and tried Madison's cell. It was dead. It was standard procedure to deactivate all phones before the start of a raid, of course, since if they were live the phones could be tracked even if they weren't in actual use.

Andrew checked his watch. Yep; the Bitches were due in

position before 5 o'clock; cocktails would precede the 6:30 dinner at the Dupont Center ballroom. Madison and her crew would be inside by now, taking the role of fill-in waitresses, waiting for the senator to show up and take her seat.

He dialed Jean-Claude again, reached him this time, told him to go to full alert; start scanning for any cell phone traffic from inside the building. He was to grab and hold and isolate Nguyen and meantime keep trying to raise Madison or Ratzo to warn them it was a trap, though it was unlikely there'd be any way to do that without blowing their cover completely.

Meantime, as soon as they got back Hideki would start assembling an extraction team. Even as they were securing the Gotham Building he intended to send a team to try and bring out Madison and ... anybody else who survived.

Of course, they could all be killed or captured by now. But Madison was strong and resourceful, and he had to try. He pictured those girls fighting and dying against insurmountable odds. Yeah, forget the "captured" part. Madison wasn't likely to just put her hands up.

He clicked Joan back onto the line. They discussed the fact that — even if he and Jean-Claude could locate and neutralize two spies inside the building — the very failure of two agents to report would tip off their handler. He'd know which two agents were missing; he'd know where they'd been assigned; therefore he'd know by default that the Gotham Building was his target.

And now came the only good news. The mayor had been upset because the handler had not yet told anyone where these two agents were. The handler — the cut-out — was Newby, the former mayoral assistant who had done so well bringing in the Arts Center job that they'd rewarded him with a curious pocket commission into the Grays. Of course, if he was actually the Gray spymaster, that would explain a lot. ...

So *if* they could eliminate the two spies, they'd be okay ... providing someone could also take out the mayor's personal favorite, the man who had finally gotten the Brackley Arena finished, Christian Newby ... deep inside SonicNet headquarters ... in the next couple of hours.

Newby had to be grabbed or killed — which meant killed, if you were going to be practical about it — and it had to be done tonight. And they only knew one person inside SonicNet headquarters who *might* be on their side. ...

⚜ ⚜ ⚜

5:26 P.M. THURSDAY, OCT. 16, THE YEAR 2031

There was a knock on Jack's apartment door. He opened it, and his dreams came true.

Well, maybe.

It was Joan. Petite, freckled, the Bjorn earring on her high, sharp, elven ear, the bright blue eyes, those brunette bangs, so beautiful he could just eat her up. She carried a long cardboard tube, the kind you'd use to store a rolled-up movie poster.

"Babe," he said. "This is great. But I thought you couldn't be seen —"

"You need to invite me in and close the door," she smiled, though she seemed a little nervous.

"Sure." He closed the door. And they kissed. It was not like kissing your grandma. Without realizing it, he lifted her off the floor. She wrapped her legs around him.

"Oh baby," was about all Jack could get out, as he finally let her slide down to the floor. (He had to hold her a little off to the side.)

"Turn on the radio real loud," she said into his ear. "We need to talk."

He did. She steered him into the kitchen, away from any windows, past the bookshelves she'd been filling up for him

409

with H.L. Mencken and Frederic Bastiat, John Ross and John Taylor Gatto.

"Jack, I love you and I want to make love to you and I'm going to make love to you but I need to talk to you first, because I don't ever want you to think I just made love to you to get you to make this decision."

"Joan, honey. You want to relax a little. I think the decision you're talking about was made a long time ago, in that day care center downtown. I've just been dragging my feet a little, not sure when the time would be right to do something about it."

"I wish I didn't have to ask you this. I wanted you to come over to us on your own. And what I have to ask could put your life at risk. You have to know that I want you more than anything. And if you say no, if you can't do this, I'll understand and I'll still love you. Honest I will."

"I think you'd better just tell me, honey."

"The Grays have two spies in the Black Arrow's headquarters. Had. They're being taken care of. But when they don't report in, their handler will know where the headquarters is, and he'll report it to your uncle. So eliminating the spies isn't enough."

"Who's the handler?"

"Newby."

"And he has to be ... killed."

"Today. This evening. Before midnight."

"Jeez."

"They had to ask. They had to send me to ask. I couldn't let anyone else do it."

"Joan, I'm a soldier. At least, I'm supposed to be. I never thought 'joining the resistance' meant all I had to do was sign a petition and march in a parade. Soldiers kill people. They put their lives at risk to kill people. I'm good with that. It's just shooting someone in the back that I've got a little problem with."

"Good. Because you're not going to shoot him in the back." She opened the end of the cardboard tube, tipped it so the article that had been rattling around inside there could slide out into the light of day, handling it gingerly.

"Assuming you can get this in there, you're going to shove this through his heart."

It was about 33 inches long, with its warhead, which was wrapped in white paper. It was an arrow. And it was, of course, solid black.

Jack took it, tested the strength of its polyfiber construction, felt its weight and heft, started to peel the paper off the warhead.

"Not till you're ready to use it, hon. Poison."

She was right. It wasn't fair that she had to be the one to ask him. It wasn't fair that he had to decide, at all. But who ever promised life would be fair? Now he had to choose — stay on his uncle's career path to fame and fortune, that seat in Congress his dad had never lived to run for ... or follow his heart and join a resistance that was probably doomed ... the resistance his father had given his life trying to start, he reminded himself.

"Listen, Babe. I know the circumstances are a little weird, so if you gotta leave, I understand. But I'm not due in till seven, which means we've got more than an hour before I have to leave. Actually, it would look funny if I went in early. So, um, since I've got some time to kill before I take this little thing and go make myself the world's most wanted criminal, if you'd have any interest in ..."

She kissed him again. He held her as tight as he could. She tore open his shirt, and wrapped her legs around him. He carried her to the bedroom. They both knew their first time might also be their last. Well, that wasn't quite true, actually. She was so beautiful with her clothes off — Jack simply couldn't believe those magnificent thrusting little breasts, the smooth curve of her butt, the marvel of the delicate downy hair guarding the most beautiful and perfect part of her, could all actually be his — that the first time didn't really take all that long, truth be told. He was amazed just to find that — as petite as she was, and as large and hard and throbbing as Jack had become — she could nonetheless take him entirely inside her without any trouble.

He marveled. He'd been afraid of hurting her. She laughed, kissed him gently. "Silly. I have to be wide enough there for the heads of our babies, don't I? Anyway, it probably helps that just kissing you makes me so wet I feel like I need a diaper. So why don't you just not worry about it, darling? You just keep doing what comes naturally, and I'll tell you if you hurt me. Because right now I'm loving every inch of you."

Of course, such talk only made him harder. So it was their second time that might be their last. No, their third. That was it. Their third time might be the last time they would ever make love in this world. OK, the fourth time. She had her legs draped over his shoulders now, to give him a better angle of entry, they were both laughing and crying at the same time, and Jack and Joan agreed the fourth time might be the last time they would ever make love in this world ...

CHAPTER 12

The most difficult struggle of all is the one within ourselves.
Let us not get accustomed and adjusted to these conditions.
The one who adjusts ceases to discriminate between good
and evil. He becomes a slave in body and soul. Whatever
may happen to you, remember always: Don't adjust! Revolt
against the reality!

— MORDECHAI ANIELEWICZ (1919-1943), WARSAW, 1943

Kill one, terrify a thousand.

— SUN TZU, "THE ART OF WAR"

6:44 P.M. THURSDAY, OCT. 16, THE YEAR 2031

All hell had broken loose in the Dupont Conference Center ballroom. Kiera had gotten the senator, alright, walked
right up behind the whore while carrying a tray of iced tea
and put two shots through the back of her chair, head down
in her endive salad, snorting her last breath through balsamic
vinaigrette. There were two rounds "safely stored," you fascist

bitch.

But then the whole back end of the room had come alive with undercover cops who had been disguised as regular dinner guests in evening wear, drawing down from their tables.

A suppressor wasn't really a "silencer," of course, except perhaps on a little .22. The first round of .45 had been clearly audible, like a champagne cork being popped. The second shot added the beginning of the louder cracking noise the end of a rug sometimes makes when you take it outside to shake out the dust. The bullet had started to go supersonic just before entering the back of the chair, even though the low-powder rounds in Kiera's gun weren't supposed to.

Madison's backup team had sprung into action, laying down covering fire from the kitchen doors as most of the diners shrieked and dove for the floor. They'd set up a radio jammer in the basement, as usual, and at least one or two of the cops kept removing and reinserting their pistol mags, indicating the device was doing its job and that this pair of bollocks still carried the absurd "personalized" issue pistols.

But not all of them, unfortunately. Kiera had taken a round in the belly, point blank, from a cop who'd been posing as one of the waiters.

Madison had lined up and drilled him through the back of the head as soon as she spotted him bringing out his piece, but he'd fired into Kiera a split-second sooner.

Kiera made it to the kitchen. Madison directed her and the rest of the squad to rally at the freight elevators as she stayed behind, prepared to stand her ground there behind the warming tables, buying them time.

Sure enough, two undercover cops, their enthusiasm or zeal for promotion outracing whatever brains they had, came through the door. Madison double-tapped them both, and then again. One of them got off two rounds as he went down; she heard the chunks of lead clang into some kind of kitchenware on the shelf behind her.

That'd slow down the pursuit. But it also called for a magazine change.

It didn't occur to her at the time there was anything unusual about the fact she'd just put down three professional government men. There were reasons. She'd taken the first one in the back of the head. For the second and third, she knew the ground and was behind partial cover; they had no idea what they were going to find as they came through that door. More importantly, though, police officers were trained to shoot only in certain circumstances — even the quickest of them spent valuable fractions of a second making the trigger decision. Madison had decided at the outset that, if their quick exit was delayed, she would kill anything that moved.

She reloaded, pocketed her empty, backpedaled out through the rear kitchen door and into the service corridor that led to the timecard room and the freight elevator.

Where she met her team coming back the other way. With Ratzo.

"What the hell?"

"Grays in the tunnels," Ratzo panted. "I barely got out in time to warn you."

"Alternate routes?"

"I tried them all. No good. They're everywhere."

"How's Kiera?"

"On my feet."

Beautiful Kiera, fairest of them all with her ski-slope nose, Kiera whose hair shone like copper in the sun, was pale as a ghost now. Blood from the belly wound had soaked her pants all the way to the knee. Her breathing was growing more shallow. They all knew she was likely to die, and not pleasantly. She might live a couple hours without treatment, but she'd be in a world of hurt pretty soon. She seemed to have trouble focusing her eyes, as though she were gazing off at the horizon, seeing the black coach and four.

Madison had wanted to do the tap herself. But Kiera had actually worked as a hotel waitress, back in Ohio. It made more sense to use someone who could fit in with the work force without looking lost, work the floor without dropping her tray. Still, if it had been Madison, she might have taken out that damned cop before she'd been hit. ...

And then, before she could second-guess herself any further, something in Madison clamped down. She wouldn't have known how to explain it, she just knew one of two things was about to happen, and which one it was to be depended on her. Four able-bodied fighters stood there, watching her for a sign, any sign. Either she was going to lose it and panic and they were all going to die, or she was going to pretend to have everything under perfect control, and make them believe it, and maybe — just maybe — some of them would walk out of this alive.

"OK, everybody reload, unscrew those suppressors, and pocket 'em. This time through, we want to be nice and loud."

"What are we doing, boss?"

"We're going right back the way we came."

"You're kidding."

"It's the last thing they'll expect. Kiera, can you shoot, or should Ratzo take your gun?"

"I wouldn't miss this for the fucking world." Her pale skin glistened with sweat.

"If we take your gun and you sit on the floor right here they'll get you to a hospital, jewel. Coming with us, I can't promise how soon that'll happen."

"You're kidding, right? I stick with my family. I die with you guys."

"OK. Just giving you the choice. Ratzo, once you're seen with us you can't be captured. You're like a living map; you know too much. So: Any way for you to slip out of here?"

"No, they were right behind us."

"Are you packed?"

"What?"

"Do you have a gun?"

"No."

"Stay right next to Kiera. If any one of us goes down, you pick up that gun and keep moving with us, moving and firing. You know how to change a magazine?"

"I'm not sure."

She showed him the mag release button on her .45, how to seat a fresh mag with the heel of his hand, made him do it himself, then made him rack the slide. 50-50 chance he'd manage it, but she was out of time.

"Hey, what's the difference between a woman and a gun?" Ratzo asked.

"What?"

"You can buy a silencer for a gun."

"That's great, Ratzo."

"How else is a gun better than a woman?"

"Ratzo."

"The gun you keep at home doesn't mind if you have a spare that you use when you're on the road."

"Jimmy, we'll continue this later. Right now I need you to focus. You can't let yourself be captured, Jimmy. I'm sorry you're here, but you can't let yourself be interrogated. Do you understand what I'm saying?"

"Yes." Ratzo said. She couldn't tell if it had really sunk in. Even if it came to that she'd give him less than a 50-50 chance of pulling it off — it wasn't like they had handy little cyanide pills — but what could she do? She wasn't going to just pop him; it wasn't like she had extra shooters. Ratzo was only doing his best; none of this was his fault. Besides, it would be terrible for morale. Now, if he went down and he couldn't walk but it looked like he was going to survive and be captured ... well, hopefully that was one decision she wouldn't have to make.

"And a gun functions normally every day of the month."

"Ratzo. ... Jimmy."

"Yeah?"

"We're all nervous, too. And we all love you. OK?"

"OK."

"Now shut up. You're going to fight your way through with us. Most of us will make it because they'll be taken by surprise, and because the jammer in the basement has taken out a few of their weapons. Not all, but some. Now, we're not running, ladies. We're walking briskly back through the kitchen and into that dining room. Once you're through the doors, fan out a little so no one can put a single round through any two of us. Hold your guns straight down against your thighs, understand? Straight down. They may not spot them right away, or they'll waste time yelling and threatening. They're men, after all.

"Do not fire first. If they do start it, you should each have two or three mags left. Remember to change magazines when you're dry. Drop your dead mags, there are no fingerprints, that's why we're wearing Latex fingers this evening.

"Slow and steady, just like we drilled. This will take about 40 seconds, so if they do start the dance there's plenty of time for aimed fire. No shooting at the damned wall panels, understand? Aim for the guns first, but everyone in there is an asshole, there are NO civilians. If they start it, we aim, aim, aim; every shot kills."

She paused. She smiled. "Hey, there were only four Earps at the OK Corral, right? Remember your training, now. It'll be like slow motion in there, easy as pie. Index along the frame, right above the trigger guard, thumb those safeties off, and ... briskly, ladies."

She led off, without looking back. Three Earps and a shotgun, she thought. A shotgun would have been nice, right about now.

Before they could exit the kitchen one of the "dead" cops on the floor — decked out in full evening wear — moved his gun, trying to line up a sight picture on one of her team. Madison kicked him in the nose with her right heel. It made a loud crunching noise; blood spattered. He went down nice and hard. Have a nice day, asshole.

And ... they were in the dining room. It looked like there were half a dozen cops with guns out, still all blemmed up in their formal evening wear, in varying states of readiness. Fortunately, she'd been right — someone coming back at them out of the kitchen was the last thing they expected. And they were mostly focused on a small group gathered around the state senator, anyway. Someone had pulled her up out of the vinaigrette, now her head was flopped back over the back of her chair, her arms out to the side, her blind eyes staring up at the ceiling. Looked like someone was contemplating starting mouth-to-mouth.

Vision across the room was also blocked by various dowagers in skirts who were just picking themselves off the floor, dusting themselves off from the first round of shots. Fortunately, no one had thought to boost the dimmer on the chandeliers; they were still down at half power.

Madison set the example, not running but striding briskly down the center of the room toward the main rear doors, not making any eye contact, .45 down straight against her right thigh.

They were a third of the way across the room. Small miracles. Then "Stop! You! Stop!" and the crack of a 9mm. A warning shot?

No matter. Madison turned, swivelled her piece at the end of her extended arm like the main gun of a tank, spotted the asshole with his own weapon pointed at the sky like a starter's pistol, double-tap, a reassuring deep "Boom, boom." JESUS a

.45 was loud in an enclosed space. And God, she loved it. He'd been standing right next to the dead senator, which would have made a good name for a rock band. Figuring "two for the same price," Madison steadied and put two rounds into the top of the dead bitch's head while she was at it, just to make sure. "Store that for me, will you, sweetheart?"

There was more firing, now, though to her perception, the volume seemed to drop. Madison was in the zone. She kept moving and scanning. She heard a grunt behind her but none of her crew fell, so she ignored it. Of course they'd take hits. People had walked and fought for hours with two, three, even four rounds in them. Keep moving, that was all they had to remember. Move and shoot. You could die on your own time, after the news at 11.

One hit, two, she was double-tapping now to increase her chance of knockdowns. Kiera and Caitlin and Brawny were scanning and firing, as well. She saw people diving for cover, at least two cops lurching from hits. Well, she assumed they were cops. They were suits, anyway, which was the same thing.

And ... drop that magazine and plug in another. She shot a distinguished looking silver-haired man with a gun in his hand — no, it was a silver gravy boat. Bad choice, asshole. Another guy in a waiter's uniform fired at her and missed. Three rounds into that ill-set smugger. How many tries did you think you'd get, dead-eye?

Behind her, Kiera was hit twice more, fell to her knees. Did they just find it easier to hit a slow mover, or was it some kind of inherited, pack instinct to finish off the wounded prey? From her knees, Kiera handed her Para-Ordnance to Ratzo. "Go get 'em," she said. Then, finding a reserve of strength somewhere, Kiera struggled to her feet again ... and Madison saw blood and flesh exploding out of her chest and shoulders as she took multiple additional rounds from behind.

Up by the stage, a single blonde woman in a black dress

sat bolt upright at her table, while her chunky little bald escort, whoever he was, dove under the tablecloth. Chivalrous bastard. As Madison's vision scanned past her, weirdly enough, the blonde was staring directly at her, her face almost expressionless. She was Scandinavian, Madison thought, maybe Russian. And she actually looked ... serene. For some reason, she was not afraid to die ... and so Madison did not shoot her.

Ratzo was hit. He walked right up to the bartender/cop who'd shot him, pointed Kiera's pistol at him. But he did not pull the trigger. So the cop shot Ratzo in the chest, point blank, three more times.

Now Ratzo returned the favor, though it looked like he flinched, pulled low and left as he finally yanked the trigger. So the cop shot him three *more* times. This was absolutely predictable, Madison realized with a curious detachment. Ratzo had not trained with his weapon, whereas the cop had. And the main thing that was accomplished in training was not so much improved accuracy as a willingness to make that trigger decision quicker — sometimes as little as a vital half-second quicker.

Ratzo went down like a tree in the forest. Down on the floor, Kiera was still moving, dragged herself over to Ratzo, leaving a trail on the carpet. Lots of blood, thick and crimson. Curious. Madison had never known there was anything between Kiera and Ratzo.

Madison and Caitlin and Brawny made it through unscathed. As their last action before pushing out through the main doors at the rear of the room, they all fired at once at the barman who had taken out Ratzo. Ten to 15 rounds in the course of less than a second and a half; it sounded like a burst from a machine gun. The guy's chest exploded into pink mist. Forty-five caliber semi-jacketed hollowpoints — don't leave home without them.

And ... they were out in the main entrance hallway, where

the "greeting" table, still bearing a number of forlorn-looking unused plastic nametags for invited guests who had failed to show up, now sat abandoned. In fact, there was no one in sight but a confused little Puerto Rican waitress, crossing herself, and a white-haired old lady on her way back from the powder room.

"This way," Madison said, still pretending to have some idea what she was doing. "Holster up."

Kiera and Ratzo. Neither of them would have gone down from any mere piece-of-shit flesh wound. Sure enough, behind them in the dining room they heard three more booming rounds of .45, followed by a half dozen sharper cracks of police 9mm. That's what Kiera had been dragging herself towards; not Ratzo himself, but the Para-Ordnance she'd loaned him. She'd waited for someone to come over and make sure she was dead before taking out a final asshole at close range.

Madison smiled through her tears. And Hideki had said these bitches weren't pros.

They heard men running at them from up ahead — from the direction of the main hotel lobby — so she calmly turned, led Caitlin and Brawny through another "Employees only" door. That was looking good for awhile, but then she heard shouting voices from ahead of them down that service corridor, as well. Their choices were being dictated for them, now.

They entered a storage room just before a mob of Grays turned the corner into the service corridor they were using. The room had a turnbolt which Madison latched behind them as she turned on the light.

And they were done. Dead end. It was a glorified janitor's storage closet with a high ceiling, some air conditioning ducts about 12 feet overhead, and a single window, also 12 feet up.

Their best chance was that no one had actually seen them come in. But they'd be checking all the doors soon, regardless. Oh, this was getting on just gallant.

"End of the road," said Brawny.

"Who's got rounds left?"

Both showed her the slides on their pistols, locked back and empty. The three of them managed to put together two stray rounds from partially loaded mags they'd pocketed during earlier tactical reloads. Not much.

"OK," she said. "Look for a rope or a ladder. A chair, anything that'll move. We've got to get out that window."

No such luck. Two cardboard boxes of paper towels that might gain them two feet, assuming they'd hold the weight of a full-grown human.

"We can still do it. I'll climb on Brawny's shoulders, Caitlin's up next, and Caitlin can get to the window."

"No," Brawny said, breaking the spell. "There's only one gymnast here, and we can only get one person up to that window, and if only one of us gets out it has to be the one who can tell the most about the organization, and on every count that's you, Madison."

"What are you talking about? We're all going, or no one is."

"You got us this far, and it was magnificent," Caitlin said. "I never thought I'd be part of anything this great in my life. But Brawny's right. You can't be captured. Think of the stuff you know."

"None of us can be captured," Brawny said. "Once you get out, we'll use the last two rounds on ourselves."

Someone tried the door. He shouted that it was locked. Now at least two men were throwing their shoulders against it.

"OK," Madison said. "But not the bullet part. Give me those magazines. Then get up against that wall and form a basket with your hands, cross them so it's strong. I'll take a running start; you count a second and a half after my foot hits and then throw me up as hard as you can. But you live, do you hear me? You surrender and you live; I'll get help and come back for you."

She holstered her pistol and pocketed the extra mags. They formed the cat's cradle for her. The first time she didn't go high enough, but on the second try she caught the air conditioning duct with both hands, chinned herself up, swung to the window and got it open.

Something heavier was hitting the door now. Had she condemned them to torture, when she should have let them take the easy way out? No, damn it, this was not over.

"I'll be back. You're going to survive. And that's an order," she said, and dropped to the ground outside.

Well, that went rather well, she thought. Every member of her unit killed or captured, and here she was, squatting in an alley in the dark, old asphalt and broken glass, absolutely unharmed, with two rounds in her last magazine.

How the hell had things gotten so roundly fucked? They had to have been tipped. That was no run of bad luck. The whole damned set-up was a trap. Was there a way she could have gotten Ratzo out of it? He hadn't been part of the original hit, there should have been a way. And who was the staring blonde at the head table? Should Madison have whacked her?

But in the end, Kiera and Ratzo were both dead, due entirely to Madison's incompetence. She'd insisted the mission could be done, after Andrew has advised against it. It had been entirely her plan. But Fiducci was an obvious target; they should have expected extra resistance. What had been her escape plans B and C and D?

Stop it. She had to stop this right now. You mourned your dead and blamed yourself on your own time; she had more pressing problems at the moment. Above her, through the still-open window, she could hear the door shatter, the shouts for Brawny and Caitlin to lie down on the fucking floor. At least there was no gunfire.

What would be done with them? Into some kind of Lightning Wagon, presumably — she was surprised they didn't still call them Paddy wagons. Where? A rear service entrance to the hotel, the loading dock where supplies were delivered. Singlemindedly, Madison began to skirt the property.

And there it was. A rear loading dock access clogged with cop cars, all of which were currently empty, though two Grays lounged outside on the dock itself, smoking. Great discipline.

And what the hell was that? Some kind of white and blue trailer with a Transportation Security logo, backed up to the loading dock, with lights on inside.

She skunked around to the far side of the trailer, staying low and keeping the parked squad cars between herself and the guards, who'd be partially night-blinded by the glowing ends of their cigarettes, not that it mattered much in a city that was never really dark.

The concrete curb alongside the far side of the trailer got higher as she moved along it. Well, actually, the trailer sank lower into the excavated drive. Anyway, she reached a point where she could see in through one of the flimsy glass-and-chickenwire windows.

Six or seven more Grays lounged around inside, where there were desks and a portal. A goddamned portal crew, parked in back of the hotel? For what?

Ah, the bureaucratic mind was a thing of wonder. To process the anticipated prisoners, of course.

Madison backed off, found a dark corner where she could lurk and keep an eye on things. She pulled out her phone, saw it was turned off, thumbed it on. She ignored the multiple incoming messages, phoned home.

"Yeah?" It was Himself. Just the sound of Andrew's voice flooded her with a level of hope she hadn't realized she was missing.

"It's me."

425

"Thank God. Been trying to get through to you. The hotel is a trap, the banquet room and the tunnels are loaded."

"Yeah, we found out."

"How bad?"

"I got two down, including Ratzo. Two captured."

There was a slight pause as he did the math. Yes, Andrew, that's everybody. Madison fucked up completely, and then bailed and saved her own ass.

"Ratzo?"

"He came up to tell us about the tunnels."

"Where are you?"

"Outside in back. There's a trailer at the loading dock with lights on and a whole portal crew inside. Might be to process prisoners."

"How bad are those two down?"

"Gone for their tea."

It meant they wouldn't be answering roll call in the morning.

"Where have they got your two captured?"

"Sure an' that's what I'm watchin' to see." Madison was usually being ironic when she resorted to Paddyisms. This time he couldn't be sure.

"And you? Hurt?"

"Mad as hell."

"OK, we've got all kinds of other shit breaking loose here, but we'll have some backup there for you inside an hour. I'll try to send the Black Arrow. But if things get hot, pull further back and keep in touch. Do not get stupid and try anything alone. You hear me?"

"Thanks. We did our best."

"You did great. How's the senator?"

"I think she's been campaigning too hard. She's just dead."

"We still need you, mo chuisle. Don't do anything stupid.

Half an hour."

"OK."

❧ ❧ ❧

7:06 P.M. THURSDAY, OCT. 16, THE YEAR 2031

It was dinnertime. Rachel knew she shouldn't bother Nguyen; she just wanted to ask if she could see him later.

It turned out the dinner rush hadn't hit yet, though. There was hardly anyone eating at Chin's but Bob from the newsstand and Kylie, the new guitarist. And they seemed to be more intent on their conversation than their food.

The other guys were standing around the kitchen, technically chopping celery and bok choy, but actually dogging it, waiting to see if a dinner crowd would show up tonight.

In fact, Rachel could see they were agitated. She asked about Nguyen. Normally they would have rolled their eyes and said something suggestive in Cantonese. Instead, they jabbered at her with considerable excitement that no one had seen him, that Jean-Claude and Airburst Barnes had already been asking after him, and that it was very strange — he would usually be here.

Instead of turning around, Rachel went through and pushed open the back kitchen door. Nguyen had the strangest habit of wandering the back end of the building. He said he snuck out back to smoke an occasional cigarette, but although Nguyen carried cigarettes, Rachel had the strangest feeling he didn't really smoke. She'd known plenty of people who were trying to quit smoking. Nguyen acted more like someone who was trying to start smoking, but kept forgetting to actually smoke. And who had ever heard of anyone older than 15 who

427

was trying to *start?*

Sure enough, she caught a glimpse of him — it was just a silhouette in the darkened hallway, but she was sure that was him.

Behind her, on the other side of the refrigerators, the other two cooks carried on their conversation, paying her no heed. She drew back, watched Nguyen through the half-open back kitchen door. He'd pulled out something that looked like a credit card, tied to a hunk of metal about the size of a pocket comb by one of those electronic ribbons they used to use to connect computer components. He stuck it in the keypad lock of the big locked door that led to Jimmy Chin's assembly line. He was cracking the electronic lock. What the hell did he want in there?

She wouldn't have been able to explain why, but she glanced behind her, spotted a big butcher knife sitting out on the rearmost kitchen counter where they usually dealt with the frozen food, grabbed it and took it with her.

Nguyen had disappeared into the factory area out behind the loading dock. The door was swinging closed on its spring. Rachel caught it and followed him inside.

It was a heavy, soundproofed door.

A single light burned, down at the far end of the long, narrow room. The only other ambient light was from the red "Exit" signs. It took a minute for her eyes to adjust.

Shelves full of crates, held up on naked steel scaffolding, lined the wall opposite the steel garage doors that led out to the loading dock itself. Getting a little chilly here on the concrete floor — they must use space heaters, or maybe there was a blower they could crank up when they were working. A long row of metal tables down the center of the darkened room, the dim backlight silhouetting AK-47 rifles in various stages of completion.

She knew they'd started out with a big stamping press in

here, as well, stamping out the receivers to go with the barrels provided by Boris and Katia. (It was the receiver that the U.S. government in its wisdom identified as "the machine gun," while the harder-to-manufacture barrels, being categorized as "spare parts," moved without regulation, railway express.)

But the stamping press had just been too noisy, so it had been relocated down to Ratzo's caverns some time back. The receivers now came up through the basement for final assembly here.

A figure moved. From where she stood, Nguyen was a silhouette at the far end of the room. Now he was moving back towards her, speaking into a phone. "Can you hear me?"

Of course. The heavy steel and concrete walls, plus the dampening field generated by Jean-Claude's machine down in the theater, made it almost impossible to use a cell phone inside the building. Nguyen was looking for a spot from which his signal could get through.

"Can you hear me now? ..." And then, finally, he must have heard a response. "You won't believe this; I found the mother lode. Out here near the loading dock. Hello? You there?"

It occurred to her, for a split second, that she should confront him, give him a chance to explain himself.

But what would he do? Lie, say it's not like it looks, push her down, get away? That's if she was lucky and he didn't just grab this ridiculous knife that was now shaking in her hand, use it on her. He was six inches taller than she was, 40 pounds heavier, at least. And he was betraying her and all her friends. Her family. If he succeeded they wouldn't just throw Jimmy Chin in prison, but Mrs. Chin, Andrew, Madison.

Nguyen was a goddamned cop. Worse than a cop — some kind of spy, probably for the Grays.

She had no way to know that, at the other end of the line, Jack Brackley was in Christian Newby's office by now, hearing him take this call. So far as she knew, there simply wasn't any time.

She had to position the blade of the knife laterally, to slip between the ribs. He was turned with his back to her, now, less than 10 feet away. Her breathing started to come faster. That was OK; her body knew she'd need oxygen for strength. Grip the knife firmly in both hands, it would probably take more strength to get it all the way in than she expected, there was a lot of muscle and other stuff to cut through. More strength than she needed to cut through a watermelon, say. She'd done that. And then she couldn't let go right away, no matter what — she had to remember that.

Now that she'd decided what to do, she looked down at the knife in surprise. Somehow, it had gone rock steady in her hands. She'd been crouching behind one of the tables. She stood up now and took one careful step, then another. She could hardly believe he hadn't heard her. To her own ears, the pounding of her heart and the wheezing of her breath sounded like surf breaking on rocks during a storm.

"Can you hear me? It's right here in the Gotham Building."

The point of the knife was within a couple inches of his back now. Her hands were close to her own chest. Leaning forward, she rammed the great triangular blade home, up between the ribs, slightly to his left side, though the heart was not as far over to the left as most people thought. As she drove it home she had to remind herself — she had no idea if she actually shouted it aloud — "You bastard! You betrayed us all!"

Oddly enough, he didn't scream. He kind of grunted. But it sounded like he exhaled a lot of air out of his lungs. He jerked then, and she was glad she'd reminded herself to keep a firm grip on the knife, because she wasn't done. She couldn't be done. God give her strength, now.

No one died right away like in the movies, she knew that. A guy with a bullet or a knife in his heart could live a long time, could still make his phone call ... might even turn around and beat her to death before he finally died.

She took a step to the right, glad she didn't have to see his face right now — she'd actually dreamed of that face, wondering if Nguyen would become the father of her children, the way a girl will. She shifted her grip on the handle of the knife without ever letting go. She had carefully positioned the blade so the cutting edge faced out, away from the spine. Now she pushed the knife sideways, sharp edge first, like gutting a fish.

This time it was harder to get it to move, because so much of the blade was inside him — it must be a full 10 inches. But it did move another inch or two sideways before he yelled and finally jerked away.

Good. That was the best she could do. And that lateral movement would slice away more of his heart tissue, hopefully sever one of the major veins or arteries where it attached to the heart. It would also open the wound cavity, giving the blood a way to flow out around the knife.

She could hardly believe she'd remembered all this stuff, worked so calmly. But he was large and she was small and when you didn't have a gun, killing someone was difficult. Hideki had drilled that into them.

Nguyen staggered and lunged away from her now, choking, yelling, reaching desperately around his back with each of his hands in turn, trying to get a grip on the knife handle and pull it out. But it was too low. He couldn't reach it.

Then he turned around, lurched and lunged back towards her. "Rachel! What have you done? Why? You don't understand." He was still trying to reach behind him to get the knife.

"You betrayed us. You betrayed us all for Castle money, you bastard."

And then Rachel really surprised herself. She punched him in the jaw as hard as she could — swung so hard she came right up off her feet. He jerked, fell forward towards her. There was blood coming out of his mouth now. He gurgled. His eyes rolled up in his head. He grabbed for her as he fell, pulled her part way down to the ground with him, spat blood in her face and down her chest. Then he was lying face down on the ground, still not dead, but thrashing, crawling, trying to get up again.

He had dropped his cell phone. She picked it up. It was lit. She carefully, deliberately, pushed the "Off" button. Damned things could be tracked as long as they were on. Maybe even when they were off. She'd better go tell someone.

Wait. He was still alive, might still crawl away. Over by the loading dock door was a portable Stop sign, mounted in a concrete anchor which had been made by pouring cement into a plastic bucket around the bottom of the metal pole, after which the plastic had been cut away. Sometimes the Chins or Boris and Katia would set it out in the rear alley when they were doing a lot of loading and unloading. She half rolled, half carried the stop sign over to where Nguyen was still shuddering and gagging on the floor. Using all her strength — more strength than she'd known she had — she picked it up, and dropped it on his head.

It tilted off to the side. His head did not break open like a melon. But she could see the bloody indentation it had made.

She heard a noise and looked up. Kylie had come in, the little Australian from the studio. What was she doing here?

Kylie was pale and wide-eyed — at least, Rachel thought she was. There still wasn't much light. Kylie was holding open the door to the hallway.

She said nothing. She looked at Nguyen on the floor, and then at Rachel, who must be a sight, covered in blood.

"Kylie." Rachel found her voice. "I need some help here. Find Andrew or Jean-Claude."

Still Kylie stood there, staring. Then she turned and ran

down the hall.

There was something wrong with the way Kylie was responding. Rachel wasn't sure what it was. What had she been doing back here in the first place? Looking for Nguyen? Meeting him?

Still not sure what it all meant, Rachel started running after her.

Kylie ran out into the Gotham lobby, which should have been deserted this late in the day. But as it happened, Bob was standing in the entrance to the corridor that led back to Mrs. Chin's restaurant, his cane out to the side, effectively blocking that route.

And now, in through the main lobby doors, came Andrew Fletcher and Hideki.

"Kylie!" Rachel shouted. "Wait! You don't understand."

And then it dawned on Rachel that, just maybe, she was the one who didn't understand. For little Kylie, finding her way blocked on three sides, stopped. She reached into her jacket pocket and pulled out a little silver pistol. Spinning, holding her arms out straight as she tried to steady her aim, she fired two shots at Rachel.

Rachel froze. She couldn't believe it. Kylie had been looking for Nguyen ... because they'd been working together.

Rachel heard the two bullets whine past her head like mosquitos. But now Kylie had turned toward the lobby doors. She fired more shots — maybe three. Rachel's heart was pounding and she couldn't be sure.

Now Airburst Barnes came running at the sound of the shots, down the wide curving front staircase that led down from the dojo and the recording studios.

Back over by the lobby doors, it seemed Andrew and Hideki paused a moment to see if they'd been hit. Then they walked forward, closing in on the little guitar player.

But Andrew only took two steps. Then he sank to his

knees. He was looking down at his right side. Near his waist, his shirt had started to turn red with blood.

Kylie only had one direction left to go. She ran into the theater. Andrew waved them on, so after a moment Hideki and Airburst followed her. Rachel had a decision to make. Join the pursuit?

Of course not. She went to Andrew. Madison would have wanted her to help Andrew.

❖ ❖ ❖

7:08 P.M. THURSDAY, OCT. 16, THE YEAR 2031

"How goes the battle, Christian?"

Jack had heard Rennie Heydrich's voice coming from Newby's office when he first approached, so he'd waited down the hall in the alcove that led to the men's room and the drinking fountain till he saw Heydrich leave.

Group Leader Rennie Heydrich was a spooky guy. Blond, with such high, pronounced cheekbones that he looked like some kind of Halloween skull. About all people knew about him was that he worked real closely with Newby and spent a lot of time in a locked wing up on the seventh floor that hardly anyone else had access to. Interrogation chambers, according to the office scuttlebutt. Torture chambers, some said.

You occasionally saw suspects being taken up to the seventh floor. But it seemed like you never saw anyone come down.

Once he was sure Heydrich was gone, Jack sauntered into Newby's office, where Christian was watching his phone.

After successfully bringing the Brackley Center in — well, it would hardly be accurate to say on time and under budget, but nonetheless having finally gotten the damned thing done — the little guy had received a commission as group leader directly into the Lightning Squads, where he was put in charge of some kind of shadowy intelligence program.

Only now did Jack begin to fully understand what he'd been up to — recruiting agents from outside police ranks to infiltrate resistance cells, or (more accurately) any group, organization or workplace in Gotham suspected of harboring anti-government sympathies.

A whole string of men-in-the-night arrests and civilian "disappearances" over recent months now began to make a lot more sense. And to think the nerve center of the whole operation might be right here, this quiet guy with the long hair and the skinny mustache in this unassuming office with a single window, on the sixth floor of SonicNet headquarters.

"Actually, Jack, things are going great, but I'm a little busy right now."

Jack had always gotten along with Christian OK. Some of the guys rolled their eyes at his long hair and dainty manners, although there were women who seemed to like the look. Maybe it was the whole "can't-tell-for-sure" thing.

"Waiting for a call?"

"What?"

"I saw you staring at the phone as I came in."

"Oh, yeah. I am, in fact. Waiting for some reports to come in."

Jack closed the door, strolled over to take a look out the window. "You know, Christian, until recently, I hadn't realized just how important you are in this operation. This string of recent busts and arrests. That's the result of good intelligence, isn't it?"

"You have no idea, Jack. Day by day it can seem grinding, dull, routine. But the key is filtering all that information, weighing it, seeing where it points. That part of things is kind of intuitive. It's an art, almost."

"I bet."

The phone rang. Newby picked it up, said "Nguyen? You're not coming in too well. Hang on a second." Then he covered the mouthpiece with his hand. Turning part-way around, trying to figure out precisely where Jack was standing behind him, he said "If you'll excuse me, I've got to take this."

"Sure, Christian," Jack said, slipping the black arrow from under his uniform tunic. "I understand."

He unwrapped the white paper from around the warhead, which was coated with some kind of brownish goo. Now, turning his left side to Newby's back and spreading his feet wide, holding the arrow shaft with his hands spread well apart but with seven or eight inches free at the business end, he rammed it into Newby's back, just to the left of the spine, as hard as he could. He threw his hips into it, the way you'd gaff a big fish on a charter boat.

He'd meant to do it while they were face-to-face, but finally decided it was an absurd superstition to cling to the notion that that would somehow make it "a fair fight." None of the hundreds of families who would never hear from perfectly innocent husbands and dads "disappeared" into the prisons — or worse — at Christian Newby's orders had been given a "fair fighting chance."

Besides, if he gave Newby a chance to struggle, there was a chance Jack himself would be cut on the poison-impregnated warhead. Like a lot of smaller guys, Newby was probably damned quick. Once you'd decided to kill somebody, only an asshole gave them a sporting chance.

Newby made a sound that was between a hacking cough and a long sigh as one of his lungs collapsed. He didn't die immediately. In fact, he put his hands on the desk and tried to stand up. Jack patiently pushed his shoulders down until he gave up. Then Jack took the phone from Newby's left hand

and placed it back on its cradle. Pulling from his pockets some paper towels that he'd already dipped in cleaning solvent, he wiped clean of fingerprints both the shaft of the arrow in Newby's back, and the phone set he'd just replaced on the desk.

The warpoint had gone all the way through Newby and scratched the top of his desk. It didn't stick into the top of the desk, though — the angle was too oblique and the desk's surface was some kind of impact-resistant plastic composite. It caught on the bottom of Newby's computer screen, though, as he attempted to stand up.

"Jack?" He asked. "What the hell, Jack?"

He tried to stand again. Jack held him down again. He exerted a lot less strength on his second try. Extract of nicotine was a fairly fast-acting poison if you got it right into the arterial bloodstream. Not that having a triangular razor-steel warhead pushed through your aorta was good for your long-term prospects, all by itself.

"Sorry, Christian," Jack told him calmly. "You're fighting a war, you know. And in war, there are gonna be casualties."

"But you work —" it came out now as little more than a whisper.

"Right here beside you? That's right, Christian. Just like all those agents you're running out there, busy betraying people who took them in and trusted them."

Quietly, stealthily, Newby's right hand had slid out to open his right-hand desk drawer. Now he tried to slide out a pistol he kept there. Jack used his right knee to slam the drawer shut on his hand. He took the gun from Newby's weakening right hand, held it with the paper towel so as to leave no prints.

It took more than a minute before Jack was convinced Christian Newby had lost consciousness. Just to be safe, he decided to set the pistol on top of a filing cabinet at the back of room, out of Newby's reach in case he should briefly recover consciousness — though that seemed highly unlikely, what with his heart having stopped and all.

Jack saw there were two text files open on Newby's computer screen. He moused up to "Database," pulled down to "Route" and shunted them to "Trash." Then he emptied the trash. He decided he'd better not do any more than that, or it would be obvious someone had been in the room. Then he used the solvent-soaked paper towels to unlatch and open the single window behind Newby's desk. They were six stories up, and all the rooftops and facing windows from which an arrow could have been fired were nearly a hundred yards away. Jack wasn't sure anyone could actually make such a shot, and the evening was a bit chilly for wide-open windows. But what the heck. At least he'd give them a believable scenario.

Remembering the white paper that had covered the poisoned warhead, he wadded it up, dropped it out the window, watched it flutter away in the wind.

His hands smelled of tobacco. He'd have to wash them.

Now he slightly repositioned Newby's chair so the angle of the arrow in his back pointed directly at the window.

And then, wiping the doorknob on his way, he left and went back to work.

It had been disturbingly easy. In fact, as the mayor's nephew and a person who had been on at least passably friendly terms with Newby, Jack was never even questioned.

⚜ ⚜ ⚜

Kylie the guitar player had taken to stopping by and talking to Bob a lot. They'd even had lunch together a few times. A real lunch, not just a sandwich at the newsstand. Bob had to wait till after 1 p.m., of course, hang up his "Back in an hour" sign.

He was getting his hopes up that she actually seemed to like him. And so he'd tried to push the other thing to the back of his mind.

His old friend Andrew had been one of the few people to pay attention when Bob would tell him things about people they'd just been talking to. Someone would stop by, engage them in a seemingly casual newsstand conversation, and leave. Then Bob would tell Andrew something about that person's state of mind — when they had lied, what they'd avoided saying ... sometimes even why.

It was a gift which they both agreed was tied at least in part to Bob's loss of sight, which had happened when he was very young. He didn't merely recognize voices, he could tell things from their timbre and intonation that other people seemed to miss. He held little factoids and bits of trivia in his mind; he was able to put together a puzzle and see a larger picture from a surprisingly small number of clues.

It had started out as a game, just to keep his mind occupied. He listened not only to what people said, but to how they said it. He could tell when they shifted thoughts in mid-sentence to avoid saying what they'd been tempted to blurt out next.

And — although he'd been trying to ignore it — there was something wrong with Kylie's voice. She seemed cheerful and bubbly, but still she would steer the conversation around to Bob's role here, to Andrew, to what everyone in the building did, even to questions of security. She seemed unusually interested in Jimmy Chin and what was going on back near the loading dock and payroll arrangements and why the building needed so large a security staff.

At first Bob put that down to her being a foreigner, not understanding the history of how Franklin Roosevelt had promised Social Security and those nine-digit numbers would never be mandatory, would never become a "national ID number" like the ones people had to carry around on their internal "travel papers" or get tattooed on their arms in Nazi Germany.

But that wasn't it. Finally he couldn't deny it any longer. Kylie was pumping him for information, and her curiosity went way beyond what should have been appropriate for a musician thanking her lucky stars that she'd caught a break and was now doing some part-time work — *paid* work — at Rebel Records, which should have been her dream come true.

So this evening Bob had arranged to meet Kylie for supper at Chin's and had done some directing of the conversation on his own, got her to talking about the Black Arrow, the assassinations and the Resistance.

And what he had heard in her voice had actually made him sick to his stomach.

She was one of them.

He'd been devastated — not just at Kylie's betrayal, her smiling, bubbling fakery, but most of all at his own failure, the way he had let down the very people who counted on him.

And so he'd followed up his stupidity with more stupidity.

He should have kept his mouth shut and gone to Andrew and confessed that he'd screwed up when he allowed Long Shot to bring Kylie aboard despite his reservations. Instead, he'd confronted her about her politics, and why she was really here.

They'd had a fight. Kylie had stormed off. And now she would suspect Bob was wise to her.

He'd tried to follow her, deftly sweeping his route with his cane.

She'd moved toward the back of the building and he'd lost her. But now there were running footsteps. Someone — yes, Kylie — was running back towards the lobby from the back of the building.

"Kylie!" came Rachel's voice. "Wait! You don't understand."

Rachel was chasing Kylie. Bob froze. What was happening? At the other end of the lobby, he heard the lobby doors
open. Someone else was coming in. Footsteps on the marble.
Hideki and ... Andrew?

Bob started to say something. But then, incredibly, shots
rang out. Loud little cracks — he thought that was a gun. Not
a big booming gun. Who among these people would be shooting, and with some kind of little pocket gun?

Had Rachel discovered what Bob feared most, that Kylie
was a government spy? Had Rachel shot her so she couldn't
get away? No, the shots hadn't come from the same place as
Rachel's voice.

Kylie was shooting. But shooting who?

Belatedly, Bob pulled his arms in tight to his body to make
himself a smaller target. Had she been shooting at Bob?

Now there were more running steps — someone coming
down the stairs from the dojo. He should have been able to
pick out whose steps, but Bob was experiencing an aural over-
load. His ears were ringing from the shots.

"What's happening?" he shouted. He was almost in tears.
Here he was, right where it was all happening, and he was
helpless to do anything for his friends. "Who's shot? Is anyone
shot?"

"Andrew's been shot," came Rachel's voice, suddenly
small and childlike.

Oh dear God. No. All because Bob hadn't been doing his
job, because he hadn't said anything.

"Did Kylie shoot him?"

"Yes."

"I'll be OK," Andrew said, although he didn't sound OK.

"I'm going to go get the doctor," came Rachel's voice.
Her steps came toward Bob, walking fast. She'd be heading to

the freight elevators and the caverns.

Bob was trying to replay the events in his mind, sort out the sounds.

"Who went into the theater?" he asked quickly, reaching out to stop Rachel as she passed him.

"Everybody," Rachel said. "Airburst and Hideki followed Kylie in there."

OK. Then Bob would go there, too. He let Rachel go.

"You really OK, Mr. Fletcher? Anything I can do?"

"She didn't hit anything vital, Bob. Go ahead; I'll be fine. And knock off the 'Mister.' "

Bob knew the layout of the theater by heart. He really didn't need his cane to run down the aisle toward the front of the house. Before he got there he heard the loud snap of the main circuit breaker being thrown. It was followed by echoing snaps in a dozen other circuits, and then that strange silence you got when a noise you'd become accustomed to suddenly stopped. Bob knew what that noise had been. The humming of the lighting fixtures. It was evening. The theater would now be pitch black. *Was* pitch black.

With the lights off, he could already feel the air starting to cool.

"Hideki?" came the voice of Airburst Barnes.

"I didn't do that. She has to be close to the main breaker board."

Bob could hear the two men, moving tentatively. Especially now.

As he understood it, for a short time — before their pupils had a chance to dilate and pick up a little information from any ambient light that might be slipping in — Airburst and Hideki would both be blind.

Blinder than Bob.

He climbed the stairs to the stage, effortlessly. Then he paused, lowered his head, extending his senses.

The guys had been building flats and risers for the Crows' upcoming New Year's Eve concert. The whole place smelled of sawdust and paint thinner. Pine sawdust. Even so, and despite all the renovations, to Bob the old theater still had a slightly musty, mildewed smell. Maybe he just remembered the way it used to smell before it got all fixed up ... but he didn't think so. Some places had a smell that told their history, a smell you could never quite cover up.

That beeping noise. Varying tones, Someone was dialing a cellular phone. Kylie.

"She's trying to make a call," he said.

"Lots of luck from in here."

"Hello? Are you there?" came Kylie's voice.

"Kylie?" Bob asked.

"You again? You're such a big dummy," she taunted, as she clicked off and redialed, obviously having trouble with her connection. "I was ready to do a whole lot more to find out what you knew, but you sang like such a bird, I never even had to put out. Thank God."

She was, indeed, over near the circuit breaker board. Bob could hear the other two trying to move towards her, but they kept banging into things.

"I think I'm out of here, gentlemen," she said. "It's been nice."

"She's heading for the stage door!" Bob shouted. "Stop her!"

"In case you didn't know, Bob, it's pitch dark in here," replied Airburst Barnes.

"Hurry. She's a police spy. We can't let her get out and make that call. There's got to be an Exit sign right over the backstage door, right? They run on emergency power. You should see it as soon as you're past the curtains. Just watch out for the —"

Airburst Barnes fell with a bang. "Shit."

"— new risers."

Now Kylie shrieked. If Airburst hadn't made it to the rear alley door in time, evidently Hideki had — and damned quietly, at that. He and Kylie had run into each other. But either he wasn't wearing a blade or he'd opted not to draw it, possibly concerned that he might slice Airburst or Bob. There was a brief tussle and some grunting noises. Then Kylie's feet came running back toward the front of the stage — towards Bob.

And once she got past the worthless cripple, who would stop her? Andrew was wounded, maybe even dying, and Rachel had gone for the doctor. Kylie might even have more shots in that gun. Did she know Andrew was the Black Arrow? Was she here to assassinate him?

What could Bob do? After all, he was ...

No ... he wasn't.

Here in the darkness, everyone else was blind. Everyone *but* Bob was blind.

He could smell the freshly cut ends of the pine lumber. Right here at his feet. He reached down. Wide sheets of plywood. Worthless. But wait ... there ... a two-by-four. He picked it up. Felt like it was three or four feet long. Here came Kylie's running feet. Kylie, who he had loved. Who he had hoped might love him. Kylie, who had shot Andrew and who would betray them all if she could get out of the building with her phone.

If she could just get past the one cripple.

But the noise of her footsteps made her as visible to him, here in the echoing darkness of this silent theater with its perfect acoustics, as she would have been to anyone else in the bright of day.

He reminded himself that she was short — her head only came up to his chest. Time the steps, here she came. He hauled back and swung with all his might, using his shoulders, as though he held a baseball bat, trying to hammer a line-drive single through the infield before they could respond —

To Airburst and Hideki, the sound was like a watermelon being chopped in half with a cleaver, followed by the bang of a heavy dead weight being dropped on a loose sheet of plywood.

"Bob?"

"Yes?"

"What the hell was that?"

"That was Kylie."

"What?"

"Kylie?" Bob said, kneeling and feeling for her where she'd gone down.

She was warm. But she didn't seem to be able to move. Something important had broken.

Now came the snapping of the big circuit breaker again, the noise of all the follow-up couplings coming alive to the power, and then the humming of the lights. Here on stage, where so many of them were focused, Bob could feel their warmth clearly.

"Bob," she said, as though surprised. "Honey."

But that was all.

"Kylie," he said, taking her in his arms. Her head flopped loose, so he tried to hold it up where it should be.

"Kylie, why did you do it? You could have had a home, here. I could have loved you. We could have worked it out."

He heard Airburst and Hideki approaching, but then they stopped. That was bad. That meant they could see there wasn't any sense trying First Aid. Instead they just waited, giving him time.

He should have been angry at someone — at Kylie, at himself. The heat of anger would have been better than this icy cold. But who was there to be angry at? He held her and stroked her hair. She felt so tiny and perfect, like a little doll. Kylie was still soft, and warm.

He jerked a little, then, as something else touched his hand. Something cool and small and — damp. The little back-stage kitten that Madison's girls had adopted was here, licking Bob's hand.

"Her music was so beautiful," he cried. "How could it be so beautiful?"

CHAPTER 13

Prudence, indeed, will dictate that governments long established, should not be changed for light and transient causes... But, when a long train of abuses and usurpations, pursuing invariably the same object, evinces a design to reduce them under absolute despotism, it is [the people's] right, it is their duty, to throw off such government, and to provide new guards for their future security.

— THOMAS JEFFERSON: DECLARATION OF INDEPENDENCE, 1776

I believe that liberty is the only genuinely valuable thing that men have invented, at least in the field of government, in a thousand years. I believe that it is better to be free than to be not free, even when the former is dangerous and the latter safe. I believe that the finest qualities of man can flourish only in free air — that progress made under the shadow of the policeman's club is false progress, and of no permanent value. I believe that any man who takes the liberty of another into his keeping is bound to become a tyrant, and that any man who yields up his liberty, in however slight the measure, is bound to become a slave.

— HENRY LOUIS MENCKEN (1880-1956), OF THE BALTIMORE SUN

8:06 P.M. THURSDAY, OCT. 16, THE YEAR 2031

Madison had no idea how much time actually passed. But sure enough, just as she'd expected, here came Brawny and Caitlin being led out onto the darkened loading dock by four "arresting officers."

Each of her bitches had blood streaming down her face — they'd obviously been roughed up and kicked around — but they were walking under their own power. They had their hands bound behind them, though whether with traditional cuffs or plastic ties Madison couldn't make out.

Their four escorts led them to the back of the Homeland Security trailer, shoved them inside, and laughed as one of them apparently fell down inside. No way to catch yourself with your hands tied behind.

Then, miraculously, the four gray-suited goons turned and re-entered the building.

Brawny and Caitlin were now guarded by however many Grays were inside the trailer ... how many had she seen? Six? Seven? ... and the two guards on the loading dock itself, armed with MP-5s. And as soon as the excitement of shoving the two girls into the trailer had passed, these two paragons of watchfulness immediately re-lit the cigarettes they'd extinguished when company showed up.

What were they thinking? The answer, of course, was that they were glorified security guards. The idea of a counterattack to free prisoners simply never occurred to them. Once someone had been arrested, she was "processed through the system." This was why John Dillinger and Billy the Kid had repeatedly escaped from jails guarded by dozens of officers. Each guard diligently guarded the area immediately in front of him, trusting in bars and locks and — in the end — the notion that everyone would surely follow procedure, wait to talk to his defense attorney, cop a plea. In their view of the world, that was the only sensible and reasonable course.

But how long would this situation prevail, before someone wised up and remembered to reassign another dozen men to guard the prisoners, or until the paddy wagon — what a fine word — showed up to transport them somewhere downtown with *real* security?

Madison couldn't wait to find out.

And there was no sense calling for help. Andrew had already said help would arrive as soon as anyone could be spared.

Madison had a pistol with two rounds. She rechecked her magazine, racked the slide to seat the first cartridge. Other than that, only the 18-inch falcata in the fringed leather sling across her back, under her silly waitress costume.

Of course. She was still dressed as a waitress.

Shifting the pistol to the rear of her waistband on the right-hand side — her shooting hand — she simply stood up and walked back to the loading dock.

The two guards looked down at her curiously. She was a waitress, young and pretty and alone.

"Is it over?" She asked. "Is the shooting over? Did they get them?"

"Yeah, miss. They got 'em, alright."

"What about Anna? My friend Anna? Is she alright?"

"Dunno, Miss. You'd better go around to the front of the hotel and ask there."

"I ran when I heard the shooting start. I'm supposed to be inside. Can you help me up?" She lifted her left hand to the nearest trooper. Gallantly, he pushed his weapon aside on its sling, gave her his left hand so their palms would meet, and lifted her up to the loading dock, showing off his strength.

"Thanks," she said, once her feet were planted. Then, bringing her right hand around — while keeping a firm grip on his left so he couldn't raise it — she placed the newly re-fitted suppressor on the barrel of her Para-Ordnance 45-12 to his head, and blew his brains out.

Since the sound wasn't nearly as loud as an unsuppressed gunshot, the second guard froze for a second, not sure what had happened. Madison improved her grip to a two-hand stance, leveling her weapon at the second trooper's head. He was about eight feet away. It was an easy shot, even out here in the half-light. For some reason, he froze, did not bring his weapon up.

Of course, she only had the one round left. Assuming it had seated properly, that there wasn't a low-brass jam in her weapon, which wouldn't reveal itself till she tried to fire again. Also assuming the round wasn't a dud. Assuming she didn't flinch when she pulled the trigger, and miss. If any of those things happened, she would have to throw the gun aside — no, directly at him, hoping he'd duck — and go to her sword. Against his submachine gun.

But she was eight feet away. Slowly, she stepped over the corpse at her feet, moving towards the surviving guard. He did nothing. She took another step. Any closer and he'd be able to reach out and grab her gun. What was he thinking? That she was afraid to fire? That any moment now she'd tell him to lay down his weapon and put his hands up? Sighting on the bridge of his nose, she squeezed the trigger ever so carefully, willing herself not to flinch.

And shot him in the right eyebrow. Pulling a little high and left; she'd have to remember that.

Two down, but she had no time to go hiding the bodies. It was unbelievable that no one had yet remembered to send an extra dozen men out here to guard the prisoners. And that run of luck couldn't last forever. She shoved the empty .45 back in her waistband at the small of her back, ignoring the second guard, who was now thrashing and wetting his pants at her feet as he finished dying. She reached over her right shoulder and shifted the handle of her falcata, making sure it would slide out smoothly when needed. It was the 18-inch pattern-welded blade with the dark hardwood handle that Hideki had sold her at the Renaissance Faire — could that have been only a year ago? Seemed a lifetime. And then, with a brisk and self-assured stride, shoulders squared, she walked into the door of the blue-and-white trailer.

A middle-aged woman with short gray hair and eyeglasses was sitting at a table, filling out paperwork. People lay dying and bleeding in the hotel ballroom, not a hundred yards away, and this bitch was filling out paperwork.

"Can I help you?" she asked, as though Madison had simply walked in the wrong door, looking for the ladies' room.

Madison recognized the type. This was one of the older women who sat at the table looking through the gray plastic tubs of wallets, checkbooks, eyeglasses, condoms, birth control pill dispensers ... the ephemera of a people who no longer possessed any privacy. And her response to Madison's presence was thus fully predictable. For the only people who strode boldly up to a team of the Lightning Squad were inspectors or agents of some other branch of government — someone who was duly authorized. The lowing herd did not act this way; they held back and averted their eyes as long as they could.

Reaching up behind her back in mid-stride, Madison slid out the razor-sharp blade that was sheathed there — designed with its weight forward, like a huge cleaver or machete — set her feet wide, and swung the weapon with supreme confidence, like a baseball bat, lopping off the uncomprehending woman's head in a single bone-shivering blow.

Blood streamed up from the woman's neck like red wine from the fountain of a Roman orgy.

Skirting the table, Madison spun like a striking tiger as she approached the Lightning Trooper who had doubtless just finished hustling Caitlin and Brawny through the metal-detecting portal, probably feeling them up for good measure on their way through.

Her turn lent the sword enormous momentum as it came back around from her right again, swinging upwards through part of the surprised trooper's chest. Then, rather than trying to halt the momentum of the heavy weapon and bring it back from left to right, she spun completely in the air again, letting out a piercing shriek like a cornered cat turning to defend her cubs as she lopped another head clean off.

The speed of this was dazzling, as was the simple fact that it was happening. It was one thing to practice the tiger on the dojo floor, quite another to take on six men with firearms as the blood spurted.

Armies spent months and years training soldiers — and only their best soldiers — to do this. Getting draftees to shoot a rifle from behind a wall at a living target is hard enough. Training young people who are not clinically insane to wreak such havoc at a range close enough to smell the garlic your opponent had for lunch as you slice into his gut is something else again.

An amateur not drilled through repeated, conditioned re-sponse will freeze in shock and confusion for as much as four full seconds when confronted with such unexpected violence. These Grays, for all their fancy uniforms and reputation, were accustomed to "fighting" only docile sheep, and so fell into the category of untrained amateurs. Madison was still just within that four-second zone of opportunity as she leapt through the portal — her blade and the gun in her waistband setting off the red light and the beeper — and approached the third trooper, who was posted in standard position to take custody of any detainee who set off the portal's alarms.

The Gray held up one arm, pointing at her as though to say, "Wait, you can't do that." Without hesitation, she set her left foot, finally reversed her direction of swing, and the vicious 18-inch falcata with its curved edge took off his arm — left to right — at the elbow as she went past. Then she was on the two guards behind him, one of them stupidly clutching his metal-detector wand while the other tried to clear his weapon to fire.

It was as though some supernatural force descended on

them. Madison held her weapon in both hands to keep her grip from slipping on the blood. She set her feet wide, hacked and swirled, snarled and slashed at their chests and arms as blood sprayed around the three of them like a fountain in the park in a little girl's jungle gym summer.

Downstrokes would have bounced off their ribs, but by slashing from side to side she opened up their chests and stomachs till their intestines and other internal organs plopped and burbled out to spill on the trailer floor at their feet. They were soon down on their knees, sloshing in what seemed an improbably large pool of fresh, frothing blood. Madison recognized the smell from the only other time she'd ever seen so much — like a copper pot boiled dry and overheating on the stove.

The smell and the memory it triggered made her keen. It was not a normal human sound. It was a noise to make grown men shiver. The Irish had named a fearsome spirit for that sound. And all men knew that to hear the cry of the banshee meant death was at large in the land. Death with brown eyes.

They were not fighting men, now. They cried like children, begged for mercy, alternated between holding their hands out in supplication and trying to scoop their entrails back into their slashed and sundered bellies.

But once Madison, full of fury, was on them, they never had a chance. She continued to let out a little cry like a wounded bird at the end of each stroke, payback for Ratzo and little Kiera — and for her mother and older sister, about the manner of whose deaths she had vowed never to speak, unless and until God decided to let her bear girl children to replace them — woman warriors to avenge their clan — tears of rage in her eyes, setting her feet now and slashing from side to side as though cutting through sugar cane.

"Sons of bitches!" she shouted.

She knew nothing but her fury. You could have struck her a killing blow and she would have kept doing this till the blood drained completely from her body or she ran out of enemies.

When you came upon someone capable of being possessed like this, all you could do was hope to stay out of her way ... and pray she was on your side.

Even Brawny and Caitlin, off to the side in a makeshift holding area, their hands bound behind their backs, stood wide-eyed at the spectacle of this dervish hacking and slashing her way through to them.

But there were still two more Grays untouched in the trailer, and by now they'd had plenty of time to recover from the initial shock of Madison's attack. Standing directly between her and Caitlin and Brawny, an older trooper, obviously some kind of officer, smiled the smile of a snake as he shouldered his weapon now, lowered his head to his rear sight, prepared to put a burst of 9mm right through Madison.

Bronwyn, wide and mighty, put her head down and prepared to ram the officer with her shoulder from behind, hoping to take him down, or at least spoil his aim.

And then came a chill breeze. Something whirred within inches of Madison's ear, and the strangest look of surprise came over the Gray company leader's face. A black arrow had neatly segmented his skull, entering through the left temple.

Watch for the Black Arrow, he'd told her.

Madison had also bypassed a pale, balding and overweight inspector who sat behind the X-ray screen, prepared to scan each prisoner's purse or other belongings for hidden discs and weapons. He had an MP-5, as well, though he'd left it hanging on the side of the machine, confident that their mere numbers would keep him from ever actually needing it.

Evidently unsure whether it had a round chambered, he had grabbed it and was coming up behind Madison now, sweat pouring off his pale flesh as he reluctantly approached this apparition, preparing to use the finely engineered firearm to bash her over the head.

But Hideki had entered from the loading dock now, even as The Black Arrow had let fly through the open door. Sprinting from behind, Hideki slashed this final trooper as he closed on Madison's back, using the Wakizashi that Hideki wore at his own back to open the hesitant fellow from neck to mid-dorsal. His pattern-welded blade easily sliced down through the shoulder and collar bone, but then glanced off the spine as it descended, severing three ribs from the spine before his stroke ran out of momentum.

That left it stuck but good. Hideki had to put his foot high against the sagging Gray's back to extract his blade. Then he spun to his left, coming around to remove the head of the guard whose pointing forearm Madison had amputated at the elbow on her way past, a fellow who had now adequately recovered to have begun shrieking quite inconveniently, adding to the din created by Madison and the portal gongs.

Hideki landed with a soupy splash, his feet set wide apart, scanning quickly right to left for another target.

But it seemed they were done. In front of Madison, kneeling on the floor, one of the two Grays she had disembowelled sagged on his side, blessedly unconscious. But as Madison paused now, panting, one last young trooper remained conscious and upright on his knees, just at her feet.

He had given up any thought of defending himself, now. Instead, he worked with a wide-eyed singleness of purpose at the hopeless task of scooping up his own entrails off the trailer floor and attempting to place them, fastidiously and with an almost touching gentleness, back into his own belly, pausing to look with amazement at the sheer quantity of blood on his hands, as though the liquid had appeared there from some source unknown.

He clearly had trouble catching his breath — both his diaphragm and his lungs had been seriously impaired.

The Black Arrow joined them in the trailer now, as Hideki punched the big "Off" button to silence the blaring portal alarm. This also shut down its flashing red light, reducing the impression that someone had opened the gates of hell. He crossed to slice the plastic ties that bound the hands of Bron-wyn and Caitlin.

Then the old swordsman found some wet towels, some-where, and rubbed the blood from their faces till they were at least mildly presentable. He asked them if the operators had yet photographed them, suspiciously eyeing the Gray equipment, wondering if he'd know how to erase the images if they had. The pair assured him no, they'd been just about to start photo-graphing them with Madison had marched in. Hideki opened the covers on the stacks and slashed the hard drives, anyway.

As the last young Gray looked up at Madison and The Black Arrow, words formed on his lips. They were barely au-dible.

The Black Arrow stooped down in front of him. The kid couldn't be more than 20. A mere child, he still had traces of his teen-age acne, looked like he'd just begun shaving. His face was wide-eyed with shock, the words a mere whisper.

"Why? We're just here to keep people safe."

Unbidden, Andrew felt tears welling up in his eyes. "Son," he replied, "it doesn't say 'to keep us safe.' It says 'To secure these rights, governments are instituted among men.' I know they filled your head with a lot of other nonsense, but that was the important part. That was the part you're not allowed to miss. You took away the people's rights. Their freedoms. Their God-given right to bear arms — any arms, any time, anywhere. And the penalty for that ... is death."

The dying young man cried with him, now. But his face still bore a look of incomprehension. So many would die, with-out ever understanding why.

"Tell Ellie —" the young man said. But he never finished. Tell Ellie he loved her? Tell Ellie he was sorry? That she should keep the baby? That the diamond was at the jewelers? That dinner was in the oven? No one would ever know.

Madison was not crying. As she came down off her adren-alin rush, she was emerging from her own alternative reality.

Her peripheral vision would return gradually, along with her hearing. But at this point she had no sense of time and place, was still looking around for someone else to kill.

Good. The resistance didn't need more tears. It needed more soldiers. No, Andrew corrected himself. More captains. And Madison would do. How many had she just killed, here, without waiting for orders?

Incredibly, it had all taken less than 90 seconds, and not a shot had been fired. Andrew and Hideki had seen Madison entering the trailer just as they'd arrived, Tommy Chin racing them here in his cab from the battle on the darkened stage of the old Gotham Theatre.

They stood there for a moment, in awe of what Madison had done. Though in truth the Grays — a bunch of draft dodgers who never really deserved their fierce reputation — had grown into a lazy and complacent bunch after years of dealing with nothing but cowering sheep. They hadn't fired their guns because they hadn't *trained* to fire their guns; they never actually believed they would *have* to fire their guns.

"OK, kid," The Black Arrow said, risking a gentle hand on Madison's shoulder, "... They're done. Time to go."

"You OK?" she asked, her head clearing. "Anyone hurt?"

"Just staying out of your way," he smiled as they did a quick wipe of their weapons on the still shuddering back of the last trooper.

"Airburst is with Tommy at the cab," The Black Arrow said, handing his bow and quiver to the blademaster. "You three go with Hideki; we'd better clear out of here fast. You got the plastic bags, Hideki-san, in case Tommy had to move?"

"I do."

"It'll be hard to get out of here without tracking some blood," he reminded the girls. "Soon as you're out of sight, pull the bags over your shoes and change direction. You know the routine. No straight lines."

"What about you?" Madison asked.

"Morning's not far off, and there are Grays in the tunnels. Not a good time for me to go running around the streets dressed like this."

Of course. Deprived of the tunnels, and if this was an area where the new, taller buildings had uneven roof lines with bigger set-backs, he'd have to shed his bow and take off the black mask to make his way more than a block or two.

"You sure you're alright?" Hideki asked his masked companion.

"Good as new," The Black Arrow replied.

"You three get going," Madison said. "I know a place where The Black Arrow can lay low for a few hours — for the day, if need be. And I already know what our friend looks like without the mask. Go!"

They did. Madison had that effect on people, now.

The Black Arrow looked a question at her for only a moment. Then they followed Hideki and the girls outside, jumped down from the loading dock — though the Black Arrow staggered for a moment as he landed, came up wincing, which was odd. The pair of them quartered off in a different direction from the other three.

"I met you when I bought my first sword from Hideki. And you touched me when you were teaching me how to shoot the bow. Think I could ever forget your touch, your voice ... Andrew?"

His mask went into a dumpster a block away. They walked together, careful not to appear to be in any rush. He put his hand on her shoulder, casually. Madison took his hand from her shoulder, swung her hip against his, pulled that arm around her waist. They walked that way for a while, hips locked, like lovers.

She led the way, obviously had a planned route, finally ushered him down a half staircase to a basement apartment in a brownstone indistinguishable from the row of brownstones

458

on either side.

"Nice place," he said, gazing about as she locked the door behind them, turned on a small lamp. Actually, it was plain and dim and a little musty. But clean.

"Belonged to a friend of ours. Got killed by the cops. So an under group leader in the Grays ended up with the key."

"And is the under group leader likely to be stopping by?"

"No. No one's going to be hearing from the under group leader for a long time."

"That's kind of what I figured."

She led him back to the bedroom, turned on the sound system, not too loud.

"You've got blood all over you. Madison, you should wash up."

"Yeah, in a minute."

And then little Madison was in his face, once again an inescapable force of nature, giving him that serious stare they all knew so well by now. And the wave of pheromones washing over him was so tangible Andrew actually shivered, felt himself knocked back as by a wave. If they could have bottled the scent that was filling the room they could have sold it for plenty — but what would the warning label have read, "If you wear this in public you *will* be raped"?

There is a power women have when they're ready to give themselves. She herself might have no idea why, but something in Madison told her this was the time. Without asking permission even with her eyes, her fine small breasts were against him as she pushed him back till he fell backward on the bed, stretched herself up to press her lips to his ear, climbed on her knees, half straddling him.

"Listen," she said, urgent to speak while the power was on her. When she got serious like this two parallel vertical lines formed between her heavy, expressive eyebrows. He knew the lines were there even though his face was buried in her hair, which smelled of fresh air and vanilla and ... Madison. "I know

I'm not for you. I know about her; I know all about her. She's smart, and beautiful, and classy and educated, and I'm not. I'm none of those things. I don't know French literature and I don't know which wine goes in which glass — I understand all that."

"Don't talk yourself down, Madison. You've got talents even you — "

"Shut up. I'm sorry, Andrew, but shut up. What I'm telling you is there's no promise here to break. You're not taking advantage of a teen-age crush; you're not going to screw anything up. I swear it. What I'm asking you to do is save my life, here, Andrew Fletcher, Mr. high-and-mighty Black Arrow. Right now.

"I'll never reach for your hand in public, nothing, I swear. No one will ever know from me, till the day I die. Only I want it to be you, see. I need it to be you. I'm asking you please. Do me this one favor, OK? Only just do it. Don't talk about it; don't think about it; don't try to be my guidance counselor and work it all out; and don't say no, OK? I mean, I know you can do this. I feel it in you, I smell it on you. Cassandra doesn't disappear upstairs three, four hours at a time because you guys are practicing your flower-arranging."

"I didn't know I was being timed."

"Anything over half an hour, women notice, dude. Don't let 'em fool you. Unless you think I'm ugly. I mean, I'm OK to look at, right? I'm young enough, I'm not fat, I've got regular features, right?"

"You're beautiful, Madison, now more than ever. And you're my best fighter; someday you'll lead armies. But — "

"Yeah, whatever. So what I need now is for you to make love to me, Andrew. Not someday. Right here, right now. I got the only key to this place, so we're all alone till we get, you know, really hungry. So just drill me. Fuck the bejesus out of me. Just this once, OK? Can you do that for your best fighter? I've never asked you a favor before and it's all I'll ever ask of you, I swear. I'm healthy and everything, I haven't been with anyone for a long, long time and I am really, really ready."

She was breathing heavily, randomly interspersed with shudders. Her breath was vanilla and her hair smelled of cinnamon and fresh air and something else ... .

It was one of those moments, like coming on a fawn in a clearing in the deep forest. You went still, and you and that magnificent creature gazed at each other and shared a moment that you wanted to hold for all time. And once or twice in a lifetime, that wild creature might come over and stick its cool nose in your hand. You didn't want to count on a lot of miracles like that. You just left yourself open to them, and allowed yourself to be occasionally amazed.

He reached down and unfastened the buttons on her burgundy vest and bloodstained white shirt and she let out the breath she'd been holding. As she did so she shuddered, giving up the last of her control, and he believed what she said, about her need, and what it would do to her to refuse her, now.

Her heavy sword in its fringed leather scabbard thudded to the floor. She was his, then, completely. She had large, white teeth between those full dark lips, he discovered, and she'd been getting a little more to eat — she wasn't quite the skinny child he remembered. Her breasts and hips were fine, ample, perfectly proportioned. She had the well defined arm muscles of a fighter, now — her arms must be aching from what she'd just put them through — and she'd obviously been a gymnast, in that earlier life she would never talk about. In addition to which, she had another quality he'd never before been able to pin down. Madison was a volcano ... steaming ... sultry.

She straddled him. She clearly had her first orgasm as she shrugged out of her own shirt — she wore no bra — seemed ready for another as his own shirt came off.

But then she spotted the bandage on his side.

She stopped.

"You're hurt."

461

"Like I told you, we had a little trouble back at the Gotham. Sorry we were late."

"Trouble?"

"Kylie and Nguyen were spies. We got to 'em just in time. At least, I hope we did."

"So they're ..."

"Gone for their tea."

"Oh my God. Poor Raitch. Does she know?"

"Rachel had to kill Nguyen, Madison. She didn't have any choice."

Madison sobbed. Tears welled in her eyes.

"Was she hurt?"

"Rachel's fine. Considering. She's the one who fetched Doc Stauffer for me."

"And Bob? Does he know about Kylie?"

"Bob was there."

"I didn't know. Honest." She touched his side, near the bandage, wincing for him.

"Bullet didn't hit anything vital. Helmut shot me up with a local. Although he did say I should spend the day in bed."

A smile curled Madison's lip. She tried to stop herself, but it didn't work. They both laughed.

"Look, I guess this was a mistake," she said. "You should rest."

He kissed her on the lips. It was soft, like being brushed by the petals of a flower. Slowly, gently, he placed his arms on her shoulders.

"No," he said. "This is perfect."

She leaned forward till their foreheads touched. Closing her eyes, she breathed deep. He kissed her again, longer. Harder. She gave up trying to be noble, collapsed against him.

Yes, she murmured in her fever, rubbing desperate hands over his arms and shoulders firm and huge, just as she'd imagined them, and the hair of his chest was not curly but straight and flowing all in one direction, like the hair of some sleek water creature. Oh, yes, thank you God. If there was only this one night it would be enough for her, she swore it.

"Deanaibh mi gu cruaidh," she gasped, her always raspy voice deeper and throatier than usual.

"My pleasure," he smiled, helping her shed her black waitress slacks. Underneath, as she straddled him again, she was soft and sleek and warm and wet. She was perfect.

"You have no idea what I just said," she panted.

"You must have grown up by the sea, to hear such talk" he smiled. "I'd make that 'Do me hard, sailor.' "

"Close e-nough." And she was on him, finally, her hips rolling and stroking, seemingly independent of the rest of her, like the gyroscope of a spacecraft, suspended in gimbals so it could move in any direction without locking up. And she was so beautiful she glowed.

"Jesus," he said.

"What?" she asked, stopping in case she'd hurt his wound, in case something was wrong.

"No, it's fine. I mean, 'Jesus, where *you* been all my life?' "

She smiled then, a smile that lit the room. He wasn't sure he'd ever known she had those huge dimples. Leaned forward till their foreheads touched, stared him in the eye, and began again, slowly.

The radio played "Naked," by the little French Canadian.

You see right through me
And I can't hide
I'm naked
Around you
And it feels so right

⚜ ⚜ ⚜

Andrew dozed off. She woke him. He didn't mind. She was breathing those hot shuddering breaths in his ear again, searching his body with her hands and mouth until he aroused again, to his surprise if not to hers, till she could slip onto him, grabbing his hands and placing them on her breasts, desperate in her heat and her need.

"You're beautiful, Madison."

"Don't."

"What?"

"Don't tell me all those lies women want to hear. I don't want the promises, I don't want the fantasies. I know my legs are too short and I've got a funny nose. Don't put any of that bullshit between us, Andrew, please. This is enough; it is what it is and it's everything it should be and I thank you, I thank you. God, I thank you." She was finding her rhythm now. God, she was like a well-lubricated cricket pump. She acted like she could do this forever.

"Madison, I get some say in all this, and you're just going to have to take the word of an expert, here. You were beautiful when you bought your first blade, and you're beautiful when you go to war. I love your voice, I love your smile, I love the way you throw yourself into life; I'm allowed to tell you you are truly beautiful. It's a prerogative a guy gets, OK? Great hips, too." This little one had made him as large as he could ever remember being, though he didn't mention that to her.

Ask any man what made a woman attractive and chances were you'd get a hierarchy of physical features: tits, ass, legs, preferably taut and perky — a relatively flat belly — and then the far more inscrutable symmetry of a beautiful face, though no one had ever succeeded in explaining why just a few of them could take the breath away, make men stare until they walked into walls.

Accurate as far as it went. For the male animal had hundreds of thousands of years of bred-in experience recognizing these symmetrical shorthand signs of youth, health, fertility.

And the male hormones were strong enough that this really could suffice, absent any affection whatever. Oh, a smile always helped. But the reproductive act did remain the prime imperative.

In all these categories, Madison was beautiful. Her eyes were huge and dark. Her hair was dense and full. Her voice was soft and cool. That sardonic smile that said she always knew more than she was letting on. The energy and freshness of youth. Lithe and strong, her warm, smooth skin glistened and slid, begged to be caressed. What little fat she carried was in her butt and her fine protruding breasts, perfectly proportioned, nuzzling him like eager week-old puppies.

But what turned him into the growling beast, what made her the most beautiful woman in the world this day, the woman he would kill to keep, was her hunger, her passion, her need ... for him. Just for him.

She had held it for him, and now it filled the room like a thunderclap. She seemed honestly amazed by the rush of unimagined pleasure when he caressed and nibbled and then sucked her nipples and ears while he was inside her. She laughed, she moaned, she giggled, she gave herself over entirely till they lost all sense of time and place and could no longer tell for sure where one body ended and the other began.

"All right, mo mhuirnin," she laughed that throaty laugh that would always thereafter harden him into a car jack. "You can say anything you need to, if it helps keep you hard. Just so you know I'm not calling you on any promise you make here. Next time we meet, introduced as friends, I'm just one of your fighters. No flowers, no candy; I won't come runnin' to your arms. This is all I want, see? But right now I do need all you've got."

"Oh *that's* not going to be a problem," he smiled.

The Veronicas came on the radio, backed up by a tasty little snare, covering the Chiffons' previously obscure "Just

For Tonight."

Just for tonight (Just for tonight)
Let me love you warm and tender
Just for tonight (Just for tonight)
Be my love and you'll remember

(Each kiss) showin' you how much I want you
(Each word) tellin' you how much I love you
(Each time) I ask you to be mine.

And then that wonderful bassoon solo, backed up by Long Shot's horn section.

They were together when, as the poet would have it, they slipped the surly bonds of earth, and danced the skies on laughter-silvered wings. And they did laugh, in their binding. And then Madison buried her face in his shoulder, so he would not see her wipe away a secret tear. She had asked for just the one day, since that was all she felt she deserved, and all she had seen in her vision.

Though she wanted so much more.

⚜ ⚜ ⚜

Andrew awakened and looked at the clock, couldn't believe it'd been only two hours. "No way you made me this sore in two hours."

"Silly man," she said as she finished drying her hair — she'd been in the shower; her skin felt clean and glowing and she smelled of mint as she climbed up on him again, went to work with a small tube of lubricant. If they'd once had clothes, neither of them could now remember when. He reached for the glass of water on the nightstand — the refrigerator had offered only watery pale beer and some noxious lemon-lime crap full of artificial sweetener. At least there were ice cubes for the water.

Doc Stauffer had passed him a handful of codeine pills. He popped a couple. The local had long since worn off and the bullet wound felt like a cramp in his side.

"Fourteen."

"What?"

"It's been fourteen hours, mo chuisle. I chose well."

He moaned. She laughed.

"Do you know what you called me on the phone?"

"When?"

"Before, when I called you from the hotel and told you they had Caitlin and Brawny."

"No."

"Mo chuisle."

"No. Did I?"

"You did."

More commonly anglicized as macushla, sometimes used with a touch of irony, the original Gaelic "a chuisle mo chroí" meant "my heart's beloved" — "pulse of my heart."

"It's alright," she laughed. "I'll not hold you to it. Though it was nice to hear, all the same. But now I have a question for you, my love."

"Yes?"

"When you said we could do the mission, that we could go to the Dupont, you had the strangest expression on your face. You saw something, didn't you?"

"I don't know what you mean."

"I'm your best soldier, Andrew. And I don't think you have anyone else you can tell. Do you trust me?"

"With my life."

"And my life is yours, Andrew — I would willingly give it up before I would betray you. So tell me ... mo chuisle. I'm your Irish bitch now, yours to command. But I'm also the one person who can understand, I think. You see things, don't you?"

He said nothing, searching her face.

"It's between us two, love," she promised. "I'm not one of your mall rats, you know. It's not a sin, where I come from, to spey the future."

"Things as they might be, nothing more than that."

"You saw death."

"Yes. I thought you'd survive, but that we would take losses. I saw death."

"And you let us go, anyway."

"It's a war, Madison. This is what we do. We send people out to kill, and to die. Every commander knows some of his men will die. If I'd known anything specific, that they were ready for you, I would have pulled you out, believe me. But that's not the way it works. I can't tell you tomorrow's lottery number. It's more an ability to see patterns unfold, sometimes a single moment in time, frozen in a lightning flash. But can I tell you what caused that moment, or whether by changing my plans I can prevent it, or instead whether that's how I caused it? There's something they call the butterfly effect. Change one thing now, you can never be sure exactly how it'll change the future. ...."

She kissed his face, then, kissed his eyes. He was surprised at her gentleness. Who was this woman? How had she come to him? She seemed to grow chilly, then, for the first time. He pulled a blanket up around her shoulders. Smooth and beautiful. Why did they ever need clothes? He could have made love just to her shoulders, just to her eyes. She had given him the treasure of her smile.

"I know, Andrew. You misunderstand me, love. I'm not blaming you. I was in command; I'll always be grateful you gave me a command, even if it turns out to be my last. I lost Kiera and Ratzo. I'll never blame anyone but myself for that.

"Brawny and Caitlin? I'm so proud of those bitches. And

what got them through was training. Ratzo died because he had no training.

"I should have had more escape routes planned. I didn't know the floor plan of that building the way I should have. I was smug — I made mistakes I'd never make again. But I'm asking about something else. Something important, I think. About something I saw in your eyes just before you told us that mission was a go. Hideki said you should cancel or else send Jean-Claude and his boys. I thought you were going to say no. But you looked into the future, and you sent us. You wouldn't have taken those losses just for Bambi Fiducci. Make me understand, Andrew. Trust me."

"You needed that battle, Madison."

"What?"

"You said yourself that we needed to keep up enough normal operations so they wouldn't suspect we've got something bigger planned. But it was more than that. As much as I wanted to protect you from it, I had to give you that battle. You just said it. You made mistakes you'll never make again. How does a person learn to command, except by commanding?

"What you did to get yourself and Brawny and Caitlin out of there will be a legend. You think only of your losses, now, and that's good, that's to your credit. But you have no idea what a victory that was, last night. People will sing songs about the way you fought your way out of there, four girls against an army. It will mobilize a nation.

"The little, 'safe' missions Hideki wanted to send you on? One of them would have taken your life. A stupid, meaningless death. Because there are no 'safe' little missions. Now, you'll plan harder than anyone. You're learning how far troops can be pushed, how they're motivated, how to plan for contingencies, where the backups have to be waiting. Troops will flock to serve under you. You'll command armies, Madison, because you'll win. That's what I saw. It's your curse, allana. You'll become a legend."

"But only if you sent me into that bath of blood."

"Yes."

"Thank you, my love. Thanks for trusting me enough to tell me. And thanks for trusting me enough to send me. Because you see, I have the sight, too. Sometimes, anyway. It's what brought me here to you.

"And now," she asked, cocking her head coquettishly, "are there any more shots left in that barrel? Do you suppose you can do me just once more, for old times' sake?"

He laughed. She shrieked and giggled as he rolled her over.

And so they forgot their pain. They forgot their lives. They loved, and slept, and loved again, and dreamed of lives that might yet be, and lives that might have been.

And she knew then, for sure, that he had the sight. Because he had not asked her what future she herself had seen, as anyone else would have asked.

And why would that be ... unless he knew?

CHAPTER 14

*Men submit everywhere to oppression, when they have
only to lift their heads to throw off the yoke; yet, instead of
asserting their birthright, they quietly lick the dust and say,
Let us eat and drink, for tomorrow we die. Women, I argue
from analogy, are degraded by the same propensity to enjoy
the present moment; and, at last, despise the freedom which
they have not sufficient virtue to struggle to attain.*

— MARY WOLLSTONECRAFT (1759-1797)

*The humblest citizen of all the land when clad in the armor
of a righteous cause, is stronger than all the hosts of Error.*

— WILLIAM JENNINGS BRYAN (1860-1925)

*He that hath no sword, let him sell his garment,
and buy one.*

— JESUS THE NAZARENE, AT LUKE 22:36

Winding into the caverns in long descending chains of
torches, they held a memorial service for Ratzo and little Kiera.

Their growing numbers surprised everyone, except Andrew and his captains.

471

Madison's troop were all there, again down to seven in number: Bronwyn pureheart; Morgan the sea-born; Rachel, lamb of God; Fiona the fair; Caitlin the Pure; slender Caelan, Gray-eyed Shayla the wanderer.

Madison had always figured them far too independent a lot to ever submit to anything so regimented as a uniform. But a number of the gallai had taken to wearing hooded green pullovers against the chill of the tunnels — with shamrocks sewn on the back, as a private joke among the Irish Bitches. Riding the subways, they'd actually gotten a good laugh more than once at being mistaken for Catholic-school girls. They joked that it must make Madison their mother superior.

Now Rachel approached Madison, asking if she thought it would be OK for the girls to adopt something more closely approaching a uniform for occasions like today's.

Someone had once said that if you paid attention long enough, you could learn something. Maybe there was something hard-wired into the human spirit that craved this kind of emblem, a symbol of allegiance and belonging. Madison told Rachel she thought it would be fine. And so the Bitches had come in their colors ... and with their bows, of course. They formed up on the left.

Bronwyn and Caitlin stood at the front. But the men treated all of them differently, now — regardless of whether they'd actually been at the Dupont. It was subtle, but unmistakable. They weren't just cute hangers-on, anymore. They were fighters. Kiera had bought them that. Bought it in blood, for everyone who wore the green.

Jean-Claude and Quart Low and Airburst had their own army of more than 40, every one a combat veteran. They comprised the largest element of the Order now assembled, forming up in a rectangle in the center and coming easily to parade rest out of long habit. The black and green camo the Army had revived to fight in the pine forests of the West had proved far better at breaking up a human outline in the tunnels and the alleys than the more homogeneous "chocolate chip" pattern some of these old timers had worn, fighting off the towelheads in the desert sands.

Anyone who knew fighting men could size up their well-worn boots and load belts — not to mention their beards and scars — and recognize something far more ominous in the quiet ease of this over-the-hill gang than the spit-and-polish perfection of some teen-age barracks brigade. They were quiet, for starters. There was no wasted motion. Like frogs waiting for flies.

Jimmy Chin had relocated his complete AK-47 assembly line down to the caverns, where it now joined the metal-stamping press.

Jimmy's factory crew made up another dozen here today, nearly all Asian, each thoroughly re-screened and background-ed after the incidents with Kylie and Nguyen.

In fact, all who now remained had been recruited by Hideki out of the dojos — primarily at the Gotham, though the offshoot neighborhood self-defense clubs were now starting to feed some talent up the line. These "factory boys" were the troop deployed only when the utmost stealth and silence were required — they trained with Hideki, fought only at night and almost exclusively with the blade.

They were dressed today in loose and flowing exercise clothes. Where they would normally have worn all black, however, today they wore white — the Asian color of mourning — set off with black belts and headbands.

Even little Timmy Chin was there — his Uncle Jim had been designing him a special pair of crutches, showing him how to use all the fancy metal fabrication gear.

And so, with no one to tell them otherwise, the Order of the Arrow had fallen to building an army along lines which would have been familiar to any commander from Alexander to Wellington.

The technologies might change, but armies for thousands

of years were built up of small units of varying size, each hailing from a single geographic locale, sharing the same weapons and tactics, language and beliefs ... and thus, inevitably, their own colors and flags. Recruited by a single captain, they answered first to him and only through him to a higher chief, whether it be for clan allegiance, mercenary pay ... or, yes, even some abstract cause.

Sometimes lost was coordination among units — though the measure of a great commander was his order of battle, his ability to understand each unit's strengths and weaknesses and employ it appropriately.

What was gained, though, stemmed from the understanding that fighters always fought first and foremost for their comrades and the reputation of their unit. Who could sing around a roaring campfire of the exploits of anonymous cannon fodder thrown together at random, men with some numeric designation instead of a proud unit name, their own traditions and colors?

It was only the arrival of the mass collectivized state, first under the tyrant Lincoln, then spreading to Europe by the time of the First World War, that had changed warfare from the specialized pursuit of small companies of proud and skilled professionals into a test of the willingness of whole nations to feed the better part of an entire generation of their young into the gaping jaws of death's meatgrinder.

The modern state adopted as the dominant symbol of this conversion of the individual into expendable, interchangeable machine parts a uniformity of costume, of weaponry, of tactics, until the only discernible difference between the brigade thrown into battle yesterday and the one coming up the road today was that the newcomers were still alive, standing upright, in possession of all their limbs ... and wondering what in hell was about to happen to them. All to prove that our side's devotion to suicidal collectivism was more devout — and thus bound to prevail — than that of the bastard across the field.

Even the colors of their uniforms came to serve as a kind of metaphor for what their parents had allowed the mighty state to make of these endless trains full of boy-children. Chosen to be less visible to snipers, of course, the uniforms also had the effect of giving the living a look startling similar to that of the dead. Call it beige, khaki, or gray, what living and dead now most closely resembled was ... mud.

Doctor Stauffer attended the service. Joan Matcham came, though they decided it would be better if Jack Brackley kept a low profile. Madison was a little surprised to see Long Shot Jones, several of his sidemen including Connor the drummer and Mustapha the bassman, and all the Veronicas. Hideki was there.

Madison had asked Hideki what she should say. His advice was not to prepare anything to say. "Tell them what it was like when you met her. Was it sunny, or did it rain? Remind them about her smile, the sound of her voice. A long speech is not good. To describe a butterfly, use 17 syllables."

She tried to stick with that. She had met Kiera in the sunshine. Her hair had shone like copper. Kiera had never seen a marmalade cat that she hadn't insisted they take in and feed. They would never be able to see an orange cat, now, without remembering.

They waited a moment after Madison made an end and rejoined her crew. But the Black Arrow did not keep them long. He appeared out of nowhere — as ever — slightly over their heads and off to the side, nestled in the waist-high folds of a natural outcropping formed by the confluence of two rows of the cavern's stalagmites, a twisted stone pulpit out of Antonio Gaudi, all red and yellow flowstone that flickered translucent from within like a huge candle from the light of the torches above and behind.

"Death is an ending, and a beginning," said the man in black. He spoke quietly, but his voice carried strong, reverberating in the dripping stillness of the ancient cave.

"We will all remember and honor Kiera and Ratzo — Jimmy — in our own ways. In ancient days, her captain would have told you that a warrior like Kiera, dying in reckless battle against a superior foe, went straight to Valhalla, to feast forever among the champions. I won't pretend to know any different.

"Jimmy Rizzolo? Jimmy discovered these caverns. He was the trailblazer of our revolution. Without him, none of us would be here today.

"Jimmy and Kiera are free now, of the pain and tears of this world, which those of us gathered here still share. And now we bear the added burden of their loss.

"Grief is natural. Grief is OK. But both Jimmy and Kiera got to choose with whom they wanted to fight, and die. You helped give them that choice, which others would have taken from them. They decided they would rather die as part of this struggle than live in a world without sunshine, without hope, without freedom. And that's how they should be remembered — for the things they valued enough to fight for. And to die for. For the things that — in their memories, and thanks in part to their sacrifice — we are now bound to attain.

"For the best way to honor their memory is to see to it they did not die in vain.

"This much I know for sure. Kiera and Jimmy willingly gave their lives, without regret or protest, for our cause — fighting so that other men and women will live free. They also gave their lives — willingly and without protest — for their friends. As each of us would have done for them. There can be no stronger bond.

"We will miss their spirit, and their smiles. But at the same time they live on in us, in all of us who knew them. So that as long as even one of us lives and remembers, they are not truly gone.

"The time came for them to put down their burden. The dark angel came to comfort them, to gather them up in her velvet wings, and carry them to a better place, beyond our world of grief and care.

"In our selfishness, we wish we could bring them back from that better place, to see their smiles, to hear Kiera's laugh and Jimmy's wonderful, terrible jokes just one more time. God in his wisdom understands, and forgives us that selfishness.

"But let us rather turn to those we cherish, now — realizing how precious and fleeting is the time we have with them — and resolve to better appreciate this life we have been given, the freshness of the wind, the gentleness of the rain, the smile of a lover and a child.

"Honor them by leading your own lives to the full. Know that life is but a passing moment. Choose well with whom you spend your life, and how you use it. Glory in the rain, as well as the sunshine. We only get the one time around.

"Kiera and Jimmy lived well, and they died well. They shall not be forgotten. God's will be done."

They lit a great fire, then — they did not actually have the bodies for burial, of course, their enemy not being the kind to surrender such rare trophies.

Many had noticed before that — through some trick of the cavern's acoustics — the Gotham Theatre's old Wurlitzer organ could be faintly heard, even this deep. Someone was playing it now — "Amazing Grace," followed by "When Will I Be Loved?"

They watched the great blaze burn down to cherry embers, and hugged one another. Then the torches were extinguished, one by one, and by the pale glimmer of the electric bulbs they went their separate ways.

⚜ ⚜ ⚜

Quart Low's younger son had once been a big-time drug dealer. It had started when Todd was a teen-ager. An elderly neighbor asked if Todd could get him some marijuana to help him keep down his chemo medicine.

Todd retired at 27, a multi-millionaire, veteran of a fair number of hair-raising encounters with the federales on clandestine Baja airstrips, and married a nice Christian girl. They went into a new business, wholesaling sporting goods which they arranged to have manufactured in China.

Todd still lived a lavish lifestyle, though, and remained friends with many of his former associates.

He was driving his new red Ferrari on the night he slowed down, about to turn into the driveway of an opulent beach home owned by one of those young men, when he spotted the clutch of police cars up by the front door, lights flashing.

Todd turned back into the travel lane and drove on. The cops gave chase. Todd could have outrun them, but he was innocent.

When he pulled over and rolled down his window, six cars slid to a stop around him. Eight narcotics officers leapt out and started screaming orders at him at the top of their lungs.

"Put your hands where we can see them!" they shouted.

He placed them high on the steering wheel.

"Open the door and get out."

Todd lowered his left hand from the wheel to reach for the interior door handle. The clicks of eight pistol safeties coming off sounded like a fresh hatch of crickets.

"I told you to keep your hands where I could see them!"

He put his hands back on the wheel.

"Now open the door and get out!"

He lowered his left hand to reach for the interior door handle and open the door.

"I told you to keep your hands where I can see them, motherfucker!" shouted one of the cops, his face turning bright red and the cords standing out in his neck.

"If you assholes weren't so ignorant," Todd shouted back at the top of his lungs, "you'd know these Ferraris have an anti-carjack device which keeps the door from being opened from the outside while someone's in the car. So either I can keep my hands where you can see them or I can open the door, but I can't do both, and if you can't figure that out then I guess you're just going to have to fucking well shoot me, you fucking brain-damaged morons!"

There is no outrage like that of the former felon who finds himself falsely accused.

Todd Cavanaugh was not caught with any drugs. Chemical tests on him and the car showed they had not been in contact with any drugs. But he was in possession of a lot of cash, which — coupled with his history — was all the narcs needed to win an indictment.

What they wanted Todd to do was to testify against his former associates. Even if he'd been willing to do that — which he was not — it would have reduced his life expectancy to a matter of weeks or months.

He refused. So they trotted in some jailbirds eagerly in search of sentence reductions who gladly testified Todd had confessed his crimes to them in his cell, in the prison cafeteria, while hunting Yeti with them in remote Nepal, anything they thought the jury might buy.

Not only that, one of these gentlemen of high character even swore Todd had tried to hire him to assassinate the chief state prosecutor, who had indeed been shot and wounded while Todd was in jail.

Coming from a tattooed hophead who regularly swatted at invisible butterflies, this was the equivalent of a panhandler down in front of the post office claiming the head of the Gotham Stock Exchange had approached him about helping out with a billion-dollar insider trading scam.

All the money Todd and his wife had borrowed from friends and relatives to start their new sporting goods business was confiscated as "drug proceeds." All those friends and relatives — including college professors and retired military officers — were warned that if they tried to put up money for Todd's lawyers or his bail, they'd be indicted as co-conspirators, on the theory that the computer list of investors in Todd and Marsha's new sporting goods business was actually a list of members of his new drug cartel.

Three local lawyers in a row accepted $100,000 retainers and then — two weeks later, like clockwork — said they would not be able to continue with the case. None returned their retainers. The court said that was fine.

Anyone opposed to the drug war was carefully removed from Todd's jury. Todd got life.

Quart Low took a few days to visit his son in prison in the Southwest. Todd had been in the hospital infirmary several times. Broken arm. Skull fracture by the ocular orbit. Inside, if you were good looking but you didn't want to be someone's toy, you had to fight. Todd had won. The former king of the yard had not fared as well.

They were difficult conversations, through the glass in the prison visiting room, father and son knowing every word was being recorded, would later be reviewed and parsed by prosecutors looking for "coded messages."

Todd was fiercely jealous. He wanted to know why his young wife hadn't been to visit him more often.

"They keep moving you around," Quart Low pointed out. He wanted Todd to tell his lovely Marsha that she should get on with her life, find someone new. Better for the decision to come from Todd than for him to get the eventual letter. She loved him, but she was young and pretty. To the young, a year is an eternity. Ten years? Twenty? Without love, without children?

But he couldn't tell his son that. He couldn't tell Todd to give up hope.

They'd taken away Quart Low's wallet and keys before he could meet with Todd — despite the fact father and son weren't allowed even to shake hands through the bulletproof glass. Afterwards, he had to stand in line to get them back. They tried to give him the wrong ones. No one seemed to care.

That afternoon, heading back, Quart Low shuffled through the airport, his mind a hundred miles away. At the security portal they told him, "You might want to remove your shoes and send them through the conveyor belt to speed things up as you go through."

Quart Low's knees hurt. There was nowhere on this side of the portal to sit down and take off his shoes.

"Is it mandatory?" he asked.

"No," snapped the young man with the mustache.

The alarms remained silent as he passed through. But the man who had advised him that he "might want to" remove his shoes nodded and caught the eye of the goon who was watching to see if the alarms would go off. The second guard stepped in front of him and waved him out of line, into the special search area. The extra humiliation was to punish him for asking whether removing his shoes was required.

After asking the others, "Search or assist?" the young Mexican with the crewcut and the electronic wand instructed him to sit on one of the gray plastic chairs. "Extend your right leg," he said. "Extend your left leg. Now stand on the mat facing in that direction."

The young Mexican had a nametag that said "Ramon."

They made Quart Low take everything out of his pockets, including his change, his wallet and his ballpoint pen. Even though he had not set off the alarm. Ramon fondled Quartlow's asshole and crotch. He made him undo his belt.

"Do you want me to take off my pants?" Quart Low asked, his voice a dull monotone, standing out in public view of a dozen staff and as many sheeplike, obedient passengers.

"No," Ramon said, cheerfully. "Just undo your belt and hold it out like this."

After asking "Search or assist?" an older, smaller Mexican with a gray mustache carried away Quart Low's wallet.

Quart Low didn't know what "search or assist?" meant. It didn't appear likely anyone was going to tell him.

"Do I get a receipt for the money in the wallet?" Quart Low asked.

Ramon, who wore a necktie designed to look like a partially furled American flag, laughed. Quart Low had fought for that flag. Friends of his had died.

"We're just going to X-ray it," Ramon said.

"You're not going to count the money?" Quart Low asked. "If I come up short, I don't get a signed receipt that shows how much was in it when you took it away?"

Ramon laughed again. His expression indicated incredulity at just how confused and paranoid some of these old Anglos could become. "We're just going to X-ray it," he said again, in the tone of voice you'd use to reassure a panicking child.

Finally they dropped what was left of Quart Low's life at his feet in a big gray plastic tub. He re-fastened his belt and put everything back in his pockets, very slowly, as the busy staff of wand-waving Mexicans worked around him, obviously impatient that he wasn't clearing the area fast enough.

At last, he shuffled off in the direction of his gate, dragging his carry-on bag on its little wheels. They ignored him now. He had become invisible. It was as though he had been erased.

On his right, as the corridor narrowed, was a men's room. Quart Low did not go in.

Proceeding a few yards further, struggling with his knees, he sat down on the carpeted floor, opposite the men's room door, his back to the wall. He had a few minutes before his flight would board. The other passengers had gone on ahead. Foot traffic was light.

He went down a checklist in his mind. The Fourth Amendment had not been repealed. It couldn't be, anyway, since it did not "grant" any rights. It merely acknowledged a pre-existing liberty — one Americans had insisted on seeing codified as a condition of their agreeing to authorize the existence of the central government, in the first place. No Bill of Rights, and the whole deal would have been off.

Quart Low was not in a war zone. No warrant had been issued to authorize his search. Refusal to remove one's shoes did not constitute probable cause for a search.

They had once argued these searches were a matter of "private contractual arrangement" between the airlines and their passengers. But Ramon was a federal employee retained by the Transportation Security Administration — older brothers to the black-booted Grays — not by any airline.

And it was now illegal for any commercial airline to change its ticket contract to encourage passengers to wear their sidearms, or allow them carried aboard, or to alter or attempt to waive the federally mandated search protocols. So the "voluntary contract" part was now reduced to transparent bullshit.

That was the checklist.

Soon, he saw the young TSA guard with the American flag necktie leave the screening area and enter the men's room, walking briskly. He was alone.

Quart Low struggled to his feet and — wheeling his carry-on bag behind him — entered the men's room.

There was no one inside but Ramon.

Ramon was washing his hands. He turned to glance at Quart Low. He smiled and said hello. A polite young man. Quart Low nodded, smiled, said "Howdy." He hobbled up to the sink next to Ramon as though he, too, were going to wash his hands.

Then he hip-checked Ramon into the wall as hard as he could.

Quart Low had boxed middleweight. Ramon was skinny. No bulk to him. And he was taken completely by surprise.

Ramon struggled to keep from falling. The floor was wet and the counter was soapy. Quart Low set his own sneakers wide, grabbed the young man's head in both hands, pulled it toward him, and then straightened his arms as though throwing powerful inside jabs. He slammed the young man's head into the tile wall next to the paper towel dispenser three times, as hard as he could.

Not the mirror. The wall. Broken mirrors attracted attention.

Ramon was still conscious, but dazed. They rarely expected any counterattack. Heck, the signs said it was illegal just to tell them a joke. The young Mexican's face still registered some surprise, but his muscles were going slack.

He would have fallen to the floor, but Quart Low maintained enough control of the young man's head to make sure that as Ramon went down his jaw slammed into the countertop with a loud crack.

Quart Low could feel the jaw break up near the TM joint. It wobbled, like a loose luggage handle. A little blood came out of Ramon's mouth. Now he was unconscious, sagging to his knees. Quart Low pulled the young man's head into Quart Low's crotch. The head was warm. An intimate moment. He stepped one leg over Ramon's kneeling form, still holding him by the hair. Then he shifted his grip on the head, turning the neck till he felt the point at which the vertebrae locked up, resisting any further movement of the head in that direction.

Quart Low reached as far around the head as he could, so when he pulled his arm back he would get full rotation, his arm acting like a car's fanbelt.

Taking care to shift his shoulders along with his arms, Quart Low broke Ramon's neck. Then, holding up the loose head, he punched the young man sharply in the larynx, breaking the small bones there to block the windpipe.

The hardest part was dragging Ramon into the toilet stall. They don't call it "dead weight" for nothing. Then he had to be seated in a stable pose so he wouldn't slip to the floor.

In his younger days, Quart Low might have locked the stall door from the inside and climbed out the top. Now he had to content himself with folding a piece of paper towel thick enough to wedge the door tight, so it would look as though it were latched from the inside.

Quart Low wet some paper towels and cleaned up the small amount of blood on the counter and the floor. Then he washed his hands. He recovered his carry-on bag and proceeded slowly to his gate.

More than 15 flights departed the airport before Ramon's body was discovered. Subsequent departures were then delayed while the terminal was locked down and passengers currently at the gates were re-searched and questioned. But by the time the body of the TSA screener was found, Quart Low Cavanaugh was asleep in aisle seat 6-C of a cramped Boeing 737 that was nearing the end of its extended service life, somewhere over eastern Kentucky. Smiling at the obviously exhausted old man, a steward inobtrusively slipped a small pillow under Quart Low's head.

The next day, Ramon Gutierrez did not violate the Fourth Amendment.

⚜ ⚜ ⚜

Ratzo was irreplaceable.

Over the months he had taught Andrew and particularly Jean-Claude and his Army Brats enough of the tunnel map in his head to enable them to move around with relative ease. But there simply wasn't anyone else who — shown a spot on a map — could immediately tell you how many tunnels ran there at what depth, how many were well lit, which were dry, how far any given tunnel would run before you had good access back to the surface without emerging in the middle of some teeming bank lobby ...

Still, Ratzo's loss served as a punctuation mark. For the

whole texture of the rebellion was already changing.

Jean-Claude now had enough recruits that he could easily put a dozen experienced archers on a rooftop at any given time. That meant an entire isolated portal crew, working in some armpit of the city late at night, could be killed from above in less than 20 seconds, before they could even send out an alarm.

Just to prove he could do it, in fact, Jean-Claude put together two such crews, one led by Airburst Barnes and the other by Quart Low Cavanaugh. They allowed extra time for Quart Low — now returned from time off to visit his family — to climb the stairs on those ancient knees.

The two crews eliminated three to four portal squads per night, every night for five days. Thirteen Lightning Troopers ran away and 39 survived their wounds. But that still marked 18 portal crews incapacitated, 65 dead, in less than a week.

Brackley went batshit. Like Churchill adding up his convoy losses in 1941 and '42, he could do the math. They could hush things up, but they couldn't change the numbers.

Mayor Brackley called in Christian Newby's buddy, Group Leader Rennie Heydrich, who responded by quadrupling the size of each portal crew, dedicating 15 of those 24 troopers to perimeter security with floodlights and .30- and .50-caliber gun emplacements. He lit up every surrounding rooftop.

This trimmed to a quarter the number of portal locations they could man. Meantime, the amount of noise and light involved in setting up such a location now guaranteed no foot traffic would move within a block of a portal during the whole time it was set up. The night portals became little more than a gesture of defiance.

Quietly, over a period of weeks, the Grays drew back till they were attempting to cover less than 15 percent of the city at night. The rest of Gotham was abandoned from dusk to dawn. The rebellion had won freedom of movement through 85 percent of the city — at least at night — without taking a single additional casualty.

Brackley's PR operation publicized the great police victory over the Black Arrow's terrorist gang at the Dupont Conference Center ... and found the effort backfiring.

Yes, they'd killed two of the assailants, one a strange man named James Rizzolo, a loner who lived in the same apartment where his mother had died some years before, and who seemed to have survived by moving from job to job as a janitor in commercial buildings on the West Side, a trade not requiring much in the way of people skills.

The other dead assassin had also been identified, as a waitress from Cincinnati named Kiera Kelly who had migrated to Gotham after her family died subsequent to a little Drug War mishap.

The cops had struck the Kelly family in the hours before dawn, as usual. Clad in black and without any visible badges, warrants, or insignia, they broke down the front door of the suburban middle-class Cincinnati home which they believed to be a clandestine methamphetamine lab, and poured in, shouting. (Of course, methamphetamine would not have been manufactured in suburban neighborhoods if not for government drug Prohibition, in the first place.)

His two scantily clad young daughters screaming as strange men crashed into their bedrooms with flashlights and guns, Sean Kelly came running down the hallway with his shotgun. After he'd been shot and was bleeding to death on his living room carpet, his naked wife Melinda tried to protect him from further harm by covering her dying mate with her own body. The officers picked her up and threw her against the wall, causing her to miscarry her third child — the boy the Kellys had been trying for so long to have.

Turned out the search warrant bore the wrong address.

Frustrated, the cops tore the Kelly house apart that night as Kiera and Cathy sat shivering in terror on the living room couch, still half naked, with the muzzles of loaded machine

pistols poised inches from their temples as the men continued to scream "Where are the fucking drugs?!" The searchers
caused more than N$20,000 in uncompensated damage, addi-
tionally stomping to death the family cat and her three orange
kittens.

Melinda Kelly never recovered from her miscarriage. Six
weeks later she was dead. An overdose of sleeping pills. Over
the next year, Kiera's younger sister — previously Christmas-
card sweet — attempted to set the combined Ohio 13-year-old
record for tattoos, body piercings, prostitution and felony arrests. Weirdly, given her previous love for animals, she also
took to maiming kittens.

Little Cathy died almost exactly a year later, of self-in-
flicted knife wounds. "Regrettably, we could not find any common drug of abuse to which Cathy tested negative," said the
Hamilton County coroner.

Kiera Kelly left town the day after her little sister's funeral, and had not been seen again by anyone who knew the
family till her photo showed up in the papers following the
Shootout at the Dupont ballroom.

But the public took a quite different view of the massacre
at the Dupont Center than the authorities anticipated.

Despite massive police protection, Bambi Fiducci had
been assassinated while eating her endive salad. At that point,
four waitresses — four girls — had proceeded to kill seven of
her professional police bodyguards and a retired federal judge
who had apparently made the mistake of reaching for a stainless steel gravy boat during the gunfight. Actually, they'd killed
15, if you counted the Grays shot or hacked to pieces in the
trailer and on the loading dock out behind the hotel, a report
eventually confirmed by the Mirror, despite continuing official
insistence that those deaths were somehow "unrelated."

A dozen others — including the wife of a city councilman
— had been seriously wounded in the melee, in which the attackers had lost two killed ... and from which at least three of

the assailants had *escaped unscathed.*

This is what could be done by four young waitresses and a misfit janitor? Mere girls? Against a hotel full of undercover cops and elite, gray-suited Lightning Troopers?

Strange things now began to happen. In at least six documented cases, zoning code inspection officers writing up citations for citizens with cars on blocks in their driveways, or for allowing children to build treehouses without a permit, were killed in broad daylight.

The neighbors, in each case, came out and helped finish off the shrieking G-man with hammers and shovels, loaded him into his official car, drove it a mile or so away, parked it by a fire hydrant, and then repaired to the closest tavern for a celebration.

The authorities responded indiscriminately, as always, with roadblocks and searches. A trip to the supermarket became a two-hour marathon.

Thousands of Gotham men who had foolishly applied at some point in their lives for a government-issued license to hunt deer with a bow were rounded up. Heydrich figured even if none of them actually *was* the Black Arrow, surely one of them had to *know* who he was.

("Well, frankly, I feel a whole lot safer now," explained the lady from Newsweek in the red dress on the Sunday morning TV talk show. "I don't know why they were ever allowed to stalk and kill defenseless animals in the first place. Once life is so cheapened, it's no wonder these rednecks turn to killing their own wives and children.")

Where the TV talking heads had once referred to events "since September Eleventh" they now began referring to developments "Since the Gunfight at the Dupont Center."

Poetry began to be written about Jimmy and Kiera. Arms began flowing back into the city. Four teen-age girls and a janitor had shown it could be done.

✤ ✤ ✤

Cassandra came in through Chin's, rather than through the lobby, bypassing Bob's newsstand.

Everybody used the building that way. If your shortest route took you through the theater, or through the glass and bronze empire of Boris and Katia, you said Hi, fetched along a cup of coffee from Bob's if you remembered, asked if anyone needed any help. It was like living in a tight-knit little village.

Rachel was in the kitchen, helping out the Chins. They'd told her she didn't have to come around, if it bothered her, remembering Nguyen. But it didn't. It was like a bad dream. It only bothered her at night.

For reasons she wouldn't have been able to explain, Rachel caught the kitchen door after Cassie went through, preventing it from swinging closed. She watched Cassandra stride down the corridor and take the turn which would lead her through to the lobby.

Gosh, it was just natural for some people, wasn't it? If Rachel had tried to make her ass and hemline sway like that, people would have laughed. With Cassandra, they just stared. Because she didn't have to try. All the weight just went to the right places. You could really hate a woman like that.

Then the funniest thing happened. The door that led out to the loading dock, where Jimmy Chin had previously had his assembly line (how well Rachel remembered), opened — just part way. It was Madison. She was looking down the corridor after Cassandra. Looking at what?

Then Rachel realized. Cassandra wasn't heading for the lobby. She knew the access code to take the rear elevator up to the penthouse. She was going to see Andrew.

It was quiet in the hallway after Cassandra's footsteps stopped at the elevator. Although they were out of sight around the corner, Rachel could hear the elevator doors open and close. Still Madison stood, watching. No, not just watching. She was clutching the door so hard her hand had gone white. Rachel took a hesitant step towards her. Then another. Madison was doing something no one had ever seen her do. Something so unthinkable Rachel was almost up to her before she realized what it was.

There were tears streaming down her cheeks. Her breath was coming in long shudders. Madison was crying.

"What is it, girl?"

Madison looked at her, shook her head, was about to turn and head back out into the empty loading dock.

"Oh, my God," Rachel said, unable to stop herself. The realization was that lightning-clear, so unexpected and yet ... not at all surprising, now that she thought about it. It was something they'd all joked about. But precisely the fact they all joked about it, all agreed they certainly wouldn't kick him out of bed, had given it a certain reassuring ... distance. It was an entirely theoretical form of speculation.

But not for Madison.

"It's Himself," Rachel said. "My God. You got it bad for Andrew."

The way the fury came on Madison, the kind of vehemence she could channel without raising her voice, would have shocked anyone who hadn't known her as long as Rachel. But Rachel had seen it before. Only never, now that she thought about it, never over a man.

"You shut up, bitch. You don't say a word to anyone, you hear me?"

"My God, girl. Have you ever told him?

"We've got it good here. Andrew has done a lot for everybody. This whole place exists because of him. But he's got a lady, and it's not our place to meddle in that."

"Funny. Andrew Fletcher is the last person in the world I'd ever imagine telling a woman to mind her place."

"It's none of your business, see? You don't breathe a word."

"OK. Calm down, alanna. You say to hush up, that's good enough for me. I just think you owe it to the man to tell him, that's all. Give him the choice."

"Yeah. Some choice."

In tears, Madison waved her off and headed to the rear stairs that would take her up to the studio, looking for someplace to be alone.

Upstairs it was blessedly quiet. Everyone was on break, all the monitor lights glowing red. Madison brushed her hand over the cymbals, picked up a live Gibson, pulled on a set of phones so she could hear what she was doing, started to pick out a tune in G, sliding to B-minor and E-minor, then to C and C-minor. Something Kylie had helped her work out. Kylie.

Long Shot had been out on break with the Veronicas and their sidemen. He and Tropicana wandered into the booth, carrying Cokes from downstairs. In that way Long Shot had of hearing something others might miss, he quickly gestured for Trop to roll tape, toggled the studio speaker on, asked, "That thing got any words?"

"Oh. I thought everybody was gone. Sorry," Madison said, wiping her eyes and starting to lay the guitar down.

"No, hon, I need a sound check. Do me a favor and give us a piece of that with some words."

"I don't think so," she said. "I'm a little, um, emotional right now."

"Oh. I understand. We wouldn't want to record anything when the singer was experiencing any, you know, emotion."

Madison sniffled and smiled.

Nobody knows, what it does to me
Nobody knows
No one should ever see
Nobody knows

What it does to me

and up to the high harmonic on the E-string then, the way Andrew would have played it.

Now those tender looks upon his face
Are meant for someone else who's in my place
And she's his lover the way I used to be

Now two of the Jones daughters, Sahara and Flamingo, were at the mike in studio B, coming in on the chorus

Nobody knows, what it does to me
Nobody knows
No one should ever see
Nobody knows
what it does to me.

The last notes rang and faded. The Jones sisters giggled. "You should record that, dad."

"We just did, hon. But I think you're right. Madison, honey? OK if we sync up the bass and drums and try that all together?"

❧ ❧ ❧

Upstairs, Cassie asked, "Do we have to have the fight, or can you just hold me?"

He touched her arm. He leaned over and kissed her ear.

He was gentle. That was nice. He could have taken her right away — she wouldn't have stopped him. Just thinking about him on the way over made her ready. More than ready. But he did her the courtesy of touching her, holding her.

It was really about respect and consideration, wasn't it? So why did they have to keep having the fight?

They loved the feel of each other's bodies — loved to bring each other to a peak of panting anticipation and desire. Then all they had to do was let it happen.

And so the other thing was pushed aside. It sat like a big black bird, perched patiently on the dresser, looking down at their desperate passion and their need. Biding its time.

⚜ ⚜ ⚜

NOVEMBER ...

While the assembled Brackley Arena roof was still on the ground the inspection agency notified the engineers it had found excessive deflections in some of the nodes. Nothing was done. After the frame was completed, hydraulic jacks located on top of the four pylons slowly lifted it into position.

But as they hoisted the roof it started to warp. A photograph taken during construction showed obvious bowing in two of the members in the top layer. So Jerry Burgess' guys were called back in to bind it in place with steel cables as thick as a man's thumb.

When this was questioned at a much later date, the contractors contended these were merely cables that had been accidentally left behind after being stretched to hold up the platforms used by the painters. When it was pointed out that this much woven steel cable of that thickness would be worth tens of thousands of newdollars — hardly something likely to be left behind by mistake — they merely shrugged.

Once the frame was in its final position but before the roof deck was installed, its deflection was measured as twice that predicted by computer analysis, and the engineers were notified. They expressed no concern. They said such discrepancies between the actual and the theoretical should be expected.

⚜ ⚜ ⚜

There were a couple unusual things about the middle-aged Japanese guy. He was concerned about the building's hours, security, parking — the usual. But he didn't seem to care much about price. He also didn't have much to say about what business he was in, except that it was "Import-Export."

The building agent had been around enough to suspect the fellow just needed a business address. Though there were "office headquarters" outfits that would provide you with a mailing and delivery address — and phone answering service — for less than this was going to cost him.

But in the end, a commission was a commission. She told the fellow they'd need two letters of reference and a bank draft for the first and last months' rent. He didn't bat an eye, told her she'd have them by morning if he found a place to his liking.

He wanted to see a list of all the available offices. She told him that was proprietary information. Obviously, the company didn't want their competitors knowing their vacancy rate. If he would just tell her what he was looking for ...

Something on the top floors. No problem. Marci made her living selling that Gotham skyline view.

Now, the 12th and 14th floors, along with the first three floors, were rented to the phone company — it was the phone company *building,* after all, she laughed. But she would happily show him what was available on 10 and 11.

And that's when Marci received her next-to-last surprise. The western suites always went first — great view of the Gotham skyline to the west. Instead, the fellow coolly picked out a small 11th floor office facing east. That was to say, facing nothing at all, except the little brick church with its graveyard, and then miles and miles of extremely flat Long Island.

Took all kinds. The bank draft showed up first thing in the morning ... and one of the letters of recommendation was from the president of the bank, indicating Golden Lantern Imports of Hong Kong and Macau could be extended "as much credit as required."

Now, how often did you see that? Out came the "Approved" stamp, and the lease, bearing the signature of lessee Isoroku Yamamoto, went into the files. Marci told the girl to hand Mr. Yamamoto his keys whenever he showed up to ask for them, and decided to treat herself to a three-martini lunch. You didn't want to look a gift horse in the mouth.

❖ ❖ ❖

Reporters had put in whole careers at The Mirror without being called into Mrs. Jacobs' office.

Oh, they all *knew* the publisher. They'd all *seen* the publisher. But alone in her office? You didn't even get called in to see the publisher to get *fired* from the Mirror.

Cassie closed the door behind her.

"Cassandra, thanks for coming. Sit down, dear. You probably have some idea why I've called you in."

Emily Jacobs was gray-haired and small. But Cassandra had never heard anyone call her weak. Yes, she'd inherited the paper. But there were plenty of other members of the Jacobs clan who had never made it into this office. Fireplace. Windows. Photos of the publisher's great-grandfather fishing in Vermont with Cal Coolidge. Nice hats.

"Not exactly," Cassie said.

"Well, you're a busy person, I'll get right to the point. I got a phone call yesterday from Herman Blumenthal. He runs

Blumenthal's Department Store. They're this newspaper's biggest advertiser."

"Yes, ma'am."

"Seems Herman has been under some pressure from the city government. Class action suits for age and gender discrimination which could be made to go away. Still no transvestites on his board of directors. An anti-trust action, even the threat of an insider trading allegation concerning his company's stock. No truth to it, you understand. But still the kind of thing that can cost millions in legal fees, and even more than that in bad publicity. You've seen this kind of thing, I'm sure."

"Yes, ma'am. I have." Blumenthal's, though. That was huge.

"I'm not telling you this on the record, you understand. If you ever want to write about it, you'll need totally different sources. You'll have to talk to Herman, yourself."

Write about it? She was about to be transferred to the goddamned gardening beat. Assuming she still had a job, at all.

"Um ... OK. Yes, ma'am."

"Oddly enough — or maybe not so oddly — Herman was calling me about your columns. It seems there are people in our current city government who are very upset about your columns. They don't like them at all. They worry that some people who read your columns have gotten so upset with the politicians and bureaucrats you write about, that they've been going around and killing them."

"Yes, ma'am. I mean — yes, I'm sure they think that."

"In fact, let's simplify that. They have been killing them. Haven't they?"

"Yes, ma'am."

"Well. I thanked Herman for expressing his concern, naturally. But I had to ask how this involved him, directly. And do you know what he told me?"

"That unless my columns were suspended, he'd have to

withdraw his advertising."

"More than 300 full pages a year. Do you know how many millions of dollars that is?" Mrs. Jacobs got up and went to look out the window. She looked so small, to carry the weight of as large an enterprise as The Mirror.

"Um ... not without the bulk line discount charts, ma'am."

"I had to check, too, dear. But it's a lot."

"Yes, ma'am.

"As a matter of fact, we recently bought a group of radio stations for less than that amount of money. Well, what could I do? What would you have told Herman Blumenthal?"

"Um ... I guess that would depend on how well I knew Mr. Blumenthal."

And then Emily Jacobs laughed. She actually cackled.

"Yes. It certainly would depend on how well you knew Mr. Blumenthal. Oh, I like that." She laughed again.

"Well," she said, returning from the window. "I have known Herman Blumenthal since we were children. He was born into his family fortune and his family business, as I was born into mine. We were children of privilege, wealthy Jews of this city, a prince and princess of the merchant class. It was never expected that we would make the kinds of sacrifices our grandfathers made to build these business empires, of which we are now the enfeebled and degenerate caretakers. Have you ever heard me called that?"

"No, I don't believe I ever have."

"Well, you don't read that kind of right-wing periodical, I dare say. But I have been called that, believe me. That, and worse. But I digress. I reminded Herman that this has been tried before, in other times and other lands. I don't usually mention race or religion; they're usually irrelevant. But in this case, I believe I reminded Herman of things my grandfather knew about in the 1930s, things that were happening in Germany, and which we did not publish, because we had advertisers with business connections in Germany, and because we had correspondents in Europe for whose safety we felt some responsibility, and most of all precisely because this was and is a Jewish-owned newspaper, and there was a concern that we didn't want to be seen as pleading a special case for Europe's Jews. Did you know that?"

"Yes, ma'am. I did."

"Good. You're a smart girl. Actually, I was tempted to call you in and tell you to be very careful in your reporting, because it's being watched very closely. But that would be redundant. For that is what we retain editors for; that is the standard we expect of everyone at the Mirror."

"Yes ma'am."

Mrs. Jacobs was looking off into space.

"Mrs. Jacobs?"

"Oh. Sorry. I told Herman Blumenthal we would be sorry to see him depart as an advertiser, of course, but that I would publish this newspaper on a mimeograph machine in my garage before I would tell a reporter of mine to stop digging up dirt on the bums who are currently in charge of this city, and reporting exactly what they're up to. The Mirror's editorial page will continue to lament people taking the law into their own hands, of course ... right under the editorials where we will continue to lambaste the gutless judges and prosecutors of this city for failing to put the Brackley gang in prison, where most of them belong. And do you know what Herman Blumenthal did?"

"He thanked you."

"He thanked me. Herman Blumenthal cried, which I don't believe I have heard him do since we were children. And then he thanked me. There will be a special full-page ad from Blumenthal's Department Stores in the local section Sunday, congratulating the editorial staff of The Mirror for our fine work in continuing to root out and expose corruption and official violations of civil rights in this city, and vowing his intention to continue advertising in this newspaper regardless of what

SUPRYNOWICZ

pressure the city government sees fit to place on his corporation. Needless to say, it will be highly dignified."

"I never doubted it."

"Do you know what percentage of people you have written about in your column in the past two years have been attacked or assassinated?"

"No, ma'am."

"About eight percent. We checked. Do you know what percentage of government officials assassinated in this city in the past year had been written about in your columns?"

"About the same?"

"Considerably less, actually. And, although I will never repeat it outside this room, some of the sons of bitches got just what was coming to them. Strip-searching people on the streets? Arresting people who protest or ask questions or tell a joke? Grabbing teen-age girls off the streets and telling their families they have no 'need to know' what's become of them? Jailing doctors who prescribe painkillers for terminal patients? And justifying all this as part of their endless 'War on Terror'? I ask you. Who are the terrorists, now? What kind of people do they think we are? These things aren't supposed to happen in America."

Cassandra was crying.

"Oh, dear. I've upset you. No, no, please don't do that."

"I'm sorry. It's just —"

"There, there. This won't do." The old lady handed Cassie some tissues. Actually some Kleenex, although you always wrote "tissues."

"Now, Cassandra, we need to do two things. First, I need you to go back to work, and keep doing just what you've been doing. Will you do that for me?"

"Yes, ma'am."

"Good. And now, I wonder if you'd be willing to join me for lunch."

"For lunch?"

500

"For lunch. You know, I don't think I've eaten in the company cafeteria in years. But somehow I feel this would be a good time to make a fresh start. You don't think I'll make anyone uncomfortable, do you?"

"No. Of course not."

"Do they still serve ham and bean soup on Thursdays?"

"Yes, ma'am. I believe they do."

"You won't say anything about my eating ham, now."

"No, ma'am."

"It was my father's favorite."

❖ ❖ ❖

Nicole!

Andrew lurched to a sitting position, instantly awake, his hand reaching under the pillow to grasp the reassuring weight of the rubber-gripped Smith .45.

He scanned the room, struggling to control his breathing. He was bathed in sweat.

It was only the dream, the old dream. He thought he'd banished it, finally. What had brought it back?

He'd gone to sleep timing out in his mind the coming operation at SonicNet headquarters. Something in the plans had made him dream of Nicole, after all this time.

It had to mean something. Someone was in danger. Someone who had worn Nicole's face in his dream.

A woman? But that didn't make any sense; Cassandra had no part in the raid. What woman?

Recovering, he replaced the .45 under the pillow, and stood up. Opening the dresser drawer, he pulled out Nicole's nickel-plated pistol. He dropped the magazine, checked to make sure the chamber was empty, re-seated the loaded mag, as he had done so many, many times.

She had always carried the gun. Except when she flew, of course. It was a federal felony to exercise your Second Amendment rights and carry your handgun on a plane. A federal felony to defend yourself ... or anyone else.

And so the hijacker had killed them all. Such a little thing. A few ounces of steel. But she could have killed him — saved herself, saved their child, saved them all — if she'd had the gun.

She never missed inside 50 feet.

Andrew knew it. He was sure she had known it. And thus no one had to tell him her final thoughts. That she loved him. That she was sorry there was nothing she could do to save herself, or the child. But that she knew *he* would do something. He would figure out a way, so the government that had disarmed his Nicole — killed her and their child — would also not survive.

She would have smiled, and nodded, going in peace, trusting him to find a way. To find the right tool.

He dialed the phone. Hideki answered.

"The day of the big operation," he said.

"Yes?"

"Who stays here? Who's security here at the Gotham?"

"Who do you want?"

And then Andrew knew. The key wasn't at SonicNet headquarters, at all. The key was right here. The key was who would stay behind.

CHAPTER 15

What country can preserve its liberties if its rulers are not warned from time to time that their people preserve the spirit of resistance? Let them take arms. ... What signify a few lives lost in a century or two? The tree of liberty must be refreshed from time to time with the blood of patriots and tyrants. It is its natural manure.

— THOMAS JEFFERSON, LETTER TO WILLIAM STEPHENS SMITH, 1787

Once you get them running, you stay right on top of them, and that way a small force can defeat a large one every time. ... Only thus can a weaker country cope with a stronger; it must make up in activity what it lacks in strength.

— THOMAS "STONEWALL" JACKSON (1824-1863)

"Before a revolution can take place, the population must lose faith in both the police and the courts."

— ROBERT HEINLEIN (1907-1988)

Joe Crosby had begun passing out Fully-Informed Jury brochures on the chilly sidewalk in front of the Gotham federal courthouse at 7:30 in the morning. Upon being asked by the U.S. attorney at 8:15 to show the attorney what he was passing out, Mr. Crosby walked up to the prosecutor and a federal marshal who were on the courthouse steps, handing one of his yellow FIJA brochures to the prosecutor.

The brochure explained that "When you sit on a jury, you may vote on the verdict according to your conscience. ... If jurors were supposed to judge 'only the facts,' their job could be done by computer. It is precisely *because* people have feelings, opinions, wisdom, experience and conscience that we depend upon jurors, not machines to judge court cases. ... American colonists regularly depended on juries to thwart bad law sent over from England."

The brochure quoted John Adams, the nation's second president, saying of the American juror that "It is not only his right, but his duty ... to find the verdict according to his own best understanding, judgment, and conscience, though in direct opposition to the direction of the court."

"The jury has a right to judge both the law as well as the fact in controversy," added John Jay, first Chief Justice of the U.S. Supreme Court, in 1794.

"All laws which are repugnant to the Constitution are null and void," the high court had ruled in its watershed 1803 decision in Marbury v. Madison ... cited by the yellow brochure as "5 U.S. (2 Cranch) 137, 174, 176."

Nor did the little brochure leave the authorities any room to argue this right of jurors to refuse to convict under bad, stupid, or unconstitutional laws — even if that meant directly violating the judge's instructions — had somehow gone away during the 19th or 20th centuries. The little brochure next quoted Harlan Fiske Stone, Chief Justice of the U.S. Supreme Court, stating in 1941 that "The law itself is on trial quite as much as the case which is to be decided."

Further, it quoted the District of Columbia Court of Appeals in its decision in the Dougherty Vietnam War "draft dodger" case, holding as late as 1972 that the American jury still had "an unreviewable and irreversible power ... to acquit in disregard of the instruction on the law given by the trial judge. The pages of history shine upon instances of the jury's exercise of its prerogative to disregard instructions of the judge; for example, acquittals under the fugitive slave law." (473 F. 2d 1113,1130.)

For bringing to the attention of prospective jurors these irrefutable, unreversed truths — from the mouths of authorities with far higher standing in the law and the conscience of mankind than any judge who had ever served in the Gotham federal courthouse — the federal marshal promptly arrested and handcuffed Crosby, informing him he would be charged with contempt of court, obstruction of justice, and jury tampering.

A crowd then began to gather outside the courthouse, chanting their demands for the FIJA pamphleteer's release. Most of these people were overflow from the crowd that already couldn't fit into Judge James McNair's courtroom for the scheduled trial of former police officer John Comiskey, on charges of being unresponsive to the IRS.

(Numerous judges and other officers of the court had long and consistently and prissily explained the reason they could bar TV cameras from their courtrooms to "maintain order and prevent a circus atmosphere" without violating the constitutional requirement for a *public* trial was that "Anyone who wants to come down to the courtroom and watch will still be allowed, so how can you say the trials are no longer open to the public?" Three hundred fifty people had shown up to watch what "justice" was in store for the popular John Comiskey; 48 were actually allowed into the courtroom after being strip-searched and disarmed, there to be supervised by three armed marshals.)

John Comiskey, aged 47, a deeply religious man who had

505

quit the Gotham police after eight years because he couldn't stand the corruption he saw there, stood indicted for failing to file income tax returns for the two previous years. (Actually, he filed Fifth Amendment returns as specified by Oliver Wendell Holmes in the Sullivan decision, in which the great justice ruled individuals could invoke their Fifth Amendment rights in connection with any question on the return.)

After hundreds of hours spent researching the intricate tax code and with Comiskey's power of attorney in his pocket, Norbert Bachman — arguably the most knowledgeable man in the United States on the subject of the federal income tax and the court decisions pertaining thereto — took his seat just before 9 a.m. at the counsel table in the modern, beige and oak courtroom of District Judge James McNair.

Comiskey and his wife were in the gallery with their 46 supporters. Bachman filled out the court's attorney form, listing himself as defendant's attorney in U.S. v. Comiskey.

The assistant U.S. attorney charged with prosecuting the case did not recognize Bachman as belonging to any of the local firms and asked Bachman where he "practiced."

"I do not practice, I do this for real, but not in any particular location," the stout little man with the unmistakably nasal Rhode Island accent replied. If you could say one thing about Norbert Bachman — beyond his encyclopedic knowledge of a tax code which most federal judges had never even attempted to read — it was that he was always well-dressed, well-groomed, and exasperatingly civil.

When he realized Bachman was not a government-licensed lawyer, the prosecutor quickly leapt to his feet and sped out the back of the courtroom, presumably to circle around and hold a thoroughly illegal ex parte strategy session with the judge, who was therefore 15 minutes late appearing.

When the judge did arrive and the court finally convened, the prosecutor moved to amend the indictment, which he claimed contained a technical error.

Bachman objected on the grounds that the whole indictment was in error because it indicted the wrong man.

"Mr. Bachman, are you an attorney?" asked Judge McNair.

"Yes," Bachman replied. "I have Mr. Comiskey's power-of-attorney right here." He held it up.

"But are you a member of any bar?" Judge McNair asked.

"No, your honor, I'm only an attorney-in-fact, not an attorney-at-law. I'm here merely to explain to the court why it has no subject matter jurisdiction over Mr. Comiskey in this matter and that if indeed a crime has been committed the government has indicted the wrong man."

"Only members of the bar are allowed to represent individuals in his court," the judge said.

Bachman replied that he had the rules of procedure and case law from McNair's own Circuit (he held them up, offering to bring them to the bench), clearly establishing Comiskey's right to have Bachman represent him. The circuit rules, of course, were adopted at a level higher than McNair's court, and were binding upon him.

Predictably, Judge McNair refused to look at or discuss this evidence, instead insisting Bachman remove himself from the counsel table.

"But your honor, it's Mr. Comiskey's intention to challenge the jurisdiction of the court. All members of the bar are officers of the court, and it would be pointless to have an officer of that court defend his contention that the court had no jurisdiction. Such a representation could not be effective, since the court could and has punished its officers for arguing against the court's jurisdiction. Not only that, I guarantee you it'll take only 10 minutes to prove that the court is without subject-matter jurisdiction over Mr. Comiskey."

"Mr. Bachman, again, I'm ordering you to leave the counsel table."

"But your honor, how will justice not be served by your allowing me to show you why you don't have jurisdiction in this matter?"

"Mr. Bachman, I'm warning you for a final time: I shall hold you in contempt if you speak another word from the counsel table," the judge warned, motioning to the U.S. marshals.

What made the 46 spectators in Judge McNair's courtroom different, that day, is that they had attended a number of seminars conducted by John Comiskey and Norbert Bachman over the months leading up to the trial, learning just what the law said about the income tax, and about the conundrum these tactics were likely to place any judge in, since the Sixth Amendment guaranteed every defendant a right to counsel — which had been consistently held by higher courts to mean knowledgeable, competent counsel.

If it were the court's intention to help the accused have the best possible counsel, Judge McNair could easily have interviewed Norbert Bachman, who had a number of documents laid out on the table, including the Internal Revenue Code. The crowd well understood how absurd it was to assume any yo-yo who had passed his generalized bar exam was "competent" on a matter as arcane, detailed, and purposely difficult to decipher as the tax codes.

Now spotting Comiskey at the back of the room, Judge McNair demanded, "Mr. Comiskey, would you please come up here."

Comiskey stood and shouted back, "Your honor, my attorney is in court to represent me in challenging the court's jurisdiction. As I'm sure the court knows, jurisdictional questions have to be resolved before any other questions can move forward. Since I'm not persuaded the court has any jurisdiction over me — and the court can't make any such ruling until it's heard the substantive arguments — I have to respectfully decline your invitation to come forward."

Judge McNair then told the marshals "Arrest that man."

For the first time, the audience actually started to make some noise, uttering gasps of disbelief and outrage.

"Silence in the court, or I'll clear the gallery!" McNair snarled, banging his gavel.

Two federal marshals dragged the former police officer before the bench. Although John Comiskey did not resist, he also offered them no help, going limp so that his feet dragged behind him.

"Let the record show that the defendant is being dragged before the bar," Comiskey said loudly, knowing that the court transcriptionist would have to write down his words, where they would become part of the formal record of the case.

"You're not being dragged, you're being escorted!" Judge McNair shouted.

The crowd laughed and jeered. McNair rapped his gavel some more.

The judge asked Comiskey if he wanted to represent himself. Comiskey said no, his attorney was present and he'd rather be represented by his attorney.

Despite repeated goadings, he refused to relent.

"Do you understand the charges against you?"

"No, your honor. I do not understand the charges against me, since the IRS has no jurisdiction over me, the taxes in question being levied only against resident aliens. I am also being denied the counsel of my choice by this court."

Judge McNair knew damned well he couldn't continue if the defendant had no attorney and kept insisting he didn't understand the charges against him — that was reversible error.

So the judge sent for the public defender, over Comiskey's objections that this would "force incompetent, ineffective counsel on the defendant, not for my protection, but merely to protect the court by creating the colorable impression that I'm provided with competent counsel."

This also went on the record, which did not please McNair one bit. Now the case couldn't be published. He could still send Comiskey away for decades. He just couldn't get his name published as the victor in the law journals.

Finally the public defender, his hair uncombed and his tie askew, came rushing into the back of the courtroom. "That man can't represent me, he's already told me that I'm going to jail!" Comiskey shouted.

With this new "counsel" present, Comiskey still refused to plead or accept any advice from court-appointed "counsel," so the judge finally entered a plea of "not guilty" on his behalf.

And now the government sought to have John Comiskey explain why he had not given any information on his earnings, bank accounts or assets to the IRS pursuant to the Section 7602 summons that had been legally served upon them.

"Well, your honor, I feel I complied with the summons by actually appearing at the place indicated and I have answered questions in this regard. I have imposed my Fifth Amendment privilege as to the fact that my answers might incriminate me."

McNair replied that the defendant was not allowed to impose a blanket Fifth Amendment claim "as to the documents or parts of them. ... You may state what the basis of your claim is."

(As the audience knew from Bachman's seminars, in all other cases up to and including treason, the courts had repeatedly ruled that the plea of self-incrimination cannot be challenged nor can the grounds for the belief that testimony might be incriminatory be questioned by the court. To compel a witness to explain the grounds for privilege would nullify the Fifth Amendment protection. The witness can only be compelled to explain why testimony would be self-incriminatory if he is granted immunity.)

The judge then explained "I am required to make the determination as to whether or not your claim is, in fact, valid. You have to relate it to some specific offense which you believe disclosure of documents will expose or will tend to incriminate you in connection with, but I may not accept a blanket claim of Fifth Amendment privilege. ... The burden is on you to establish that you do have a valid Fifth Amendment claim."

Comiskey asked, "Can you grant me any kind of immunity that will clear me from any kind of prosecution?"

Judge McNair replied "I have no authority to grant immunity. That may be done only under the statute which places the responsibility for granting immunity with the attorney general of the United States."

Of course, the judge could simply have asked the prosecutor if he'd grant immunity, giving him the choice of otherwise dismissing the case and sending everyone home.

It was perfectly obvious to everyone why Comiskey's testimony as to his wealth, assets and bank accounts could incriminate him and why the government wanted that information: If he hadn't filed for the years in question, the money in his bank accounts could provide prima facie evidence of "income." On the other hand, if he had filed, information about his wealth and bank interest could bring a charge of tax evasion or providing false or incomplete information to the government.

Of course the Fifth Amendment made it harder for the government to prove tax cases — often, downright impossible. But a mere argument of inconvenience didn't allow them to overrule the Bill of Rights, or there was no longer any Constitution, at which point the only remaining rule of government would be "We take as much of your stuff as we want because we've got the guns."

According to McNair, however, the only way Comiskey could keep from testifying against himself was to testify against himself by explaining why he believed the testimony might incriminate him! McNair was attempting to extract a confession from Comiskey in open court. A Mafia informant suspected of murder would have been granted immunity immediately or been excused, because nothing could compel him to reveal any information — including why he was pleading the Fifth.

Comiskey tried again: "Can you explain to me how I can answer that question without the possibility of incriminating myself?" Comiskey asked.

"Well, you are not testifying against yourself. You are testifying to establish your claim. ... If you refuse to testify to establish your claim, then I must find that the claim was without merit and order the documents to be turned over."

"Aren't you asking me to be a witness against myself?"

"I will tell you again, to answer the question."

"I don't understand how I can forfeit my Fifth Amendment rights."

"All right, I am telling you to answer it. If you shall not answer it, I will order that you be held in custody until you purge yourself of civil contempt. I will throw you in jail."

This despite the fact that in its Miranda decision, the high court had ruled the Fifth Amendment is available even "outside of court proceedings and serves to protect persons in all settings in which their freedom of action is curtailed," and that an individual is "guaranteed the right to remain silent unless he chooses to speak in unfettered exercise of his own will."

Furthermore — as the audience well knew from Bachman's seminars — in Garner vs. U.S., 424 US 648, the Supreme Court had affirmed Garner's conviction on the grounds that Garner supplied the incriminating evidence on his tax return "voluntarily," since he could have withheld the information by claiming the Fifth!

And then Judge James McNair made his third and final error.

His first error had been joining the conspiracy designed to keep the U.S. people believing that they owed an "income tax" on domestic wages or salaries, when no IRS agent had ever been able to answer the simple question of where in the Internal Revenue Code such an in-country wage-earner was defined as a "taxpayer" with an obligation to pay and file.

(They couldn't show where it was because it wasn't there. It couldn't be there because that would violate the high court's Brushaber and Baltic Mining decisions. Instead, the populace had simply been hornswoggled into "volunteering" to participate in the payroll withholding tax as a wartime emergency measure in the early 1940s — there was even a custom-made Donald Duck cartoon ginned up for exhibition in the nation's theaters to encourage them to sign up — after which the "emergency" tax simply never went away. If it was mandatory, why did millions of Americans sign a Form W-4 "Request for Withholding" every time they started a new job? Why wasn't the form called a "Registration for Mandatory Withholding"? Was there any other "mandatory" government enactment to which you had to "request" to be subject?)

McNair's second error had been his failure to clear the courtroom at a much earlier stage.

But now he did something Norbert Bachman had coached John Comiskey's friends to listen for. He cited Carlson.

"Under U.S. v. Carlson, you cannot claim this privilege!" McNair shouted.

The crowd, which had been muttering, now fell deathly silent. He had done it. He had cited Carlson.

In U.S. vs. Carlson, 617 F.2d 518, the court had ruled "There is little doubt that a truthfully completed tax return, stating his gross income, the lack of federal income taxes actually withheld and the true number of available deductions would have provided 'a lead or clue to evidence having a tendency to incriminate ...' The government concedes that Carlson could have been prosecuted under 26 U.S.C., Sec. 7205 for filing a false withholding form ... (and that the) privilege is asserted to avoid incrimination for past tax crimes."

And then the court had written what amounted to nothing less than an astonishing formal charter for a gang of lawless thieves to steal in utter violation of the very law the court had just acknowledged:

The Supreme Court ruled: "If Carlson's assertion of the privilege were valid, it would license a form of conduct that would undermine the entire system of personal income tax collection. ... We are thus confronted with the collusion (sic) of two critical interests: the privilege against self-incrimination, and the need for public revenue collection by a process necessarily reliant on self-reporting. ... The character and urgency of the public interest in raising revenue through self-reporting weighs heavily against affording the privilege to Carlson. ..."

(It was a right, suddenly it had become a "privilege" — the same word McNair had just used — and all to protect approximately 40 percent of the federal government's income, without which the government would merely shrink to the size it had been 15 years before.)

Since the government's power "to raise revenue is its life blood," the Carlson court had continued, if other taxpayers were "permitted to employ Carlson's scheme ... (this would) seriously impair the government's ability to determine tax liability," making the government's ability to collect income taxes "inordinately burdensome if not impossible." The court thus concluded that since "The record clearly discloses that Carlson was a tax protestor. ... Carlson failed to assert the privilege in good faith."

"You're citing Carlson?" Norbert Bachman shouted, leaping to his feet and violating the rules of decorum in a courtroom for the first time in his long career of constantly losing to the IRS despite knowing their own code 50 times better than they did. "But in Carlson, the court ruled 'a truthfully completed tax return' was self-incriminatory!"

"Shut up!" McNair shouted, pounding his gavel. "You're not allowed to say that!"

"I'm not allowed to say what? That neither you nor anyone else from the government has ever been able to show us anywhere in this Internal Revenue Code that makes in-country wages subject to the income tax?"

THE BLACK ARROW

"If I have to tell you one more time: promoting the theory that the income tax does not apply to wages and salaries is forbidden. It's forbidden!"

"Your honor, I've read the law and it never applies the income tax to wages and salaries earned by U.S. citizens within the United States — it can't do that, because that would be in violation of the constitutional ban on direct taxes not apportioned, Article One, Section Nine."

"That was repealed by the 16th amendment."

"No, your honor, the U.S. Supreme Court, in rulings that bind you, said both in Brushaber and in Baltic Mining that the 16th amendment created no new taxing authority, it merely prevented you federals from shifting an income tax into the category of an indirect excise, instead requiring them to collect it as a direct tax apportioned among the states by population, placing it smack dab in the category where it had always belonged."

"I told you you're not allowed to say that! The law says everyone has to pay the income tax!"

"Of course it can't say that. It doesn't apply to Frenchmen in France or bushmen in Africa or congenital idiots in Idaho. Have you actually read the law?"

"Of course I've read the law!"

"Well, fine. If there's somewhere in the Internal Revenue Code where it says a U.S. citizen has to file and pay an income tax on wages and salaries earned within the 50 states — in the continental United States — just tell us where. To get around Brushaber and Baltic Mining, the statute says that 'For purposes of this statute, the United States shall include Puerto Rico and the island possessions.' It doesn't say Montana. It doesn't say Michigan. It doesn't say Maryland. They could have said 'and the 48 contiguous states' if they wanted to. Heck, they've had a hundred and fifteen years to put it in there, if it was just an oversight.

"Every time we demand that one of your courts require

515

the IRS to answer this question, everyone goes and huddles in chambers and comes back and says the question has already been answered and we're out of order and we're guilty. You never answer the goddamned question, and you never make the IRS answer it. We've got the whole code right here on the table, including all the parts they keep re-numbering. Just tell me the goddamned section."

"I don't have to! It's the law!"

"Your dishonor isn't allowed to just blurt something out and claim it's the law. It has to be written down. This is a government of laws and not of men! Written laws! Show us where it's written down. This is the whole code right here. Come down here and turn to the page and read it to us, you old windbag! You said you've read it. We're waiting."

"Shut up! I warned you! Arrest him! Arrest that man and throw him in chains! I know the law. I'll tell you what's the law!"

The marshals started to move on little gray-haired Norbert Bachman. And then something happened which free men had been waiting to see for 80 years.

No one could ever explain precisely why it happened that day, any more than they could explain why it had failed to happen on ten thousand previous days when by all rights it just as well could have. Although it certainly was critical that Judge McNair had allowed his courtroom to be packed with people who'd been well-enough informed through Norbert Bachman's seminars to actually be able to follow all the cryptic gobble-dygook the judge was muttering — purposely constructed as a kind of code talk usually only comprehensible to other "officer-of-the-court" attorneys.

But more than that, there was something else new and different in the air, in that autumn of 2031. The Black Arrow had been fighting his war of rebellion in the city for a full year. And while no one could definitively say he'd been winning, it was equally obvious that he was not losing.

Not only had The Black Arrow not been captured, but his rebellion had spread. The pace and frequency and extent of the assassinations and episodes of civil disobedience had grown exponentially. Motor Vehicles offices burned in the night, now — and if they were outside the ever shrinking government "safe zones," no one even showed up to rake through the ashes till morning.

The 47 spectators had been listening in silence and fascination, apparently as hypnotized as rabbits watching the swaying head of a cobra. But when Judge McNair, his face red and twisted with fury, actually ordered the always polite and civil Norbert Bachman to be led away in chains, it happened.

First two, then four, then all 47 spectators en masse flowed up over the backs of the benches in front of them, like a tidal wave breaking through a fractured dike.

There was no other physical barrier between them and the court personnel. They closed the gap in less than six seconds.

One of the marshals managed to present his weapon and fire a warning shot into the ceiling, but by then it was too late. The outraged crowd had had enough, and they had the prosecutor and the three marshals outnumbered 10-to-one. They simply mobbed them, knocked them to the ground, started kicking them in the head. Judge McNair came up off the bench and headed for the little door to his chambers, knocking down the overweight court stenographer as he tried to get past her, his robe flowing out behind him like the judge in some old Gustave Dore cartoon.

But the crowd caught him, as well.

The marshals and the U.S. attorney were beaten to unconsciousness — two of them to death — with their own chairs and, in the end, pieces of their chairs. The freedom fighters found the chair legs worked particularly well. But Judge McNair, still wearing his black robe and — ridiculously enough — still carrying his gavel — was wafted out of the courtroom and down the corridor on the upraised hands of the cheering

517

throng, down to the courthouse cafeteria, where a few of the more knowledgeable members of the audience managed to disable several safety devices on the baloney slicer before picking it up off its counter and using its spinning blade to slice off Judge McNair's still shrieking and babbling head, which someone then carried outside and stuck up on one of the spikes of the iron fence by the front gate, its lips still forming silent curses.

Now the crowd went systematically from one courtroom to another, looking for other federal popinjays in black dresses.

Usually public access to the judges' chambers — a long, narrow series of offices and corridors behind and parallel to the corridors that allowed public access to the courtrooms themselves — were blocked by electronic locks on a series of doors so designed as to be virtually invisible, free of windows and even coated with the same color wallpaper as the courthouse walls ... the same way the Wizard of Oz used to hide behind his curtain.

But thinking ahead, John Comiskey's closest friends — some of them fellow ex-police — had removed from its hinges the door that led from McNair's courtroom back into his chambers, which gave them access to the whole rat warren of otherwise inaccessible judges' hidey-holes.

Catching another judge and getting him down on the ground, John Comiskey's brother-in-law, who had finally had enough of seeing friends and family sent up the river for nothing but demanding that a court show them the law, shouted so everyone in that wing of the building could hear:

"Hey, motherfucker. We're here to remind you of something. The only purpose for which governments are established among men is to 'protect these rights' ... not to keep the government's attempts to seize the bread from the mouth of labor from being 'inordinately burdensome if not impossible.' And you know what? In the Garner case, the court ruled Garner had provided the information on the tax return voluntarily, since he COULD HAVE WITHHELD IT BY PLEADING THE FIFTH! Do you HEAR ME?"

Learning of what was going on inside, the 300 additional people who'd been waiting outside for word of the outcome of the Comiskey trial now surged into the building, pinning copies of the Declaration of Independence and the Bill of Rights to the chests of two captured judges, including one who had been found trying to sneak out a rear exit wearing his female clerk's fur-collared overcoat and quite jaunty feathered hat. Breaking the glass with his elbow and pulling a large red fire-axe from its case on the wall, Comiskey's brother-in-law chopped off both of the screaming men's feet, and then their hands.

"Now, in the few remaining minutes before you die, you motherfucking traitors may just want to crawl around in little circles or something," he declared, as young boys were sent to stick the hands and feet up on the fence next to Judge McNair's still-bleeding head.

As they did so, Judge McNair's eyes moved to watch them.

Inside, the scene now resembled something out of bedlam. Not sure how far down the chain of command the axe-wielders intended to go — apparently hoping they'd be spared if they could cast off any trace of their government employment — the massive cafeteria ladies ran shrieking down the hallways, pulling off and throwing away their uniform maroon shirts and white plastic nametags, their ponderous breasts heaving and swaying in their enormous white support bras as they crashed into each other in their scramble, like buckboards in the Calgary stampede.

Here and there a frail and elderly unarmed bailiff in a brown uniform positioned himself in the hallway, putting up his hand in an attempt to stanch the mad torrent of pursued and pursuers — and was hurled aside like so much driftwood dashed on the rocks by the storm tide, left washed up against the baseboard, broken and moaning.

Outside the building there were rifles among the crowd now, a fair number of them AK-47s out of Jimmy Chin's factory in the cavern. Master Adajian's neighborhood self-defense clubs had obviously been busy with their distribution duties.

The crowd in the courthouse section of the building was having good success running down judges who were cowering either in their chambers or in the ladies rooms or trying to slip out the side exits. Fortunately, so massive had the so-called "justice" system of extortion and imprisonment become that plenty of people in the crowd had been through their sausage-grinder justice system personally or else sat crying in court as they watched one or more loved ones sent away in the current mockery of "justice," with its 98 percent stacked-jury "conviction" rate in the federal courts, which saw no robbers or burglars or murderers tried, but almost entirely non-violent citizens who had merely offended against the regulators and the taxmen.

Enough, anyway, to recognize the assholes on sight. None was spared, including the clerks when they were recognized, and the number of heads displayed on the spikes of the front fence — several of them women with really expensive frosted hairdos — started to grow.

The mob was thrown back, though, when they tried to breech the east entrance, which led to the cells and holding pens, where Fully-Informed Jury pamphleteer Joe Crosby was being held. The guards were more numerous there, and they were police officers of the jail division, not mere marshals or bailiffs. The guards here had sidearms which they were not afraid to use, and they were also forted up behind doors and room dividers made of steel bars and bulletproof glass.

The crowd, frustrated, responded by starting fires. The first attempts were amateurish and the guards put them out without much trouble, though in doing so they had to expose themselves, and a few were brought down by aimed rifle fire from the crowd.

A couple of fire engines showed up, but were unable to talk their way through the teeming throng. When one of the drivers tried to part the crowd by simply driving through them at walking speed, he was shot for his trouble. The engine drifted to a halt with the dead driver slumped over the wheel, a stalled island of flashing lights in a sea of angry citizens.

The rifle fire was picked up by the SonicNet and brought a Lightning Squad racing to the scene. But as soon as the 10 Grays saw the size of the disturbance they withdrew to a safe distance in their van and tried to make phone contact with the security forces inside the building, while also radioing in for instructions and backup. For some reason no one could now recall, this tactic of falling back and waiting for instructions had long ago become known as "doing a Columbine."

It was at that point that the voice came on the building's loudspeaker system.

Someone had managed to wire him into the external speakers on an emergency basis, so his voice could be heard all 'round the block.

"Your attention, please. This is Patrick Reilly, I'm a senior federal prosecutor."

The crowd booed and jeered.

"I have taken temporary command here. And I've been authorized to negotiate an orderly transfer of control of this building."

There was a puzzled pause, and then some scattered cheers. Most in the crowd seemed unable to understand what he'd just said. Of course, he was lying; Pat Reilly had no direct orders from anyone, unless you counted the ongoing, life-changing revelations he'd been experiencing since his run-in with Doctor Death in that hospital basement.

He'd been forced to turn to the black market to get his beloved Charlene the drugs she needed to live out her final days at home with the boys in anything approaching normalcy

— drugs that were cheaper to manufacture than aspirin, drugs acquired from poppy plants whose existence and usefulness mankind had known about for millennia, plants which could be grown with ease anywhere that enjoyed a relatively warm climate. Yet the sap of these flowers was a "drug" which could have gotten him or Charlene or the people who supplied them thrown in prison for life.

He had expected he'd have to deal with vicious armed drug gangs — drooling Colombians with gold chains and gang tattoos who would demand anal sex or worse as part of their payment. Instead he'd discovered a community of brave, non-violent superannuated hippies who tooled around in rusty, aging vans — one step ahead of the Lightning Youth "Turn in a Clunker" patrols — making it their mission to bring relief to the suffering ... all felons considered worse by the law than child rapists, all people Pat Reilly himself would previously have locked up for the rest of their natural lives without a moment's hesitation.

He owed them the last month of Charlene's beautiful life. And then, at the end, when she told him she couldn't stand his running the risk of prison any longer because the boys would need him now more than ever, when Charlene turned out to be the strongest of any of them, assuring him she would do it with his service pistol if he didn't help her, they all said their good-byes, and Patrick Reilly had committed one last state and federal felony, helping her take the final overdose that ended her pain in this world, helped her become the angel he had always known she deserved and longed to be.

"As many of you know," he sobbed now into the microphone, fighting to bring his voice back under control, "I submitted my resignation some days ago. I can no longer send people to prison for exercising their civil, legal, constitutional, and human rights to possess firearms, or to buy and sell and use any drug or plant extract they please, or to keep the money they earn by the sweat of their brow. Especially when the tax in question is written so as to apply only to American citizens living overseas, and to foreigners earning money in America, and the IRS just lies about it and puts us in prison if we don't pay."

Now the cheers were more extended.

"Chief Judge McNair, and a number of other judges whose courtrooms were in this building, are now dead. Their heads are on display on the fence at the north entrance. May they rest ... well, no. But may God have mercy on their souls."

This time the mob cheered for itself, and for something most of its members already knew. But it was different hearing someone publicly announce and confirm what you had accomplished. The main reason Pat Reilly announced this, of course, was to convey the true situation to most of the guards, who had been locked inside the jail section of the building the whole time and would have no idea how far things had gone. He now continued along that line, with those listeners in mind.

"Lieutenant Kaufman — Larry — you've got a lot of brave men and women under your command. They'd fight to the death if they had to, you and I both know that." Only because anyone would fight to the death if cornered, of course. But Reilly didn't say that.

"But you're not National Guardsmen, and you're not Marines. You're not assigned to protect this building. That's not your duty." That was technically true.

"Your duty is to protect the more than one hundred prisoners we have locked up in the cells and holding rooms in this building, all of whom are required by law to be presumed innocent. I know most of you people outside have friends and family among those men, who are locked inside this building, like trapped rats. If this building burns while they're still inside, you will be murdering them, murdering your own."

He paused a moment to let that sink in.

"Some small fires have already been started. We've got most of those fires under control. So far. But the fire engines have not been able to get through. If we lose the battle against these fires, the prisoners as well as all the guards are going to burn to death."

The guards probably wouldn't have thought of that. And needless to say, they'd be a lot more concerned about having their own personal selves burned than the damned prisoners, who they considered to be all guilty, anyway.

"We don't want that. No one wants to see those prisoners die in their cells. But the fire engines have not been able to get through." He paused to let the impact of that fact sink in among the guards locked inside the windowless cell areas, now prisoners along with their prisoners.

"So here's what I'm ordering:" he said, pushing his bluff, since he had no real authority to order anything. "Lieutenant Kaufman's men will need about 10 minutes to unlock all the internal doors. I'd like you folks outside to delegate two or three leaders to meet me at the east entrance in about 10 minutes, under a flag of truce. If we can all agree, I'm going to lead the prisoners and the guards out that door in about 15 minutes. I'm asking you all to be patient for that long, so we can let these prisoners go, so we can spare their lives."

That drew some additional scattered shouting and cheering.

"The guards are going to keep their weapons, and march out in good order and with their heads held high. Once everyone is safely outside, I will escort the guards as a group to the fire station around the corner, and the prisoners will be free to go."

So far, with the one exception of the fire engine that had tried to breach the crowd, no one had started killing garbagemen or firemen. They were among the only municipal employees anyone still liked, largely because they never arrested anyone. So with any luck, the firehouse would be respected as neutral ground.

"At that point, this building will be surrendered to you

folks, whose taxes built it in the first place. You can turn it into a drug store, or you can burn it to the ground, it's up to you."

From the shouts and cries, it sounded like Option Two was considerably ahead on the Applause-o-meter.

"Give us 10 minutes, and send two or three delegates to meet me at the east door."

Two of the crowd's negotiators were Norbert Bachman and former police officer John Comiskey. Reilly had jury activist Joe Crosby brought from his cell, as well — he wanted the most prestigious and recognizeable group he could assemble for the front of their column; he hoped no one would want to shoot these guys.

It was a pale and somber group. No one had expected things to go this far so quickly — least of all John Comiskey, who was, after all, a former cop.

There wasn't much to negotiate, really. They all agreed the main object was to get everyone out of the building without further loss of life.

And so — with bald-headed Norbert Bachman holding up his hands in a victory salute, and bearded jury activist Joe Crosby flanking him on the other side — Patrick Reilly led them all out with no further loss of life, a bizarre kind of pied piper operating on some indefinable mixture of insight, instinct, and inspiration.

Within an hour the now-empty federal courthouse was a funeral pyre of flames, a Viking burial for Judge James McNair which was probably better than the old fascist deserved, but which immediately gave a focus and a concrete television image to the rebellion which had been simmering in the city for months.

By nightfall another courthouse and the downtown Gotham IRS building were also in flames, and the remaining portals of the Lightning Squads that had been left out and publicly accessible were being torn to pieces by angry mobs in a number of neighborhoods.

But the government did not fall.

Mayor Brackley was on the evening news that night, announcing at a press conference that anarchy would not be tolerated, that police and the Lightning Squads would track down the ringleaders of this outrageous wave of violence and would deal with them as required by law, that his men would be using their machine guns to make a violent example of anyone they caught, in order to demonstrate that "guns and violence never solve anything."

It was as though two football teams had withdrawn to their locker rooms after playing to a tie score in a bruising first half, licking their wounds and still snarling defiance.

But even if the victor had yet to be decided, at least everyone was now on notice: the rebellion was no longer just some guy in a black suit flitting across the roof at midnight.

This one was for real.

❖ ❖ ❖

"You're rich, Andrew. Couldn't you just have put it all in a trust, moved to some island?"

They were having the argument again.

Cassie knew they shouldn't. She was losing him and she didn't want to lose him. They said arguing was good because it cleared the air, but what were you supposed to do when it just spiraled down and down? If it wasn't resolved then it would always be there, waiting to lunge out of the darkness at them when it was least expected. Some couples just left the monster to grow in silence, pretending it wasn't there. Her parents had done that. Till the bitter silences and the list of things they didn't dare talk about expanded to fill their lives. She wouldn't do that.

"I tried, once." Andrew was trying to be patient. He didn't

yell. It didn't help.

"Good people died. If everyone with the capability to resist goes and hides on an island, what happens when they've eaten out all the storehouses here, and they start picking off the islands? They are parasites, you know; they're never satisfied. Anyway, my family's been in this city almost 200 years. We helped build it. It'd be like seeing them rape a beautiful woman, and just walking away."

"But you're just picking off the foot soldiers. It's the judges and senators and presidents who give the orders."

"The people you're talking about don't go out and ruin people's lives in person. They do it from behind big mahogany desks; they do it over the phone as they sit on the pot in their gold and marble tax-funded bathrooms. They send the guys in the blue uniforms with the sweatstains under the arms, and when the poor bastard who just wanted to live free and not be searched and numbered and tracked burns up with his dog or hangs himself after being buggered a dozen times in his holding cell, these bastards don't even have to watch the mess getting cleaning up."

Graymalkin was trying to climb Andrew's leg. He picked up the huge cat, who immediately snuggled up against his neck and started purring.

"If we set out to kill everyone who believes it's OK to take from the productive and redistribute to the lazy, the shiftless, and the drunk, I'd have to kill 95 percent of the graduates of your modern government schools. We'd run out of garbagemen to haul away the corpses; wolves would roam the streets.

"You can't do that. All I can hope to do is teach the enemy's foot soldiers that there may be a price to be paid for forgetting their only job is to *protect* liberty and property. All we can hope to do is show a few of the downtrodden that there's hope, they can fight, the enemy *can* die.

"And the lack of due process ..."

"Should we hold kangaroo courts, like they do, just to

maintain good form? Try them before a jury of their fellow tax collectors, bring in trained monkeys in black robes to rule you can't put them on trial for just following orders?

"What they've declared on us isn't justice, it's war — war to the bitter end, a war of tyranny and slavery against property and freedom. Hundreds have already died, Cassie. You've written about some of them. How many years have you been trying to convince them to change their ways?"

"Andrew, you could be killed."

"Then I'll die a free man, fighting for what's precious to me. To fight and die, or live as a slave licking their boots, paying their taxes, apologizing for everything good and true and brave? That's supposed to be a tough choice?

"I know. I just wish ..."

"That it could all be done by the rules? They perverted the rules decades ago. When was the last time any one of them did a single day in jail for exceeding his constitutional authority — hell, even for killing someone?"

"No. I just wish it didn't have to be you."

She was crying again, now. She didn't want to cry. He would hold her and it would feel good but then they'd have it all to do again, later. Graymalkin got upset and jumped down.

"I'm sorry," she said. "I said stupid things. I keep saying hateful things, and I don't mean to. I don't want to. I felt betrayed. You didn't trust me enough to tell me what was going on."

"I was waiting for you to finish the courtship dance and come to stay."

"When you start sleeping with someone, I think that's when you're supposed to start trusting them. You're not supposed to be lying to them."

He said nothing.

"Do you think we can ever get it back, what we had?"

"I don't know, Cassie. I admired you. Still do. Then we met and we had so many things in common, it seemed perfect.

Maybe that's the problem. It seemed like such a natural fit to me, I took some things for granted. A guy wants his woman to be proud of what he does."

"I'm amazed at what you've done, Andrew. It's like you've had the lives of three normal people. You're rich; you're famous; you're talented and successful ..."

"So I should have left it at that ... not gone out at night to kill cops and taxmen?"

She laughed, a trace of the old soft and gentle Cassie creeping through. "You'll have to admit, it's an unusual hobby. When a guy says, 'I need to spend a few nights out with the boys' ..."

She touched his arm — stroked it gently.

"There's someone else, isn't there?" She couldn't look at his face. She wanted the truth. But she didn't want that to be the truth.

"There could be someone else," he said. "But that's not the point."

" 'Could be'? There can't 'could be' someone else. And why do men always say it's 'not the point,' goddammit? If you want out because there's someone else, say so."

"I haven't made anyone a firm offer."

"You made *me* a firm offer."

"Yes I did."

"And now you're throwing me away? Why? Because I got mad when I found out; I yelled at you about the killing? Goddammit, Andrew, you can be so cold and inflexible; you're such a bull. We had a fight, OK? We disagreed about something. What couple on earth hasn't had a fight? I'd been shot, for God's sake."

"I didn't want you to say the things you were saying. That you keep on saying. In a million years, I never saw it coming. I tried to stop you."

"Did you ever really love me?"

529

"This is not just some misunderstanding, Cassie. I wanted you to be part of my life, part of what I do. But you rejected that."

"And because I didn't put on a black vinyl suit and be your Catwoman, now you've found some little chippie who just thinks you're Superman, who'll never question anything you say or do? Who is it, one of those little Irish bitches? You should try little Madison, she'd be perfect. Moons after you like a sick calf."

"I told you a long time ago, Cassie, life is short and there's no surplus of joy and passion in this world — when you see something that's right you need to grab it, to hang on tight.

"I wasn't the one who decided to take things slow and have some kind of courtship by the rules where you don't kiss till the third date. You expect life to be some kind of formalized ritual, Cassie, but it's not. It's messy and inconvenient and risky. You throw yourself in and take chances. You do crazy things because they just feel right even though you can't possibly know where they'll lead."

"That's the way children see the world, Andrew. Then you grow up you *do* have to consider the consequences. Grownups plan ahead."

"And yes, Cassie, sometimes it doesn't work and your heart gets stepped on and you end up with new bruises. I would have cooked for you and we could have made love and you would have never had to leave."

"A nice dream."

"When the dream is in front of you, Cassandra, you reject it; you walk away. You've always done that, haven't you? There's less risk; you stay in control; you can't be hurt. But you settle for the pale echo, a faded Xerox copy of the real passions that end up defining life for the rest of us. It's a question of whether you're ready and able to commit, to throw yourself off that cliff and know I'd catch you."

"But you wouldn't be catching me right now, would

you?"

"And when someone finally walks away, when they *all* eventually walk away — that validates the things you did that drove them away, doesn't it? All tidy and hermetic. You always held back, Cassandra. I always felt like, 'Well, I might have to write a story about you someday, so I have to maintain my objectivity, here.' Measuring what you said, like someone who'll only wade in up to her knees.

"Part of you always hung back and watched, as much as you were really there in the moment, like you were using half your mind to figure out how you'd describe it all in a paragraph, searching for the right adjectives. Does being a reporter mean you have to let the whole world go by, your whole life go by, just hanging back on the sidelines scribbling notes, without ever picking a single thing you're going to commit to — that you can never live wholly inside a single day, without thinking about which parts you could use in an article?"

"Maybe. It doesn't make me happy about myself."

Cassie rested her forehead against his arm.

"Old habits come from old disappointments. How do you unlearn old lessons? We can't change who we are. And you, Andrew — you still think you can find someone who'll take a leap like that?"

"Because my life depends on it, I go on looking."

"Would you really have made me supper, and let me stay forever, if I'd gone home with you and let you make love to me the first night we met?"

"If you'd been the kind of person who could have done that, if you could have committed, yes. It's what I wanted more than anything. No rules. Just the passion of the unknown."

"I would have been just another one-night conquest in a long line, and you know it. You would have gotten bored with me and thrown me out within a week. You can't find out enough about someone in one night."

"Some things aren't about logic. The one who fills you

with longing and makes you come in your pants has cut right through to a much more basic selection program."

"I love you, Andrew. As much as I can love anyone, I love you."

"I know that."

"How often do you find someone who likes to cuddle in the morning, who can hump like a bunny all night long?"

She looked out the window at the winter street.

"I'm leaving the city," she said. "I'm going to the West. I was hoping you'd come."

"When?"

"Soon. Days — a week. I tried to quit; they gave me a year's leave of absence instead. Sullivan says they'll print any dispatches I send back. I'm going to write a book. About ... all this. I need to do this to sort things out for myself, mostly. But my main obligation is to the truth, the truth as well as I can put it together."

"I know that."

"As much as I can love anyone, Andrew, I loved you. I love you still. I hate this thing that came between us. I hate it. I don't understand it myself. I want to be with you. Can we try to put it behind us, to get back what we had? Will you come with me?"

He did not reply.

"Damn it, you say you hate the killing."

"I do."

"Then give it up. Come away. Do you think you can kill them all? Do you think they'll never kill *you?* Who is it you owe this to? How can you owe it to anyone to keep doing a thing you hate? Do you really think they appreciate it?"

He was silent.

"Andrew, I feel like I'm going crazy, here. I'm going crazy without you. I want you back — I want back what we had. Just tell me what to do. Put a gun in my hand and I'll shoot the mayor on TV, whatever I have to do. Just tell me what I have to do. Only don't be like this to me anymore, I turn to you and there's just this wall of cold. Oh, God, please!"

It was a wail from the prison of loneliness. No one could hear it and not be moved. But it was a self-imposed prison, the loneliness of a life of rules, carefully learned and carefully followed. Intricate rituals replacing the real, messy, agonizing life of the heart. He'd offered her a chance to throw herself into life, his life, a new life they could carve out together. Instead of seeing it as a chance to escape a prison built of someone else's rules and grab the passion she'd always craved, she'd acted like he was trying to shove her into a wild, strange sea where she would surely drown.

She'd kept her pride, and her dignity, and her independence. Of course, he'd never wanted to take those away. But now, would they be enough for her?

She cried. "Can we?" she asked. "Can we get it back, Andrew?"

He relented, then, and took her in his powerful arms. They both loved the way it felt. It was a long time before they spoke again. A very long time.

❧ ❧ ❧

Madison was ashamed. She was doing a thing she'd told herself over and over again that she must not do. It was a task few others could have pulled off, for he moved like a big cat, changing his pace, stopping or doubling back when he passed into an alley full of shadows, so anyone with lesser instincts would have either stumbled right into him or else lost him a dozen times.

At first she'd lied to herself, told herself she followed him sometimes, staying out of sight, in order to be there to protect him in case anything happened. After all, he WAS the revolu-

533

tion. They had all spoken from time to time about the nearly suicidal way the boss refused to travel with any bodyguards.

But there was no point kidding herself. She did this as self-torture. She'd known almost immediately he'd been heading for Cassandra's apartment. From her vantage point she'd been able to see him rung in, and now Madison was at it again, imagining him in someone else's arms — the perfect bitch's arms — as she counted the long minutes: five, 10, 15. Finally, she could stand the churning in her stomach and the ache in her throat and eyes no more. And so she turned and stumbled away, recovering her street sense in a moment, checking all sides for danger as she moved. She wouldn't know how long he had stayed, this time. She was glad she would not know.

⚜ ⚜ ⚜

After Andrew had gone, Cassandra pulled on her robe and went and stood in the middle of the kitchen floor, looking at nothing, microwaving hot water for tea. Graymalkin arrived on the counter, looking at her curiously, asking to be picked up. It was earlier than usual, but he knew the dawn couldn't be far off. She shoved him gently aside. He'd been a good traveler when he was young; hopefully he could make one more great journey with her.

She could never quite remember how or why she managed to fuck up every good thing in her life, but there it was. Probably he was right — lack of courage. She pretended to want the bold, the dramatic, living life on the edge. She tried to convince herself. But in the end, when the chance was there, she always pulled back, settled for what was safe. Somehow she knew that if 10 people tried to jump the precipice and only nine made it across, she'd be the one who'd fall. And so she held back. Her courage was only on paper.

She would go to the West.

Maybe there, somehow, she could do her penance, make amends for a life of pointless promise, predictable failure. Maybe there, at least, she could do something that had been given her alone to do, help give birth to a new race, born and bred in freedom.

And then Cassandra did what she'd been doing every morning for days. She threw up in the sink.

⚜ ⚜ ⚜

It was late. Everyone had gone home. Madison should have locked up and gone home, too. But there was peace for her here, in the big exercise room with its gray floor mats and familiar smells, the high dark windows from which you could catch an occasional glimpse of the dark, quiet river to the west.

In her old age, life had returned to the old lady that was this building — life, and meaning. And now the dance of new life had begun. She was content. As Madison's music was cueing up, the quiet was interrupted only by the occasional banging and clanking of the old steam radiators, once so lovingly maintained by Jimmy Rizzolo.

Madison felt herself walk to the middle of the room. She liked the way it felt, the confidence in her muscles. She could feel them separately, now, as they worked. She remembered doing gymnastics as a little girl, before her world had been ripped apart. She'd been confident, then, too, assured by her coaches that she had talent. It was enough then to get a move right, to put three moves together, then four, then seven — to hit her mark and bask in their approval. How little she had known of the world beyond that cozy little spotlight, where she had allowed herself to believe in her own competence. How little power she had actually possessed to deal with the insanity when it came.

This felt different. That had been a little girl's body, so light, so forgiving, so easy to push around. Her musculature was different now, not quite as flexible and forgiving. But there was a compensation. Power.

She was already sweating from her workout. She shed her sweats now, down to her shorts and halter top. When her music cued up again she would do the dance of the tiger one more time, with the falcata. The sword was heavy and made the routine less graceful ... unless you were very strong. Unless you were very, very good.

Madison was good. And of course, the weapon was part of her body now.

The song began again, Anne Wilson's "How Do I get You Alone?"

Till now I always got by on my own
I never really cared until I met you
And now it chills me to the bone
How do I get you alone

The first step. Ever so slowly. It was tempting to show off her speed, but speed could be added later. Speed was of no value if the form was not right in the first place. The form was everything. And slow was actually harder, took more control. Feel the muscles in play. For the first time spin, slash, recover, straighten. Every landing mattered. A damaged knee could be for a long time. Gradually her body picked up its pace, unbidden. It was like this in any activity committed to muscle memory, even sex. Start right, and eventually the body took over and dictated its own pace. Not only was the control of the conscious mind not necessary, it was actually helpful to turn it off.

Except for the breathing. Some moves were easier if you

held your breath. But then the oxygen deficit would start to tell, and you'd end up panting. Instead, she'd had to train herself to breathe in flow — inhale as you climbed, so you'd always be exhaling when you landed, which naturally contracted the diaphragm, anyway. That had taken the longest to learn, like a piano player learning to play seemingly mismatched parts with both hands at the same time.

> *You don't know how long I have wanted*
> *to touch your lips and hold you tight*
> *You don't know how long I have waited*
> *and I was going to tell you tonight*
> *But the secret is still my own*
> *and my love for you is still unknown,*
> *Unknown*

So familiar was the routine now that she could distance herself from it, almost as though her mind and eyes were floating above, watching Madison's body at work. Not a beautiful body — too skinny and wiry, except that the breasts were finally large enough now to require the sports bra, the legs a bit too short in proportion — but taut, competent ... right.

And because she was able to go outside herself, she knew then that there was someone else in the room, watching.

For an instant she thought of turning her head, but she opted not to let this intrusion interfere. It would just be another test of her concentration. She had the blade. And whoever it was, she did not sense him as a threat. That was interesting, because it came unbidden: "him." She decided to see if she could extend her senses any further from the whirling form beneath her. As she breathed more deeply, she sought for his smell in the room. In between the inevitable scuff and squeak of her feet on the mats, she listened to see whether he moved. Didn't he, at least, breathe? Who did she know who could be there, yet remain that silent?

There, she smelled his familiar smell. As she slashed the air a final time, completed her high spin, landed with both feet together, dropped to her knees, panting and enjoying the sheen of the cooling sweat on her flushed and heated skin, she waited before raising her eyes. How had he watched her? With satisfaction, knowing she was his, could be his at any time, just for the asking? Even with pride, perhaps? She had kept herself fit, for him. Pushed herself beyond the limits, pressing more weight than some of the guys, especially with her legs. More than once he had called her his best fighter, said it in front of the others. More than that, she was a captain now, her Bitches assigned on equal terms with Jean-Claude's veterans and Hideki's nightfighters.

Good. That would be good. It wasn't much, but it was something. Better than to be ignored, spurned, cast out. If that's all he wanted her for, then she would be the best fighter she could be. Stand at his side one day, in that way at least, if not any other. Maybe that was all the dream meant.

Smiling, confident, she raised her chin to look him directly in the eye. And found that he had gone.

The room was empty, once again. Had she imagined it? No, the papers on the bulletin board still fluttered where he had passed, his faint scent still unmistakable to her heightened senses.

To the emptiness, she whispered his name.

CHAPTER 16

Those who have been once intoxicated with power ... never can willingly abandon it. They may be distressed in the midst of all their power, but they will never look to anything but power for their relief.

— EDMUND BURKE (1729-1797)

The whole aim of practical politics is to keep the populace alarmed — and thus clamorous to be led to safety — by menacing it with an endless series of hobgoblins, all of them imaginary.

— H.L. MENCKEN, OF THE SUN (1880-1956)

To preserve liberty, it is essential that the whole body of the people always possess arms, and be taught alike, especially when young, how to use them.

— RICHARD HENRY LEE (1732-1794),
PRIMARY AUTHOR OF THE BILL OF RIGHTS, 1788

The Griffin Mansion — for 90 years the official residence of the mayors of Gotham City — stood on the far East Side, uptown at 88th Street, in a park above Hell Gate, a roaring stretch of tidal race where the Harlem and the East Rivers meet.

The gray fieldstone Federal-style mansion was faced with wood — now painted yellow on the ground floor and white above — and was renowned for its three-sided porch and trellis railings, sweeping around the house at the second-floor and attic levels.

The joint had apparently been the cat's pajamas in the early 19th century. Archibald Griffin, a Scottish shipping magnate and prominent member of Gotham society, threw lavish parties attended by the likes of Louis Philippe of France, John Quincy Adams, and Washington Irving. But Griffin never recovered from debts incurred thanks to the government shipping embargoes and subsequent unpaid claims of the War of 1812. He had to dissolve his firm and liquidate his assets — including the house — in 1823.

Subsequent owners saw the surrounding farmland yield rapidly to encroaching urban development. By the late 1880s a municipal sea wall and promenade had been built along Hell Gate. The city fathers then began to cast covetous glances on the old Griffin property itself, mewling that this last piece of open space needed to be "preserved for all the people."

In 1896, beginning a proud tradition, the city of Gotham "condemned" the property and and grabbed it from its private owners, incorporating the Griffin Mansion's 11 acres into the city's newly-dedicated William T. Sherman Park.

Over the next 30 years, the once-proud house was used for children's carpentry and home economics classes, then as an ice-cream parlor, then as the park's concession stand and toilets, and finally as a storage building for silage for the animals of the adjacent zoo.

Finally, in 1942, Parks Commissioner Robert Moses convinced city authorities to designate it as the official residence of the mayor. Somebody swept out the hay and moved in Fiorello La Guardia.

The building was now thoroughly restocked with a positively hideous assemblage of early 19th century furnishings — austere, fragile, uncomfortable pieces of craftsmanship which the antiques dealers raved about and which Jack and Tanya both agreed would be better suited to a museum devoted to the artifacts of the Spanish Inquisition.

The holiday gala on which Eustace "Buffy" Summers and the rest of the committee had been working all fall was intended as a fund-raiser for the latest set of renovations to the two-century-old barn. But with the accelerating progress of the insurrection, it had become far more than that.

A vast security cordon had been thrown up — all the way out onto the river, where patrol boats guarded against amphibious attack — in an attempt to demonstrate that the city's social and political elite were still in charge, could still gather for a holiday merriment when and wherever they pleased.

Of course, the floodlit no-man's-land surrounding the place gave the lie to this whole premise. But the TV reporters would be discouraged from emphasizing that part of the show ... instead it would be all the stars of the social and political firmament, parading out of the limousines to spend a festive political evening with the mayor and his dashing young nephew. (Jack was asked to wear his best dress uniform, with the new medal for his fine "suicide prevention" work during the raid at the day-care center downtown.)

This was also the social event at which his uncle had decided to announce Jack's betrothal to his "intended," Eustace Summers — who, in a highly considerate gesture, he would finally be allowed to meet some minutes beforehand.

Jack had told Joanie he was going to finally have it out with the old man, put his foot down, tell his uncle there was someone else in Jack's life and it was unfair to lead along this wealthy socialite — who probably wore horn-rimmed glasses, weighed 250 pounds, had moles and a goiter — whom Jack hadn't the slightest intention of even dating, let alone marrying.

Joan had surprised him by the vehemence with which she'd argued against this plan.

"It's OK to seem reluctant, Jack. Blush and go all nervous, that'll work. But if you mention there's someone else in your life your uncle is going to want to know who. And when you won't tell him he'll get suspicious and put detectives on you — on both of us — and God knows what they'll find. The best thing to do is just go ahead and meet this Eustace Summers. It can't do any harm. Honey, I'm not worried about losing you, honest."

"You ought to be jealous as hell over my meeting another woman who my uncle wants me to marry," Jack had responded. "What's up, hon? Is this your way of telling me I should start shopping around? That it's not gonna work out between us?"

She'd had to cuddle up to him, then, to convince him he was wrong. As a matter of fact, when they were done cuddling up and she was tucked in under his arm and asked him "You convinced now?" he'd said "Well ... almost," which had caused her to punch him in the shoulder several times before cuddling up all over again, at which point he'd loudly insisted "OK, I'm convinced, hon. Honest I am. I'm totally convinced. I'm not likely to need any more convincing for, jeez, at least another hour or two ..." Problem was, she was actually quite a hard little puncher, and his right shoulder soon started to go noticeably black and blue.

⚜ ⚜ ⚜

Biff Harder was there — the fellow Lightning Trooper who'd shown Jack the ropes on the SonicNet screens, could it really be almost a year ago? Biff had been assigned to the security detail. Jack had kept up the acquaintance — Biff knew a lot of technical stuff about the system and had been happy to find a kindred soul when Jack had expressed an interest.

Truth was, Jack couldn't understand half of it. But he had a good rote memory — it had always come in handy at exam time — so he was able to repeat most of it back to Joan, verbatim. She then told him what to ask about next.

Biff had originally been assigned to the checkpoint down at the end of the driveway. But Jack pulled a few strings and got him shifted inside the house, where at least Biff would be able to get something to eat and avoid freezing his ass off.

Biff had expressed gratitude somewhat in excess of what was required, took the opportunity to show Jack the latest photos of his wife, Darla, and 4-year-old Cindy. They were pretty cute, Jack had agreed — especially the kid.

Folks started arriving shortly after 6 — his Uncle Dan stationed Jack near the front door as part of the welcoming committee. He didn't have to take coats or announce people — various uniformed footmen were assigned this duty, which was a good thing, since Jack didn't know who most of these self-important and oh-so-stylishly costumed folks were.

So it mostly came down to shaking hands, introducing himself, pointing people toward the food and drink. His uncle said it would be good practice. He meant for politics — Jack had even heard some talk of running him for the congressional seat Bambi Fiducci had been angling for, prior to her unfortunate run-in with the endive salad.

Jack answered all such speculation by saying he was much too young; such an office should go to someone experienced, someone who'd already paid his or her dues in the party. His uncle smiled and said, "That's perfect; I knew you'd be a natural at this."

"But I mean it," Jack had protested.

"Even better!" his uncle had beamed.

The place was done up in almost medieval splendor. Christmas wreaths and red satin bows and baroque synthoplaster angels hovering in pastel gossamer gowns from the same guys who did up the decorations for the big department stores downtown — massive things that it took a crew of six to anchor to the walls.

Jack often wondered where the fancy limousines and town cars all came from — you hardly ever saw them out in the streets, any more than you saw all these fur coats and tuxedoes.

He remembered reading about the way the decadent kings of 17th and 18th century Europe had competed to see who could throw the most extravagant costume balls — the queen of France done up as Little Bo Peep, shepherding little lambs all dipped in gold gilt, or whatever.

He wondered if some of those parties would have felt like this.

Oh, there was plenty of holiday cheer, all kinds of inside jokes about politics and society, all damned witty, Jack had no doubt. Though most of it was Greek to him.

But there was something wrong here, a kind of crackling brittleness. And they'd made him read enough history in school that he thought he recognized it.

The French aristocracy didn't all just pack their bags and flee after the storming of the Bastille in 1789. There were still plenty of powderheads left around to arrest and behead during The Terror, three years later. So what on earth had all those fancy land barons in their silks and powdered wigs been doing over those three years? Trying to come up with some compromise republican government that would retain some kind of orderly protection of property rights? No. They'd been throwing parties.

What had the redcoats done, right here in Gotham, for the two years between their loss at Yorktown and the time they finally got around to pulling out?

Held masqued balls, of course, and humped their American mistresses with enthusiasm and aplomb.

One of the German mercenaries who were essentially the only good soldiers the French had in Indo-China in the late 1940s and early 1950s had written a book where he told all about how useless the French commanders were, pulling on their white gloves and escorting the latest sweet young thing to that evening's party at the ambassador's mansion.

"But if you don't listen to us and pay attention to the kind of tactics we need to use out there in the jungle you're going to lose this war and get kicked out of the country," the sweat-stained Germans, fresh from the back country, would insist.

"Yes, probablement," the French generals would agree with a smile. "C'est la vie."

Was that what he was seeing here?

Tanya Petrov showed up at his arm, looking good. She was blonde and pretty ... though just a little, um, stout for Jack's taste. He saw where his uncle had finally bought her some nice jewelry. Getting soft in his old age.

After some initial awkwardness, he'd gotten to like Tanya. She was free of the bullshit that infected almost everyone else near the center of power. They'd become friends.

"Jack, aren't you going to offer me a drink?" she asked.

"Oh, sure."

"Unless you just can't tear yourself away from your position of honor here, directing people to the bar."

"Yeah, right. Black Russian?"

"Of course. A double," she said. Behind her smile, there was always something else in Tanya's expression. For a long time, Jack had thought it was sadness. Recently he'd changed his mind, though. She could actually laugh at the way things were, sometimes. And sad people don't generally laugh. Which meant it had to be something else, some other emotion lurking there, waiting its time.

Which was just a little scary.

By the time he returned with her drink the people at the door were whispering and looking his way. "What's up?" Jack asked.

"It seems your intended is about to arrive," Tanya smiled. Jack's stomach did a somersault. Tanya actually seemed to be enjoying his discomfort.

Sure enough, the door opened, someone was handing over some giant fluffy coat which appeared to be made of wolf fur — fake, he assumed, wondering briefly how he'd feel about a woman who wore real wolf — and then the uniformed doorman announced the arrival of Miss Eustace Summers.

She strode in, clicked right up to Jack and Tanya on her stylish spike heels, gave them each a huge smile, and held out her hand for Jack to kiss ... or shake ... or something. He completely forgot what it was he was supposed to do.

Given how well he'd prepared himself to treat Miss Eustace Summers in a polite but cool manner, aiming not to hurt the poor dear's feelings but still intent on getting the message through to her as quickly as possible that he had no intention of marrying anyone chosen by his uncle for social and political reasons — nothing personal, mind you — Jack was, basically, dumbstruck. His mouth was open, his tongue was presumably lolling out like the village idiot, drooling on himself as he worked his brain real hard to try and figure out how many pennies it might take the buy the nickel pack of gum.

She was petite and elegant. She had the most perfect legs, and a slim waist. He didn't know anything about clothes, but he was sure this shimmering bottle-green piece of iridescence must have cost a fortune, precisely because it appeared so simple. And her perfect face would have brought tears to the eyes of a statue.

No one could possibly be that beautiful, that pert and captivating. The huge blue eyes, the big dark bangs against her pale skin, the high, elflike ears, the perfectly sculpted nose ... even a few freckles. His heart would have melted, even if it weren't for the other thing.

Which was that — except for the fact that she had inexplicably long hair tonight, pulled stylishly over to one side, dark brown all the way to her shoulder, and that the iridescent stud she usually wore on the left side of her nose had inexplicably vanished, not even a little hole where it had been, some kind of trick with the makeup, presumably — there was something else about this "Eustace Summers" that had just rendered him completely ... literally ... speechless.

She was Joan Matcham.

"Joan," he said, as she finally solved his "what to do with the hand" problem for him by taking his big mitt in both of hers, a handshake which managed to be somehow both direct and feminine.

"Jack, it's Eustace," she said clearly enough for anyone nearby to hear. "I've been so looking forward to our meeting; I've heard so much about you." And then, under her breath, but without ever breaking her smile, *"Do smile just a little, Jack. If you frown at me like you've just met the village monster, these women* will *gossip; you have no idea."*

"Um, Eustace, you're even more lovely than I'd heard," he managed to croak.

"You're too kind, Jack. But your uncle has such a lovely house. Won't you show me around a little? Hi, Tanya, delightful to see you. We have to catch up later. But now you'll excuse me if I steal away this big hunk of man, won't you?"

Tanya's laugh covered them as they got away from the immediate crowd near the door, which now turned its collective attention to the next arrival, carefully calibrating each attendee's social status in relation to their own.

"For God's sake, Joan, what have you done with the real Eustace Summers? There are bound to be people here who know what she looks like."

"Jack, honey, I love you, but think about it. Rich society debs are supposed to play tennis and attend fund-raisers for African charities and the Disease of the Month. Eustace Summers trying to find work as a programmer was just considered cute, and the hacker world certainly wasn't going to take in some dizzy debutante in a tennis bracelet. And the furniture, is it original to the house, or are these restorations? So Eustace cut off her hair and became Joan Matcham."

"What?"

"I'm your actual fiancee, Jack. I'm Eustace Summers. At

least, in places like this I am. Are you disappointed?"

"Uh ... stunned."

"I know, dear.

"Where'd you come up with the name?"

"Joan Matcham? Out of an old book by Robert Louis Stevenson. You probably read it as a child."

"Weren't you worried somebody would notice?"

"Of course not. Nobody reads any more. Hideki goes around telling people his name is Akira Kurosawa or Isoroku Yamamoto or Toshiro Mifune — no one bats an eye. I could call myself Margaret Mitchell; the only place they'd give me any trouble would be in the old-age home."

"Who?"

"My, this house just reeks of history, doesn't it? Just to imagine it dates all the way back to the Eighteenth Century, to the founding fathers, the greatest men in our history — James Garfield, Rutherford B. Hayes."

"I liked you better in short hair."

"That's good, Jack. Because you see, when this dress comes off, so does the hair."

"Oh."

"You mustn't think too much about the dress coming off till after dinner, Jack. You're a healthy young lad and you'll embarrass us both. The idea tonight is to find me potentially acceptable, not to bend me over the dessert table. Though I'll admit I'd love to see their faces. I'll try not to mention it again."

"I didn't mind."

"I know, dear. You are charming. Absolutely certain you don't want to get married?"

"What? Well, yes. Just not to some socialite named Eustace. I mean, not to —"

"I was teasing you, dear. Now, I've seen about enough of this insufferable 18th century kindling that I wouldn't dare straddle you on; I hope to God you never expect us to actually live in a wind tunnel like this."

"Well, that's a relief. Like hanging out in a damned museum, no place to put your feet up."

"*That's my Jack.* Now, I don't suppose there's a source of nourishment here? Some lovely little canapes, perhaps, and some Fiji? *Since I'm sure a nice rasher of bacon and a Guinness stout would be too much to hope for.*" She put her arm around his waist, then, and gave him a little squeeze, and Jack fell in love all over again.

Which was convenient, now that he thought about it, if this was the girl he was going to marry.

"What is it, Jack?"

"Your name is actually Eustace?"

"Old families have old names. No one actually calls me that."

"What do they call you, then?"

"Buffy."

"Your name is Eustace *and they call you Buffy?*"

"Are you making fun of me?"

"No. This is just going to take a little ... getting used to."

"So now you're going to reject me because of my name?" she pouted.

"Who said anything about rejecting you? This is just going to take a little ... getting used to ... Buffy."

"You *are* laughing at me."

⚜ ⚜ ⚜

The dinner would be served buffet style, which was better than a formal service with assigned seating, though it would still put a crimp in what Jack could accomplish. He confided to Joanie — um, Eustace ... he was never going to get this straight — that his main goal for the evening was to track down Oliver Oates, who he hadn't managed to spot at the front door but who he was assured would be here. Oliver had been his uncle's campaign manager and confidante from Day One. He aimed to get the guy alone somewhere and put a little pressure on him to see what he knew about the death of Jack's father.

He was half expecting Joanie to try and talk him out of it. Instead, she agreed they should get going right away.

Joan could be such a pleasant surprise.

They found Oliver Oates in the library, which was all oak and beveled glass. There was an actual fire in the actual fireplace. The old man — Jack hadn't remembered him looking so old — was alone, and he was already half ossified on a bottle of one of Uncle Dan's best unblended malts — Knockando, in this case.

Come to think of it, Jack had heard his uncle more than once, lately, making cryptic references to the fact that Oliver might have become more of a liability than an asset. He'd give good odds the drinking was part of it.

"Jack!" the old college professor was in good spirits. "Come on in, have a drink! And who's this fine creature with you?"

"My fiancee, Uncle Oliver. May I introduce Eustace Summers. Eustace, my uncle's campaign manager, Oliver Oates. I used to call him Uncle Oliver when I was a kid."

"Of course. Should have recognized one of the Summers kids. We've always been able to count on your family. But I thought I knew all the girls ..."

"They call me Buffy, Mr. Oates. I'm sure that's how you —"

"Of course! Little Buffy? Well, you've filled out just fine. And you've got a fine young man, there. I remember playing with Jack when he was little enough to sit on my knee, hard as that may be to believe."

"Uncle Oliver, we've got to talk to you. It's important."

"Oh, that sounds serious," said the old man in the red V-necked sweater and the red plaid holiday bow tie, not mimicking seriousness very well as he opened a door with beveled cut-glass panes in the big oak bookshelf, pulled down two more whiskey tumblers, held them up to the light to make sure they were reasonably dust free. "And serious talk calls for a serious drink. You'll join me?"

"Of course," Buffy beamed. Joan, rather. Eustace.

"Seeking advice about your forthcoming marriage, no doubt," Oliver nodded seriously as he diligently shared out a double for each of them ... and another for himself.

"I'm afraid I can't be as optimistic as the occasion usually requires," he said, settling into one of the oversized green leather chairs near the fire. They pulled up two more to sit near him. Oliver Oates' once-blond hair and bushy eyebrows had long since gone white, and his hair was overdue for a trim — it hung a bit shaggily over his ears and the back of his collar.

"Ice?" he asked as an afterthought. Jack bobbled a couple of cubes for each of them with the stainless steel tongs out of the silver plated ice bucket. He assumed it was plated, anyway. Oliver waved him off; continued to take his straight.

"You've probably noticed I'm no longer a member of your uncle's inner circle. Funny how the numbers man is a genius when the numbers tell us how to win, but suddenly persona non grata when the numbers no longer tell a happy tale."

"Oliver —" Jack started to interject, looking to change the subject. But Joanie kicked him with the side of her shoe.

"What tale do the numbers tell?" she asked, leaning in close to the old man, sharing her big eyes and her perfume. If it had been anyone else, Jack might even have said she leaned forward far enough to show some tit, though he was sure his Joanie would never have done *that*.

"Well, Buffy, it's no state secret that the mayor — our entire political leadership — see the problem on the national scale as the rebels in New Columbia, and the problem on the local scale as The Black Arrow. So essentially all their thinking is tactical, all based on the premise that if we can win just one big battle out West, if we can get just one person on the inside to sell out the Black Arrow so he can be cornered and killed, the problem's solved, from there on we're back in control and it's just a matter of time."

Oliver Oates reached for the bottle. Joanie beat him to it; poured him a stout refill. The label said it was 21 years old. It occurred to Jack he wasn't sure if his Joanie was as old as the Scotch.

"What they forget is, if Montana or Idaho had tried to secede 30, 40 years ago, it wouldn't have lasted three weeks. If someone had tried what the Black Arrow is doing — hell, forget about 'if,' people *did* try that kind of thing 30, 40 years ago. It wasn't as politically directed, but some asshole sniper would start picking people off, and what would happen? The public pulled together, everyone called in their tips, vehicle descriptions. It was hardly ever the cops who caught 'em. It would always be some truck driver or senior citizen with time on his hands, spotting the guy asleep in his car in some highway rest stop, calling in on his cell phone, trying to get the 9-1-1 operators to listen to him.

"Why doesn't that happen now? Why do people cheer the Black Arrow and put him on those goddamned T-shirts? Why do we have so many copycats out there? Because the Black Arrow isn't the problem, that's why. He's just a symptom. If your skin erupts in big boils, sure, you treat the boils. But that's just at the surface. If you don't want them coming right back you have to look for the underlying cause — the boils are just the symptom of some deeper problem."

"And the numbers show the problem?" Joanie prompted.

"Inflation so out of control they had to devaluate 10-to-one, but they didn't change any of the underlying problems with the money supply or the government handouts and payrolls and pensions — do you have any idea what the unfunded pension liabilities look like? We call them "the Red Tide." But they still didn't go back to a gold or silver standard, they just keep printing up their colored confetti as fast as they can, so it's no secret they're going to have to do it all again.

"Why would anyone invest in that environment? I invest a hundred newbucks today, you promise me a hundred forty newbucks in three years, but by then the newbuck is worth a dime — which 30 years ago people would have called a penny?

"In three more years the private economy will be essentially gone. Sooner. Anyone who can move their operations offshore either physically or electronically has almost finished the job. New Washington is going nuts trying to tax the Internet, but it's like trying to scoop water with a sieve. How do you ban software? How do you ban code?

"Now that oil is priced in Euros or Rupees the Europeans and South Americans who hoarded dollars in their mattresses for generations are panicking, shipping them back over here in bales like we used to ship them our used bluejeans, saying, 'I'll take whatever I can get.' We thought we could flood the world with worthless dollars and they'd never come home? Well, New Washington is about to declare they'll no longer redeem the old dollars at any rate, and at that point what do you think is going to happen to the overseas value of the newbuck? Think we'll still be able to buy spare helicopter parts from the Indians and the Chinese for colored paper? When the New Columbians are buying machine tools to build whole new factories, paying in bullion silver and gold?

"They think they can fool people by rigging the numbers. Well, Argentina tried that. They're already means-testing Social Security, which they said they'd never do. More and more people working in the black market, refusing to accept a paycheck with 60, 70 percent deducted off the top. That means there's nothing flowing in at the other end of the hose, at a time when we've got more seniors on the dole than ever in history, huge medical costs, sucking on a hose with less and less going in the other end.

"The schools have become nothing but an exercise in denial and fancy footwork. They re-name Algebra "Algebra 3" and reclassify playing with blocks as "Algebra 1 and 2" so they can claim a lot more kids are taking algebra now. A course they used to teach in the seventh grade, by the way, and now the kids struggle to pass one algebra course to graduate high school, while the Europeans take statistics and calculus. They dumb down the tests and give each kid four tries so they can claim everything's fine, but even so the number of kids scoring above 700 on both SATs has dropped to almost none. That's your top 3 or 4 percent, the ones you need if you're going to keep a technological society up and running, no matter how far you dumb down your worker drones.

"We've become a Third World country, honey; we're importing our engineers from China and India. Can you believe that? The average kid coming into college now thinks we fought the Civil War against either the Germans or the Spanish, and *then* he can't tell you which side won. These kids don't even know how to count change; I doubt they know how many cups there are in a quart. You can't make *up* questions so simple they know the answer. 'Name one person who has ever served on the United States Supreme Court.'

"There's no more jury trial now, the process is so stacked even the innocent are advised to plead out — they'll get 10 times the sentence if they dare to fight, and they won't be allowed to mention that the law in question is unconstitutional, anyway.

"Our incarceration rates are the highest in the world, and to clear enough cells for the doctors who treat the pain patients, the women who tried to defend themselves against rapists with knives, and the people who were smart enough to ask about the geographic jurisdiction of the tax laws, they're having to cut loose the murderers and the rapists, put them in uniform and send them to the front.

"Well I've got news for you, they don't stay at the front. They don't make very good soldiers. They desert and they roam wild. We haven't seen it bad here, yet, because we're two thousand miles away, but it's spreading. You should read the reports I see from Minneapolis and Kansas City and San Francisco, almost every day now.

"Tax compliance is plummeting. Has been for decades.

They think it's just the Black Arrow killing taxmen and regulators? If he had an army of a thousand he couldn't account for what's going on. They used to say the system was based on 'voluntary compliance.' We laughed about it, back then; a really good cynical joke. But now it turns out they were right. People started asking 40 years ago, 'What happens if everybody just stops volunteering?' Now we're finding out.

"Don't stay in this city, kids. Nobody wants to hear the bad news, but you can go outside at night, any place high up, and watch the lights flickering out, like the last campfires of the Romans as they got ready to pull out of London. You know what happens to this city if the water pumps fail? If the trains full of fresh produce stop arriving? And we let this happen. We always said, 'Sure, it'll happen someday, but that'll be on somebody else's watch; we won't be here.' Well, that's our curse. Our curse is we're still here."

Joanie nodded to Jack.

"Oliver," he asked. "Who killed my father?"

"Oh, God," Oliver Oates said. He stared at the floor. His breath came in great lurches. A tear rolled down his cheek.

"We know my Uncle Dan had it done. But I need to know now, while you can still tell me. We just don't have any more time, Uncle Oliver. Were you there?"

The old man was actually crying, took out his handkerchief to blow his nose.

"I swear to you, Jack, boy, I had no idea what they had in mind. I had no idea Christian was going to do that. We all knew the way your father had been talking. You've got to understand what it would have done, politically. Your uncle had been trying to convince him not to go public. I just thought they wanted to put a scare into him, to show him how serious it was. As God is my witness."

"Christian Newby?" Jack asked, very quietly, with his teeth clenched. Without realizing it, he'd been feeling guilty about the way he'd killed Christian Newby, up in his office at SonicNet Headquarters. But if this was true — and it made sense, it was exactly the kind of job his uncle had kept Christian around for — the only thing he regretted now is that he hadn't cut off the little bastard's balls, first.

Oliver Oates leaned his head back now, tried to regain his composure. "I knew it would come out eventually. I told them it would. And you deserve to know, Jackie. But I swear to you I didn't know they were going to do it."

"You knew it would come out ... because of the evidence," Joanie said.

"Yes."

"Jack's father, Tom Brackley, left a statement," she tried.

"The disc. The disc he was recording when they killed him."

"Yes. And where is the disc now?"

Oliver Oates seemed to have recovered himself, then. He dried his eyes, sat up, steadied himself, looked at them with some calculation. He checked to make sure there was no one else in the room. He held out his glass. Joanie poured him the last of what was in the bottle. It glowed a lovely amber.

"That's the strange part," old Oliver said. "The part I could never understand. Why would your uncle keep that disc? It's almost like he wanted it to come out, in the end."

"Where is the disc now?" Joanie asked.

"Always kept it in the wall safe above his desk, upstairs," Oliver Oates said. "Probably still there, as far as I know."

"And do you know the combination?"

"Hell no. There are some things you're better off not knowing. I'm probably only alive today because I don't know stuff like that. Alive so far."

Jack and Joan stood to go back out to the dinner.

"Don't you kids mess with it," said the old college professor, quietly, almost as though he were speaking to himself. He leaned back in his chair. "I doubt Dan Brackley would harm either one of you. But he still has some people working for him who wouldn't hesitate. Even if The Black Arrow did get rid of Christian Newby. The Black Arrow, or ..." he looked directly at Jack "... someone. I'm serious. Let it go. Go find yourselves a nice farm someplace, raise horses and babies, have a good life. Funny thing is, when Tom Brackley died, it was as if Dan Brackley killed himself — that part of him that could ever have been redeemed, the part that could still have done some good. The end is nearer than you think, kids. I'm serious."

He picked up the empty whisky bottle, then, holding it to the light. They left him in the library, alone with the future.

⚜ ⚜ ⚜

Dinner had started. Joanie put enough food on her plate to be polite and sat down across from Tanya and the mayor. Jack wasn't feeling very hungry, either, but he had to try some of the pork chops in Madeira sauce, just to be polite. They'd fixed it with some kind of huge black mushrooms. And the green beans, of course. They were actually bright green, not mushy gray, and they had little sliced almonds on them. Must have cost the world. And the potatoes were au gratin, his favorite. But he only filled the one plate, since he had no appetite and was only being polite.

And the fresh dinner rolls, of course. Still hot, with real butter. Only three, though.

Someone had gotten the mayor started on feminism and equality for women.

"Sure, they say they want equality, but I've never seen a woman yet offer to pick up the check after dinner. I'm a single man, I've handed out a thousand business cards; no woman has ever called to ask *me* out."

"Maybe they just couldn't get through the switchboard," offered one wag.

The mayor laughed along with the rest of them. But he wasn't done.

"Women say they want 'equality,' but only so long as the

557

men are still stuck doing the asking and suffering the rejection and paying all the bills. If they feel like taking off, the courts give them their alimony and child support and turn a man into a fleeing bankrupt felon if he refuses to pay up."

As he spoke, the mayor tipped his coffee cup to look in it. Finding it empty, he slid it over in front of Tanya, with a tilt of his head that indicated he'd like it filled.

"Why?" he continued. "Where's the written contract that requires that? They'll tell you it's a tacit unwritten common-law contract, dating back thousands of years. OK, fine. But show me a man who's ever succeeded in going to court and getting a court order that the little lady had to provide him with sex and a home-cooked dinner three times a week."

Tanya had been staring fixedly at the coffee cup in front of her. Her face revealed no identifiable expression. Deliberately, she extended her left arm, placed the back of her left hand against the cup and saucer, and slid both slowly across the white linen tablecloth to the edge of the table between her and the mayor, where they fell to the floor with a clash.

Instantly, one of the uniformed waitresses was kneeling down to gather up the remains, as another darted in to set a new, full cup of hot coffee in front of the mayor.

Everyone at the table, including the mayor and Tanya, acted as though none of this had happened.

"Suddenly this same, thousand-year-old, unwritten common law contract that's so binding on the man for *his* part of this unwritten deal turns into a horrible, barbaric throwback to benighted times," the mayor continued, "a target of nothing but revulsion, not the kind of thing you could *possibly* imagine our modern, progressive courts would ever enforce ..."

"That's telling 'em, Mr. Mayor," said a male guest who'd been going through the wine rather resolutely. Judging from the look on the face of the stout lady sitting next to him, Jack had a fairly good idea where he'd be spending the night.

Joan made eye contact with Tanya. They both excused themselves to head for the powder room. Someone had changed the subject, asking the mayor about an op-ed piece in today's Mirror that had complained about the new tax rates, quoting Jefferson and Adam Smith about leaving men free to enjoy the fruits of their labor.

"Adam Smith and Jefferson sound great," Dan Brackley replied, "but in the real world, the poor require the most services and are able to pay the least. That may all be OK in some ethereal world, but here in this world there are real people with real needs and real expectations who demand services and require services, and that's why we need government."

There was general agreement around the table, including some energetic clinking of silverware on the wine glasses. One of the waiters came over and whispered in his Uncle Dan's ear. The mayor signaled for the waiter to hand him the phone.

The mayor listened for a moment, his face glowering progressively darker.

"What?!" the mayor finally exploded. "That doesn't make any sense. The new facility is open; we gave him every goddamned thing he wanted! Where? Indianapolis?! In Indianapolis the goddamned traffic jams are caused by farm implements, for christ's sake. When you ask for the elevator in Indianapolis they take you out to see the grain silo. Are you fucking kidding me? In Indianapolis they have the priests bless their goddamned basketballs before the game."

The mayor's face was a contorted mask of red. He thrust himself to his feet and stormed out of the room, still shouting into the phone, though if he had choicer epithets from which he wanted to spare his guests, chances were most of them would have paid dearly to hear what the heck they might be.

So the rumors were true. Joey Cantalupo's Gotham Seminoles had snuck out of town in the middle of the night, decamping for Indianapolis and leaving the just-completed Thomas Brackley Hockey Arena and Performing Arts Center without its sole major league tenant.

"Arrest him," the mayor's voice carried from the half-darkened sun porch. "Get men across the bridge and arrest the son-of-a-bitch." There was another pause. "For violation of contract, what do you mean 'For what?' What do you mean they're gone? Everything? Oh Jesus. That mother fucker!"

Jack decided this diversion offered the perfect opportunity to go break into his uncle's safe. Laying his linen napkin down on his plate, he gazed for a brief, forlorn moment at the remaining half porkchop, palmed his two remaining dinner rolls, and slipped out through the kitchen, heading for the back stairway to the second floor.

Biff Harder was sharing dinner with some of the kitchen help. Jack was pretty sure Biff did not see him slip by.

❖ ❖ ❖

Biff Harder did spot the two women heading up the back stairs, a few minutes later. The blonde in the black dress had been with the mayor, so she had to be kosher. And he really wasn't supposed to be concerning himself with the conduct of the guests, anyway — his job was to keep in touch with the guys out on the perimeter, deal with any threats that might penetrate as far as the house.

Yes, Biff was supposed to patrol a bit, but only to watch for anyone breaking in.

Nonetheless, he wasn't sure who the little brunette in the iridescent green dress was. And besides, there was something furtive about the way the two of them had looked all around before heading up those stairs. He couldn't put his finger on it, but he decided to investigate.

You couldn't be too careful, these days. The Black Arrow seemed to have agents everywhere. Hadn't Christian Newby been killed, alone in his office on the sixth floor of their own building?

Upstairs, Tanya showed Joanie the door that led to the mayor's home office. In the bedroom across the hall, from the sound of things, another couple had sneaked away from the party and were doing things you really shouldn't do in someone else's house — especially the mayor's.

But what the heck. Perhaps they were married and never got a chance to see each other at home. Tanya smiled and offered to stay in the hall, running interference should anyone grow too curious.

Joanie slipped into the office, where she was surprised to find the lights on.

Jack was already there, eating a dinner roll, using his other hand to work at the safe, which he had easily located by taking down some kind of framed citation or diploma from the wall behind the desk.

"Jack. What were you doing?"

"Same as you, babe."

"You have the combination to the safe?"

"Um ... no."

"And you were planning to get in there, how?"

"I thought I'd just try some numbers, my uncle's date of birth ... you know."

"And how many bad combinations does this model allow before it shuts down and sounds a silent alarm?"

"Um ... I don't know?"

"Jack, you're a dear lad, you're strong and handsome and brave; I wouldn't want anyone else fathering my children or covering me when the shooting starts. But sometimes I wonder if you didn't play too many games with your helmet off. Here, let me try." Joan dug into her purse and produced a little black box connected by a wide electronic ribbon to a computer plug, while from the other end extended a standard phone cord with jack. She plugged the wide end into the "security test" port on the safe, disconnected the handset from the phone on the desk, and popped the computer jack into the phone, at which point, from the sound of things, it immediately began speed-dialing a number. Soon her little portable modem was humming and clicking.

"What is that?"

"I'm dialing into our mainframe."

"Where?

"Someplace far, far away. Finland, the Isle of Man? You can never be sure."

One at a time, the red lights on her little display started to turn green. Finally the last one flickered over, and the lock on the safe released with a satisfying click.

"Remind me never to try to keep anything secret from you," Jack sighed.

"That would be a good policy, dear."

"Did the combination begin with 4-26?"

She looked. "Yes."

"Birthday."

"Ah. The Taurian enigma."

There were a number of electronic discs in the safe. They knew better than to trust the labels. Joan activated the player on the desk and they started loading them in one at a time, running just a few seconds of each.

The first two showed his uncle sitting in hotel rooms, talking with two different women. One of them looked like Tanya. Jack didn't want to think too much about what the rest of those discs might show — or how many there were. But he set aside the one with Tanya.

The third was paydirt.

Jack's father sat at a desk in a library. The very library where they had sat drinking with Oliver Oates not an hour ago, Jack noticed with a shiver. Thomas Brackley faced directly into the camera, which must have been resting on one of the bookshelves across the room, preset for a zoomed-in medium close-up. He held a sheaf of papers in front of him — a prepared speech, presumably — but he consulted them only occasionally. Mostly he seemed to be speaking from the heart, directly through the camera lens to his audience. Jack thought it would have been riveting, even if it wasn't his own dad — the longest recording of his dad's voice he'd ever seen or heard.

Col. Thomas Brackley wore a crisp green uniform, but no hat. It was a dress uniform, with the chest card of little colored silk devices that indicated the medals he'd won, at home and abroad. He wore only one actual medal, Jack noted. He'd never actually seen his dad wear it — the old man had always scoffed at the guys who wanted to brag about such stuff; more than once Jack had heard him say the CIB was the only one a real soldier looked for. Well, the Combat Infantryman's Badge, and maybe the purple hearts.

The one medal he was wearing hung around his neck on a blue watered silk ribbon. He must have figured it might help add some weight to his words.

And what words they were. Jack's dad talked about the things he'd seen and done in the West — not all of them things to be proud of — about the courage his men had shown, how proud he was of them, and the heartbreak of their losses. But even more he talked about what he had seen it do to his men, as they realized they were killing their fellow Americans, freedom-loving Americans who were fighting for the same things George Washington and Francis Marion and young James Monroe had fought for in 1776 — freedom and independence; the right to set up their own government, spend their money as they saw fit and raise their kids as they saw fit, without bowing to the orders of some arrogant capital full of greedy lawyers and paid-off politicians, thousands of miles away.

Tears rolled down Jack's cheeks as he watched. Then his father paused and looked off camera to his right as he heard the door to the library open. On the disc, they saw him ask "What's up?" as he stood and walked off camera. It sounded casual. Was there an edge of concern? But the camera kept recording, of course. Then his voice, again: "What the hell? Danny, you can't be serious." Then two loud noises, in quick succession, a longer pause, and then a third. They didn't sound loud enough to be gunshots — the microphone on the disc recorder obviously had some kind of limiter. But Jack knew they were.

It had happened off camera. Jack was sure he'd heard his

dad say his Uncle Dan's name. Whether that would have been proof enough, all by itself, he wasn't sure. But now there were other voices, asking where he wanted the body moved, assuring his Uncle Dan that he didn't have to worry, because they knew how to clean things up. He recognized his uncle Dan's voice, telling them not to touch a thing.

"Don't be stupid. I know these forensic guys. If they come in here and figure out we've been cleaning up, there's no way to explain that. And it's not like he won't be missed, or they won't know where he was staying. The key is to make it look like somebody else did it, the damned rebels getting back at him for all those guys he killed in Denver." Then his uncle Dan walked into the pre-focused frame, picking up his dad's sheaf of papers from his desk.

The image was framed for someone sitting at the desk. But his Uncle Dan stood behind the desk. So the top of his head was cut off. But it was still clearly him — he wasn't all that tall, and his bald head was especially recognizable as he bent down to gather up the pages.

What was it, then, that he noticed? Was the recording device making some kind of noise? Probably it had a small red light on in the front, indicating it was running. But actually, Jack knew exactly what it was. His Uncle Dan had a sixth sense about these things. He could see it, like watching the gears turn in some old clockwork machine at the museum. His uncle stood there, looking down at those papers, sensing something was wrong. Why had his brother been sitting here at this desk, in a full crisp uniform, with all these lights on, facing across the room at a blank wall of bookcases?

Then that devilish awareness came across his face. He smiled, and looked up directly into the camera. His eyes didn't dart around, searching. He just looked up directly into the lens. He pointed with his chin. "Over there. Shut that damned thing off and bring me the disc."

"Yes, sir" came a voice from off camera. And Jack recognized that voice, now. The late Christian Newby, just starting to work his way up in the world.

"Couldn't help himself," his Uncle Dan said. "Had to tell everyone. ..."

And then the image bloomed and went to roaring gray static.

⚜ ⚜ ⚜

They could hear Tanya's voice from outside the door.

"And there is nothing I have to offer that you find of any interest?" she said, obviously wide-eyed with innocent disappointment.

"Ma'am, I'm a married man," came a male voice. "I don't do that sort of thing. But I do think there's something going on in this room that you don't want me to see. Now stand aside!"

Everything but the disc they'd come for — and the second one Jack had set aside — was already back in the safe. Jack closed the thick steel door, turned the locking handle, and replaced the framed document. Joanie looked from the door to the French windows that led out to the balcony. But they were out of time.

"Trust me?" Jack asked, quietly.

"Of course," Joanie said.

"Come over here."

Biff Harder pushed past the blonde Russian, opened the unlocked door, and leaned into Mayor Brackley's office, where the lights were already on.

Jack and Joan were standing by the desk. He was leaning her over and kissing her. He was kissing her real good. In fact, she had one of her knees up, and Jack was in the process of laying her down *on* the desk.

"Jack?" asked Biff Harder, more than a little shocked.

Without letting Joanie fall, Jack straightened and turned

to look at the cause of the interruption. The top of Joan's gown had slipped down around her waist. She wore no visible undergarments.

"Oh, Jeez. Sorry," Biff blustered, pulling the door closed. He blushed a serious shade of red, turned and headed quickly along the hallway and down the rear stairs.

Tanya covered her mouth, doing her best not to laugh out loud.

Across the hall, the amorous couple punctuated Biff Harder's retreat with a suitably dramatic conclusion.

As they were heading back downstairs, Jack slipped the extra disc to Tanya.

"We didn't watch this," he said. "But I think it might belong to you."

CHAPTER 17

"It is a mistake to assume that government must necessarily last forever. The institution marks a certain stage of civilization — is natural to a particular phase of human development. It is not essential, but incidental. As amongst the Bushmen we find a state antecedent to government, so may there be one in which it shall have become extinct."

— HERBERT SPENCER (1820-1903)

"Government is the great fiction, through which everybody endeavors to live at the expense of everybody else."

— FREDERIC BASTIAT (1801-1850),
"ESSAYS ON POLITICAL ECONOMY," 1846

"All our liberties are due to men who, when their conscience has compelled them, have broken the laws of the land."

— DR. WILLIAM KINGDOM CLIFFORD, ENGLISH PHILOSOPHER
AND PROFESSOR OF MATHEMATICS AND MECHANICS AT
UNIVERSITY COLLEGE, LONDON (1845-1879)

By the time Deputy Chief William Flanagan arrived at the scene it already would have qualified as a full-fledged disaster by the measure of any such fuck-up in previous department history.

It had started typically enough, with a tip from a source whose leads had proven solid before, to one of his undercover men in the neighborhood, that the one-story free-standing house at 7304 Queen's Court was more than just your typical drug lab or fake ID processing center.

This, the undercover detective was assured, was nothing less than the headquarters of the Black Arrow gang here in Queens. Surveillance had indeed revealed an unusual level of comings and goings, including panel truck deliveries to the back door. And although the phone tap had been unable to penetrate the perps' encryption technology — which in and of itself was illegal and gave more confirmation this was a live one — the sheer volume of calls had been judged sufficient all by itself to justify a raid.

The location was odd — a pocket of four free-standing single-family red brick homes dating from the 19th century, now surrounded on one side by a matching red brick church and its cemetery (sloping down to an old creek bed drained since the days of the Second World War) and on the other three sides by light industrial and warehouse buildings which now towered over the well-preserved old houses by several stories. A block to the west, a telephone company office building towered far above the older, lesser structures. But that was too far off to be of any immediate concern to Flanagan.

The very unlikeliness of the locale must have made it seem a safe hideaway. The houses on either side of 7304 turned out to be vacant; a preliminary title check had run into a tangled web of front companies reminiscent of the Mob.

It wouldn't be accurate to say a search warrant was "obtained." The idea that nervous cops still stood before a skeptical judge trying to convince him there was enough "probable cause" to break down a citizen's front door was a useful myth in which to keep the populace believing. But the fact was that any number of "tough on crime" municipal and superior court judges had long since begun issuing the cops sheafs of pre-signed warrants which they could fill out as they saw fit, simply calling the judge's clerk to report the serial numbers on the forms being used today, so the court would have a matching record should anyone check.

Flanagan actually had cause now to wish the process had taken a bit longer, in this case. The SWAT team had deployed as usual in the pre-dawn stillness, shouted "police" as they took down the front door with their battering ram, at which point five officers of the seven-man front door team had — according to the sketchy reports from the survivors — raced down the restricted hallway that led from the front door into the living room, finding directly in their path a fully manned and sandbagged gun emplacement right between the fireplace and the television set.

His officers were estimating the damned thing was a 20mm or even 30mm cannon — the kind of beast mounted in attack helicopters and A-10 warthog attack jets. Given the limited structural damage to the building across the street, though, Flanagan was guessing a .50-caliber machine gun, or even one of those semi-automatic .50-caliber Barrett rifles the Canadian snipers had used to such good effect in Afghanistan in '01 and '02 — an example the New Columbians had learned to copy all too well.

With his targets coming straight toward him and lined up like rubber ducks, a skilled operator could have emptied that weapon's 10-round magazine in a couple of seconds. And Flanagan knew from personal experience that there was no such thing as being "wounded" by a .50-caliber hit. Designed to penetrate engine blocks, those things took off limbs. They simply blew men apart.

Though that in itself was odd. If this was the Black Arrow

gang, what were they doing using a gun? And then, even as he formed the thought, Flanagan realized what a dangerous trap you could fall into, assuming there were "rules" when there were never any rules, assuming that because an adversary had never previously used firearms he therefore wasn't "allowed" to use them ... might not use them, in fact, at precisely the time when the surprise would be most effective.

Besides, the Black Arrow's harem had used suppressed .45s at the Dupont ballroom.

Anyway, the officers covering the back yard had obeyed their standing orders and not returned fire into a building which they knew their cohorts were infiltrating from the front. The last two officers in the seven-person front door assault team had pulled back, which was also according to the pre-assault briefing, though Flanagan noted with disgust that these two "by the book" gutless wonders were policewomen — none of the men *he'd* trained with would have left their own dead and wounded littering the hallways and front stoop as they scampered back to the vehicles to radio for help.

More than an hour had passed, now. The sun was well up and that seemed to be pretty much where matters had remained till Flanagan got there. A lieutenant with a bullhorn had tried to get the occupants of the house to agree to a truce so they could at least recover the two uniformed officers who lay sprawled on the front door step — no way to know for sure whether they were alive or dead, though the pools of coagulating blood and the fact that they were not moving was hardly encouraging.

But there'd been no reply from the house.

Shit. Five officers down — some if not all of them probably dead — in a single raid, and it wasn't even lunchtime. Even as he watched, the first TV wagons were arriving and setting up their satellite towers, while his own helicopter was joined by one of those goddamned Channel 7 "Eyes in the Sky." Mother fuck. Good luck keeping this one under wraps. He'd have to contact headquarters and have someone there start to work up a cover story. ASAP.

There'd been a day when the loss of just one or two officers in the line of duty had warranted a huge public funeral, caissons and flags and rifle salutes and thousands of officers in all their brass and finery trucked in from the five boroughs and suburban forces from as far as 100 miles away. But this damned Black Arrow gang had finally completed the transformation of the force from a "civilian" unit to a completely militarized force, operating more like an occupying U.S. army in some foreign enclave like Bosnia or Iraq or Venezuela.

That made his men more anonymous and less sympathetic to the general populace, Flanagan and his superiors knew. No more bobbies on the beat rescuing kittens from trees. That, combined with their reluctance to admit just how effective the Black Arrow had become, had argued against publicizing just how many men they were losing now, by the steady drip of night-time attrition. But still, with the exception of the Dupont Center Massacre and the nightmare week shortly thereafter when the Grays had lost 65 men in five nights, it had mostly remained individual incidents, in retaliation for police operations against specific Black Arrow tunnels and other lairs in Manhattan. Never five blue-suit cops dead in a single day.

They could try to keep it quiet. But regardless of how they handled the mostly lapdog press, Flanagan had some idea what this would do to morale within the force, where the grapevine was quick and usually deadly accurate. One or two officers are martyrs — you could use their loss to motivate the rest of the troops. But five?

The Black Arrow had warned, only a week or so ago, that the death of a couple suspected Black Arrow henchmen during interrogation in an East Side precinct house would be repaid "disproportionately." But Flanagan still refused to believe this had been a set-up from the start.

After all, the bad guys were still in there — this wasn't the main island, with its network of interlocking basements and tunnels under practically every building, where these damned tunnel rats could be counted on to slip through your fingers almost every time.

This was Queens.

Flanagan pulled back the command post behind a couple of parked cruisers where they could be partially screened by the corner of a solid brownstone warehouse building almost a hundred yards from where the two motionless, uniformed figures could still be seen on the front stoop of 7304. One of his guys informed him the phone company was having no luck ringing through to any phone inside there — the occupants appeared to have simply pulled the plug.

Now Kenko, head of the six-man sniper detachment, checked in and asked for orders. Finally, enough resources were arriving on the scene for Flanagan to start getting something done. He told Kenko to make his own choice of the best positions from which his men could cover three sides of the house from above — he wasn't going to stick anyone out where they'd be exposed in the cemetery — instructing him to "get a move on" and check in when ready both with Flanagan's own radio guy and with the helicopter unit which had also just checked in, arriving from nearby LaGuardia.

Lack of phone contact short-circuited a lot of the traditional negotiating tactics — getting to know the loser, chatting him up, telling him how much we care, tracking down his wife or mother and getting her on the phone to remind him how she packed his lunchbox with peanut butter and Twinkies when he was a kid, all the usual hogwash designed to stretch them out and wear them down, get the loser weepy about how mommy had put quarters under his pillow when he lost his baby teeth till he'd drop his guard and amble into the line of fire from one of the rooftops — end of *that* happy reminiscence.

Flanagan paused for a moment. The scene was strangely peaceful. Incongruous birds sang — it was warm and sunny for early December. He'd meant to put the training wheels on his grandson's new bike today, hoped the kid didn't try taking it out for a spin without them. Damned kid reminded Flanagan of himself at that age — a boundless future, no limits, always rarin' to go.

Then he remembered the cops down on the doorstep of the house. Would any of them ever get to spend a day with the grandkids? So he sent his guy back to the bullhorn, trying to explain to the still-mute occupants of the house that things would go a whole lot better for them if they at least allowed the wounded to be cleared away from the front door. Meantime Flanagan had them deploy Archie, the little caterpillar-tracked robot, to carry a note under a white flag right up to the front of the house. The unit had a video camera that would give them a closer look at their downed officers as well as anyone who came to the front door. It also carried a loaded, remote-actived 12-gauge shotgun, though that would be removed later if the occasion arose to show off the cute little robot to the ladies of the press.

The occupants did not respond or come out to take the note attached to the front of the little robot, but at least they didn't shoot it. A second SWAT team was now on site, and Flanagan ordered them to deploy stealthily from the flank, only as far forward as they could maintain concealment, counting on the little robot to at least distract the perps' attention as it buzzed randomly around the front door. He made sure the guys newly deploying had "thumper" 40-mm grenade launchers and a good supply of tear gas, smoke, and flash-bang "ferret" grenade rounds.

Now two and then three of Kenko's six snipers were checking in from their vantage points on the roofs of the nearby buildings. The two of them who were most directly to the west of the house reported there was some kind of big black hole in the west roof of 7304, though they couldn't see any smoke or other immediate signs of the cause of this newly detected structural defect. Weird. A hole in the roof. Flanagan tried to remember the last time it had rained. Who would pick a building with a hole in the roof?

⚜ ⚜ ⚜

Quart Low Cavanaugh had been camped out in the janitor's closet near the stairwell on the top floor of the warehouse building since before midnight.

There was a little heat in the building — about enough to keep the pipes from freezing.

He had a canteen and a little food. He'd snuck across to use the men's room twice. His bladder wasn't as strong as it used to be. Urine left in a can could be DNA tested.

He'd had longer waits, under a lot worse conditions.

The problem was his knees — especially in this cold. He was too damned old. He couldn't sit for too long, and he couldn't stand for too long. He had to switch back and forth. And what was really a struggle was to get his eye down to the level of the peephole that allowed him to watch the stairway that led to the roof.

He'd heard all the shooting earlier — the boom of the .50-cal clearly distinguishable from the police popguns.

And now came the sniper, right on schedule. The stairs coming up from below rang with the police sniper's boots. This was the second toughest moment. One man, or two? No military sniper would ever deploy without a spotter who could glass for targets but also cover his tail.

One, as expected. Or rather — as they'd hoped. Though Quart Low's instructions were to proceed, even against two.

This shooter looked like a serious man, but he wasn't taking much pain to be quiet. He felt safe here. Rifle still cased.

Quart Low could have stepped out and taken him in the back. What the plan called for actually put Quart Low and the rest of the boys at slightly more risk. But the decision had been made to take them out once they were in position on the roofs. That way Long Shot, almost half a mile away in the window of the office Hideki had rented in the telephone tower, could back them up with his own heavy-barrelled M-21.

After the sniper had climbed the last flight of stairs, opened and closed the door to the roof, Quart Low counted. Allow time for the sniper to cross the roof — the last 15 yards on his belly, in order to avoid skylining himself. Now he'd be getting into his final position, scanning the area for unanticipated threats. He'd unzip his rifle case, check the sling, remove the scope covers, open the bolt, check the load. Sling up. The man who had passed looked like a kid compared to Quart Low, but he'd have more than 10 years in. He would be methodical, but not leisurely. Before long, he'd be reporting himself ready.

Quart Low emerged quietly into the hallway, checking his six. Stand still for a moment, listen for anyone else coming up those stairs.

Nope; clear.

Last check to make sure he'd left nothing behind. Then up those stairs to the rooftop. Other than the creaking of his knees, quiet as a cat.

Quart Low was dressed in the full regalia of a Gotham PD SWAT team member, though he carried no long gun. The regulation black police boots, dark blue outfit, matching military coal-scuttle helmet, were all purchasable by mail from numerous police supply catalogues. They'd been cracking down on "civilian" access to the heavy Polykev outer vests, but Boris and Katia had come up with plenty.

You just ordered on some convincing-looking police letterhead stationery. Stenciling on the "GPD" logos was all the hand finish work that had been required.

Emerging onto the brightly sunlit roof, Quart Low took two deep breaths, squinted till his eyes started to adapt to the glare. He left the door ajar and started across the roof at a fast walking pace, bending from the waist to keep his head down as though he was taking some half-hearted precaution not to be seen from the street below.

They'd worked this out. If he had tiptoed, then the moment he was spotted the sniper would have gone alert. Why would a fellow cop be sneaking up on him?

Crunching across the gravel of the flat roof at a modest pace, making a moderate amount of noise, would actually seem less alarming.

Sure enough, the sniper had an unconcerned expression on his face as he half rolled to see who was coming up behind him with new orders. The sniper had been lying belly down on the roof, legs well apart, only the stainless steel muzzle of his .308 — no, probably .338 — rifle positioned in a convenient slot in the shallow parapet. He'd started to work the sling around the left arm of his shooting jacket, but was not fully slung up. He wore a sidearm, but the flap on the holster was still fastened. He made no move to reach for it.

"Yeah?" he asked.

If a military sniper had done that, without his sidearm in his hand to deal with the unexpected, he would not have lived to be an old military sniper.

That was the difference between soldiers and cops. No matter what a cop's individual talents, no matter how soldier-like a cop might dress, cops grew used to the comfortable assumption that they always had their prey outnumbered, outgeneraled, outthought, and surrounded. This fellow was ready to receive fire — unaimed, incompetent fire — from down in the surrounded house. He could not conceive of a threat to his life arriving in the form of what appeared to be another uniformed cop — even if he didn't recognize the face — sent up to bring him some new instructions.

Quart Low gave him a half smile, nodded his head in acknowledgement, pulled the silenced black Colt .22 from the waistband behind his back, clicked off the thumb safety, clamped on the second hand to steady the weapon, put four rounds into the police sniper's throat and face without breaking his stride. Never rush. Four to six seconds. Two had gone into the mouth, which was ideal. Cerebellum.

The sniper gave one great heave, his back muscles suffering a spasm as powerful as if he'd been hit with a pair of cardiac paddles.

Quart Low noticed the officer's radio with the little rubberized antenna was out on the roof within easy reach of the sniper's right hand. Either he'd just checked in to report himself in position, or he'd been getting ready to.

The .22 had an advantage over the larger calibers. The round was truly subsonic, which means a properly suppressed .22 really was "silent" — at least in a situation like this, with the ambient noises of the city to distract those below.

So Quart Low was in no great hurry.

He knew the cop was done, but it had been decided they'd all go ahead and make sure, since you never could tell when someone might get excited and leave a breather behind. And survivors could remember and talk about all kinds of things, even if they didn't shoot you in the back as you left, just out of spite.

Quart Low went to one knee, and that knee was actually on top of the rifle. Wounded guys could whack you pretty good with the side of a rifle.

Unscrew the suppressor, a surprisingly heavy tube of blued steel about the size of the cardboard cylinder that came inside a standard roll of toilet paper. Tuck it into your shirt pocket, seal the Velcro.

Now his own pistol went into his holster, instead of back into his waistband where it could have fallen out if not carefully positioned. Thumb safety on. Snap the holster closed. Out came the old K-Bar, dark gray-green parkerized metal that wouldn't reflect the sun, tang covered in thick, non-slip leather.

He did not slice the throat. Instead, using his left hand to hold the head so the left cheek was pressed down into the gravel of the roof — the little .22s had stayed inside and not messed up the back of the skull to speak of — holding the knife underhanded, he stuck the blade all the way through the neck, forward of the spine. The cutting edge was pointed out, to the right, toward the front of the throat. That's the way he pushed the knife, now, laterally, till it cut its way free.

Blood gushed out in a good wave. The heart had not yet stopped. The man's life formed a large crimson pool on the roof, spreading in a growing but not quite symmetrical circle. The dying sniper still shuddered a little, under Quart Low's gentle but firm left hand.

Quart Low looked at the face for a moment. Still frozen in an expression of surprise. He could still remember most of the faces. Poor sap had probably figured he'd be barbecuing ribs and playing with the kids by 5 o'clock. Quart Low wondered if the family would hear about it before suppertime. Phone call, or the car at the door?

Then the last part. Wipe the knife on the guy's sleeve, into the sheaf, snap the band. Then, from inside his own shirt, the five-inch green Day-Glo sticker. Peel the backing, wad the backing into your pocket, roll the guy the rest of the way back over on his tummy, replace his helmet, and slap the sticker on the back of the helmet.

The smaller one on the back of Quart Low's own helmet was red. It meant: "Stop: Don't shoot this one." The one on the dead sniper was green. It meant: "This is now a Good Cop."

From the telephone building, Long Shot was watching five or six of these simultaneous little dramas through his scope. Hopefully.

If a scuffle developed on any of the rooftops, he'd go ahead and take any clear shot at anyone not showing a red sticker. Hopefully. But he also understood there was no need to give himself away, to make any noise shooting any officer decorated in lime green.

Then, once they were all off their respective roofs, Long Shot would give them two to three minutes to get down the stairs to the waiting vans inside the loading docks at the rear, before popping some cops down in front to stir up some panic, give the hit team some cover for their getaway.

And that was that. The house down below was nothing but a lure, a stratagem, a ruse of war. The real point of this whole operation was simply to take out the sniper squad once they deployed onto the roofs, so there'd be no one competent to man the roofs surrounding SonicNet headquarters the following Thursday night when the Order of the Arrow attacked, just six and a half days away.

Down below stretched a nice panorama of the old brick church and the churchyard, full of the peaceful dead. But there'd be time enough to think deep thoughts about mortality and the cruelty of mankind some other time.

Quart Low Cavanaugh had a schedule to keep. And he had to do it all on the one extremely creaky set of knees.

⚜ ⚜ ⚜

Two members of the SWAT team had volunteered to put on orange vests and play the role of paramedics as they moved up to the front of the house to clear the two dead or wounded cops who were still visible outside the door from the initial raid. For all Flanagan knew the occupants of the house had already committed suicide or died of wounds sustained in the initial pre-dawn assault, so he had to take a chance if it meant getting one or both of those officers out alive. The two volunteers switched clothes with the real EMTs out of sight around the corner and then brought the ambulance — strobes flashing but siren quiet — slowly along the street until they were parked almost directly in front of 7304.

The lieutenant with the bullhorn explained to the occupants — if anyone was still listening — that these were unarmed civilian ambulance drivers operating under a white flag and that they would merely be removing the officers by the front door and then withdrawing. The little tracked robot gave Flanagan a video image from up closer to the house, and additionally they had the 12-gauge on the robot which could be fired if anyone came out to threaten the officer/ambulance techs.

The two officers in the bright orange vests pulled a stretcher out of the back of the ambulance, dropped the wheels, looking very competent and professional, deployed a white flag on the overhead I.V. arm, locked the undercarriage down and wheeled the gurney up the access walkway in a brisk professional manner. Reaching the first downed officer, they stooped over to pick him up.

And the .50-caliber rifle opened up from inside the house, blowing the chests out of both men with four rounds at point-blank range.

After a moment of stunned silence, the forward SWAT team started pouring rounds into the house without orders, giving away their positions. Rifle fire was returned from at least two visible windows of 7304. The yellow muzzle flashes were clearly visible inside the darkened rooms, and at least one more forward officer spun to the ground.

"Kenko, have you got shots?" Flanagan shouted. "All snipers are cleared to fire. Cleared to fire. I want suppressing fire into the house. Forward team, launch grenades. Whatever you've got loaded, pour it in there."

Smoke and incendiary grenades did arc gratifyingly toward and into the windows, now, but so far there seemed to be no response from the rooftop snipers.

"Kenko, where are your men? Open fire."

"Sir, the snipers are no longer responding," shouted the radio man, pulling down and closing his fist around his lip mike so he wouldn't broadcast to anyone who might be listening.

"What do you mean, not responding? Is the whole channel down?"

"That's the thing, sir," the radio guy actually looked frightened. "Their mikes are live. They're just not responding."

"Goddammit, get somebody up to those rooftops and ask Kenko what the hell is going on. I need fire support. Forward team, pull back! Fire as you come but get out of there!"

There was dense smoke pouring out of a couple places in the house now, as well as from the hole in the roof, indicating the smoke grenades were working, and probably some incidental fires had been started inside, as well. Flanagan had his back-up units keep up the volume of fire into the house to cover the withdrawal of his forward teams. His second in command was back now, signaling him to pull off his headset so they could speak without being overheard.

"What's going on?" Flanagan shouted over the reassuringly constant gunfire being poured into the single-story brick house.

"Sir, the snipers are dead," shouted Ed Dudley.

"Which snipers?"

"All six, sir. Kenko too."

"That's not possible. There hasn't been enough aimed fire returned out of the house."

"Right, sir. From the look of the first two, I'd say they were each shot at close range with a suppressed handgun, pretty much the minute they'd assumed their positions on the roofs, and then had their throats cut."

"Are you nuts, Dudley? It's broad daylight. We've got, what, eighty police officers here. Who cut their throats? Where'd they go?"

"Don't know, sir. If they were pre-positioned up on the roofs it stands to reason they had escape routes planned in advance. Bastards could be dressed as cops, firemen, Good Humor ice cream guys, anything."

Jesus Christ. Kenko and two of those men had taught rifle courses at the academy. This was impossible. Six snipers plus the five original SWAT team members — Flanagan no longer held out much hope they were alive — plus the two brave officers who'd gone in dressed as ambulance techs. This was going to mean his career. He could have explained the first few — they died before he got here. But no one commands an operation where you lose 12, 13 cops, probably more. Jesus. Flanagan felt the bile rising in his throat. He was suddenly short of breath. What the hell else could go wrong?

Dudley looked like he was going to say something, but then he reached up and grabbed his throat, crimson blood flowing out between his fingers. The "thwack" of the bullet penetrating his throat was followed what seemed like several seconds later by a distant boom, almost lost in the ambient traffic noise. Jesus. That was *long* range.

Flanagan's combat training took over and almost certainly saved his life as he dropped and scurried around the fender of the nearest marked unit. Another bullet slammed into the vehicle where he'd been standing, little more than a second later. Then he saw two officers who'd been sharing coffee out of a thermos hit in quick succession over behind the corner of the sandstone building — where they had to be completely invisible to the perps in the now-burning house at 7304 Queen's Court.

"Where's that fire coming from?" Flanagan shouted into his throat mike, to no one in particular. Damned fast and accurate fire. Somebody had a semi-auto rifle and knew how to use it.

"Sir, upper floor window of that phone company building a block to the west. It overlooks all our positions here."

And was a perfect position from which to back up the assassins on the roofs, who had obviously been pre-positioned by someone with the expertise — police training? — to eyeball this set-up and guess precisely where Kenko would position his shooters.

If any of those assassins were still around, they'd sure make good their exits now, under this kind of covering fire. Jesus Christ, it had all been carefully set up, hours, days, maybe even weeks in advance — it had to be — and they'd been ahead of him every step of the way, knowing exactly what he'd do and when he'd do it. Regulations. By-the-book Flanagan. It was fucking brilliant.

"Tell the snipers to return fire and pin that guy down."

"No snipers left, sir."

"Goddammit, we've still got their rifles, don't we? Somebody show some initiative, here. Return fire."

"Sir, into a building full of civilians? I'm not sure any of our guys can hit with any accuracy at that range."

He meant "any of our remaining guys," of course.

"OK, OK. Where's the helicopter?"

"Sky 27, sir, I've got the sniper spotted."

"Well get over there and draw fire; buzz him."

"Yes, sir."

He heard the helicopter's chatter change pitch as the pilot banked into a steep turn over the house and headed due west toward the sniper in the telephone tower, the chopper passing right over the hole in the roof of 7304, the strange hole for which there had been no explanation, in a house full of professional killers with modern, military equipment.

"Belay that, 27. Veer off, veer off," Flanagan shouted.

"Say again?" asked the pilot.

But it was too late. The surface-to-air missile looked six feet long — though Flanagan knew that had to be an optical illusion, it was probably only half that length — as it rocketed out of the hole in the roof on line toward the telephone company office tower, an angle at which it had probably been pre-positioned since the beginning of the battle, waiting for the chopper to pass over the house on a due westerly heading. Flanagan could only look on helplessly as the missile's smoky contrail corkscrewed slightly, the warhead locking onto the helicopter's heat signature. The missile and the helicopter merged. There was a cherry-red fireball, a loud "crump," a wave of searing heat, and then only the silhouette of the suddenly unattached rotor blade remained, arcing slowly to earth like some aborigine's abandoned boomerang.

Flanagan had the strangest realization. This was the feeling in the pit of the stomach that George Armstrong Custer had felt, and "Chinese" Gordon when he lost that battle in Ethiopia ... or was it the Sudan? They had all fallen into the habit of thinking the bad guys would always be doped-up long-haired losers holed up without options or obligingly charging the white man's machine guns on camelback, that all you had to do was get them on the phone and pretend to be their buddy while you got your snipers in position. He had allowed his own behaviors to form a predictable pattern. And he had finally encountered a field general smart enough to plan a counterstroke for every goddamned predictable, by-the-book thing that he knew Flanagan would do.

Please, God, he thought. At least let it be someone who'd fought in the West. At least let it be a veteran. Not some 20-year-old girl.

The house at 7304 Queen's Court burned to the ground. The forensics teams found no bodies inside, except for the cops killed that morning — including the two by the front door. It turned out there was indeed a tunnel exit from the basement, a century-old passageway leading under the churchyard and down to the old dry creek bed, once an estuary that had carried barge traffic during the Prohibition era of the 1920s, and possibly as far back as the days of the Underground Railroad, when escaped slaves had passed through on their way to Canada — a concept only recently revived as the people again found their government tracking them, exploiting them, giving them reason to have to sneak out of town in the dark of night as uniformed enforcers pounded on the front door.

That was doubtless why the bad guys had chosen the house in the first place — that and the fact that any rookie could stand in the front yard and point out precisely the six positions to which Kenko or anyone else would dispatch their snipers.

The source of the original tip had disappeared, of course — seemed his several-month career slipping information to the undercover guys on minor offenders had been manufactured just to set up this blow against Gotham's Finest.

And the sniper nest in the upper floors of the telephone tower was abandoned by the time they got to it — rented a month back to some Asian guy who actually signed his name Isoroku Yamamoto — didn't anyone read their history books anymore? — the money coming out of an impenetrable maze of fronts in Hong Kong and Macau. Guy never bothered to move in anything but a rented desk and a wastebasket, along with some blue and gray moving blankets which had doubtless cushioned the weapon where it lay across the windowsill. Rent-a-truck company said a few hundred blankets a month didn't get returned; they were generic and identical.

The sniper himself? A large, older black man had been seen exiting the building just before Flanagan's men sealed off the lobby, carrying the kind of white box florists used for delivering long-stemmed roses. Nice red bow. Had the army trained black snipers back, say, around the time of the first two Iraq wars? Sure. Not many, but some. Or he could have been carrying the weapon — broken in half — out for someone else. Then again, maybe the flower-sender's lady love was out sick for the day, and the rifle that killed Dudley and five others was still jammed in a wall someplace, not to be found till the building was demolished in, oh, about 50 years.

Another dead end. Who was it who'd said the Order of the Arrow were a bunch of amateurs, that they'd be rounded up inside 90 days?

Twenty-one sworn personnel — including the entire sniper squad — plus the helicopter pilot. Police departments didn't take those kinds of casualties. Armies took those kinds of casualties.

Armies with a problem.

⚜ ⚜ ⚜

Tom Sullivan got Mrs. Jacobs' permission to hire 20 additional armed private security officers to guard the Mirror's printing plant and loading docks.

In addition, without any formal orders, many of the pressmen showed up that night with brickbats or iron bars, ready to defend the presses should the police or the Lightning Squads try anything.

The suburban edition started rolling at 11 p.m. But as was so often the case these days, the 11 p.m. television newscasters actually broke the story, holding up early proof copies of the Mirror's front page, as though to assure their viewers they weren't making this up.

"New evidence implicates Mayor Brackley in his brother's death," read the lede headline;

"Plot motivated by Thomas Brackley's
plan to denounce War in West as
'last resort of ruthless tyrants' "

The Tom Brackley video disc Jack and Joan had smuggled out of the mayor's mansion was released to television in time for their breaking 6 a.m. broadcasts. Without the disc, the reports could have been dismissed as a scurrilous political dirty trick. But martyred war hero Tom Brackley denouncing the war on disc, in his own words? Why would the rebels have killed Brackley if he'd been about to publicly embrace New

Columbian independence? And besides, there was the mayor's face. How were they going to explain that?

By 8 a.m. the City Hall staff was engaged in full-court damage control. The main theme was the only available theme: "Let's not have a rush to judgment; these overblown and politically motivated allegations will work themselves out through the proper legal channels."

Dan Brackley holed up in his office, taking no outside calls and coordinating the staff damage control efforts. He finished reading through the Mirror stories for the third time, parsing out what they had and where it had likely come from. He considered it highly significant that he hadn't yet been able to get through to Oliver Oates. He'd been at the Christmas party. With Newby dead, who else even knew that disc existed? Then he paged briskly through the rest of the paper as he focused his mind on prioritizing his counteroffensive.

His eyes latched onto a three-inch story on an inside page in the Business section; an odd little report the rim editors had thrown in as a "bright." Seemed Gotham's costume rental stores had run out of Santa Claus outfits. Not that they were merely all reserved for Christmas Eve, mind you ... that would hardly have been a big surprise. No, it was still a full week before Christmas, and the racks were bare.

Dan Brackley couldn't be sure why, but the story struck him as one of those little puzzle pieces that might turn out to mean something. He clipped the item and stuck it up on the edge of his computer screen with a piece of Scotch tape, in case it should jog some memory or connection, later on.

What he needed now was a major coup, a major victory to shift attention back onto the War on Terror. And fortunately, that plan was already well underway.

What Daniel Brackley had was a secret, and from that secret he had hatched his infinitely subtle plan.

Newby had been a great loss. He had combined an almost unlimited deviousness with an ability to lay down the law and get things done — look how he'd managed to get the Brackley Arts Center finished when all the architects and engineers and building contractors seemed to want to do was squabble about imaginary design flaws and whose fault everything was. "Just put the bolts in the holes!" Newby had insisted. And lo and behold, the job was done.

But Newby had also kept good records. It had taken them awhile — a few relevant files had been erased, indicating Newby had either been killed by someone in SonicNet Headquarters in the first place, or that a co-conspirator had been on hand to open the window (window wide open on a chilly fall evening?) and make sure the long-range archer did his job, then to trash whatever files Newby had up on his computer the evening of his death.

But eventually they'd pieced together the coded records of his spy network.

Out of his hundreds of agents, two had stopped reporting on the very night Newby died. And by cross-referencing the locations of those who were still operating against early, unencrypted lists of locations where Newby had judged it important to place agents, a very interesting location and suspect had popped up:

The two agents who had disappeared the same night Newby had been killed were the Vietnamese and the little Australian that Newby had placed at Daniel's request in the newly renovated Gotham Theatre block — recently purchased and restored by billionaire record executive Andrew Fletcher.

It made sense. Fletcher had the wherewithal to help fund the Order of the Arrow. The terrorist killed in the Dupont Center shoot-out, James Rizzolo, seemed to have a carefully laundered background — no one could have so *little* information on file unless he'd spent most of his life hiding in a cave — but he had grown up and lived less than six blocks from The Gotham Theatre. And his last known job had been as a janitor ... in the Gotham Building.

And while Andrew Fletcher himself was no longer politically active, there were plenty of links between his family and extremist organizations dating back almost a century — now banned free-market "think tanks" that had channeled funds into any number of dangerous anti-government outfits dedicated to promoting so-called "Austrian economics" and the insane ramblings of the long-discredited anarchist cult leader Alissa "Ayn Rand" Rosenbaum; studies of so-called "government waste" actually slanted to imply government did more harm than good.

Why, Fletcher's grandfather had actually known a lot of these people personally — Ludwig von Mises, Murray Rothbard ... mostly anarchist Jews who believed things as innocent and normal as central reserve banking were nothing less than ancient Masonic conspiracies. Brackley wouldn't have been surprised if it turned out they'd all been involved in the Rosenberg A-bomb spy ring.

And Andrew Fletcher himself had been a thorn in the side of city government for years, running what amounted to his own private goddamned "legal aid" charity to fund court cases by those who wanted to practice medicine without a license or who didn't want to pay their fair share of taxes, who wanted to spend years stalling and blocking the sensible progress of redevelopment projects which could help everyone by creating new jobs and tax revenues — all based on absurd arguments that filthy immigrant slumlords with rat-infested tenements and flophouses, catering to drunken, unsanitary whores, drug peddlers, and half-breeds, had so-called "property rights."

Oh, it was going to be a pleasure taking down this Andrew Fletcher. And there was little doubt the Gotham Theatre block was some kind of nexus of the rebellion. Brackley could seize the whole place under the asset seizure laws, either board it up to stop it competing with the Brackley Center or lease it out to be operated by someone who would gladly kick back to him some percentage of its gross. And who knew what they'd find once they got in there — Newby had even believed there was some link between the building and all these new-made AK-47s which had been pouring onto the underground market in recent months. A basement factory, perhaps? Right in the middle of downtown?

But the rebels obviously had spies somewhere in his office, or in the SonicNet. They'd gotten to Newby, after all. He had suspected Tanya Petrov; she had seemed awfully energized when she overheard him talking about the ambush they'd set up at the Dupont Center. But she'd gone and sat right there at the table beside him. And the assassination of Bambi Fiducci had proceeded without interruption — had she just not had a chance to call in a warning?

Nah. He was getting paranoid. Over the months, Tanya had come to look forward to their little ... sessions. And she was a woman, after all. Only a cruel God would have given them any more intelligence than they needed to cook, clean, breast-feed and hump their little brains out.

At any rate, Daniel Brackley was far too wise to plan a big raid on the Gotham Block well in advance, with all the opportunities for leaks that would create.

The plan he came up with was much subtler.

He would hold a much-publicized awards rally for the Lightning Squads at the newly opened Brackley Arena, only three blocks from the Gotham Theatre. This would present an obvious opportunity for the rebels to try and pull some kind of raid, while defenses at other locales were at skeleton levels.

Of course, Daniel would have everyone on the alert for just such a raid, with orders to simply pull in like a turtle into its shell until help could arrive. The only really sensitive target was SonicNet Headquarters itself, up in midtown. He frankly doubted even the Black Arrow would have the strength or the chutzpah to throw himself against such a target, but Brackley prepared, just in case.

Three full squads — at least 20 men — would be set up

with machine guns along intersecting arcs of fire to stop any-one who tried to enter that building though the basement tun-nels, long the rebels' chosen means of entry.

He armed the lobby guards with machine pistols, had them finish replacing the building's front plate glass windows and doors with bullet-proof glass, and ordered the front doors equipped with locks which engaged every time the doors closed — locks which could be opened only by the guard on duty behind the front desk.

Finally, he had Flanagan assign the police sniper team to man the roofs surrounding SonicNet Headquarters on the eve-ning of his big rally at the Brackley Center. If the nightcrawlers were foolish enough to try and strike the headquarters, and if they tried a ground-level entry in lieu of their preferred tunnel approach, they'd find a considerable surprise in store.

But it really didn't matter where the Black Arrow chose to deploy his forces that night. At the conclusion of the awards rally, the mayor would simply stand up in front of all those troops, exhort them with a rousing speech, and then tell them the rebel headquarters had just been discovered, only three blocks away.

They would take to the streets by torchlight, march the three blocks to the Gotham Theatre Block, and seize it. Be-cause the whole operation would be impromptu and seemingly spur-of-the-moment — because there would *be* no advance planning — there could be no security leaks.

He would have an army of thousands, against rebel forces probably not numbering above 50. Assuming they were even home.

And if they *did* go for the bait and attack SonicNet Head-quarters during his awards rally, imagine their plight: thrown back with heavy losses from his prepared ambushes, they would turn tail and try to run back to the shelter of their pre-cious Gotham Theatre ... only to find it had been *seized!* That their last place of refuge had become a heavily manned Lightning Squad fortress. His pursuing forces would shatter them against the anvil of the very place where they thought they could find shelter!

God, his talents were wasted here. After a victory this massive, surely his name would begin to circulate on the national stage.

⚜ ⚜ ⚜

Daniel Brackley was right about almost everything.

Hideki's Big Operation did indeed target the capture and destruction of SonicNet Headquarters itself, and it had indeed been scheduled to take advantage of the fact that the vast majority of the Homeland Defense Special Forces — the Grays, the Lightning Squads — would be gathered at the new Brackley Arena for the mayor's awards ceremony. Nor did anyone in the Black Arrow's organization know about the mayor's plan to conclude his rally by leading the Lightning Squads out of the Brackley center, three blocks on foot, to storm and seize the Gotham Theatre Block.

So when that assault came, Hideki, Jean-Claude's veterans and most of their forces would be several miles uptown, at SonicNet Headquarters.

The main thing the mayor did not know, of course, was that the Gotham Police Department's sniper squad had been eliminated some days before, in the disastrous raid at 7304 Queen's Court.

The police had decided to keep that quiet until they could rebuild the unit. Completely quiet. The city council was known to be full of leaks, so the mayor was not told.

And so, as a light snow began to fall late in the afternoon of the big awards rally at the Brackley Center, there were no snipers ... no police presence at all ... on the roofs surrounding

SonicNet Headquarters.

Now, this wouldn't have mattered much if Hideki had been planning on bringing his troops in through the tunnels, which would have been their standard modus operandi of days past.

But he was not. Jean-Claude's team would assault across the rooftops, entering the building through the roof stairwell, while Hideki led the main assault, directly through the front doors.

The big challenge had been finding a way to get a number approaching a hundred fighters — carrying not bows and arrows, but folding-stock fully-automatic AK-47s from Jimmy Chin's factory in the cavern — onto the sidewalk in front of SonicNet Headquarters, on an early weekday evening when the streets of midtown would be crowded with cheery Christmas shoppers — without sufficiently alarming the guards inside the lobby that they would immediately lock the building down.

The doors and the front plate-glass windows had just been retrofitted with bulletproof glass, young Jack Brackley reported. How to get and keep those front doors open?

Hideki had gone to Andrew. They'd even brought in Madison and Jean-Claude, Quart Low Cavanaugh and Jimmy Chin. They'd racked their brains. It would be a busy Thursday night full of Christmas shoppers. How could they get close to a hundred fighters right up to those front doors without arousing anyone's suspicions ...

The people who came up with the solution, in the end, were Boris and Katia.

SUPRYNOWICZ

CHAPTER 18

When the resolution of enslaving America was formed in Great Britain, the British Parliament was advised by an artful man, who was Governor of Pennsylvania, to disarm the people; that it was the best and most effectual way to enslave them; but that they should do it not openly, but weaken them, and let them sink gradually. ... I ask, who are the Militia? They consist now of the whole people, except a few public officers.

— GEORGE MASON (1725-1792), VIRGINIA'S U.S. CONSTITUTION
RATIFICATION CONVENTION, 1788

What, Sir, is the use of a Militia? It is to prevent the establishment of a standing army, the bane of Liberty! ... Whenever Governments mean to invade the rights and liberties of the people, they always attempt to destroy the militia, in order to raise an army upon their ruins.

— REP. ELBRIDGE GERRY OF MASSACHUSETTS (1744-1814),
DURING FLOOR DEBATE OVER THE SECOND AMENDMENT,
1 ANNALS OF CONGRESS AT 750 (17 AUG., 1789.)

SUPRYNOWICZ

THURSDAY, DEC. 18, 2031, 11:40 A.M.

Madison came up to the penthouse a little before noon, the morning of the big raid on SonicNet headquarters.

Andrew was looking out the big balcony windows. His back was turned to her. He was playing his hollow-body Gibson, to no one. It was a pretty song, but sad. Clapton's "Wonderful Tonight." His song for Cassandra, no doubt. He played the lead and the rhythm parts at the same time — the kind of thing that would make a beginner quietly return her axe to its case, hoping no one would ask if she played.

"Madison," he said, without turning around. How did he *do* that?

"Sorry to impose," she said.

He set the guitar in its holder. Colorful images flashed on the TV in the corner, but the sound had been turned down. They repeated the same story over and over, about the front page revelations on the death of Thomas Brackley. Though no one seemed to realize the story had been slipped to Cassie and the Mirror by Joan Matcham and Jack Brackley.

Maybe the revelations would generate enough excitement to keep everyone's attention off the cryptic little report buried deep in the Business section, indicating Gotham City's costume rental shops were entirely out of Santa Claus outfits. Not that it was likely anyone would attach any significance to the little news item. Still, she knew Andrew would have expected it to be anticipated and avoided.

"I hope you can always talk to me, Madison," he smiled.

"Jesus. It really is a castle in the sky you live in, isn't it?" she asked, wonder and delight capturing her face as she gazed up at the skylights, down at the deep-pile white and brown rugs, striding over past the display cases of red and bamboo Japanese arms and armor to join him, gazing out across the balconies at the city below.

"I suppose it is," Andrew said, smiling as he saw it, afresh,

596

through her eyes. Irrepressible Madison.

She'd been up before, of course. But always for some meeting, never when there was time to take it all in, never alone ... with Himself. She glanced toward the bedroom, then averted her eyes and brought herself back to the business at hand. "Hideki says there's no part for my girls in the big raid."

"I know."

Not "I'll look into it." Just "I know."

"Andrew, if it's because of Ratzo and Kiera — because of the Dupont Center — put someone else in charge. Punish me, if you have to, but not my girls. They've worked hard. They're ready. They deserve to be part of this. Do you know what he's got us doing? Pulling guard duty here at the office."

"Do you have enough bodies?"

"What?"

"To guard this building?"

"Against what? And then, when I told him, 'If there's nothing else for us, let us stand bodyguard for The Black Arrow,' he tells me The Black Arrow isn't going, either. The Black Arrow, not going on the biggest operation we've ever staged? What's going on, Andrew? If you have a problem with me, I can take it."

"Madison, The Black Arrow was a lone guy on a rooftop, reminding people there was still hope, that the bastards weren't invincible. He was Batman. He was Zorro."

"Was? He is."

"There's no place for him in this kind of operation. I'd just draw fire; we'd have to devote more manpower to protecting me than I'd be worth. And what if our people did see me get hit? Symbols work both ways. The resistance has changed. That time is coming to an end."

"An end? If this attack succeeds, we'll have them on the run."

"We don't have the numbers yet, Madison. That time will come. But you'll build that army somewhere else. Vermont, maybe. Somewhere we can breathe, and recruit from people who've already left the city for a new life. We can't get lured into set-piece battles here, when they still outnumber us the way they do. We can be proud of what we've accomplished, but don't fall into the trap of believing the people will rise up behind your banner and make the kinds of sacrifices you and your girls have made. They won't. Not enough of them. Not yet.

"We still have to hit and run — hit and disappear. Push Brackley's boys to the edge, and they'll act like trapped animals. You think the kind of people we're fighting would stop at leveling whole sections of this town, if they thought it would keep them in power?"

"So what do we do now?"

"That's the right question."

She fought down her old frustration with Andrew's Zen-like calm. Like trying to get a straight answer out of a damned monk. She took a deep breath, tried not to react emotionally. He did this for a reason. Lives depended on her now. She had to think deeper. "You only stop fighting when you've won. So the question answers itself."

"Define 'win.' "

"We kill them all."

Madison was going to make such a great commander. It wasn't that she was stupid — not at all. She was just so refreshingly ... unassailed by ambiguities.

"The line to that gallows would stretch for miles" he sighed. This smile was the sad one. "Every asshole who ever worked at the clerk's office, every zoning code enforcement officer? Then what? We take up our orbs and scepters and sit on our high-backed thrones and rule over streets littered with the crunching bones of our enemies, backed by our personal fedayin? Ever read about a guy named Pol Pot? Do you know why the French called the year 1792 'The Terror'?"

Madison's heartbeat had just doubled. She had to take

deep breaths. Stop being such a goddamned schoolgirl. So he'd said "We." It was just an expression. He hadn't meant "we," we. Get a grip.

"Nobody takes the Black Arrow for a would-be dictator," she said.

"Good. But if they're right, at what point is it OK for me to hang up my bow and go start a family out in the Free Lands somewhere? There comes a time when you've gone too far down that road and you can't stop. Lots of people don't figure that out till it's too late. When did I sign the contract that I can never do that, because now I'm supposed to be the New Boss ... same as the old boss?"

Tears came to Madison's eyes. So that was it. Running off to the West with Cassandra. She looked away. Now she systematically quartered and examined the room as she listened. Madison could no more help herself from doing this than a dog could stop itself from sniffing tree trunks. So much space, it was like a temple. There was the kitchen where Cassandra cooked him his breakfast. No, she corrected herself. Not the domestic type. He would cook for her. A few dirty dishes in the sink. Madison would quickly have put that to rights. And there, in that corner, the walled-off space would hold the bed ... where he made love to Cassandra, hour after hour.

She hoped at least the bitch took good care of him there. Madison would never have Cassandra's gorgeous body, she understood that. Those curves. But where was she? Men didn't need it just once a week. If they were normal and they weren't hitting on you every other day they were finding it somewhere else — either that or they'd eventually go bad and turn into very twisted puppies, everyone knew that.

Andrew was saying something about George Washington and the Whiskey Rebellion. She listened not so much to the words as to his voice. He hated it, she realized. He hated the killing. And though it hurt him, the fact that he did not love the slaughter — that he had never come to glory in it — is what had kept him what he was. Kept him from becoming ... like them.

And what did that say about her? For there was no denying Madison gloried in what she had discovered about herself — the talent she had found within herself, for deathmaking. What was Jean-Claude's toast? Rum, rebellion and revenge.

"... and he's the best case. Look at all the lives the French sacrificed to get rid of the Bourbons ... only to end up with Napoleon. And they loved Napoleon; they practically worshipped him. You think that isn't tempting?"

"You're right, Andrew." That was his Madison. Once she got it, she didn't feel any need to keep going over the same ground.

"You have a right to a life. To go start that new life. But without you to lead us, who will they follow? Hideki? Me? Now that we've come so far, we're just going to send everyone home? If we quit now, you think they won't come tracking us down, rooting us out of our holes, one at a time?"

"We couldn't end it if we wanted. I've just looked ahead and seen what happens if The Black Arrow allows himself to be set up as the new Maximum Ruler, that's all. And I won't do it. You do not want to initiate the Glorious Rule of The Black Arrow. You have no idea. Which means I've got to put away the suit.

"There are a thousand Black Arrows out there, now. Young Black Arrows, old Black Arrows, practicing midwifery and pharmacology and marksmanship without a license. We just have to find the courage to embrace the chaos, to let the waves wash over us. It's the only way there's ever going to be a real cleansing.

"If the Black Arrow disappears down a dark alley and isn't seen any more, they still have the hope that he can rise again — they're still free to fight in his name. But if he puts on a nice suit with medals across the chest and starts making speeches about how we're opening this new water treatment plant in the name of the New Collective, then there hasn't been any revolution, Madison. Not really."

Madison wiped a tear.

"Anyway, there's something going on. There's something wrong, and I don't know what it is. My vision has gone dark. I just knew that I had to ask Hideki to keep you here."

"Close to you."

"Yes."

So in the crisis, he had wanted her near. She was glad for that much, even if there was to be nothing else. Here at the end, he trusted her and wanted her near, even if it was only for her bow and her sword.

"What is it, Andrew? What is it we need to guard the Gotham against? What's coming?"

"I can't tell. But it's all too easy. Brackley pulls his manpower off and gives us a clean shot at SonicNet Headquarters ... or anything else we'd like to hit. Meantime, he's got fifteen hundred, two thousand Lightning Troopers at the Brackley Center, three blocks from here.

"They sent in Kylie and Nguyen. And since then, nothing? What kind of sense does that make? Even with Newby dead, they've got to have noticed those two never came home. And someone would know the last place they were sent was here."

"You think he's going to hit us here at the Gotham, tonight after his rally, when his men are all pumped up, like taking them out for pizza and beer after the game." And she was supposed to hold the block with her crew of seven. "That would explain why the museum is closed for inventory. I assume Boris and Katia are packing everything in boxes to go into the tunnels?"

"I don't know what he's going to do. Something so big it just blacks everything out for days. I can't get far enough away to make it out. It wouldn't take another spy for them to figure out we're here. So many people now, there's bound to be loose talk. ..."

"You could call off the attack. We could dig in here."

"Madison. Hideki is taking, what, a hundred fighters? Dug in here, how long would we last against 2,000 Grays, once they started calling in the attack planes? That would be Dan Brackley's dream come true. If they attack, we scatter into the tunnels. You know that. We've been all over this. If Hideki and Joanie can pull off what they have planned, that alone will be worth whatever it costs. If there's any fighting here, it's a rear guard action — we hold them off while the rest get away."

"And that's how you see yourself? Standing alone on the barricades with your last arrow, going down in a blaze of glory while everybody else runs like rabbits?"

"I don't see anything, Madison. It's all gone dark."

She took a hesitant step, halving the distance between them. She had always kept her word, never treated him as though he owed her any of the acknowledgement and affection — not even the casual touch — that a lover expects. But he looked so lost now, so alone. He must know. Surely he knew how she felt, how much she wished he would take her in his arms, how much she wanted to stroke that brow, kiss his eyes, offer some comfort, whatever he needed. Where was the other bitch, when he needed that? Where was the always perfect and beautiful Cassandra?

"Andrew," she started, and then hesitated.

"Madison, about you and me —" he tried.

"No," she said, putting her fingers to his lips, smiling the sad smile without using her eyes. "Tell me tonight, love. Tell me after."

If he were to tell her now that the two of them could never be, she wasn't sure she could go on, do what needed to be done this day. For she knew now this day would be the day she had seen in her vision, when the two of them would face the enemy, side by side.

With any luck, perhaps she would die in battle today, as

was her destiny, the brave death she had craved so long, so that she would never have to hear the words she could not bear to hear.

Now the elevator began to move behind her. That would be Hideki, coming up to report that all was ready for the evening's assault. Good.

"So," she said, suddenly businesslike, "if I'm supposed to defend this fortress of yours with whatever dregs of humanity Hideki sees fit to leave me, it's going to be a busy day. From these balconies you can actually see the Brackley Center — Jesus, all the way to the river. Can I put one of my girls up here as a lookout?"

"Of course."

"Someone will have to show 'em how to make coffee on your fancy Italian equipment without burning the place down. They're not exactly Suzy Homemakers. I'll rotate them every two hours, to keep a fresh set of eyes. As a matter of fact, I want two bitches up here from the time it gets dark. I think there's some night vision equipment down in Ratzo's Caverns, and I'll want to send Brawny for some good binoculars — not cheap stuff, something German — the big Zeiss babies like they use in the Navy, put 'em on a tripod, that'll pick up some damned light. I'm sure they cost the world, can Fletcher Industries stand it?"

"Get some cash from Bob, or have Melody in accounting set you up with an EPO. Talk to her soon, though, I'm sending the office staff home early. We'll call it a half day for Christmas shopping."

"You mean 'holiday' shopping?" Madison smiled.

"Yeah."

"And I'll want everyone on live headphones so we're not trying to dial each other up in case things start jumping."

"Talk to Long Shot in the studio; we should be able to do that. Have him scramble a local channel so the other side can't tune us in like the evening news. *If* they come."

The elevator doors opened; Hideki arrived.

"Now tell me you don't mean for us to defend this building with nothing but our bows and arrows," Madison continued.

"What did you have in mind?" Andrew asked.

"If they come, we'll let them see a few of us outside with the bows. Maybe we can thin their ranks with some long shots, make them think a minute, slow 'em down. But once they're inside two hundred yards we've got to switch to the AKs, or we'll be swamped in minutes." Madison grew animated as she looked down to the street, started to visualize her deployments.

"There have to be plenty of extra rifles still down in the caverns. I'll need half a dozen with the longer, heavier barrels. Hideki says he only needs a hundred for the raid, right?"

Hideki nodded.

"We've never used concentrated firepower before. If they come they'll be expecting an old Robin Hood movie; we'll give 'em 'Saving Private Ryan.' Can I move some hardware up as far as the basement this afternoon? With plenty of ammo?"

"Sure," Andrew smiled. "You know the way to the caverns, right?" Of course Madison knew. Madison knew everything.

THURSDAY, DEC. 18, 2031, 5:30 P.M.

By nightfall she'd inventoried and assigned what few personnel she had.

An early nightfall.

The day had gone silent, shortly after noon. The air took on a glowing, sepia cast, like one of those fading black-and-white snapshots with serrated edges out of the old family album, a bathing suit with a skirt worn by a lovely young woman

604

with funny short hair and an uncanny facial resemblance to grandma, cars with their windshields divided in half like you saw in the old gangster movies, the men with oiled-up pompadours wearing the oddest double-breasted, two-tone suits.

The swallows would have flown low if there'd been any swallows. As it was the pigeons made low noises, pecked at each other to vent their anxiety, shuffled nervously for position as they settled back into their aeries on windowsills and inside the rusting steel frameworks of the billboards. When a distant cabbie did honk his horn the sound bounced off the low, iron-bottomed clouds, till they all felt they'd been sealed inside some kind of airtight steel drum.

Something was coming. The air filled with foreboding. The foreboding smelled like diesel and the sooty sulfur of garbage burned yesterday on the far-off Jersey downs.

Old-timers watched the wind go still. Then it shifted till it blew from the northeast, and they knew. By 3:30 it had started to snow — first flurries, then a driving snow that stuck. That would help cover the ground-level entry up at the SonicNet building, but it would also make things harder on Jean-Claude's team up on the roof — especially as the wind picked up and the snow started to mix with freezing rain.

Those who thought they might still escape the city in time turned on their headlights early, their tires crunching and thrumming, then slowing as they found they had to gear down and use more torque to muscle through the thickening blanket of white. The windshield wipers sang a diastolic song, like the clopping of horses' hooves.

They'd already closed the museum and antique shop "for inventory." Now Madison ordered Chin's closed early, as well, "due to storm" — though she asked Annie Chin to solicit a few kitchen volunteers to keep them in coffee and feed her bitches a hot supper to go. You didn't want to underestimate the value of a hot meal, especially if later on she was going to ask them to play hide-and-go-shoot-your-ass outside in the sleet, lying around with their feet going numb, pretending to be snowdrifts. Speaking of which, she made a mental note to send someone out to buy up longjohns, heavy polywool socks, scarves, gloves, waterproof boots ... they'd have to run a quick inventory of sizes. Troops could handle a lot if you could keep them relatively warm and dry.

Closing the restaurant also let her set up a quick deployment position for Morgan and Fiona, their AKs waiting with spare mags and ammo cans just inside the doors — a pair of locked doors which she now had them partially block with a portable dishwashing unit from the kitchen. Inside the machine they wedged bags of uncooked rice — it wouldn't stop an anti-tank round, but a couple feet of hard dry rice should defeat your basic pistol ammo, as good as a sandbag.

This would give them some coverage on the far northern flank when she gave the word. Rachel and Shayla she sent to the south, into the theater, with orders to prop open one of the fire doors into the alley and prepare a quick-deploy position from which they could cover the square from their far left flank.

They had nothing belt-fed, so in essence she was deploying half a dozen of the heavier-barreled AK-47s as fixed Light Machine Guns. That meant setting up bulletproof emplacements — in the alley outside the theater she had them pile actual sandbags from backstage, carrying any extras across to Chin's. The downside of using magazine-fed rifles this way was that in sustained fire you could burn a 30-round magazine in seconds. So Madison was adamant that they spend the afternoon loading mags, "and I don't want to hear anything about your goddamned fingers bleeding." A pile of 40 mags per gun was her minimum — 60 apiece would be better.

Tommy Chin was out driving cab but little Laurie Chin volunteered to hang around and load — even insisted she'd stay to reload mags if it came to a fight. So did Bob in the newsstand. But no one could reload as fast as you could shoot 'em. The somber, brooding afternoon was soon filled with the cryptic clicking of rounds being fed into banana clips, against the pressure of the follower springs.

And then, after Rachel and Shayla had built their position, Madison took one look and had them tear it down again and move it forward, to the very end of the alley. They'd need the wider field of fire.

"We'll stick out here like a sore thumb."

"Not after dark, especially if we get the kind of weather they're predicting. So move a couple of trash cans up here for now to conceal you; we can push 'em aside when we need to. And where are your damned vests?" She clicked her throat mike. "I want everybody in polyKev and trauma plates right now."

"Madison, we're six stories up," came Caitlin's predictable argument.

"Oh, gee, I guess they couldn't hit you then ... if they were throwing really big rocks. And what if I need one of you to come down here later and man a gun? I said now."

Caitlin and Caelan had just taken over the latest shift as their spotters, up on Andrew's sixth floor balcony. Andrew and Madison stashed their own bows with Bob in the newsstand and stood watch from the main lobby doors. Annie and Carole Chin took up a coffee-and-egg-roll run to keep everyone supplied. Bronwyn got assigned to go out and buy up all the wool and waterproof outergarments she could find.

As Boris and Katia suited up and left to join Hideki's raid they mentioned all the antique firearms were still in place in the museum, in case they wanted any — except for the M-21 sniper rifle, which had mysteriously disappeared a few days before.

"Those are just non-functioning replicas," Annie Chin pointed out

"Yeah, right," Andrew replied. "Built into the wall down near the floor under each gun you'll find a locker that swings open from the bottom, with a couple thousands rounds for each weapon, in cans. Get those down here, too, but keep the right ammo with the right gun, because a lot of 'em are different." Mismatched, incompatible ammo had been the terror of army quartermasters for centuries. "Bring any magazines you find in there, too."

Dr. Stauffer's new assistant, Herbert West, was off with Hideki and Jean-Claude and the main body. Helmut busied himself setting up a makeshift trauma center in the museum, which had no windows but good overhead lights. Originally, the plan had been to have it ready for anyone injured in the SonicNet raid, upon their return.

Unhappy with the lack of cover should the six of them have to start out doing any actual firing from the front doors, Madison had the bitches roll the big sand-filled ashtrays out from the lobby and position them on the sidewalk just outside the main lobby doors to give them some cover, pulling in a few stray newsracks from along the sidewalk as well. One bore a faded picture of Cassandra Trulove, she noted, her lovely red hair and lips turning blue and green, the red inks always being the first to fade in the sun.

Quickly blanketed with a few inches of snow, this motley lineup of urban flotsam would actually pass for a little breast-works.

Then she did a final inventory of who was left in the building.

"The Veronicas are still up there in the studio with Marvin."

"They're not fighters," Andrew advised. "Send them home out the back."

"So they can hunt us down one at a time, hiding like rats?" asked Flamingo Jones, who had evidently commandeered her own headphone, upstairs. "I had a Scottish grandfather who told me their fighters used to go into battle to the sound of the pipes. Well, I may not be much of a fighter, but I've got pipes.

Dad, can you wire the studio mikes through the outside speakers?"

"Sure. Heck, I can do better than that." Upstairs, Marvin dug into his mighty duffel bag, from which he had been known to haul a bassoon if that's what was called for, and produced a weird looking fur sack with various wooden beads and what looked like hacked-off clarinets dangling from it. "Young Connor, did I once hear you brag you could play one of these things?"

"What I said was I didn't have the wind to play the longer pieces," smiled the long-haired young percussionist. "But I might manage a few light airs."

And so it was that as darkness fell, as Andrew withdrew so the Black Arrow could later put in his appearance in full regalia if needed and the Irish Bitches settled in behind their makeshift barricade of newspaper racks and sand-filled ashtrays, there came skirling through the sidewalk speakers the haunting melodies of "Dark Island," "The River Ara," and "The Waters of Kylesky."

⚜ ⚜ ⚜

THURSDAY, DEC. 18, 2031, 6:40 P.M.

A lot of people didn't realize Gotham actually shared the same latitude as Rome. But in mid-December the sun still set shortly before 5 p.m., thanks to Daylight Savings Time, enacted in 1917 to save coal for the war effort. A war no living soul could now remember.

Gotham also lay at the southern end of a snowbelt. Oh, a southeast breeze could push the advancing winter back up the river for awhile. But when the gale shifted and blew from the northeast — as it did this evening — the old sailors knew

Gotham could be a freezing, snowy harbor.

A thin dusting of snow had already begun to fall by the time the 4 o'clockers started to get off work. (As an answer to surging unemployment, the 30-hour work week had been mandated by federal law, for everyone but security forces, in 2017.) But on this Thursday before Christmas, the afternoon exodus was somewhat postponed, at least in midtown, as droves of gift-buyers finished up their Christmas shopping at the great and still-glittering retail emporiums, all of which guaranteed to stay open till 9.

Typical of a decaying culture now reaching back into the past in nostalgia for its former greatness, the first-run theater down the street was now playing a Christmas movie in that hot new genre, the simulated double feature. For your modest 9 newbuck admission — double that if you wanted a popcorn and a caffeine-free Coke (caffeine having been technically banned in 2019) — you got the same cast assuming different roles in fast-paced 45-minute end-to-end remakes of two, count them two, classic old films — upgraded with today's requisite car chases, partial nudity, and sexual situations, and spliced up together with a six-minute Dufus Duck cartoon.

The crowds — conditioned by the government schools to have trouble focusing on any single story line for longer than an hour — lapped them up.

This week's 100-minute "double bill" featured debonair leading man Jason Justin with porn-kitten-turned-mainstream-hottie Monica Manifique playing dual roles in twin remakes of "It's a Wonderful Life" (every time one of the little bells hanging off Monica's hooters chimed, you knew a fresh angel had earned his wings in heaven) and "Miracle on 34th Street," the story of a young girl who enlists the aid of Santa Claus and the spirit of Christmas in sparking a romance between her two previously cynical and embittered "uncles."

Crowds of people moved up and down the sidewalks, many with gaily wrapped Christmas boxes or those heavy coated-paper store-logo bags designed to accommodate them. A spirit of good fellowship and conviviality seemed to have resurfaced among many, who actually called out Christmas greetings to total strangers, offered to hold cab doors open for overburdened dames and dowagers, and stepped aside rather than forcing a bundled-up young pregnant woman into the freezing slush of the gutter ... as they probably would have, without a thought, two weeks before.

Across the street from the huge Homeland Security and SonicNet headquarters, a fully costumed Santa in red suit and white beard had set up what appeared to be a Salvation Army collection tub on an iron tripod as he rang his bell in front of the neon-lit bail bond office and storefront Afghan restaurant there.

And now from the west came two more Santas, setting up similar collection pots on little tripods along the sidewalk directly in front of the two swinging glass entrance doors to SonicNet headquarters. They commenced to call out deep and booming expressions of holiday cheer to the passers-by, a few of whom dropped spare change or even paper bills into their iron kettles.

From somewhere over on the avenue half a block to the east a loudspeaker could be heard playing "Let It Snow." And now — one of those otherwise incongruous sights you could only encounter at this time and place — here came an actual troika of three more big-bellied Santas in full red-and-white felt costume, approaching from the east on the side of the street opposite SonicNet headquarters, either just getting off the afternoon shift at Blumenthal's Department Store over on the avenue, or perhaps grabbing a last smoke before they reported back to duty for the final three hours of terrified tots shrieking in horror and peeing their legs.

These three appeared to know the Salvation Army Santa in front of the little kabob house — who knows, perhaps they were union brothers. And so they stopped to chat, turning their heads in unison to watch in appreciation as a young creature in a short haircut with high, elflike ears and sporting the green tights of one of Santa's helpers ambled past, the fleece-lined collar turned up on her brown leather jacket, but still swinging her little miniskirted green hips quite provocatively.

And now, down the north side of the street where the SonicNet building sat, came a gaggle of Christmas carolers in Victorian garb, moving along slowly in company as they sang songs from plastic-coated sheet music in the black three-ring binders they held open in their hands.

The men wore tall black or tan beaver hats in the 1840s style, white ruffled neckcloths, white gloves, and long black or burgundy frock coats with shining black silk collars. The ladies wore an assortment of early Victorian caps and bonnets, and either long black coats with red Salvation Army piping or else floor-length dark blue or green coats with turned-out powder blue or mint green lapels.

There was no way to discern their actual figures under such garb, of course, though even a charitable observer might have noted none of the ladies appeared to be suffering from anorexia.

There was even a young lad hobbling along with them — which might help to explain their slow pace — Tiny Tim with his crutch, or so it would appear.

In this day of Political Correctness, it would have been considered impolite to point out the anachronism of the fact that virtually all of these carolers appeared to be of Asian descent.

"O Come All Ye Faithful," they sang, easily drowning out the competing carols wafting from the department store loudspeakers over on the avenue. Then "God Rest Ye Merry Gentlemen." And then, as they approached the SonicNet building itself, "Good King Wenceslaus Looked Down, on the Feast of Steven ..."

No one knew what the hell "Good King Wenceslaus" was

actually about, of course, or who he'd been, or what the hell the "Feast of Steven" was. But the song had been carefully chosen as Jean-Claude's cue by the simple expedient of testing various tunes on the men at a distance across Ratzo's Cavern, to see if they could tell "I'll be Home for Christmas" from "Holly Jolly Christmas" from "Have Yourself a Merry Little Christmas."

Sure enough, half the guys turned out to be tone deaf, and could not. But for some reason, nearly all of them could pick out "Wenceslaus" from the rest of the clutter. So "Wenceslaus" it was.

Up on the rooftop across the alleyway from the rear of the SonicNet building, even through the wind and the now-thickening snow, Jean-Claude picked out a snatch of the distant tune and knew the carolers had arrived at the front of the building.

Security had been their salvation, of course. The police had decided to clamp down a lid of absolute secrecy on the embarrassing fact they'd lost their entire sniper unit out at Queen's Court a few days before ... at least until such time as they could field a replacement squad. The Grays and even Mayor Brackley were not on the need-to-know list, so Mayor Brackley was still assuming there was a full team of police snipers on the nearby rooftops to cover all entrances to SonicNet headquarters during the three or four hours when skeleton staffing levels would prevail, as the bulk of his forces were gathered for their "Awards Ceremony" at the new Brackley Arena.

Of course, Flanagan would probably have warned Brackley the roof was uncovered, regardless of "need-to-know," if *he* had the slightest hint Brackley was expecting a rebel raid during the awards assembly, at which point he planned to spring the jaws of his trap by marching his gathered forces directly from the Brackley Center three blocks east to the Gotham Theatre to cut off the withdrawing rebel forces from their secret base of operations.

But — equally concerned with security leaks — Brackley

and the Grays had not shared *that* information with Flanagan and the Gotham P.D.

And so Jean-Claude's men found themselves alone on the adjoining rooftop from their arrival at nightfall, free to bolt together the little sliding plank bridge they would use to throw a dozen heavily laden breach-and-blow technicians onto the roof of the Homeland Security headquarters itself.

The song was their cue. Careful to keep plenty of weight on the near end so the leading edge would cantilever out across the gap — obscured from observation from the alley far below (in the remote event anyone might walk through the alley at night, anyway) by the darkness, the wind, and the snow — they rolled their makeshift drawbridge out across the abyss, to a safe touchdown on the other side.

Jean-Claude himself was first across.

They were bridging the alley behind the building, far narrower than the access streets on either side. Still, he was crossing a gap of more than 15 feet, at an elevation more than 100 feet off the ground.

Jean-Claude had mentioned to no one his lifelong fear of heights. He'd always had it; it was why he never became a paratrooper.

There was a great secret never revealed by those with the fear, of course. The standard explanation — that looking down from a height made them dizzy, disoriented, afraid they would fall — was only half the truth.

The true terror lay in the fact that looking down from a height made them dizzy and disoriented, and made them afraid they would ... jump. That was the part you never dared speak, lest they lock you up somewhere. In that tantalizing urge lay the real terror. Some part of your mind actually dared you, wondering how exhilarating it might feel to fall.

He hadn't mentioned all this because the crossing was the most dangerous and important part of the mission. It had to be done if they were to succeed, and who else would do it? Quart

Low, with his hobbled knees? Even if he made it across, how fast could he get down the stairs on the other side? Yes, logically, he could and should have given the job to Airburst Barnes. But he hadn't. Why? Because it was his place, by honor and by duty. Because of the distance he had traveled, and the losses he had suffered, to find himself in this place, in a position to strike a crippling blow at their enemies — striking at their weakest underbelly — to do some serious damage this day to the Motherfuckers in Charge.

So now he would be first across, and not on a calm and windless day, but in a snowstorm quickly changing to freezing rain, buffeted by unpredictable wind blasts of up to 70 miles an hour, more than a hundred feet up in a black and freezing sky that had now come alive with malice, gathering its strength, daring him to risk it, warning him with the shrill cry of the banshee.

Nor was their little gangplank entirely rigid. In fact, it was bowing considerably by the time he got to the middle — forcing himself across, foot by foot, on his hands and knees — the little bridge bending sufficiently that those watching from behind worried it might compromise the horizontal interface on the far side, like a kid's soda straw finally buckling if you bent it too far.

If he had looked down — which he knew better than to do, since just refocusing your eyes could disorient your equilibrium — Jean-Claude would have seen nothing but wet black asphalt. He held no illusion that the wet snow would have formed enough of a drift, down there in the protected alley eight stories away, to break his fall.

He was clipped to a safety cable, but whether that would hold, exactly how far he would fall before it engaged, and how hard he would hit the wall of the near building if it came to that, he'd decided he would just as soon not find out.

And so he gritted his teeth, and did what it most terrified him to do, inching out over the dark abyss, the wind howling

615

about his ears like a malevolent spirit, angry at him for all the lives he'd ever taken — or allowed to be taken — a spirit that would laugh with joy if he were to relax his grip, her sharp sleet driving into his face and hands, daring him, go ahead, bring up your knee, shift your hand ...

And NOW she gathered her strength and slammed him her hardest blow, just as he'd passed the mid-point on their makeshift bridge.

Just as he released the grip of his right hand and extended it to move the next 18 inches, the wind struck, throwing that loose arm out into the indigo void, where it found nothing to grasp but the frozen starlight of the abyss.

With only his left hand and his knees he clung to that slender, swaying plank. Behind him, his men held their breaths.

Moving forward again was the hardest thing to do. Tears were in his eyes. The voices in his head told him not to move, that the only safety lay in freezing here in place. But he had a whole crew behind him, and each passing minute served to numb all their hands, not just his.

Ninety percent of being a soldier was pressing forward, doing things you would never do for yourself, doing them so that those behind you might live and succeed. And so, focusing on the memory of his dead — the pale, blameless faces of Louise and their son — he twisted his face into the dark scowl of purpose.

He pulled his right arm back against the force of the wind until it again gripped the edge of the gangplank. Then, dragging along his hook and cable, the men paying it out behind him, he inched ahead one more foot, then another, until — so quickly, the moment he thought would never come — he was across.

He rolled off onto what he expected to be the reassuring solidity of the roof. Instead — the storm having shifted almost entirely from snow to freezing rain — he splashed down into half a foot of freezing wet slush.

Rolling to his knees, knowing the key now was to keep moving, he paused only a moment to shudder and catch his breath. Then he was up and splashing across a surface no unauthorized foot had ever before trod, securing the cable to the thrust-up housing of the rooftop stairwell entrance of SonicNet Headquarters, giving those who would follow him the ability to clip their load-bearing vests to a guide cable now anchored on both ends. At that point, in theory, even someone blown or slipping off their makeshift gangplank would find himself dangling from a solid quarter-inch woven steel wire, along which he could still be reeled to safety.

No one wanted to find out if this would really work, of course. So they all aped Jean-Claude's example, scrambling across on hands and knees, even if they were glad for the added comfort of being able to keep that cable under their armpits as they made the transit.

These men had not gotten old by confusing courage with bravado.

They left two men on the far roof, to keep an escape route clear in case they should have to pull back the way they came. These two were extremely solicitous of the last member of the team to cross the plank — a person so small she looked almost like a child next to them — making sure she was firmly clipped to the safety line.

Within four minutes they were all across, soaked and freezing, huddling up as they tested the stairwell door. Locked, naturally.

But then, incredulous, Jean-Claude waved off the team with the C-4, the fuzes and the crowbars, kneeling down to take a closer look at the lock.

He looked up at them. Even in the darkness and the freezing sleet, they could tell from the gleam of his gold front tooth that he was smiling. He felt around in his pocket for a credit card, but of course they'd all stripped themselves of any personal ID for the raid. Catching on, one of the boys handed him an anonymized, throwaway long distance phone card. Sliding it into the jamb alongside the lock, Jean-Claude popped the door open.

The Gotham City headquarters of the Special Forces units of the multi-billion-newdollar Transportation Security Division of the Homeland Security Department of the United States of Freaking America had been protected by pushing in the button on the back of the doorknob to engage the sliplock. They could have opened it with a butter knife.

⚜ ⚜ ⚜

Down at the front of the building, Company Leader Delgado took note of the crowds on the street as he reported to start his 7 p.m. shift. The line outside the movie theater down the street was just starting to file in for the 7 p.m. Monica Manifique double-bill, which told him he was a few minutes early, as usual.

Allowing the Christmas carolers right in front of the building struck him as damned poor security, but it was Christmas, after all. "Good King Wenceslaus" came to an end, and the smiling carolers started "Santa Claus is Coming to Town," always one of his favorites.

They had stopped and turned to face the building, obviously offering a special acknowledgement in this Christmas season for the brave work of his boys in the Lightning Squads. Delgado chided himself for being such a grump. After all, if you couldn't trust a Christmas caroler ...

He's making a list
He's checking it twice
Gonna find out
Who's naughty and nice

Santa Claus is coming to town

One of the bell-ringing Santas wished him a Merry Christmas as he entered through the west door, calling him "Sarge." Funny, he didn't recognize the man's voice. Great makeup job, though. He would have sworn the full white beard and long, wavy white hair were real.

"Merry Christmas, Kovacks," he said to the guard on duty at the desk, who gave him a big smile and the usual slightly limp salute. Delgado had pretty much given up trying to teach these men a proper salute. It wasn't the Air Force, he kept reminding himself. "Who are the Santas?"

"What?"

"The guys we've got right outside in the Santa suits. I didn't recognize the one who spoke to me as I came in. Couple of our guys volunteering for the crippled children's fund?" As he spoke, Delgado turned to look behind him. As the door had started to swing closed behind him, the Santa who had wished him a merry Christmas had taken a few steps, reached out, and caught it. Over on the east side of the lobby, he noticed the other Santa had similarly abandoned his donation kettle to grab that door and keep it from closing behind another trooper arriving for the 7 p.m. shift, which would be even thinner than usual, what with the bulk of the men being away at the awards assembly just getting started down at the mayor's new Arts Center.

Kovacks' attention was drawn somewhat further away, to the other side of the street, as he absently answered. "Hm? Beats me. They didn't check in here."

He was looking through the building snowstorm — starting to mix with freezing rain — at the Santas across the street, stomping their feet and rubbing their hands together in front of the bail bond place and the little Afghan kabob house, which had recently raised its prices. Kovacks was trying to remember what that reminded him of. Oh yeah. A scary movie he'd seen as a kid. The lady had been waiting to talk to a teacher in the school, so she had sat down out in the playground — somewhere up along the Northern California coast, he seemed to remember. As she sits down, she notices a couple of crows sitting on the rungs of the kids' jungle gym behind her. Then she looks up to notice a few more crows flying in to land on the jungle gym behind her. But when she turns around there aren't just four crows, there are like a hundred. Really creepy, 'cause of course in the movie the birds had started attacking people.

Across the street, laughing and chatting like factory workers waiting for the morning whistle to blow, where he'd noticed only three or four a few minutes ago, there had to be, what, 30 big-bellied Santas in full red-and-white outfits? Forty?

Who the hell had ever seen 40 Santa Clauses, all suited up, at one place? What were they waiting for, the Santa Claus bus? What if a kid saw that? How was a mom going to explain to that kid how there could be 40 different Santa Clauses? That just wasn't right.

"Are you listening to me, Kovacks? We've got two total strangers wearing fake beards right outside our front doors, and you don't know who the hell they are or who gave them any clearance to be here?!" Company Leader Delgado reached right past him to trip the red "Emergency Lockdown" switch. A klaxon started to sound.

But by this time the Santas at the doors had reached down, placed some big hard rubber wedges in place to hold the doors wide open, and booted them soundly home.

Yes, the locks would now prevent the doors from opening again the next time they closed. But the question was how Kovacks and Delgado were going to get to the doors to close them.

Then both Santas reached up and ripped away their big false bellies, revealing ugly black folding-stock AK-47s slung across their suddenly slimmer red-flannel chests, with those hefty black ribbed 30-round banana-shaped magazines already in place.

They both dove inside to clear the doorways, the one with the natural flowing white beard kneeling down a little stiffly.

To his right, the second Santa sprawled prone behind the big concrete planters along the front window. Needless to say, Boris from the museum was the only Santa with professionally tailored bell-bottom red felt trousers, a cut-away, toreador-length Santa jacket with double rows of brass buttons, and a wide-brimmed red felt Santa Claus fedora. Close behind him came the dozen costumed Christmas carolers led by Katia and Hideki, also pulling short-stocked AKs from beneath their long Victorian topcoats.

"Jesus Christ!" Delgado yelled. They could have had fucking 40-millimeter grenade launchers under those coats, for all he could tell.

Even as the thought formed in his mind, and the leading elements coming in through the doors were spraying the lobby with their first hundred rounds of fully automatic .30-caliber fire, Tiny Tim stopped square in the east doorway, lifted his crutch, sighted, pulled the pop-up trigger, and sent a 40-mm fragmentation rifle grenade directly into the hard plastic map of the world behind the front desk, where it detonated, spraying Delgado and Kovacks the front desk guard with hot shrapnel from above and behind.

From the loudspeakers out on the avenue the familiar strains of "Winter Wonderland" came wafting as what was actually a company of 50 Santas — each armed with a fully-automatic AK from Jimmy Chin's factory in the caverns, initially tucked beneath their fake Santa Claus tummies but now deployed and ready to rumble — poured across the street in a red felt stampede to complete the breach of the SonicNet lobby.

A reserve force of 15 more Santas led by Quart Low Cavanaugh came trotting up from the west (if a geezer like Quart Low could ever be said to actually trot), positioning themselves strategically in doorways on both sides of the street to repel any counterattack and to keep the line of withdrawal clear in case their cohorts inside should find the need to beat a hasty retreat.

Like Airburst Barnes, Quartlow had refused to wear a fake beard, instead growing out his own red-and-mostly-white peach fuzz over the preceding weeks. Now he shifted his AK-47 on its sling to point down and to the right, freeing his hands to pull out his lighter and a fine Cuban cigar. On second thought, though, he reluctantly tucked it away, deciding to save it for later.

What if a kid were to come along, after all, and see Santa puffing on a stogie? What kind of example would that set?

Upstairs, Jack Brackley heard the carolers start to sing "Santa Claus is Coming To Town." He knew this was the cue for Jean-Claude's boys to start breaching the door from the roof. And that, in turn, meant it was also his cue to pull the suppressed Para-Ordnance high-cap .40 from his desk drawer and saunter over to the DARPA code room, where the TIA boys were under strict orders to lock themselves inside by slamming the vault-like door and commencing the destruction of all sensitive code disks and files the moment they heard the alarm klaxons from downstairs, which should be sounding right about ... there you go.

The alarms were followed by the sound of automatic weapons fire, only faintly audible from the lobby six floors down, and then the hollow crump of a 40-mm rifle grenade killing Group Leader Delgado and Kovacks the desk guy.

A red lightbulb on their console started to flash. The boys in the code room leapt to their feet — and right into the muzzle of Jack Brackley's .40-caliber persuader.

"Gentlemen, please return to your seats and keep your hands where I can see them. I believe you both know me, my name is Jack Brackley, and I'll be your hostage-taker for the evening.

"As you can probably hear, this building is in the process of being temporarily occupied by The Order of the Arrow, and I'm part of the new management team. The original plan, I'll admit, was to kill you both, and I've got plenty of firepower here to get the job done, believe me. Additionally, please be aware that if either of you tries anything, it's just as easy for me to pop two as to pop one.

"But fortunately for you gentlemen, there was a change of plans, which explains why — as you may have noticed — you're still alive. I know you boys signed up for all the crypto magic code-word stuff; you're more mathematicians than shoot-'em-up soldiers. So the current plan is, we're just going to sit here nice and calm, hands away from those keyboards, please, we don't want to be tempted to delete anything or send out any more alarms and get ourselves shot to hell for nothing. Remove your earphones and your throat mikes, please, and ... yes, here come those lovely USO girls, now."

A gust of cold air had told him the stairwell door was opening — cold air from the roof, where the outside access door would be wedged open as well.

From out on the street, interrupted quite regularly by automatic weapons fire, could be faintly heard the loudspeakers down the block at Blumenthal's department store, playing

In the meadow we can build a snowman
Then pretend that he is Parson Brown
He'll say are you married
We'll say no man,
But you can do the job when you're in town ...

And now pouring forth from the stairwell came the first of Jean-Claude's boys, all of whom had met and spent a little time with Jack, in hopes of reducing the chance he'd be whacked for nothing more than the color of his uniform.

"Now, boys, I do need you to stand up very slowly," Jack

advised his two guests, "no sudden motions with those hands, and back away from your consoles. I assure you, there's nothing you can do to prevent this temporary change in building occupancy — think of it as a leveraged proxy call. But you will survive if you cooperate. A little car ride, an interesting little interactive seminar about a bunch of computer crypto stuff I can't even begin to pronounce, and you'll be free by morning, unless of course you decide to sign up for the longer hours and lower pay on our side of the fence. But hey, it's not a job — it's an adventure."

One of the young men betrayed a foolish notion by darting his eyes rapidly to a red button next to his computer screen — whether designed to erase data or to send out some radio alarm was not immediately clear. But he hesitated a second too long.

Jack took a step to place his pistol barrel in a position where it would take the pimply young fellow full in the chest without hitting his buddy, firmed up his two-hand grip on the weapon, and thumbed off the thumb safety with an audible "click" which made both code room boys visibly flinch.

"Make my day," he smiled.

Realizing he'd been read like a map, the crewcut little weasel backed down. Jean-Claude's boys handcuffed both and led them out to the stairwell without further incident.

The pair of crypto geeks would have a little chat with Joan — either blindfolded or from behind a two-way mirror — later on, far from here. They would never even suspect she'd been in the building.

When the coast was clear, the smallest member of the raiding party emerged and walked to the code room, still wearing her fleece-lined leather jacket above her green tights and miniskirt.

Everyone cleared the way. She gave Jack a nervous smile. He nodded, but found he couldn't touch her. Too many brave men and women had died to make this moment possible. Downstairs, the boys would corrupt the SonicNet computer system and trash the place. The purpose of the whole raid would be explained as bringing down the SonicNet — the symbol of federal oppression and gun control in Gotham. It was a worthy enough goal. But Andrew would never have risked so many lives just for that.

Jack felt himself shiver. There were tears in his eyes. If it worked, tonight would change the world.

Joanie didn't dick around. A counterattack could come at any time. She pulled up a chair, sat down at the alpha monitor and hit the return key to refresh the screen. It was pristine. No alarms. She let out a breath. From the hard case that she carried next to her heart she pulled one of the golden discs — she carried a second for backup. It bore no visible writing but a black letter "S." She slid it into the reader.

E-mail program. Most recent message from the Pentagon's Defense Advanced Research Project Agency in New Washington. Hit "return." Now open the latest item on the desktop, where her disc had just been read. Cut-and-paste Samson into the body of the e-mail message, where it would look like random clutter. (This was the genius of what they'd done. No attachment to raise any alarms.)

Send.

And then the most wonderful thing happened — the thing they'd all been hoping for, the first concrete proof of what they all believed, that Joan Matcham — Eustace Summers, whoever the hell she was — really was that rare genius who was worth a hundred divisions, the Queen of Codes.

Nothing.

Nothing happened.

In New Washington, in the heart of the most secure redoubt of DARPA's Total Information Awareness program — a computer system that, for its very purpose, had to interface in real time with the computers of every other government agency — the e-mail was received. Apparently just a mistaken bounce-back, without the traditional acknowledgment attached. No anti-virus alarms sounded. Nothing unusual had been detected.

This was the genius of Samson, which would not do anything for 84 hours. Nothing, that is, but burrow itself into the system, attach itself to every outgoing message, begin to replicate itself in every government computer all around the globe.

Eighty-four hours during which it would be captured on every back-up disc — even if some sleepy logistics base in Alaska or Diego Garcia failed to back up their data over the long weekend — so that when they finally did discover it and try to erase their drives and restore data from the back-ups ... Samson would lurk there, too, like a fang poised against the jugular of the tyrant.

Joanie even knew when they would start to suspect. DARPA's most sophisticated sniffer was a raw volume counter, which in about 24 hours would start to flash a yellow light that something was writing too much new code — Samson duplicating himself in the bowels of their systems.

In about 24 hours they would start shutting down, purging, and backing up from disc. They would think they had it under control. And then, 60 hours after that, just like the hero in the Bible ... When you awake you will remember not a thing.

All the data of the federal government — the IRS, the DEA, the BAFE, Homeland Security, the goddamned market orders for undersized California apricots at the Department of Agriculture — would begin to erase. The invincible strongman would be blind. He would no longer be able to count the number of his slaves. He would not even remember their names.

She had done it. She stood up, turned to face Jack, and then her knees gave way. He caught her. She was shaking. He carried her outside the room. Jean-Claude's boys went to work, reprogramming the lock on the room's vaultlike steel door. When they left they would close the door and it would lock itself from the inside. When a recovery team did arrive they would assume the TIA operators had locked themselves inside when the raid began — as ordered — and that any failure by them to respond to communication attempts simply meant they thought they were still under attack and that the attackers were mimicking the rescue codes. DARPA would consider its Net still secure. For at least 24 hours.

Once Jack made sure Joan was going to be OK, he didn't stand on ceremony. He took off his uniform down to his shorts, folded it so she could carry it away for him in case he should need it again on some unforeseen future occasion. Then he slipped into the spare pants, shirt and heavy coveralls Jean-Claude produced for him out of his haversack. No sense getting shot by the good guys on his way out the door.

"The seventh floor?" he asked.

"We found a locked wing, just like you said. We've got the door wired to blow; they're waiting for us."

Once Jean-Claude had arrived back on the top floor his men backed off, covered their ears, detonated the charges. The heavy steel door — painted white — blew quite satisfactorily off its hinges, was left hanging at an angle by what was left of its lock.

The first old-timer from the explosives team was shot dead as he went through the doorway — just dropped like a stone. Jean-Claude was the next man through, sweeping the hallway relentlessly with his AK. Two gray-uniformed guards showed themselves, firing handguns. After he'd killed them, Jean-Claude calmly dropped his magazine with a clatter, jammed home another, racked his slide, and rendered their faces and upper chests unidentifiable with a further series of four-round bursts.

Jean-Claude believed in being thorough. Jack was impressed.

The guards' frothing blood flowed down the hallway floor beneath the folding table where they'd been playing cards. From the table, Jack grabbed their key ring. He slung it over his left arm, resumed his grip on the wooden handguard of the extra AK-47 they'd brought for him.

There were 16 single-prisoner cells with small double-glass windows, set up like the quarters of a psychiatric hospital. A few were empty; about a dozen contained prisoners. The rooms were soundproofed; the prisoners couldn't be heard moaning till they got the doors open.

Jean-Claude sent a man downstairs to bring Dr. West. Serious damage had been done to these men. Only one was coherent enough to tell them anything of use.

Further down the hallway were the procedure rooms — the torture chambers. They were surprisingly modern and well appointed, their dentist's chairs and stainless steel operating tables upholstered in a tasteful beige to match the tile floors. There was even piped-in music. Only the propane blowtorches and some of the electrical equipment looked out of place.

"Why are you here?" they asked the prisoner who was able to talk.

"Letters to the editor," he said. "They thought I knew something about the resistance. But I didn't"

"Where is everyone? The medical staff?"

"Some kind of big rally. They're all out getting awards for the fine work they do here."

"Who ran this place?"

"Heydrich and Newby. Haven't seen Newby in weeks, though. Group Leader Rennie Heydrich is in charge. We call him The Skull. Who are you?"

"It's OK. We're getting everyone out."

"The girls," said the old man, trying to point with a hand that was missing several fingers.

"We haven't found any women."

"Down at the end of the hall. The big room. They call it Heydrich's Harem."

As they passed the last torture chamber a deafening mechanical snarl emerged from the room, the noise itself knocking them sideways. Behind it came lunging a huge, pale man in the white clothing of a hospital orderly. The smell of smoke and gasoline fumes came with him. He had just pull-started a huge and roaring orange chainsaw, with which he now lunged at Jean-Claude.

Quick on his feet, Jean-Claude ducked and dodged. Behind him, Jack triggered all 28 rounds from his magazine into the hulking albino. Some kind of safety shut down the chainsaw as the dead orderly dropped it and sagged against the wall. The saw bounced, still smoking. The hallway stank of gasoline exhaust.

"You OK?" he asked Jean-Claude.

"Jesus Christ! What kind of fucking chamber of horrors are you guys running here?"

Once they got the door open, the room at the end of the hall was about as bad as Jack had imagined.

The fact that it was relatively clean and uncluttered and well-lit made it worse, somehow. At least it was heated. There were five girls. They were slim, should have been attractive, if they were fed and cleaned up, and if they hadn't been ... here. Four of them were huddled against the walls, on stained mattresses which were the room's only furnishings, except for the common toilet facilities. The oldest — the one who stood to meet them — might be 17. The youngest was probably not yet 13. They were naked, and most had bandages over old cuts and bruises.

Except for the oldest, they all had something wrong with their eyes. Their pupils were dilated and they didn't seem to be able to focus. Whether from shock, or from being kept on some kind of drugs, the men couldn't immediately tell.

The mattresses were stained yellow and brown from semen and blood. More blood, though.

"Get blankets," Jean-Claude told two of his men. "Blankets and clothes, whatever you can find. Socks and shoes, too. Take them from the goddamned prisoners downstairs; let *them* go barefoot. Take the smallest they have"

"Water," said the oldest girl, who also seemed the most coherent. "Bring them water."

He sent two more of his men running with a motion of his head.

She was tall and slim. She had an ugly knot below her left eye. Someone had clouted her when she resisted. The swelling was not new. It had already gone yellow and purple. She crossed her arms across her naked chest, but she did not cower. She stood tall, glaring defiance. Her courage and her anger were a relief. The nakedness of the other girls, curled up against the walls and shaking, was not erotic.

Jean-Claude's face went pale as he met this one's eyes. Her stare was direct. He knew exactly who she reminded him of. His heart stopped. There were tears in his eyes. Not in hers.

"They only give us food and water and blankets when we cooperate," she said, calmly. "Where did you come from?"

"The roof," Jean-Claude said, feeling clumsy and stupid as he pulled off his heavy jacket and wrapped it around her shoulders. She started to bristle and pull away, then stopped herself. It took an effort for her to let him put his arm around her, even briefly. But she made the effort. Not to pull away.

"Who are you?" she asked.

He took the keys from Jack and searched for the proper one to undo the chain that bound her ankle to the wall. This close to her, he could smell her sex. Any other time, it would have been good. Now it embarrassed him. "I am Jean-Claude Renaud," he said. "The Black Arrow sent us."

"To get us out?"

"To destroy this facility," he replied, watching her lift her foot to rub her chafed ankle. She balanced effortlessly, like a wading bird. "But we will get you out, too."

"Good," she said. "Can I have one of those?"

He read her eyes more closely, then. Though it wasn't his

own safety he was concerned about.

"We still have need of our rifles," he said. "Here, take this."

He reached to the rear of his waistband, pulled out his old VZ-52 pistol. He reversed it so he could hold it out to her, grip first, the muzzle pointed toward the floor. She took it.

It was a brutal triangle of overengineered Czech steel, two pounds heavy with a terrible trigger. But it was capable of sending a round of high-speed bottlenecked .30-caliber Russian ball through almost any Kevlar vest. And it had never jammed.

"This is the safety," he said, showing her. "Push it down before you fire. It reloads itself seven times. Aim for the middle of the chest."

"I know how to shoot," she said, her right thumb hunting for the mag release.

"It's European style," he explained, showing her. "Down here at the bottom."

She dropped the mag, eyed the top round, felt its leaden heft, slammed it back home with the heel of her hand the way any shooter would.

"My name is Tamlyn Scott," she said.

And then she was no longer naked.

This room was not entirely soundproof. From outside the barred windows they could faintly hear the sound of Christmas music from the street far below.

When Jean-Claude left he had his rifle in his hands, and he was striding in a way that left no one inclined to block his path. Behind him, the girls were being dressed and released from their chains. He passed Dr. West, who was standing in the hallway outside one of the prisoners' cells, speaking firmly into his phone.

"Morty, I don't have a lot of time to explain. Bring at least two other people you trust — other residents, RNs, whatever. Just competent people who aren't going to freak out. The scene is gonna look kind of strange when you get here, but you walk right up to the Santa Claus with the rifle, keep your hands in plain sight — yes, you heard me — and tell him I called you. The seventh floor. I've got severe shock, second and third degree burns, some compound fractures that have started to knit without being properly set, some amputations that have been treated by gross cauterization, and the biggest problem we've got is what looks like heavy sedation but only partial charts.

"Gee, Morty, do you think so? Do you think that's what it sounds like? We can decide that later. I don't know. I need you here first. Because there's still gunfire here, Morty. Yeah. No, it's not safe. Who ever promised you safe? Come save some lives."

⚜ ⚜ ⚜

Hideki's crew had cleared the ground level and started systematically working their way up toward Jean-Claude's team. The rooftop boys had secured the code room and grabbed the stairwell and elevator doors on the rest of the top three floors, as well as the interrogation wing, though they were spread mighty thin to do even that, especially as they now tried to scrounge up enough blankets and clothes for the prisoners.

Jean-Claude's team were the only ones who knew about the TIA coderoom on the sixth floor. As far as the Santa Claus force had been told, the main targets were the 78 actual SonicNet monitoring consoles on the second floor.

And there was little question the destruction of the SonicNet would have a huge psychological effect on the populace at large.

Elements of Hideki's team had been carefully trained to round up the operators, who didn't even wear sidearms when on monitor duty. Then they systematically shoved a custom-designed virus disc into each unit's auxiliary reader.

The machines brought up a sequence of three "Not scanned for viruses, are you really, really sure you want to open this thing?" messages, the last requiring a service technician's clearance code. Jack had sent the service clearance codes weeks ago. Once the discs were running, the team's instructions were to allow a full four minutes for the virus to reduce the entire SonicNet computer system to gibbering idiocy. Only then did they pull the covers off the processing stacks and weld the enclosed wiring and memory chips into an indistinguishable mass with their portable propane blowtorches — close matches for those found in the seventh floor torture rooms, weirdly enough.

Yes, the system could be rebuilt. Anything could be rebuilt. The question was, given the expense and considering what a jaw-dropping failure the SonicNet had been — heck, it couldn't even protect *itself* from armed assault — would anyone bother?

Fortunately, as they had hoped, the building was otherwise nearly empty. The bulk of what Gray strength remained was positioned in an ambush around the basement tunnels. It was thus the wall of Santas descending from the main floor into the basement level that encountered the heaviest resistance.

Of course, when they'd come up with the Santa gambit, Hideki and Jean-Claude were thinking only about breaching the front doors. What the psychological effect would be on the basement Grays when they found they were under assault from above and behind by a seemingly limitless horde of jolly old elves in full red-and-white outfits and blazing AK-47s was something they hadn't bothered to stop and gauge.

Hideki's team had suffered two wounded in the front lobby — three more guards cooling their heels in the break room had attempted to deploy back out into the lobby with their H&Ks. The Santas suffered two more wounded now. Fortunately, the Grays were still depending on their little 9mms, manufactured by a former German typewriter company.

Tiny Tim had to be called in with his 40mm crutch to ply them with a bit of shrapnel and white phosphorus before they finally showed a white flag.

Jean-Claude reached the bottom of the basement stairs just as the remaining Grays came out with their hands up, abandoning their weapons. The safety on an AK-47 makes a loud click. Jean-Claude strode far enough forward that he was at no risk of hitting their own men. Then he opened up on the Grays, emptying a full 30-round magazine.

A ball of yellow flame was clearly visible emerging from the barrel of his weapon. In the enclosed space, the noise was deafening. About half the surrendering Grays fell to the floor, some spinning like bowling pins. Most had survivable wounds, though four or five looked good and dead. The rest backed up against the wall, peeing their pants. One tried to run, was quickly butt-stocked to the floor by the closest Santa.

"Jean-Claude, those are prisoners. They've surrendered," said Hideki, over the sound of Jean-Claude's shellacked .30-caliber brass empties bouncing and rolling on the basement floor.

Hideki's voice was soft, but had a distorted sound to eardrums still ringing from the Kalashnikov's .30-caliber assault.

"Oh, pardon me. And what prisoner-of-war camp were you planning to lock them up in? Who is it, here, who's going to volunteer to cook them three square meals a day while they play cards and dominoes in your make-believe prisoner-of-war camp for the next couple of years? Hey?

"We have no way to hold prisoners. They won't talk to us about exchanging prisoners. Do they? Do they? Either you have to kill them or you let them go. And if we let these bastards go, they'll be back to killing us tomorrow. Won't they? Back to killing us and running their little torture chambers. Am I wrong? Somebody convince me I'm wrong."

Nobody but Hideki would meet his eyes.

"We have our prisoners upstairs, from the computer rooms, people who might be able to tell us something — more prisoners than my men can safely handle, already. And you haven't seen the seventh floor. You haven't seen what these assholes did to the people we found there ... the ones that are still alive.

"These scum? Can't you see how they were deployed? To ambush us as we came out of the tunnels. You think they would have given us the chance to put our hands up and surrender and become 'prisoners-of-war' if we'd come in this way? Do they treat any of our people with the respect of 'prisoners-of-war' when we're caught? Name rank and serial number? Geneva convention? Do they?

"Did they treat my wife and baby — my only son —" his voice broke, "as 'prisoners of war'? Fuck your 'prisoners-of-war.' They've been murdering people for nothing but trying to live our lives in peace for what, 40 years? Ever since Waco and Ruby Ridge. Ever hear of those? And we're supposed to let them put their hands up like little kids playing on the playground? 'I give up; I get a do-over; but first I get some cookies and juice'? Does my son get to grow up and get married and have children, do his kids ever get to play their little playground games?

"You've been watching too many goddamned TV shows, where no one ever dies and they always let the bad guys go after they've been taught their lesson. Well here's a lesson."

He punctuated his remarks by removing the old mag, tossing it to the floor with a clatter, inserting a fresh and fully loaded black 30-rounder in his rifle, and drawing back the bolt.

Quietly, Hideki took a single step forward. He slid his foot, actually. Bringing his right arm up across his chest, he reached under his right arm with his left, laid the left hand gently but firmly across the receiver of Jean-Claude's rifle, to keep the bolt and its carrier from closing — though it would still be pretty painful for that left hand if Jean-Claude released the bolt.

"It's enough, my friend," he said. "Let it go now."

Jean-Claude stood a full head taller than Hideki. He out-weighed him by 40 pounds. But everyone in the room had their eyes on Hideki's right hand. By crossing his arms he had left his right hand free access to the hilt of his sword. No one who had ever seen him use it — including Jean-Claude — had any doubt who would win such an extremely brief contest.

"Let it go, my friend. We won today. This one is ours."

Jean-Claude narrowed his eyes. Pride and rage warred with his common sense. Hideki knew better than to predict the outcome of such an internal struggle. He nodded slightly, focusing, trying to reassure his fellow captain, as though there were only the two of them here in the room.

Jean-Claude pulled his rifle barrel up to the vertical, away from Hideki's hand. The bolt slammed closed, but he no longer had the prisoners in his sights. He let Hideki hear the safety click on — a loud and deliberate sound on the Kalashnikov. Then he turned and walked back up the stairs.

"Sir?" asked one of the Santa Clauses, all of whom were breathing shallow.

"These men are prisoners," Hideki said, still speaking softly. "Most of them will live. Have them carry their friends upstairs. Doctor West will patch up those in the greatest need; we'll call ambulances as we leave."

"Bastards," said the Gray's ranking officer, who wore silver eagle badges and sat on the floor with a bullet in his side.

Hideki squatted to speak to the man at his own level. His usually soft voice was now even quieter. The effect was more chilling than if he'd shouted.

"Everything my friend said is correct. If our roles were reversed, would you be patching up my wounded and setting them free? You were put here to kill us without mercy.

"What I just did here was not to save you, it was to save my friend. I did not want him to become the kind of man who kills prisoners. I did not want him to become ... like you.

"I don't know what they found upstairs. But I'll bet you do. Now if you take my advice, you'll think of your men, and hold your tongue."

The Santas herded their prisoners — wounded and otherwise, the able-bodied carrying several who looked like they weren't going to make it — up the stairs behind Hideki, who didn't look back.

"Thanks," said one of the Grays, who'd been figuring he'd never see the sky again, to the last Santa behind him.

"Merry Christmas," the Santa replied. But he did not smile.

SUPRYNOWICZ

CHAPTER 19

*"When the government fears the people there is liberty.
When the people fear the government there is tyranny."*

— SAMUEL ADAMS, REVOLUTIONARY (1722-1803)

*"He that knoweth to do good and doeth it not,
to him it is sin."*

THE BOOK OF JAMES, 4:17

"Rebellion to tyrants is obedience to God."

— THOMAS JEFFERSON: HIS MOTTO

"The future will be better tomorrow."

— DAN QUAYLE (1947 -), 44TH VICE PRESIDENT
OF THE UNITED STATES

"All we are saying is ... give war a chance."

— SYNDICATED COLUMNIST CAL THOMAS, SEPT. 26, 2001

THURSDAY, DEC. 18, 2031, 7:23 P.M.

Daniel Brackley couldn't believe it. The surviving Lightning Squad company leader up at SonicNet headquarters also wasn't coming in very clearly — he must be phoning from somewhere in the basement — making what he was saying almost as hard to understand as it was to believe.

"The building was invaded by what? Phantoms? What did you say? Santas? As in Santa Claus? What are you talking about? What's your situation now? In the basement? But you were set up to repel any assault from — What? They came in from above?"

He had a police sniper team on the roofs, goddammit. This made no sense at all.

He beckoned for someone to call Deputy Chief Flanagan out of the wings to join him here in the snack bar and rest room concourse, which was the only place in the new Brackley Arts Center where he could make out enough of this call to even start to piece things together.

"Flanagan, it's one of our guys at SonicNet Headquarters. One of our last remaining guys, unless I'm talking to some kind of escapee from the loony bin. He says the building has been overrun, that they came in on the ground level and from the roof. Apparently he's one of a small number of Grays still holding out in the basement. That make any sense to you? Don't we have a full sniper team on the roof?"

"No, sir. The department's entire sniper squad was wiped out in that mess out in Queens a couple of days ago. I thought you knew."

"The entire squad? How do you wipe out the entire squad? What happened, their bus went in the river? Why wasn't I told, goddammit? I was supposed to have overhead cover for that building tonight."

"Sir, who took the building?"

"The Black Arrow, of course. Who do you think took the

building? It wasn't the goddamned French Army, I can promise you that. Dammit! How long have we got left on these ridiculous awards?"

"Maybe 40 more minutes, sir."

"That's too long. Have you got a unit standing security here?"

"Not really, sir. Gotham P.D. was told to back off so this could be an all-Homeland Security affair. I've got eight or 10 guys handling traffic, but most of those hundred uniforms covering the entrances, the parking lot, the perimeter and the rear doors are Lightning Squad, under Group Leader Heydrich.

"Pull them together and tell Heydrich I'm instructing them to march on the Gotham Theatre building, three blocks east."

"Sir?"

"It's the Black Arrow's headquarters. It's what Newby was working on when he was killed. We put together his notes and worked it out. But all the rebel fighters are up at SonicNet Headquarters, which would have held if your asshole Gotham Police Department hadn't left the roof uncovered without telling me. Hello?!" he shouted into his phone. "What? Christmas carolers with machine guns? They're bringing in what? Hello?"

"Sir?"

"Cut off. The connection was breaking down anyway. Sounded like he said they were bringing in Tiny Tim, and that can't be right. See if you can open some other line of communication to SonicNet Headquarters, Flanagan, and then pull those men together and get them marching over to the Gotham Theatre. Heydrich is a little scary; you'd better go along with him and get the place secured. And don't forget to check all the basement levels, God knows what you'll find. The idea is to seize their base before the rebel forces turn for home, see. Then I'll lead the bulk of the Lightning Squads over there, right behind you, and crush the returning terrorists against your anvil as soon as we wrap up here. What's the weather like outside?"

"That snow got pretty heavy, sir, and now it's turned to a freezing rain. A little nasty."

"What are you saying? Your boys afraid to walk three blocks in the rain?"

"We're police officers, sir. We're out in the rain every night. That's the only reason you've still got a city, sir. I was thinking of you."

"OK, Flanagan. Point well taken. You're a good man. Get Heydrich to round up as many men as he can and get over there and secure the Gotham Theatre block, I'll see you there."

Flanagan left. Daniel Brackley flashed his own badge and ordered an orange drink from a concessionaire who'd been about to shut down for the night. Almost time to go back inside and pump himself up for his closing remarks. Let them give out the big medals and promotions, a bunch of mutual back slapping designed to boost morale. Then he'd make his surprise announcement, tell the men he'd just discovered the location of rebel headquarters, just three blocks away! And then he, Daniel Brackley, would lead them in their triumphal march. All arranged. Except for this damned freezing rain. So much for the torches. Torches would've made good video. Well, it was a tough job, but somebody had to do it.

Biff Harder didn't recognize the mayor as he brushed right past him, his little Cindy in his arms, on his way back into the auditorium. Cindy had had to go to the bathroom.

As Biff re-entered the hall the guy from New Washington was still into his stem-winder about how important the contributions of the Lightning Squads were here on the home front, backing up our brave boys in green as they took the war to the terrorist enemy on the far Western frontier and in the treacherous jungles of Venezuela. The guys were cheering at the appropriate places. Hell, he'd cheer anything that kept him off the snowy killing fields of Wyoming, too. Biff shifted his daughter to his other arm and checked his watch. Darla wasn't supposed to get off work till 8 and the rally had been set kind of early, so there really hadn't been any option but to bring Cindy along. There were other wives and kids, so she wasn't alone, although it did look like she might be about the youngest here.

Once Darla got off work she might try to stop by, although he'd warned her it would probably be nuts, trying to find each other. If he left for home now he could call her and tell her not to bother trying. Biff slowed his walk back to their seats, seriously considered just ducking out on the rest of the event — he certainly hadn't done anything that was going to get him awarded a medal here tonight; those were going to the guys who'd risked their lives taking the war to the resistance, putting themselves in harm's way on the big day-care and home-schooling raids, not to some drone of a dispatcher who just sat in front of his console all day, flipping buttons.

They reached the bottom of the concrete ramp. The place wasn't even full to a third of capacity, so they'd roped off the seats to concentrate the crowd closer to the stage. Their seats were still well up ahead of him.

That's when the roof made its first noise — a loud, high-pitched, metallic shearing sound like a big ship scraping up against the pier as it came in too fast for docking.

Biff took a few more steps toward their seats. Both he and Cindy craned their heads upwards to see if they could find the source of the noise. There were nets suspended from the ceiling and in the nets were red, white, and blue balloons. They were obviously designed to be released when the event reached its grand finale. Some of the ropes holding the nets in place gave way now and about half the balloons started to float down. The speaker at the microphone had fallen silent, looking up like everyone else to see if he could figure out what that terrible noise had been.

The band leader must have been told the balloons coming down were his cue. Not sure what the change in plans meant, he nonetheless followed his instructions, tapped sharply three or four times on his music stand for the band's attention, and with a great motion of his arms started them in on the opening bars of "Don't Stop Thinking About Tomorrow."

Something else was going on with the roof now. All around the circumference, like the dominoes falling in one of those contests where people work to see how many they can line up next to each other and then knock down in sequence, the diagonal metal support struts were snapping. They were made of solid steel and the noise of their giving way was loud. What this meant pretty much seemed to dawn on everyone at once — the diagonal braces might not literally hold up the roof, but they surely kept it from warping or twisting or buckling or whatever the hell it had just decided to do. And they surely weren't supposed to all be snapping and breaking like that.

The band was quickly drowned out by the shouting as people — uniformed Gray officers and men and women and their family members — leaped from their seats and tried to run for the exits.

But of course, they'd all been crowded into the area near the stage, so the crowd wouldn't look thin and scattered on the videos of the event — shots which would easily be framed to cut off the large empty sections of the room further back. So they were pretty much all in each other's way, the narrow rows channeling them like panicked passengers trying to get out of a sinking airliner.

The usual mob trampling began.

Biff Harder didn't have that disadvantage. He and Cindy were almost back to their seats, but he hadn't yet gone through the hassle and contortions of asking people to stand up and let him through.

He thought of Darla. He was glad he'd refused to let her take the day off to join him. Then he realized he held their precious child in his arms. He turned and started back up the ramp, first at a fast walk, then running, picking up speed as he felt, actually felt the press of people from the aisle seats start to rise up behind him.

From overhead now came a series of bangs that hurt his eardrums. Real pain. At least the right eardrum was broken, he suspected. Felt like blood trickling. Cindy shrieked and covered her ears with her hands. And then it was as though his whole world twisted. It was very disorienting. Pieces of the roof — not just the support braces under the roof, but the roof — shifted and slid together, like pieces of an accordion. There was a blast of cold wind and a quick vision of night sky where you definitely should not have been able to see the cold night sky. Large pieces of stuff — lighting fixtures, a huge box-shaped electronic scoreboard which must have weighed tons — all kinds of stuff started to fall from the ceiling. It looked like slow motion but Biff knew it would all hit in a matter of seconds.

He turned and glanced behind him as he ran. It was a vision from hell. He couldn't tell whether the band was still playing — it looked like they were. On stage people were backing away, pointing upward, screaming. It seemed that all around him people's mouths were open to scream, like one of those old paintings by that weird Norwegian guy. Their screams seemed silent, though, as all such human sounds were drowned out by the one great noise. Stuff from the roof was landing among the crowd, now, stuff so huge and heavy it was like watching insects being stomped.

They were just squashed where they stood, unidentifiable liquids jetting across the floor around the periphery like the remnants of one of those little plastic fast-food ketchup packs squished underfoot on a hot summer sidewalk, the occasional stray arm or head spinning up in the air as it was severed from whatever had stood beneath the tumbling beams and heating conduits. And this was still just the ancillary stuff, the stuff that had shaken loose, that had merely been suspended *beneath* the roof. What was coming now, propelled by and bearing with it who knew how many thousands of tons of icewater and snow in one huge freezing mass that would hit with the force of concrete, was *the roof.*

❖ ❖ ❖

Darla had hoped to surprise them. She'd gotten off work early, fought the traffic, but was finally pulling into a space in the half-empty parking lot just at — she checked her watch — 7:30. She locked the car, turned to walk briskly toward the new Brackley Arena, where the awards event was already half over ... and that's when her world collapsed around her.

The roof. That noise. Oh, God. It was *the roof.*

Biff Harder realized in a moment of eerie calm that they weren't going to make it. The roof was coming and he wasn't going to make it. To his right as he started up the ramp his eye caught a shape, a dark triangle of deepest black. At the point where the staircase came down from the higher seats to his right and the two inclined planes of reinforced concrete met, there was a gap, an empty triangular space barely two feet on a side.

The roaring consumed everything now, the ground shook, the noise filled his ears till he couldn't hear. Shouting, "Crawl, Cindy, crawl!" he dove for that black triangle. Holding little Cindy at arms' length before him, with all the force and strength of his being he willed that small child into that small black hole.

Dan Brackley was turning to re-enter the arena with his orange drink when he heard the great shearing noise. The building shook and then came a series of explosions, like sonic booms. His first thought was that there'd been a bomb. Jesus, had the Arabs managed to smuggle in another nuke, even after what happened in Damascus?

No, if it had been a nuke he'd be glowing dust by now ... right?

Looking up, he noticed a huge black crack opening up on the lateral concrete support above the portal he'd been about to re-enter.

❖ ❖ ❖

THURSDAY, DEC. 18, 2031, 7:30 P.M.

Seven stories up, the wind blowing across the Brackley Center roof from the northeast was now a steady 70 miles per hour.

This caused what engineers call a "ponding effect." As the rain and melting snow accumulated in the southwest quadrant of the roof, far from the inadequate drains, that part of the roof began to sag. And the sagging allowed more water to accumulate.

The depth of the water at the drains along the edges of the roof remained two inches. But out nearer the middle, the sagging roof allowed the water depth to reach 12 inches, 16 inches ... 20 inches.

The load-bearing ability of the main 30-foot cruciform roof beams had already been cut in half by the late Christian Newby's approval of the shortcut of bolting the diagonal braces to the little "stubs" sticking out below the beams. The change also invited flexing. The computer simulations had simply not been designed to measure the Brackley Center roof design's extreme susceptibility to buckling.

At the time Biff and little Cindy Harder re-entered the hall at 7:28, the top exterior compression members on the east and the west faces of the roof were overloaded by 852 percent. At 7:30, the most overstressed members in the top layer of the roof buckled under the added weight of the rain and snow, forming two major "accordion-like" folds.

With a series of booms audible for miles, the accumulated water collapsed the Brackley Center roof in a cascading structural failure which is complicated to describe but which, in the event, took less than 10 seconds.

Not much time to figure out what was going on, to stand up, and to leave the hall. Not much time at all.

The arena's roof proceeded to plummet the 87 feet to the floor. The air pressure increased by the rapidly falling roof caused some of the walls to blow out. Mayor Brackley, for instance, was lifted off his feet and thrown approximately 20 feet, though he survived, suffering only a sprained shoulder.

Very few of those inside the auditorium proper were so lucky. Given the kind of weight involved, when the plane of the roof met the plane of the floor, neither the auditorium seats nor anything in them presented much of a palpable obstacle.

Outside, Deputy Chief Bill Flanagan had already given Group Leader Heydrich his marching orders. Once the roar came and — to their collective astonishment — the roof collapsed, he immediately reversed his instructions and urged the Lightning Trooper to keep his men on site to help coordinate rescue efforts, which Flanagan immediately began to organize, not waiting to find out if anyone else in the area outranked him. But Heydrich insisted on carrying out his last order from the mayor, whom he now assumed to be dead.

Flanagan kept his own handful of men on site, calling for emergency help and beginning to marshal rescue and emergency medical operations. Thus, the Gotham P.D. took no part in the ensuing march to the Gotham Theatre, by somewhat under 100 Lightning Troopers, who Mayor Brackley had expected to back up with the rest of his nearly 2,000 Homeland Security forces at the end of his awards assembly.

For all intents and purposes, as a cohesive fighting force, and in a period of a mere 10 seconds, the local units of the Transportation Security Division Special Forces of the Homeland Security Department — Gotham City's Lightning Squads

— ceased to exist.

⚜ ⚜ ⚜

By 7 o'clock Bronwyn had come back and distributed heavier winter gear to everyone. Barring anything unforeseen, Hideki's raid on the SonicNet headquarters should be beginning.

The studio crew played 20-minute sets over the speakers. In between, the minutes dragged by. Madison had readied everything she could. The driving snow changed back and forth to sleet, then turned into mostly freezing rain, on a stiff 50 mile-an-hour wind. It'd be stronger than that up on the rooftops. Motor vehicle traffic on the streets thinned to almost nothing as more and more people decided to hole up wherever they were for what was obviously going to be the season's first substantial winter storm.

And then, at 7:30 p.m. precisely, from the west, a noise like a nuclear blast — like God's own sonic boom.

"What the hell was that?"

"The Brackley Center for the Performing Arts," came Caelan's voice from up top.

"OK, I've got a noun. Would anyone care to buy us a verb?"

"Hell if I know." Now it was Caitlin's voice from up on Andrew's balcony. "Somebody blew it up, I'd say. Walls blew out, big column of dust and crap going up into the air despite this storm. Jesus, did we do that?"

"Not that I know of. Fire?"

"No, I don't see any flames. But we've already got emergency vehicles heading in from all sides." Three fire engines and as many ambulances came directly past the Gotham within a few minutes, all heading west.

"Jesus, were there *people* in there?"

"Unless they cancelled their big awards gala, I'd guess about 2,000 Homeland Security special troopers."

"Jesus. Trooper sandwich, anybody?"

"Sloppy Joes."

"Oh, please. A little compassion?"

The bitches really didn't like the Grays.

"Everybody hold your positions," Madison warned. "But send me Laurie Chin. I need to get somebody over in that direction with an earphone who can tell us what's going on. And Marvin, anybody up there got anything like a police scanner?"

❖ ❖ ❖

"OK, I've got a mob of Grays heading right toward us."

"Refugees from that mess at the Brackley, or assault troops?"

There was no answer.

"Caitlin? Kind of important that we have a little detail, down here."

"It's not like a summer day in the park out there, you know." The girls upstairs were obviously exasperated by their inability to see clearly through the dark and all the weather — made worse by the way the city's ambient lights would reflect off driving rain or snow. "We're trying to make something out. There! You see that?"

"Yeah," it was Caelan's voice now. "I've got 'em, too. Short rifle barrels. The Grays are packed. They're hunkering down in this sleet, not marching in any particular order, stumbling into each other. They look more like a damned lynch mob. But they're slung up with MP-5s and they've got some officer in a real nice hat up front, a Group Leader — heading this way and they're looking to party."

"How many?"

Another exasperating pause. You tried to count a group of ten and then multiply.

"Eighty."

"A hundred."

"Make it Ninety."

"How far?"

"Two-fifty."

"Yeah. Short of three hundred."

"I'll be drawing a lot of fire, if they spot me," Andrew said to Madison. He'd shown up in full Black Arrow splendor just at the time he was needed, of course. Set your clock by it. "Safer if you go with your girls when they shift out to the flanks."

"No. I stand here, right by you. That's the way I saw it."

"Really?"

"Lots of times. Starting that night in the alley."

"You sure?"

"Absolutely."

"How did things turn out?"

"None shall pass," she said. And then she smiled. "Andrew, there's something I have to tell you, while there's time."

"I know."

"I love you."

"I know that."

Her throat mike was off, but a couple of the bitches were close enough to hear. She didn't care. They pretended to be stone deaf, of course, busy tuning the stabilizers on their bows.

"You do?" she asked.

"I do."

Madison smiled, lifting her shoulders as a shiver of pleasure and exhilaration played up her neck and spine. Anyone else would be peeing their pants about now. Instead, she was like a runner before the starting gun. It wasn't that Madison didn't realize she could die. She just turned it into exhilaration. She could see them, now, a surging gray line through the rain, about 250 yards out; Madison drew her bow, elevated it to 45 degrees, tried a ranging shot.

The wind was gusting from behind them and the right. The wind caught the fletching at the rear of the arrow, drifting the tail to the left and pushing the warhead high enough that it almost stalled in mid-flight. Then it passed into the more sheltered space of the street across the square, corrected itself, drifted left and hit one of the buildings on the south side.

"That surely sucks," she said.

Andrew drew his bow, set to a heavier draw weight, and held a little lower. It looked as though his shot was going to hit the facing building to the north of the street along which the mob of Grays was approaching, but the north wind pushed it left, back onto course, and it vanished into the gloom and drifting sleet between them and the advancing troops. From its trajectory, it had probably fallen a little short.

"OK, girls," Madison said. "Get out here; we shoot kneeling. Try to stay behind an ashtray or one of those news boxes — the ashtrays are better. Everybody try a ranging shot to see how they fly. Hold right for the wind, and only try about 40 degrees high or they'll stall."

Their first round looked far from impressive, six thin and lonesome shafts fighting their way against the wind. The second shots were a bit more consistent.

"Caitlin? Caelan? Two hundred?"

Another pause.

"Two hundred."

"Ladies. Fire for effect. Pour it in there; they could close that distance in about a minute if they decided to run."

She and Andrew did the same, and now the flow of their arrows into the gaping maw of the street across the square did look considerably more impressive. Six of them firing a razor-sharp broadhead every three to four seconds — 15 to 20 shafts in the air at a time — should start doing some good, if the advancing body was within range.

Shooting a bow is not like firing a rifle. All the muscles of the arms and shoulders and the strong side of the back — in fact, all the muscles down to the buttocks and thigh — were engaged in a cadence of motion. The rhythm had to be constant.

And because Andrew had taught Madison the Samurai cadence — not merely drawing the right arm but simultaneously extending and lowering the bow — their rhythms were the same. The instructor and the student now moved in unison. Kneeling beside him, even without touching him, she could sense every motion of his body. Their bows fully drawn, she knew he felt the rush of pleasure up his neck from the full compression of the trapezius at the exact instant she did — the moment just before release.

She had known it would be like this. Just like this. Even the warm rhythms of their breathing were matched. Like making love.

No. Better. Anyone could make love. This ... was theirs alone.

"Yes!" Caitlin quickly recovered. "Scoring some hits. Looks like it took 'em a few seconds to figure out what was happening, but now I can see some spinning and going down. Only on the left flank, though — their right. You might see if you could slice a few of your shots closer to that north wall."

It didn't last long, though.

"They're breaking up now, pulling back."

There was a thin scattering of cheers in their headsets. But there was also a scattering of return fire back up the street — enough to discourage anyone from standing up for a stretch. It was highly inaccurate, but stray rounds and 9mm ricochets could kill you just as dead.

"Dial up Laurie and ask if she's close enough to see what

653

they're doing."

Sure enough, after a few seconds Caitlin was back on.

"Yeah, she's laying low in a storefront, waiting for them to go by. Laurie says they're breaking into two groups, one moving north and one south. Looks like they're going to work up the side streets, come at us from both flanks at once."

"OK, girls." Madison sounded reassuringly calm. "I think it's about time to bid a fond farewell to Robin Hood and Friar Tuck. Shift out to the flanks — no, no, pull back inside and move through the building. Let's not show them everything we're doing. Sling up tight on those AKs, now, check your magazine stacks, and stand by — I'm gonna let 'em come well out into the square before we introduce them to our new lawnmowers. Move!

"Annie, get whoever's left in the kitchen to help reload mags out of the ammo boxes. Keep them well back under cover. And try to spread out a little, babes, I don't want to lose two of you to a single grenade. We'll just assume for now the numbnuts remembered to bring grenades — every now and then one of them lets loose of his dick and does *something* right."

"Leaving us a little thin here in the front, aren't you, Madison?"

"Hey, me and the Black Arrow. What army's gonna come through that?" she smiled. Madison lived for this. Her face was flushed now and the hair was standing up on the back of her neck. "Besides, we need back-up, we got Bob."

"That's right, Madison," came Bob's voice on the headsets. "Course, I'm not much of a marksman. But I can sure reload these magazines. Plus, we got gallons of coffee."

"De-caf?"

"Want some illegal stimulants, babe?"

"Sounds good to me."

Andrew finally heard from Hideki, then, up at SonicNet Headquarters.

"Mission accomplished," he said through considerable interference from the storm.

"That's great. Losses?"

"Lost one of Jean-Claude's. Five or six walking wounded. Jack says Hi. And someone needs to tell I.T. we're sending over a few new applicants for their, um, interviews."

So they'd gotten to the DARPA boys before they could lock their vault. Joan's technical crew was all set up, in a safe basement not far from the SonicNet building, to "interview" the captured technicians, see if they had anything to share that was worth their lives.

"Listen, Hideki-san, we need you back here as soon as possible. We've got 80 or 90 Grays coming at us from across the street to the west. And not much to hold 'em with."

"Damn. Well, we've got the manpower freed up, except Quart Low is keeping a rearguard here to cover the doctor till he can deal with some prisoners we found. Only problem is, we're like, 30 blocks away. And in case you didn't notice, we got snow flurries."

"Yeah, we're singing Winter Wonderland here, too."

"OK, we're coming. Subway?"

"What's fastest?"

"Cab."

"Take a cab."

"I got a hundred guys here, Fletcher-san."

"Take a dozen cabs. Did I mention it's just me and Madison's Bitches?"

"Hey," came a deeper voice from upstairs.

"And Long Shot. I got Long Shot."

"Well then, I don't know why you'd need any back-up. You got 'em outgunned, already."

"Quick as you can, old friend."

From over their heads came a resounding boom, and one of the enemy troops who had found a position in the third-floor window of a facing building across the square pitched forward through the shattered window in front of him and flopped to the ground. The Black Arrow looked back over his head to see Marvin Jones positioned in a second-floor window of his own, scanning for another target with the military-issue scope of the M-21 sniper rifle.

"Is it breakin' some rule to use a rifle?" he shouted down.

"Ain't no rules," the Black Arrow laughed as he picked off his own Gray — a junior officer who'd left himself exposed at what they foolishly thought was "long bowshot." Madison was also still on her bow, driving back a few scattered Grays who had started moving foolishly out of shelter both to the left and the right. But the bitches followed orders and held their fire — Madison wanted the fully automatic 7.62-by-39s to come as a nice surprise when the time was right.

"Is that one of those 'deactivated war trophies,' Long Shot?"

"That's right," Marvin laughed, picking off his own Gray with junior officer's bars who'd stood up to issue a command a good 100 yards down the street. "Deactivated to BAFE specifications. The kids should be down there with the rest any minute now."

On cue, here came the Jones sisters, offering Madison a German MP-44 and a thousand-round can of rare 7.92-by-33. Andrew told them to hold the 1928 Thompson with half a dozen drums of .45 as a back-up in the lobby, opted instead for an FN-D, the Belgian version of the Browning Automatic Rifle, this one a special late Israeli contract job in .308.

Boom.

"Hey, this thing shoots a little high," Marvin shouted down.

"Well how damn far were you shooting the last time you used it, a thousand? There are other lines in that scope, you know."

"Already figured that out." Boom. Another head exploded in a window across the way as another Lightning Trooper made the mistake of showing himself. A spray of purple under the streetlight glow, as though Long Shot had picked off a gallon can of tomato sauce.

"Where'd you learn to shoot, Old Marvin?"

"Told you. I was in Iraq, baby."

"Told me you spent a year wandering around in the desert."

"That I did, brother. Just me and my spotter, wandering around in that god-awful hot, flat country looking for Iraqi generals in their fine, fancy uniforms."

But the enemy was not done, and those shooting from cover now had the range.

"Need a medic here," shouted gray-eyed Shayla.

"That's down in the theater, doc," Madison clarified, not mentioning that if it was Shayla's voice calling then it was Rachel who was hit. "You got it?"

"On our way."

"Brawny, get over there and back Shayla up."

That was her only front-line reserve. After that, they'd be down to throwing in her lookouts, followed by the kitchen help and back-up singers — all brave and willing, but a little short on training. Madison tried not to wish Jean-Claude had left Quart Low Cavanaugh and a dozen Santas. They'd already succeeded in their mission, three miles uptown — the question now was whether the bitches could do the same. A question for anyone else, that was to say. Madison had no question at all.

❖ ❖ ❖

At the crowded Belmore cafeteria, Tommy Chin folded his cell phone, looked around, and climbed up on top of his table.

657

Even in the usually raucous Belmore, this was a little unusual.

"Excuse me," he said. Then louder, "Your attention, please! I just got off the phone with my uncle Jimmy. The Order of the Arrow just captured SonicNet Headquarters, up in midtown. They've destroyed all the SonicNet computers. The SonicNet is down ... permanently."

The initial response was, predictably, silence. Even though most knew Tommy Chin well enough to say Hi in passing, they had no way to be sure this was true. And in any group this large there were bound to still be a few snitches and government sympathizers, ready to take down the names of anyone who started dancing in the streets.

But then, finally, some scattered applause and cheering did begin.

"The problem is, those fighters need to get down to the lower West Side in a hurry. About a hundred guys in all, so I need 20, 25 cabs. It's a paying fare, but I don't have to tell you guys this is some dangerous. They've got to move right now, to head off a Gray counterattack down at the Gotham Theatre.

"This is the one we've been waiting for, guys. The big battle is happening right now, this minute. If you've ever wished you could do something to help the Black Arrow and the fight for freedom, this is it. So anybody who's willing to come uptown with me to SonicNet Headquarters and drive these resistance fighters to where they're needed, you're only gonna get the one chance.

"OK? ... Let's go!"

Tommy jumped down off the table and started for the door. He saw a few men he knew rise to follow him, but not enough. The rest seemed to be looking at one another, checking to make sure this wasn't a joke.

Well, there was certainly no doubt where Tommy was going. So all there was to do now was to stride for that door like he was confident every soul in the place was at his heels.

Until he got outside in the snow, he wouldn't know whether the taxicabs of New York were ready to join the revolution, or not.

⚜ ⚜ ⚜

Understandably reluctant to hang around any longer in the freezing rain — especially with Long Shot Jones picking off strays with his .308 and Andrew and Madison still scoring with an occasional arrow from the front doors — Lightning Squad Group Leader Rennie Heydrich did the best he could. A burning red highway flare thrown end-over-end into the square was their obvious signal, at which point the bulk of his men came storming out in two groups, one across from each flank of the Gotham block.

They avoided the front doors, from which they'd received all the defenders' fire to date. Instead, the two flanking groups, of approximately equal size, were heading directly for Morgan and Fiona inside the doors of Chin's restaurant on the right, and for Shayla and Rachel — no, Shayla and Brawny, Madison corrected herself — in the alley next to the theater on the left.

Heydrich had counted their bows. Against greater resistance he might have taken longer and sent men around to envelop them from the rear. But his ad hoc command was already short on training and communications — he couldn't afford to send men off through a blizzard on uncoordinated wild goose chases where they'd fall out of direct contact. He wanted to use his numerical strength to end this quick.

His decision made sense. He expected Long Shot might pick off a few men, and that half a dozen archers might take down another handful during the time it took them to storm across the square. But they fired as they came — that could generally be expected to keep any mere civilians cowering on the floor. He'd swamp the defenders with sheer numbers — it should all be over in minutes.

"Wait," Madison urged into her throat mike. "Let them all get well into the square. You should be on full auto with plenty of spare mags ready. Until they start to fall back, we've got to pour it into 'em."

The Grays were scattering 9mm fire at the building as they came. But Rachel had apparently been hit by sheer bad luck — until the Bitches opened up the Grays wouldn't be able to spot any specific targets in the blowing rain and snow.

Madison let them get a third of the way across. Then: "OK, you sweet bitches, let 'em have it!"

The Black Arrow peppered the advancing grays on the right with his Israeli BAR, a lovely stout 22 pounds of finely crafted Belgian steel; Madison fired left with her World-War-Two vintage MP-44 — light, handy, reliable, still the most ergonomic of its breed. It was the weapon on which Mikhail Kalashnikov had based his Model 47.

And it was with the heavy-barrelled Model 47, of course, that from each flank the Bitches now opened up. Prone in the snow, Shayla and Bronwyn remained invisible except for their muzzle flashes. Fiona and Morgan, on the other hand, could be more easily seen inside the doors of Chin's — they had to duck the flying shards till all the glass had been shot out of the front doors.

Six machine guns can make pretty fast work of 70 or 80 men — especially when the very presence of modern full-automatic weapons was catching the attackers by surprise. Across their ragged front Grays started to spin and fall, the wounded dropping to their knees. Their advance slowed momentarily. But then their remaining non-coms came up, exhorting them and pushing them forward. They knew this ill-trained group would be unlikely to mount a second charge — they had to get this job done the first time.

The yellow and orange muzzle flashes of the six defensive gun positions gave the attackers somewhere to focus their fire, and at this short a range their hail of 9mm rounds started to have some effect.

The Bitches' fire faltered on the left. Shayla again called for the medics.

"That's on our far left, again" Madison clarified for the doc. "I still need some fire over there, Shayla." In answer, a single rifle sputtered back to life. That meant that in addition to Rachel, even big Brawny had now been hit, and presumably hit bad. Shit.

Now the Grays were advancing again, employing a more sensible tactic in which half the men lay prone and lay down covering fire while the rest popped up and advanced in short dashes, diving for the ground again by the time the Bitches could traverse their barrels and pick them up. Now the miserable weather and the foot of wet snow blanketing the pavement started helping the attackers — once they flopped down in the street they were completely invisible; you could only target them during the brief seconds when they stood and ran. Even the fact that they slipped and staggered erratically in the slush made them harder to lead.

Madison worried about ammo consumption, of course, but the attackers had to be stopped while they were still out in the street; that's why she'd made them peel their fingers raw loading mags all afternoon. Once it was hand-to-hand her meager force would be outmanned at least six-to-one, by men who would often outweigh her girls by 60 pounds. "Keep pouring it on!" she insisted. "Fire till they're red hot! Shoot shoot shoot!"

Most training with these weapons concentrated on using short bursts to avoid wasting ammunition. But that's because most modern enemies weren't suicidal enough to charge you like First World War Zouaves coming up out of the trenches. On the few occasions where they did — like the Chinese human wave attacks in Korea — the tactic could still work based on sheer superiority of numbers.

Few who didn't work with them truly grasped how powerful an explosion it took to drive a lead-and-copper bullet down a rifle barrel at 2,700 feet per second — better than 1,800 miles an hour. The rifle barrel was exposed to those pressurized and superheated gases every time the weapon fired, and heat transfer, particularly into the thin steel out by the muzzle, was fairly efficient. Many a new recruit had raised a blister on his neck by coming into contact with his weapon's barrel after firing a quick 20 rounds and re-slinging his weapon over his shoulder.

But full-auto fire could throw hundreds of rounds per minute. Overheated machine gun barrels could literally turn orange-hot, then cherry red, and fail. Good mobile machine guns like the old British Bren came with spare, easily replaced barrels and an oven mitt for changing them. Unfortunately, Andrew's FN-D was the only weapon here with that capability. But they had no spare barrels ready for it, and it was too late to shift the heavier piece over to Shayla on the left now, anyway.

"Caitlin? Caelan?" Madison ordered. "Get down here and give Shayla some support over on the left. I think I got more medics than shooters over there."

"On our way."

"I'm not done yet," came Brawny's voice, as a reassuring second weapon resumed fire on the left. "Just tie somethin' around it," she said to whoever was dealing with her wound. "What do I look like, a goddamned China doll?"

But now from the right, Fiona called in to report both she and Morgan had been hit, multiple times, by flying glass. Not only that, they were almost out of ammo.

"Bob, did you hear that?" Madison asked into her neck mike.

"I've got ammo," he replied. "Lots of it."

"I'm a little short of runners. Can you get it over there yourself?"

"Sure can."

Back in the newsstand, Bob gathered both arms full of the banana-shaped 30-round steel magazines he'd been loading all day. He bent to pick up his cane, but realized he couldn't manage it without reducing the load he carried. And so he leaned it back in its place, took a deep breath, and set off at a run across the lobby and up through the museum, the shortest route through to Chin's, carrying his load of brass and lead.

It was so exhilarating, he wondered why he'd never done it before. He knew every yard of the building by heart. Why did he insist on carrying the cane around with him in places he knew perfectly well? Now that he thought about it, he couldn't remember. Old habits, old crutches.

As he entered Chin's he shouted for the girls to tell him where they were. As they answered Morgan and Fiona turned and saw him coming toward them at a dead run, dodging tables as though he knew precisely where each one was. Which he did, of course. But around him the air was a cloud of bursting glass as subgun fire from out in the street tracked along behind him, taking out the last of the windows along the west wall.

Madison could do the math. The enemy was within 40 yards on each flank now; point-blank range. It would all be over soon.

And then, like the distant trumpets of the cavalry in some old John Wayne movie, they heard the snow-muted blare of taxi horns, as though it were New Year's Eve or the Yankees had just won the pennant. Louder and louder the beautiful atonal symphony grew, the fire of the attackers slackening as all turned to see what was coming.

What came around the corner from uptown was, in fact, some two dozen yellow taxis, a phalanx of taxis three abreast and filling the entire street, moving fast enough to lift their wheels as they took the corner, skidding and banging into each other on the freezing snow and slush like old-fashioned dirt-track stock cars, correcting and barreling on into the open left flank of the remaining Lightning Squads. They all had their high beams blazing; it was like turning around in a rail yard and seeing nothing but the sweeping headlights of three advancing locomotives, line abreast and coming directly at you.

Out in the square, the Grays faltered.

As the cabs came on, a red-clad Santa leaned head and shoulders out of the right front and left rear windows of each taxi, each Santa in turn bearing a fire-spitting AK-47 set on full auto. Most of their red peaked caps flew away in the wind of their passage. In the lead cab, Airburst Barnes' long white hair streamed out behind him like the tail of a white stallion at the charge.

With a little help from Tommy Chin, Hideki and his fighters had taken a cab.

Those Grays who didn't move fast enough were hit — first by the gunfire and then by the hoods and fenders of the speeding yellow cabs themselves. They went tumbling into the air like bowling pins.

The right flank relieved, Andrew was able to step out onto the sidewalk, swivel left to avoid placing her in his line of fire, and join Madison in pouring their combined weight of lead against the Grays who'd been advancing against Shayla and Brawny on the left. Their combined fire took the remaining Lightning Squads there directly in the flank.

Thus hit on an exposed flank, already freezing and drenched by the rain, shot up and dispirited, most of their junior officers picked off by the legendary Long Shot Jones, the remaining Lighting Squad troops broke and ran, chased down from behind by Yellow Cabs bearing Kalashnikovs, like lancers running down the fleeing infantry at Waterloo.

And as the Taxicab Army shot down the fleeing Grays like panicked rabbits, over the loudspeakers the Veronicas sang "Sweet Talkin' Guy":

Stay away from him, stay away from him

THE BLACK ARROW

Don't believe his lyin'
No you'll never win, no you'll never win
Loser's in for cryin'
Don't give him love today, tomorrow he's on his way
He's a sweet talkin' (sweet talkin') sweet talkin'
(sweet talkin') guy ...

Group Leader Rennie Heydrich was infuriated, disgraced. But then, from the position where he'd taken shelter, huddled at the base of the Francis Marion equestrian statue halfway across the square, he spotted a familiar form near the front door of the Gotham. There could be no mistake — it was the Black Arrow! He carefully positioned the front sight of his subgun, pressed the trigger, and ... nothing. His last magazine had run dry.

The rattle of some scattered 9mm fire still came from the storefronts across the street, as well as from some wounded men lying where the taxicabs had bowled them down. Three more deep booms from Marvin's M-21 on the second floor soon brought that to an end. Any remaining Lightning Troopers who couldn't figure out a quick way to withdraw were soon coming out with their hands up, or showing makeshift white flags. A few even surrendered to the young Indian couple from the restaurant across the street, who brought them out, covering them with a butcher knife and their own surrendered weapons.

"Where's Jean-Claude?" Hideki asked as he walked up to Madison and The Black Arrow, an edge of concern in his voice, looking faintly absurd in his Victorian Christmas carol get-up.

"I am here," the Frenchman waved as he approached from up the street, herding in a small group of shivering Grays, their hands held high. Jean-Claude and his roof team were the only friendly troops now scouring the street, taking prisoners or identifying wounded to be hauled in for triage, who were not Santa Clauses. Jean-Claude's long hair had come loose during the evening and was now plastered down the sides of his face, giving him the appearance of a drowned rat.

But he was smiling.

"You're taking prisoners, now?"

"These Cub Scouts seem to have lost their way," he laughed. "Perhaps we can put them to work shoveling the sidewalks, hey?"

And then, lunging at them out of the wet snow, a bayonet held out in front of him at the end of his short rifle like a lance, came the Gray group leader, Heydrich.

Madison's perception shifted to slow motion. Out in the street, Jean-Claude and his bedraggled prisoners looked shocked. Jean-Claude was strong, but his prisoners were in his way; he would not be quick enough. The Gray officer, his face twisted in his desire for revenge, pushed past Hideki, who stumbled and dropped to one knee. The assailant was heading right for Andrew. Bringing her AK-47 up to guard position, Madison stepped in front of Andrew to take the charge, guarding him with her life. Behind her, The Black Arrow, who had been prepared to open up on the Gray with his FN-D, checked fire and brought his own muzzle up so it wouldn't cover Madison's back. His hands full, it was too late for him to reach for his own blade.

Madison braced herself to catch and deflect the onrushing bayonet with the metal top handguard of her short rifle. If she caught it right, she would push the blade high and left, step to her right and follow up with her gun-butt to the back of the asshole's head. If her timing was off, of course, she'd take the blade somewhere — probably high in her left chest or shoulder.

The Gray officer in his visored cap was a scary looking guy, pale, with cheekbones so pronounced he looked like some kind of Halloween mask. She could even see the skulls and lightning slashes on his collar. He made it to within three feet of her. Then he folded like a cheap umbrella in a high wind.

Madison's eyes shifted focus as Group Leader Rennie Heydrich flopped, lifeless, out of her plane of vision. Behind the collapsing Lightning Squad officer, incongruous in his long two-toned wool Victorian Christmas get-up with the high starched white collar, Hideki rose from his one-knee stance with the grace of a gymnast, spun with the mighty blue-black blade O-Takahira still extended for balance, wiped it dry in one pass, and gracefully returned it to its blue silk scabbard.

Madison smiled. Yeah, Bizen Hideki nokuni Takahira had stumbled and fallen in the snow. Right. When monkeys flew out of her ass. The charging Gray officer had run straight through the cutting edge of O-Takahira, like a chunk of cheese fed into the slicer. Not a bad way to go. Clean, at least.

Morgan and Fiona came limping out of Chin's, helped by Bob, who wore no shirt despite the cold. He'd torn his shirt into strips to bind their wounds, kneeling beside them as they kept feeding his 30-round magazines into their rifles, feeling their bodies for wounds in what would have seemed an unduly intimate manner, under other circumstances.

"I thought we'd had it till we saw this big lunk come running at us through that cloud of broken glass," Fiona smiled. "Then I figured, hell, if *he's* not afraid ..." She grabbed him around the neck, gave him a big Killinchy muffler.

Bob responded to the kiss with a huge smile. Somewhere along the way he'd lost his cane. He didn't seem to miss it.

⚜ ⚜ ⚜

And so the chronicles record that 10 stood with him that day. Like clouds of hornets their arrows flew, and none was allowed to pass.

Bronwyn, pure of heart, fought on despite her wounds. There was Madison, mighty in battle, wise in counsel, who would later lead the army of the North with her daughters beside her. Morgan the sea-born; Rachel, lamb of God; and Fiona the fair, all shed their blood that day, as did Robert the Blind, who that day put aside his cane. And with them stood Caitlin the Pure; Caelan the slender; black Marvin with his M-21; and Gray-eyed Shayla, the wanderer who would find no peace this side of heaven.

It became a company of legend, a tale long told and not forgotten. For even as the call came upon them unexpected, and against all odds, they stood fast, and would not be moved.

⚜ ⚜ ⚜

Annie and Carole Chin and the rest who'd been sheltering inside the Gotham ran out now to tend to their wounded, which was just about everyone. Only the Black Arrow and Madison stood completely unscathed. But it was to tiny Rachel that Dr. Stauffer turned his full attention, leaving the minor injuries to Dr. West, who had returned with Hideki and Jean-Claude and the force that history would remember as Tommy Chin's Taxi-Cab Army.

"Came as fast as we could, boss," Hideki said, looking down at the pale body of Group Leader Rennie Heydrich, who had not been cut completely in half, but close enough. His blood still oozed out into the packed-down snow. "Looks like you managed OK."

"The Bitches were magnificent. As expected."

Hideki turned and pointed to the west, where even at this distance the flickering glow of the flashing strobes of a hundred squad cars and fire engines could be seen painting the low sky red and blue.

"Whole damn roof fell in during their rally. They say it was the rain; roof wasn't designed to shed the rain. Nobody's sure how many dead, but it was thousands. Basically the city's whole damned Gray force, except for the ones we killed or captured up at SonicNet Central, and these you took care of, here. They're done for, old friend. Act of God, if you ask me. They say there were like a hundred survivors — not counting your Welcome Wagon committee, here."

"Brackley?

"The mayor got out. They said on the radio he was out in the lobby making a phone call, one of the few. And the radio says unorganized gangs are using the cover of the storm to attack the portals wherever they can find them, all over the city, just tearing them to pieces. I'm afraid they're doing the same to any Grays they find still manning them, too."

"You need to go find Tanya Petrov. I promised her you'd pick her up and take her along when the time came — she knows there's one more thing we need to do, and she has all the access codes to City Hall."

"You think Brackley will go back there?"

"The wounded beast returns to its lair. That's where he'll go. Unless she changes her mind, we promised Tanya she could be there at the end."

"Sure boss. You're not coming?"

"My part's done. Never been much for tickertape parades. You guys will do fine from here. Don't get suckered into joining any interim 'unity' government. They'll try two or three, after which New Washington will probably send in the troops and arrest everyone for their trouble.

"Leave the water department and the garbagemen alone; burn down planning and zoning, police headquarters, the tax office. Keep handing out guns. After that, people are just gonna have to work things out on their own.

"But no, the Black Arrow disappears now. ... I'd look kind of silly sitting at some big desk issuing orders, anyway."

669

They had tears in their eyes. Hard as it was to believe, they realized they might never again see the man in black, silhouetted by the moon.

Madison pulled herself up to kiss him then, the man with the great strong arms who she'd first seen on a moonlit rooftop so long ago, a kiss that longed for what might have been. She put her lips to his ear as the tears washed her cheeks, and spoke for him alone, one more time. "If you ever want to come back, pulse of my life," she said slowly, to make sure it was clear, since she only planned to say it the once, "you come back to me. Because you're the only man I've ever loved, and I will love you always." She stayed there to breathe for a moment, sharing the perfume of her fertility and her secret — the secret she would never speak, the one secret that might have caused him to stay. For that night had been the one spotless and perfect thing in her life, and she had made a solemn promise never to cheapen it by using it to try and hold him.

She turned and pulled away, then, but found he still held her left hand, their fingers having intertwined without her realizing. She yanked but he did not let go.

And then he was close behind her again, his chest and shoulders huge against her back, his right arm around her belly.

"You weren't going to tell me," he said into her right ear.

"Tell you what?"

"You're walking around here, glowing like a Christmas Madonna. There's color in your cheeks that no one's seen before. When you think you're alone and no one's watching, you hide behind your hair and close your eyes and smile; it emanates off you in waves. Your fine little breast has grown an inch, not that anyone's complaining. You even smell sweeter. Guys hold doors for you, Madison; they don't know why. And you weren't going to tell me?"

She arched her head back into his shoulder. Her hair smelled of sweat, and vanilla, and Madison. "Don't know what you're talking about, aroon."

"Madison?"

She sighed. "Most guys don't notice such things."

"The guy you picked wasn't most guys."

"No, he wasn't."

"When did you first know?"

"Some time now."

"This is myself you're talking to."

"About the time you were putting on your pants," she said. And then they both laughed, though she laughed through tears.

"My Madison."

"Oh God." He shouldn't have said that. She turned and her tears were buried in his shoulder, now.

"What we had that night was the one perfect, spotless thing in my whole fucked-up life, don't you understand? I want to keep it that way, OK? I told you I'd never use it to hold you. I didn't plan it this way, I swear. I just couldn't stand to have you stay because of this, to look up one day and see you staring off in the distance, thinking of places you could have gone, things you could have done, if I hadn't held you, if you hadn't been trapped. I won't do that. I won't live that. I know you have your plans."

"Madison, there's more work to be done here, now. You don't need to answer me right away. But I have to tell you something, even though it may screw up all those wonderful plans you've made to be strong and handle this all alone."

"And what would that be, mo chuisle?"

"It's not her I want, Madison. It's you."

She sobbed. It was the cry of a wounded animal.

"You, Madison. Just the way you are. Tonight and next week and next year, if you're willing, you. I want you in my bed, I want you in my arms. I want you by my side for everyone to see, beauty. Providing you don't mind making love every day, breeding little Amazons as long as we're able."

She pushed back to eye him at arm's length.

"By all that's holy, you haven't used your powers to steal into my dreams and tell me what I long to hear? You honestly want all the wains God can give us?"

"Precisely the number I had in mind."

"Why? Because of what's in my belly?"

"Partly. That makes me the happiest man in the world."

"You're serious?"

"Foolish woman, where do you come from that a man doesn't want to sleep with the mother of his children, make love to her all night long?"

"I'll get fat."

"Not for long. And when you do I'll lie you on your side so I can love you every day. But mostly it's because of what you are, Madison. The way you throw yourself into life without a net. The way you loved me, holding nothing back. I'd give anything for another night with you, beauty. I'd give my very life."

"And have you told all this to her?"

"I have."

"Oh, God."

"Will you have me, Madison?"

"And give you big strapping sons," she laughed through her tears.

"And give me great bonnie daughters, I think. For it's a race of warrior queens I mean to get on you, mo mhuirnin, raised to the sword."

"Aye, you've got the sight. I thought it was a dream I could never live to see. I still don't know shit about antiques, alainn."

"But you can shoot them just fine."

"Mo luaidh," she said. Her beloved. She kissed him then, long with her lips and teeth and tongue, and let out a breath she felt she'd been holding all her life.

"Mo nighean donn," he replied. His brown-eyed lass.

"You never told me how you learned the old tongue."

"For I am old, allana, and have traveled many lands, winnowing the comely maidens for the likes of you."

"And yet you didn't pick the beauty."

"Ah, but I did."

She laughed, and cried. And then she shook her hair, stuck out her chin, and once again was Madison, mighty in battle, who would command the Army of the North, ordering Jean-Claude's troops to search among the bodies in the street, still careful of ambush, hauling in anyone who the doctors could help before they froze in place ... anyone, she was careful to specify, regardless of the color of his shirt.

No one questioned her. She commanded here, and had not been relieved.

Hideki took a squad of his best bowmen, then, and went to find Tanya Petrov and escort her downtown, carrying their Oneida Black Eagles one final time.

For there was still one job left undone for the Order of the Arrow.

CHAPTER 20

Among the many misdeeds of the British rule in India, history will look upon the act of depriving a whole nation of its arms as the blackest.

— MOHANDAS GANDHI (1869-1948), IN 1927

If ye love wealth greater than liberty, the tranquility of servitude greater than the animating contest for freedom, go home from us in peace. We seek not your counsel, nor your arms. Crouch down and lick the hand that feeds you. May your chains set lightly upon you; and may posterity forget that ye were our countrymen.

— SAMUEL ADAMS, REVOLUTIONARY (1722-1803)

Helmut Stauffer would not be interrupted. He would not be relieved. Others came to help him, and one by one they had to drop away to gulp water and pace off their cramps before returning to the table.

Finally Herbert West arrived to join him, stopping only briefly for a word with Jean-Claude.

Dr. West had been late returning from SonicNet Head-quarters. He'd stayed till they could find places for all the rescued prisoners where they would be treated without being chip-scanned. All but one.

"Someone waiting for you over at Chin's," he told Jean-Claude as he washed his hands and held them out for the gloves. "Well, what's left of Chin's. Watch your step in there till they sweep it out."

"Who?"

"She stayed to make sure all the others were safe. But she wouldn't go, herself. Says she's got something of yours she wants to return."

Jean-Claude's hand went to the small of his back, where the two pounds of Czech steel would usually have been. He nodded then, and went to find her.

She wasn't in Chin's, where a chill breeze moaned through shattered windows and glass still crunched underfoot.

He spotted her out in the frozen street, the breeze twisting her hair. She stood unmoveable, still wearing Jean-Claude's oversized green field jacket, though by now someone had also found her some baggy uniform pants and unlaced combat boots.

She had the big Czech pistol out and pointed down toward the ground at a 45-degree angle. There was something there, in the snow.

Jean-Claude hurried his pace out the door and down the sidewalk.

She'd found Group Leader Rennie Heydrich. He'd bled out into a pile of deep crimson snow from the massive gash inflicted by Hideki's blade. But he was not yet dead. The cold must have slowed his metabolism, and with it his dying. Now he held up a hand in supplication.

Jean-Claude took another step toward her. He had no right to interfere. Sometimes, though, even a dying man could find the strength to lurch to his feet. Sometimes, an inexperienced shooter would hesitate too long.

They stood like that for a moment, a silent tableau, the prey finding her fangs, turning on her tormentor.

In his heart, he must not have been expecting it. And so Jean-Claude flinched when the pistol discharged, only a few feet from him.

The bottlenecked .30-caliber Tokarev cartridge of the bulky VZ-52 was a high-speed round. Sixteen hundred feet per second. It made a loud, flat crack that echoed back from the buildings across the street. The muzzle flash was a ball of orange and purple fire the size of a football.

Neither her expression nor her posture changed. She fired again. She did not rush. She took three or four seconds between each shot, regaining her sight picture and squeezing the terrible, mushy trigger of the old Czech weapon gradually, surely, just the way her father had taught her.

Jean-Claude decided he'd like to meet that guy.

She would have hit with every round at 10 times the distance. She fired until the magazine clicked empty — for the follower did not lock the slide back on the VZ-52.

She turned to face Jean-Claude. The gun remained in her hand, pointed at the ground. There were tears in her eyes. Then she threw her arms around him, heaving great sobs into his shoulder.

Jean-Claude paused. It had been one year, one month, and 28 days since they had killed his Louise. In that time, not a day had gone by when he had not thought of her, and of their child. But life went on, and everything was for a purpose.

He had not heard Louise's voice for some time. Now he felt her presence, one final time. She was smiling.

And so he put his arms around Tamlyn Scott, and took her to his heart.

⚜ ⚜ ⚜

They rigged up Helmut Stauffer's pride and joy, the cast-off X-ray machine, to track where the bullets had bypassed Rachel's vest, entering on a downward trajectory past her collarbone — not downward at the time, of course, but laterally as she lay prone behind her gun.

For Rachel was small and frail, and the challenge was to remove the offending projectiles and patch her back together from the inside out when there was so little expanse of flesh to start with, so little blood left for the tiny heart to pump, almost as though they were doing surgery on a child.

Most of their other wounded had minor injuries from flying glass, but even those with gunshot wounds gladly waited their turn. More than that, they volunteered their blood, if their type might help.

In the end, more of their blood was pumping through Rachel's veins than her own.

She looked so pale and peaceful, lying there under the anaesthetic. Her translucent skin seeming to glow, with blue veins that could actually be seen to pulse. The guilty thought crossed more than one mind that she was more than half-way to her rest already — why prolong her pain?

But Helmut Stauffer would have none of it. She had done her part, and now he would do his.

It was hours later — nearly dawn — before Madison finally saw a lone tear running down the surgeon's cheek. Her heart stopped. Behind the mask, she could not make out his expression. She looked across at Herbert West, who had joined his colleague in the seemingly endless clamping and sewing once the worst of the other cases were patched sufficient to the night — all treated in the order of their injuries, and not according to the color of their shirts, just as she had ordered.

And then, on the younger man's face, she saw the faintest of smiles. The artery was patched. The lung was closed. They were almost out. And still that brave and tiny heart, somehow, no one could say how, continued to pump.

They were all still gathered around her — all save those who had gone to meet the mayor one last time at City Hall, and save for Helmut Stauffer, of course, who allowed himself one cup of coffee before moving on to follow up Dr. West's work on an injured Lighting Trooper they'd been unable to transport to one of the hospital ERs — when the gold ring of day colored the Eastern sky, and they were finally sure Rachel was coming back to them.

"We won, didn't we?" she asked, weakly.

"Yes, macushla. We won," Madison told her, smiling and crying.

"You're my family. All of you. The family I never had. I'm so happy. I'm so happy I was with you. God bless you all. We did OK, didn't we?"

"Yes, Rachel. You did fine."

"I was so afraid I'd let you down. But in the end, I wasn't afraid. Not at all."

"We know."

"We kept putting snow on the barrels, but they still got red hot. I think I burned my hand."

"It's going to be fine, little one."

"You'll light a candle on my birthday, won't you?"

"You'll light it yourself, you poor innocent. Dr. Stauffer says he didn't spend all night on his feet for nothing. You're going to live, jewel, and you can tell your grandchildren to light the fires each year for the heroes of this fight."

"Really?"

"God's truth."

"I thought you were all here because I was dying."

"You don't get off that easy, allana. We'll have more work for you once you've slept."

Rachel smiled then, and cried, and squeezed Madison's hand for a time — with her good hand.

And then, just as she was ready to fall back asleep, they

all watched as a little marmalade kitten, his ears laid back with the intentness of his purpose, manfully hoisted himself, paw over paw, up the trailing blankets from the floor, trotted up Rachel's torso on unsteady legs, and snuggled down to sleep under her chin.

"Nguyen," she said, finally giving the big-eared creature a name, as he purred outlandish loud and she kneaded the loose skin at the back of his neck.

All took turns standing watch over her, the rest of that day, all save two, whose absence brought only smiles. For the last time anyone saw Madison and the Black Arrow he had swept her off her feet like a child, her face buried in that great shoulder. Then they were gone. And the Veronicas sang "These Dreams."

❖ ❖ ❖

Arriving back at his office at City Hall, Daniel Brackley found no one there but his loyal assistant Wimley, who urged him to rally the troops.

"Milton, I've always valued your loyalty, but there comes a time to face reality and look out for your own skin. There'll always be a place for a good administrator who doesn't ask too many questions. You just need to make yourself scarce for awhile, then sniff the air to see which way the wind blows. You'll be OK. Now go home; take a few days."

"Sir, there's pretty much no one else here. Security was cut back to a skeleton staff what with everything else going on tonight. I think there are just two guys working the guard station on the ground floor."

"Check with them on your way out, have them re-set the alarms. Much good it'll do."

"But sir, if I call around, things are never as bad as they

seem. The governor called. Now, he reminds us the National Guard was deployed to Minnesota ..."

"Montana."

"No, sir, we lost Billings to the rebels a week back. They've crossed the Powder and the new plan is for the regulars to hold them at the Missouri. I know you've been kind of busy to follow the news, and they kind of tried to keep it quiet, anyway. The point is, he says he doesn't have any troops to help us. But I'm sure the reason he called was —"

"To gloat, Milton. Six months ago they were talking me up as a sure thing to replace him in the capital. Now I couldn't get re-elected mayor if we rigged every machine in the city."

"Um, there was a call about that, too, sir. The warehouses where we store the new electronic voting machines? They're on fire, I'm afraid."

"SonicNet headquarters was gutted tonight, Milton. Attacked, ransacked, destroyed. Everyone there massacred, as far as we know."

"Yes, sir."

"By a bunch of mole people out of the sewers, Wimley. Do you understand?"

"Yes, sir."

"The Thomas Brackley Performing Arts Center and Arena collapsed, Wimley. Roof blew in. I still don't know how they pulled that off. All those brave boys. We lost thousands. I escaped by seconds. Do you hear me? Seconds."

"Sir, about that, this is a perfect opportunity to attribute that to sabotage by the rebels. It'll be months before an official inquiry can issue a report, and we can control the makeup of that panel. This could gain us enormous sympathy, if it's handled right. You know the old saying, if all you've got is lemons, you just make lemonade."

"Milton."

"Sir?"

"Thanks for everything. Now go home."

"Yes sir."

"Here, Milton, take this." He handed the younger man the silver-framed photo from his desk. Daniel and Thomas Brackley, smiling. Younger brothers in a happier world.

"Sir?"

"I'd just as soon it didn't fall into the wrong hands. You can give it to my mother, if you see her. Now get your ass out of here; that's an order."

"Yes sir."

Absently, Daniel Brackley noticed someone had left a radio playing in an office with an open door down the hall. It wasn't very loud, but he thought he recognized the tune.

Outside, the rain had changed back to a freezing sleet, which played off the windows like a jazz drummer working a snare with metal brushes. Once his men had owned the night, had cherished the hours before dawn as the best time to stage their SWAT raids, breaking down doors and terrorizing the sheep as they cowered in their beds, seizing guns and drugs and the counterfeit IDs and ration cards the greedy bastards were always using to cheat the system. Was it Brackley's fault they refused to work hard enough to pay their taxes and still feed their kids?

New banks of spotlights now illuminated their remaining strongpoints, his watchmen peering out through bulletproof Plexiglas, their video cameras sweeping back and forth, back and forth, sleepless in their slow-motion vigilance.

But now the night belonged to the other side. Whatever men he had left, isolated in their islands of artificial, sodium-vapor dawn, were terrified of the increasingly frequent power outages. Desertion and early retirement were running rampant, outright mutiny on occasion, though so far he'd managed to keep that out of the papers. And his brave boys would no longer move at all after nightfall, except in the strongest armored convoys. His own city and they felt more and more like the Airborne, outgunned by a bunch of half-naked froggy boys slinking through the alleys of Mogadishu or Baghdad or Caracas.

Out there in the storm and the shadow, indistinguishable shapes already moved. Live long enough, and eventually your monsters would come to life. Who had told him that? His little brother Tommy, of course. A shiver ran up his spine. His shoulder was hurting from where he'd been thrown on his back when the arena roof came down. He turned back to the desk, opening the drawer to reach for his bottle of unblended scotch, black market of course, thanks to the new thousand-percent liquor tax.

The Macallan. Pretty good shit. He needed it.

It was almost empty. Was he really going through them that fast now, or was some rat looting his stash? The former, in all likelihood. No one would dare steal his good stuff — certainly not Wimley.

Well, so what? Did anyone in New Washington ever listen to him, understand how fast things were degenerating down here on the front lines? Must they always drag their fucking feet on approving the new steps that were necessary to catch these traitors once and for all? The Germans who'd fought for the French in Indochina in the 1950s had had it right. Wherever Brackley has been allowed to demolish the homes and execute the family members of the troublemakers he'd made good, rapid progress.

But no, there'd been a "public relations" backlash after it hit the press. Well, what was so special about the press, that they should be allowed to work openly for the enemies of law and order? They'd let that damned woman write her rabble-rousing columns far too long. That was where this whole thing started, turning this "Black Arrow" into some kind of hero, for chrissakes. Damned sewer rats.

"Milton?" he said into the intercom. "Milton? Is that you? You still here?"

The intercom just hissed. Something was moving in the

darkened outer office. Quietly, but definitely something. Something that was not Wimley.

Brackley buzzed for the guards on the ground floor. No answer there, either.

He felt no panic. In fact, it brought a refreshing clarity. What the hell was he worrying about? All of it was someone else's problem, now.

So it had come, finally. OK. He'd played the game by rules established by others, and he'd scored his fair share. He wasn't going to whine and beg and plead for a "do-over" if his string had run out.

Life was short and dangerous and complicated; you played it out as best you could, cried your tears in the darkness, enjoyed your trophies in their time. When your day came, what was the use of shrieking and cowering and peeing yourself like a bitch, running around flailing your arms and begging for mercy? He'd never had any mercy on his enemies and he didn't expect any now.

So his little brother had won, in a way, after all. Maybe he'd been right and they should have joined the rebels. Tommy would have made a good street general.

Nah. Danny Brackley was too old to go hide in the sewers and the subway tunnels with the rats and the mole people.

Would his nephew be one of the team they sent to take him out? He hoped not. He'd kind of hate to kill his own nephew, or be killed by him, even now. Though the kid had some spunk, he'd give him that. At least he wasn't some simpering queer. Had probably stabbed Newby in the back, one on one. Nobody else in that building had the balls, that was for sure. They'd needed a Brackley for that.

Well, he sure wasn't going to sit here quivering like a bowl full of jelly, get himself captured and tortured, videoed whimpering and blubbering for the Rebel News Service.

He opened his right-hand desk drawer, pulled out the old blued automatic he kept there, a top-of-the-line Kimber with a checkered walnut grip, checked the magazine, made sure it had a round chambered and the safety off. The peasants could die disarmed in their beds; not Danny Brackley.

From the outer office, he heard the sound of the wind moving the weighted curtains at the balcony windows.

Scotch-taped to the side of his darkened computer screen, flapping gently now in the unexpected breeze, he spotted the little news item he'd clipped out of the paper — had that been only this morning? Gotham costume rental shops running out of Santa costumes.

The group leader on the phone had said SonicNet headquarters was under assault by an army of Santa Clauses. Was that how they'd gotten to the front doors? Resourceful bastards, he'd give 'em that.

Brackley looked at his calendar. On any other Thursday night his regular bitch would be showing up with her leash & harness, about now. But from the outer office tonight came only the metallic hiss of steel blades being drawn from wood-and-silk scabbards, and the faint flash of the streetlights on blued steel.

Good. If they'd sent fewer than four guys he'd be insulted. He finished his scotch and, without further ado, strode briskly into the shadows of the outer office.

That was the last thing they'd expect from a fat, balding bureaucrat — for him to go straight at them. At least he'd go down fighting, just like he always had.

The arrows came from at least four directions. They felt like a boxer punching him in the chest. Where were the bastards?

He opened fire, scattering five shots at the shifting shadows. There was at least one yelp of pain. Good. Got one of the slimy SOBs. Time to move. He turned to his right, went to stoop behind a desk, but found himself puzzlingly short of breath. The sound of more feathers coming at him, like the noise of a flock of pigeons taking off together from a roofline.

At least three more arrows hit him. Two hit him and seemed to disappear — it took him a moment to realize they'd gone clear through, shattered something in a glass frame on the wall behind. He hadn't realized these modern bows had that much power.

He fired some more shots. Then the weapon jammed. No, the slide was locked back. Empty. Did he have a spare mag?

Suddenly, he didn't care. He was tired, very tired. He put his back to the wall and slid down till he was sitting on the floor.

From the shadows, someone came forward and hunkered down in front of him. His nephew Jack.

"So, they decided to let you do the honors," the old man said, smiling as though at some secret joke.

"You killed my father," Jack said.

"He could have had it all, Jack. Threw it away. Just like you."

"But that wasn't your biggest crime. You destroyed the hope for peace and freedom that he could have represented. That's the part you've never figured out."

"Spare me your pathetic lectures. You think your precious Black Arrow is going to be any better, once he crowns himself Lord Regent and Protector, interim Fuhrer, Revolutionary President for Life, whatever the hell it's gonna be? Ever lived in a city governed by some kind of peasant revolutionary council? Read your history. The bloodshed has hardly begun. And they always turn on their own. Always. Watch your ass, Jackie, boy. Do you know what happened to Napoleon's two co-consuls?"

"Napoleon ruled alone."

"Got that one right." He coughed blood. "Ah, hell, get it over with, Jack. Assuming you're actually man enough to get it done. Finish me. These damned things are starting to hurt."

"Sorry, Uncle Dan. Not my honor."

A different-shaped figure with a quieter tread stepped forward out of the shadows then, where a line of silent archers stood watching, still as a line of statues along the wall of some ancient temple. Fuller hips.

"Hello, Daniel."

Daniel Brackley, his life leaking out of a dozen wounds, struggled to refocus his eyes. "Tanya? That you?"

"Yes, Daniel." Tanya Petrov was dressed in black pajamas, like the rest of them. Damned nightcrawlers. But what was that she was holding? Long. Curved. Sword.

"Tanya," he forced a smile and a soft laugh. "What are we playing, 'This is Your Life'? Such elaborate choreography, to pull off one dirty little hit. Who else is waiting in the wings, my third grade teacher? Hey, we had some good times, didn't we?"

"Do you remember the first time I met you, Daniel? It was right here in this office. I was so terrified. I had nowhere else to turn. I tried to tell you my Yuri hadn't done anything wrong. And you told me that day that it didn't matter. Do you remember?"

"Yeah, yeah, whatever. I lived my life settling grudges, Tanya, don't teach your grandma how to suck eggs. I did you a favor, whether you know it or not. I gave you something to hang onto, didn't I? And we had some good times. Think of everything I taught you."

"The reason I'm here tonight isn't because of what you did to me, Daniel, or a dozen others like me. Rape us, kill us, make us hate ourselves so much we want to die — so what? We don't matter so much. What matters is what you said that day. Do you remember? I told you my Yuri hadn't done anything wrong, and you said it didn't matter.

"But it does matter, Daniel. It's the only thing that matters. It's called justice. Can you still hear me, Daniel? I just wanted you to know that. That's why they said if I helped them, if I told them all your plans and helped destroy the Lightning Squads, destroy everything that mattered to you, then I could be the one.

"I don't know if you'd heard yet, but some men from the Free Forces went to the prison and broke my Yuri out, almost two weeks ago. They broke a lot of people out. What I'm doing here tonight is for them.

"I was due to leave and go join him in New Columbia three days back, if he'll still have me. Because I'm going to tell him everything, you see. I would have killed myself a long time ago, except the Black Arrow saved my life. The way he did that was, he sent a friend to tell me no matter how hard it was for me, there was a way I could make myself your favorite by calling you little pet names and giving you presents and acting as though I really enjoyed being brutally raped by a smelly, awkward little dwarf twice a week, helping you act out your pathetic fantasies. That if I did that you'd trust me, and let down your guard, and I could learn everything about your security, which I did, which is how we got in here tonight, and knew just where every guard was, so we could kill them all so very quietly.

"I stayed around because they said I could be the one, Daniel. You see, we've had an appointment. We made our appointment a long time ago, right here in this office. We made an appointment that I like to think of as our final date — an appointment for me to meet you here, tonight."

"A woman." He laughed a little, coughing. "I guess it had to be. Makes good sense. You want me to say I'm sorry? I'm not sorry for anything, little Tanya. I took the world as I found it, I played by rules I never made. What would you know? Man makes this world; woman just lives in it, second-class intellects, second-class grifters, every one of you. Manipulative little bitches.

"I did what God put me here to do. Did I ever beat you up? You came to me willingly, the same as any woman who makes a calculation, chooses a man because he's rich and powerful, because of what he can do for her. I made sweet love to you. I did my very best to get you pregnant and procreate the race. Doesn't it say in the Bible to be fruitful and multiply? If you've been doing something to poison your own fertility it was none of my doing.

"Tell your Black Arrow he owes me one. I bet he doesn't have any trouble getting the girls, does he? You've probably been screwing him on the side, yourself.

"You tell him he owes it all to me, little Tanya. What the hell is a hero without a good villain? A cardboard cutout in tights, that's what. When they make the movie, which part do you think the great actors are going to fight over? The stud in the costume and the mask?" He tried to laugh then, choking for a moment on the blood in his lungs. "Me, Tanya. All the great ones will want to play me. The Black Arrow is nothing but a German bodybuilder, a lifeguard in a jock itch commercial."

He closed his eyes now. The pain of his wounds was good, not nearly as unbearable as he'd expected, more like the way your stomach rumbled, thinking it was hungry, when you were trying to fast and just telling it to consume some of your own stupid extra fat for a day or two.

He'd always been such a stupid coward about physical pain, when in fact it was the other kind that killed you in the end. Soon sweet death would come, and he would be haunted by the faces of his lost loves no more. His dead lovely Barbara, and all those fake painted bitches who had teased him and denied him, scorned his offers to love and provide and protect. What had he wanted that was so dirty and obscene, that they should all laugh when he so much as asked them out to dinner?

"You think you're killing Daniel Brackley here tonight?" he managed to ask, a small smile of joy and revenge curving his lips. "I was killed years ago, my heart and soul ripped out by one of your kind. You're just finishing off a wounded kill that the lovely Carmilla should never have allowed to wander off in pain. I'm the walking dead, Tanya, thanks to your kind, thanks to bitches like you.

"God bless you, little Tanya. Kids will be terrified around the campfire by stories of my name, long after you're forgotten dust. I die thinking of your beautiful sweet cunt, Tanya. It never made up for the sweet love I could never have. But it was good enough, for awhile. Just do me a favor and see if you can do something right this one time, love, and make it clean, will you?"

She stepped up close to him, then, crouched down so she was on his level. She drew the glistening blue sword from the scabbard. Clutching it with both hands, she drew her arms back like a batter waiting for the pitch.

And then ... she couldn't. Her eyes filled with tears and she just couldn't. Weeping, rocking back and forth on the balls of her feet, she handed the great sword back to Hideki.

"No?" Daniel asked, opening his eyes to a squint. "I didn't think so. You don't have the heart for it. That's women for you. They go along, let men take all the risks. Oh, they'll spy and cheat behind the scenes. They always consider themselves the victims. You know all about that. But when it comes time to actually get something done, whether it's building a building or paying the bills or finishing off a wounded dog ... get a man to do it, it's just too hard. Right, babe?"

"He's right," Tanya sighed as she rose to stand next to Hideki, looking down at the bald-headed little man, a tear trickling down her cheek. "I am weak."

"No," Hideki said. "You are the strongest of us. It's just that you're not a taker of life. There's no shame in that, especially for a woman, born to give life. Allow me to do this for you. It's my trade."

"Will the arrows kill him?" Tanya asked.

"These weren't poisoned. But yes, he'll bleed out, now. There's blood in his lungs. He has an hour, probably less. We'd only be putting him out of his pain."

"Then leave him," she said. "It's enough. There's been

enough killing."

Hideki looked at her, and down at the mayor, whose breathing was labored now. Then, silently, he re-sheathed the great sword, put his arm around Tanya, and led her away. The others followed, one limping with a makeshift bandage around a gunshot wound to the leg.

Jack Brackley was last. He stood for a moment, looking down at his uncle. Then he left, too.

Daniel Brackley was in considerable pain. He couldn't seem to get comfortable. But it wouldn't be long. What a waste his life had been. Never any kids of his own. Well, whose goddamned fault was that? Now that it no longer mattered, a silent tear rolled down his cheek. Down the hall, he could still hear a radio playing. And through his tears, Daniel Brackley smiled a bitter smile. They were singing:

> *When I call you up*
> *Your line's engaged*
> *I have had enough*
> *So act your age*
> *We have lost the time*
> *That was so hard to find*
> *And I will lose my mind*
> *If you won't see me ...*

⚜ ⚜ ⚜

FRIDAY, DEC. 19, 2031, 2:00 P.M.

The rescue workers at the Brackley Arena site had been at it 18 hours when they finally took a break. All the injured from the concourses had been extracted and sent off in the ambulances by dawn. They didn't want to actually bring hearses to the site, but as the day progressed that's what most of the ambulances came to be used for. Then, as the sun rose and the weather started to clear, the cranes had been brought in to lift and remove the major roof structures. And that was when the job had gotten a lot more depressing and stressful. Because there were no survivors at the level at which they were working now. Just bodies.

Two in the afternoon would be the warmest part of the day, with sunset due again at 4:53. The supervisors decided to give their men 20 minutes for coffee and a breather. They also ordered all the machinery shut down so the special teams could go in with the dogs and the listening gear. The sensitive microphones were lowered down wherever there was a gap in the rubble, listening for what no one had heard from down below in at least six hours — a human voice.

One of the dogs, a shepherd crossbreed named Goldie, climbed up on a little mound of rubble, walked around and around in ever tighter circles, her nose to the ground. Then she sat and barked. Her handler went over to pet the poor creature, who had been known to alert on some pretty strange stuff.

"What you doing up here, girl?" he asked. "Don't you want to come down where they've dug a little deeper?

The dog wagged her tail — actually she wagged the entire lower half of her body — and barked.

"Where?"

She pushed aside a patch of roofing material with her nose and began to dig strenuously.

"OK, guys, over here. She says she's got something."

From behind the temporary fence, which was as close as they'd let her stand, Darla Harder had been watching the golden dog intently. A funny color for a shepherd — she had hardly any black to her coat. Not purebred. Part retriever, maybe. There was something different about that dog, anyway. The other animals seemed very businesslike, snurfling along with their noses to the ground like bloodhounds.

692

This one was goofier. Younger, maybe. She looked up, bounded around, sniffed here, sniffed there. She seemed much less organized in her efforts. Darla instinctively liked the goofy creature. The others were like robo-dogs. This one had personality.

Darla had a blue-and-gray moving company blanket pulled tight around her shoulders — one of the firemen had brought it during the night. She'd snuck off once to pee. Otherwise, despite being soaked and freezing, she had refused to leave, to take a break, to change her clothes, anything.

They'd tried to push the families further and further back. But a few of them who'd been there right from the start, helping to move the rubble, had managed to stay inside the security cordons. The fire and rescue guys just didn't have the heart to make them leave.

Finally, around nine in the morning, as the weather cleared and started to warm up and the bigger cranes moved closer in, some guy in a suit and a white hard hat had come and told them some fancy stuff about how they should go rest and get washed up and come back later because "The rescue effort has entered a new stage." Some of the others had looked at her, waiting for her to explain what it meant. She'd played dumb, although she knew exactly what it meant. The "rescue effort" had "entered the stage" where all they expected to be rescuing from here on in were dead bodies.

Whether they got it or not, most of the others did finally relent and walk back to the police lines, succumbing to the lure of coffee and sandwiches and a place to wash up and get some dry clothes.

Darla Harder did not. She knew what her father would have said. He would have said it was "magic thinking," that there was no possible rational reason to believe that as long as she stood here, picturing Biff and their darling Cindy alive, there was a chance. That as soon as she turned away and hung her head and accepted their deaths ... they would, indeed, die.

Ridiculous, superstitious, magical thinking. But she didn't care. It was all she had, that hope and belief. All she had.

It was mostly hand work, when they suspected they might be onto a breather. No one wanted to shift a big piece of wreckage and find they'd actually let it slip onto a surviving victim, snuffing out a last hope. But eventually they did have to attach cables to some of the bigger pieces, use some power assist from the cranes to lever some of the twisted roof beams out of their way.

Incredibly, what they found was a full seven feet below where Goldie had begun to dig. It was after 4 p.m. — the sun was low on the horizon and the day already cooling toward another freezing night — when they found Biff Harder, cold and dead, in his full dress uniform. He'd made it part way up the ramp, but not far enough. He was wedged up against a little triangular niche formed where one of the descending staircases met the main concrete ramp out to the refreshment and restroom concourse. It looked like he'd tried to squeeze in there — had almost made it — but not quite.

Funny thing, though. He couldn't have had more than a few seconds. You'd think he might have tried to throw himself into the little space head first. Instead, he'd wedged his back into that niche, as though he was trying to seal it off.

Well, they said it had all happened in a flash. Who could explain the way a person might act when the end came that way?

They wrapped him up before they tried to lift him so nobody out on the perimeter would see anything except another one of the somber black bags coming out. Nothing unusual about that — there had been hundreds already and there would be a whole lot more to come. The ones that could be pieced together well enough to fill a bag, anyway.

Goldie's handler was trying to talk into his cell phone, to report they'd found no one alive and the heavy equipment could be brought back in. He banged the phone against his hard hat. He was getting nothing but static.

In the break room where the Red Cross had set up their coffee and donuts in one of the portions of the Arena concourse that remained standing, the bimbo in the golden hairspray helmet on the 24-hour news channel had broken away from her coverage of the big funeral for those 21 cops who'd been killed in the big terrorist ambush the week before, and was now talking to a slowly gathering crowd.

"... say earlier reports of a rebel attack on the nation's telecommunication systems were unfounded. Rather, Homeland Security and the Defense Advanced Research Project Agency now say this is a routine and temporary shutdown ordered by the government itself, likely to last about 12 hours at the most, as they root out and destroy the last remnants of a virus that managed to find its way into a limited number of government computers yesterday, a new supervirus which authorities have dubbed 'Samson' ..."

Giving up on the phone, her handler reached down to pet Goldie, congratulating her on a job well done, and to slip the lead back onto her collar.

Which is when she bit him.

She didn't break the skin. But she flipped her head with a speed he couldn't remember ever seeing, and she took his hand in her teeth. Pretty hard. In three years, Goldie had never done that.

"Goldie?"

She growled.

"Goldie?"

And then, releasing his hand, she turned back to the little triangular niche, still half-clogged with powdery gray rubble that had sifted down long after the late Biff Harder had punched his final timecard, and once again she began to dig.

She dug like an animal possessed, whimpering and tossing rubble out between her hind legs in a cloud till the handler coughed, stepped to the side, had to wipe the grit and crap from his face.

"Goldie, honey, it's too small," the handler said, as he stepped up to her side to get out of the way of all the choking dust coming up between the dog's hindquarters. "He tried to get in there but he couldn't. Nobody could fit in there, girl."

He again reached to attach her lead chain to her collar. She turned, growled, snapped her jaws with a loud clack only inches from his hand. He jumped, involuntarily.

Jesus! Now he was starting to get pissed. He was tired, and cold. This had long since turned into a thankless, depressing task. And now this. You trained a dog, babied her, took her into your home with your kids, and now she acted like this? What was wrong with the nutty bitch? The kids had always loved her, even though she had a reputation for being a little loopy — as likely to take off down last night's rabbit trail as to lock onto the suspect you were after.

But this was too much. This was more than he could tolerate.

"Goldie, we're done here, dammit!" he shouted.

He shouted it really loud. Loud enough that even someone with damaged eardrums could hear.

And that's how they found the last survivor of the Brackley Arena roof collapse. And figured out that Biff Harder hadn't been trying to get into that little angle between the slabs of reinforced concrete, at all. He'd been trying to do just what he did — use his last effort in this life to plug it with his body, to keep it free of rubble.

"Mister?" said the small, clear voice from inside that little triangle of darkness, which was much too small for any adult human. The voice of the girl who would visit the dog named Goldie every Sunday for as long as the police dog shared a place on this earth. "My name is Cindy. Is my daddy going to be OK?"

Darla couldn't explain why she pushed down the fence, then, pushed it right to the ground — which she hadn't imagined she'd have the strength to do — and started picking her way across the rubble to where they were bringing out the latest body bag. She just knew, that's all. The dog was barking and the men started to shout and wave their arms and she just started to run because she knew. The dog's handler was reaching down and pulling something out of a little black triangular hole in the ground. Something with the tiniest little pale white hands. And then those hands did something she would never forget. They reached around that big man's neck, and they grabbed hold and held on tight.

⚜ ⚜ ⚜

After that night, the Black Arrow was seen no more. Some say he simply vanished into the dark from whence he came.

Others say he died in the final battle at the Gotham Theatre, his body secretly carried away and buried by torchlight in an unmarked grave in the twilit caverns far below — a place known only to the original members of the Order of the Arrow — protecting his true identity even in death.

Some insist he escaped to the free lands with Cassandra Trulove, who later bore his son. While others insist he withdrew into the permanent night of the caves after he lost his true love, Madison the captain, hero of the Dupont ballroom, who would go on to marry Andrew Fletcher and lead the Army of the North, bearing the Cailini, the legendary warrior daughters who would first fight beside her — then, finally, complete the battle for freedom.

Yet some there are who believe none of these things. They insist he has not gone at all, that in the dark of the city's night, wherever the weak or the oppressed cry out in pain or fear, a quiet footfall can be heard on the roof, the owlshadow passeth before the moon, a shiver again runs up the spine of the oppressor. The twang of the bow, the quiet gasp of feathered death ...

The Black Arrow lives.

SUPRYNOWICZ

POSTSCRIPT

In the social event of the season, Eustace "Buffy" Summers married Jack Brackley outdoors on the grounds of the Summers family estate in Sunnyvale, L.I., the following spring. Buffy Brackley went on to found the Internet shopping service Cryptomart (see Thomas Chin's "The Code that Killed the Taxmen," Regnery) and the GravityNet wireless communications system. She currently resides on the island of Nantucket, a sizeable portion of which she purchased outright in 2039.

Jack Brackley and Helmut Stauffer, Surgeon General of the Army, were awarded separate decorations of the Columbia Cross by Gen. of the Army Madison Fletcher for valor in command of elements of the Army of the North at the Battle of Newburgh on Dec. 15, 2034. Helmut Stauffer subsequently died of wounds sustained when he refused to abandon his surgery in the face of enemy fire. Jack Brackley now lives with his wife and numerous grandchildren on Nantucket Island, where he has taken up beekeeping and the crossbreeding of more potent strains of opium poppy, one of which has been officially recognized as subspecies papaver somniferum staufferii.

❖ ❖ ❖

Who are the militia? Are they not ourselves? ... The militias
of these free commonwealths, entitled and accustomed
to their arms, when compared to any possible army, must
be tremendous and irresistible. ... Congress have no
power to disarm the militia. Their swords, and every other
terrible instrument of the soldier, are the birth-right of an
American. ... The unlimited power of the sword is not in the
hands of either the federal or the state governments, but,
where I trust in God it will ever remain, in the hands of the
people.

> - TENCH COXE (1755-1824), FRIEND OF MADISON
> AND PROMINENT FEDERALIST, IN THE
> PENNSYLVANIA GAZETTE, FEB. 20, 1788.

The most foolish mistake we could possibly make would be
to allow the subject races to possess arms. History shows
that all conquerors who have allowed the subject races to
carry arms have prepared their own downfall by so doing.
Indeed, I would go so far as to say that the supply of arms
to the underdogs is a sine qua non for the overthrow of any
sovereignty.

> - ADOLF HITLER (1889-1945), EDICT OF MARCH 18, 1938. H.R.
> TREVOR-ROPER, HITLER'S TABLE TALKS 1941-1944 (LONDON:
> WIDENFELD AND NICOLSON, 1953, P. 425-426)

Before a standing army can rule, the people must be
disarmed, as they are in almost every kingdom in Europe.
The supreme power in America cannot enforce unjust
laws by the sword because the whole body of the people
are armed, and constitute a force superior to any band of
regular troops that can be, on any pretense, raised in the
United States.

> - NOAH WEBSTER (1758-1843), AUTHOR OF THE FIRST
> DICTIONARY OF AMERICAN ENGLISH USAGE (1806).

Those who make peaceful revolution impossible will make violent revolution inevitable.

- JOHN FITZGERALD KENNEDY (1917-1963)

ATTRIBUTIONS

The tale of Jack Brackley and Joan Matcham is based on Robert Louis Stevenson's "The Black Arrow," 1888, copyright expired.

The list of symptoms of a city under seige on pages 94-95 is drawn in part from the 2003 "Signs of Dictatorship" essay by Wayne Madsen, senior fellow, Electronic Privacy Information Center, found at www.prisonplanet.com/123003yearsend. html.

The court discussion of the Fifth Amendment in Chapter 15 is drawn from Irwin Schiff's "The Great Income Tax Hoax" (Freedom Books, 1985), pp. 268-290. Used with permission.

The author thanks Nevada blademaster Jim Hrisoulas, author of "The Pattern-Welded Blade" and other books on the subject, for his forgeside discussion of the comparative strengths and weaknesses of Japanese and Europeans blades.

THE AUTHOR GRATEFULLY ACKNOWLEDGES
THE CREATORS OF A PRICELESS LEGACY — SOME OF THE
GREATEST SONGS OF ALL TIME:

"Casey Jones," by Jerome Garcia and Robert Hunter, copyright © Ice Nine Publishing, used by permission.

THE BLACK ARROW

ABOUT THE AUTHOR

A graduate of Eaglebrook (where he lettered in football), E.O. Smith (where he lettered in track), and Wesleyan University (where he played Orsino in "Twelfth Night"), Vin Suprynowicz worked his way through school as a disc jockey, short-order cook, motel night clerk, and member of the relentlessly unsuccessful rock & roll band "The Four Shadowings of Doom."

He began his writing career with the alternative weekly Hartford Advocate (writing part-time and driving the delivery truck at night), eventually giving up honest work entirely to become an award-winning reporter for the daily Willimantic Chronicle, news editor of the daily Norwich Bulletin, and managing editor of the daily Northern Virginia Sun — all before he turned 27.

He now works as a newspaper columnist and editorial writer in Las Vegas, Nevada, where he is still searching for his Madison. His non-fiction books include "Send in the Waco Killers" and "The Ballad of Carl Drega." He is at work on another novel.

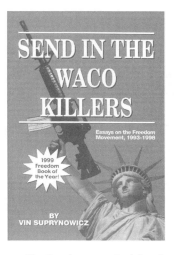

Guess what? It's not about Waco!

Your right to trial by a randomly selected jury — not one stacked with jurors who swear to convict in advance — is gone.

The IRS can now seize your bank account, paycheck, and house — without so much as a judge's order. Your banker will cooperate fully.

People who never sold, touched, or even saw a single gram or cocaine or marijuana are in federal prisons on "drug" charges — including plastic-vial manufacturers and hydroponic-supply store owners.

The Founders guaranteed Americans the right to keep and bear arms for defense against their own government. But the meager legal arms of the Branch Davidians were no match against government tanks and helicopters at Waco. And today, our rulers are more afraid of arming airline pilots than of having 767s fly into skyscrapers.

How did we get to this point? Is there any peaceful way back from the toboggan ride to tyranny? The answers are in *Send in the Waco Killers* (1999's Freedom Book of the Year), by America's syndicated Libertarian columnist, Vin Suprynowicz.

"This volume by Suprynowicz is why words exist. It is the seminal work of the last five decades. It will change lives. It will direct nations. ... The hand of Suprynowicz ... points to hope and the brillant possibilities alive in the human heart. ... It does what words were meant to do: inspire and teach. This book works a slow magic. Suprynowicz has given us the lyrics to freedom's song. It is up to us to make the music."

— Bill Branon, author of "Let Us Prey"
(a New York Times Notable Book of the Year),
"Devil's Hole," "Spider Snatch," and "Timesong."

Order your copy now.
Use the handy order form at the end of this section.

And be sure to check out our Web site at
www.theLibertarian.us and
www.LibertyBookShop.us

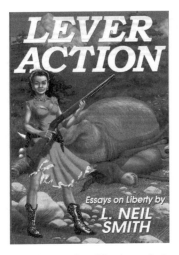

Non-Government Warning:

L. Neil Smith's vision of liberty is highly contagious and incurable. Exposure to his ideas will changes your life.

This warning from the back cover pretty well sums up most people's reaction the first time they read any of L. Neil's work.

L. Neil Smith is the most prolific Libertarian writer of our time. He's the author of more than 20 science-fiction novels, including *The Probability Broach*, and *Forge of the Elders*, named the 2000 Freedom Book of the Year by Free-Market.net.

In *Lever Action*, his first book of non-fiction, Smith again demonstrates that he's one of the strongest voices putting pressure on the Archimedes lever that will eventually lift the world to freedom — and the stars.

"Smith is best known as a science fiction author, and he's also an essayist, editorialist, activist, and speaker, and Lever Action *is the first ever print collection of his non-fiction offerings.*

It's about time.

Few books are so compelling that placing them in the hands of a friend becomes and act of revolution. Thomas Paine's Common Sense *and Vin Suprynowicz's* Send in the Waco Killers *have previously been the chronological bookends of that canon.* Lever Action *is the latest addition to it."*

—Tom Knapp, Free-Market.net

Order your copy now.
Use the handy order form at the end of this section.

And be sure to check out our Web site at
www.theLibertarian.us and
www.LibertyBookShop.us

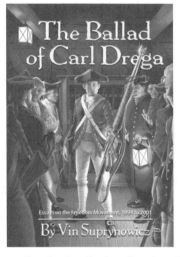

ORDER FORM

Use this form to order copies of Vin's non-fiction books *Send in the Waco Killers* and *The Ballad of Carl Drega*; L. Neil Smith's collection of non-fiction essays *Lever Action*; or additional copies of the trade paperback edition of *The Black Arrow*.

(Prices quoted are in U.S. dollars drawn on a U.S. bank. For other currencies or to pay in hard metal or other legal trade goods, please inquire.)

Send in the Waco Killers .... ____ @ **$17.95**

Lever Action .... ____ @ **$13.95**

The Ballad of Carl Drega .... ____ @ **$24.95**

The Black Arrow (trade paperback) ____ @ **$24.95**

The Black Arrow (leatherbound limited collector's edition)
___ please inquire re. price & availability

Add $3 S&H for first book, $1 for each additional _____

TOTAL ENCLOSED: $ _____

Name _____

Address _____

City, State, Zip _____

❏ Visa ❏ Mastercard #: _____

Exp. Date: _____

BIG DISCOUNTS ON BULK ORDERS!

Quantity	Discount	S&H
4-7	20%	$1.00 per book,
8-15	30%	$50 maximum up to 80 books.
16-32	40%	
48 or more	50%	
80 or more	50%	Free Shipping

To order with credit card visit Web site **www.LibertyBookShop.us** or **www.theLibertarian.us**. Make checks payable to: Mountain Media, 3172 N. Rainbow Blvd., Suite 343, Las Vegas, Nev. 89108, U.S.A.